Scruples Two

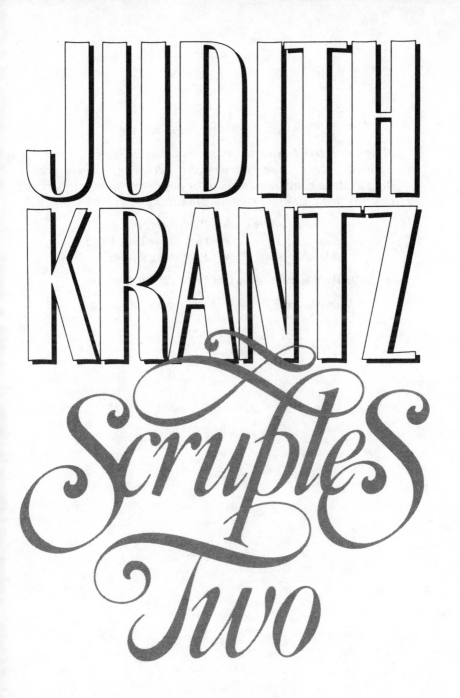

JUDITH KRANTZ

Scruples Two

CROWN PUBLISHERS, INC.   NEW YORK

Dedication

For my granddaughter, Kate Mattie Krantz, my youngest, most adorable and most promising heroine.

For Steve, first, last and forever my one and only—without him I would never have written Scruples *and there most certainly would never have been a* Scruples Two, *fourteen years later.*

Acknowledgments

*I owe a special debt of gratitude to these two friends who
helped me by sharing inside knowledge of their professions:*

Emily Woods, President of J. Crew.

*Gordon Davidson, Artistic Director/Producer of the
Mark Taper Forum in Los Angeles.*
and to
Edwina Lloyd, my wonderful, unflappable assistant.

Scruples Two

*I*n the momentary wait before the presentation of the Oscar for
Best Picture, that pause during which Oscar fever reaches its
height, while the presenters walk out of the wings and downstage
to read the list of nominations, Vito Orsini began to sweat. What if
Maggie MacGregor's information had been wrong? What if Mirrors
hadn't won Best Picture? Jesus—he'd have to buy the rights to The
WASP come what may, according to the terms of his bet with Curt
Arvey. But what the hell. He shrugged his shoulders and smiled. Right
or wrong, he had to have that book. It had been written for him to
produce. He knew it.

Billy Orsini, squeezing his hand tightly, had no such last-minute
panic. Dolly Moon had called her first thing that morning, unable to
hold back the good news. But Billy hadn't wanted to tell Vito because
she suspected he might feel that in some way it diminished the Oscar
he was about to get if he knew the secret of the envelope had been

revealed before the actual presentation. Nor would she tell him that she was pregnant until tomorrow, when the glory of this night was less fresh. The news, for her husband, childless at forty-two, would upstage whatever industry recognition he could ever be given. And as she felt Vito's hand tense more firmly than ever over her own, she told herself to be honest. She, Wilhelmina Hunnenwell Winthrop Ikehorn Orsini, did not have the faintest intention of sharing the particular spotlight of glorious maternity with any little gold-plated statuette that the Academy of Motion Picture Arts and Sciences, in its infinite wisdom, might ever bestow.

I

*B*illy woke reluctantly from a dream of such poignant happiness that she tried to cling to it as long as possible. She was running in the dream, bounding effortlessly up a flight of circular steps that led to a platform at the top of a tower from which, she knew even as she ran, she would see a radiant springtime woodland leading to the adventure of a beckoning turquoise sea. She opened her eyes with a sigh and waited for the emotion of the dream to fade, but all the joy stayed with her.

Blissfully disoriented, confused even as to the date and place, she mistily consulted the high ceiling until memory floated back. She was in her own bed in her own house in California. It was April, it was 1978. Last night Vito had won the Oscar for Best Picture and Dolly Moon, her dear friend, had won for Best Supporting Actress. Four hours later Dolly had, with dispatch and composure, given birth to a magnificent baby girl. Billy and Vito, with Lester Weinstock, Dolly's publicist, had skipped the post-Oscar party and waited at the hospital together. Then they had all returned here, to celebrate with scrambled eggs, English muffins and champagne. Billy remembered cooking the eggs and she had a clear vision of Vito opening champagne, but after that everything blurred into a haze of toasts and laughter. Perhaps both men were in bed with her? A quick peek revealed that she was alone, and on Vito's side of the bed the covers were thrown back.

Yawning, stretching, groaning with pleasure, Billy eased herself cautiously upright. Her bedside clock told her that it was past noon, but she didn't feel at all guilty. If a woman couldn't sleep late after enduring the many nervous tensions of yesterday, when could she? Especially in her condition, her incredible condition, her excessively interesting, newly discovered condition that was still a secret. But now the time had come to make her announcement. She heard Vito's voice on the phone in the sitting room next to their bedroom. Good, that meant she could throw some water on her face and brush her teeth before he realized she was awake. As Billy brushed her hair, dismissing as always the bugle call of her insistent beauty, even she couldn't fail to notice the vivid freshness of her skin, the artless brightness of her smoky eyes, the deeply gleaming abundance of her dark brown hair. She looked ten years younger than her thirty-five years. It must be hormones, she thought, up to their notorious tricks.

When she emerged from the bathroom Vito was still on the phone, so Billy was inspired to take a quick shower. From the instant she told Vito about this baby, he'd be so excited, so thrilled, so blind to distraction that everything else would become unimportant while they spent hours talking and planning, so she might as well grab this opportunity. A few minutes later, still damp from her hurried shower, barefoot and all but dancing in eagerness, Billy threw on a peignoir made of almost transparent crêpe de chine and flung open the door to the sitting room.

In quick, reflex confusion, she stepped back into the bedroom. What the devil was Vito's secretary, Sandy Stringfellow, doing sitting on Billy's favorite chair in her very own, very private and off-limits sitting room, murmuring discreetly into Billy's private phone, whose cord Sandy had dragged over from Billy's desk? Neither Vito nor Sandy had noticed her, so absorbed were they in their separate conversations. Billy shrugged out of her indiscreet peignoir and put on slippers and a robe made of heavy toweling.

"Good morning," she said, beaming at Sandy and Vito. Sandy made an apologetic grimace and continued talking. Vito looked up quickly, waved, smiled, blew her an abstracted kiss and continued listening intently.

"Yes, Mr. Arvey, Mr. Orsini will take your call as soon as he gets off the other phone," Billy heard Sandy say. "Yes, I know how long you've been waiting, would you rather he called you back? No, I can't say exactly when, that's the problem. We don't have a switchboard here, and the phone hasn't stopped ringing all morning. Mr. Orsini hasn't even had time to dress to go to his office. It shouldn't be long now, Mr. Arvey, but this phone doesn't have a hold button. Yes, I know that's ridiculous, but I'm on Mrs. Orsini's private phone."

Billy scribbled a question mark on a piece of memo paper and thrust it at Vito. He shook his head at her and pointed toward Sandy.

"Who's he talking to?" Billy asked.

"Lew Wasserman, about *The WASP*," Sandy answered, putting her hand over the mouthpiece of the phone. The two women made wide-eyed faces of mutual congratulation at each other. The combination of the most influential and powerful man in Hollywood and Vito's cherished new project, in which he hoped to star Robert Redford and Jack Nicholson, explained everything about Vito's intensity.

"Where's Josie?" Billy asked. Surely Josie Speilberg, her own secretary, should be running herd in here.

"Terrible stomach flu. She called in sick," Sandy answered.

"Great," Vito said, "that's great, Lew. Yeah . . . yeah . . . uh-huh . . . I understand your point . . . . Right. Listen, Lew, thanks again for the advice. Breakfast tomorrow morning? You're on. Seven-thirty? No problem. Good-bye, Lew." He hung up and gave Billy a quick, violent hug and a brief, hard kiss, triumph and victory making him move twice as quickly as usual. "Sleep okay, darling? No time to talk, I absolutely have to take the other phone and talk to Curt Arvey. That miserable sucker should never have bet me that *Mirrors* wouldn't win. Now he's going to shell out the million and a half for the rights to *The WASP*, and I want to make sure he's closed the deal with that New York literary agent. If ever there was a hot property . . . ." He had picked up Billy's private phone and was deep in conversation with Arvey while Sandy jumped to answer the other phone, which had started ringing the minute Vito put it down.

Billy looked at the two of them and realized they had forgotten her. Well, her news would wait, she told herself, and she needed breakfast. She waltzed down the staircase and through the sun-dappled double living rooms of her very large yet supremely comfortable house. It was an old house, as houses go in California, built in the 1930s, and in spite of its size it managed to retain an intimate, human scale. It was a house rich in personal, non-fashionable accumulation. Each room beckoned the passerby with asymmetrical bouquets of up-holstered furniture, interestingly covered in slightly faded, succulently flowered English linens and ribbon-striped French cottons; there were fine old needlepoint rugs on the irregular, polished floorboards; no room was without several working fireplaces in which firewood was newly laid. Clusters of blooming plants, ferns and small trees stood in nooks and corners and were grouped near the French doors, piles of books overflowed the bookcases, everywhere a multitude of paintings stood propped up and against the walls. Small, splendid bronzes, well-used silver candlesticks, inlaid tea caddies and birdless birdcages covered the tabletops; baskets brimming with magazines stood by the chairs and everywhere were gloriously idiosyncratic antiques, bought for their charm and exuberance. There was no gilt, no formality, no grandeur or opulence, not so much as one jeweled snuffbox among the hundreds of whimsical objects, yet it was obvious that Billy had never refused to be tempted when she happened across something she wanted. In spite of their fascinatingly disorganized clutter, the rooms were so big that they were characterized by crisp space and carefree freshness. It was not the house of a woman who had to please or impress anyone but herself, yet only huge expense could keep this great house in the customary immaculate perfection of unstudied dis-order that Billy loved.

She made her way through the library and the music room and the dining room, on her way to the pantry, smiling gaily at her three maids as she crossed their busy paths. Two of them had their arms filled with flower arrangements that had just arrived, and the third clutched sheaves of telegrams.

In the kitchen Billy's chef, Jean-Luc, concealed his surprise at the appearance of his employer; twice a week he conferred with Miss Speilberg about menus for the week, but Mrs. Orsini rarely visited the kitchen, and certainly never in her bathrobe. Billy asked him to send Vito and Sandy a platter of club sandwiches and make her a dish she saved for very special moments: three slices of white toast covered thickly with Tiptree's Little Scarlet strawberry jam and topped by carefully layered slices of very crisp bacon. This combination tasted like sweet and sour Chinese food for infants, and was a masterpiece of empty calories.

Sugar, salt, white flour, and animal fat, Billy gloated while she waited in the breakfast room for the bacon to be browned to the point of almost burning. This would be her last hurrah before she began her pregnancy diet, a bravura farewell gesture that could be appreciated only by a woman as compulsive as she was, a woman who knew the value of every calorie she had ingested since the age of eighteen, when she had lost a lifetime's accumulation of fat and determined success-fully to stay thin forever.

Nothing but melon, broiled tomatoes and steamed fish tonight, Billy thought, without regret, as she sipped orange juice and con-sidered the scene in her sitting room. This phone marathon couldn't go on much longer. Presumably it had started hours ago, since Vito, an early riser under all circumstances, still hadn't had time to shave or dress. Soon the calls would taper off, most people would be out to lunch, Sandy and Vito would go to his office to handle things more efficiently. Of course there'd be more calls to the house and more flowers and telegrams, but this post-Oscar frenzy couldn't last more than a few hours. After all, the world had a million really impor-tant things to focus on, no matter how significant this big win was to Vito and her.

She'd finished her sinful lunch without tasting it, Billy realized as she hurried back upstairs to the private part of the house, hoping to hear Vito busy in his own dressing room, expecting to find her sitting room empty. But both Vito and Sandy were exactly where she'd left them. "What the hell?" Billy wrote and shoved the paper under Sandy's nose. The secretary grimaced in semi-desperation and wrote, "He's talking to Redford—I'm keeping Nicholson *waiting*."

"No shit!" Billy said to the air, in a mixture of mystification and exasperation. My God, those actors had perfectly good agents. Why was Vito talking to them directly? Or had they called him? *The WASP* had been at the top of the best-seller list for seven months, it was the hit book of the decade, everyone wanted to be involved in it, but such a breakdown in Hollywood protocol was something she'd never heard of before. She'd settled down to listen when Sandy waved another note at her.

"Maggie's on her way here now with a camera crew . . . a special day-after-Oscar roundup show for tonight's news. Shouldn't you dress?"

Billy's jaw dropped. This was a goddamned invasion of privacy. She'd turned over her house to Vito and his band of workers without a second thought for six weeks of postproduction when it had been a question of getting *Mirrors* edited and mixed without the studio's interference. She'd worked eighteen hours a day as a script girl; she'd never complained about the damage to shining floors or the breakage of her most delicate bibelots during the entire mad and feverish process, but Maggie MacGregor and her gonzo camera crew were something else again. She didn't give a damn for the fact that Maggie's television show from Hollywood was, week in and week out, one of the five most widely viewed programs in America. Nor did she care that Maggie had tipped Vito off about winning the Oscar. Maggie was Vito's friend, not hers, never hers. She and Maggie never met without reinforcing their cordial mistrust. They couldn't afford to allow themselves to become enemies—the town and the business were too small for that—but they'd never trust each other. Her house wasn't a soundstage, for Christ's sake, she didn't want strangers inside it, she'd never allowed a single magazine to photograph it, and Maggie damn well knew that.

For the past three years, from the time she had bought her Holmby Hills estate, on Charing Cross Road, on the coveted south side of Sunset Boulevard just beyond Beverly Hills, Billy's property had been discreetly patroled twenty-four hours a day by armed men with Dobermans; barbed-wire fences were concealed in every foot of the thick perimeter hedges of her eleven acres; there was a tall iron gate at the beginning of her driveway and a gatehouse guarded by two uniformed men who waved away anyone who stopped a car to rubberneck. All that security went with being one of the richest women in the world, as sensible and necessary as it was to any boss in organized crime, and now Maggie MacGregor, without so much as a by-your-leave, was thrusting her way in with a camera crew. Why couldn't Maggie interview Vito in his office?

Still unwilling to disturb Vito, Billy scribbled the question and plunked it down in front of Sandy, who stopped flirting with Jack Nicholson for a second and murmured, "Human interest, she's shooting everyone at home."

Billy retreated to the absolute privacy of her thirty-foot-square dressing room and the deep window seat on which she'd huddled yesterday when she realized that she was pregnant, when hours of soul-searching had revealed to her stubbornly disbelieving mind that she had wanted all along to have a baby without knowing it.

It was two in the afternoon, more than twenty-four hours later, and she still hadn't told Vito. *Nobody* knew. She was quivering, bursting, palpitating with her great news, and Vito couldn't be pried away from the phone so that she could tell him first, before anyone else, as was right and proper. Until he knew, she had to stay silent. It was getting a little hard to hold on tight to that otherworldly happiness she'd carried intact from her dream into her life, Billy realized, and then she brightened. She would go and spend the next few hours at Scruples. If she didn't actually see the camera crew invade her house, it would be as if they'd never been there.

Billy dressed rapidly and managed to leave without causing Vito or Sandy to look up from their phones. During the eight-minute drive from her house to her sumptuous boutique on Rodeo Drive in Beverly Hills, Billy realized that the exciting weather of early spring was the perfect match for her mood. Oscar weather, like Rose Bowl weather, was uncannily dependable. No one in the world-wide television audience had ever seen less-than-perfect weather in California on those two particular days. No one had ever seen the gloom of those endlessly foggy June mornings when the sun doesn't fight through the clouds until afternoon; no one had ever seen the dark chill and frightening floods of the January rains or, far worse, the glare of the dangerous, flat white sunlight in the late-summer forest fire season . . . no, Hollywood always primped itself silly and presented its best face when the world was watching. Typical, thought Billy, typical. She was still enough of a Bostonian to be able to sneer slightly at a city that managed reliably to fool the public.

She drove down Rodeo Drive and turned into the underground parking lot at Scruples, feeling the familiar, proudly swelling warmth of ownership. Scruples was the extravagant fantasy she had brought to life four years earlier, the most opulent and successful specialty store that had ever existed. Last night, during the Oscar ceremonies, Billy had decided to open new branches of Scruples all over the world, in the great capital cities where those rich women lived whose lives revolved around shopping and entertaining, that tiny but endlessly greedy consuming class born to become Scruples customers.

She'd made a resolution, Billy reminded herself, not to jump too quickly into building the new branches, not to make a single important move without the advice of Spider Elliott and Valentine O'Neill. She intended to make them her partners in the new Scruples company that Josh Hillman, her lawyer, would set up. Spider, the former fashion photographer who now managed Scruples, had been the one to supply the key inspiration that had set the right, lighthearted tone for the store's success, and, God knows, she couldn't operate without Paris-bred Valentine, her head buyer and designer of the brilliant custom-made clothes that gave Scruples much of its cachet. She couldn't wait to tell them her plans, Billy thought, as the elevator mounted to the third floor, where the executive offices were located.

Strangely, neither Spider nor Valentine was to be found. Spider's secretary ventured that he and Valentine had gone shopping. Of all the bizarre ideas, Billy thought, gone shopping *where,* she'd like to know, when Scruples was the shopper's chief mecca in the world? Frustrated once more but clinging doggedly to her good temper—probably they'd gone to buy Vito a victory present, something you couldn't find in a woman's store—Billy decided to tour her domain as she often did, pretending that she was an out-of-town visitor seeing it for the first time. But no sooner had she begun to drift as inconspicuously as possible through the ground floor of Scruples, conjuring up the mindset of a tourist from Pittsburgh, than she was besieged by a dozen women, some of them acquaintances, some total strangers. Each of them wanted to share vicariously in Vito's Oscar by congratulating her, by being able to go home and say to as many friends as possible, "I told Billy Orsini how thrilled I was for her and Vito today." Instinctively, with polite smiles scattered in every direction, Billy fled to her own office and locked the door behind her.

Billy sat at her desk and considered the situation. She couldn't possibly go home for hours, she didn't feel like doing a Joan Didion and taking her classic Bentley on a long freeway drive to nowhere, so clearly she had to remain sequestered in here simply because she couldn't face the barrage of women downstairs. Wouldn't another woman, on a similar winning day, have stayed to bask in the generous, largely well meant babble of goodwill from which she had just run away?

Damn it to hell, would she *ever* stop being shy? Billy asked herself, finally admitting why she was unable to enjoy compliments and congratulations without painful self-consciousness. She'd had good reason to be shy while she'd been growing up, a chubby, embarrassingly dressed, motherless poor relation of all the aristocratic and financially secure Winthrops of Boston, exposed to a score of happily adjusted cousins who, at their kindest, ignored her, and, at their frequent worst, made her into a laughingstock. She'd had more than good reason to be shy when she'd been sent off to Emery Academy, an exclusive boarding school for future debutantes, where she had spent six unendingly cruel, searingly lonely years as the designated outsider, the butt of jokes and freak of the class, a girl of five feet ten inches who weighed two hundred and eighteen pounds.

But then she had spent an all-important, transfiguring year in Paris and returned, thin, grown at last into possession of her dark and dominating beauty, returned to go to New York and work as a secretary for Ellis Ikehorn, the mysterious multimillionaire whose Ikehorn Enterprises owned businesses all over the world. She had made the very first friend of her life, Jessica Thorpe, with whom she shared an apartment. Jessica lived in New York now, but Billy still spoke twice weekly on the phone to one of her only two real women friends in the world. Dolly Moon was the other.

Two close women friends, Billy mused, not much for thirty-five years. When she was twenty-one she had married Ellis Ikehorn, and from that day until his stroke seven years later, she and Ellis had led a life of international travel during which Billy, with her staggering sense of style and princely jewels, had become a fixture on the best-dressed list. When they weren't roving on business they settled for pleasure at their villa at Cap-Ferrat, they visited their ranch in Brazil, they stayed weeks at a time in London in their suite at Claridge's, then flew off to their seaside house in Barbados or the manor house of their vineyard in the Napa Valley. Their New York headquarters were in their Sherry Netherland tower apartment; their photographs appeared constantly in scores of magazines, they were among the few who had entry into the Olympian level of society around the globe, and it would seem that they had dozens of friends.

However, no one but Ellis and Billy ever penetrated to the single important truth behind the screen of the stardust of privilege that radiated across their life. The closeness of their relationship was the only thing that mattered to them. Entertaining and being entertained, they never made a meaningful new friendship, for no one really caught their attention but each other. The charmed circle they created of their life, as surely as it protected them, kept other people severely out.

When Ellis had the stroke that incapacitated him in 1970, Billy had just turned twenty-eight. For the next five years, until his death, she had lived almost as a recluse in a Bel Air fortress where all life gravitated around the semiparalyzed man. Her contacts with other women were limited to the members of her exercise class, women whose poorly concealed curiosity about her had warned her off any possibility of a deeper friendship. Yet, Billy thought, naturally they had been curious, for had she not still been a freak? A supremely well dressed, thin and beautiful freak whose wealth actually created her freakishness?

Face it, she was a born outsider; she just didn't fit into any of the groups that formed among the women of this one-industry town. She was too preoccupied with her dying husband to join in their gossipy, dressy luncheons, which were often based on the excuse of planning a charity ball. She didn't belong to the set formed by the wives of studio executives in which each woman's position was totally determined by her husband's power in the film business, a fierce Hollywood version of Washington, D.C.'s political wives' pecking order. She couldn't remotely be a member of the guerrilla wives, the early-thirtyish, firmly fleshed, desperately calculating beauties who had married rich, divorced men twice their age, who had signed prenuptial contracts that eliminated a division of community property, and whose chief interest in life was trying to get pregnant so that they would have hostages when their husbands began to consider dumping them for still younger flesh. And she would never make a friend among the handful of women writers, producers and stars of the film business who respected only their working peers and had no time for civilians.

She might have discovered potential friends in Hancock Park or Pasadena, Billy thought, where the quietly elegant, old-money set lived, rarely deigning to cross to the ''Westside,'' where all the movie money settled, but even without knowing them she was sure they'd be California versions of those conservative, predictable Winthrop cousins who had made her childhood so miserable.

When Ellis had died and she had been released from her solitude, rather than accepting the role of new widow and ''extra'' woman, she had thrown herself totally into making a success of Scruples, until, two years later she had married Vito and been immediately caught up in the whirl of making *Mirrors*. She hadn't been shy with Dolly Moon when they met on the set, because Dolly had no idea who she was and didn't let it make a difference when she found out.

Dolly and Jessica. Two true, eternal women friends out of a lifetime. Perhaps that wasn't really such a low number. Perhaps it was about average, perhaps most women fooled themselves about how staunch their good friends were? Billy put her feet on her desk and hugged her knees. She was just feeling like a misfit because this day, which was to have started with her telling Vito about their baby, had gone so abruptly and immediately off course. She was a fool to remember the ghosts of so many lost and lonely years, to allow them to intrude on the wonder of her new life. Just because she wasn't at ease in groups of women didn't mean that she had no capacity for friendship. Her Aunt Cornelia would have told her to pull up her socks, Billy reflected, as she swung her feet back to the floor and bent over her desk, where there was more than enough work to do to keep her busy until the coast was clear back home. She was glad to have the work to distract her a little from feeling the growing, feverish ache to be with Vito, to have his full attention, to lie in his arms and tell him her news and watch the happiness on his face, to get him off the fucking phone!

As she drove up to the gatehouse at five-thirty, one of the gatemen assured Billy that the television people had just left. But some other visitors had arrived, he added, people Mr. Orsini had told them to admit.

Who in holy hell could they be? Billy asked herself in a wave of disappointment and irritation. It was evening, she had been gone for more than four hours, the business day was finished even for Oscar winners. Visitors! She'd throw the pack of them out, whoever they were, double quick! She didn't care if it was Wasserman, Nicholson, Redford, and the ghosts of Louis B. Mayer, Irving Thalberg and Jean Hersholt, with Harry Cohn and the brothers Warner thrown in for good measure. She'd have them out of her house!

Billy glared incredulously at two dozen cars parked in front of the house, threw open the front door and stood riveted at the sight and sound of at least forty people talking and laughing at the top of their voices, beginning to fill up the double living rooms. She refused to believe what she was seeing. A roaring party, what promised to be a hurricane of a party, was taking place and Vito was the center of it. In the mob she spotted Fifi Hill, the director of *Mirrors,* the stars, the editors, the composer and a score of others who'd been involved in the making of the movie from the beginning. And behind her, pushing their way through the door, came more people, all crew and cast members, every one of whom kissed and hugged her quickly before they rushed over to Vito.

Billy pushed through the crowd until she reached her husband.

"How . . . . why . . . Vito, what the hell . . . . ?"

"Darling! About time! I wondered what had happened to you. We're having the wrap party for the picture—remember, the first one was cut short, so I had an inspiration and decided to have it over again. Everybody's still as high as kites. Don't worry about the food, Sandy called Chasen's and told them to send over everything. Isn't this a great idea? Listen, I've got to find Fifi, I still haven't congratulated him on getting Best Director."

"You do that," Billy said to the spot where Vito had been standing. Had Alexander the Great ever been as blazingly sure of himself, as triumphant, as consumed with energy and excitement after any of his victories? she wondered, following her bold, bronzed Caesar of a husband with her eyes as he dashed into the throng. She had married Vito on a great wave of passionate love, hardly knowing him. Only after their marriage had she realized how much of his own passion was reserved for his work, how obsessed he was by filmmaking. Now, after ten difficult months of compromise and adjustment, Billy thought she had come to terms with it. Yes, she certainly *had* come to terms with it, she assured herself as she slipped through dozens of people to reach the staircase; she accepted him exactly as he was, and tonight was as it should be, a blaring, riotous celebration of a unique achievement no one but Vito had believed possible for a low-budget movie.

As Billy threaded her way across her sitting room she noticed teetering piles of unopened telegrams tossed between the baskets of flowers that covered every surface, including the floor. Tomorrow the telegrams would all be sent to Vito's office, she determined, tomorrow Josie would open all the cards on the flowers and make a list of people to thank. But right now she'd put on something festive and join the party. Sooner or later the guests would have to leave and she'd be alone with Vito and the only other news that could possibly matter on this day of jubilation and rejoicing.

Vito and Billy were wearily saying good-bye to their last guests when one of the gatemen called the house to say that another person had arrived, asking for Mr. Orsini.

"Tell whoever it is I'm sorry but it's too late, Joe, the party's over," Vito said. "*What?* What? You're sure? No, it's all right, let the taxi through."

"Totally impossible," Billy muttered, "even the catering crew on the picture was here tonight. Vito, make an excuse, don't dare let anyone in this house. If I can find the strength to climb the stairs I'm going to bed, I'm beat."

"Go on, darling, I'll handle it."

Ten minutes later, when Billy had stripped off her clothes, put on a robe, and was starting to take off her makeup, Vito entered her dressing room and closed the door behind him.

"Who on earth was it?" Billy asked, drooping with exhaustion in front of the mirror.

"It's . . . . a long story."

There was a note of utter disbelief and shock in Vito's voice that told her this had nothing to do with a guest who was too late for the wrap party.

She spun around and looked at him searchingly. "It's bad news, isn't it?"

"Don't look so frightened, Billy. This isn't about us, this isn't about you."

"Then it's about you! Vito, *what's wrong?*"

"Oh, Jesus," he said, dropping onto a chair and looking past her, his eyes seeming to focus on the wall. "There are so many things I've never told you . . . . it's unforgivable. From the second we got married I've been so fucking preoccupied with the picture, not a minute to spare, I kept promising myself that as soon as all this craziness was over I'd tell you the whole story, the minute we had some peaceful time together . . . . I should have told you the day we met, but it was the last thing on my mind, it didn't seem to matter then because I didn't know we were going to get married . . . the only thing that I could think of was the present, the past was the past, and then everything happened between us so quickly . . . . "

"Vito, if you don't get to the point—"

"My daughter's here."

"You can't have a daughter," Billy said flatly.

"I can. I do. I was married before. It didn't last a year. We were divorced and she's lived with her mother ever since."

The shock of his words kept Billy's voice almost even. She struggled so hard to keep from shouting that she almost whispered.

"*A child?* I wouldn't care if you'd had ten other wives, but a child, Vito? In the year that we've been married, are you trying to make me believe that there was never, *ever* a single minute when you could have told me this, for Christ's sake? My God, so what if you've been divorced, but a child! We've had hours and hours, you could have told me during any one of hundreds of meals, before we went to bed, when we got up in the morning . . . . Don't tell me there was never any peaceful time!"

"I was always going to tell you, it just didn't happen," he mumbled.

"Vito, give me some credit for intelligence. You let it go too long and then you didn't want to rock the boat. You should have told me before we got married, it wouldn't have made any difference, but *now*, springing it on me now? I just can't believe this is happening. What's her name?"

"Gigi."

"Why did she come here tonight?" Billy asked, fighting the desire to scream. She had to remain calm because Vito looked as if he was going to faint. "Because of the Oscar?"

"Her mother . . . . her mother died . . . . she was buried . . . . yesterday. In New York. Gigi sent me a telegram. It must be with all the others. When she didn't hear anything from me, she got on a plane and just . . . . came."

"Where is she now?"

"In the kitchen. I gave her a glass of milk and some cake and told her to wait until I'd talked to you."

"How old is she?"

"Sixteen."

"*Sixteen!*" Billy screeched. "Sixteen! My God, Vito, that's not a child, that's a teenager! Practically a woman. Don't you know anything about sixteen-year-olds? Vito, get me a brandy, a large brandy. Never mind, just bring the bottle." Billy scrubbed off the cream that was still on her face and hurried toward the door.

"Billy . . ."

"What?"

"Shouldn't we talk more before you meet Gigi?"

"About what, Vito?" Billy asked incredulously. "She wouldn't be here if she had another place to go, would she? She hasn't seen you in at least a year because I'd know if she had, so if she flew all the way across the country without even hearing a word from you, you've got to be her only refuge, wouldn't you say?''

"Oh, Christ! Billy, you're not giving me any credit for anything. This is an old story, it was over fifteen years ago, and you're being as judgmental as if it had just happened."

"I'm being realistic," Billy said. "It *has* just happened—to me." Billy turned and quickly made her way down to the big kitchen. She hesitated only a second before pushing open the double doors, hearing Vito still on the staircase.

A small figure was sitting very still on a high stool behind the big butcher-block table. In front of her were an empty glass and an empty plate. On the kitchen floor was a small, battered suitcase. When Billy walked in, Gigi looked up and slid off the stool, standing wordlessly, without moving. Billy's first thought was that Vito must be wrong, she didn't look old enough to be a teenager. And she didn't look like Vito. What was visible of her face through a mess of plain brown hair was delicate, oddball, somehow immediately and indefinably elfin. In the several baggy, rather ragged sweaters she wore layered indiscriminately over her jeans, she seemed to be a waif, a scrap, a sprite, blown into this grand, bright kitchen by a teasing gust of wind.

Gigi remained still and speechless for a long minute, enduring Billy's inspection. In her straightforward stance, poised squarely on her cowboy boots, standing as straight and tall as she could, there was nothing of apology or of defiance, yet somehow, tiny and nondescript as she was, she had presence, immediate, undeniable presence. She was tired and very sad but not pathetic, she was alone but not needy. Something about her was deeply interesting. Gigi's eyes met Billy's, Gigi smiled—and a piece of Billy's heart she didn't know she possessed fell in love.

The main thing, Billy told herself frantically, as soon as the necessary, conventional words of greeting and comfort had been said, was to postpone absolutely everything, every explanation, every plan, every bit of discussion, until tomorrow. None of them was in a condition to think clearly. Vito, steadily nipping brandy, was silent and visibly utterly confused in a way she had never imagined he could ever be; she herself was in the grip of a combination of so many conflicting emotions that they merged into pure bewilderment, which her own large brandy did nothing to minimize, and Gigi, who had just downed the first brandy of her life, was clearly knocked out from fatigue and grief.

"We've all got to get a night's sleep," Billy announced, sweeping them out of the kitchen. "Gigi, do you want to take a bath before you go to bed, or are you too tired?"

"A bath, please." Her voice was so young, Billy thought. No regional accent that she could detect, a clear, pure and innocent sound with just the hint of a promise of a lilt, a musical note, in spite of her weariness.

"Vito, take the suitcase," Billy said, and putting her arm around the girl's almost childlike waist, she led the way to one of the many guest rooms, which were always kept in immaculate readiness.

"I'll show Gigi where everything is. Vito, say good night to your daughter and get out of here," Billy said as Vito stood staring blankly and unhelpfully at the suitcase he'd carried upstairs. Billy ran a bath while Gigi unpacked her few things, and as the girl soaked, Billy turned back the bed, opened the windows just enough and closed the curtains. Finally she lay back in a deep chair and had another brandy since she couldn't think of anything else to do that was useful, appropriate or sensible, and she couldn't let Gigi put herself to bed all alone.

Billy closed her eyes and drifted, her mind refusing to deal with the problems the girl's arrival created. What she really needed, she thought, was one of those French fatigue cures where they keep you fast asleep, except for meals, for three weeks, and you wake up looking twenty years younger, only they seemed to have closed those clinics. Perhaps they'd found out that three weeks of a steady diet of barbiturates wasn't good for people? Or maybe she should go to one of those frightful, cruel spas where they made you run five miles up a mountain before a juice breakfast and gave you only chopsticks to eat with so that each tiny meal of chopped vegetables would seem to last longer? In any case she needed to do something to rouse her from the spin her mind was in. She swallowed another brandy.

"Billy?"

She half opened her eyes and saw a diminutive, forlorn figure enveloped in white, who looked exactly like Casper the Friendly Ghost.

"You're singing," Gigi said.

"I am?" Billy was amazed. "I must be drunk."

"'Look for the Silver Lining.' My . . . my mom used to sing that song."

"Betcha all women do . . . . betcha a couple guys wrote it to string them along."

"Yeah, Jerome Kern and some other guy."

"How come?"

"How come what?"

"How come you know that?"

"My mother was a gypsy."

Billy's eyes popped open.

"Do you . . . . well, don't you . . . . what I mean is, wouldn't you have a . . . *tribe* . . . . or something?"

"I wish. No, not that kind of gypsy. She was a dancer. She was touring with a revival of *Annie Get Your Gun* . . . she'd been dancing with pneumonia, she didn't let anybody know, she didn't see a doctor . . . she wouldn't pay attention to it because she couldn't afford to lose the gig, so by the time she couldn't hide it anymore it was too late for antibiotics . . . gypsies . . . they'll do dumb things like that every time." Gigi tried to speak matter-of-factly, but all her words poured out in a shaking rush.

"Oh, Gigi," Billy cried, holding out her arms and drawing the bundle of towels down onto her knees. "I'm so terribly sorry. I can't even think of how to tell you how sorry I am. If only I'd known! I had no idea, not the slightest, not a word! And I would have helped if I'd known, you know I would."

Gigi sat stiffly upright. Her voice quavered from her attempt to sound in control. "Mom always said she was sure you didn't know about us. She was too independent . . . she never counted on Dad, never tried to keep in touch. It had been—a while—since we'd heard anything from him. A long while. But it's always been that way."

"How—how old was she?"

"Thirty-five."

My age, Billy thought, just my age. She felt a bolt of pure rage shoot through her. Vito's career had been up and down, at times he'd been what passed for broke in producer circles, but nothing, not one single reason on earth, could excuse neglecting his child.

"Gigi, I promise you, it's never going to be that way again," Billy vowed, smoothing the girl's hair. Gigi allowed herself to be caressed, but she remained awkwardly perched on Billy's knees, obviously willing herself not to give in to emotion. With Gigi's wet hair covered by a towel, Billy could see the details of the girl's face. She had a straight, small nose that just missed turning up at the tip; small ears that just missed coming to a point; light brown eyebrows that formed a decided point over beautifully formed eyelids and large eyes of an indeterminate color in this dim light. Her mouth was small, her lower lip fuller than the upper. Her upper lip curled upward at the corners so that even when she was as grave as she was now, she wore the slightest tantalizing promise of a smile. Her forehead and chin were nicely rounded and her jawline oval, so that her entire head seemed cunningly and carefully made. She could be pretty, Billy thought, she just doesn't know it, or doesn't care. Without her messy hair hiding her face, Gigi reminded Billy of illustrations of flappers from the 1920s, with their sleek, pert, impish look.

"Is that your real name, just Gigi?" Billy asked, searching for a neutral topic, respecting her desire to be grown up.

"It's what everybody calls me. I never tell my real name."

"My real name is Wilhelmina, so there's no chance that yours can be worse than that," Billy probed, curious.

"Oh yeah? How about Graziella Giovanna?"

"Graziella Giovanna." Billy said the words slowly. "But that sounds so beautiful, it's melodious, like an Italian princess from the Renaissance."

"Maybe to you, but not in grade school, not in high school, not anywhere in this century. Those were Dad's grandmothers' names. Mom insisted on them, I don't know why. Her own grandmothers were called Moira and Maud. Moira Maud . . . 'Come back to me my darlin' in the evenin' in the gloamin' '. . . it sounds like an Irish love song —I'd rather be called Gigi, no matter what."

"Graziella . . . Graziella . . . I wonder what I'm going to name my own baby?" Billy asked dreamily. "I only have six or seven months to decide."

Gigi jumped to the floor. "You're going to have a baby!" she exclaimed.

"Oh my God, I've told you! I wasn't going to tell anybody until I told Vito. I just found out yesterday. But, Gigi, what's wrong, why are you crying?"

Billy staggered, getting up from the chair, and with determination grabbed Gigi and fell back down again, cuddling her tightly. It was good for her to cry, to cry her heart out. Many minutes passed as Gigi wept in Billy's arms. Finally she stopped and let Billy pat her wet face dry.

"I never cry," Gigi muttered at last, sniffing fiercely, "except for good news. I've always hated being an only child."

By the time Billy had tucked Gigi in and returned to her bedroom, Vito was sprawled all over the bed, plunged into a heavy sleep. Billy stared at him, her elbows akimbo, her rage returning and mounting. Suddenly he was a total stranger. This man who had not told her, in almost a year of marriage, that he had a daughter? It was not an omission that could be explained away. She didn't know him, she had never really known him. He hadn't seen or mentioned Gigi in a year. *Must that not mean he wouldn't want their child?*

Fired by the brandies she'd drunk, Billy knew that she had to confront Vito before another second passed. She was going to have this out with him if it took all night. If he didn't want a child, their future was impossible. She couldn't wait till morning. It would be as difficult to get him alone as it had been all of this endless, infuriating day. No, it would be worse, since he would want to avoid the issue. Vividly she imagined Vito sequestering himself in one meeting after another for the next week, the next month, the next six months, then in preproduction, then production, then postproduction, unable to give her his precious attention until after the wrap party for *The WASP*— and even that minute of concentration in the far future wasn't guaranteed, she told herself, punching him viciously in the arm, prodding him on his shoulders, pulling his ears, pinching his nose, pounding on his chest in a rising tide of violence, not giving a damn if she hurt him, finally hoping to hurt him. Just as she was beginning to think he was completely insensible from the effects of the brandy, he opened one eye, lifted his head an inch from the pillow and squinted at her.

"Vito, we're going to have a baby. I'm pregnant," Billy shouted furiously.

Vito's eye closed, his head fell back, and just before he passed out again, in a voice that she could barely hear he murmured, "Yeah, Lew . . . sure, Lew . . . seven-thirty . . ."

2

*B*illy had acted as if he were a serial killer, a child molester, a man who put cherished pet poodles to death slowly and painfully, Vito thought with fury as he drove too quickly to his breakfast meeting, blinking impatiently at traffic lights through the thundering gray fog of the most intense hangover of his life. So what if he had forgotten to tell Billy about Gigi? There were thousands of things he'd never yet had time to tell her, never would tell her. Okay, it was thoughtless, careless, incredibly embarrassing, but it wasn't malicious or deceptive, he hadn't been trying to put anything over on anyone, he just had been too *busy*. Busy with a man's work, busy with the most crucial thing in his world. Why couldn't any fucking woman he'd ever met in his life understand *busy*?

Trying and failing immediately to achieve a detached state of mind, Vito told himself that he was paying the too-high price, no less humiliating because it was inevitable, of marriage to a rich woman.

When they'd met at the Cannes Film Festival last spring, when they'd fallen in love so immediately, when he'd let Billy talk him into marrying her in spite of all his convictions, he had been chasing his erection, nothing else. He had to look at the facts; his powers of reason and resistance had disappeared, vanquished by a hard-on. Vito remembered too well how he'd allowed Billy to convince him that if her money had been his, their marriage would be perfectly normal. Damn right it would have been normal. And it would have *remained* normal! But over the last ten months, from the day of their marriage, while almost all of their joint attention had been involved in the production of *Mirrors*, something powerful had solidified inside the internal, unseen structure of their marriage, something that he had ignored, willfully or not, until this morning when it became inescapable.

Only this morning, Vito thought, had he become keenly aware that he lived in a magnificent house he would never have been able to afford unless he'd been one of the old-time giants of his industry, a house that was maintained at an enormous weekly sum that had nothing to do with him, a sum at which he couldn't even guess. His servants, including the second cook, whose only duty was to cook for the rest of the staff who lived in their own wing, were paid by Billy's accountants, as were the restaurant bills, the flower bills, the entertainment bills, the travel bills, the insurance, even the dry cleaning. His car was always filled with gas by an unseen employee who kept it immaculate on a daily basis. When was the last time he'd so much as stopped at a drugstore and paid for a package of razor blades? He and Billy hadn't been married long enough to file an income tax return, but since his income for this year had been next to nothing and hers had been in the tens of millions, the joint signing next month at her accountant's office would be a farce, carried out because she *wanted* it that way. The vast, meticulous, luxury-freighted tempo at which their entire life was led existed because she *wanted* it that way, Vito said savagely to himself. *Want*, Billy's middle name. The first time she'd asked him to marry her, he'd told her that it was impossible because it would mean living in her style, not his—when had he forgotten that? How long had it taken him to take his present life for granted, and when had he begun to accord Billy's wants a never-mentioned power?

He'd felt the weight of that power this morning, felt it in the size and freedom of Billy's anger, as if she were a queen who had been betrayed by a serf. Why couldn't she understand that his long-ago first marriage to Mimi O'Brian, Gigi's mother, carried no more real importance than a brief affair? Except for the child, of course, a child she'd insisted on having even though Vito had never wanted one. He'd told Mimi from the day she announced her pregnancy, a few months after he'd somehow entered into that impulsive, quickly regretted marriage, that he was moving too fast to have a child. He'd insisted that it was impossible, out of the question, a major mistake, but she'd been an Irish devil of stubbornness, she'd believed that a child would make their faltering marriage last, although he'd warned her that he wouldn't be blackmailed. Her insistence on naming the kid after his grandmothers, Giovanna and Graziella, had been another form of blackmail, but Mimi had no living family to object, and she'd whisked Gigi off to be baptized before he'd even known about it. It had been a pathetic and meaningless gesture, since he'd never known either of the two old women.

But he'd done the right thing by Mimi after the divorce, more than the right thing, no matter what Billy thought. He'd waited to get the divorce until the baby was six weeks old and Mimi was back on her feet, he'd managed to keep up his child-support payments, and whenever he was in New York he tried to remember to drop in and see how they were doing, no matter how inconvenient it was, not that it was anything but inconvenient, to be honest. Half the time Mimi had been out of town with a show and Gigi had been living with one or another of a family of temporarily unemployed gypsies, all friends who took care of one another's kids when it was necessary . . . . nothing wrong with that life at all, he'd decided. She was growing up in a dancers' kibbutz, one big family in which all the kids got along just fine.

But, Jesus, when he struggled out of bed this morning, Billy had been already awake and in full fury. She must have been up all night planning how to accuse him of every crime any father had ever committed. Luckily he'd had to rush out of the house to make his early date with Lew Wasserman or he'd still be pinned down, listening to her enumerating a list of his faults. Right after the total joy of yesterday, she'd destroyed every particle of his well-deserved afterglow, Vito thought bitterly. He'd won the ultimate prize for which he'd worked all his life, he was about to put together a deal he'd yearned for, his whole career had been validated, he'd made the giant step and the future was his.

He had every right to be on top of the world, but Billy had spoiled everything with stinging recrimination for faults he wasn't guilty of. She knew nothing about it, she hadn't given him the benefit of any doubt. If she'd allowed him time to explain in any kind of detail—but no, she'd been transformed overnight into a hanging judge. He'd always known that Billy had the capacity to turn into a bitch. What woman didn't? But he'd be damned if he'd stand for her announcing that someone had to start being responsible for Gigi even if he had never had the fundamental human decency to be a father, as she'd hissed at him while he tried to shave. Sure, Gigi was welcome to stick around for a little while, until she got over her mother's death, but then she was going to be shipped right back to New York, where she'd live happily in one of the gypsy families and go back to her school and grow up the New York kid she was. His life wasn't about *teenagers*, for Christ's sake! Fatherhood had been forced on him, but that didn't mean he had to like it, then or now. Did Billy think she could make pronouncements about his daughter? She had a lot to learn, Vito thought grimly as he turned his car over to the valet parker, and the first thing was the limitation of her power over him.

When Gigi woke up at ten, she found a sheet of paper on the carpet next to her bedroom slippers. "Gigi, I'm so glad you're here! I'll be home all day. Just dial 25 on the intercom on the phone next to your bed whenever you're ready for breakfast or lunch or whatever and I'll join you." The communication was signed with a scrawled, "Love— Billy."

Gigi sat up in bed and considered the note with amazement and respect. It was real, a perfectly real sheet of paper, the ink smudged when she wet it with her finger, so logically everything else in the room must be real. She'd seen rooms like this in old movies, but the person in the bed was dressed in a satin or chiffon negligee, an actress playing a grand lady, toying with a cup of tea and a triangle of toast from a tray that a butler had just placed reverently over her knees. If she didn't have to pee so badly she'd just stay all day long, right here under the lace-bordered, monogrammed sheets in this sure-enough, honest-to-goodness, four-poster bed hung in acres of flowered cotton, a bed too thrilling for ordinary sleeping, a bed that deserved to be appreciated as a theatrical experience. She might even ring for that butler who was sure to be lurking around somewhere, Gigi thought, knowing she would never dare to do such a thing, but first things first. She scampered into the bathroom in the ripped T-shirt she wore to sleep in. She emerged in a few minutes, her face shining from the scrub she'd given it—she dimly remembered that she'd had a bath the night before, so there was no need to waste time on excessive cleanliness—and cautiously approached the intercom for the first time in her life. As she had anticipated, the phone was white. The only thing she wouldn't do was swallow the contents of any bottle labeled "Drink Me," Gigi vowed. This was Wonderland enough.

"Oh, Gigi, terrific, you're up! Did you get a decent night's sleep?" Billy asked.

"Marvelous, but I don't remember anything. Did I drink brandy last night, or is that just my imagination?"

"It wasn't a big drink . . . at least not very, purely medicinal," Billy said guiltily.

"I guess I haven't lost my memory entirely, but where am I? Where are you? What do I do now?"

"Just put on your bathrobe and I'll be there in a few minutes."

Gigi looked at her ancient plaid robe, and hastily put on the jeans and sweater she'd arrived in. Clothes didn't matter to her, but the robe looked kind of gummy. In fact it was filthy, now that she inspected it carefully. In New York it had seemed within the limits of acceptable, but the golden morning sunlight that streamed into the blue, white and yellow flowered bedroom showed stains and spots she'd never noticed before. In fact, everything in the sumptuously large bedroom existed in a different dimension of reality from anything she had ever known was possible, a dimension of never-imagined luxury that brought a shocking refreshment to her senses, as if she had wandered in the night through a black-and-white world and awakened to find herself in a Technicolor Oz. She was Alice in Oz, Gigi thought giddily, as a tap sounded on the door and Billy walked into the room, grabbing her in a firm hug.

"What do you want to eat more than anything in the world?" Billy asked.

"Oh, anything, I'm starving," Gigi said, trying to throw the robe over the foot of the bed.

"No, really. We have everything."

"Bagels, cream cheese and belly lox, please."

"There speaks a true New Yorker. I guess we don't have everything, after all. Try again," Billy laughed. Ellis Ikehorn had always truculently maintained that belly lox was better than caviar.

"Corn flakes, fried eggs sunny side up, white toast? Orange

juice?'' It was the most normal breakfast Gigi could think of on a moment's notice.

"Done." Billy picked up the phone and relayed the order to Josie Speilberg, now recovered and back in her office. "Come on, Gigi, we'll eat on the terrace."

"Haven't you had breakfast yet?"

"I'm going to watch you eat, and Josie is going to call Art's Deli in the Valley and order the best belly lox west of Manhattan."

"I don't want you to go to a lot of trouble, honestly," Gigi said in far less confusion than she would have believed possible. She had often imagined what her father's new wife would look like, but nothing could have prepared her for the breathtaking reality of Billy's height and beauty and powerful glamour, for her queenly assumptions and casual but absolute authority. Billy Ikehorn was totally outside of Gigi's experience, yet somehow she had managed to make her feel uniquely wanted. The vast inequalities between them just didn't seem to matter.

"It's fun for me," Billy said honestly. She yearned to fatten Gigi up. At sixteen she couldn't possibly have stopped growing, but even at her present, decidedly modest height she looked too fragile.

During breakfast she questioned Gigi gently, and by the time the meal was over, Billy realized that there was no one in New York with a family claim on Vito's neglected daughter. Gigi had never even known any members of her father's family, and her mother hadn't had any siblings or living parents. She was a sophomore in an average public high school, and although she knew a lot of boys, she hadn't had a romance past or present. In fact she didn't think she'd ever been in love except with James Dean in *East of Eden*, which she'd seen fifteen times. She liked all the three or four families she had stayed with when her mother was touring, but she hadn't adopted any particular one as her favorite. Gigi had the subway map of New York City engraved on her heart, and she knew a surprising lot about cooking and shopping for food, tasks she'd taken over from her mother at least five years ago.

"Gypsies don't eat right," Gigi explained, warming to her subject under Billy's interest. "They never have the time to buy fresh food and prepare a decent meal from scratch. Most of them live on Cokes and cigarettes, like ballet dancers. Mom used to worry that I wasn't getting the proper nutrition for a growing girl, so I figured it was something I could help her with. Then I found out that I loved doing it and I'm good at it. I know a lot of the out-of-the-way markets in the city—I cook Italian, American and pretty fair Chinese—I learned from friends and cookbooks. I haven't started French cooking yet, but I plan to. The thing is, even if you never make a career out of it, there's always a job for a cook. And it's a wonderful hobby.''

"Do you have any other hobbies?'' Billy asked, impressed by Gigi's enterprise.

"Not unless you count going to old movies and humming off-key. I was brought up on show tunes, original cast albums mostly, the real old stuff, Rodgers and Hart and Lerner and Loewe, *good* music. Art is my favorite class in school—I love to draw.''

"Have you ever thought about being in show business, Gigi?''

"No way. My mother . . . . died of being in show business and it certainly doesn't leave Dad with much of a life. Look at the way he's a victim of his work. It's totally pathetic.''

"I guess you could put it that way,'' Billy murmured. Vito, a victim! What a pack of lies that bastard had sold her.

"He's such a great guy,'' Gigi said with a small resigned sigh. "Of course I understood that he had to be out here where the business is, or away on location, and that there was never any reason for him to come to New York except to see me. He and Mom never got along, right from the beginning, I always knew that much. She explained to me, ever since I was old enough to understand, that Dad loved me a lot but his life was awfully difficult. Sometimes, when he was trying so hard to put together the financing for a picture, he was late with the child-support payments, but he always came through for me, no matter what. It's so wonderful that it's finally all happened for him at last,'' Gigi concluded. "I guess this is the first real home he's ever had.''

"I guess,'' Billy said, realizing that Gigi's mother had created a splendidly false picture of Vito so that his daughter would never suspect how little a part of his life she had been. Obviously she had been a woman who had put Gigi's emotional welfare ahead of what must have been her own bitterness and disappointment. Billy shuddered at the thought of what Gigi's mother's life must have been—years of a far deeper anger than she had been living with ever since Vito rushed out of the house this morning. Only the need to distract Gigi had enabled her to put it at a moderate distance, where it lurked, unfinished business ready to pounce. Until she and Vito somehow resolved the miserable argument that his breakfast appointment had cut short this morning, there was no possible way to tell him about their baby.

"I didn't know people really lived like this." Gigi finished breakfast quickly, and as she looked around her, her voice was full of an innocent, gentle wonder, as lacking in envy as if she'd found herself sharing a cave with a hermit.

"Well . . . California . . . it's sort of another world," Billy said, suddenly seeing her familiar surroundings through Gigi's eyes.

Gigi looked all around her, into a world of mythic freshness, and drew a breath of astonishment. The house was located at the highest point of the estate and so placed that from where they sat, no other houses were visible. All around them stretched romantic vistas that led the eye into tantalizing distances lit by the midmorning sun, a multitude of greens and a softness of many colors. There was a mellow European splendor to the scene, a European ripeness of bloom. After Billy had bought the charming, rambling old mansion, a well-ordered mass of white bricks, climbing vines, chimneys and the occasional, well-weathered half-timber, she had persuaded the greatest landscape designer of his age, Russell Page, an elusive legend, an English gentleman sometimes described as "taller than God and twice as frightening," to redesign the entire eleven-acre property, creating gardens of lyric harmony. Dozens of tons of earth had been moved; thousands of full-grown trees had been brought in on huge cranes; magical woodlands, olive groves, and airy glades had appeared, watercourses and reflecting pools had been threaded through the gardens; richly planted flower borders illuminated the paradise of green, the triad of sky, trees and water.

"Those men over there," Gigi said, pointing toward a group of gardeners who were visible at a distance, crossing midway down a long path created by two rows of majestic sycamores that divided a perfect sweep of lawn. "What *exactly* are they going to do, for instance?"

"Exactly?" Billy smiled at her innocent precision. "I suspect they'll sweep up dead leaves, water, deadhead the flowerbeds, weed any weed that has had the nerve to spring up overnight, remove annuals that are past their bloom and plant new ones."

"How do they know what to plant?" Gigi's question was accompanied by a look of candid curiosity. Her knowledge of plantlife was limited to parks and sidewalk flower stands.

"There's a head gardener who tells them what to do. Every week

I get together with him and we walk around and plan things—we make lists. Something always needs work. Years ago this part of California was a desert, and without constant attention and water it could revert in no time." Billy shuddered at the thought of nature.

"Do those men come every week?"

"Actually . . . every weekday." And they were just the basic work crew, Billy thought. The head gardener, who had been trained by Russell Page himself, and his assistant lived at the house. In addition there were two men in charge of the orchid house and the greenhouses in which the blooming houseplants were boarded between seasons; another man did nothing but lawns; a part-time specialist kept a sharp eye on the temperamental rose gardens, and two women fed, watered and groomed the hundreds of houseplants three full days a week. Even a few days without intensive maintenance of her gardens was unthinkable . . . . but hard to explain, especially to Gigi.

"Wow. That's neat. Never a dead leaf, is that the idea?" Gigi's smile, now that she thought she understood how it all worked, was enchanted and amazed, like a child seeing its first huge, helium-filled Mickey Mouse balloon.

"Right, dig we must for a better Holmby Hills," Billy answered, remembering that Josh Hillman, her lawyer, had standing orders with every major realtor in town to let him know before anyone else if one of the properties on the street came on the market. She intended to snap them up, one by one, bulldoze the houses, and lure Mr. Page back to extend her gardens. In addition to the unique pleasure of living with his work, these purchases would put even more distance between her place and Hefner's Playboy Mansion, which was located down her street, Charing Cross Road. Billy couldn't actually hear the inmates there doing whatever it was they did, but she didn't like living on the same winding, narrow street as the Mansion without the widest *cordon sanitaire* money could buy.

As they talked, Billy observed Gigi as casually as possible. Her eyes, which had seemed a neutral gray last night, were discovered to be an unexpectedly fresh and hopeful pale green, as young as an opening bud on a New York tree in the early spring before a speck of soot has fallen, a green that lasts only a day in nature. Billy remembered that particular green from the days before her marriage, when she and Jessica and their boyfriends would come staggering home at daybreak and realize that spring had arrived overnight. But Gigi had pale eyelashes that didn't call any attention to her eyes, and her incredibly uninteresting mess of dull, plain brown hair flopped over her eyes and hid them most of the time. First: Haircut, Billy thought, beginning a mental make-over. Next: Light brown mascara, I don't care if she's only sixteen, it's criminal not to wear a touch of mascara. After that, clothes. Everything, from the sneakers up. It didn't matter if Gigi chose to live full-time in jeans and ratty sweaters, but the girl needed new ones, or at least new ones that looked worn and tattered in the right way instead of the wrong way. Billy didn't know how she was so sure that Gigi's clothes were beat up in the wrong way, since teenagers were an enigma to her, but she was never mistaken about clothes. She was certain that she could walk through Peking and tell you which Chinese women had done a certain secret and invisible—and probably forbidden—little something to their identical jackets to give them an extra allure.

But it would all have to wait. She didn't want to impose on Gigi, she didn't want to make her feel that there was anything that should be improved about her. Billy tried to put herself in Gigi's place. She was a girl who had just lost her mother and was trying valiantly not to impose her own deep pain on a stranger; a girl who found herself transported overnight into what must be an overpoweringly grand atmosphere; a girl whose father had left her alone for the day without saying good-bye; alone with an unknown older woman who Gigi had to have learned from the media was not just plain rich but famously, *abnormally* rich. Far more famous for being rich than for owning Scruples or being married to Vito Orsini.

And yet . . . . and yet. Suddenly Billy knew whom Gigi reminded her of. Spider Elliott, of all people. He had always treated her exactly like everybody else, as if she didn't have a bean. He talked to her with the same openness as Gigi did. Her money had never impressed him worth a damn, and she felt that it didn't impress Gigi either. She *knew* it didn't impress Gigi. The house and the grounds interested her, she was curious about details and how things were done, but they didn't awe her. She wasn't mentally pinching herself, and at the same time trying to act as if her surroundings weren't new to her. This was passing strange, to say the least.

"Gigi," Billy heard herself saying with the same stealthy seductiveness as the snake in the Garden of Eden on the subject of apples, "have you always worn your hair long?"

* * *

Sara, currently the hottest hand with scissors at Vidal Sassoon's Beverly Hills Salon, was delighted to give Mrs. Orsini an appointment in half an hour. For anyone else, as Billy well knew, the wait would be a week.

"Holy Father, what have we here?" Sara asked in her quick Cockney deadpan when Gigi sat down in her chair.

"A golden opportunity for you, kiddo," Billy snapped. She wasn't going to have any of the cheeky Brits Vidal brought over from London putting Gigi down as they managed to do with half the population of the city, male as well as female. "I want you to give my young friend here a look that will do her justice, not illustrate any of your pet theories, or Vidal's either, for that matter. One trendy slash too much —just one—and we're going to find ourselves with a serious problem."

"I take your meaning, Mrs. Orsini," Sara said, lifting up the weighty mass of Gigi's totally unshaped head of hair in both hands so that she could see her hairline at the back. "Full, isn't it? Nothing you can't do when there's plenty to play with."

"You're working today, kiddo, not playing," Billy said severely, sitting down next to the hairdresser's chair.

Sara looked at her sideways and ground her teeth. Billy's grim policewoman's expression reminded her of her own mum's when she started to practice cutting on her younger sisters. The only thing worse was a mother with a handsome little boy. For the next half hour she put her scissors aside and combed and brushed Gigi's hair into dozens of different styles. Gigi and Billy watched, mesmerized. Nothing worked.

"Mrs. Orsini, I'm going to have to cut quite a bit to get anywhere," Sara said finally. "Cut and thin."

"A half-inch at a time, Sara. Just don't surprise me."

"Rightio." She set to work, as cautiously as a sculptor cutting directly into a precious piece of marble. Gradually Gigi's neck was revealed, a very white neck that, for all its extreme delicacy of shape, was exactly as strong as it needed to be to form the perfect base for her head. More and more hair fell to the floor and was swept up by an assistant almost as soon as it fell. Repeatedly, Sara partially wet Gigi's hair and blew it dry to estimate her progress. Basically it was ever-so-slightly wavy hair, she thought, and it wanted urgently to flip upward at the sides. She couldn't think of anybody who had emerged from

Sassoon's with a flip since the day he went into business for himself and produced the straight, severe, geometric, face-hugging cuts that made his fortune. On the other hand, Vidal was six thousand miles away and horrible, scary Billy Orsini was almost sitting on top of her feet.

"Mrs. Orsini, the only way to keep this hair out of the young lady's eyes is to give her bangs. There's just too much of it to hold back off her face any other way. And it wants to turn up a bit at the sides and back."

"That's what I had in mind," Billy said, smiling for the first time. "The flapper look. Louise Brooks with a flip."

"Louise Brooks?"

"Before our time. An early movie star who disappeared after a few films. Her hairstyle was famous all over the world."

"You don't say," Sara mumbled in relief, bending over Gigi now that she had Billy Orsini's accord. Talk about your control freaks! Her rival, Dusty Fleming, was welcome to her.

Ten minutes later the haircut was finished. Gigi's green eyes, under their pointed eyebrows, looked out at the world from a frame of wispy, multilayered bangs that revealed the shape of her oval forehead. When she moved her head quickly her hair moved too, with an enchanting, swaying freedom, and her pointed ears appeared and disappeared. When she held her head still, her hair still looked vitally alive down to the tips of each upward-flipping strand, each hair a tiny, independent arrow that seemed a lighter brown where it caught the light.

"Wow," said Gigi in awe. "I look . . . Wow! There's no word for it, is there? But better . . . so much better that I can't believe it. Oh, thank you, Sara!"

"It's my personal best," said Sara proudly. "Mind if I take a Polaroid? I want to send it to Vidal. Wish I'd thought to do a 'before' shot."

"Of course not," Billy said, giving her a fifty-dollar tip. Gigi looked perfect. Her elfin quality was clearly visible now. She wasn't pretty in any usual, ordinary, average way, but she was deeply intriguing to look at. Or was she just deliciously impish? Elfin, impish? Impen? Elfish? In any case, she was astonishing and undeniably chic, which was something Billy simply hadn't had the imagination to foresee. Chic at sixteen, *chic*, by God and by golly, the last thing Gigi had been at breakfast, chic, one of the great, good, miraculously permanent things you could never buy with any amount of money. That neck and head could go out to lunch in any great restaurant in the world for the next seventy years, if you wrapped the rest of Gigi in a cape down to the floor. *Lunch*.

"What time is it?" Billy asked, incredulous at her sudden hunger.

"Almost two," said Sara.

"Oh Lord, sorry, kiddo," Billy said and gave her another fifty dollars for not complaining as she had been entitled to do. "'Bye, Sara. And thanks. Maybe I'll come in next week and let you do your damnedest on me."

Billy and Gigi left the shop and a hairdresser who was both gratified—she never ate lunch anyway—and determined never to be trapped into a personal booking with Billy Orsini. But she'd do that kid again any time.

"I feel like somebody else, as if an alien has taken over my head," Gigi said to Billy after they had wordlessly gulped two small sandwiches each at the little lunch place hidden away in the gift department on the third floor of Saks Fifth Avenue. "I wish my mother could have seen me like this." Her voice was full of sadness.

"I do too, Gigi." And it could have so easily happened, Billy thought regretfully, if only her blindly self-centered husband had brought his daughter out to visit while her mother was alive. But she mustn't let the girl start looking backward or she might begin to ask some pointed questions about her father, and Billy knew that, try as she would, she might not be able to lie about Vito as effectively as Gigi's mother had over the years. She was still far, far too angry.

"You know, Gigi, you actually are somebody else," Billy said, handing her the menu for dessert, "or starting to be. Imagine Marilyn Monroe as a brunette with a bun and a center part. Well, you're twice as different as she would have been. Hair . . . is . . . destiny." Billy produced the last three words solemnly.

Gigi giggled, her expression changing. "Look, I'm just a kid, but I know you didn't really mean that."

"No, but it's the sort of thing ninety-nine percent of the people I know would let me get away with," Billy said thoughtfully. She realized that she hadn't brooded about her wrenching fight with Vito—

their first fight—since Gigi had awakened. Nor had she been fixated on telling Vito about the baby. All her attention had been focused on Gigi. She'd even forgotten to limit herself to one sandwich. This girl was addictive. And honest and smart.

"Listen, Gigi, let's just sit here for a while and sort things out."

"What things?"

"Your future plans. I know that when you got on that plane yesterday you were obeying a blind instinct to be with your father because he was all you had left. I doubt that you were thinking any further ahead than that. Am I right?"

"I just knew I had to tell him. I don't even remember what I thought about during the flight except getting here."

"But now you are here, and he does know. Have you thought about a next step?"

"Not really." Gigi shook her head in surprise at how easily she'd forgotten the future in the tumble of new impressions. "I've just been going on automatic pilot. Maybe I could spend a few more days here, if it's all right with you, before I go back. I can make up the homework I'm missing in a few hours . . . it's not exactly a school for major brains. And I think I'd like to live with the Himmels. She's an ex-gypsy and he's a stage manager. They have daughters almost my age and we're all pretty tight. My child support would cover my expenses until I'm eighteen, but I'll be out of high school and working somewhere as a sous chef by that time anyway. I can even take summer school, add a few classes next year and graduate by the time I'm seventeen and a half."

"What if you didn't go back to New York?"

"Huh?"

"What if you stayed with us, lived with us, went to school out here?"

Gigi was without words. Everything she'd seen and done since she'd arrived at Billy's had been part of a dream that had nothing to do with life as she knew it. Alice hadn't gone to live in Wonderland, she'd visited. Dorothy had returned from Oz.

"Gigi, it makes perfect sense!" Billy cried. "You *have* a father, you can't just go off and live with strangers when you have a perfectly good father. I'm sure he won't even consider letting you do it." When she saw that Gigi's expression hadn't changed, Billy summoned her most authoritative voice. "And you're going to have a brother or a sister. Last night you said you'd always wanted one. And you'd get to love California even if it isn't New York and you can learn French cooking from my chef and . . .''

"But—" How could she tell Billy, Gigi wondered, that she didn't want to be a sponge, a taker? She guessed that Vito would make a lot of money from *Mirrors*, and maybe someday he'd send for her, but right now he and Billy obviously lived on Billy's money. Her mother had speculated out loud on the subject of Dad's rich new wife many times, but she couldn't have imagined what the reality of those newspaper and magazine digits translated into. Nobody could.

"But what?"

"It's all so . . . . you're so, well, incredibly generous—but it's so much . . . you probably don't realize how . . . *much*, that's the only word I can think of." Gigi stumbled, but she knew she had to say what she thought. "Your life is so . . . . your gardens, your beds, your sheets! Even the way you talk to hairdressers, I mean, I'm just not a part of all of that, am I? I'm a New York kid, I'm a worker bee, and this place is a foreign country."

"Generous!" Billy picked up the key word, the only word that mattered in Gigi's speech. She hadn't been a poor relation for twenty-one years without learning every painful lesson about the hated feelings of obligation and not belonging. "Nonsense! Generosity had nothing to do with it. It's normal, Gigi, absolutely normal for you to come and live with us! And I promise you'd get used to living here, it's just a sort of super suburb, and all the kids go to public school just like in New York . . ." Billy fell silent, thinking nervously of the notoriously spoiled youth of Beverly Hills High. She brightened, realizing that she didn't live in Beverly Hills, so Gigi couldn't go there anyway.

"Billy, this idea of yours—it's so . . ." Gigi thought of another way to protest. "I'd be completely changing my life. How can I make that kind of decision?"

"Your life changed when your mother died," Billy answered gently. "She was your family. Now your father is your family, and I'm . . . . well, listen, I have some rights here too, I'm your wicked stepmother."

"How corny can you get?" Gigi couldn't suppress a spurt of laughter.

"I know, but it's legally true. You can't deny that your father's wife is your stepmother."

"You don't feel like a stepmother."

"What do I feel like?"

"A friend."

Billy's eyes filled with tears and she turned her head so that Gigi wouldn't see them. They sat silently for a moment until Billy reached out and grasped Gigi's hand.

"Please stay, Gigi. Stay for me. I don't want you to go away. I want a friend. I need a friend."

"Oh." Her voice was small and strange.

"'Oh'?" Billy repeated the word in confusion.

"That makes it different. Completely different. I didn't know if you wanted me or if you felt it was something you ought to ask."

"There's no 'ought' about it. I never do anything because I ought to."

"No kidding."

"Gigi, stop teasing me. Yes or no?"

Gigi turned quickly and her lips pressed firmly on Billy's cheek. "Yes! I must be crazy, but how could I possibly say no?"

After an intense hour and a half in the Saks teen department, Billy had arranged for Gigi's old clothes to be disposed of and all the new ones delivered to the house. Gigi was now clad in severely faded jeans that looked as if they had belonged to her for years of sailing and riding with Ralph Lauren, Calvin Klein, Gloria Vanderbilt and dear old Mr. Levi of Levi Strauss. Her baggy cardigan, an unnameable green between sage and emerald, had obviously been hand-knit for her great-grandmother, the young duchess, by a crofter in an Irish cottage. Her open-necked white lawn shirt had almost certainly been found in a flea market off Portobello Road and her slightly shabby, faintly tattered black velvet vest, with a jet bead or two still hanging by a thread, had been left to her by an eccentric transvestite uncle. Everything but the jeans was just a bit too big, and the jeans were the essential bit too small. The general impression was of a girl who not only hadn't the faintest idea how she'd chosen her becoming clothes, but didn't care, had never cared, couldn't be forced to care, a girl who had simply put on the first things that came to hand from a pile of stuff she kept on her floor, since she was too busy on the phone to put anything away neatly. Billy decided that Gigi should keep her canvas shoulder bag and dirty sneakers. They had an authentically cheap and utilitarian throwaway quality that couldn't be duplicated. Just as good shoes and a good bag were essential for a woman, they could be a sign of over-calculation on a teenager. New sneakers could ruin everything.

"You're sure?" Gigi asked, thrilled but still looking at herself suspiciously in the mirror.

"Positive." After the first ten minutes of browsing in the teen department, Billy had caught the wave. Her years of dedicated devotion to clothes had been focused on the stock of the department, and as she looked she mentally discarded everything that wouldn't do justice to Gigi, as well as everything that was over the top, too much of a costume. Gigi was wearing the most original of their purchases; most of the others were more standard teen gear, although Billy hadn't been able to resist some deeply funky bits and pieces.

Billy looked at her watch. It wasn't even half past four yet. She'd just phoned Dolly at the hospital and had been told that she had a "do not disturb" on her phone and regular visiting hours weren't till after dinner. She'd planned to take Gigi to see Dolly and her new baby girl as soon as possible and now, frustrated, she decided that she couldn't go tamely home after all this excitement, she had to show Gigi off to somebody who could properly appreciate her. Clearly that left only Valentine and Spider. What's more, they hadn't been in yesterday when she went looking for them, they hadn't even called to congratulate Vito, and she wanted to know exactly what they thought they were up to, neglecting the store and ordinary politeness as well. It was time for a little trip to Scruples, the one thing she had promised herself this morning that she absolutely wouldn't do because the store would just be too much for Gigi to absorb.

But that was then and this was now and Gigi had already absorbed so much new experience without being the worse for it, that a touch of Scruples couldn't hurt, Billy decided in an adrenaline high.

"I really should stop by Scruples," she said to Gigi. "You're not tired, are you?"

"Tired? I'm so excited I won't sleep all night, maybe not all week." Gigi thrust her thumbs in the pockets of her jeans and slumped. Yeah!

They walked the two blocks to Scruples, the tall, magnificent woman and the small, graceful, distinctive teenager who obviously belonged on Rodeo Drive, drawing appreciative and curious glances from dozens of passersby. As they walked, Billy told Gigi about Spider and Paris-bred Valentine, explaining briefly that they had been good friends for six years, meeting in New York in 1972 and working there, Valentine as a fashion designer and Spider as a photographer, until, two years ago, she'd hired them to help her at Scruples.

"Spider's a born-and-bred Californian," she told Gigi. "He has that typical California hair, streaky gold, like a lifeguard, and those outrageous beach blanket eyes, so blue you simply can't take them seriously, his taste is sublime but in some ways he's still a big rambunctious kid even though we're about the same age. Still, all my best Scruples customers refuse to buy a single dress if he hasn't approved of what it does for them. Valentine's something else entirely, a very passionate, serious kind of person, and very private. For reasons they haven't shared with me, they've been barely talking to each other lately, some sort of misunderstanding between co-workers, I guess, but normally they're pretty good pals and totally professional." There was no need, she decided, to confuse Gigi by any mention of Spider's underground but well-established reputation as a seducer, a charmer who knew—and kept—the sensuous secrets of a hundred women.

As they arrived at the store, Billy hustled a foot-dragging Gigi through the temptations of the first floor, heading directly up to the executive offices.

"Did they ever get back from shopping?" Billy asked Spider's secretary.

"Yes, Mrs. Orsini, they're both in their office."

Billy turned and hesitated before going in. As she'd warned Gigi, Spider and Valentine had been visibly on the outs for weeks. She didn't want their glum humor to affect the girl, but on the other hand, who else could appreciate Gigi as much as they could? And didn't they need cheering up? Didn't Gigi, far more than they? Didn't she herself, come to think of it? It would be a kindness all around. Without knocking, Billy opened the door to the office where Spider and Valentine shared an antique, leather-topped partners' desk. Billy took two long steps into the room and stopped dead, Gigi bumping into her heels.

"Oh. Sorry," she mumbled automatically and turned to flee, grabbing Gigi by the hand. Jesus Christ Almighty! Valentine was sitting on Spider's lap and he was kissing her on the lips, his arms wrapped so tightly around her that he was actually cupping her breasts. Jesus Christ Almighty! She'd seen it with her own eyes, and so had Gigi. An impressionable child. Jesus Christ Almighty!

"Billy, come back here, you idiot," Spider commanded, laughing so hard that he almost made Valentine fall off his lap.

"Not right now, I don't want to interrupt you," Billy said in desperate confusion, trying to sound as if this were something that happened every day. "I'll be back later, I'll knock next time."

"Will you get your ass in here, or do I have to come and make you?" Spider shouted while Valentine shook with laughter.

"I thought you'd gone shopping," Billy said, turning reluctantly. Oh God, Valentine was still cuddled up on Spider's lap. Billy had never seen such a look of blissed-out contentment on Valentine's alert face, such a flashing of joy in her mermaid's eyes. Had they no shame?

"Just what the hell is going on here, anyway?" Billy asked, beginning to get over her shock, but still holding Gigi's hand for moral support.

"We got married yesterday," Valentine said.

"Oh, bullshit," Billy said indignantly.

"I told you," Valentine exclaimed, delighted. "I told you that's what she'd say! You owe me twenty dollars, Spider."

"Congratulations," Gigi said, uncertain at these developments but automatically polite. "I'm sure you'll be very happy."

"You don't even know these people!" Billy said to Gigi, even more indignantly. "Why did you say that?"

"They look married to me."

"They do?"

"Definitely."

"But they can't just get married, not just like that, not without telling me, anyway they've known each other forever, they're not in love with each other . . . they . . . they . . . . they got married." Billy sat down weakly. Why was she talking to Gigi instead of to Spider and Valentine, she wondered, unable to grapple with more important questions.

"We went to Vegas, we eloped, we didn't tell anybody. You're the first to know," Valentine said, jumping off Spider and coming to kiss Billy. "You and . . . ?"

"Gigi Orsini, Vito's daughter."

"Sure, Billy," Spider said indulgently.

"Graziella Giovanna Orsini, Vito's daughter and my stepdaughter. Gigi's come to stay." Billy stated these simple words in a multileveled complexity of tone combined with a certain unmistakable look with which they were both deeply familiar. They were immediately informed that not only was this girl undoubtedly Vito's daughter, although, incredibly, they'd never heard of her, but they had better not ask any questions or display the slightest surprise at her sudden appearance.

"I'm enchanted to meet you, Gigi," Valentine said, shaking Gigi's hand and, on second thought, kissing her on both cheeks. "Welcome to Scruples."

Spider got up hastily and approached Gigi with the ease of a man who had rarely encountered a female mind he couldn't see through. "Hi," he said, looking down at her with unfeigned interest, taking both her small hands into his and holding them carefully as he inspected her with warm curiosity. "I'm happy you're here. And I know we didn't shock you. Something tells me you're more sophisticated than Billy."

"Come on." Gigi smiled up at him. "It's just that I'm from New York."

"That would explain it." Spider wondered what would account for the look in her eyes that contained an inexplicable sadness, the slight trembling he felt in her hands and the vulnerability she radiated? "Has Billy been showing you the town?"

"I have a haircut and a whole new wardrobe. If there's more to this town, I'm not ready for it."

"It takes a bit of getting used to. But since you're going to live here, Gigi, you have all the time in the world. And one day you'll wake up in the morning and wonder how you could ever have lived anywhere else and you'll look at all the people coming out of the tourist buses and taking pictures of each other on Rodeo Drive and you won't know why they're doing it when it's all so ordinary."

"That sounds like being brainwashed," Gigi said, laughing at his nonsense. How could such a spectacular-looking guy make her feel reassured, protected and appreciated, when, as a rule, exceptionally handsome men made her nervous, Gigi wondered, not knowing that hundreds of women had asked themselves exactly the same question. Maybe it was the laughing crinkles at the corners of his eyes, maybe the broken nose, maybe the chip missing on one of his front teeth, maybe just the genuinely involved tone of his voice, but magically he'd made her relax more than she had all day.

"It is being brainwashed, only we prefer to call it the California lifestyle. Gigi, you look hungry to me, and Billy, you too."

"Oh, Spider," Billy protested, "you always think women look

hungry. Gigi, believe it or not, practically the first thing Spider made me put into Scruples was a complete kitchen so our customers never had to leave for lunch and break the rhythm of their shopping."

"Didn't it work?" Spider asked.

"It tripled our business and paid for itself in two months," Billy admitted, "and I'm famished. Gigi and I had a pitiful lunch, and then we wore ourselves out shopping."

"I'm feeling faint," Gigi said hopefully.

Spider picked up the phone to the kitchen and ordered high tea, complete with cakes, scones and sandwiches for all of them.

"Spider, you forgot to ask for champagne," Billy said. "I want to toast you and Valentine, even if I still can't get straight how this happened or why I didn't even have a clue, which is what really irritates me."

"Oh, Billy, it's such a long story and it was all my fault," Valentine said joyfully. "I was so suspicious of him—he was too frivolous, this big, blond creature, this typical American beach bum with all his adoring girlfriends, too sure of himself—so I decided he could never be more than a friend."

"No, it was my fault," Spider objected, as a waiter appeared with a heavily laden tea cart and four bottles of champagne. "She frightened me off with her French superiority, so I got involved with the wrong people because I couldn't get anywhere with her."

"Oh, nonsense," said Valentine, "practically the first thing you said to me was that I was a bad-tempered bitch who lacked gratitude. Does that sound like a frightened man?"

"No, you said I *thought* that's what you were. Don't put words in my mouth," Spider corrected her.

"This sounds like the first draft of a script I'm going to be listening to for the next fifty years," Billy observed dryly. "Or is it more like a *Cosmo* article come to life? 'Men and Women, the Communication Gap'? Could we save the next installment of your mutual divine blindness until after the toast?"

Spider opened the champagne, offering a glass to Gigi with a question in his eyes. How old was she, he wondered. Fourteen, maybe?

"I started on brandy last night," she assured him, "so I'm an old hand at this."

"To Mr. and Mrs. Spider Elliott, together at last and not a minute too soon, it would seem. But let's not bother with details, I love both of you and I always will. Long life and great happiness to you both.'' Billy raised her glass and sipped deeply as the others raised theirs.

For a minute all four of them drank champagne peacefully, feeling a warmth envelop them that had nothing to do with the level of alcohol in the Dom Perignon. Spider poured more champagne, thinking that he'd never seen Billy look so glowingly beautiful. Perhaps it was Gigi, although the idea that Billy had been longing for a stepdaughter of her very own seemed farfetched, even considering that Billy had an immense capacity for hankering for things she didn't yet have.

Billy waited until the others started to circle the tea cart before picking up a phone and calling her secretary at home. No, Josie told her, Mr. Orsini hadn't called in. There were literally dozens of other messages for her, more flowers, more telegrams, but not a word from him.

"If he calls, I'm at the store," Billy said abruptly, hanging up and drinking another glass of champagne to douse the flames of her renewed anger. Normally she and Vito checked in with each other by phone twice a day, no matter how busy he was. So he was going to go out in the garden and eat worms, was he? Well, that wasn't going to stop her from enjoying herself, she vowed. Gigi was going to stay and be cherished by her, and cherish her; Spider and Val had found each other at what they insisted was long last, and what's more, Lester Weinstock, her darling Dolly's personal publicist, had just arrived in time to join the party, looking as happy as he deserved to be and carefully bearing a crumpled mound of sparkling fabric in his arms.

"Dolly sent me," Lester said, his voice almost hesitant as he looked around at the festivities, but his smile as cheerful and reassuring as ever. "Here's the dress Valentine made her for the Oscars. It finally dried out and she thought that maybe if it was sent to the cleaners . . ."

"Of course it can be rescued," Valentine interrupted, "and there's so much fabric in it that I promise when I'm finished with it she'll have two dresses instead of one, a short and a long." Billy, remembering the sight of Dolly leaving the Oscars after her water broke while the memorable wet patch of amniotic fluid on her miraculous dress was televised all over the world, drank another glass of champagne to Valentine's talent.

"She made me promise to deliver it to you personally," Lester added.

"Quite right, a dress like that must not be allowed to pass into any hands but those that understand it. But how is the baby, Lester, and how is Dolly?" Valentine vowed never to tell anyone that she and Spider hadn't watched the Oscars.

"They're both absolutely perfect. Incredibly perfect. I didn't know anything could be so perfect." Lester just stood there, never so much a tall, bespectacled, somewhat overstuffed rumpled teddy bear as at that minute. But, thought Billy, there was something very different about him from the young and unseasoned PR man she had made the studio attach to Dolly six weeks ago, after her Oscar nomination. What accounted for his new self-assurance, his visibly unbounded pleasure with all things in life, including himself?

"Lester, get yourself some champagne, sit down, say hello to Gigi Orsini, Vito's daughter, and tell me how Dolly is besides perfect," Billy ordered. "I couldn't get through to her on the phone a little while ago, they wouldn't let me. Was she sleeping, is she exhausted, will it be all right to visit her tonight?"

"She's not a bit tired," Lester said. "I had to cut off the phone. Hundreds, really hundreds of press people from all over the world want to interview her. There were a couple dozen photographers around the hospital, but they couldn't get in. Normally there's a lot of interest in the Oscar winners anyway, but with Dolly . . ."

"The circumstances were unusual," Billy said, beginning to grin as she remembered the saga, known only to her and Dolly, of Sunshine, the rodeo rider, with whom Dolly had followed the circuit for a year before they broke up. Their reunion for a Fourth of July fling had resulted in Dolly's baby.

"As her publicist, I think it's a mistake for her to talk to anybody, anybody at all," Lester declared. "It's not as if she's married."

"You know you won't be able to stop her," Billy said. "Dolly's such an innocent, short of sitting on her head . . . ."

"Yeah, and she'd probably tell them about Sunshine too," Lester said firmly. "Except I've put the lid on that."

"She told you about Sunshine?" Billy asked, stunned.

"We've told each other everything," Lester answered, beaming with pride.

Billy looked closely through his heavy glasses into his nearsighted eyes. "Lester Weinstock, I think you are trying to tell me something, so will you stop beating around the bush and spit it out, we're talking about my best friend here."

"I love Dolly and she loves me and we're going to get married as soon as possible," he declared.

"Good God! Has everybody gone crazy? You've known her only six weeks, and she was pregnant the whole time. Lester, is this a rescue fantasy?"

"If it is, she's the one doing the rescuing. Aren't you happy for us?"

"I'm . . . overjoyed . . . I think it's wonderful beyond words," Billy said, feeling the tears begin to rise. What was wrong with her today? She, who almost never wept, was leaking tears all over the place.

"Dolly's decided on the baby's name," Lester said, putting an arm around her shoulders. "Wendy Wilhelmina Weinstock. Wilhelmina for you because you're the godmother and Wendy because it goes with Weinstock. Do you approve?"

"W. W. Weinstock," Billy said slowly. "She sounds like a studio head. Very Hollywood, Lester, in the grand tradition. Of course I approve. You're marrying the best girl in the world."

Billy stood up and took the floor. "Order in this room, I demand order here! We will now drink a toast to the engagement of Lester Weinstock and Dolly Moon and their baby daughter, my goddaughter, Wendy Wilhelmina Weinstock."

In the uproar that followed, Gigi tried to count all the things that made up the California lifestyle. A stepmother who had become a friend, a major haircut, a totally new wardrobe, a promise to move three thousand miles from New York and live in the most beautiful house in the world, an elopement, an engagement, a new baby, about four glasses of champagne—and that was only since breakfast. She *adored* it here, she thought giddily, as she toasted Lester and Dolly and the newborn baby with such an impressive name. These people were even crazier than gypsies.

Billy poured herself another glass of champagne. Dolly was a wonder, she mused, a miracle of nature. She and Lester were exactly right for each other. And now that the proof was before her eyes, Spider and Valentine were exactly right for each other too. Obviously she had no natural matchmaking instincts or she would have seen it all coming long ago. If it weren't for Gigi she'd be feeling intolerably out of things, sitting here with her secret while the others drank to marriage, engagement and childbirth.

Imagine having a husband who passed out after you'd told him in plain English that you were pregnant! Vito hadn't had the decency to phone all day. If there had been a mere message that he'd called, she'd have known that he wanted to make up their quarrel. One item of faith on which Billy would bet her last dollar was that if you truly want to make a phone call, no matter how busy you are, no matter how important you are, no matter how the weight of the world is resting on your shoulders, you can do so if there's a phone available. Years ago Billy had stopped believing anybody who said, "I was going to call you, but I couldn't get a minute." But who was she to moralize, she asked herself, she who still hadn't made her apology to Valentine, who had informed her that she was pregnant two days ago when her Oscar dress wouldn't zip up. She drank more champagne, brooding, while Spider, Valentine and Lester excitedly discussed wedding and honeymoon plans, and Gigi tried to take it all in.

Gigi was used to the theatrical excess of dancers' lives, but these people made dancers look drab and ordinary. Spider Elliott was like . . . . like . . . if her beloved James Dean had grown up into a man and become two feet taller and moved like Fred Astaire and been combined with the young Gary Cooper in one of the old movies she loved so much . . . yes . . . that might almost make a Spider Elliott, Gigi decided in a haze. He had the kind of splendor she associated only with Marlboro Country and Viking sea captains or college football stars, never with real people. And Valentine . . . she was the most French thing Gigi had ever imagined, her hair the most enviable firecracker red, her eyes the most brilliantly green, her face the most expressive . . . . everything about her was perfect down to the freckles on her nose, Gigi thought, carried away by a fever of hero and heroine worship.

As Gigi looked from Spider to Valentine and back again, Billy told herself that some things demanded to be made known. Some things were ripe for the telling and would only lose their flavor if they were kept back. Some secrets were made for sharing at certain moments when a crucial mass of energy developed, when you were in the right place at the right time with the right people, or at least all of them but one. Anyway, Gigi knew and Valentine had guessed, so it wasn't really a secret anyway.

"I have another toast to propose," she said, getting up rather unsteadily from her chair. "To Valentine O'Neill, who told me something I didn't believe two days ago, Valentine, darling Valentine, as usual, you were right."

"Billy! Oh, Billy, how wonderful!" Valentine ran and hugged her, leaving Spider and Lester mystified. "You silly men, she's going to have a baby, at least give her a kiss!" Valentine laughed at their expressions as they began to comprehend what she had said.

Vito, frowning, appeared in the doorway a moment later as Billy was standing, bathed in glory, surrounded by a pandemonium of exclamations and congratulations. When he had arrived at the house and found it empty of everyone but the staff, Josie had directed him to Scruples, where, as he had expected, he had walked in to find Billy the center of attention as usual.

A small, mysteriously familiar figure flung herself at him, crying, "Dad, I'm not going to be an only child forever, and I'm coming to live with you and Billy!"

"Vito, terrific news! Do you want a boy or a girl?" Lester demanded. "I hope it's a boy, since you've already got Gigi."

Spider clapped him on the back. "Well done, Vito! Gigi arriving for good and Billy having a baby all in one day—you're a hell of a fast worker, fellow."

"Vito, it's thrilling! I'm so excited about your baby and Gigi is so delectable—you must be on top of the world! Did Billy tell you I was the first to guess?" Valentine asked.

"Vito, you'd better have a drink," Billy drawled. "You're pretty far behind the line of scrimmage."

Automatically Vito accepted a glass of champagne, automatically he arranged his face in a smile and shook his head in a way that indicated that he couldn't answer such a barrage of excitement, that he was speechless with delight. He sat down, with a look of a man in control of his life, and asked himself what kind of witch he had married, a woman who had metamorphosed herself into a prospective mother without the slightest communication with him, without a word of consultation or warning, without mutual agreement that they both were ready for a child or, at the very least, some private announcement. What kind of way was this to hear such news, having it babbled at him from everybody but Billy? And meanwhile, in a few hours, she had used her crafty wiles to put her unmistakable stamp on his daughter, at least he supposed it was still Gigi who called him "Dad," to take it entirely upon herself to arrange Gigi's life, and to announce her future to everybody.

"Cheers," Billy said so quietly that the others couldn't hear. She looked at him hard and raised her glass.

"Cheers?" Vito replied. "Cheers to the winner? I guess I'm the only one who didn't realize that this was a contest."

3

A week later, Maggie MacGregor and Vito sat having lunch in the Polo Lounge of the Beverly Hills Hotel. Maggie had her customary command-center booth, placed to the left of the door, so that she could observe everyone who came and went. However, when she didn't want to be interrupted by greetings she positioned herself with her back to the door, in a way that indicated to everyone in the industry that she was doing an interview and would welcome no intrusion. As she and Vito drank white wine and consumed their Cobb salads, a double operation was taking place in Maggie's alarmingly alert mind. On the one hand she was listening intently, her round, Coca-Cola brown eyes focused and serious. In her capacity as a journalist she was the first, as was her right, to hear Vito's earliest plans for the film production of *The WASP*, now that all the contracts to the rights to the book had been signed and Curt Arvey's studio's check for the down payment of half a million dollars had cleared the bank. On the other hand, in her capacity as a female, and one who had hankered after Vito for the four years after their affair ended, she was trying to figure out the exact nature of his mood. She was too tough an interviewer and too shrewd and intuitive a woman to be entirely convinced that Vito's new project was the only thing on his mind.

There was some other quality, a kind of an edge or shadow, coupled with a forced over-intensity, an overinsistence in his apparent singlemindedness, that made every inquisitive hair on her head rise slightly off her scalp. The Vito Orsini she had first met in Rome four years ago, with his formidable aura of invincibility, was here in the flesh but not entirely in the spirit. Something was up with Vito, something not quite kosher, and she suspected that it didn't have to do with movies or their production. Vito's energy level, usually twice that of other men, lacked its full focus. His tone of voice sounded a shade less vibrant than usual, as if he'd forgotten to consume plutonium for breakfast. He still radiated the control of a maestro, a virtuoso, a man for whom the words "make haste slowly" would be utterly meaningless, but there was something . . . . something bitter? . . . . about him. Bitter or gloomy? Or possibly disappointed?

But how could he be any of these things, Maggie asked herself. He had received the ultimate accolade of the industry, and with his new picture still in the earliest, blue-sky phase of development nothing yet could have dimmed that glory. Hell, if a Best Picture Oscar didn't give Vito total joy for at least a week, what would? And now he was about to make a film of the book for which the record-breaking price of a million and a half had been paid by Arvey's studio. He should be flying. Well, she wasn't the most powerful woman in television reporting because she hesitated to ask questions, Maggie reflected, and spoke with her usual tact.

"Vito, what the fuck's wrong with you?"

"Nothing! You're absurd, Maggie."

"Have I ever been absurd since you've known me, pal?"

"A fool, yes. Infinitely foolish. But absurd . . . well, there's always a first time."

"Maybe so, but it hasn't happened yet. What's going on? And I'm not asking as a reporter, just as your friend."

Vito drew a deep breath, put down his fork and allowed a silence to hang between them. Finally he spoke in an altered tone, acrid and touched with self-pity. "Maggie, could you just explain to me why it is that at the minute, at the absolute point in time that one thing finally goes right, something else goes wrong?"

"It's the first rule of the universe. The double Big Bang theory. I think I was about ten when I figured that one out. Aren't you a little old for such revelations?"

"Apparently not."

"So it's Billy."

"I didn't say that!"

"What else could it be? You only have time for one and a half things in your life at the same time, and since it isn't the new picture it's got to be your home life."

"You want to know what her problem is?" Vito exploded. "She's never found out that a man can't possibly be successful and competitive in this business without being an egoist, without self-interest driving him every minute of every day, without a full measure of toughness and ruthlessness and utter determination to let nothing get in his way. Maggie, you know this town, you know that it takes balls like that, in fact that's the minimum you have to have just to begin with. But Billy never had to fight hard for anything in her life. My God, Maggs, she's one of the richest women who's ever lived! Naturally she thinks that thoughtfulness and infinite consideration and floods of warm, emotional, tender puppyshit are standard equipment in a man, or if they're not, they should be. I wonder how that first husband of hers ever managed to keep those illusions of hers intact, but of course he'd made his fortune by the time they met, the man was sixty and she was twenty-one, and he made a life out of spoiling her. Before me, Billy's never known a self-made man who was in the middle of his career."

"Is she giving you a hard time because you're totally involved with the new picture? Come on, Vito, I know the amount of effort it took to make *Mirrors* a success, didn't she learn anything then?"

"I guess so," Vito said vaguely, shrugging.

"So it isn't an attention problem," Maggie said judiciously. "Sex? I never deal that out, although with you I'd really doubt it. Major, *major* doubts, Vito, all power to you. Money problems? Hardly. Hey, Vito, when you eliminate money and sex and attention, what's left? Doesn't she admire your character?" Maggie smiled wryly at her own last words. In her experience, producers' wives learned early not to judge character too closely.

"She thinks I'm not a good father."

"Oh, Vito, give me a break! I thought you were going to level with me."

"It's serious. I did a very stupid thing. I never told her that I had a kid by my first marriage—"

"You didn't tell me, either," Maggie interrupted in indignant astonishment. "Not the marriage and not the kid, but, after all, I'm not your wife. Billy must have been royally pissed."

"Damn it, Maggs, it just didn't come up, somehow. It has nothing to do with anything—the marriage was a mistake from the day it happened—the only problem was that it produced a child. She's sixteen now, a good kid, but not anything I'd ever planned on, believe me. Gigi—that's her name—showed up here unexpectedly the day after Billy found out that she was pregnant. The timing was as bad as it could have been."

"You are not, definitely not, a good father, Vito." Maggie shook her head so hard that every curly cowlick on her charming head bounced. "I have to agree with Billy."

"But does that make me a total shit?"

"Not total. Not enough to seriously bother me. But Billy probably expected more of you."

"She expects everything, Maggie, everything you can imagine, including the perfect papa, past, present and future. And for Billy, 'expect' is a verb that means 'want.' Her wants are her laws. I admit that I didn't have an acceptable excuse, but I'm not a monster. So what happens? Right underneath the surface I feel this huge current of suspicion and doubt coming from her. Billy's like a bird hatching an egg, ready to attack anyone who comes near. I wish I could just ignore it, it's the last thing I need now, but it's getting to me, even you noticed it."

"Is Billy so perfect that she has a right to expect so much from you?" Maggie asked silkily.

"Now stop that! I know you don't like her, Maggs, I shouldn't be spilling all this stuff, not even to you, but there's nobody else I trust. Obviously Billy's not perfect, nobody is, God knows I'm not, but she's my wife and she's got to take me as I am."

" 'Got' or no 'got,' she obviously doesn't."

"Do you think that's too much to ask?"

"How would I know, Vito? I've never been married."

"Stay that way, there's a lot to be said for it. Oh fuck, strike that,

Maggie, I just don't want to be made to feel that I'm in the wrong. *Even when I am.*"

"Oh, I do adore you, Vito! Not many men could say those words with such a sense of righteousness. You're a rotten father, but at least you're honest. When is Billy going to have this baby?"

"In six or seven months. As far as I understand it she's barely pregnant, although with all the fuss you'd think the baby was going to be born today."

"By the time that happens you'll have turned into a decent enough father, believe me, I've seen the process time after time, even in this town."

Maggie decided to digest Vito's personal communications at her leisure. She'd never heard Vito talk at length about himself before. He'd never discussed his marriage except in the most casual and superficial way. Her new trove of information was too splendidly juicy even to think about now. And her interviewer's timing told her it was time to change the subject.

"Tell me more about your conversations with John Huston," she asked, shifting gears smoothly. "How come you haven't signed Fifi Hill to direct the new picture? He did such a brilliant job on *Mirrors*. After all, he got an Oscar too."

"*Mirrors* was a two-million-dollar picture, *The WASP* is going to come in at twenty, if I'm lucky. I need a major, *major* name director, somebody who's made it beyond a shadow of a doubt. Fifi's got a dozen good offers to pick from, so he can't complain. But what a coup it would be if I can get Huston."

"What a headache."

"I can handle him."

Not necessarily, thought Maggie with a swell of fizzing anticipation, violent curiosity and pleasurable wickedness rising in her belly, not if you can't handle Billy Ikehorn, that spoiled, rich, ten-foot-tall twat you just had to go and marry when you could have had me.

"I've checked out the school situation, Mrs. O.," Josie Speilberg told Billy when she came back from a solitary stroll under the path of sycamores that generally restored her soul to some semblance of tranquillity. "There are only two possibilities for Gigi. She can go to Westlake in Bel Air, or she can go to Uni, that's University High, the nearest public school. I would certainly recommend Westlake."

"Will they really take her in the middle of the second semester?"

"They'd be making a big exception for you, but yes, after they'd interviewed Gigi and given her their usual tests. You know, it's considered the finest private school in Los Angeles and it's all girls. Very suitable, I think."

"What about Uni?"

"They have some three thousand students and a very high percentage of National Merit Scholarships. The children are mostly local, from Brentwood mainly, but there's also a large and definite presence of inner city youngsters, most of them bused in. Of course it's coed." Josie sniffed meaningfully at the unsuitability of such raging democracy. Whatever Mrs. O. decided was law with her and had been ever since she first started working for her back in the days when Ellis Ikehorn had been slowly dying at the estate high in Bel Air, but she retained her right to indicate an opinion, if not to express it outright unless directly invited.

"Gigi would be better off at Uni," Billy decided immediately. "She'd probably feel out of place at Westlake. It's small, with a magnificent campus, but it's filled with rich girls, the local elite. Didn't Shirley Temple go there, and Candy Bergen?"

"Westlake also has its scholarship girls, like any other private school."

"Uni, Josie, Uni. Where does the school bus stop?"

"There isn't one, Mrs. O. When I called the L.A. School District, they hadn't even heard of Holmby Hills. Nobody from around here goes to Uni, just absolutely nobody. They finally condescended to look us up on the map and said Gigi would have to take the city bus!" Josie bristled with outrage.

"She'll have to be driven. Pick some reliable man on the staff and tell him to use one of the house cars," Billy said, referring to the vans that shuttled back and forth, picking up various supplies for the kitchen and the garden. "As soon as Gigi learns to drive, she can take herself to school. I'm going to get her a little car, when she's ready."

"Of course, Mrs. O." Josie wondered what vehicle her boss meant by "a little car." An automobile, varying from a second-hand VW to a new BMW, was traditional for all the local boys over sixteen, but not necessarily the girls. Personally she thought it was silly to have such a big establishment without a chauffeur, but Los Angeles people rarely did. In Grosse Pointe, where Josie had started her work as a personal secretary, people kept their chauffeurs properly busy.

"Can Gigi start school on Monday?" Billy asked, as she left the room.

"Certainly. I'll make all the arrangements."

Who, Josie Speilberg wondered, should be tapped to drive Gigi to school? It wasn't more than a ten-minute trip, but still somebody had to be responsible for getting her there on time and picking her up every afternoon. She took out the list of live-in household staff from her desk and pondered. She had hired them all herself, when Billy had moved into the house after Ellis Ikehorn's death, and she ran a tight ship.

William, the butler, had to be available to serve breakfast and afternoon tea, so he was out. Jean-Luc, the chef, also had to be on call all morning and at teatime. Young Gavin, the head gardener, was up and out at dawn, carefully supervising the all-important watering crew before the sun had a chance to climb. She couldn't ask him to leave his precious tasks, and his assistant, Diego, served as Gavin's indispensable translator to all the Spanish-speaking workers. Except for Gavin and Diego, all the garden and greenhouse workers lived out, and she didn't want to mess with their schedules. It was too hard to find careful, consistent people, and Mrs. O., otherwise far from godlike, would notice every wilted flower petal, if not every bird that sang. Any one of the three maids who lived in the house, or the second cook or the full-time laundress-cum-seamstress, both of whom lived out, could manage to add the chauffeuring to their duties, but Mrs. O. had specified a man, so a man it must be.

Which left Burgo, the full-time, live-in handyman. Burgo washed the cars, gassed them up and kept the garage spotless; Burgo touched up paint on almost a daily basis; Burgo knew, almost before something went wrong, how to fix the glitches in the plumbing or electricity, and when the problem was too deeply rooted for his talents he knew the professionals to call. He had a special ability to rustle up the overburdened phone repairman to service the antiquated system they had never had time to modernize since Mrs. O.'s marriage, he oiled squeaky doors and replaced light bulbs and oversaw the weekly window-washing crew. Burgo, in effect, was the husband—or perhaps the wife?—of the house, and how other people managed without a Burgo, bless his heart, was a question Josie never dared ask. However, ever since she had lured him away from the Playboy Mansion by a substantial increase in his wages, Burgo seemed perfectly happy with his room and his food and the company of his co-workers. Burgo O'Sullivan it was, then. After all, what was a handyman for?

"Oh rats, Burgo, is there anything worse than starting in a new school?" Gigi was plaintive and suddenly homesick for New York. Burgo, a cozy, cheerful, middle-aged man with faded red hair and a good smile, inspired her confidence, which was in short supply this morning.

"It's a big place, and there's safety in numbers," he said.

"I used to go to a big school, and every new kid stood out as if she were standing in a spotlight, so don't soft-soap me, Burgo."

"You look just like the rest of them, and you're probably just as far ahead in your classes as they are."

"Great, that's supposed to make me feel better?"

"No, just not worse. I know it's tough, but after today you won't be new anymore, think of it that way. Make just one single friend and that's all you need to start you out on the right road."

"Ah, Burgo O'Sullivan, you're an Irishman all right."

"And what would you know about that, may I ask?"

"My mother was an O'Brian. She used to drag out the same kind of traditional blarney."

"And wasn't she right?"

"Most of the time. All right, Burgo, me boy, I feel better. Happy now? I can't wait to be looked over by a whole class of new kids, all of them dying to be my first friend. If only I were about five inches taller, blond and a surfer."

"Yeah, but the smaller girls catch more boys," Burgo said thoughtfully. "Boys your age are mostly too short for the girls, but you can have your pick."

"I don't like boys," Gigi said, annoyed. "They have zits, they smell and they don't know how to have a conversation."

"You will. In fact I'd lay odds. Here we are," Burgo said, pulling up and stopping curbside near the driveway to the school. "That's the faculty parking lot, over there. I'll be back for you there at three-thirty on the dot." He leaned out of the van and greeted a maintenance man who was standing nearby.

"Stan, I didn't know you started work so early," Burgo said. "This is Gigi Orsini, she's starting school today."

"'Morning, young lady. I didn't know you'd become a driver, Burgo."

"New assignment. I'm coming up in the world. You on for poker night, Stan?"

"When have I ever missed a game?"

"Never."

"Poker!" exclaimed Gigi. "I *love* poker! And I'm good! Can I come?"

"Guys only, Gigi, and you'd have to be a little older." Burgo chuckled at her eager expression. At least she looked in a better mood than she had when they'd started out. "Now out you go. Good luck!"

"Top of the mornin' to you, Mr. O'Sullivan." Gigi thumbed her nose at him, raising her eyebrows fiercely, and produced as false and toothy a grin as she could. She jumped out of the car, shrugged her shoulders, took a deep breath and sauntered away, in no visible rush to find her new homeroom.

A week later, in the early evening, Billy returned to the house after an appointment with her gynecologist, Dr. Aaron Wood. Her exhaustion was perfectly normal, he'd told her. The first trimester of pregnancy was often the most tiring, and she wasn't into her fourth month yet, as far as he could determine. Her projected due date would vary by as much as several weeks, he warned her, since she couldn't be certain when she'd become pregnant.

Billy sank down onto a chaise longue in the yellow and brown sitting room of the suite she and Vito shared. The smallish room, with its walls entirely hung with shirred paisley, was decked out today in a great abundance of flowering spring bulbs; baskets of jonquils, daffodils and fragrant yellow and white freesia stood on the tables, and potted white azalea trees in full bloom banked the sides of the fireplace in which a fire had been lit an hour before her return. She closed her eyes, let her shoes slide to the floor, and tried to relax in the warmth and perfumed air, but weary as she was, her body refused to unwind and her mind rejected the efforts she made to let it float. Instead she found herself yet again circling around the situation with Vito.

Since the morning after Gigi's arrival, she'd been careful not to confront him with any additional reproaches about his past treatment of the girl. Gigi was too dear to her now for her to get into any fruitless discussion with Vito about what he could have done better in the past.

Part of her silence was due to her reluctant realization that she'd been carried away that afternoon at Scruples. Even all the champagne she'd drunk, even the forty-eight hours of silent frustration while she'd guarded her secret, didn't excuse the fact that she should have told Vito about the baby before anyone else. But what difference would it have made? she asked herself for the hundredth time. That night, after they'd come home, he'd said all the conventional things about being happy about her pregnancy, but to her ears his words had sounded like a formula. She didn't know what she'd expected, Billy thought unhappily. Vito was such a volatile man that he might have danced for joy or burst into tears or . . . or . . . anything but the totally conventional response he'd made. And since then he'd been so busy that he hadn't arrived home until right before dinner with her and Gigi. In fact he'd skipped dinner several times for meetings with various potential scriptwriters, agents and other such gentry. After dinner Vito went back to the phone in his office in the house, reaching the people he'd missed during the day. His working life, or what he referred to as "being in development," seemed to have degenerated into one phone call after another, each blending into the next, interrupted only by meetings that gave birth to more phone calls to arrange more meetings. When was the last time they'd had a quiet hour alone together? Billy wondered, just as Vito walked into the room.

"I didn't expect you before eight," she said in surprise.

"Redford's agent had to catch a plane," Vito explained. "Drink?" he asked, heading toward the butler's pantry.

"No, thanks. I can't touch alcohol without a headache. Anyway, the doctor said not to. How's the picture going?"

"So far, so good. It's too soon to celebrate, but I'm almost certain I have a lock on Nicholson, and Redford's just about in the bag. We're down to negotiating the pieces of the profit, so it's basically a question of money and I'm willing to give them what it takes, I just don't want to make it too easy. Of course, what they both want to know is, who plays the girl?"

"Who plays the girl?" Billy inquired, wishing she gave a damn, wishing she weren't mortally tired, wishing she didn't feel slightly sick to her stomach all the time, not just in the mornings, wishing Vito would ask how she was, wishing she and Vito weren't being so damned unnaturally polite to each other, wishing, in spite of her fatigue, that they had to dress and rush out to a party so they wouldn't have to continue to be polite all through dinner alone together because Gigi had been invited to a sleep over by the girl she described as the neatest of her five—or was it fifteen?—new best friends.

"Dunaway or Fonda on the one hand," Vito answered. "Streep on the other. I won't even take a call from any of their agents until the actors' contracts are signed, but I'm ready to bet that I can get whoever I want. The question is, which one is most obviously the right wife for Redford?"

"It's a problem," Billy agreed, thinking that none of them were obviously right for Redford, in fact they all seemed obviously wrong, but Vito was only interested in casting one of the top stars in the business. On the other hand, what did it matter? Streisand had been obviously the wrongest possible wife for Redford, but Billy had cried buckets at the end of *The Way We Were.*

"Maybe Streisand?" she suggested, trying to show an interest.

"Streisand!" Vito put his drink down with a bang. "For Christ's sake, Billy, haven't you *read* the goddamned book? Redford marries a girl from his own background, she's a bigger WASP than he is, if such a thing is possible. *Streisand!*"

"It was a joke, Vito."

"The hell it was," he said accusingly. "You weren't even paying attention."

"You're right. I must have been thinking about something else," she said coldly.

"And what's that supposed to mean? As if I didn't know."

"As if you didn't know what, Vito?"

"That you're sitting there building up your grudge against me," he said, suddenly ferocious. "Every single day since Gigi showed up, you've been working on that grudge, nursing it, building it up; Vito Orsini the terrible father, Vito the irresponsible, Vito the man without a heart, Vito from whom you rescued poor pitiful Gigi and turned her into a princess with a wave of your magic wand, Vito who isn't so totally gaga, so worshipful, so thrilled out of his mind that he's unable to think about anything else but you and your sacred, world-shaking pregnancy, Vito who will unquestionably turn out to be a dreadful father to this child, just as he was to Gigi . . ."

So this was what had been brewing, Billy thought. She should have known. He was full of guilt, and now he was turning it against her. Her exhaustion vanished as she pushed herself up from her reclining position.

"I get the picture," Billy said in an infuriatingly temperate tone.

"You really don't have to keep on and on like that, Vito, working yourself up into a lather. You can't imagine how utterly childish and ridiculous you sound."

"You're incapable of seeing yourself at all." Vito's voice got louder as he was stung by her words. "You think you can scream accusations at me at the crack of dawn one day and then give me the cool, calm, superior treatment for the next two weeks as if nothing had happened and that makes it all right, we can just go on from there. Well, I have news for you. I won't stand for it! I won't put up with it! I don't intend to live this way!"

"Well, aren't we having a nice little tantrum? Why don't you just lie down on the carpet and kick your heels in the air?" Billy stood up, collected and icy. "I don't intend to try to talk to you when you're like this."

"We're going to talk about this now, so sit the fuck down, Billy," Vito raged, putting both of his hands on her shoulders and forcing her back in the chaise. "Now you listen to me. I don't *owe* you any excuses. I am exactly the man I was when you met me, nothing's changed, and I refuse to apologize for anything in my past. There are explanations—not excuses but explanations—that I could have given you so maybe you'd understand why I was less than a good father to Gigi, but you never asked me about them, never gave me a chance. No, you jumped right away to the worst conclusions and you rushed like a fireman into a burning building to save her, make her over, fix her up, turn her into *your* child—"

"Forgive me for interrupting, but that simply isn't—"

"Shut up, I haven't finished. So now you're pregnant. I wasn't consulted, I wasn't part of the decision, but fine, swell, when you wanted a baby it's typical that you wouldn't have bothered to find out how I felt about it. Whatever you want, you get, that's your pattern. I'll attempt to be a decent father, try to give me that much credit at least. I didn't like hearing about it after everybody else in the world, but what the hell, what's done is done. No, don't interrupt! What I want you to understand, what I insist that you understand, is that the fact that you're pregnant *does not* make everything else in *my* life unimportant—oh no, that's where you're dead wrong, Billy."

"Vito, I don't think—" Billy interrupted.

"Shut up, I'm not finished," he shouted. "I've got a movie to make. *WASP*'s going to be a major movie, a big picture, the biggest one that'll be made this year. It's the chance I've been struggling for since the first day I've been in the business. I'm making this movie twenty-four hours a day, the way you're making a baby, and I'm just as involved with *WASP* as you are in being pregnant. That's the way it is—the way it would be with any man in my position—and you've got to accept it and stop acting like a fucking Sacred Vessel. Your money totally isolates you. You don't live on the same planet as ordinary mortals, you can't possibly realize or even care how vital this is to me. There's no big stake in it for you—whatever happens, it won't change your life one little bit, will it? Do you think producing pictures is just my *hobby*, for Christ's sake? It's been my life for eighteen years, *my life*, understand? You'd better get out of that ego-centered, self-absorbed, sable-lined, solid-gold space capsule of yours and start trying to turn into a real human being, because otherwise it's going to be one hell of an impossible year.''

Billy stood up, as tall as she was, and looked him in the eye without a hint of an expression on her face. "It seems to be starting out that way, doesn't it?" she said calmly, and walked out of the room, shutting and locking the door to the bedroom firmly behind her.

Billy sat in the window seat in her dressing room, to which she had retreated after Vito's tirade, so dumbfounded that she didn't move for an hour. Finally she picked up the phone and dialed Josie Speilberg at home.

"Josie, I have to fly to New York unexpectedly tomorrow on Scruples business. Can you possibly do me a great favor and sleep in one of the guest rooms until I get back? Mr. Orsini's schedule is irregular, and I don't want to leave Gigi here alone with just the staff after you go home."

"Of course, Mrs. O. No problem. There's no reason to worry about Gigi. She's got Jean-Luc totally in her power. After school they're working on the basic steps that go into making French sauces. She's on the phone with her friends for hours every day. I don't know when she finds time for her homework, but she does. I'll keep Gigi company at dinner, and get her to bed on time."

"Could you call my pilot for me, please? Tell him I'll want to take off by nine, and send a car and driver here at eight. I'll be all packed and ready to go. And order another car in New York."

"Shall I make hotel reservations?"

"Not unless I call you back. I'll probably stay with Mrs. Strauss. You can reach me there."

"Certainly, Mrs. O. Have a good trip."

"Thank you, Josie. Good night."

Billy hung up and dialed Jessica Thorpe Strauss on Fifth Avenue.

"Jessie, darling, I'm terribly sorry to call so late . . . Oh, good, I was afraid you might be asleep. Listen, I've got to see you. Can I come tomorrow and stay for a few days? Oh, wonderful! I'll get there just before dinner. No, I can't talk about it now. See you tomorrow."

Galvanized by having taken action, Billy started to put a few things into a suitcase. When she was packed she unlocked the bedroom door. There was no one in the sitting room. She got some tomato juice, fruit and crackers from the butler's pantry, and returned to her room, not bothering to lock the door. Where Vito would sleep tonight was of no concern to her. After his charming little performance tonight she assumed it would not be in any house of hers.

"I'd have bashed him with a bookend," Jessica exclaimed, "and if I'd killed him by accident, no jury in the world would have convicted me. How *could* you have listened to all that load of vile crap and stayed so calm?"

"I still can't figure it out," Billy answered, as unnaturally calm as she had been for the entire flight to New York. "The worse he got, the more I froze. Every word seemed to sever a nerve, a connection between us. I looked at him raving away, twisting everything that had happened, making up stuff that hadn't happened, and there seemed to be an actual sheet of glass between us . . . . . as if we were in different rooms . . . . as if he was on a stage and I was in the audience. It was Vito, but it wasn't Vito. I couldn't believe I was married to that man. And I still can't. It's so eerie. I don't know how I *should* be feeling. We've never had a fight like that before. I still feel more numb than anything. All I could do was mock him, I couldn't get up any fight. And now I can't seem to feel as angry as I know I should be. Do you suppose it's because of the baby? A protective cocoon or something?"

Billy sipped on a cup of the mint tea Jessica had brewed in the lush little boudoir she called her "office." It was the one room in her large apartment overlooking Central Park where no one was allowed to enter, a necessity considering the constant importuning of her five children and her husband, David, who was away at an important investment-banking function in Boston. Jessica trained her myopic eyes on her friend. Billy's last bewildered words alarmed her more than any of the vile things Vito had said.

"Do you remember," Jessica said carefully, "when I came out to visit you last summer and you told me how desperately you hated having to be the producer's perfect, invisible, useless wife while Vito was shooting *Mirrors* on location?"

"I'm not likely to forget."

"And I asked you why you didn't get a divorce and you said you were absolutely mad about him—in fact, your exact words were that you 'couldn't live without the fucker'?"

"And then you told me it was just post-honeymoon depression and that in a few months I wouldn't even remember it," Billy said. "Maybe you're *not* the person I should always flee to for advice."

"Possibly, but who else is there?"

Billy smiled quizzically at her tiny friend. She'd been getting advice from Jessica Thorpe since 1962, Jessica Thorpe from the oldest of Rhode Island families; Jessica Thorpe of the Pre-Raphaelite hair, the lavender eyes, the summa cum laude, Vassar-trained brain and the irresistible droopiness of each of her delicate little features; Jessica Thorpe, who had turned into her best friend in the first five minutes of their meeting, who had educated her thoroughly about men and sex and seen her safely through all the affairs she'd had before she met Ellis Ikehorn.

"Nobody. You're stuck with me," Jessica said briskly. "Tell me this, if you weren't in a foaming rage, how come you jumped into your plane and came straight here? We could have talked about it on the phone."

"No, I had to see you. I had to have a reality check. *Am I* that person he said I am? You're the only grown-up I trust to be honest with me except—well, maybe Spider Elliott, and I certainly couldn't ask him. I know that my money keeps me from having to deal with the problems everyone else has, so . . . . well, could he be right? Am I that self-righteous and self-absorbed?"

"Your money doesn't stop you from being human, Billy. Don't start thinking that way. Money can only prevent you from having to worry about the material things that everybody else worries about, money gives you more time to worry about the essentials."

"Ah, Jessie . . . ."

"No, I'm not saying that just to make you feel better. I knew you when you didn't have a bean, and you haven't changed in the important elements of your character, except you've grown up a little. Sure, you have your own jet and a hundred and twenty-five gardeners and the biggest, best-stuffed closet and fanciest store in the world. You're demanding and perfectionistic and obsessive, but you were that way when I met you, you just couldn't afford to act on it. You're still Billy Winthrop, you're generous and loyal and your instincts are basically decent and you've never been self-righteous in your life. You were a wonderful wife to Ellis and you've tried like hell to be a wonderful wife to Vito. Of course you're self-absorbed from time to time, but tell me who the devil isn't the center of her own universe? I still am, and I'm proud of it. With five kids, my healthy self-interest is the only thing that keeps me sane. Do you think they aren't each the center of their own personal universes?'' Jessica blew her permanently too-long bangs out of her eyes with an indignant puff.

"When you get pregnant for the first time at thirty-five,'' she continued, "it's totally normal to be involved with how you feel. What's not normal is Vito's *anger*. That's what bothers me the most. Everything he said came from anger, and I just don't see what right he has to be angry at you. I wonder . . . is it possible that he's afraid of something and is covering it up with anger?''

"The only thing in his life now is *WASP*. . . . Why would he be afraid?''

"He's made nothing but low-budget pictures for eighteen years, right? When you met Vito he had some successes and some failures behind him, but basically he was hanging on by a thread. Remember how you told me that when he met you he cheerfully admitted that his last three pictures had lost money? *Mirrors* was a fluke, a lovely little picture, but a very long shot to win the Oscar. Suddenly, literally overnight, Vito's a giant success. Could it be that? The change, the challenge?''

"From being *afraid* to being *angry* to being *mean* . . . to me? Really rotten, shitty mean? Would success cause that? Is that a logical progression in any way?''

"I just don't know. I don't know Vito at all, Billy. It certainly wouldn't work that way for my David—I'm just asking questions, playing detective.''

"No.'' Billy shook her head decisively. "Vito's always been so fearless, Jessie. That was the first quality I recognized in him, a fearlessness. He's a man who never worried about *if*s, he just forged on with it, making it happen. That's been the way he's been working on *WASP*, full speed ahead, no questions asked, a sense of his time having come at last. No, it isn't fear, I wish it were that simple. Then I could begin to understand him."

"We may never know what's going on with him, since man is not an animal that chooses to communicate with its mate," Jessica sidestepped, too angry with Vito to trust herself to speculate further on him without saying something Billy might never forgive her for. "Tell me more about Gigi."

"I can see that she's mourning her mother, even though she keeps so busy that someone else might not realize it," Billy said slowly. "It'll be a long time before she gets over that loss . . . maybe you never do. I never knew my mother, but I have such respect for the woman Gigi's mother must have been . . . she brought her up to be so self-reliant, so straightforward, she's interested in the whole world, at ease with all kinds of people. She fit into her new school right away. She's wildly popular already, and thank God, she's not interested in boys yet. That's when I'll have to start to worry."

"Just don't come to me for advice about adolescents," Jessica said. "Each one of mine presents a revoltingly different set of problems. They ought to meet Gigi, it might shape them up."

"Wait a minute, Jessie! Wouldn't David junior be just about the right age for Gigi, not now, but when she gets interested in boys? They could get married, have lots of children and we'd be the joint grandmothers!"

"If she'd take David junior off my hands, consider it done," Jessica laughed, delighted to have taken Billy's mind off Vito for a minute. She went to make more tea, remembering how worried she had been when her friend had decided to marry someone she had known for only a week. Talk about asking for trouble!

Last summer, when Billy had been so unhappy, feeling like an outsider on the *Mirrors* location, she had spoken to her sagely of the necessity of making compromises in married life, even quoting Edmund Burke to her. But now, Jessica thought savagely, she'd be incapable of advising Billy to compromise with a man who had, by Gigi's own account, spent almost no time at all with her during her entire childhood. If he hadn't given a damn about his first child, why should he turn into a good father to Billy's child? What a brutal bastard he was to abuse her verbally at this vulnerable time in her life. How could Billy not be as furious at him as she was herself? Or was Billy unconsciously preventing herself from getting as enraged as she damn well should be, because she was pregnant by the son of a bitch and didn't dare admit to herself how bad the prospects looked?

If she really spoke her mind, Jessica thought, turning off the electric kettle as it boiled, she'd have to tell Billy that Vito had become a shit *because* of his success, not because he was afraid of it. She'd have to say that he'd behaved decently so long as he was in a down position, but now that he was top dog, he was able to express his resentment of Billy's wealth. Few men, if any, wore well in marriage to women who were far richer than they, much less a woman as rich as Billy. But she wasn't going to speak her mind, because maybe, just maybe, she was wrong and everything was going to work out. Maybe the Oscar wasn't a curse.

"Mint or chamomile, Billy?"

"I'll live dangerously. Make it instant espresso this time, dearie. Decaf, of course."

Josie Speilberg's relationship with Vito's secretary, Sandy Stringfellow, was a cautious one. Sandy had worked for Vito for seven years, almost as many as Josie had worked for Billy, and they treated each other with all the punctilious protocol of ambassadors from neighboring countries that live in peace with each other yet remain on guard for any power play, any frontier invasion. They were too totally loyal to their respective bosses for them to regale each other with the inside gossip that made the mafia of Hollywood secretaries so strong, yet they kept each other informed of Billy's and Vito's whereabouts as a matter of course, without specific instructions to do so. Hollywood secretaries need to know, on a twenty-four-hour basis, where to reach people, and after hearing from Billy the morning after her arrival, Josie called Sandy to tell her that Billy would be in New York for a few more days.

"Shopping for maternity clothes?" Sandy asked.

"I imagine Mrs. O.'ll have them made at Scruples," Josie answered.

"And why not?" Sandy was tart.

"That's what I'd do, if I weren't beyond my childbearing years."

"I can't wait to be safely postmenopausal like you, Josie. It's such a bore to have to worry about getting pregnant, even with the Pill."

"Cheer up, it won't be long. A year or two, maybe three at the outside?"

"I'll get you for that someday. 'Bye, Josie. Keep in touch."

Three days later, Josie called Sandy again, to tell her that Billy was arriving home sometime that evening.

"Mrs. O.'s planning to leave New York after dinner, so even with the three-hour time change, she'll be in late. She told me to go on home after dinner with Gigi. I guess she doesn't want Mr. Orsini to wait up, she didn't say one way or the other."

"He's out for dinner with Maggie MacGregor anyway."

"Right. 'Bye, Sandy," Josie said, thinking that it was interesting to know where Mr. Orsini was dining for a change. He'd been out for dinner every night since Mrs. O. had left, although without information to the contrary, Jean-Luc had prepared dinner as if he were going to be there. Each morning of Billy's absence, by the time Josie Speilberg made her way downstairs for breakfast, Vito had left for his office. Although he'd called once to say hello to Gigi, she hadn't seen him come in at night before she'd retired to watch television while Gigi finished her homework in her own room. The upstairs maid had reported to Josie that Mr. Orsini had moved from the master bedroom to one of the guest rooms, although the house had so many that Josie hadn't laid eyes on him.

Mrs. O. must have been having trouble sleeping, Josie thought, although she hadn't mentioned it. Her own parents had never shared a room except on their brief honeymoon because her father snored so loudly. She understood that the Queen of England and Prince Philip's bedrooms weren't even on the same floor of Buckingham Palace. Even for royalty, that *was* just a bit odd, but separate bedrooms were a luxury she thoroughly understood and approved of, even for heavy sleepers. They kept the romance in the marriage as nothing else could except separate bathrooms, Josie concluded. If she'd ever been married, she would have insisted on the bathrooms even if she'd had to do without a closet.

When Vito had discovered that Billy had left for New York, he'd called Maggie for dinner. He had no intention of eating with Gigi and Josie and playing daddy, no inclination to eat out alone, no dinner meeting planned that night, and he could count on Maggie to sense his mood and not ask him questions he didn't want to answer.

They'd gone to Dominick's, the dark, smoky, cramped, uncomfortable, undistinguished grill without a sign over its door that was one of the best-kept secrets in Hollywood. Dom's served only a short list of basic steaks and chops, although on rare days a favorite customer could get grilled chicken. Its limp tablecloths were authentically red and white checked, you had to pay cash or have a house account, they wouldn't take a reservation unless you were a regular, you left there with your hair smelling of cooking, wondering why you'd gone, but every night a number of the power players in Hollywood congregated at Dom's, where there were no civilians to be seen. Like the Polo Lounge, it was a place at which you were guaranteed to be noticed, and when Maggie and Vito had dinner there three days in a row, nobody, not even Dom, thought anything of it. You couldn't carry on anything you shouldn't at Dom's because it was a part of the industry, and you couldn't carry on with Maggie MacGregor for the same institutional reason.

Or so people reasoned, Vito thought. The first night he'd had dinner with Maggie, he'd gone back to her house for a drink, and there they had resumed the affair that had kept Maggie in Rome for two weeks in the fall of 1974, supposedly interviewing him for *Cosmo*. They had both known, all through dinner, that it was going to happen, and the clubby, nothing-to-hide atmosphere of Dom's had only enhanced an anticipation that had needed no questions or answers to guarantee it.

Vito had never forgotten how lusciously erotic Maggie was, once she took off her clothes. In the four years since he'd last seen her naked, she had learned how to dress but she had lost nothing of her voluptuousness. There was not an inch missing of Maggie's ripe, heavy breasts, and her plump, inviting bottom was as round and creamy as ever. She was wonderfully quick to attain her orgasm, coming almost as soon as he started to touch her clitoris, even before he entered her, and then insisting that he take her just as quickly and ruthlessly as he chose, urging him on without words, her movements unmistakable, her body juicy and open. Making love to Maggie was like fucking the best whore in the world, Vito thought, and he found himself capable of coming more often than he did with Billy because he could please Maggie so quickly and frequently, with so little preliminary attention. Between bouts of lovemaking they gossiped and laughed casually, in an offhand camaraderie he relished, without any of the sticky palaver of two people who are in love. And all along Vito was aware, with a lordly assurance, that if and when he chose to feel Maggie's soft lips close around the tip of his cock, all he had to do was put his hand on the back of her neck and push it down between his legs. She liked it like that, she liked it any way he gave it to her, she wanted him hard and she wanted him soft, so that she could make him hard, and thinking about her readiness to please aroused him at odd times during the day in an urgent, inconvenient way that hadn't happened to him since he was in high school. Fucking Maggie MacGregor involved no big fucking deal, Vito thought, and that was what made it so exquisitely addictive.

When Sandy informed him of Billy's plan to return to California late that evening, Vito knew that he would be at Maggie's house that night. Fed up with the limited cuisine at Dominick's, they had decided to eat pizza at her place. He sat at the desk, wondering if he should leave Maggie sleeping, as he had been doing, to return very late to the guest room in the house on Charing Cross Road where he still slept, dressed and breakfasted, or whether or not he intended to be at home at a reasonable hour. A "reasonable" hour of return, for anyone out for dinner in Hollywood, would be eleven or eleven-thirty at the latest. People didn't linger in restaurants here as they did in all civilized cities of the world. They ate no later than seven-thirty, and parties broke up soon after eleven; even successful parties held on weekends were over by midnight.

He couldn't make up his mind what he was going to do, Vito realized at last. If he came home by eleven-thirty he would probably see Billy, and if he saw Billy they would have to talk and if they talked, he didn't know what they'd end up saying. If he came home at three in the morning, there would be no explanation but the obvious one. Perhaps something would happen during the day to make him make up his mind one way or another, but right now it was in the laps of the gods, if there were any of them still hanging around, he thought, and picked up the phone on which Sandy had been buzzing him patiently.

It was nine o'clock by the time Billy reached her bedroom. There was no sign of Vito, and she had no inclination to look for him. The flight had been smooth, she'd done nothing but sit and read, yet she felt extraordinarily tired, too depleted to even tiptoe into Gigi's room, where the light was out, and take the peek at her that she'd promised herself during the trip. She was simply too frazzled to do anything but strip off her clothes, put on a nightgown and crawl into the bed. It was midnight in New York, Billy realized, but it was some other, utterly drained hour in her body. Could a mere three-hour time difference produce jet lag, she wondered, as she drifted off to sleep.

Hours later, Billy woke in the dark, woke abruptly, as if from a bad dream, with her heart pounding, and the absolute conviction that something was wrong. She listened intently for a second, wondering if the house was on fire, until a fearsome cramping ache began to mount in her belly. She wrapped her arms around herself as tightly as she could, pressing into her stomach with all her power, and the ache, which felt like a very severe menstrual cramp, gradually receded. Now Billy knew what had awakened her, and a rush of fear enabled her to get out of bed and switch on the light. There was blood on the bottom sheet, and another cramp was beginning. Billy shut her eyes and bowed her head and waited, moaning, until it was over and she could move again. She had to get to the hospital, and quickly, was all she could think. Vito! No, she didn't know where he was. She dialed Gigi on the intercom.

"Hello . . . hello, who is it?" Gigi's voice said confusedly.

"Gigi, it's Billy. I'm back, but I'm in trouble. Wake up whoever drives you to school on the intercom and tell him to have a car downstairs right away. I'm going to the UCLA hospital, got that, tell him UCLA, it's the nearest."

"Okay, hang on, I'll be right in."

"No, Gigi, no, I don't want you to see this."

"Billy, just put on your slippers and a warm robe," Gigi said and hung up.

A minute later, as Billy was in the bathroom, stuffing Kleenex into a pair of panties she'd put on under her nightgown, she heard Gigi open the bedroom door.

"Do you need me in there?" Gigi called.

"No, I'll be right out." Billy emerged, ready to go, and saw Gigi standing watchfully by her bathroom door, clad in jeans and a sweater she'd pulled over her pajamas, slippers on her feet.

"Lean on me," Gigi said. "Burgo's waiting downstairs. I didn't think you'd want him up here in your room."

"Oh, Gigi, Gigi, I'm losing the baby."

"It's probably not certain, not yet. Come on, put your arm around my shoulders, we have to walk downstairs and get to a doctor."

"Oh God, why did this happen?"

"Come on, Billy, just put one foot in front of the other, you can lean on me, I'm strong."

"Wait . . . wait, I can't move . . . . all right now, hurry, before I have another cramp."

Together they quickly managed the stairs and walked through the house, stopping only once when another cramp hit Billy. Burgo took over as soon as they appeared at the front door, helping Billy into the car. Gigi slid in next to Billy, her arm around her protectively, as they sped the short distance to the emergency room of the hospital. But although they reached the UCLA emergency room in minutes and every measure was taken to save Billy from having a miscarriage, within an hour it was over. Dr. Wood, Billy's own doctor, arrived too late to do anything but confirm the fact.

"But why, why?" Billy asked again and again.

"It's not at all unusual, Mrs. Orsini. You were barely three months pregnant, perhaps a week more at the most. If a miscarriage is going to occur, it's most likely to happen during these first three months. It doesn't compromise your future capacity to have children. There was some good reason for this pregnancy not to continue. We doctors consider it nature's way of correcting a mistake."

"Oh God," Billy said flatly. She would never ask again.

"If you feel strong enough, I'd advise you to go home in an ambulance. The hospital will only depress you. I'll send you a private nurse to care for you there. A few days in bed and you'll be as good as new."

"Don't bother about the ambulance. I have Gigi, and Burgo's still waiting. They got me here, they can certainly take me back."

The doctor looked at Gigi sharply. She was holding Billy's hand, as she had been for the last hour. No one had been able to prevent her from staying by Billy's side. "Fine, Mrs. Orsini, but stay here for another hour at least. I'll wait outside and go home with you and settle you down. May I ask who this young lady is?"

"My daughter," Billy said.

"At least you have one child, and you'll certainly have another. You're only thirty-five."

"Yes," Billy agreed, "this one . . . at least."

4

*A*fter her return home from the hospital, Billy stayed in bed, sleeping deeply, waking to a half-doze, and then sleeping again. Several times she rang for orange juice and toast with jam, occasionally she read for a half hour, but for two days and one night she managed to lull herself into forgetfulness, into a willed calm, a sheltered place where nothing was allowed to enter her consciousness but the smoothness of the sheets, a few pages of an unmemorable book, and the rapid recuperation of her body.

Long after midnight following the second day of rest, she opened her eyes, feeling strong and so wide awake that it was impossible to stay in bed for another minute. She looked out of the windows and saw that the moon was full and high in the sky, the night was unclouded, and the garden paths were softly illuminated by the concealed lights that went on automatically every night. Billy hastily pulled on a warm sweater, slacks, a trench coat and waterproof boots, picked up a key and went outside to prowl around and try to walk off her alertness so that she could go back to sleep again till morning.

She walked slowly but deliberately out onto the terrace, testing her body's willingness, and found that the motion felt welcome, necessary. She began to stride briskly, enjoying the sound of her firm tread on the paths that lay bathed in the heavy dew that came in from the ocean every night. Taking the long gardeners' walk that had been planned to circle the outer borders of the property, passing the cutting gardens, the vegetable gardens, the greenhouses, the tennis courts and the pool, occasionally exchanging a silent nod with one of her security men, she headed toward the hidden garden, to which only she and Gavin, the head gardener, had keys.

Within ten minutes, Billy unlocked the wooden door to the walled garden that lay concealed behind a screen of dark cypress. It was an all-white garden at every season of the year. Tonight the first roses of spring bloomed, flinging their new canes high over the twelve-foot-high stone walls, their sprays mixed with climbing trumpet vines and rampant jasmine that was in its full glory. The square garden had been Billy's special request of Russell Page. She had first seen an all-white garden at Sissinghurst Castle, in Kent, on a day in earliest spring when she had visited there with Ellis Ikehorn. The only bloom at that time of the year in England had been a bed of enormous white pansies with violet centers. They had given her more of a shock of beauty than if the entire garden had been at its summertime peak.

Billy closed the gate behind her and walked forward, through the beds planted in drifts of white alyssum and primroses, narcissus, iris, tulips, lilies-of-the-Nile, cyclamen and ranunculus, all the flowers of spring dazzled by the moonlight that reached so softly into their hearts. She was a little tired now and she welcomed the old wooden bench that waited beneath an arbor of wisteria. The bench was her favorite place in the world, the place she came when she wanted to be alone, away from the house, from phones, from any hint of noise or hurry.

She hadn't come here in weeks, she realized, more weeks than she could count. The roses hadn't yet received their annual post-Christmas pruning the last time she remembered visiting the walled white garden, and now they were reaching the apex of their late April bloom, always their finest display of the year, after resting for three months during the short California winter.

The roses told Billy what she already knew. It was time to stop and think, one of her least natural occupations. It was time to take an inventory of her life instead of just rushing through it, time to leave the mental safe house of her restorative sleep.

Start at the beginning, she told herself, start at that dinner party at the Hôtel du Cap that Susan Arvey gave just a year ago; start with meeting Vito Orsini that night and falling in love with him; start with those short, urgent hours of courtship in which she had quickly declared her intention to marry him; start with the lunch at which her determination had carried the day and he had agreed to marry her; start with their flight back home, eleven uninterrupted hours, the longest stretch of time together they were to have until . . . . the longest stretch of time they were ever to have alone together, period, in bed or out.

Vito had plunged into casting *Mirrors* the day they'd returned from Cannes. After six wildly busy weeks, with a script almost finished, and casting completed, Vito had left her alone while he went location-hunting, and once the locations had been found in Northern California, she had joined him for the actual hurry-up-and-wait, frantically boring, slow-motion frenzy of film production, feeling so neglected by Vito, so overlooked, so barely tolerated as long as she didn't make a nuisance of herself, that she had fled to Jessica in a fit of self-pity and rage, just as she had done only a few days ago.

And between trips to whine and complain and pour out her troubles to poor Jessica, Billy asked herself acidly, just what had she done with her life? She'd made friends with Dolly Moon, she'd watched from the sidelines as Spider and Valentine ran Scruples very competently without her, and she'd served as an emergency script girl while *Mirrors* was edited in her house. That script-girl stint, using her old secretarial skills, had been the only truly useful thing she'd done all year, besides demanding that Vito find a publicist for Dolly and thus, unknowingly, introducing Lester Weinstock into Dolly's life. Other than those two good deeds, she had nothing to be proud of unless she counted rescuing Gigi when the reality was that Gigi had rescued her.

For months on end, she'd waited around endlessly, patiently, impatiently, but hanging around nevertheless for Vito to land somewhere for a few minutes so they could say hello, she'd been supportive and a good sport and a cheering section, a devoted, loving wife whose life was wrapped up in her husband's success . . . . and an asshole. She was no more necessary to him than a third leg, a third arm or a third ball. Two of each made sense, three were unmanageable.

Vito wasn't her husband, he was her lodger, Billy thought, someone who took up room in a highly superior boardinghouse and occasionally threw the landlady a quick, thorough and expert fuck. She had to grant him that. He made great love when he found a spare wedge of time, so long as the phone was disconnected. Why hadn't she ever objected when he reconnected it immediately afterwards? She'd begged him to visit this garden with her, just once, but he'd never managed to free himself for the half hour it would have taken. Why hadn't she tried harder to get him here?

Why—why bother to ask herself why, why bother to analyze what she'd done wrong and he'd done wrong? Why not just recognize that what she'd felt for Vito was infatuation, not love. She couldn't be sitting here, reckoning up the past, her heart beating steadily and without anger, if she loved him now. She couldn't think about him with the cold indifference, the vast contempt she felt, if she loved him still. The passing of infatuation left a barrenness of heart, a bruised soul. It was "an extravagantly foolish or unreasoning passion," as Jessica, the dictionary freak, had once called it. Yes indeed, that just about summed it up, Billy thought, without a tremor. Everybody has to eat a peck of dirt in his life, or so she'd heard, and she supposed everybody had to go through an infatuation and out the other end. She just wished she'd gotten it over with earlier, at fourteen instead of thirty-five.

Except for Gigi. Billy felt a sudden surge of savage rage rise up and fill her with such heat that she couldn't sit still any longer. She paced rapidly around the flower beds, tearing a rose apart with trembling fingers and flinging the petals into the small central pool. Gigi. The way Vito had behaved toward Gigi was unforgivable, permanently and forever unforgivable. Even now he ignored her except for one or two isolated, perfunctory phone calls. There were no possible *but*s, no extenuating circumstances, no defense. If Gigi hadn't had a great mother, God only knows what would have happened to her. Yes, Vito was a busy man, Vito was preoccupied with his career, but none of that could explain how he had overlooked Gigi. The only explanation —not an excuse but an explanation—was that, in one very basic sense, he was a bad man. A bad man who made a bad father. Any good man, any decent man, might not necessarily have what it took to be a good father, but he wouldn't have allowed himself to be a *bad* father.

Billy quickly closed the door to the walled garden behind her and locked it. She took the most direct path back to the house, not noticing the moonlight filtering down on her through the old trees, not paying any attention to the archways and glades and ponds and meadows, the hedges and vistas that stretched on all sides as she almost ran in the eagerness of having reached a decision. How early, she wondered, would it be all right to telephone Josh Hillman? It was almost four in the morning now, and her lawyer was an early riser. Still, she had to wait at least two hours until she could call and instruct him to put into motion the steps toward a divorce and, most particularly, the steps that would make her Gigi's legal guardian. By California law the divorce would take just six months, by next October she'd be Billy Ikehorn again, thank God. Waiting till six to phone Josh would test her patience, but at least she was certain of the essential element of her plans. Vito wouldn't put up the slightest opposition. He wouldn't dare.

During the next year Billy was deeply immersed in the construction of the new Scruples in New York and Chicago. True to her vow, she had made Spider and Valentine partners in the new stores without any other investment than their talent. It was her way of showing them how much she valued them, of finally thanking them properly for their indispensable roles in the success of Scruples in Beverly Hills. It also served the purpose of making certain that she'd never lose them to her envious, always opportunistic competition. Josh Hillman maintained that there was no legal necessity for her to be so excessively generous, but she had insisted, and no one knew better than he when it was useless to argue with her.

Spider was now hard at work night and day, dealing with the architects and designers Billy had hired to create the new stores as quickly as possible. He used her executive jet to shuttle from New York to Chicago to make sure that the basic Scruples concept of a store as a shopper's perfect playground, a great caravan of choice, a never-ending source of real and fantasy gratification, was maintained in every detail. Valentine hired a cadre of buyers to assist her in covering the European collections, although she still had to make the final decisions in Paris, Milan and London, a rigorous test of judgment she couldn't leave to others, for Scruples' customers were buying more foreign designers' ready-to-wear than ever. Both she and Spider were often needed in the Beverly Hills store, she to design custom clothes and he to put his stamp of approval on the most important purchases of their biggest customers, to whom his unsparing advice had become indispensable.

Billy's travels took her to Europe, Hawaii and Hong Kong, where she spent a vast amount of money buying superbly located sites on which future Scruples stores immediately went into the planning stage. She was so busy that when she came back to California she was eager to spend most of her evenings with Gigi, although she forced herself to accept an occasional invitation to a party. Her interest in meeting an attractive new man, should such a rare bird be flying free in Los Angeles, was nonexistent; emotionally, Billy felt as if she'd found a comfortably refrigerated room and shut the door behind her with relief. If a healing process was taking place, she was unaware of it; it seemed to Billy that her marriage to Vito had been essentially too shallow a union to require major repair. Its loss left her feeling empty rather than bitter. Vito's open liaison with Maggie MacGregor was a matter of no interest to her, which surely proved that she was cured of him. The very fibers of her heart seemed to have dried out, she knew she had become more cynical about the possibilities of happiness, but reason told her that she was not wrong. Mentally she shrugged and turned to the constant interest and excitement of the expansion of her retailing empire.

Spider and Valentine didn't have the time they needed to look for a proper house, so Spider had sold his small bachelor place and moved into Valentine's West Hollywood penthouse. About once every two months, Valentine found a minute to fret that they weren't living a proper bourgeois married life, that her spices were growing stale and she hadn't made a decent *pot au feu* for him since leaving New York, but Spider was enthralled with the penthouse in which Valentine had magically reproduced the mood of the Manhattan apartment in which she had lived when they first met. There they had confided in each other the disappointments of their romantic problems during the years in which they had been loving friends, but never lovers.

That first tiny apartment, its furniture covered in faded pink and white toile de Jouy, lit by red-shaded lamps, in which the powerful nostalgia of Piaf's singing was so often heard in the background, had never failed to remind him of Paris. Now he had a piece of Paris in Los Angeles, a make-believe Paris in which the single most authentic and unmistakably French element was Valentine herself, a sorceress whose green eyes were filled with whimsical, witty life, her ever-changing fund of expressions crossing her white face under her curly, unmanageable toss of hair that looked as if she'd dipped lace in paprika. He could live on take-out and restaurant food forever, he assured his wife, he hadn't married her for her cooking—well, not entirely—and certainly he hadn't married to live the bourgeois life. What was that all about anyway, he'd ask, since neither of them was what he thought of as bourgeois? Comfort, she'd answer, and regular habits and a sense of being really and truly settled down. Not this almost-bohemian existence, not all this travel, and certainly not, *no never ever*, take-out food.

The first public screening of *The WASP* took place on a night in late April of 1979. Susan Arvey had made a print of the picture available for a gala preview for the Women's Guild of St. John's Hospital, at five hundred dollars a ticket. This annual fund-raising event traditionally consisted of a black-tie dinner followed by a preview of a yet-unreleased and unreviewed, but major picture. The dinner had been a quick sell-out since everyone who had read the book, which included everyone who still read current fiction, had been itching to see the movie, the filming of which had taken place with a tight lid on publicity that only made them more curious.

After the evening had ended, as Susan Arvey settled down to remove her makeup, she found that she was still humming the music from the picture. She unpinned her long, naturally blond hair, which had been arranged in the smooth, elegantly prim chignon that was her trademark in a town of full, tinted, teased, sprayed hair, and inspected herself carefully in the mirror, as meticulously as she did after she'd finished dressing, for she held herself to a standard that decreed that her makeup be as impeccable when she returned as when she left home. She was not disappointed, nor had she expected to be, although she would never fail to double-check her immaculate prettiness, a prettiness so complete that it made many genuine beauties seem unfinished and raw. Her features were small and dainty and perfectly sculptured, set in a delicately rounded baby face, a legacy from her mother, an actress from Minnesota whose Swedish ancestors had made her one of the few genuine blondes ever to reach Hollywood.

At forty, Susan Arvey looked like a woman whose thirty-fifth birthday lay somewhere in the future, but her mental processes and her thirst for power were inherited directly from her father, Joe Farber, once a redoubtable leader of the film industry. Susan was Joe Farber's only child, born to his second wife when he was in his late fifties. Her parents had brought her up to the ermine and the purple, her father imparting lore of the golden days of Hollywood to her while she was still a small child, her mother, hastily retired from an undistinguished career, watching exactingly over her chick to ensure that she made full use of her advantages. Susan had been taught to run a house with the fastidiousness of the Duchess of Windsor, she had been groomed to marry well, marry young, and, above all, not to marry "a piece of talent."

At nineteen she had accepted Curt Arvey, son of a studio owner and an established, rising executive of thirty-three in his father's business. Joe Farber had approved. Now, twenty-one years later, Susan had long been in possession of all the necessary traits and equipment for dominance in Hollywood society. She was one of the industry's most accomplished and feared social leaders. The coveted invitation to her black-tie dinner parties, at which she casually used her mother's huge collection of priceless Chinese export porcelain, placed a couple within a circle that made up, in Hollywood, the equivalent of a regal court. Thereafter the favored couple lived on the point of a sword, for Susan was capable of making intimates of them and then, after years of friendship, dropping them without their ever knowing why. In point of fact, she didn't need any good reason for her actions, except to prove once again that she could exercise an authority that she was prevented from using openly at her husband's studio.

Did any of the women at tonight's benefit realize that although she could produce a print of *The WASP* at will, her ability to influence her husband's business decisions was severely limited? Susan wondered as she continued to check herself in the mirror. After Billy Ikehorn she was the best-dressed woman in Los Angeles; she possessed the most respected backhand on any tennis court in Bel Air, and she owned one of the finest collections of first-rate French Impressionists on either coast, yet she knew herself as an unfulfilled woman as she turned from side to side to study her delicate profile.

Her days were full. Every morning she had a seven o'clock tennis lesson. At eight-fifteen she took her shower, and by nine-thirty, after she'd skimmed the *L.A. Times* and the *New York Times*, she and her social secretary began two hours of phone work, steadily calling the women with whom she lunched, planned charity galas, and dined. Afternoons were devoted to shopping for new clothes for these lunches, balls and dinners, for fitting the clothes she'd already bought, and for a strenuous daily two-hour workout in her private gym, followed by a massage.

Yet in spite of this life in which not a minute was solitary or unemployed, Susan Arvey lived with constant frustration, for her birthright had been a giant appetite for business ascendancy that had been thwarted, not just by her gender but by her father. By the time she had reached the age of twenty-six, both Joe Farber and his wife were dead. She had inherited a vast fortune, but it had been left in a trust so constructed that it was unbreakable. Her trustees had invested a good portion of her inheritance in the studio her husband had now taken over from his father, and when Curt Arvey took his company public, Susan found herself her husband's largest stockholder. However, all meaningful, heavy-duty muscle in the film business had been denied her because her father hadn't trusted her to manage her own money. Only through the unsatisfying proxy of marriage could she try to impose herself on the doings of the studio, an influence that at best could never give her a position of equality.

As Susan brushed her hair she couldn't keep from brooding on this permanent grievance, the galling, infuriating, thwarting prohibition of a lifetime, an impotence for which there was no cure. As the mere wife of the boss, not the boss herself, she was forced to sugarcoat her demands, indeed to stifle all but the most important of them. If she hadn't been married to Curt, her stock would have guaranteed her a recognized, major position in the studio's policymaking. However, if she wished to stay successfully united to a man as stubborn and prickly as Curt, it was necessary to restrain herself, to stay within certain well-marked boundaries, for he could take umbrage even at her most tactful interventions. Yet divorce was not an option, even if she had wanted one, for a stable marriage is essential to a woman who intends to continue to rule within the film community.

Although Curt had now far surpassed her father's financial success, Susan often reminded herself, with an inward sniff that it was only in today's devalued dollars, her father's money had been made when you could keep it. The Arveys' twenty-one-year marriage existed in a state of turbulence. Curt Arvey couldn't reject out of hand his wife's deftly disguised reactions to his decisions. Yet, like two soldiers from opposing armies, cast up alone on a desert island, their sniping at each other made for a more distracting and interesting interchange than if they had been making a predictable common cause around a campfire.

During the period that Vito Orsini had been in production of *The WASP* for Curt's studio, the film had received more than Susan's usual critical scrutiny. Ever since Vito had practically abducted Billy Ikehorn from her party during the Cannes Film Festival two years ago, she had distrusted him. Even the Orsinis' divorce, which proved that she had been right all along, hadn't restored Vito to favor with her. Yes, she'd kept a particularly sharp and authoritative eye on *The WASP* every step of the way.

Now, her hair drawn back from her face, Susan moved around her bathroom, getting ready to go to bed. She was so delighted with the events of the last few hours that she couldn't resist breaking into a dance step from time to time, still humming the music from the picture in a gleeful monotone. As she settled down and began to remove her makeup, Susan Arvey reviewed the evening against the background of other charity galas. The hotel ballroom dinner had gone as planned; the food had been up to its routinely boring but perfectly edible standard; the service had been deft; the usual women who didn't know how to dress for a formal screening had outdone themselves in bouffant dresses that overflowed into their neighbors' laps; the audience had received the picture with a great show of enthusiasm.

Susan herself had been enthralled by the novel from which *The WASP* had been made. When Curt told her of the unheard-of sum he'd been forced to pay for the film rights, she had contented herself with nothing more than a side-to-side motion of her head that indicated he'd been suckered. In truth, she was glad that he was to make the film rather than any rival studio. The storyline of the book wasn't complex —that was one of the beauties of it, Susan thought as she methodically creamed her face.

The action took place over a period of twenty-five years, beginning in 1948 when the WASP of the title, Josiah Duff Sutherland, entered Princeton. He was a descendant of a wealthy Rhode Island family who numbered Presidents of the United States, senators, and presidents of universities among their ancestors.

Sutherland, a veteran of Korea, fine looking, upright, and virtuous, was possessed of a decent intellect and a charming, gregarious disposition. He became a roommate of Richard Romanos, the great-grandson of the country's most important and long-established Mafia family, a magnetic figure who had been designated by his proud, powerful father to emerge totally from the Mafia and take a place among the American aristocracy.

Rick Romanos was as witty as he was forceful, and possessed of an intelligence far superior to Sutherland's. He and Josh instantly became friends, attracted by their differences in personality. Forming a tight pair, they went on to Harvard Law School after graduation, always rooming together, double-dating, sharing everything but the secret of Romanos's true background. Together they joined an important law firm and together they planned how Josh Sutherland would run for the New York City Council, for Congress, then for the Senate and eventually for the Presidency.

Sutherland married a lovely, suitable girl, Laura Standish, descended from one of the great Charleston families, but Romanos remained a bachelor, the ultimate man about town. In the course of the twenty-five years between graduation from college and Sutherland's attaining the Presidency, Rick Romanos found himself, against his will, growing more and more envious of his friend's success, a career that he believed was only possible because Sutherland was a WASP. He became equally envious of his friend's possession of a perfect wife. With Laura he carried on the kind of casual, aboveboard flirtation that can flourish under a husband's very nose, if the husband is blind enough to be unthinkingly sure of his wife's devotion.

Eventually, Romanos set out to betray Sutherland, gradually finding ways to use Mafia money to ensure Sutherland's elections and reelections, slowly placing him under obligations to Mafia interests, encircling his friend with the Mafia so tightly and secretly that there could be no escape for the politician. When he had accomplished all this, he took Laura away from Sutherland in the course of the election campaign itself.

When Josiah Sutherland woke up on the morning of his inauguration, he was not sure whether his wife would be by his side or not. At the last moment she appeared and stood next to him, but even as he took the oath of office, he did not know the nature of her future relationship with Rick Romanos, who was destined forever to remain his closest associate, nor did he know what would be the first favor his friend would require of him, the first of many favors he would have to repay.

Well, they couldn't have started out with a better cast, Susan thought, as she gently began to wipe away her discreet eye makeup with an oiled pad. Diane Keaton for the girl had been a perfect choice, physically far better suited to Redford than Dunaway or Fonda, and totally believable as a politician's well-born wife. Yes, the ordeal of making *The WASP*, the ordeal that had been visited on Vito Orsini, the ordeal she had watched unfold with mounting fascination and pleasure, had begun with a perfect cast.

The first glitch came when the location scouts had bad luck with the Newport "cottage," the mansion that was to serve as the Sutherlands' family summer home, and the scene of much of the action. Too many canny, rich Newporters refused to rent their homes to a movie company at any price, and Vito had been forced to settle on an estate that was simply too small. The ballroom and other large sets had had to be built on Hollywood soundstages, but not even an expert could tell when an actor moved from one room in the real house into the next room, built on a set three thousand miles away. He had lost that authentically perfect Newport view, but who among the audience would know the difference? she wondered.

Yet it was there, with the location failure in Newport, that the budget had started to get out of hand, way back there, Susan thought, before a finished script had been delivered. Or rather when the first of the five scripts that were eventually written was still in progress.

Susan paused, one eye made up, one naked, and considered the nature of the four top scriptwriters Vito had approached. Naturally each of them, faced with a completed book, saw a way to tell the story with a shade of difference from the author's own viewpoint, each had had a series of minor insights of his own that he fought for, insisted on. But no, Vito Orsini would never allow one of them that relatively small amount of creative freedom, that *necessary* amount. His ego growing larger by the day, he had become as protective of the absolute integrity of the book as if he'd written every word of it himself.

True, Susan admitted to herself, after fighting to a point of rupture with four of the top screenwriters in the United States and England, Vito had indeed managed to find an unknown writer who'd made a totally faithful and workable translation from book to script, she couldn't deny that. Of course, by that time the budget had grown yet larger than expected, but writers weren't your chief expense on a picture, not when you emerged with a good script on which everyone could agree.

Susan completed the removal of her eye makeup and reached for the bottle of rosewater she had made up for her at a local pharmacy. There was nothing as gentle for removing the thin film of oil that remained on her skin. Now directors, she told herself, looking back in delectation at the suffering that directors had managed to inflict on Vito, directors were, of course, notoriously impossible, far worse than screenwriters. She'd been doubtful when Vito went after Huston, and when that deal had fallen apart, she hadn't been surprised. The two men weren't destined to get along, even Curt had agreed with her on that.

Of all the egomaniacs who band together to make films, directors are unquestionably the worst, but wouldn't you have thought, she asked her pale, clean, perfect face, that *one* of them would have suited Vito, bloated with self-importance though he was? Milos Forman, John Schlesinger and Sir Carol Reed had all read the script, had all been eager to direct *The WASP*, until Vito made it plain that he would attempt to dominate them, until they came to understand that this producer, this mere producer, had every intention of coming to the set every single day and breathing down their necks as they plied their trade, instead of taking himself off to an office somewhere, hopefully deep underground, from which he would devote himself to making their lives easy.

She hadn't tried to resist telling her husband that it served Vito right for not having signed Fifi Hill who had directed *Mirrors* and won the Best Director Oscar last year, but of course by the time Vito tried to get Fifi he was unavailable. Yet, even then, Susan thought, breaking into a wide smile at the memory, Vito had made another of his last-minute saves. From somewhere he had gotten his hooks into a young director, Danny Siegel, who had been responsible for two low-budget films, both critical successes, a director still so new to the business that he'd jumped at the job of tackling a huge picture in spite of the specter of Vito's control looming over him.

Yes, at that point even she had almost decided that the movie was out of the woods from a preproduction point of view, Susan remembered. With the stars signed, the character parts cast, a good finished script, a talented if untested director, and an experienced producer who had just won an Academy Award, the number of things that could go wrong seemed to have diminished. Her good humor had faded as Vito seemed to have overcome his problems.

By that time the budget had been thrown away, of course. With so much time wasted on the aborted scripts and finding a director, Siegel would be forced to shoot in "platinum time," which starts after double time is over, paying everyone on the picture triple time to finish the picture on schedule, to work twelve-hour days, to work weekends and holidays. But what did millions of dollars in additional crew costs matter on what was going to be the picture of the year? Wasn't that how Curt had put it? Her father would have put it more pungently, perhaps Joe Farber wouldn't have put up with it at all, but directors in his day weren't as powerful as they had become.

Susan Arvey began to slowly brush her hair. Getting ready to go to bed was a calming ritual with her and she never rushed, no matter how late it was. She brushed and brushed, all but grinning now at her reflection in the mirror, remembering the way in which young Danny Siegel had immediately made Redford and Nicholson like him, trust him. The man had a way about him, a dynamic force, an all-but-irresistible youthful imagination that was so fresh, so inventive that when he'd had his brainstorm, his stroke of genius, when he'd hit upon the most unexpected and challenging way to use the actors, they had immediately responded to him.

She'd never forget the day Curt came home and told her that on Siegel's suggestion Redford and Nicholson had decided to *exchange* roles, that Redford was going to play the Mafia prince and Nicholson the WASP. Vito, Curt said, had been totally caught up in their wave of excitement, Vito had completely agreed with Siegel that it was a brilliant idea, Vito had been utterly convinced that only a young jerk of a film student would cast Redford as a WASP, that only a hack producer would cast Nicholson as a Machiavellian mafioso, but that to let them play against type was an act of courage, of daring, of sheer brilliance that would never be forgotten in Hollywood.

The makeup people had done their best, particularly since the two men had to age twenty-five years during the picture, but with stars like Redford and Nicholson there was a strict limit to the amount of makeup you could use to change their internationally famous faces. Susan Arvey walked into her closet to put on her nightgown, shut the door behind her and gave herself over, doubled up, into a fit of laughter that would have turned into hysteria in a less well controlled woman.

Redford, with his blond hair darkened, but burdened with his saintly blue eyes, his indestructible good-guy smile, his entire personal baggage of Anglo-Saxon heritage, his *aura* of built-in sweetness, his beatific *teeth*, for Christ's sake, plotting corruption against his best friend with an assortment of sinister mafiosi, each one of them supposed to be a member of his very own family; Nicholson, in that perfect WASP toupee over his toned-down but unmistakably diabolic eyebrows, his wickedly gleaming eyes, his marvelously crazed smile, his cacklingly naughty laugh, supposedly having no problem at all in earning the trust of the American voters . . . . both actors doing their excellent best, God knows, but quite unable to escape from the power of those essential and uniquely personal qualities that were the bedrock reason they *were* stars, not mere actors. Christ, she hadn't dared to look at the screen during most of the charity showing, for fear that she'd start to shriek with laughter and not be able to stop.

She'd had to concentrate hard on her contempt for the benefit crowd, civilians every one. They were so excited by having secured their coveted, expensive tickets, so awed by the scenery and the elaborate sets, so sucked in by the guaranteed star power on the screen, so pleased by the faithful rendition of the plot of the book, that they hadn't dared to trust their own judgment about the casting, even assuming that they were making judgments. Critics, she told herself, they weren't. The critics, the real critics, would have their say soon enough.

You're dead meat, Vito, Susan Farber Arvey told herself cheerfully, and blew a kiss to herself in the mirror.

"Susan? Where the hell are you?" Her husband was prowling around outside her bathroom, never daring to violate her inner sanctum.

"I'll be right out," she called. After all, she reminded herself, twenty-one years of marriage . . . . she'd have to take pity on the poor schmuck, as her father had called him to his dying day. Tonight at least.

"Tired?" she asked sympathetically, as she emerged, tying the sash of her satin robe.

"Yeah, beat. These previews take a lot out of you, even when the press hasn't seen the picture yet."

"I thought Diane Keaton was a revelation, darling, I had no idea she could be so overpoweringly sexy. When a woman can be made to understand that another woman's sexy . . ."

"That scene where Romanos seduces her in the suite at the Marriott while Sutherland is making his big campaign speech in the ballroom . . . ."

"It was as lowdown and dirty a scene as you can get on the screen

. . . everybody will be talking about it . . . I could see it again and again.''

"I never thought we'd get so many clothes off her," Curt Arvey said.

"All her clothes were a triumph, darling. The Annie Hall look is gone forever. In fact, everybody who had anything to do with the wardrobe should get a raise."

"And the music, Susan, was it great, or was it great?"

"It's still going through my head, the theme in particular."

"What about the sets, Susan? I told you they'd work, even without those damn places we couldn't rent in Newport."

"Who'd ever know? If I hadn't been to Newport myself, I would swear that you'd shot there. Vito had a brilliant set designer, Curt, not just Newport, the whole picture was drop-dead gorgeous."

"And that Diane!" Curt Arvey whistled. "When I think that Vito wanted Fonda . . . I'm glad I talked him out of it."

"Amazing that you actually talked Vito out of even that one detail, dear. The entire picture is his, you realize, totally his. A Vito Orsini Production, never forget it. Vito's vision, dear, his responsibility, his final imprint, his every last one of the important decisions." Susan fussed with the pillows on her bed until she had them arranged in the way she liked them, which no maid had ever quite learned. She turned to Curt, who was sitting on his bed, looking into space.

"You know, Curt, I'd be the last person ever to underestimate the importance of a studio, you financed it, it's part of your yearly product, but let's face it, darling, Vito Orsini is going to grab all the credit, there's no way out of that. I have to admit, in all fairness, that he's the final creative force on this picture, whether I like him personally or not, and I still don't, no matter how well this picture does. Just as Vito lapped up all the credit on *Mirrors*, I assume he'll do the same with this one, and, as usual, we'll just have to stand by and watch him get the glory, while nobody even remembers the name of the studio that financed it."

"Yeah, you're right about that, Susan." Curt Arvey smiled for the first time in five hours. "Yeah, it's Vito's baby, all right, from beginning to end, every last frame of the picture. I think I'll try to go to sleep now, Susan."

"Sweet dreams, dear." Susan Arvey gave her husband a kindly kiss. She would go straight to wife heaven for this night's work, she thought, as she planned her visit to Geoffrey Beene's trunk show at Magnin's the next day. Beene was her favorite designer, and she rather thought she might just order one of everything, in fact she was sure of it.

On the day Curt had come home and told her of the exchange of roles between Redford and Nicholson, on that day which marked the exact minute when Danny Siegel took over the picture and Vito, megalomaniac that he was, had not seen the trap he was falling into, had, incredibly, been so puffed up by his illusion of his personal infallibility, that he had climbed on board little Danny's bandwagon of lunatics, Susan Farber Arvey had told her husband that he must cross-collateralize the profits of *Mirrors* against the future profits on *The WASP*, and do it at once. She had not bothered to sugar-coat her words that day, she'd said "must" and she'd meant *must*. Curt had listened to her without objections. Vito had made no difficulty about the change in the deal, as carried away by the conviction that he couldn't make a mistake as he was convinced by Curt's threat to shut down the picture and write it off as a tax loss.

The Arvey Studio's yearly balance sheet wouldn't suffer by so much as a penny from tonight's delicious debacle, she thought blithely, for *The WASP*, a thirty-million-dollar movie that would lose everything it cost, was completely covered by the profits on *Mirrors* that continued to roll in steadily from all over the world.

In fact, as this happy financial truth sank in deeper and deeper, Susan Arvey decided that the day after tomorrow she'd commandeer one of the studio's jets, fly to New York and do some meaningful shopping, antique shopping, for there was a limit to how much serious money you could spend on clothes. Perhaps she should consider redecorating the entire house. On reflection, it cried out to be done. She'd call Mark Hampton in the morning. She deserved her little rewards.

Redford and Nicholson wouldn't lose. They would easily laugh their way through such massively ridiculous miscasting . . . no more than a glitch for each of them, not even that. But Vito! Vito had had the power to stop the exchange of parts as soon as it started. Vito could have fired that criminally insane Siegel boy, replaced him with any competent nonentity, and the picture, as written and originally cast, would have been a classic, a huge moneymaker for all of them.

Ah, Vito, you persistent overreacher, you've finally made the fatal mistake for which Hollywood will never forgive or forget you . . . your first major picture, your first giant chance, your opportunity to lock in the success of your fluke Oscar, and you've screwed it up totally. No one in this town will fail to be delighted by your failure. Haven't you been asking for it for a long, long time? Susan Arvey mentally crossed Vito Orsini's name off the list of people with whom she intended to get even. There was nothing she could do to him that he hadn't done to himself.

Would Curt, she wondered, ever openly acknowledge that she had been the one to insist on the cross-collateralization, that she had seen the iceberg that sank the *Titanic* in time to save the ship? Possibly he would never give her the credit due her. It was late in life to realize you'd married a man as nonvalidating as your father, but there was no help for making such a classic mistake.

Still and all, she was one up on Curt for two or three years—maybe four—and he knew it. When you resort to assuring each other how good the music had been after a screening, you've touched bottom. As Susan Arvey moved happily toward sleep she wished that her father, that blindly chauvinistic old bastard, had been here to listen to her performance tonight. But no, he was probably too busy turning over in his grave. In his day you could have bought a huge chunk of L.A. with thirty million dollars. And in his day he had.

5

*M*aggie MacGregor shoved her desk chair back on its
rollers and put her legs up on her littered desk. The
weekly meeting to plan her show was over; her execu-
tive producer, her line producer, her assistant producers, her writers
and the rest of the drifting flotsam and jetsam who seemed necessary
to the network to make the show work every week, had gone, taking
their ceramic mugs and leftover doughnuts with them.

Alone for the first time in hours, Maggie forgot the show they had
all been busily planning, and considered the most important fact of the
meeting. Not one person had so much as mentioned *The WASP*, not
even in passing.

The picture had not yet received a single review, not even in the
Hollywood trade papers, whose reviews appear before those in the
daily newspapers. Full-page newspaper ads had been appearing for
two weeks, and first-run movie houses had been showing *WASP* trail-

ers for several months. The picture was scheduled to open in three days in eight hundred theaters across the country and nobody, not the lowest of gofers present at the meeting, seemed to have heard of its existence.

She would have sworn, Maggie thought, that none of her staff was capable of tact, but obviously she was mistaken. They had been supremely tactful, a roomful of people managing to totally ignore the presence of the decaying corpse of an elephant in their midst, an object that weighed a ton more than all of them put together and produced a frightful stench.

Of course, if they had been great actors, they could have dared to just mention the picture in passing, lightly, as if it had no connection to her, but lacking that much talent they had wisely opted for blindness. Had they all gathered together before the meeting today and decided how to behave? They must have, she realized, for not one of them had put a single toe wrong, and such discipline from her usually irreverent and unruly troops was unthinkable unless it had been planned. In these meetings nothing was sacred, the lowest and most scurrilous of industry rumors were treated as ordinary fodder, there was no star big enough to inspire their respect, no potential story too scandalous or vulgar for them not to consider it within their territory.

Maggie had assumed that they had all known about her and Vito for many months, probably longer, most likely since the beginning, since no such secrets could remain hidden to the people who worked for her, people who had been trained by her. Her own wide, well-established spy network, which stretched into every corner of the film business, would have reported on her to them—it was a matter of course. What she hadn't realized was that the news about *The WASP* had circulated so widely without a single industry screening.

If it had just been a disappointing but nevertheless iffy picture, bound to garner some bad reviews and some good ones, a picture that many people would go to see because of the cast and the lavishness of the production, regardless of conflicting reviews, *The WASP* would not have been taboo as a subject of conversation, not even if Vito and she had been married.

Her people had worked for her too long to think that Maggie would be offended by their speculation on the future of such a picture, in fact they would have been busily presenting ideas to help give the film some positive publicity.

Therefore their silence meant that it was even worse than she had thought. "'Tis ill talking of halters in the house of a man that was hanged." Wasn't that the way it was put? Who would think to find such delicacy among her staff? So Vito's picture was indeed going to be The Turkey That Ate Hollywood, and the news was out.

Maggie was surprised, but only at the depth of the lack of surprise she felt. Being in love with Vito hadn't turned her brain to sweetbreads. She'd listened to his vivid stories of his conflicts with that parade of writers and directors, convinced that Vito, as she had always known him to, would somehow make it all come together in the end. Preproduction problems were as normal to making a movie as burping is to bringing up a baby.

But when he had told her of the exchange of leading roles, she had had to turn away to conceal her shock. Later that evening she had managed to say, very casually, that she couldn't imagine Gone With the Wind with Rhett Butler played by Leslie Howard and Ashley Wilkes played by Clark Gable.

"That wouldn't have worked, Maggie," Vito had agreed. "But this isn't the same thing, not at all." And that had been his only response, for his passion for what he now thought of as his own idea had been too blinding to make him even stop to consider her warning.

Was it then, Maggie wondered, as she listened to the silence of the building in which everyone but she had left for lunch, was it then, at that moment, that she had started to fall out of love with Vito?

Probably. She knew herself well enough to be fairly dispassionate. She was nothing if not self-protective. She could never have lasted in this business, she could never have come as far as she had, if she hadn't consistently guarded her ass.

Love was a luxury she really shouldn't let herself afford in her job, but she had decided to indulge herself when Vito and Billy came unstuck. It was too wonderful to pass by. Love was like one of those great dresses that you knew, was far too expensive, a dress you knew you wouldn't get enough wear out of to justify the price, a dress you knew you should leave in the store for some other sucker—but bought anyway because life was too short and you'd regret it forever if you didn't.

She could afford to fall in love, overpriced item though it was, but she couldn't afford to be linked to a loser. She had two publics, Maggie told herself: the television audience who wouldn't know or care if Vito Orsini fell flat on his face, and the important circle of insiders in the industry, who would respect and fear her much less than they must, when they learned that she and Vito were still together in spite of *The WASP* and the reception it was going to get.

Thank God, Maggie told herself, Vito had never suggested marriage. She might have accepted, and where would that leave her now? She shuddered, thinking of women who had to keep smiling through, women who were forced to be loyal, come what may. That particular line of work was not, never had been, for her. Thank you very much indeed, but she wasn't bucking for the Mrs. Norman Maine Award.

Maggie dialed the New York office of the network, reaching the direct line of the powerful vice-president of the network and director of television specials, Fred Greenspan, who had just returned from the perquisite of his own leisurely Manhattan lunch, almost as long as the dinners enjoyed by Romans. Within ten minutes they had worked out a series of shows she would do from Manhattan. There were enough films being shot on the streets of the five boroughs of New York to keep her busy for months. When would she be ready to start?

"Gosh, Fred, you know me . . . once I get an idea I can't wait to get at it. Let's see—I can pack this afternoon and grab the red-eye tonight. So send a limo to meet the plane, okay? I'll be on it. Dinner tomorrow? Why, Fred, I'd adore it! You promise not to talk shop? I'll hold you to that, Fred. I know you've always had a funny little itch for me . . . but I bet you're still not ready to do anything about it."

Gigi sat in the chintz-cushioned bay window of her room with her best friend, Mazie Goldsmith, both of them cross-legged, both of them in deeply relaxed jeans and faded T-shirts with their enviable and honorable history displayed by their well-washed tattiness, like the battle standards of forgotten regiments. They were eating steadily through a plate of the special triple fudge brownies with fresh coconut icing that Gigi had just baked on a Saturday afternoon in mid-April.

Mazie and Gigi had fallen into a routine that suited Billy and the Goldsmiths. On most Friday nights they slept over at the Goldsmiths' Brentwood house, where Mazie's father, a highly placed MGM executive, invariably gathered a small group and screened a new movie in his projection room, followed by a buffet supper and another movie, very often a classic or a foreign film. On Saturday morning the two girls drove over to Billy's and spent the day there. Mazie slept over, leaving on Sunday in time to rejoin her family for dinner.

Mazie Goldsmith was a girl who one day, to any adult's eye,

would turn into a classic brunette beauty, although nothing could possibly convince her of that now, with her awkward height, her extra fifteen pounds of baby fat, and the thick glasses she was too squeamish to trade for contact lenses. Mazie got excellent marks, almost as good as Gigi's, and the two had picked each other out as kindred souls in the crowd the very day Gigi started at Uni.

Gigi, at seventeen and in the middle of her junior year of high school, had grown two inches since she had arrived in California, so that she was now five feet four. She retained all the delicacy of form that had made her seem wispy at first sight, but there had been a subtle transformation in the way she held herself. Her determinedly straight-forward stance, which had once seemed a defense against her smallness, now announced itself as downright self-confidence. Although she never thrust herself forward in any group, her upright carriage, the compact directness of the way she unconsciously stood and moved, attracted attention she didn't notice.

In whatever casual position Gigi arranged herself, she formed a vital and memorable pattern, like a dancer who can't sit or stand without grace. Her brown hair, which Sara's scissors had continued to experiment on until her close, straight cut, with its slight outward flare, had reached perfection, was streaked with the vivid tones of a variegated marigold, hues that ranged from downright orange to deep terracotta. Gigi had learned to use brown pencil to darken the light hairs of her strongly pointed eyebrows, and she skillfully coated black mascara on her long but invisible lashes. Now her eyes, shadowed under their deep lids and dark lashes, inspired instant curiosity. People who met Gigi found themselves drawing closer in involuntary curiosity so that they could determine the color of her leaf-green irises. Her eyes were eloquent yet artless, her glances still shy, still unaware of the uses of coquetry. Her clear, creamy skin betrayed her emotions, for she flushed easily. She had more than a touch of the theatrical about her, and the sleek 1920s flapper look, which Billy had first recognized as a potential for her to grow into, had been accentuated charmingly. Gigi seemed to command a reservoir of laughter so that even when she was serious she carried the perfume of mirth on her lips.

On this particular afternoon Gigi and Mazie had decided that it was still too damp and cool to drive down to the beach, too early to start the math homework they were supposed to be doing together, too much fun hanging out together to bother phoning around and finding out what everybody else was planning for tonight. All of their many friends went around in packs; no girl went out alone with a boy on a date; a bunch of males and females from Uni would just gravitate together on the weekends, summoned by the jungle drums of the adolescent world.

"I felt my dad getting a little uptight last night while we watched the uncut version of *Last Tango in Paris*, he hadn't expected it to be so hot," Mazie mused. "Our being there made him nervous, but what could he do, once it had started? Send us out of the room in front of everybody and ruin his record with the ACLU? He gave me a worried look when the lights went up, but Mom was cool."

"Didn't you think it was terrific?" Gigi asked. "I did."

"I'm not sure I exactly followed it entirely, there were some obscure moments . . . . but Brando's butt . . . hmm . . . well, what about Brando, Gigi, does he make your team?"

"Absolutely. The first team, the Dream Team."

"You're absolutely sure? That picture's seven years old and he's gained a ton since then. He's the Godfather now. You can still change your mind," Mazie offered generously.

"Maze, if you don't want to see Brando's equipment, you have not a shred of genuine curiosity, we're talking one of the great beauties of all time here, one of the great actors, one of the great personalities, forget his weight, forget his age, think of his *essence*."

"Remember, you're only allowed ten nominations to the Dream Team, Gigi."

"Well, he's made the cut on mine. Yours?"

"Take it easy, I'm thinking it over. Maybe . . . maybe Belmondo. After Dad screened *Breathless* I began to obsess about him. He's seriously sexy, he has crazy bedroom lips . . . wouldn't you take Belmondo over Brando?" Mazie inquired seriously, her dark eyes squinched up behind her glasses.

"Nope," Gigi was quick to reply. "I can perfectly well *imagine* Belmondo's stuff so I don't have to waste space for him on my team. I'll bet anything he's your basic, well-hung—*bien pendu?*—hunk, if the French have a word for hunk. Why don't you put him on the second team?"

"Ah, the second team," Mazie said, lighting up. She took off her glasses and unfurrowed her brow. Mazie loved to make nominations for the second team because they didn't commit her as deeply as the Dream Team. For the second team you could nominate a man who might turn out to have a disappointing penis without worrying too much about what other penis you were losing the opportunity to choose. Like a picky collector in an antiques shop who has finally made that difficult first purchase and now starts to look around with liberated avidity, Mazie felt freed to plunge into a Dream-Team nomination. "Woody Allen," she announced.

"Just a minute, Maze, just one little minute," Gigi objected. "Woody Allen's been on my Dream Team for months. You can't suddenly want him too, that's not fair."

"Why not? You'd still get to see it first. You wouldn't have to tell me anything."

"Oh, sure. I could take a good long look, maybe even a Polaroid, and then I'd keep the information a secret from you. What kind of crummy friend would that make me?" Gigi looked laughingly at her ever-rational companion and offered her another celestial brownie.

"You mean you'd share? You wouldn't mind?"

"Sure, I'd share. Think how much more we could enjoy his movies if we knew the ultimate truth, what *really* is there underneath those rumpled boxer shorts he's forever walking around in? There's got to be a reason he never wears Jockeys."

"But sharing isn't in the rules," Mazie objected.

"Listen, this game was my original idea, so I'm making up a new rule today, a sharing rule, it gives us each double opportunities."

"But isn't the point to have to narrow it down? To agonize?"

"Maze, you take it too seriously, you've got to loosen up. We're never going to get to see their stuff anyway, so why not be greedy? Let's get going. I'll take Sinatra. Dream Team." Gigi snapped her fingers triumphantly at Mazie's expression of horror.

"Good God, Gigi, they're getting older and older with you! Is this some sort of gag, or are you just being perverse?"

"Historical interest." Gigi looked as superior as Gloria Steinem, as she tried on Mazie's glasses. "Maybe Ol' Blue Eyes has an ol' blue dick. Remember, in his youth hordes of women would have killed for it."

"Yeah, well, I'll take Richard Nixon, in that case, I can be weird too."

"That's beyond weird, Maze, I don't advise it, I really don't. I'll pretend you never said Nixon," Gigi said generously.

"Okay. And I won't count Sinatra. Now down to business. Dustin Hoffman, I wanna see Dustin Hoffman. Dream Team."

"Me too, ever since *The Graduate*. We're sold solid on Dustin

Hoffman. He's a double Dream Team if there ever was one, a gotta-see," Gigi agreed. "But moving on into the world of fiction . . . . Norman Mailer?"

"Never! Not even on the fifth team."

"I was just testing you. He's not on the playing field, not even a water boy, him and his sacred sperm."

"Philip Roth?"

"No argument," Gigi said. "Except that it's a totally banal choice, it's too obvious. And once you've read *Portnoy* you're on such familiar terms with his horny horror that it's lost the charm of novelty. A wasted vote. I wonder if old J. D. Salinger is still in business?"

"Oh, Gigi, stop! The man's a hermit!"

"Yeah, but he could write. Golden oldies, Maze. Oldies but goodies."

"Gigi, if you bring up Walter Cronkite again, we're through."

"I'll bet he's gorgeous. He's on my Hall of Fame team . . . . you can retire, but you're always a member for life."

"Another new rule," Mazie complained.

"I'm feeling rebellious today. If I could, I'd repeal the Constitution and start this country all over again. I pick Andy Warhol. Dream Team."

"Gigi!"

"Warhol, I say! It's my choice, my right, my team."

"That's literally *disgusting*! Oh, Gigi, you *revolt* me!"

"But you'd never have thought of him, would you?" Gigi crowed triumphantly. Her fun came as much from Mazie's reactions as from her choices. "Don't I get points for originality?" Gigi made her eyebrows jump under her bangs in fierce triumph, a trick Mazie's nerves could never resist.

"Sometimes I worry about you." Mazie ate the last brownie with a sigh of concern. In the last few weeks Gigi had streaked her hair without warning, using the contents of an entire bottle of peroxide on a comb and running it repeatedly through her nice brown hair; she'd taken the spotless new white Volvo that Mrs. Ikehorn had given her, because it was the safest car going, and had it spray-painted shocking pink; and now her fantasy life was getting out of hand. Sinatra . . . Warhol . . . was this a bad sign?

"Gigi," Mazie ventured cautiously, "the Uni football team?"

Gigi made loud, convincingly real retching noises. "Yuck! *No boys!* You know we said no boys! Feh, phooey, double feh!"

"Right," said Mazie, relieved. Gigi hadn't abandoned their major principle. "And the coach?" she asked slyly.

"Ah, the coach, the eternal problem, my Maze, my old pal, whether to go for the coach or not. I'm still sitting on the fence on that one. There's something so banal about picking the coach, but . . . still, he *is* gorgeous. I can't seem to figure out if I really want to see a real person's penis, a person I actually see walking around campus, a person I personally know, or whether that'd be too much of a . . . responsibility."

"I don't get why you'd feel responsible. It's not as if you'd have to tell him you'd seen it."

"But there'd be this terrible temptation. Let's say I saw it and I liked it. I wanted it. Then my responsibility would be to try to seduce the coach, to make actual . . . contact."

"Want it? Who ever said anything about wanting it?" Mazie cried in alarm.

"But clearly that'd be the next step. After seeing, wanting, after wanting, touching."

"No, no!" Mazie shrieked in outraged denial. "Absolutely not . . . you've changed one rule too many. You've gone too far! *Touching!* You know we said no touching!"

"No touching, never ever, I promise," Gigi agreed hastily, having succeeded in frightening herself. "The coach is *out!* Just don't bring him up again, don't remind me."

"Don't worry, I won't."

"Girls? Girls? Are you doing your math homework?" Billy's voice called to them through the door.

"Yes, Mrs. Ikehorn," Mazie said quickly, "we're in the middle of it."

"Good, because if you've made some real progress you can take a break. I thought maybe you'd like to try to get into the early show of *Kramer vs. Kramer* and then grab a hamburger at the Hamlet—that is, if you're still interested in seeing Dustin Hoffman."

"Oh, we are," Gigi answered quickly, "we definitely are. We'll be finished in time, Billy, count on it."

In the course of his career, Vito Orsini had been up and he had been down and yet no one could say that they had seen him crestfallen. His bold, energetic countenance never collapsed into a look of weakness, he bore trouble with the same self-assertion with which he encountered prosperity. Thanks to his Italian heritage, his aristocratically aquiline nose, the fullness of his well-marked mouth and his air of easy prosperity in his endeavors, any signs of insufficiency or disappointment were foreign to his exterior. It was easy for Vito to look strong. When he telephoned Maggie, expecting to set the time at which they would meet for dinner that night, and discovered a message from her answering service to tell him that she had left town and could only be reached by leaving his name and number, he received the news with nothing more than an irritated twist of his lips and an angry frown.

No one watching him would have realized that he had just received an authoritative announcement that *The WASP* was doomed, as clear as if he'd read it in a headline on the front page of the *New York Times*. The meaning of Maggie's sudden departure was unmistakable, or would have been to anyone but Vito.

Maggie, who thought herself so clever, was a fool after all, Vito told himself as he hung up the phone, she'll feel like an idiot when the picture became a success. Worse, she'll know she was a coward, and it was he who was the fool to have expected more cinematic intelligence from a twenty-seven-year-old television gossip who had been nobody but a women's magazine writer only five years ago. To hell with her, he thought, and dismissed her absence from his mind. He had never loved her, but she had been, or so he had believed, that rare woman with whom he could be honest, that female friend he could fuck and trust. So he'd been wrong about her. Life was full of mistakes where women were concerned, and Maggie would be the loser.

In the next few days, as the reviews began to appear, Vito, as was his habit of long standing, refrained from looking at a single newspaper or discussing the reviews with anyone who had read them. In the early days of his career, when he had gone to Italy and produced a string of critically reviled spaghetti westerns, Vito had decided once and for all that the public knew what it wanted to see, and no reviewers could keep them away. The westerns, so despised, had brought in amazing profits. However, a number of his later films, which he had considered to be among his best, films that had been the darlings of the reviewers, had failed to attract a paying audience. The whole thing was, always had been, a crapshoot, he told himself, and this time he felt lucky, he smelled success, the success in which he had never failed to believe throughout the struggle to produce *The WASP*.

By the end of the first week after *The WASP* was released, Vito no longer felt lucky. He felt almost nothing but total panic. So great was the fall from his expectations that there was no gradual spread of creeping disillusionment, no slow, relentless realization that the picture was falling off too quickly from a good start. The drop was as swift as that of a head from a guillotined neck.

On the first day, a Friday, the box office had been strong as the diehard Redford and Nicholson crowd showed up with a morbid curiosity to see for themselves just how bad the picture was, unable to accept the critics' unanimous and ferocious recommendations that no one waste a single minute watching the atrocity that had been wrought on a brilliant book. The reviewers, all of whom had admired the book, overlooked anything good about the movie in their eagerness to condemn the desecration that the corrupt devils of Hollywood had visited on it. It was a bloodletting without precedent, an eagerness to destroy that not even Susan Arvey could have anticipated. However, on the second day, at least until the first 6:00 P.M. show, box-office receipts had been acceptable, and until the evening there was always the hope that on Saturday night business would pick up.

But word of mouth, that extraordinary force that is stronger than any ad campaign, stronger than any star appeal, had done its work. It was as if everyone in the country who had seen *The WASP* on Friday and Saturday afternoon had decided to call ten people to tell them how bad it was, and as if each of those ten people had called ten others, a verbal chain letter that kept the audience out of the theaters except for a few movie-buff deathwatchers who wanted to see the picture before it was yanked so that they could report exactly how much worse it was than they had been led to believe.

Everyone who actually paid to see the picture *hated* Redford as a scheming bad guy, and *loathed* Nicholson as a helpless good guy. They felt personally insulted by every scene in the picture because they felt so bitterly cheated by the use that had been made of two of their favorite stars, a use that made them falter for a while in their necessary belief in the Redfordness of Redford, the Nicholsonness of Nicholson. It was as if Vito had scalped and eviscerated Santa Claus in an orphan asylum on Christmas Eve.

By Sunday it was all over; the picture would play to empty houses only until the theater owners could scramble to replace it. Vito had cut off all communications to anyone involved in the movie from the moment it opened. He had spent the time driving alone in an orbit of Los Angeles, from San Diego to Santa Barbara to the far reaches of the

San Fernando Valley, searching out the theaters that had booked *The WASP* to see if there were any signs of life from the outside of the marquees, knowing that this occupation was futile and ridiculous, but unable to stop. By Sunday noon he knew there was only one thing left for him to do.

"It's your father," the butler, William, said, calling Gigi to the phone.

"Hi, Dad," Gigi said, trying not to sound too surprised. "How are you?"

"Couldn't be better. Listen, if you haven't got anything else to do tonight, how about having dinner with me?"

"Oh! Well . . . . sure . . . terrific! I'd love it. Where are we going —I mean, what should I wear?" Gigi knew she sounded confused, but she hadn't had a phone call from her father in two months or more.

"Don't bother to get all dressed up, just look nice. Ask Billy, tell her it's Dominick's, she'll figure it out. I'll pick you up at a quarter of seven sharp."

Vito hung up before she could say another word. Gigi contemplated herself in the dim glass of the painted and carved Venetian wood mirror that hung over the phone table in the hallway where William had found her. She made astonished eyes at herself and shook her head solemnly as she made her calculations.

She and Mazie had remained in their respective homes this weekend to study for a major English exam that was being given tomorrow, and was too important to study for together. Gigi had spent all of Saturday at her books, and intended to do her last-minute cramming on Sunday evening. She had planned to spend the coming afternoon in the kitchen with Jean-Luc. Billy had been in New York most of the week and wouldn't arrive back at the house until after dinner, so Gigi and the chef had laid elaborate plans to use his free time to make a whole poached chicken in the fashion of François Premier, with wild mushrooms, truffles and heavy cream.

Forget the chicken, Gigi instructed herself, cram until a quarter of six and then get dressed.

"Jean-Luc," she asked the chef, after she'd apologized and called off the lesson, "have you ever heard of a restaurant called Dominick's?"

"Here in Los Angeles?"

"Yup."

"Never. So you abandon me for a Dominick?"

"You know I would abandon you only for my father."

"Have a good time, Gigi," the chef said, showering Vito with mental curses, this so-called father who inconsiderately snatched away the most promising pupil he'd ever had, just before he intended to expose to her the ten most important things to know about truffles and their passionately interesting possibilities in conjunction with the meat and juices of a chicken.

Gigi managed to stay immersed in her books until just past five o'clock. It had never taken her an hour to dress in her life, but she was too excited at the prospect of seeing Vito and too anxious about how she looked to spend another minute with Elizabethan poetry. She took a shower and shampooed the hair she had shampooed yesterday. When it was blown dry she judiciously added a few new streaks to her bangs, thin but bright ones, using a paintbrush dipped in the peroxide instead of a comb. She marshaled all her favorite clothes and separated them into groups, discarding everything that looked remotely "dressed up" or suitable only for a high school girl. She tried on several different combinations before she arrived at a compromise she thought would fit any restaurant that Jean-Luc, who knew all the best places to eat in the city, had never heard of. She pulled an off-white cashmere sweater with a high turtleneck over her head and stepped into a wide skirt of supple suede in a shade that matched the darkest of the ochre streaks in her hair. She tucked the sweater inside the skirt and added a wide belt and cowboy boots, both made of a fine rust-colored leather.

No earrings, Gigi thought as she put on her eye makeup. She had a dozen pairs to choose from, but she wasn't comfortable yet with the rules of the great earring code. Earrings could make or break anything you put on. Earrings meant so many different things in so many different contexts that you had to be as experienced as Billy to penetrate the language of earrings, to know which pair was right to wear on what occasion, and why. Although the easy, non-statement way out was to have your ears pierced and wear simple studs made from silver or gold, she, who wasn't chicken about many things, broke out in a sweat at the idea of anyone getting near her earlobes with a needle.

Gigi grabbed a leather jacket to sling over her shoulders and settled in the semicircular entrance hall, perched on a chair that would give her an immediate view of Vito's car. He was prompt, and she dashed out of the house as soon as he arrived, opening the car door, sliding in and greeting him with a quick kiss on the cheek, as if this were something they often did, instead of the first time she had ever had dinner out alone with her father in her whole life.

They drove the relatively short distance to Dominick's, on Beverly Boulevard, chatting about the weather. Vito headed straight into the hidden parking lot behind Dominick's, as did all habitués, and helped Gigi out of the car, entering the restaurant through its back door and passing through the tiny kitchen before they reached the dining room proper. Vito and Gigi were, as he had planned, the first to arrive for dinner that evening. He had requested a particular booth, one slightly removed from all the others, at the far end of the small room and off to one side, so that Gigi faced into the room and his back was toward it.

While he drank several honest 1940s-style gin martinis that Dom made for him at the bar, Vito explained to Gigi what the significance of the restaurant was, the clubbishness of it, the insidership that it conferred. Behind him he could hear the room filling up quickly, for Hollywood ate especially early on Sunday night, but he never glanced around to see who was there.

Vito directed his attention entirely toward Gigi, his dark head with its distinctively short cut, thick cap of tight curls bent toward her as if she were the most fascinating woman alive. He asked her about school in detail, nodding in absorbed concentration to her animated answers; he wanted to hear everything about Mazie and her other friends and he made her giggle repeatedly as he commented on everything she told him. As they ate their lamb chops and French fries, no detail of Gigi's life was too insignificant to interest Vito, no description quite full enough for him not to pose a series of sensitive, often droll questions. He was utterly absorbed in her, preoccupied as only a man can be when confronted by a beautiful and alluring woman, made oblivious to his surroundings by his thirst to communicate with her.

Gigi grew more and more at ease in the glow and gallantry and solicitude of his attention. Her low, authentically joyous laugh rang out time and time again, cutting clearly through the discreet mumble of gossip that filled the smoky room, echoed by Vito's deeper but equally sincere amusement. Gigi bent her sophisticatedly sleek, chic head toward her father, the simplicity of her sweater making a startling point of her vivid hair, her lovely neck rising from the turtleneck to her oval chin in such a beautiful shape that every woman envied it. Gigi was so obviously unaware of everything but the high pleasure of being with Vito that no one at a single one of the booths and tables in the room was able to escape noticing that a very special kind of excited fun was taking place at Vito Orsini's table, a fun from which they were entirely excluded.

After dessert they were ready to leave the steak house before anyone else had finished dinner. Once Vito had signed for the check, he and Gigi walked back the entire length of the restaurant, arm in arm, Gigi flushed and, in her own delicately demure way, thrilled with herself. At each table Vito stopped to introduce her briefly, with the proudest of smiles, the happiest of looks, his expression, as ever, that of a conquistador. "Sid, Lorraine, my daughter, Gigi Orsini . . . . Sherry, Danny, my daughter, Gigi Orsini . . . . Lew, Edie, my daughter, Gigi Orsini . . . . Barry, Sandy, Dave . . . my daughter, Gigi Orsini . . ." By the time they found their way out through the kitchen and back to the car, Gigi had met a sizable percentage of the most important people in the film industry, people who would have laid heavy money against seeing Vito Orsini having a splendid, carefree time on this particular night, people who had never known he had a spectacularly adorable daughter with whom he had such a loving and close relationship.

These people gave each other meaningful looks that expressed two sentiments: Bewilderment at Vito's carefree acceptance of the disaster of the year, and an equal, slightly grateful acknowledgment that there was, after all, something more important in life than the success or failure of a single motion picture. Didn't they all have families, if not children? Wasn't that what counted in the long run? What about a man who wouldn't let *anything* spoil his evening with a daughter like Gigi? You had to admire the guy. For many minutes after Gigi's exit from Dominick's, a number of the leading citizens of Hollywood found themselves thinking of Vito Orsini as a lucky man.

Gigi didn't notice Vito's silence as they drove back to the house. She was basking in the afterglow of an evening such as she had never known before, the kind of evening she had never thought to spend with her father.

As they reached the gatehouse, Gigi noticed that the limo that had brought Billy back from the airport was just leaving.

"Billy's home," she said warningly.

"I won't come in, then," Vito replied. "We'll say good night outside. I'm going out of town tomorrow."

"For long?"

"Yeah. Probably for months."

"Oh, Dad," Gigi said, suddenly forlorn.

"I didn't want to spoil dinner by telling you sooner. I have to go to France to fulfill a commitment I made before *Mirrors* came out. I signed a two-picture deal then with a group of foreign businessmen, extremely well financed, serious Lebanese with money to burn, who want to get a toehold in the international film business. I have to make those pictures for them before I can go on to anything else. I'm meeting them in Paris the day after tomorrow. Chances are we'll do a lot of the filming in France and England."

"Damn."

"I know. I'm not anxious to go, but that's the name of the game. As Willie Sutton said, he robbed banks because that was where the money was . . . . and right now it's in Paris. Maybe you can come over during the summer for a few weeks . . . I could give you a job as a gofer, start you out in the business. I'll call Billy from Paris and discuss it with her."

"Oh, don't forget, I want to come, I really do!"

"I won't forget," Vito promised. He opened the door for her and kissed her good night quickly, waving as he drove away.

Disconsolate, Gigi entered the house and made her way upstairs to Billy's room.

"Darling!" Billy turned around and hugged her. "You look perfect! But so sad! What's wrong? Did your father say something awful? William told me you were out for dinner with him."

"He just told me he's leaving for God knows how long, making pictures in France."

"Well that's understandable, isn't it?" Billy asked gently.

"I think it's a good idea, I just hate to see him go."

"Did he say anything about that . . . the picture?"

"Not a single word."

"So you didn't have to say anything either," Billy asked, looking at Gigi closely.

"No, thank goodness. I was really worried at the beginning of dinner, but then I understood that he was going to act just as if nothing had happened, so I relaxed. I've never had such a fabulous talk with him! Oh, Billy, he was so interested in everything about me . . . it was as if he was discovering me for the first time! Maybe I'm finally old enough for him, do you think that's what happened? I had so much to tell him, and he was such a good listener that I completely forgot all about the picture. I can't believe that it just went right out of my mind."

"Hmm." Billy was thoughtful. When she and Mazie and Gigi hadn't been able to get seats for *Kramer vs. Kramer*, they had popped into the first Friday-night screenings of *The WASP* in Westwood. Neither of the two girls had dared to suggest leaving as the film began to unfold itself in all its misbegotten embarrassment, until Billy, suffering keenly for Gigi, had insisted on going, pleading a terrible headache. Gigi had read every single one of the reviews over and over, grieving so much that Billy had finally had to take them away from her and tear them up.

"Where did you eat?" Billy asked curiously.

"A place called Dominick's. That's why I smell as if I've been barbecued. But I met a bunch of Dad's friends on the way out . . . he knew everyone there. They all were awfully nice, very friendly, just as if nothing had happened. Nobody said a word about it."

"That's the way it goes . . . in public. No one in the business knows when he's going to be in the same position as Vito, so there's a code of behavior," Billy explained, putting her arms around Gigi.

You are a truly accomplished swine, Vito, she thought bitterly, using the daughter you've never bothered about as your shield, taking her to the most public possible forum, bombarding her with your charm, playing the adoring father, parading her in front of Hollywood, knowing that she would deflect the difficult moment, confuse the crowd, throw some temporary stardust in their eyes. I can just see you operating tonight, giving Gigi the same treatment that worked on me, making your daughter fall in love with you at your convenience. What plans will you have for her, now that she's an asset?

6

*V*alentine O'Neill sat at the drafting desk of her design studio at Scruples, sipping the strong French coffee she brewed for herself each morning, and considered a variety of subjects. It was spring of 1980 and she was entirely happy. How many women were entirely happy, she wondered. And at the inconsequential age of twenty-nine, at that? It was her impression that most women at twenty-nine were worried about their boyfriends or their husbands or their children or their jobs, or their lack of them, or their problems in managing all of them at once. Most women didn't achieve entire happiness—which meant a kind of serenity that allowed you to actively observe yourself being happy, did it not?—until they became grandmothers and could retire from the fray of life and just enjoy themselves, or so her mother had assured her. Her poor mother, Valentine thought, who, for all her wisdom, had died much too soon, working almost until the last minute at her highly skilled job as a fitter of haute couture clothes at the House of Balmain.

No, she was, of course, not *entirely* happy, Valentine realized, for she would always miss her French mother, who had married an American she'd met the day of the Liberation of Paris and gone to live with him in New York, where Valentine had been born. Only after his early death had the young widow taken her half-Irish, half-French child back to her own native Paris, where the workrooms of the great dress house of Balmain had become Valentine's second school. There Valentine had learned so much that she dared, after her mother's death in 1972, to return alone to New York and seek a designer's career for herself.

And now here she was, eight years later, she and Elliott, incredibly, married and almost as incredibly partners with Billy Ikehorn in two ever more wildly successful boutiques, the new Scruples in Chicago and New York. If only her mother had lived to see her happiness, Valentine thought, almost unable to comprehend it without someone to discuss it with besides Elliott himself, who spent so much time being charmed in his carefree way at her wonderment that she wasn't sure he truly understood just how surprising it all was.

Valentine kept her feet on the ground by continuing to design clothes for individual women, custom-made clothes in the grand tradition. No amount of other work had made her relinquish her absolute control of the couture department that existed only in the California Scruples, a luxury to which many rich women could only aspire, no matter how much money they had, for Valentine had only so much time to give them, and her earliest customers received preference. She had a visceral need to continue to work with her hands, to invent, to sketch, to handle fabrics, to create clothes for special occasions, clothes that expressed her own imagination and talent. Her waiting list had been closed for a year now, although, like every other closed waiting list, it always had just one or two openings for women with special connections.

Like Gigi Orsini. Of course she was going to make Gigi's senior prom dress, Valentine thought with a tilt of anticipation, even if Billy, as fussy as a typical worried mother, thought it risked spoiling her. How could you spoil a girl whose idea of heaven was to be initiated into the secrets of Valentine's own kitchen? How could you spoil a girl who had spent an entire Saturday shopping for and cooking a five-course dinner in their own apartment and presented it to them as a second-anniversary present, a supremely classic dinner that Valentine had admitted gladly she herself could never possibly have equaled on her best day? Her own cuisine, learned from her mother, was that excellently comforting but essentially middle-class cooking that you could—should, if possible—eat every day. But Gigi had learned from an accomplished French chef, and her elegant, complicated cooking was to ordinary French food what one of Valentine's own designs was to a garment off the rack.

Even if Gigi had been a horrid brat, how could she not design a dress in which the girl would be seen to her greatest advantage at such an important occasion as a senior prom? Any designer who had to work day after day with ordinary flesh and blood, with women whose raw material it was necessary to conceal, enhance or disguise, would jump at the chance to take a busman's holiday and make something exquisite for Gigi, that delectable young person who combined such whimsical freshness with such an air of innocent swagger. Gigi, it seemed to Valentine, brought with her the sound of distant music whenever she appeared, joyous snatches of carefree tunes that had filled the air in another time in the history of the world. She looked as if she had danced out of another era, now a half-century in the past, danced to the beat of jazz; she looked as if she should be smooching in the backseat of a convertible with a Yale boy and drinking bathtub gin in honkytonks, whatever they were, and smoking forbidden cigarettes and driving entire squads of young men crazy with unfulfilled passion—this girl who had just barely started to date, who had, according to Billy, no bad habits, which in itself was enough to worry Billy.

Was it the half-Irish heritage they shared, Valentine wondered, that made her feel such an affinity for Gigi? Or was it that they were both, she believed, hardworking and logical respecters of a status quo that they would rebel against immediately and effectively if it struck them as the right thing to do? One thing was sure, they were both of the green-eyed, white-skinned, redheaded type of female, no matter by what artifice that red—or rather orange—was obtained in Gigi's case, no matter that Valentine felt that she towered over Gigi, who seemed to have finally stopped growing. Designing for Gigi would be like designing for herself if she had ever had a senior prom, an institution that would surely have been forbidden in her own Paris lycée, if it had ever been heard of at all.

But she could not begin to think about Gigi's dress now, Valentine realized as she glanced at her watch. She had an appointment with a new client in two minutes, another exception to the waiting list. She frowned, thinking of the request—impossible to refuse—that Billy had made, asking her to design a wardrobe for Melanie Adams, who was to star in Wells Cope's new film, *Legend*.

Cope, the most envied, secure and tasteful producer in all of Hollywood, had spent a year waiting to find the absolutely right second vehicle for Melanie Adams, who had leapt into international superstardom in the first picture he had made with her.

Legend, a story that skillfully combined the Dietrich and Garbo success stories, could indeed only be made with the one actress of today who had nothing to fear—at least physically—from comparison with those immortals. Nevertheless, Valentine would have refused, in spite of all the wooing, all the publicity she stood to gain, for she needed no additional press and she was impervious to the most skillful importuning.

However, Melanie Adams was the former fashion model who had broken Elliott's heart when she left him flat, with a viciously cruel note, four years ago, leaving Valentine to put the pieces back together.

Elliott, her own Elliott, was a man who truly enjoyed and appreciated women, who celebrated the female presence in the world, who gave himself to them as warmly and sweetly as they gave themselves to him, healing their hurts and understanding their problems. But before he had fallen in love with Valentine, he had fallen truly in love only once, with Melanie Adams.

And that girl had been brutal to him, she had used him ruthlessly, she had lied to him consistently, and she had treated his emotions with nothing but contempt. Elliott had never blamed Melanie when he talked about her with Valentine, he had always sought to try to understand her, to explain away her actions, but Valentine knew the truth and she burned with a desire to punish the creature who had caused Elliott such desperate pain. Melanie had done unpardonable things to the man she loved. Elliott was a gentleman. If Melanie Adams came to him today he would be kind to her, he would never seek any revenge, but she, Valentine, was too much of a woman not to.

And also, to be honest, Valentine asked herself with a half-amused shake of her head at her own answer, wasn't she a little bit curious about this Melanie Adams? Wasn't it normal to want to see with her own eyes, in the flesh, the only other woman Elliott had ever loved?

* * *

Melanie Adams arrived at the studio just as Valentine buttoned the
last button of the strict white smock she always put on over her own
clothes when she received clients. She was surrounded by an entou-
rage: Wells Cope himself, a fair-haired, handsome man in his early
forties, slim and superlatively groomed, accompanied by his executive
producer, two publicists, Melanie Adams's personal hairdresser, and
a secretary. These six people huddled around the actress protectively,
so that at first Valentine couldn't pick out Melanie standing among
them with an air of not being present at all, like a captive queen among
the savages, while they introduced themselves to Valentine.

"I regret, Mr. Cope, that I cannot say welcome to my studio,"
Valentine declared. "I had no idea that you personally intended to
accompany Miss Adams, and I cannot imagine why you've brought so
many people with you."

Wells Cope laughed easily, not taken aback by Valentine's frigid
tone.

"I should have warned you, Miss O'Neill, but of course the costumes for *Legend* are entirely too important for Melanie to walk in
here by herself, just like anybody. We came to make your job easier,
to help you, to—"

"Mr. Cope, you can add nothing to my job. I have read the script,
I understand exactly what is necessary in the way of costumes. I need
only Miss Adams."

"But . . . you don't understand. Miss Adams—Melanie—expects us to be here to pave the way, to give her feedback, to—"

"To hold her hand, Mr. Cope? If she cannot entrust herself to me
with confidence, there is no use in proceeding. Obviously I intend to
work with you eventually, naturally you will expect to approve my
designs, to edit them with my assistance, but today I need Miss Adams
by herself. I have less than two hours for her this morning. Are you
going to leave her quite alone with me, or are you departing—all of
you—and taking Miss Adams with you?"

"You might have warned me, I had no idea you'd be so . . ."
Wells Cope was no longer smiling.

"'So' . . . what?" Valentine asked, pleased by his consternation,
but showing no change in her severe expression.

"So . . . positive."

"Take it or leave it, Mr. Cope, just don't waste my time."

"Melanie?" Wells Cope turned to her questioningly.

"For heaven's sake, Wells, will you all just please get the hell out of here?'' Melanie Adams's voice still contained faint, maddeningly sweet cadences of her native Louisville, Kentucky, but her delivery was curt.

Wells Cope had discovered her, he had invented her, he had turned her into an actress, and he had signed her to a four-picture contract. The deluge of adulation her personal success had brought had soured her on his mentorship and ownership, which, as yet, she saw no way to escape.

"I'll be back for you at noon," he said, frowning. "Come on, everybody, let's leave these two ladies to get on with it."

"Well," said Valentine, when they were alone, "that's better, I think."

"I admire your style, Miss O'Neill. I've never seen anyone throw Wells out before. I enjoyed it."

"Please call me Valentine. I'm not normally so abrupt, but their presence was entirely unnecessary. I'm surprised they didn't know that in advance."

"I told Wells that you didn't design by committee, but they're all so nervous about having the clothes right, with *Legend* being a period piece . . .''

"For which, of course, I would never design strict period clothes, since what women actually wore in that era would be shockingly unattractive to us now."

"Oh yes! That's exactly what I thought when I looked at all those early photographs of Dietrich and Garbo when they first came to Hollywood . . . they both dressed like frights, everything was too long or too bulky or just plain tacky, and those dreadful hats! I didn't want to do the picture because I couldn't bear the clothes."

"Have no such fears," Valentine said, as she observed Melanie Adams closely, watching the way she used her hands, the way she turned her head, the way she held her shoulders. She was, naturally, smaller than she photographed, but even more beautiful in the flesh than on the screen, if such a thing was possible, Valentine admitted to herself.

"I will approximate the period," she told Melanie, "interpret it, design whatever it is that your own look demands, and still give the audience the impression that you are dressed in the height of fashion of those years. What I will avoid—the reason Mr. Cope will pay me so well—is the disillusionment of reproducing reality."

" 'The disillusionment of reality' . . . I like that, I understand that," Melanie said slowly. Reality had always eluded her never-ending search. All of her life, no matter how many people told her she was beautiful, no matter how many men had loved her, she had never been able to experience an inner perception of herself as a real person. She was only certain that she was real when she had a streaming head cold, she sometimes thought with the fretfulness of a child.

When Melanie Adams had turned from modeling to acting, she'd found that during the time the camera was rolling, she felt real. Like somebody else, of course, yet *actual*, *there*. But the camera had to stop eventually, leaving her beached and sad, absorbed again by her core of emptiness, her ever-renewed quest to break out of an intense, inescapable connection with her own image and emerge into the world, like a chick trying to peck its way out of an unbreakable eggshell. Melanie's need to take and take in order to create the smallest, always fleeting sense of selfhood had taught her how to inspire love, but no amount of adoration had ever been enough to release her from the chains of narcissism.

"I said, of *reproducing* reality," Valentine said softly, correcting her.

"Oh, I suppose, but it's the same thing, isn't it?" Melanie said vaguely, running her fingers over the bolts of fabric that leaned against the wall near Valentine's desk, lightly touching the panne velvets, the melting cashmeres, the icy satins. She turned to Valentine with curiosity, seeming to come out of a dream.

"You're married to Spider Elliott, aren't you?" she asked. She had seen photographs of Valentine in *Women's Wear,* but she'd never come across her in person. She hadn't anticipated that Valentine would be so sympathetic, so understanding. In fact, she hadn't wanted to meet Spider's wife, and only Wells's insistence had brought her here today.

"Elliott and I have been married for two years," Valentine answered matter-of-factly.

"I used to know him . . . in fact, he took the first test shots of me when I started modeling. In a way, I guess you could say that he started me on my career."

"You could say that," Valentine agreed, "but any other photographer could have done the same—Elliott said it was impossible to get a bad shot of you. I remember when Harriet Toppingham first saw those test shots at *Fashion and Interiors*—Elliott said that she called you 'killingly beautiful'—did you know that?"

"No," Melanie laughed, delighted. "Harriet was always over the top, absolutely excessive—but a great editor. Goodness, you must have known Spider well for him to have told you that, such a silly detail, and it happened at least four years ago. I'm amazed that he still remembers."

Valentine took out her tape measure. "Let me get some measurements before I forget," she said. "Just stand still." Deftly she began measuring the crucial distances from the nape to the top of the spinal column, from there to the precise end of the shoulder bone, from the shoulder bone to the point of the elbow, from the elbow to the wrist, from the wrist to the tip of the middle finger, measurements that were only the beginning of what she would need, yet measurements she trusted no assistant to take.

"It wasn't that he remembered exactly," Valentine said, continuing to speak as she plied her tape measure. "You see, we were neighbors in our little lofts, and at night Elliott told me everything that had happened to him during the day. I was weak-minded enough to cook dinner for him any evening that he wasn't going out, but it was either that or let the poor foolish man starve to death. The day he met you, he told me that he'd blurted out that he was in love with you when he didn't even know your name! He said he surprised you so much the only way he could get you to stay in the studio was to make you a great liverwurst and Swiss cheese sandwich on rye bread." Valentine's voice rang with humor. "I was frankly impressed that under such circumstances of high emotion he still had enough presence of mind to make a decent sandwich, when all he could ever think to make for me, when I came crawling to him for comfort at the end of one of my own tragic love affairs, was his eternal Campbell's cream of tomato soup with Ritz crackers."

"He *told you* about falling in love with me?"

"But of course," Valentine said with a shrug. "We had no secrets from each other. I suppose that sounds strange, in fact I know it does, a woman and a man who tell each other everything, who continue to have no secrets from each other, but that's what happens when you don't start out with love, just with plain, ordinary friendship."

"Ordinary friendship? It sounds like more than that to me."

"Oh no, truly not. In fact, at first I didn't even like Elliott . . . or rather I didn't approve of his habit of falling passionately, head-over-heels in and out of love with half of the most beautiful models in New

York. I'm sure you must have realized that was his pattern at the time you met him. How could I put my faith in a man with such a record of going from woman to woman, of loving wildly here and loving wildly there, almost indiscriminately, so long as the girl was beautiful? He had to go a long way to win my trust, fond as I became of him.''

"How . . . did he convince you . . . that you could trust him?'' Melanie's faltering question seemed to come from a distance, so thin was her voice.

"Ah, I must not tell you that,'' Valentine said, smiling gently. "You would be too flattered, and if we are going to work together well, I can't become yet another person who flatters you.''

"But it had something to do with me? Come on, Valentine, you have to tell! It's not fair to hint at it like that, it's really wrong of you. If you weren't going to tell me, you shouldn't have brought it up.''

Valentine laid down her tape measure. "You know, Melanie, you're right. There are some things that Elliott told me that he should have kept to himself. I should have kept silent.''

"But I insist! I promise you I won't be upset . . . since he told you everything, why should he have kept one thing back? What was it, Valentine?''

"Well . . . you'll remember that after you'd finished your first picture, there was a long wait before Mr. Cope decided what your next career move should be?''

"How could I forget? I went crazy with the waiting, but what does that have to do with it, with your trusting Spider?''

"At that time, Elliott hadn't seen you since you left for Hollywood, since you left him rather suddenly one afternoon in New York —ah, Melanie, I had to comfort him over that shock, let me assure you. Poor Elliott was quite broken up about it for a while—weeks and weeks, yes, as long as that before he found another love—but in the end it was good for his male ego to find that there was at least one girl who could say no . . . Where was I? Oh yes, quite a while after that time when you came to see him at home here in Los Angeles, and . . .'' Valentine's voice trailed off. She blushed and turned her eyes away from Melanie's face.

"What about it?'' Melanie demanded roughly.

"Melanie, of course it was natural, was it not, that you two made love? And that it was delicious for you? Both of you. I understood perfectly why you wanted to resume your old romance with Elliott, so many girls found him difficult, almost impossible to forget . . . but when he told me about it, and—how can I put it?—how he was forced to explain to you that his feelings for you were over for him, no matter how good the lovemaking was—well . . . I think the fact that he had been totally cured of you, which is something I imagine no other man who ever loved you could say—that it was then, at that time, that I began—slowly, I grant you—to trust him, to believe that perhaps he had grown up and had recovered from his addiction to loving every beauty who came his way. Does that answer your question?''

''Fully,'' Melanie said, in a strained attempt at humor.

''And I have not flattered you too much?''

''I'm not sure, Valentine. I'll have to think it over.''

''Bravo! So, let us begin. I've made some preliminary sketches, some rough ideas, that I had no intention of showing Mr. Cope until you gave me your own opinions. It is you, not he, who will wear the clothes, so it is you, not he, I design for. Come to my desk and I'll show them to you.''

As Melanie turned the sheets of paper over, examining them closely, Valentine felt surprised at herself, with an inner merriment that she still had so much to learn about her own emotions and abilities. She left Melanie rapt over her designs while she treated herself to a rare cigarette. She always kept a pack of Gauloises Bleus in her office for times when she wanted to retreat into thought and now she felt a sudden need for one as she sorted out her emotions. First of all, she hadn't dreamed that she could manage to so skillfully misrepresent her own Elliott as a man who had been in love with many women, not just two. And in the second place she had not known until today just how violently jealous she had been of Melanie Adams. Back when Elliott had been involved with Melanie, she, Valentine, had almost managed to convince herself that she thought of him only as a friend, although now she knew that she had loved him from the day she first saw him. And finally, in spite of all the confusion of these past emotions, she knew that she would make the once-hated Melanie truly magical clothes, that she would surpass herself.

Valentine resolved to create for Melanie clothes that would make the poor lovely creature less sad. She would never have believed, until today, that the strongest emotion she would feel for Melanie Adams was pity.

* * *

Susan Arvey left Mark Hampton's office humming, her step as light as a debutante's. As soon as the famous decorator could manage to take the time, he would be flying out to California to take a good long look at their house before he came back to New York and started to plan to redo it from stem to stern, from head to toe, from laundry room to drawing room. And what a nice man he was! His knowledge of the history of great interior design of the past was encyclopedic, yet his relationship to the needs of today was so sensitive that for someone like her, who insisted on out-and-out grandeur, yet *domesticated* grandeur, so that comfort ruled all else, there could be no better choice. He understood to their depths the uses of extravagance and luxury. And she responded deeply to the last thing he had said to her during their consultation: "The only dogma worth observing is one that is self-imposed." Actually, he'd said it about the way to decorate bedrooms, but she thought it was an observation that could be broadened and used for life itself.

Waiting in the early-evening rush for the light to change so that she could cross Fifth Avenue, she felt lightheaded and giddy as she always did when she abruptly found herself walking on a New York street after a trip from Los Angeles. She visited the city frequently, but she always forgot how many people there were in Manhattan, each one competing for his little bit of space, actually afraid that the light would change before he managed to get across in safety.

Thank God, Susan thought, as she always did on the first day in Manhattan, that she had been born on the Coast. In New York, even Joe Farber's daughter and sole heiress would only be one of many hundreds of equally rich women with an always-to-be-reestablished claim on society's attention. If she lived here she would be flung into a swarming pool of women like herself, competing, as anxiously as these people waiting for the light, for her place in the fashionable world. She would have to get in the ring, year after year, with women whose money came from ancient family fortunes, women with far more pride of birth than she, and with women with new fortunes made in banking, in industry, on Seventh Avenue, in publishing, in literally every single one of the great money-making businesses of America whose owners lived in New York.

In Hollywood, that single-industry town, where her father had been among the handful of financial giants and her husband was, in today's terms, another, she could hardly have helped rising to the top. Her success had been assured unless she'd gone out of her way to avoid it. Susan knew that; any woman who calculated as clearly as she could not help but accept that particular fact. Nevertheless, she had dedicated her energies to making sure that she was always at the top of the top; she competed for ascendancy even when it wasn't strictly necessary, aching daily for more power than male-dominated Hollywood would allow her.

Yet . . . yet . . . in New York a woman could sometimes seize her *own* power, not have it come to her as a reflection of the power of her father or her husband as it almost always must in Los Angeles. In New York a woman could run a magazine or an advertising agency or a fashion business, and owe nothing to a man.

But to do that would mean becoming a working woman, a career woman, a woman who had to risk failure, Susan Arvey realized, and such a life didn't appeal to her at all. No, she didn't mind getting up early for a tennis lesson, but to go to an office! As the British used to say, "It wouldn't suit."

When she reached the apartment at the Sherry Netherland that the Arveys had bought years ago, she phoned home. It was almost dinnertime in New York, afternoon in Los Angeles.

"Yes, Curt, I'm fine. I've just left him . . . he couldn't be nicer. Yes, darling, we decided to do the whole house. Redecorating keeps you young, out of a rut. After all, you wouldn't want me to get so restless that I'd sell the paintings and start a whole new collection of those modern artists, would you? Oh, it'll be about three more days before I can leave . . . so much to do. How are you, sweetie? Feeling better? Good. You should try to forget about that film entirely. Everyone else has. Tonight? I'm doing the usual. Natalie's discovered a play that's so far Off Broadway I think it's in Newark. Don't worry, Curt, of course I'm arranging for a limo, you don't think I'd get into a New York cab, do you? That's like shutting yourself in a closet with a maniac. I'll call tomorrow. Take care, try to get some sleep tonight. 'Bye, darling."

Her wifely duties completed, Susan Arvey took off all her jewelry and put it in the safe she had had installed in her closet. She made another phone call, had a short conversation and fixed a time later in the evening.

As she took a long, self-indulgent bath, she thought fondly of Natalie Eustace, who had been her roommate during her freshman year at college, before she left to marry. Curt loathed Natalie's artistic pretensions, her delight in plays that should never have been written, much less produced. He was always grateful when he didn't have to spend an evening with her. In fact, he hadn't seen Natalie in years, for Susan spared him, making dates with Natalie only when Curt wasn't in New York with her. Curt realized that she needed to go to New York more than he did, considering her interest in art, given her great collection. There were so many exhibits to see, so many new galleries to check out, so many auctions that were promising, to say nothing of revisiting her favorite museums. He could live without all that perfectly well, thank you, Curt told her, but if she enjoyed it, why not?

Why not indeed? Susan Arvey echoed, inspecting herself carefully in the mirror on her dressing table. She had been just thirty-eight, an unusually pretty and young-looking thirty-eight, when she'd had her first facelift.

For years she'd been on the alert for the right moment, the absolutely first instant at which she would be able to notice the effects of gravity on her chin line. Every day she automatically pulled the skin of her jaw and cheeks back toward her ears and then let it relax into its normal configuration. The day on which it relaxed a certain amount too much, an amount that was far too little to be apparent to anyone but her, was the day on which Susan had made her appointment to have a consultation with the plastic surgeon in Palm Springs who was so much more discreet and so much more expensive than anyone in Beverly Hills.

The Good Doctor, as she thought of him, had told her that very few women were as smart as she was, clever enough to come to him as early as she had. Usually they waited until repair work was necessary to the naked eye. In the past, he said regretfully, even as little as ten years ago, doctors usually considered it wise to wait to do plastic surgery until they could make a difference in their patients' looks. This meant that the work would be noticed, when the whole point was that it should never be noticed. Her facelift would be done at precisely the perfect amount of time *before* it was needed, he said, pleased at the prospect of perfect conditions. The Good Doctor assured her that he would do such a gentle, subtle job that not even the most sharp-eyed and suspicious of her friends would ever guess. In addition, the recuperation from the inevitable bruises and swelling would be exceptionally quick and easy. The Good Doctor had lived up to all his promises.

Susan Arvey told Curt that she was going to a health spa for a few weeks of diet and intensive exercise. When she returned from the desert, where she had stayed at the Doctor's intensely private postoperative clinic, seeing no one but nurses and the Doctor himself, Curt observed that the spa had put the sparkle back in her eyes. Now, at forty-one, she looked exactly as she had at thirty-four. She assumed she always would, except for those inevitable, really rather attractive "character" lines that returned sooner or later as time passed and she used her facial muscles to smile or frown. The Good Doctor was only a few years older than she, and he had two brilliant young surgeons training under him, so if she kept up her tennis and her workouts and her massage, why should she ever look much older than thirty-four?

Susan Arvey inspected her naked body, as always with an unsparing, ferocious, suspicious eye for detail. She'd started out with a splendid, slender, full-breasted body, and thanks to her never-ending attention it remained as lithe, supple and well-toned as it had ever been. Thank God she'd never had children; that damage was irreparable. She never exposed her skin to the sun after her early tennis lesson, so the skin of her body was like a girl's. She was a great deal stronger than she looked; for years her exercise had been directed at building her flexibility, and her flat abdominal muscles and long, shapely arm and leg muscles betrayed no bulk.

While she arranged her blond hair into its timeless chignon, as she applied her simple makeup, Susan chuckled at the prospect of still looking thirty-four at fifty-four. Obviously, by that time people would realize that she must have had some "work" done, simply because they would have known her for so long, but they wouldn't be able to gossip about specifics, and actually pinpoint the day and the doctor, the way they relished doing about every other woman in town who suddenly looked "rested."

Susan went to the kitchen of the five-room apartment, took out the chicken salad that room service had left in the fridge for her, and ate it quickly, without interest. She dressed in the quietest and most conservative of her expensive dresses and left the hotel, greeting the friendly doorman as she always did. As soon as she was out of his sight she hailed a cab and gave an address on Second Avenue. The taxi drew up at an unimpressive modern building with no doorman and a self-service elevator. There she went to the eleventh floor and unlocked the door to a small apartment she had owned for years, an apartment she had had furnished by Bloomingdale's design department. The apartment had been bought by her trustees at her direction, and furnished and maintained in the same way. Her trustees had as little curiosity about the apartment as her husband had access to her trustees.

It had a pleasant enough living room, she thought, as she always did, comfortable and in good taste, a living room that any well-paid, single working woman might be able to afford. She turned on all the air conditioners, for the air was stale, and went quickly into the bedroom of the apartment. There her heart started to beat even more heavily than it had been beating from the time she had left the Sherry Netherland.

The bedroom was not average, not ordinary, not easily affordable, and quite certainly not even in good taste. It was shut off from any connection to the outside world by lavish and thickly hung draperies that completely covered the walls and windows in feminine tones of light and dusky pinks, with an occasional touch of deep red. The room contained several cunningly placed screens and mirrors and a large bed with an elaborate wrought-iron headboard and footboard, piled high with pillows and made up with silk sheets, a bedroom that was entirely hedonistic and complicated, a bedroom that kept secrets.

Susan Arvey crossed it hastily, going straight to the large dressing room, where she took off all her dull clothes. She made a careful choice of one of the dozen floor-length robes that hung there, picking one that shimmered in violet tones. Each of the robes had a wide sash at the waist, a deep neckline and a full skirt. They were made of precious but light fabrics, airy enough to be almost transparent, but used so lavishly that their folds concealed any clear look at her body. Susan opened a cabinet in the dressing room and inspected five long red and brunette wigs on stands, finally choosing one that was an exceptionally long tangle of black curls. She undid her chignon, pinning her hair on top of her head, and fastening the wig securely. Suddenly Susan Arvey looked not thirty-four, but twenty-four, for the sweep of hair took away a full decade. Her makeup needed no attention; its very simplicity added to her look of youth.

For the second time that evening she stood in front of a well-lit full-length mirror and took inventory. Try to critique as she would, there was only a girl standing there, an exceptionally good-looking girl with a marvelously appealing body, of which the worst you could say was that her breasts were perhaps too large, her nipples too prominent, for every taste. No one she had ever known in the world would recognize her; the dark wig made an amazing difference in her looks, falling forward in curly bangs and shadowing her cheekbones. She took her bare breasts in her hands and pushed them forward so that the neckline of the robe framed them in their lush, white nakedness. She arranged several of the curls of the wig so that they fell over her breasts, and parted the robe at the waist so that her blond pubic hair was visible. She stood, swaying slightly, admiring her erotic image for long minutes, feeling a warmth rising in her body, a puissant liquid feeling shot through with flashes of desire. Finally, almost reluctantly, she rearranged her robe and went into the bedroom, moving around deftly, making sure that the right dim lamps were lit and that the pillows on the bed were properly arranged.

The doorbell rang almost as soon as she was finished with her preparations. Trembling slightly, she went to answer it. Part of the excitement of these evenings was that she never booked the same man twice. It ensured that he would never become too curious or posses-sive about her, and it preserved the charm of her surprise. All the men who worked for the agency were gifted, the very drunk actress who had first told her about it had confided.

"They don't send ugly men, but their looks are not the point, see, the point is that they can get it up and keep it up, they can perform, see, if you know what I mean, and believe you me, we're talking about a very very special talent, worth its weight in gold. They're all young or they couldn't do it, they can't fake it like the girls, that's why they charge such a fortune. They're squeaky clean and they're not ever going to turn mean and they cost like bloody hell, but let's face it, sometimes it's worth it, know what I mean?"

Susan had pretended not to know what she meant, but she'd kept the agency's card that the actress had pressed on her. The actress, who'd blacked out on what she'd told Susan Arvey, never had to worry about losing Susan's friendship, for Susan couldn't be certain how much the woman had retained of a conversation they never had again.

She opened the door, keeping it on the chain. Several times she hadn't cared for the look of the man the agency sent, and she had asked him to leave, phoning immediately for a replacement. Tonight she was pleased. As she let the man in, she sized him up. He had a perceptibly awkward look on his pleasant, scrubbed, open face. He obviously was new at this, Susan thought, appraising his height, which was barely more than her own, his healthy tan, his short, light brown, curly hair, his broad shoulders, his noticeable sturdiness. He wore the preppy clothes they all wore, his oxford shirt open at the neck, his sports jacket hanging over his arm. They never dressed more formally; the agency was not an escort service.

As she closed the front door behind her and locked it, she said, "You are here to do only what I tell you to do. I don't permit questions, you may not ask me anything at all, you must stay silent under all circumstances. You must please me, you must obey me implicitly." Although she spoke in a low, level voice, no one listening to her would doubt her entire seriousness.

She led the way across the living room into the bedroom, noting that the boy's bewilderment was only intensified by his finding her so unexpectedly young and beautiful. Once they had reached the insinuating deep pink cave of the bedroom, Susan took his jacket and threw it on a chair. "Take off all your clothes," she commanded, and sat down in an armchair near the door, watching him while he obeyed her, almost stumbling as he shook his feet out of his trousers and flung them on the carpet. "Now stand with your back to the door, and look straight ahead, don't look at me," she dictated. Ignoring his surprised face, she thoughtfully studied the young man's tanned, naked body. The hair of his chest and thighs was fairly abundant and the same light brown as the hair on his head. He was powerfully built, all of his muscles were unusually well developed, and his penis, dangling heavily between his legs, was considerably shorter than average but twice as thick.

As she sat impassively, betraying nothing but a steady, calm interest, Susan could feel her rising excitement at the sight of this wholly desirable boy. It was necessary that he be a stranger, necessary that he be prohibited from expressing his own personality, necessary that he be immobile, totally subject to her scrutiny, unable to act unless she allowed it. His very youth and evident inexperience made her feel a flare of inventive mischief. She gave him an order she had never given before.

"I want you to turn around and face the door, stand flat up against it and keep your feet together," Susan directed him when she had looked her fill. His back was strong, his buttocks shapely, firm and round, the only part of his body besides his penis that wasn't completely tan. She got up and stood behind him, not letting her robe touch him, and ran a finger lightly down his backbone to the base of his spine, pleased by the strong reflexive shiver he couldn't control. Without touching him anywhere else she began to finger his buttocks, teasing them with casual, caressing, roving fingertips. As her hands played with him she dictated her injunctions. "Stand absolutely still," she enjoined him, "don't move an inch away from the door. You think you know what I want, but you haven't any idea. You think you can give it to me, but I'm going to take it from you. Take it, do you understand?" She put both of her hands over the solid curves of his bottom, rotating them so that they created a warmly intimate friction.

"Don't!" she ruled cruelly as she felt him starting to press back against her. "Don't you dare! Hold still, part your feet, but stay pressed flat against the door." When he had complied, she worked her hand slowly, so slowly that he couldn't restrain a moan, into the warm place between his thighs and made herself master of his balls. For minutes, while he stood shuddering with the effort not to move, she grasped them, weighing them in her fingers, pleased with their ponderous heaviness, exploring the thickness of the coarse hair at the root of his hugely swollen, short penis that was crushed against the door.

"Touch it," he groaned.

Susan smiled briefly, but when she spoke he heard only anger. "I told you not to ask. You have no rights. Now I'll never touch it, *never*, you've just guaranteed your punishment, you've disobeyed me." She licked all her fingers and returned to his balls, moistening them and squeezing them with the most luxuriously subtle pressure, listening to his heightened breathing as she toyed ever more arousingly with him, relishing the increasing difficulty he was having in preventing himself from making any noise. "Don't you have any self-control?" she asked in contempt. "Turn around and face me. Oh, really, you should be ashamed of yourself. Look at you, you're no better than an animal. You've disregarded every word I said. Go over to the bed, lie down on your back, and get ready for your punishment. I warned you once . . . that should have been enough."

He moved stiffly toward the bed and lay down, keeping himself rigorously still, his arms at his sides, although he was panting for breath. Susan bent over him, opening her robe and freeing her hanging breasts. He bit his lips at the sight of them, but prevented himself from moving. When she saw that he was managing to obey her, she parted her robe until it was open all the way to her waist, allowing him to see what lay between her legs, swaying her hips from side to side until her provocation suddenly made him lift himself a few inches off the bed. Susan looked at his flushed face in disdain and spoke to him in a low, scornful voice. "I was going to give you one last chance," she said, closing her robe, "but now you've thrown it away. I was going to do . . . oh, such good, good things to you . . . but . . . no . . . it's over . . . you'll never get another opportunity . . . do you have the slightest idea what you missed by your disobedience? Now! Put your arms over your head, spread your legs again, and lie still."

There was a flicker of fear in his eyes as he watched her take out the long chiffon scarves that she kept ready in the bedside table. "Don't worry," she said briefly, "I don't believe in causing pain." Deftly she fastened his wrists and ankles to the graceful curves of the iron headboard and footboard, knowing that the scarves, for all their softness, were exceedingly strong. She arranged the last scarf so that it lightly covered his eyes, enabling him to see her through a layer of chiffon, but not to see clearly. Susan Arvey stepped back, looking at her captive with gourmandise. His penis was a burly, twitching, aching thing that he could not reach under any circumstances, that he could not touch for relief. He was entirely at her mercy, aroused to a point that an average man would be incapable of sustaining for long, but the agency did not send average men, and she knew she could do whatever she wished to the boy, as slowly as she pleased.

She let her robe fall softly to the floor and then she took all of the pile of pillows that separated the crown of the boy's head from the headboard of the bed, threw them to the carpet and made a fairly wide place for herself on the mattress behind his short curls. She perched lightly there, kneeling, watching his eyes as he tried to look backwards at her nakedness. Oh, but he wanted her, she thought, he wanted her so badly. Restraining him was necessary for what she intended to do to him. Even the best trained of the agency men couldn't be entirely trusted to acquiesce in the punishment she had formulated for him. Slowly, from her kneeling position, she curved forward over him until the big tips of her dark nipples swayed over his open mouth, just too high for him to reach them. His tongue flickered imploringly in the air as he watched them through the scarf. Now and then she allowed him to capture a nipple and suck on it for a while until she pulled back, ignoring his protestations, humiliating him until he begged, for now that he had lost all hope of pleasing her by docility or obedience, he implored her shamelessly. Susan played this game with him as her nipples hardened into tight points, and slowly she allowed him to take more and more of each breast into his mouth, relishing the excruciating good steady suction. Only when she chose not to continue to hold back did she lean far forward over him, resting on her elbows and her knees, her legs spread open wide above his head.

Slowly, ever so slowly, knowing that he was watching helplessly, now speechless with lust, she lowered herself toward his mouth. She sensed, rather than saw, his fleshy tongue straining up toward her. His tongue was blunt and wet and desperately eager and eventually, after much hesitation, she finally allowed him to use it between her open thighs, to use it on the soft, fragrant, partially opened lips of her lower body. She let him plunge his tongue between those lips, parting the hair, stabbing at the slickness and the wetness there, his chin raised as high off the bed as possible. She let him attempt to weaken her with his clever tricks, she felt her own congestion grow heavy while she kept her eyes on the clublike penis he was utterly unable to use. As soon as she could drag herself away from this luscious importuning, she lifted herself up again effortlessly and sank backwards on her heels so that he couldn't reach her or even see her.

"Oh no! Please!" he begged and she laughed and let him suck madly only on her flickering fingertips. Soon she bent her body down over his mouth again, this time low enough so that he was able to capture her clitoris and work on it with his tongue and his lips and the insides of his cheeks while she circled her bottom slowly, knowingly, pushing it hard into him for an instant before she lifted up just out of reach. Again and again she raised herself completely off his mouth and listened with voluptuousness at his supplications to let him put his cock in her, just to let him inside. "No," she insisted, "never . . . . you're worse than ever, you can't be trusted, you're disgusting, totally disgusting, I warned you . . . I even gave you a second chance . . . but there's no help for you now . . . you deserve to be punished." Now she stretched herself so far forward that he knew that if she chose to, she could easily reach his penis with her tongue. However, she lay quiveringly still, permitting him to explore deeply, with his mouth, the succulent bounty between her legs. She concentrated on his frantic lapping of her rapidly engorging clitoris. His penis was so sternly distended in its peak of excitement that she almost took pity on herself and on him, almost let herself touch it with her tongue, but she firmly prevented herself from yielding to that weakness. Soon she saw signs that he was beside himself with excitement, for although he couldn't touch his penis, or close his thighs over it, he was still free to use his pelvic muscles to clench and unclench his rear in a grinding up-and-down motion that was about to carry him over the top of endurance. Only then did she abandon herself to the tugging and pulling of his tongue on that heavy, hot, yearning point of her body, only then did she allow herself to give in to the waves of lust that led her so quickly into her long, drawn-out peak of release that was made all the more delicious by the sight of his sperm bursting forth into the air, but not in her, no, never in her, for that was not allowed, not while she was the boss, not while she was on top, not while she was in power.

The next day, when she met Natalie Eustace for lunch, Susan Arvey listened attentively to the detailed discussion of the best in Off-Broadway plays. Natalie loved these lunches, during which she could feel so superior to her old friend, whose life, though privileged, didn't include this artistic dimension.

"How are you spending your evenings here, Susan?" Natalie finally asked after she'd described her own doings at length.

"The usual, dinners with business friends of Curt's, people you'd have no use for. I do envy you, Natalie, going everywhere, but there are some things I just don't have the time for, alas."

"Perhaps when you're in town to buy antiques with Mark Hampton, you'll have time to devote an evening to me. But let's leave Curt at home—as usual, hmm?"

"We'll count on it, Natalie, even though antique-shopping usually leaves me wilted on the vine."

"I must say you don't look wilted," Natalie said with a note of envy at Susan's glowing health.

"It's the California life, cookie, I've always said it may be dull, but something about it is unquestionably good for you—some secret ingredient in the smog." The red wig tonight, she thought, the one that is long and straight, and two boys . . . yes, she'd phone as soon as lunch was over and reserve the two newest, youngest boys the agency had, and force one of them to watch, naked, bound and unable to move, while she taught the other to obey. Yes, with his eyes covered with one thin layer of chiffon, so that she felt completely free, he would observe everything while he waited his turn, he would watch until he understood that her orders were never idle threats. If he had learned his lesson properly, perhaps she would touch him with her tongue, even with her lips . . . or perhaps not. There would be so many other games to play with two boys instead of one, just as there were so many possibilities in a world where the only dogma worth observing was that which was self-imposed.

7

"Yes, Jean-Luc, you wanted to see me?" Josie Speilberg, busy in her office one morning in the early summer of 1980, wondered why the chef had requested a private interview with her.

"I must give my notice, Mademoiselle, with regret," the portly man said calmly.

"Oh no, Jean-Luc, you can't do that!"

"But indeed I can, Mademoiselle. There is nothing wrong with this position, you have been most kind and I have no complaints, but I must be realistic. Next year Gigi will be away in college. She has been my dream pupil, and frankly, I have stayed on here this long only to teach her everything I could. Madame Ikehorn has no real need of a chef."

"But, Jean-Luc, Mrs. Ikehorn always has a chef, she's had a chef ever since she married Mr. Ikehorn, of course she needs you." Josie was appalled at the prospect of finding another experienced chef, just when things had been going so smoothly in the kitchen that she had been able to forget all about it.

"Permit me to disagree. When Madame is here, she eats so carefully that the quality of my cuisine must, of necessity, be diluted into, shall we say, a thin broth? Nourishing but needing no special skills. If Madame ever entertains again, she can always employ a fine caterer. She doesn't need to keep a chef who has practically nothing to do. Soon I will forget the uses of butter and the taste of heavy cream."

"If it's a question of salary . . . if you're going to cook for someone else . . ."

"No, Mademoiselle, it is not that. It happens that I have a chance to realize an opportunity I have long hoped for. A friend requires a chef for a small restaurant he is about to open in Santa Barbara. The cuisine will be distinguished, the restaurant elegant, and he has offered me a partnership. I think you will agree that I would be foolish not to seize this chance."

"I can't deny we don't do a lot of fancy French eating here, Jean-Luc, but isn't there anything I can do to change your mind?"

"Short of keeping Gigi at home, nothing, dear Mademoiselle. I need not leave for another two months. I think that will give you enough time to find somebody else who will suit. Perhaps an older man, someone who will be glad to be paid to sit around in great comfort and do a minimum of work, someone who will not miss the lack of challenge, perhaps . . . . an American?"

"Oh, really, Jean-Luc!"

"I am frank, Mademoiselle, but not unfair," he said respectfully, and took his leave.

Provoked by Jean-Luc's attitude, Josie searched far and wide until she discovered a young chef, twenty-six-year-old Quentin Browning, whose father owned a fine country hotel in the Cotswolds, known for the excellence of its kitchen. The Ash Grove, a venerable hostelry near Stratford-on-Avon, offered twenty bedrooms and five suites, but the key to its year-round success was its good-sized restaurant where tables were booked weeks in advance by people from the neighboring countryside as well as Londoners who made the jaunt just for the food.

Quentin Browning had gone to Rugby and then headed straight for Switzerland for schooling in the hotelkeeper's trade. He had always known that one day he would go into the highly prosperous family business, he took a keen interest in the varied skills of hotel-keeping, and he did well in Switzerland. Afterwards he decided to train seriously as a chef. Although the Ash Grove employed a large, skillful staff in the kitchen, it was essential for him to be able to do anything the head chef could do before he was experienced enough to criticize and innovate. Unless he had that ability, he would always be at the chef's mercy, a situation that would be intolerable.

Quentin Browning worked in great restaurant kitchens in Lyons, Paris, Milan and Rome, starting with the lowliest jobs and moving upward stage by classic stage, his success assured by hard work, talent and the powerful personal charm that has twice its normal impact when it is possessed by an Englishman, a member of that island race that does not rely on charm as a job qualification. Quentin Browning had just completed a one-year stint as assistant chef in a top French restaurant in Houston and had been offered a tempting job in San Francisco. However, he had turned it down for this opportunity to work in a large private house.

A lack of challenge, he decided, was exactly what he needed after the medieval slavery of his years of a chef's apprenticeship. His father didn't need him quite yet, and would never guess that his dutiful son was enjoying the equivalent of a well-paid vacation, considering the high wages that the simple job offered. Why shouldn't he enjoy a lovely long gulp of the California lifestyle: surfboards, sunshine and his particular fancy in the female line—big, beautiful, buxom, blond broads, preferably by the dozen—before burying himself in the depths of the Shakespeare country and tackling his life's work, Quentin asked himself, with the answer implicit in the question.

Gigi said a sad farewell to her Jean-Luc, her friend and irreplaceable teacher who had stayed on long enough to see her graduate from high school, an event attended by Billy, Spider, Valentine, Dolly and Lester, Sara the hairdresser from Sassoon, everyone who lived in the house on Charing Cross Road, and half the staff of Scruples. Vito was somewhere in the South of France, and only Gigi missed him.

To cheer herself up after Jean-Luc's departure, Gigi decided to make a cake for the replacement who was due to arrive tomorrow. Nothing fancy, nothing showy, nothing vulgar, but a cake that would test this newcomer's knowledge of baking as little else could. She decided to make a vanilla génoise, the basic French sponge cake, which, to be perfect, demands such invisible expertise that only another expert can judge it. His reaction to the sponge cake was the test she devised, the trap she laid for him, for she had no faith in any Englishman who made the bold claim to be a finished French chef.

"But why a sponge cake, Gigi?" Burgo O'Sullivan asked curiously as he watched her set about her work in the kitchen that was deserted on that afternoon. "Why not something more eye-catching?"

"Burgo, I know it wasn't easy when you taught me to drive, I know you took your life in your hands when we tackled the freeways, but even you would never have the sheer reckless courage and the skillfulness of hand to attempt to make this seemingly plain cake. There are so many things that can go wrong in the process that I'd be all atremble thinking about it, if I weren't so damn good."

"I admire your modesty."

Gigi grinned at him. "Modesty has no place in a kitchen. It's like a bullring, Burgo, you don't start something you can't finish," she proclaimed as she beat eggs, sugar and vanilla with a whisk over hot water. "This has to exactly quadruple in volume, my friend, this mixture has to be *overbeaten* by ordinary standards, overbeaten with an exactitude and precision that is heart-stopping to contemplate."

Burgo leaned back comfortably. Gigi, working with total concentration, enveloped in a starched white apron that reached almost to her ankles, with a black velvet headband holding back her bangs so that they wouldn't get into her eyes, looked like an industrious, old-fashioned child bride, he thought, someone who should be drawn for an illustration in a Victorian cookbook. "I'm not impressed yet," he said, "but I know it's just a question of time. Since you're going to tell me anyway, why overbeaten?"

"Because the secret to this potential disaster of a cake lies entirely in its supreme texture, and when I add two and a half sticks of melted butter to it, as I will in good time, the butter will deflate the batter, and might even break it down. Therefore," Gigi pontificated, flourishing her whisk at him, "I must compensate in advance by overbeating in order to end up with a cake that's divinely moist."

"Makes sense," Burgo grunted.

"Wait, Burgo, wait! If I get carried away and overbeat even the slightest bit too much, the batter will become too fluffy and the cake won't be moist either."

"Too much and it'll be dry, and too little and it'll be dry?"

"A giant crumb, Burgo, one miscalculation and that's what it'll be,'' Gigi said with mock gloom, beginning to sift flour into the mixture, which she judged had reached its instant of immortality. "On the other hand, since I'm not using baking powder, if I don't fold this flour into the batter in absolutely the right way to achieve an utterly smooth combination of ingredients, the cake will be heavy and sticky, not a vast crumb, Burgo, but a huge, soggy pancake.''

"Is baking always this rough? The Betty Crocker box makes it look more like fun.''

"Burgo, I'm aiming at an otherworldly cake, something that will make this new chef's little piggy eyes pop right out of his smartass head. Betty Crocker wouldn't do it.''

"Seems to me that you're showing off.''

"Good cooking is always about showing off,'' Gigi said imperturbably. "If it weren't for the cooking instinct, we'd still be sitting around in a cave, eating raw meat and roots. Houses exist primarily to shelter a kitchen. There'd be no civilization without the cooking instinct.''

"I knew there had to be something to blame for civilization,'' Burgo said, as Gigi poured the batter into a cake pan, put it in the prewarmed oven, and began to make the butter cream combined with custard with which she would ice the cake and spread between its three layers. "I've been living in this house so long,'' he added, "I'd begun to think it was the shopping instinct. You got a date tonight, Gigi?''

"Naturally,'' she said smugly. "We're all going to the *Rocky Horror Picture Show*.''

"Who's 'we'?''

"My gang, Burgo, you dope, my gang—Maze and Sue and Betty and some guys. Why?''

"You've seen it twelve times,'' Burgo objected, knowing that they would probably see it twelve more times before the fad ran its course. What he really wanted to know was if Gigi had a date with any particular boy. On poker nights he occasionally questioned his friend Stan, the security guard at Uni, about the phenomenon of group dating. Burgo thought it was high time that Gigi had a nice boyfriend of her own instead of always being part of a swarm, for after all she was eighteen—his mother had been pregnant with her second child at eighteen—but Stan, who knew far more about teenagers than Burgo, told him it was perfectly natural. "If she went steady with one rotten stud, then you'd really have something to worry about, overprotective the way all of you are," his friend had advised him. "As soon as Gigi goes to college next fall, it'll change and you'll wish she were back in a nice, safe gang."

For a time, while the cake chilled enough for Gigi to slice and ice it, the two of them sat in companionable silence.

"Burgo, look at this cake," Gigi demanded when she had finished. "What do you think?"

"You said you wanted something plain."

"But not boring! This is the single dullest-looking cake I've ever seen. It's round and it's white and that's all you can say. It could be a whole Brie cheese if it weren't the most sublime sponge cake in the world."

"So decorate it."

"I had intended it to be immaculate, a throwaway, a seemingly insignificant cake, so that this Limey creep's reaction would be only to its quality. Anybody can decorate a cake and let the eye fool the palate. I'll ruin its purity if I decorate it, but if I don't, nobody will even bother to taste it. This is not how Sara Lee got rich."

"Hey, Gigi, you've got an artistic problem. Do you sell out or do you stand your ground?"

"I compromise. I'm going to pipe a message on the cake in the simplest possible way," Gigi said, inspired, as she melted white chocolate and fashioned a pointed paper cone. She poured the liquid chocolate, mixed with a dash of vegetable oil, into the paper, snipped off the tiniest bit of the tip of the cone, and on the surface of the cake wrote, "Welcome to Quentin Browning" in large, thin, flowing script, before she added an almost invisible, complicated loop design around its entire perimeter.

"That's grand," Burgo said in admiration. "White on white, like a gangster's shirt and tie."

"He'll have to try it, if only to be polite. And when he tastes it, I'll casually remark that I'm just an amateur hobbyist cook and baked it for kicks. Ha! Then let this Browning try to top it. Jean-Luc told me that Englishmen simply can't bake . . . it's something genetic. Now Burgo, you and I do the dishes."

"The cook does the dishes, Gigi. Do you think I'm a complete patsy?"

"I know it for a fact. Here, you can lick the icing pan first."

* * *

On Sunday afternoon, when Quentin Browning arrived at Charing Cross Road with his luggage, the great house lay sleeping. After Gigi's graduation, Billy had taken off for Munich, where clothes-conscious, deutsche mark–loaded women were thirsting for the opening of a Scruples that was still not quite ready. Since most of the staff had the day off, Burgo had been delegated by Josie to greet the new arrival. He showed Quentin to his room in the staff wing. "Do you want the guided tour or do you want to get settled?" he asked.

"I'll unpack later, thanks. I'd like to take a look at the kitchens first. When Miss Speilberg interviewed me, she didn't have time to show me around."

"Sure thing. I'll make you a cup of tea if you like."

"Thanks, I'd really appreciate that. Nobody but my mother's made me a cup of tea for years. What else do you do around here?"

"Everything but cook, clean or garden."

"I have an uncle at home just like you," Quentin said, smiling in recognition. "He's the fellow without whom the whole enterprise begins to fall apart in a few days. You're the indispensable man, then."

"That's one way to put it," Burgo said, sizing up the newcomer. For an Englishman he seemed like a regular guy. Maybe he played poker.

After a detailed inspection of the kitchens, the butler's pantry, the storage pantries, the wine cellar, and the dining rooms for staff and family, Quentin and Burgo settled down in the breakfast room with a pot of tea and the cake, which Burgo had brought out as Gigi had instructed him. Quentin read the inscription. "Not only is this very kind, but I'm actually starving," he admitted, pleased by the special attention.

"I just called Gigi on the intercom and asked her if she wanted some tea," Burgo said.

"Gigi?"

"Mrs. Ikehorn's stepdaughter. She was upstairs reading."

"A little girl?"

"Not really little, but not big, all things considered," Burgo said thoughtfully. "Little-ish, for California anyway."

"How old is she?"

"Youngish. Oh, here she is. Gigi Orsini, Quentin Browning."

Gigi shook hands automatically, smiled automatically and sat down automatically. She had never met a native Englishman in the flesh, but she was deeply familiar with them as a species, from Laurence Olivier to Alec Guinness, from Alan Bates to Sir Ralph Richardson, from Rex Harrison to David Niven, from John Gielgud to John Lennon. Englishmen in all their varieties could hold no surprises for her, she was certain. Yet somehow she'd missed seeing anyone on film who had prepared her for the reality of this particular young man. He was a tall male of the lean and adventurous type, he looked like a self-reliant explorer of the upper reaches of the Nile rather than a chef, yet his quick, slightly bucktoothed smile made her think suddenly of a schoolboy who'd just come home for the holidays. He had a long, bony nose, biggish ears, and straight blond hair neatly parted on the side, which nevertheless persisted in flopping over his forehead. He had an air of reserve, yet the expression in his gray eyes was candidly friendly.

"Come on, let's try the cake," Burgo said as Gigi sat there silently, eyes unfocused, not even sipping the tea he'd made.

"Cake?" Gigi asked, as if the word were in a foreign language.

"The cake on the table, this round white cake," Burgo said, cutting into it impatiently. He'd been mentally tasting it since yesterday. He never should have licked that icing.

Automatically, Gigi and Quentin each tasted the cake. Burgo ate a large bite of his and thought the top of his head would come off. It was more than Gigi had promised, more than any cake had a right to be.

"It's okay," Gigi said remotely.

"It's truly super cake," Quentin said absently, looking at her and taking another transcendental bite. She wasn't his big blond type, but he could always make an exception, and with her punk orange hair, her pointed ears and her just-about-to-smile mouth, she ranked high in the adorable category. "Your chef was an artist."

"He was," Gigi said on a sigh.

"I hope I can do half as well."

"Gigi," Burgo prodded, "Gigi, when did this cake get itself made exactly?"

"Who knows?" Gigi breathed vaguely.

"You don't remember? Gigi? *Gigi?*"

"No," she said, giving him a forbidding look.

"Do you cook?" Quentin asked, searching for something to say to this lovely, indifferent, laconic creature.

"Oh no," said Gigi sadly, "I've never had time to learn, not even a minute."

"But surely, at least the rudiments?"

"I've been much too busy, haven't I, Burgo?"

"What? Oh, sure . . . ."

"Would you like to learn? Just the basics, that is, enough to get by?" Quentin suggested. Giving girls cooking lessons had never failed him yet.

"Hmm . . . I suppose so . . . it's probably a good idea, just in case, don't you think, Burgo?"

"Yeah, Gigi, in case you ever have to. On a desert island, maybe," Burgo said disgustedly. Whatever complicated trap Gigi was now setting for Quentin had become too Machiavellian at this point for him to figure it out. The least she could have done was to notify him of her new deviltry.

"We could skip the peeling onions and carrots stage and go right on to . . . to scrambled eggs," Quentin offered, anxious to take away any hint of drudgery.

"Oh no, I'd want to do it right," Gigi said, eyes wide and earnest. "I'd want to start at the very beginning and work my way up to eggs . . . not skipping a single step. I have all the time in the world and nothing else to do . . . . all summer long."

"I think I'll have another piece of cake," Burgo said, suddenly hit by a wave of foreboding almost strong enough to take away his appetite, "since the two of you don't seem hungry."

That evening Gigi drove Quentin on a tour of Los Angeles, from the Santa Monica pier to Beverly Hills, from the Sunset Strip to Pink's, the famous hot-dog shack that, like many tourist attractions, thrives on humanity's attraction to thoroughgoing, shameless sordidness.

"Tell me more about the Cotswolds," she asked Quentin as they stood at a counter and ordered another round of spicy hot dogs buried under chili, mustard and chopped onions.

"Look here, Gigi, you've been asking me questions since we got into your car, but you haven't told me anything about yourself."

"Oh," Gigi demurred, looking away with a disenchanted air of mystery that only Bette Davis could have rivaled. "I don't really know how to begin . . . it's been such a complicated, cosmopolitan life, Quentin . . . traveling between New York and Los Angeles. I've had the best of two great cities, I suppose I'm considered prematurely sophisticated, and I have to admit to being unquestionably spoiled, but, damn it, it's not my fault that I was *born* restless. It's an incurable problem—forever seeking the next experience, even if it's outrageous, forever hoping to find the next sensation, even if it's violent. And the worst of it is that I know exactly what's wrong with me. You'd think that at twenty-one I'd have found something I could stick to by now— don't look so surprised, Quentin, I've always been cursed by these ridiculously childish looks of mine, they've fooled dozens of men." Gigi shook her head with deliberately theatrical exaggeration at her own deceptively ingenuous appearance, and dismissed it with a blasé gesture. "You see, Quentin, no matter how I wander, how I experiment, something always seems to be beckoning me on, some intensity of living that lies just behind the next encounter."

"How come you're spending the summer here, then? It seemed so quiet when I arrived."

"Last year I was . . . . how can I put it? . . . feverish . . . even, yes, even excessive, almost verging on self-destructive, I'm afraid. Someone at the house will be bound to gossip, so I might as well admit that I became far, *far* too involved with . . . . oh, hell . . . with a rock group . . . a bizarre episode, now that I look back at it, but not without its attractions." Gigi smiled a slow, small, wry smile that contained many secrets. "In any case," she continued, "Billy decided—insisted —that I stay home this summer so she could stop worrying about me, and since I love her, I agreed. Little did I guess it was going to be my chance to learn to . . . cook." She gazed up at Quentin through her dark lashes with such wicked naughtiness in her eyes that he was jolted into a realization that the category of adorable was far too limited to hold a personage of Gigi's worldliness.

"I understand why you said you'd been too busy to learn."

"It wasn't exactly a priority."

"Obviously not. What, ah, which rock group was it, exactly?"

"Oh, I'd rather not say, Quentin. In fact, I'm trying to forget." She turned slightly away from him and he saw the giveaway blush of memory rise on her fair skin from the bare base of her throat, which lay revealed by the deep neckline of the oversized white silk shirt she'd tucked into her white jeans. Gigi blushed all the way up to her bangs, her long Indian silver and turquoise earrings swaying as she tried to hide a rush of emotion.

"I'm sorry, Gigi, it was stupid to ask that question. I don't know why I did."

"No, don't be sorry—it's been over for months."

"Really over?"

"Completely. I'm totally recovered. In fact, as experience goes, it was as complete a one as I've had, and what more can one ask than that? *Non, je ne regrette rien.* Remember that Piaf song, Quentin, 'regret nothing'? That's my motto. Come on, let's go home."

Gigi was silent as she expertly guided the shocking pink car back to Charing Cross Road. For all of the past year she'd felt herself literally aching to grow up, fruitlessly stretching in every direction to find a way out of the silken skein of the chrysalis of girlhood, but nothing in her life had provided an opportunity. The boys in her gang were emotional children compared to even the least mature of the girls, but they'd continued to hang out together, forming a tight little crowd of their own in the huge senior class. None of them wanted to rock their enviably secure and safely familiar boat until the last year of school was over. There had been the usual amount of teenaged groping and smooching and harmless intrigue, but the boys had all been practically interchangeable as far as she was concerned, and less exciting, by now, than brothers.

As Gigi drove she couldn't believe how passively she had lived inside an old skin she had long ago outgrown, how quietly she'd remained sheltered by Billy and Josie and Burgo and the routine of the great house and her friendship with Maze. As it had turned out, she and Maze might as well have been sent to a convent school as Uni, she thought, although among its thousands of students there were gangs as wild as anyone could imagine.

With each mile the car covered, she seemed to be speeding into the landscape of adulthood. Each time she glanced quickly at Quentin's fascinatingly bony profile, her hands tensed resolutely on the wheel and she grew older and wiser and more sure of herself. He was a man and she was a woman, Gigi told herself, she had become a woman the instant she told him she didn't know how to cook. But of all the amazing string of lies she'd told Quentin, surprising even herself, one thing was true, she didn't believe in regrets. Now that she grasped just how sheltered she'd been, there could be no looking backward.

Gigi greeted the gateman, glided quietly up the long drive and parked her car in the garage. No one seemed awake in the house, to her familiar senses, as she opened the front door, trembling slightly with her intensity of purpose.

"No key?" asked Quentin.

"Not necessary with the security guards. You'll learn about them."

"But how do I find my way to my room? I'm lost without Burgo."

"I'll guide you, no problem. But come on up and see my apartment first. It's worth the trip as another tourist attraction, especially after Pink's."

"Like sneaking a look at the Queen's private rooms in Buckingham Palace?"

"My place is far more comfortable, from what I've heard." Quickly Gigi led the way through the house and up the stairs. Last year her bedroom had been expanded and redecorated into a complete suite by breaking down the wall into the neighboring guest room, so that now she had a large sitting room, a small kitchen and a dressing room as well, all done in a combination of luxury and glamour that Billy hoped would be an enticement to Gigi to attend UCLA and live at home during her college years.

"It's pure . . . Hollywood," Quentin finally said in an astonished voice as she led him around, ending up at the *pièce de résistance*, the biggest bed he'd ever seen, hung from the ceiling in such a prodigal amount of striped pale green, white and pink silk that it was fit for Catherine the Great to use as a traveling tent.

"That was the basic idea. Would you like a drink?"

"No, thanks."

"Would you like a kiss?"

"Yes, please."

Gigi reached up and put her arms around his neck and kissed him briefly on his chin.

"Well, I'd better get back to my room," Quentin said with determination.

"What's your hurry?"

"Gigi . . ."

"Yes?"

"What are you up to? Looking for the next encounter again, the next complete experience?"

"Exactly," Gigi answered in a laughing voice, relieved that he'd taken the ball out of her unaccustomed hands. "But only if you're interested. It's not part of the job."

"Jesus, Gigi, you don't mince words," he groaned.

"You have exactly five seconds to make up your mind," Gigi informed him, clenching her hands with determination and holding her breath with impatience.

"Ah . . . Hollywood," Quentin Browning whispered in surrender and took her in his arms, lifting her off the floor and depositing her on the bed. He kissed her eager, triumphant mouth over and over, and ever more deeply as he unbuttoned her shirt and freed her small, rosy, exquisitely young and pointed breasts. Quickly impatient with mere kisses, no matter how excellent, Gigi tugged on his hair so that he was forced to leave her mouth and bend down to her breasts. She took them in her hands and roughly thrust her delicately arrogant nipples into his mouth, as avidly as if she wanted him to bite them. "Wait, wait," he muttered, but Gigi chose not to hear him, and hurried to wriggle out of her jeans and panties while he was still busy learning how much the little pink tips could swell and harden. "God, you're greedy," he mumbled as he became aware of her nakedness, "a greedy little girl, so greedy," and he stripped as quickly as he could. She threw her arms around his chest and rubbed herself up and down against his bare body, as violently as if she were on fire and was trying to smother the flames with his skin, all the while kissing him ardently wherever her thirsty mouth landed.

"Hold it," he commanded, pinioning her arms so that he could look at her, so that he could examine the deep indentation of her waist, the splendidly modeled swelling of her elegantly formed hips and legs, the slight roundness of her belly and the flaunted promise of her tangle of pubic hair.

Gigi closed her eyes tightly while he looked at her, panting with impatience, breathless with expectation, but unable to free herself from this inquisition until she started to move her hips from side to side on the bed in an instinctively languid cadence of such seduction that it made him forget his curiosity.

As soon as she felt him loosen his grip, she launched herself at him abruptly, opening her legs and pushing herself forward so that he found his penis imprisoned by her warm thighs. He laughed at her impulsiveness and drew back so that he could caress her between her legs and open her properly. He traced a path through the silky, curly thicket of her gentle mound, trailing his fingers purposefully down to the lips he intended to see with his own eyes before he entered them. Gigi closed her eyes again, at his touch, clenching her teeth and writhing on the bed with such intensity that he caught fire from her eagerness and could resist no longer. He took his firm, quivering penis in his hand and thrust it all the way into her with one quick, brutal shove, too inflamed by her avidity to hold back. She was tight, he thought, because she was so small, and that was the last lucid thought he had as the movements of her body responded to his. She bit his shoulder until she drew blood as she met his relentlessness with an equal relentlessness of her own, urging him on quickly in the grip of an attack of such impetuous passion that it astonished him, experienced as he was. He tried to hold back, not sure if she was ready, but she didn't allow him any hesitation, using her body at a breakneck pace, mercilessly, even clumsily, but to such potent effect that soon he was rearing and bucking in the grip of a vast and irresistible orgasm.

Exhausted, he fell away from Gigi's body and lay speechless on the bed. Finally he gasped in weary admiration, "You really go after what you want, don't you?" When she didn't answer, he looked at her through his half-open eyes, and saw the unmistakable, flushed, expectant, suffused face of an unsatisfied woman. "Oh, shit . . . . you didn't . . . I'm sorry . . . "

"I didn't but I will . . . you're not going anywhere," Gigi said, hugging him. "I'm sorry I bit you."

"Don't do that again, that hurt."

"I won't have to . . . next time . . . it was only so I wouldn't scream with the pain of it."

Quentin sat up abruptly. "What the fuck? Wait a minute—what's that?" He pointed accusingly at the small bloodstain on the bed.

"What does it look like?" Gigi asked, tremendously pleased with herself.

"It looks like you are the biggest liar I've ever met," he said furiously.

"Most likely," she agreed happily, "most likely."

"But what about the bloody fucking rock band? What were they, all girls?"

"Oh, Quentin, don't be so literal-minded," Gigi giggled, smoothing back the hair that fell over his forehead. "I happen to loathe rock."

"Oh God, what have I got into?" he cried. "What are you, you greedy little bitch, fourteen?"

"Certainly not!" she said with spicy indignation. "I'm well past the age of consent, there's nothing to worry about. Now why don't you lie down and take a little nap? You look as if you need it. I'll be back in a minute."

Gigi took the precaution of locking the two doors to her suite and hiding the key. Quentin was sound asleep with an expression of satisfaction on his ineffably lean, long, alluring features before she tiptoed with a slightly wincing step into the bathroom. As she ran a warm bath she trusted would soothe her various bruised, sprained and stinging parts, she hummed a rollicking counterpoint to Tony Bennett singing "The Boulevard of Broken Dreams." All things considered, Gigi decided, she wouldn't tell Maze. She was too old now to reveal everything that happened to her. And the night had just begun.

If this was Gigi's idea of flirting, he gave up, Burgo thought as he watched her obediently scraping carrots and chopping celery and learning how to plunge a tomato into hot water before peeling off its skin, a minor trick she had demonstrated for him three years ago. He gave up completely; the whole silly, childish thing was none of his business, and since Gigi was so backward that she thought playing the idiot in the kitchen was the way to attract a fellow, he washed his hands of it. There had been nothing to worry about after all. He'd been afraid, for a bad half hour, that she'd learned a thing or two from Mrs. Ikehorn, a woman who wouldn't pussyfoot around peeling shallots when she had designs on a man, from what he'd heard about her past, but little Gigi was making no progress at all in that particular direction, thank the good Lord. He was the last person who had any intention of telling her what she was doing wrong.

Josie Speilberg, from her office, knew everything that went on in the house, and she was gratified to hear that the new chef had continued Gigi's cooking lessons. There was always more to learn in an evolving discipline like cooking, each chef had his own techniques, and a dedicated student like Gigi could count on soaking up something important from each new teacher who came her way. She wished Jean-Luc could see that Gigi's interest in cooking hadn't diminished because he'd withdrawn his presence. As she always said, no one was indispensable.

As for the rest of the staff, they were so accustomed to seeing Gigi in the kitchen that they had long ago stopped asking what she was working on. All cooking seemed to involve identical preparation; only the results interested them.

Billy returned from Munich and spent a few days in Los Angeles before going on to Hawaii, where another Scruples had been built to take advantage of the huge business to be done with people on vacation and the growing troops of affluent, fashion-conscious Japanese travelers.

Billy had planned to take Gigi with her on this trip, and then on to visit the Scruples in Hong Kong. She didn't like to be separated from Gigi for long, but apparently all the poor child truly craved, after the excitement and tension of her senior year, was to stay put at home, like a frog on a log, basking in an orgy of all-out laziness, sleeping hours later than she'd ever slept before, mooching around the kitchen as usual, swimming languidly every afternoon and slowly recovering from the strain of getting into college. She'd been accepted at Smith and Vassar and Berkeley, but she'd decided to go to UCLA, to Billy's joy and relief.

As they lunched together, Billy observed Gigi closely and noticed how graduating from high school had changed her. Of course, graduation was one of the great rites of passage, Billy thought, noting a new and endearingly high-spirited happiness in Gigi's manner, a new brilliance in her eyes, a heightened color on her tanned cheeks. Gigi seemed to have grown up in just a few weeks, which was clearly impossible, an optical illusion, but on returning from Munich she had been struck by it. Gigi had a sweetly thriving tartness about her that was new, a playfully minxlike quality that was new, a way of moving that was newly supple, a . . . a *female* quality that was new.

"Gigi," Billy asked, shocked by a sudden, terrible suspicion, "have you been *eating* more than usual?"

"Probably," Gigi admitted. "In fact, that's just about all I seem to do. Lazy as I am, I haven't missed a meal."

"My God! Darling, you've simply got to just watch it! You can't afford to get fat, and with your delicate bones even a few extra pounds will show. You may think you can get away with it, but believe me, when you don't exercise and you eat normally, it just adds up, until one day . . ." Billy shuddered at the awful possibility of a fat Gigi. "You happen to look particularly adorable at the moment, that extra weight is still becoming, but there's a thin line between blooming and being overblown, and you've got to promise me never, *ever* to cross it."

"I promise, Billy, on my honor, I'll start counting calories. If you don't have to go to Scruples today, I'll beat you at tennis, just to show you I can still sweat with the best."

"You're on," Billy agreed immediately. If there was one thing she dreaded for Gigi, it was the traditional weight gain of college freshmen. She'd really have to watch her closely to make sure it didn't happen, counting calories or not. Gigi wasn't diminutive or tiny or short or petite or any of the other words that might have been used in honesty to describe her insignificant person when she'd first arrived from New York, Billy decided with the true impartiality she always gave to such vital assessments. Gigi had grown enough, just exactly enough, to be, in her slender way, quite, quite perfect. Actual inches were less important than proportion, and Gigi was so well proportioned that she gave the impression of being taller than she really was, especially since she held herself with such upright, all-but-regal assurance. Still, she'd always been able to eat as much as she wanted, and everybody knew that such a state was possible only for the very young, a description that, somehow sadly, in spite of its inevitability, no longer fit Gigi at all.

While Billy was away, Gigi and Quentin sneaked up the back service staircase in the main wing to reach Gigi's rooms on the deserted corridor. During Billy's return they'd found other places to make love each night: the changing rooms in the tennis pavilion, where they threw dozens of thick towels on the floor to create a bed, and the storeroom in the orchid house, where bags of peat moss made a soft banquette and the controlled humidity and temperature were so perfect that they could lie naked and feel that they were in a forest.

Gigi was in a perpetual state of the obsession of first love, on a merry-go-round that never stopped, her head whirling, her heart yearning. During the day, too restless to read, indifferent to all her former friends, she lived in a state of breathless expectation as she waited for her cooking lesson, knowing that Quentin would soon be bending over her, showing her how to properly manipulate the blade of a chopping knife or the sharp edge of a potato peeler, for she was the most awkward, slow and ungifted of possible pupils.

He had to clasp his hand over hers a hundred times before she could learn how to crack an egg cleanly, without stabbing the yolk open with the jagged shell, and when it came time to scramble the eggs he had to stand behind her and demonstrate at length before she began to understand the coordination of grasping the pan and the spoon and the scraping, lifting, stirring motion that would keep the eggs from sticking.

In fact Gigi was unable to begin to attempt the simplest cooking technique until Quentin made physical contact with her, until he started to breathe too quickly and became mixed up in his instructions. Then she would discover that she needed to go find something in the storage pantry and he would follow her helplessly, knowing that they would stand there with their arms wrapped around each other, lost in a world of perilous kisses until the lesson was forgotten and all he could think about for the rest of the day was the coming night.

Gigi was in love with all her heart, and Quentin, who was in love with only half his heart, recognized the difference from the distance of the eight years that separated them. It seemed to him that he had not had a minute to himself to think the situation over clearly since it had begun, a month ago. He scarcely recognized himself, physically enslaved as he was to this eighteen-year-old sorceress who reigned over him with such a sovereign assumption of her domination that he wouldn't know how to dispute it even if he wanted to. Every night, night after night, he found himself rising to heights of sexual pleasure that he hadn't believed existed, and yet, during the next day, Gigi could so easily make him want her again, even when he swore to himself that just once he would manage to resist her, for once she wouldn't have her own way.

Gigi knew no limits, he thought, but he was a grown man of twenty-six who knew full well that limits existed and he was overreaching them.

In the mornings, back in his own room, rushing to get dressed and go downstairs to prepare breakfast, Quentin Browning realized that he was in danger of forgetting his own name, much less his plans for his clearly organized future. He was getting in over his head, he warned himself, and then lost his rational morning thoughts in the course of the day, as the night approached and Gigi's wonderfully low laugh sounded and Gigi's teasing green eyes enticed him, robbing him of any common sense.

One morning, early, Quentin took one of the house cars and went to Gelson's to do the shopping for a party that Billy was having the next day, before she left for Hawaii. He took the opportunity of finding himself alone for a few hours to try to sort out the situation in which he had so unexpectedly found himself.

Yes, Gigi was an enchantment . . . . but. Many buts. It wasn't merely that she wasn't nineteen yet, it was everything else about her: her gypsy mother and her gypsy past, her film-producer father, her incomprehensibly rich stepmother, all the people who had formed her, all the life experience that had created a girl who was, to him, an exotic plant that could flourish only in Hollywood.

They had no future at all, supposing that he were to dream of offering her one, he told himself, thinking clearly. He was pointed firmly in the direction of the life of a hotel owner who lived most of the year at the rhythm of a demanding business. A sound life, a fruitful, useful and interesting life for him, but Gigi could have no place in it.

When he married, he would expect his wife to help him in a steady, reliable, dependable way as he shouldered the burdens that lay ahead. She'd have to learn all the things his mother knew: become an accomplished chatelaine, able to hire and fire, able to oversee everything from the most mundane details of the linen supply to the greeting of favored clients and their comfortable placement in their preferred rooms. And she'd have to be happy doing this, year in and year out, leading an honest and responsible life, a happy life but one that lacked much fantasy or freedom. That was simply the way it was.

Gigi? Able to function like that? Gigi, his spoiled, impulsive, romantic, imaginative little sweetheart? Gigi, who could and always would choose to do anything that caught her fancy? Gigi, who was just starting out on her adventures, whose life was one vast potential—how could Gigi settle down now, when every option was open to her, settle down as he must settle down, settle down for good? Her years at college lay ahead, the whole wide world lay open to her.

Even if he were fool enough to give her all of his heart, to think of marrying her, even though she might agree to marry him with the best will in the world, no one could ever expect it to work, Quentin told himself, not a chance in bloody hell, and he knew it to the bottom of his soul.

No one had warned him, he reflected miserably as he found a parking place, that a single taste of the California lifestyle would end up giving him such problems. Why couldn't he have stumbled on that big, bovine Anglo-Saxon blonde he'd wanted, instead of a quicksilver blend of Celt and Italian with larcenous eyes and a pickpocket mouth?

Even now, after only a month, Gigi was too much for him by half, and she wasn't even trying to be reasonable. She was too eager for his kisses to listen properly whenever he made an attempt to tell her that they should slow down, go easy, cool it. Gigi was reckless right up to, and almost past, the edge, blithely braving any hazard, seizing any chance to touch him, to caress him, even when there were other people in the room, drunk on the excitement of a kind of danger that was utterly new for her. Quentin knew that one day they'd be discovered, one day, sooner or later, it was inevitable that they'd be caught if they carried on as madly as they had been doing.

The summer still stretched ahead, over two months before classes started in September, and even then Gigi would be sleeping at home every night. Quentin Browning told himself that he was running a fearful risk that mounted every day and that if—no, when—their affair came to light the blame would all fall on him, for he was an adult and Gigi had been a virgin when he came to the great house, this almost-child who was the darling of every member of the staff and the most prized possession of the frighteningly powerful Mrs. Ikehorn, who would ruin him for life.

He pushed two shopping carts to the meat section, where he would instruct the butcher exactly how to prepare the particular cuts of loin of veal he needed for tonight, and then go about his shopping, picking up the meat on his way out. As he passed a towering display of canned tomatoes, Gigi approached him, sashaying down the aisle with imperturbable poise and dancing Jazz Baby step, her marigold hair catching and holding the lights of the huge market, as if she were on center stage. As she came abreast of him she stopped and looked at him with surprise. "Fancy bumping into you here," Gigi said, swiftly bending down to pick up a can. She managed to brush his knuckles with a kiss before she threw the tomatoes into one of his carts.

"Gigi! Be reasonable, for Christ's sake. What if one of Mrs. Ike-horn's friends saw us?"

"Billy's friends don't do their own shopping," she answered, shrugging impatiently and moving toward him with purposeful intention in her eyes. "Give me a real kiss, my sweetest darling, there's nobody around. I need a kiss so badly, I have to have it."

"Stop it!" Quentin gave her an icy, angry look, abandoned the carts and disappeared around another aisle as quickly as his long legs could take him.

"I'm really disappointed about Quentin," Josie Speilberg sighed to Gigi, a day later when Gigi appeared in her office to ask her to renew her Automobile Club card.

"Didn't Billy's dinner party turn out perfectly?"

"He's resigned, is what he's done. He's leaving tomorrow—not even giving a week's notice. It's incredibly thoughtless and it just couldn't be more inconvenient, there's never anybody halfway decent looking for a job at this time of the year, but he was absolutely adamant in spite of all my advice."

"Advice?" Gigi could only echo Josie.

"Obviously I asked him to give me a single reason why he'd leave this job so quickly, particularly when he'd promised to stay for at least a year, and the only reason he could give me—at least he sort of hinted at it, in his confusion, but I drew my own conclusions—was that he'd gotten in over his head with some girl or other and he didn't know how to get out of it without hightailing it home to England immediately. I suggested a dozen different things he could say which would let her down lightly so that he could stay on—Dear Abby has nothing on me in that department—but he kept insisting that he had to leave. Maybe she's pregnant . . . I'll just bet that's what it is. I don't know what Mrs. Ikehorn will say when she gets back from Hong Kong and finds another new face in the kitchen, assuming that I can find one. Isn't it a shame when people let you down that way?"

"I won't believe it!"

"That's exactly what I said to him . . . Gigi! Wait, leave me your old card. Oh, really . . ." Josie Speilberg looked at her empty office. Why couldn't people be more organized? Why did everyone make life difficult for her? Why was everybody in such a rush and at the same time so stubborn? Now if she ran the world . . .

Gigi locked herself in her room and abandoned herself to a torrent of grief so dreadful that she had to stuff the edge of a sheet in her mouth to keep her cries from drawing the attention of the maids who passed in the corridor. She was curled up on the bed in a tight, shaking ball of frightening anguish, the bedspread covering her entirely, trying to hold herself together, hugging herself with all her strength to contain the violence of the pain that felt like a wild animal, suddenly uncaged, trying to eat its way out of the trap of her chest. Yet her mind never stopped working. She never doubted for a second that Quentin was going to leave the next day. If she hadn't happened to talk to Josie today, he would have disappeared without saying anything to her.

He didn't love her. He'd never loved her. He wanted out and he was too cowardly to face her and tell her. He thought she'd make a scene, he knew she'd try to stop him, he hadn't even been kind enough to lie to her, to invent a story, a family emergency she could believe. Why hadn't he said that he'd had a phone call from home, that he had to rush home to help out his father? Did he think she'd insist on going with him? Probably . . . probably . . . that must have been exactly what he thought. So he wasn't being entirely cowardly, just taking his precautions, to escape her unwanted . . . . attentions. Unwanted, oh yes, unwanted, with just the same cold withdrawal he'd shown her at Gelson's the other day. She could have endured anything, even his telling her that he didn't love her, if he'd only had the respect—yes, the basic respect for her—to sit down and tell her how he felt. Just because she was in love with him didn't mean that she couldn't accept the truth. He didn't owe her his love.

After a long while Gigi stopped weeping and lay still, trying to think what to do. If only she could hide in her room until Quentin was gone, stay safely here and not let anybody see her face, but if she did, no matter what health reason she gave, from cramps to a head cold, Josie would quickly put two and two together and know exactly what had happened. Such humiliation was worse than anything she could imagine, even though she was sure that Josie would never reveal her secret, never discuss it, never even look as if she knew it.

In four hours she had a cooking lesson, and if Quentin didn't want her to ask questions, he'd be in the kitchen waiting for her, just as usual. Of course she could cancel the lesson, Josie would think nothing of that, but everything in her rebelled against that thought. She could retrieve nothing now, except her pride, the self-respect that had been stripped from her. No, thought Gigi, going into her bathroom to soak her face in cold water until she could see through the slits of her eyes, no, she would cancel nothing, she too would behave as usual . . . or almost as usual.

As soon as she'd managed to make herself presentable, Gigi slipped out of the house unnoticed, and made a lightning trip to Santa Monica Seafood. She returned to the house at an hour when she was certain that Quentin would have left the kitchen and taken himself off someplace where she couldn't find him, before her cooking lesson would force him back to the kitchen.

She carried four large bags into the kitchen, put on her apron and began the long process of laying out everything she would need, as precise as a scrub nurse in an operating room, glad of the necessity to focus her mind. Deciding what she must do in advance, for she intended to do only the minimum before her lesson, she prepared a savory fish stock, using chopped vegetables, spices, wine, clam juice and water into which she put all the bones, heads, tails, skins and trimmings she removed from the many pounds of red snapper, halibut, pompano, scallops and perch she had bought. In another pot she steamed the shrimps, clams and mussels in their shells, while she plunged the lobster into a third pot of boiling water.

Gigi left the broth to simmer for a half hour before she strained it and replaced it on the stove in the largest pot in the kitchen. She retrieved the cooked lobster and, when it was cool, divided it into easily handled pieces. She made another rapid check of the kitchen table and glanced at the clock. She went to the intercom and buzzed Burgo, who always, at this hour, put his feet up in his room.

"Burgo, will you come watch my cooking lesson today?"

"I can't stand it, Gigi, not even for you. I'm sorry, sweetheart, but enough's enough."

"I won't be taking a lesson today, Burgo, I'll be giving one," she said in a tone of voice that made him put his feet down with a bang.

"All right! Got your Irish back, have you, kid? How much of an audience do you want?"

"Everyone you can round up, including Josie and all the gardeners."

"You've got 'em."

"Just come one minute early, and Burgo, if Quentin tries to leave, don't let him."

"Man bites dog, huh? High time, is all I can say."

"I'm a slow study."

"But not completely stupid, sweetheart."

"I'm counting on you."

"You always could," he said and hung up, mirthful for the first time since the day of the white-on-white cake. It took Gigi an awfully long time to understand men, he thought, but she'd been too young and innocent to realize that playing dumb wasn't the only or best answer when you wanted to get someone's attention.

Quentin Browning spent two hours on the sands of the Santa Monica beach, taking his last, desperately gloomy look at the Pacific. He'd never come here again. He'd become a landlocked man, surrounded by cold seas, with only memories of Gigi. Of course he'd marry one day and he'd be happy and the details of his month here would fade. That inevitable forgetting, he mused, was the worst part about it. He couldn't afford to love Gigi and he didn't dare to tell her. He might be a shit—okay, he *was* a shit—but he was a very smart shit to get out now, painlessly, quickly, effortlessly.

When he drove back and approached the kitchen he heard the unaccustomed sound of many voices. Good, he thought, thank God he wouldn't be alone with her. He didn't know how he could go through with another lesson alone, but he'd had no choice. He walked into the large room and saw Gigi standing at the kitchen table, barely visible through the expectant crowd of staff that surrounded her.

"What's going on?" he asked one of the maids, but she smiled at him without answering. She knew only that it was a break in the day's work, some sort of exhibition of Gigi's, like the ones she gave when Jean-Luc had been there.

"Hey, be careful!" Quentin shouted as Gigi picked up a particularly sharp knife, but before he could reach her she had started to slice leeks into the thinnest of strips, her knife moving so quickly and professionally that he stood utterly still, so astonished that he couldn't move or speak.

In seconds the julienned leeks were ready and Gigi was dicing tomatoes, mincing garlic, chopping fennel, pulverizing bay leaves, chopping onions, grating orange rind and grinding pepper. She was doing all those various operations simultaneously, or so it seemed to those who were fascinatedly watching her flying hands and her flying feet and the flash and glitter and clicking and flicker of her many tools. The expert rhythm of her movements never faltered for a second as she measured celery seed, opened a package of saffron and extracted a teaspoon of the precious spice, scraped tomato paste out of a can, and finally heaped everything she'd prepared into a large casserole in which hot olive oil was waiting. Then, with careless precision, she shook a few tablespoons of salt into the oil from the palm of her hand before giving the mixture a businesslike stir.

"Gigi . . ." Quentin began, thinking he must say something, almost anything, but she paid no attention to him or anyone else as she attacked the pile of freshly cleaned fish, fileting them with virtuoso attention, the most deft of fingers and a shining shimmy of knives that she wielded with the authority of a master and the cool proficiency of an authority. When the fish lay ready she diced those that cooked slowly into one-inch cubes and cut the rest into two-inch slices, accomplishing the task so quickly that five pounds of fish took her less than three minutes to reduce to size.

Only when she had slid the fish into the hot broth on the stove did Gigi so much as glance at Quentin. He was standing with his arms folded tightly across his chest, glaring at her as he tried and failed to conceal the anger of someone who realizes he's been the victim of a huge joke. But there was unquestioned professional admiration in his eyes, and that was the only thing Gigi needed to see.

"Did any of you know," Gigi asked the room at large, "that bouillabaisse was, or so they say, first invented by some kindly angels who brought it to the Three Marys who happened to be shipwrecked somewhere in the South of France? I didn't know that sacred personages got hungry like the rest of us, but why not, after all? Of course this soup won't be as good as it would be if I had Mediterranean rockfish that were caught fresh this morning, but I'm doing the best I can and I believe it'll be fairly tasty—there's enough for everybody. Oh, Quentin, would you bring me a lot of bowls, heat them first, please, and slice that French bread over there while I make the garlic mayonnaise—it wouldn't be traditional bouillabaisse, would it, chef, without the *rouille*?"

Quentin turned on his heel and started to leave the kitchen. "I'd bring the bowls she asked for," Burgo said quietly, blocking his path, "and I'd slice the bread too, if I were you."

In surprise Quentin glanced at Burgo, and what he saw on the older man's face made him head immediately for the cupboard in which the earthenware bowls were kept. Fool! Fool! Fool! What an utter, bloody ass she'd made of him. This must have been the hilarious running gag of the entire household, he told himself, scarcely able to see through his rage as he fumbled with the long loaves of fresh bread Gigi had left on a side table. As he looked around the crowd he saw smiling faces, all watching Gigi with the expression of people expecting a familiar treat, like theatergoers waiting for the curtain to rise on a well-loved play.

"Just in time," Gigi said cheerfully, as she put a slice of bread into the bottom of each bowl and artfully arranged the shellfish. "Now we'll all have time for a drink before the soup is ready, but with bouillabaisse it should be beer, not wine, for some reason or other that only the French understand. Or perhaps the chef can tell us? Can you explain it, Chef Quentin? No? Too bad, just open the beer in that case, and we'll drink it without a good reason."

Burgo helped find the glasses and pour the beer, taking pity on Quentin, poor bugger, although he didn't quite know why, except that Gigi had been too much for him, as she was bound to be. Soon everyone in the kitchen had a glass.

"Wait!" Gigi's voice rang out, as she hopped up on a kitchen chair. "Wait, everybody, we're going to drink a toast! A good-bye toast to our friend, Quentin Browning. He's leaving us tomorrow. Oh, stop that fuss, all of you, he has to leave and that's that—so drink up quickly and we'll all have time for another beer." She lifted her glass high and looked Quentin directly in the eye, her pointed eyebrows raised in a gallant salute, her mouth curling upward in a frank smile, her expression knowing and understanding and full of compassion, the thin steel knife in her heart quite invisible.

"Good-bye, Quentin, bon voyage, return home safely, and *regrette rien*. You know that's my own motto—I don't mind sharing it —if you should ever feel the need. Regret nothing, Quentin, *rien*!"

8

The Comtesse Robert de Lioncourt, born Cora Middleton of Charleston, South Carolina, was a *jolie laide*. As usual with certain French expressions, a direct translation is misleading. A woman thus known as a "pretty ugly" is neither pretty nor ugly in any ordinary way. She can be alluring, if she knows how to use her looks; she can be formidably fashionable, if she knows how to wear clothes; she can be famous if she has personality and talent; but her general look is never so traditionally tilted as to have a claim to prettiness, nor so ill-favored as to remotely merit the word *ugly*. Barbra Streisand, Bianca Jagger, the Duchess of Windsor, and Paloma Picasso were or are all examples of the *jolie laide* at its best, its most cleverly cultivated, its most brilliant and powerful.

Cora Middleton, whose mother was a member of the great Cincinnati family of Chatfield, had not realized that she would mature to become a *jolie laide* when she married Comte Robert de Lioncourt.

She had calculated her chances, as coldly she was to calculate all her qualities, and knew that in spite of her intelligence and her excellent lineage, she was as homely as a girl could get, destined to be first a wallflower and later an old maid.

During her adolescence her lack of physical attraction, particularly noticeable in a Southern city of famous teenaged beauties, had made Cora particularly shy and withdrawn. She had never learned to use the genuine charms she possessed—a beautiful speaking voice, perfect teeth and a mouth she hated because she thought it was too long and too thin, although it became delightful when she smiled—for she spoke as little as possible and smiled rarely. At nineteen, already a clear-eyed, opportunistic cynic, she accepted the proposal of a man of forty-nine, a selfish man who would never have considered marriage to Cora Middleton if he had not known that she possessed a fixed private income of seventy thousand dollars a year. She accepted him because she felt that marriage to a count with an authentic title was infinitely better than no marriage at all; she accepted him because he owned an enviable apartment in the best part of Paris and something of a position in French society, where he had long dined out as a useful extra man. He could offer her a life that in Charleston would seem glamorous to the popular classmates whom she had always envied so bitterly.

The count was the last of his line and wished no more from life than that it should be easy, idle, and spent in the pursuit of beautiful objects. His collection of antiques was the one passion to which he had dedicated all his time and much of his inheritance. Cora's money would continue to keep him in comfort so long as they had no children, a subject on which they agreed, for Cora had no wish to be left a widow with growing children, a certain eventuality, considering her husband's age.

The Lioncourts met and married in 1950, in Paris, where Cora had been sent to learn French, and there they made their home, in Robert's large, inherited apartment on the second floor of an ancient *hôtel particulier* on the Rue de l'Université. They traveled leisurely at least six months of every year, staying with friends as often as possible. Their travels were not those of tourists but of collectors, for Cora, like Robert, learned to worship antique furniture and porcelain, old glass, old silver and carved ivory: precious *things* became her religion, her children, her contentment.

The purchase of things, things of all sorts, so long as they were genuinely fine or, if not fine, highly original, and the arranging of them into collections that complemented each other, made up half the interest of Cora's life. The other half was concentrated on getting to know people of social importance in every city to which they traveled. Just as she had no intention of being left a widow with children to worry about, she didn't plan to become a widow without a wide circle of acquaintances.

Cora had her own connections, for the Chatfields and the Middletons had friends in Europe even though they rarely left their own cities, two of the prettiest in the United States, preferring them to anywhere else. Robert's mother had been English, the third daughter of a baronet, and he knew everyone he considered worth knowing in London and Paris. People like the Lioncourts, who collect widely in Europe, inevitably make friends in New York, among other collectors. The Lioncourts inspired the respect of visitors to France many millions of times richer than themselves, for they entertained with formal hospitality whenever their friends passed through Paris, inviting them to dine in a setting that was unrivaled for sheer charm.

Everywhere their guests looked, there were dozens of things they would give a great deal to own themselves, possessions the Lioncourts had bought at the bottom of the market, never putting a foot wrong. Every good antiques dealer in Europe shuddered when they walked into his shop, for they bought the very pieces the dealer, against his own principles, had been covetously contemplating reserving for himself; antiques that were just on the verge of coming into fashion or objects so curious, so unusual that they had been overlooked until the Lioncourts started poking into the corners of the shop. Cora and Robert de Lioncourt would fly across Europe at a moment's notice to attend an antiques dealer's funeral, knowing that on such occasions, grasping families would provide the possibility of picking up something at half its value for ready cash. They became as adept at buying well at auctions as dealers themselves, for they never allowed themselves to be carried away in the heat of the chase. Few estate sales, important or unimportant, escaped their attention, and they had cultivated dozens of little old ladies who had been collectors in their youth and now sold their precious pieces, one by one, to support them in their old age.

The Lioncourts bought no painting and sculpture. They settled the question quickly; fine art, by the time it was accepted, was far beyond their means, and when it was experimental and still affordable it was too much of a risk. They crowded their walls with remarkable engravings and mirrors, and so rich with objects was their environment that no one had ever noticed the lack of art.

Every foreign acquaintance of the Lioncourts who visited them at home believed them to be enormously rich. Robert and Cora were emotionally united, as by nothing else, in the immense gratification this belief afforded them. However, there was no titled lady in the Seventh Arrondissement who paid her bills as reluctantly as did Cora de Lioncourt. She found fault with every service she required, with every item she bought for herself or the house. She complained viciously, keeping tradesmen and professionals waiting, she delayed payment for as long as possible while her dollars were earning bank interest at the Chase in the Rue Cambon; but she paid eventually, at a substantial discount for cash. In a country of high taxes like France, where people write personal checks for almost everything including cheap bistro meals, cash that doesn't have to be declared, known simply as *liquide*, is so desirable that Cora's wad of crisp banknotes paved the way for her to keep expenses down to the bone.

When Robert de Lioncourt died in 1973, Cora was forty-two, just the right age, she thought, to begin her well-anticipated widowhood. She felt a distinct gratitude toward her husband for having left the world at such an appropriate time, without any undue lingering. She had had little interest in sex when she married, and life with Robert had not increased it; she wasted no time casting about for another husband, for not only did she calculate to the centime the high value of her title, but she knew that any unmarried man her age or older would be seeking something else in a wife, someone younger, someone sexier, certainly someone pretty. She would find greater distinction in being a titled widow with a famous collection, she realized, than in being half of a couple.

The Comtesse Cora de Lioncourt had not neglected her own development in the course of twenty-three years of marriage to a man who had nothing to recommend him but exquisite taste. Robert had insisted that she patronize the best hairdresser in Paris; he had chosen her clothes himself until she learned how to do so; he had her taught to use makeup, supervising the lessons personally, for his wife, like his apartment, was a reflection on his taste.

At forty-two, Cora had grown into a *jolie laide*: her beaky nose, her too-small eyes, her straight hair, her too-high forehead somehow combined with her superb smile to make her look immensely interesting in her sophistication and style, a worldly exotic who gave the eye a great deal to wander over. She never entered a room without people asking each other who she was; she dressed severely, in black and white in winter and in white and black in summer; she never changed her center-parted, unadorned pageboy hairstyle that reached just below her ears, nor was she ever seen at night without the finely worked, large pieces of antique jewelry that had come to her from Robert's mother. She had good legs; hand-made shoes from M. Massaro, who had invented the Chanel pump; a stringy, tall body on which clothes hung exceedingly well, and long hands with immaculate nails covered in invisible polish.

Her only problem, Cora de Lioncourt realized, was that seventy thousand dollars a year in 1973 was not enough money to live on in the style of the 1950s and the 1960s. She would have to go to work.

She sat up in bed, with her glasses on her nose and a notebook on her knees, considering the situation in the round. A job in Paris was out of the question, for she had retained her American citizenship and she wouldn't be able to obtain a work permit. She could, with much red tape, probably open an antiques shop, but the thought of becoming a shopkeeper revolted her. She was of the class who bought, not of the class who sold.

Actually, the idea of a real job, a job at which she would have to spend eight hours a day, was repugnant. Not only was it impossibly dreary to consider spending so much time in the sordid surroundings of any ordinary office, but there was literally no job she could think of that wouldn't cause her visiting friends to question her wealth, and that must never happen.

Cora de Lioncourt wrote down two words on her pad: *New York*.

She had always loved New York. She never felt so alive as when she spent time there. Everything in New York pleased her, particularly her friends who understood so little about her world and were so impressed by it, no matter how rich they were. Any one of them could have easily afforded a vast apartment or a house with a garden in Paris, but they were so ridiculously intimidated by the supposed difficulties of the language and the frightening idea they had created of the snobbishness and stand-offish character of the French, that they admired her just for being able to live here happily.

It had indeed taken a bit of getting used to, she reflected, remembering the first years of her marriage, but then she had Robert's family laundress and his family food purveyors and his family electrician and his family plumber and his family cleaning woman, all of whom were almost as valuable to her as his family background, when you stopped to consider the multitude of petty, maddening details of keeping house in Paris. Getting on with the French was a walk in the park compared to making a French electrician properly rewire a defective fuse box, Cora thought.

She wrote again on her pad: *Invisible job*.

What could she do that would be invisible, she wondered, her mind clicking as she surveyed her assets. She knew almost "everybody," which merely meant that she knew many of those key figures who could introduce her to most of the people she wanted to meet. She and Robert had never entertained without a purpose, ruthlessly choosing to invite only guests who would be satisfied to find themselves in the same room with each other. They weighed their own importance, without vanity, down to the last centimeter and never distributed their intimacy or entry to their circle unless it added to their luster. However, they had never reached true intimacy within the highest levels of French society, a constant disappointment Cora had never learned to accept.

Cora and Robert de Lioncourt had long ago realized that the expression "flattery will get you nowhere" was a downright lie. Flattery, well applied, could get you almost anything but intimate friendship. Cora de Lioncourt's greatest personal talent, by her own accurate reckoning, was the ability to use flattery. Through flattery she accumulated those acquaintances who could do her the most good, and through it she kept them. Her flattery was never obvious. It never consisted of mere compliments, but rather of enthusiastic interest in other people's doings, their comings and goings, their problems and pleasures. Her enthusiasm, combined with the smile she had now learned to use so well, flattered people who thought themselves immune to it. Since no one suspected that this rich woman who owned so many precious things might want anything from them, they never realized that their relationship with her was based on her flattery.

Slowly she wrote two more words and added a question mark. *Public relations?*

No, that wasn't quite it, but there was something . . . . something in those words that she could work around. She would never become a PR woman; they worked like dogs, which she had no intention of doing, and a large part of their work consisted, basically, in asking favors for their clients. Anyway, she didn't know the rules of that game.

She wanted to *do favors* for people and get paid for it, Cora de Lioncourt decided. Was there a name for that profession? She smiled a chilling smile none of her acquaintances would have recognized. No, whores got paid for different services and pimps for yet others . . . but surely there was room in New York City for a woman who *facilitated* things? A woman who made things happen that wouldn't otherwise happen, an intelligent, elegant, highly placed woman who just happened to be able to accomplish the impossible for a discreetly paid sum?

Indisputably, Cora told herself, there was always a need for such a woman in bumbling, uncomplicated New York, where so many women were striving to make their way upward, yearning for guidance. Only in New York did she suspect she could earn the kind of money such services should command. The French were too cheap to pay the high prices she hoped to establish. As for the British, they didn't need her. They had their own traditional arrangements for grace and favor.

So. She got out of bed and walked slowly around her apartment, gently touching an object here and there; standing at this place and that place to appreciate a happy juxtaposition of the view of one room from another; looking at herself in various mirrors, all of which gave back her image backed by a reflection of such beauty massed behind her that it was, after all, a bit sad, although no one knew better than she the unfortunate condition of the paint on the walls. But the apartment would sell in a day, considering its location and size, and the proceeds would buy another, in far better shape, on a good street in New York. And everything, every single object, every piece of furniture, would come with her. Rearranging them in their new home, contriving a new background that would show them at their greatest advantage, was exactly the kind of thing she liked best to do. Unfortunately she could never do it for anyone else, since professional decorators had to compromise somewhere to keep their customers happy and she would never compromise with the arrangement of an interior, nor would she trust a customer not to change things or add things the minute her back was turned.

Would she miss her French friends? Cora de Lioncourt snorted. No one who had not been born French, no one who had not gone through the French school system, truly had French friends. French society women made their friends in school, *en classe*, most particularly at the convents to which most of them were sent, and they consolidated these friendships at the *ralleys*, those teenaged social groups into which their mothers organized them tightly, almost as soon as they were born. She knew two hundred people who would be delighted to eat a dinner at her table, and who would invite her in turn, but unless you had been born into their circle you would always be no more than a guest in their eyes. All her French relationships had been based on Robert's family connections, and these people had always known that Robert had no money before his marriage. In French society the Lioncourts could not possibly pass for rich people. Nor was Robert's family particularly distinguished. They had never, she admitted to herself, made it to the top of the ladder, never absolutely *made the grade*. She would never forgive the French for that. She'd be glad to leave Paris, a city that had, in any case, seen its best days.

But, oh God, the sheer *hell* of dealing with French moving men!

Spider and Billy sat at Le Train Bleu, a newly opened, expensive French restaurant off Madison Avenue, waiting for Cora de Lioncourt to join them for lunch on a day in late June of 1980. They were in New York for a few days on business while the Beverly Hills Scruples, over four years old, was closed for repainting and some new construction. June was a dead month in the retail business, too late for their kind of customers, who chose their spring and summer wardrobes in late winter and bought for fall in July, so Billy had decreed that closing the store would be no loss at all.

"Why are we meeting this woman?" Spider asked.

"We can use her," Billy answered. "It's as simple as that. Anyway, I think you'll like her. I've met her here and there every time I come to New York and she's remarkably pleasant. She knows everybody . . . on my last trip she gave a small dinner for me, and I had the most fun I've had in a long time."

"Aside from worming her way into your affections, just what is it she can do for us that we need?"

"Oh, Spider, don't be so suspicious."

"Mrs. Ikehorn, there's a look on your face that tells me that you're up to no good."

"Mr. Elliott, have I ever been up to good?"

"Jesus, Billy, ask me a question I can answer."

Spider gave Billy that happy, sensuous grin to which she had tried to become immune. When Valentine had agreed to leave New York and come to work at Scruples in 1976, she had conned Billy over the phone into giving Spider a job as well. Billy had found out about Valentine's trick before she met Spider, yet he had managed to persuade her to give him a chance. The first thought she'd had about Spider was that he was one man she could never allow herself, and she repeated that thought every time she was alone with him, erecting a barrier of playfulness that kept his attractiveness, for he had only grown more attractive as the years passed, at a distance that was comfortable . . . or almost comfortable.

Billy sipped her white wine, meditating on those particular qualities that made Spider, along with her lawyer, Josh Hillman, one of the two men in the world she trusted. There was not the slightest taint of affectation to him, she thought; his raw manliness, like his outrageous masculinity, his rogue energy, was bred in the bone. He had a manly energy, a manly gentleness, a manly openness, a loyalty and a kindness that were steady and unconscious, part of him no matter with whom he was dealing. He had juice, that damned sexual juice that was so difficult for any woman to ignore, but it was his pith, nothing he turned on or off for reasons of his own. She couldn't imagine him telling her a lie, but above all else, in spite of his glamour, Spider had a manly simplicity that no amount of worldly experience had tarnished or diminished, quite probably because he had never really grown up.

While Billy sat composedly, looking over the new and interestingly decorated restaurant, Spider gazed at her reflectively. She had seemed like such a difficult customer when he'd met her that nothing could have persuaded him that four years later he'd consider her a close friend. She had never lost certain qualities that must to this day make her seem impossible to other people; she was still royally impatient, still a demanding perfectionist, still impulsive and determined to have her own way, still capable of springing into sudden autocratic rages when her detailed orders weren't carried out properly.

Unquestionably many people feared her, Spider realized, but they were not the people who knew her best. No question that there were a multitude of poorly organized architects and decorators, contractors and heads of construction crews in Hong Kong, Munich, Honolulu, Rio, Zurich and Monte Carlo who developed migraines at the sound of her name.

When Billy announced that she was coming to visit here in New York or in Chicago, Spider knew that no one who worked at either store relaxed until she had flown back to Los Angeles. Billy was one holy hell of a tough boss, no question about it, but she never remained unreasonable or unfair when conditions were explained to her, even during the difficulties of creating the first Scruples. She gave people a second chance, on occasion even a third, before she fired them, and those who performed satisfactorily were promptly rewarded with loyalty and generosity.

He was curious about this new friend of hers who had invited them both to lunch. He and Valentine often wondered why Billy had so few women friends. She created an ever-so-slight, but distinct, wall of distance between herself and almost every woman they knew; only a few, like Susan Arvey, were treated without that tiny touch of reserve, and Billy didn't even like Susan Arvey, although she respected her mind.

Valentine and Billy had grown very close in the last few years. "Today Billy told me that she feels that Dolly, Jessica Strauss and I are her three dearest friends in the world," Valentine had told him, just the other day. "I felt so touched, so pleased, and yet a little sad for her, I don't know quite why. Perhaps because she doesn't have a husband to be her best friend, the way I do." It *was* sad, Spider thought, that you couldn't be as rich as Billy was and still expect to be a normal woman, with normal friendships. Certainly not with a normal dating life, God knows. She tried to deal with the men who went after her, but she was gun-shy now, and who could blame her?

Marriage to that miserable peckerhead, Vito, had humanized her, but the divorce had made her suspicious of all men. He dreaded to think what else the divorce might have done to Billy if Gigi hadn't been there. Gigi had brought out a tenderness and a deeply feminine sweetness in Billy that Spider hadn't realized she possessed, but she could still be swept into a moody unhappiness that he sensed came from someplace in her he didn't understand.

Billy looked younger now than when he'd met her, but he knew she was thirty-seven, not quite a year older than he. It might be the haircut, Spider thought, for not long after the divorce she'd had her long, dark brown hair cut very short, so that it had shaped itself into a careless point at her nape and sprang back from her forehead in thick, blunt-cut, large, loose curls that looked as if no hairdresser had ever come near them, a deceptively casual-looking style that had to be trimmed every two weeks. Her head, held high by her powerful throat, seemed more imperious now than when it had been softened by the hair she used to wear to her shoulders. Her luscious mouth was as full as ever, her naturally rosy lips still covered only by a layer of transparent gloss, and her eyes had lost none of their smoky mystery; in fact, they had gained in their dark, unflinching challenge. If you had no idea who Billy was, you'd have to turn your head to look at her, he thought, for she carried an empire in her eyes. Billy's beauty—for she was a raging, flaming, tearing, wild-ass beauty, Spider admitted—retained its strong, verging-on-virile quality that made her seem to be one of a long line of huntresses. Today, in the fitted, belted red linen jacket and crisply tailored trousers Valentine had designed for her, Billy, oblivious of the fact that everyone in the crowded restaurant was aware of her, looked as if she could leap on a charger and lead a troop of redcoats to the sound of martial trumpets. She only needed a sword.

"Madame is late," he remarked.

"We got here early," Billy answered, looking at her watch. "In exactly one minute she'll be one minute late and there she is now, so stop your whining, you're just hungry."

Billy introduced them and as he sat down, after rising to greet the newcomer, Spider looked her over curiously. A strange and strikingly distinctive bird, he thought, reserving judgment, for he was a man who liked almost every woman he'd ever met, and he meant to give this lady a fair chance, although something told him, way down where he kept his deepest instincts, that she might turn out to be an exception to his feelings. Yet she was charming, perfectly charming, bubbling with amusing things to say, listening intently to what was said to her, and as far as he could tell, she was unimpressed by Billy's position, an attitude Spider knew was rare.

"Cora has the most marvelous apartment I've ever seen, filled with the most exquisite things in New York," Billy informed Spider.

"Do you like things, Spider?" Cora de Lioncourt inquired.

"Could you be a little more specific, Cora?" he replied.

"Antiques, objects, bibelots, great junk, 'smalls,' " she said in her lovely voice in which the Southern echoes had never died.

"What's a 'small'?"

"A British dealer's term for an addiction, a little object you hadn't intended to buy and certainly don't need, but end up paying too much for and take away with you, filled with the thrill of possession.''

"I get a kick out of great junk, but 'smalls' sound like a new kind of candy, too rich for my blood, and antiques are something I've never lived with and don't know about . . . bibelots I tend to break.''

"Then you simply must come and visit me, let me show you my things, and be converted,'' Cora said, seeming to be captivated by his indifference. "I have ten friends who say you've changed their lives by your incredibly perceptive advice about clothes—taste, in my experience, is never confined to only one area. I'm sure you'd have an instinctive knowledge about things, I'd bet money that you could tell a great antique chair from a merely good antique chair, this very minute, without knowing why, just because of your eye. Do say you'll visit me!''

"I appreciate the invitation,'' Spider said, "but I'm not much of a shopper. I like to advise women on how to make the most of themselves, but I consider that activity called 'going shopping' a kind of terrible torture.''

"Spider, Cora isn't talking about shopping, she's talking about collecting,'' Billy laughed, familiar with his deliberately obtuse manner. Sometimes, though not often, Spider could be rubbed the wrong way.

"Billy, speaking of shopping, I had an idea last night just as I was going to sleep,'' Cora de Lioncourt said, "and I wrote it down so I wouldn't forget. I thought that your Scruples ads, fabulous as they are, might possibly be made even better. I know absolutely nothing about advertising, so shut me up if it sounds ridiculous, but why don't you appear in the ads yourself, instead of using models? It would be so much more interesting for women to see you, the actual owner, wearing the things you're selling, and you're probably roughly the age of your best customers, no matter how unfairly young you look. I've seen enough photographs of you to know you could carry it off—is that a totally stupid idea, or does it make any sense?''

There was a silence as both Spider and Billy sat still, not eating. It was a bold and original idea that had never occurred to either of them before.

"Well . . .'' Billy murmured, unwilling to admit how much the idea immediately tempted her. She was almost ashamed of how proud she had become of her stores; she identified herself with them in a visceral way; they were her triumphs. She knew how well she photographed, how well she wore clothes . . . Why not?

"I don't know," she said slowly. "I would never have thought of it—Spider, what do you think?"

"Right off the bat? Okay, I think it's . . . risky."

"Why risky?" Billy demanded.

"I don't know that you'd want to be the symbol of the Scruples customer," he said, groping for words. "Look, Billy, I have to deal with them directly, and ninety-nine and nine-tenths of one percent of them can't wear clothes the way you can. They're used to seeing photographs of models looking better than they ever will, but you're a real person, and that could be annoying to them, a kind of turn-off. And there's more—"

"What?" she asked impatiently.

"You've often told me that you hated being on those lists of the ten richest women in America, and constantly being identified that way in the media, every time your name is used, right?"

"Right."

"So appearing in the ads, wearing the latest styles, would make you just that much more of a target. You'd be more envied than you are already. That's not a good idea. Ultimately it could work against you . . . women would see the pictures and think, 'Oh no, not Billy Ikehorn *again* wearing a dress that probably costs a fortune . . . it's so easy for her, she owns the damn store and she's so damn thin, but it's too expensive for me and I couldn't carry it off anyway' . . . that sort of thing."

"You're right, Spider," Billy said, hiding her regret imperfectly.

"I know you're right," Cora de Lioncourt said, hiding her disappointment perfectly. "It's that kind of sensitivity, that kind of understanding of women's psyches that makes you so unusual, Spider. I see the pitfalls now . . . . the idea goes into my wastepaper basket."

"But it's a marvelous idea for someone else, Cora," Billy protested, "probably a designer, a woman designer who happens to design for her own body type . . . someday I'm sure someone will do it. I do think you're clever!"

"Well, thank you," she said, showing her perfect teeth. "Then maybe I'll put it in my 'file and don't forget' file."

"Whatever you decide, Cora, I'm thrilled that you're going to be helping us with the big party in the fall, after Labor Day," Billy said.

Spider continued to eat his turbot. This was the first he'd heard of any party, but he wasn't about to ask questions, not right after spiking Cora de what's-her-name's guns.

"It's going to be really hard," Cora said, "to plan something that will top the party you gave when the first Scruples opened. I know that Spider was singlehandedly responsible for that huge success—it was a party that showed genius, Spider, and I doubt that I can arrange anything half as good, but I mean to try. For New Yorkers to be trumped by a big party in Los Angeles . . . well! They're going to expect the fall celebration to be incredible and they'll be picky, Billy, picky as the devil. They hate competition from the provinces. If they don't believe New York is the center of the universe, how can they justify living here?"

"Spider, I didn't have a chance to tell you about this before lunch," Billy said, "but the last time I was here, Cora suggested it."

"I see. So Cora's going to help?"

"After all, Spider, it makes sense. We never officially celebrated when we opened, and we really should have had a big party for the publicity if no other reason. New York isn't your town, the way L.A. is, and it certainly isn't my town, but it *is* Cora's town. We need someone here on the spot who knows all the right people to use for food and flowers and music and decor, someone who can add the newest interesting names to our guest list . . . I haven't any doubt that it's a good idea."

"All I want besides the fun of doing it," Cora said, "is for Spider to pick out a dress for me to buy to wear to the party. I crave that famous Spider Elliott experience."

"I think you have your own look down to perfection, Cora, you know as well as I do that you don't need me," Spider said, pleasantly but unsmiling.

As he spoke, he thought that there was absolutely no need to give such a party. It would cost a fucking fortune and the New York Scruples was already doing three times as much business per square foot than any other store in town. If they needed publicity, which they didn't, it was to be had for peanuts, but since Billy obviously wanted to throw a monster bash, why not? It couldn't hurt, not the way those ads would hurt, so why should he throw cold water on her plan?

The only thing was, there had been plenty of time for Billy to tell him about it before lunch—weeks, in fact, since Cora had come up with the idea—so why had she waited to spring it on him until Cora was there to back her up? No, he didn't like the Lioncourt even a little bit. And flattery would get her nowhere.

After lunch, for which no check was presented, as it never was to Cora de Lioncourt, she dropped in on several antiques dealers before returning home. As she had expected, she saw nothing worth a second of her time, but she wanted to reject and reject, and reject again, with pointed, spiteful, accurately disdainful words, to vent some of the rage Spider Elliott had aroused in her. Christ, she hated men like that! Handsome, uselessly handsome, dismissive, with minds of their own.

Men with influence over rich women were her natural enemies, and a man like Spider, an impervious man, a man who resisted her and didn't hesitate to speak his mind, was the worst of all. Rich women were her prey, and Billy Ikehorn was the biggest of all the big game that had ever come her way; she'd been stalking her slowly and carefully and successfully since she first met her, and she'd invited Spider to lunch with them in order to take his measure. He was distinctly bad news, Cora thought, as she returned to her apartment and made herself a cup of tea before she went to her desk to look over her accounts.

Absently she studied the list of the five expensive new restaurants in town where she had arrangements. Her fees were all paid in cash— Cora insisted on *liquide*—for bringing parties of friends for lunch or dinner, with the checks taken care of by the restaurants themselves. Le Train Bleu had waited two months for her to bring Billy Ikehorn, and tomorrow there would be a mention in a well-read gossip column; they owed her a handsome bonus. Although she charged a yearly rate, payable in advance, she made no promises to the restaurant owners. She guaranteed to bring the right people when they opened and for a while afterwards, but the success of the place depended entirely on factors she couldn't control. If a restaurant didn't catch on, she dropped it instantly, for she couldn't afford to take her friends anywhere that was half-empty.

Restaurants were the least of her business, she thought, but dependable. They closed and opened at an amazing rate in the city, and she only agreed to work with the best, recommended to her by members of the network she had built up in the past seven years of residence.

The first year had been grindingly tough, and Cora de Lioncourt had often stiffened her resolve by repeating to herself that she was in a period of investment; not a dime could be expected to come in until she had established herself. The move had been made twice as hard by the discovery that her dollars bought less in New York than her francs did in Paris, so that decorating her apartment and maintaining her standard of living forced her to take a bite into her capital. Nobody in New York gave discounts for cash, not even the shoe repairman, the apartment painter or the lady who cleaned her teeth—what was wrong with these Americans, who had taxes to pay just like everybody else? But she stuck to her plan. Her New York friends had indeed entertained for her, and once her apartment was ready, Cora promptly invited them back, in well-thought-out combinations, adding the best of the new people she had met, particularly anyone connected in any way with the media.

In Paris the media didn't have the social importance they had in New York. The French newspapers contained reviews of movies, plays and books, but where society was concerned, they were stuck in the Stone Age. French newspapers and magazines didn't contain life-style pages or society gossip columns that told people what parties were being given by which hostess; who was wearing what on each occasion; who had been seen lunching where, with whom; who had just bought a new place and intended to gut and redecorate it; who had gone on vacation with what group of friends, or what charity balls were being planned by what group of women.

The French gave almost nothing to charity; their private parties were closed to the press, ladies lunched together at home, and everyone knew where the few women who could still afford the couture dressed. People wisely played down their wealth for fear of the tax inspectors.

Ah, but New York! An event hadn't really taken place unless it was reported in the press; newspapers and magazines were rich in outlets for such news, and Cora de Lioncourt made a study of the media that covered the to-ings and fro-ings of the rich as thoroughly as an anthropologist. Her greatest stroke of luck, and she had always known she would have one piece of luck or another, had been a friendship she had developed with Harriet Toppingham, the powerful and feared editor of *Fashion and Interiors*.

The two women had met briefly several times in Paris, when the fashion editor came for the collections—they had many mutual friends —but only in New York did the acquaintanceship become an important friendship for both of them. Harriet was as totally in thrall to collector's mania as Cora, and equally knowledgeable. They developed a genuine affection and true respect for each other as they lunched together on Saturdays and then went off to the auction at Parke Bernet, or drove out for a day to investigate country dealers; not even a suburban garage sale could fail to inspire the thrill of the hunt for women who knew that you could never guess where a great or merely desirably amusing object might turn up.

Beyond collecting, they discovered that they shared a natural affinity that went right to their hearts. Each of them had grown up unattractive and ambitious, and each of them had made a successful life by imposing her intelligence and taste on the unpromising material she had been given. Each of them was cynical; each of them mistrusted men and hated all the pretty women of the world who floated so easily through life on a cloud of admiration. Each was bitter, each was lonely, each was unstoppable. Each needed the other.

Harriet Toppingham and Cora de Lioncourt collected different kinds of objects and used them in different ways in their complicated, beloved interiors, so the element of competition, which might have been a problem, was absent. As soon as Cora's apartment was ready to be photographed, Harriet devoted an eight-page color spread to it in one of the monthly issues of *Fashion and Interiors*.

On the day that issue appeared, Cora was not merely made, she was consecrated. No one in New York who mattered to her remained ignorant of the arrival in their city of the fascinating Comtesse Robert de Lioncourt, the custodian of a world of treasures, the well-born charmer from Charleston as well as a Chatfield of Cincinnati, who had conquered Paris and had now returned to her native land and created a setting of refinement and character, with a flavor so distinctly special, so wittily her own, that no decorator in town could have imagined it. The Sunday *New York Times Magazine* photographed her apartment for their decorating pages, as did *New York* magazine and *Town and Country*, all during Cora's second year in the city.

New Yorkers, who were becoming a bit tired of admiring each other's predictable art and sculpture, vied for invitations to Cora's small dinners, where they felt as if they had been transported to another country, a country that existed outside of time and space, created by Cora's brilliantly innovative evocation of her Paris apartment. She became celebrated and courted throughout the inner circle of the small world from which she intended to make her fortune.

Yes, dear Harriet had been the key, but she had underrated herself, Cora thought. She hadn't realized how the profession she had invented for herself was suited to her abilities. She got up from her desk, changed into a bathrobe, and lay down on the deep couch, covered with tapestry pillows, a couch that she thought of as her office, for there Cora had established her command center with the only tools she needed for her work: three books of phone numbers, a yellow pad, pencils and a telephone.

Her first clients had been antiques dealers, for they were the breed of tradesman with whom she could deal in the most surefooted way. Cora answered the entreaties of her new friends to "take them antique hunting" by leading them to the expensive dealers with whom she had made her arrangements, receiving a large kickback on the high prices they charged. On the other hand, she thought with pride, she never allowed anyone to buy something that wasn't worth owning. If they showed a foolish yen for an unworthy piece, she pointed out, gently but firmly, why it was wrong for them.

Next she had launched a talented young Charleston decorator, new to New York and a distant relative, who had sought her help in finding him his first big client. Cora fished about carefully, finally bringing him a recently divorced friend who was looking for someone unknown and original to decorate her new penthouse. On this transaction, and the dozens of similar deals she had made with six other carefully chosen decorators, Cora took a solid ten percent of the total the client spent. The decorators who worked with her considered the percentage reasonable since the countess never brought them clients who weren't convinced of the necessity of using fine antiques, a belief that invariably caused the clients, sooner or later, to throw away their budgets, eyes big with delight at the thought of the grandeur of the finished project.

Cora de Lioncourt entertained so well that it was inevitable for her to branch out into the field of parties. Women were always asking her for her secrets and she was generous with them, knowing that by the time they copied her she'd have found new sources to use. The florists whose shops she made fashionable, the caterers she discovered, the musicians she suggested, all paid her yearly fees with gratitude, for where Cora led, others followed.

There were several areas Cora chose not to venture into. Hair salons were too unpredictable, and she didn't intend to risk losing a friend over a bad haircut; she trusted no jewelers or furriers except the great ones, whose reputation stood behind everything they sold, and such businesses had no need for her. She never felt the slightest desire to steer women into buying clothes from any particular store where expensive errors were bound to be made.

After three years of solid success making money from antiques dealers, decorators, restaurants and all the trades that were used in entertaining, Cora de Lioncourt found herself ready to undertake the launching of people. Here all her taste and discrimination and cleverness were essential to the delicate task.

People who required launching, new people who had recently arrived in New York or natives who had finally made big money, of whom there seemed to be more and more every day, were so often simply *not* launchable, lacking the material she required. She would only accept clients who had the real possibility of swimming on their own once she'd given them a send-off. She could guarantee nothing, as with the restaurants, and she made sure that she got paid up front. Ah, but when the right client came along, Cora thought, smiling to herself, when the right couple from the hinterlands telephoned, or the right newly single woman with huge alimony presented herself, then there was an opportunity in gold indeed! There was almost nothing such people wouldn't pay for a toehold in New York society, and when Cora de Lioncourt invited them to a few of her famous little dinners, when she introduced them gradually into her wide circle, when she helped them to entertain on their own, in the apartments that had been decorated by people she suggested, they could hardly complain if they didn't click.

It all made one big, grand circle, a dance in which every move led some solid sum to drop into her lap, and from there into her rapidly increasing portfolio of stocks and bonds. And in the dance Cora had established, new leaders were always needed, stars like Billy Ikehorn who would add a glittering layer of the highest luster to the world Cora had created around herself.

A close association with Billy Ikehorn, even if she spent nothing, never bought so much as a teaspoon, would be worthwhile to Cora, but she was convinced that with the right encouragement Billy Ikehorn was on the verge of spending more money than any other woman to whom she had so generously unveiled her sources. The Scruples advertising idea would have brought her no commission at all except Billy's gratitude. Occasionally, for special people, she gave away such tips, which she thought of, reveling in the delicious lowness of it, as "loss leaders."

The fall party for Scruples would merely be a beginning. Clearly, Billy had to have an establishment in New York. It was incomprehensible to Cora that Billy kept nothing but a four-room pied-à-terre in the Carlyle, that she had only one home base in California. It was almost a scandal, Cora thought, for such a rich woman to live so meagerly, so stingily, in such a small and unpretentious fashion. She owed it to the tradesmen of New York, if to no one else, to spread some of that money around.

Her plans for Billy were going to be no less than a public service, Cora de Lioncourt promised herself, even though she would never be able to take public credit.

When Spider was out of town on business, Valentine found it doubly difficult to sleep. She'd always been prey to insomnia, but it was almost bearable when she could prowl around their apartment, knowing that Spider was sleeping. Now, when she found herself alone and awake in the middle of the night, she was more restless than ever. Thank God, Spider would be home from New York tomorrow, she thought as she went to watch television in the living room at two in the morning, for insomnia was far worse when she was lying in bed than when she was up and doing something. She could have gone to New York with Spider, as he had begged her to, but Valentine had decided to take advantage of the days in which the store was closed for redecoration to look for a house.

No man could be expected to have the patience to inspect house after house with a real-estate saleswoman, but Valentine had plunged into the process this past spring, knowing that somewhere the perfect house lay waiting them. Today she thought she had . . . perhaps . . . found it, and her sleeplessness was compounded by her excitement at the idea of taking Spider back there tomorrow to get his opinion.

She turned the television off in disgust. No, nothing so bad could be endured. There was only one remedy, to which she had recourse frequently before her marriage and even now when her husband was out of town. She must work until she fell asleep from sheer fatigue, and to do that she had to go to Scruples, to her design studio. The house she'd seen today had room for a studio, as this apartment did not, Valentine thought as she dressed hastily, room for a garden, room for a library, room for children, room . . . so much lovely space . . . it would be a different sort of life, although no life could be better than hers was now.

Quickly she drove the short distance to Scruples and let herself in. Because of her nighttime visits she had a key to the service entrance and knew all the security codes. The store smelled of fresh paint, new lumber and sawdust, Valentine noticed as she made her way to her studio, and Scruples looked huge and strange with all the inventory temporarily removed and put into storage. It had been emptied and made totally available to the crews of painters and carpenters, dozens of them still working overtime to get the job done quickly, but her studio was forbidden territory. She had allowed no repainting there, thank you very much, for she was up to her eyebrows in work on the *Legend* costumes, and could not be disturbed for anything, she had told the painting contractor indignantly.

Valentine turned on the bright overhead lights of the studio and looked around in relief. Here she could spend the night profitably and even sleep for a few hours on the battered old chaise longue she kept in a corner, half buried under her collection of fashion magazines and old copies of *Women's Wear Daily*. It was an old, friendly, familiar habit, leafing through back issues of *WWD*, looking for pictures of old friends, seeing what had happened months ago in the frenzied world of Seventh Avenue that she was happy to be part of no longer. Valentine often took a break in her daily routine, curled up there for half an hour and browsed through the papers, but she hadn't had time to do so recently, because of the press of work.

She was simply going to have to demand a larger studio, Valentine realized as she looked around, if Billy ever again asked her to design costumes for a film, as she had with *Legend*. The studio had never been so impossibly crowded before, but in order to create the costumes for Melanie Adams on the schedule she had agreed to, Valentine had been forced to have a dozen dressmaker's dummies made exactly to Melanie's measure.

The actress had neither the time nor the patience to stand still for lengthy fittings for the sixty-odd costumes Valentine was designing. Each of the dummies was presently clad in a gauzelike material, a kind of heavy, flexible tulle, that Valentine was using instead of the traditional dressmaker's muslin, which was too stiff to use as a *toile*, the working design for these 1920s and 1930s costumes she was creating, costumes that must drape softly and becomingly.

In addition to the crowd of dummies, the small studio was littered with old photographs from films in which Garbo and Dietrich had starred in their early days; piles of yellowed old newspapers that showed the two actresses as they embarked or disembarked from Atlantic crossings or posed for publicity stills, as well as books of film history that had been brought by the studio for Valentine to study. Her usually orderly studio had never been in such a mess before, Valentine thought, dismayed, but it wouldn't remain that way for long. There was just enough room for her to move around the dummies, cutting, pinning, draping and redraping the resilient soft gauze; the silent, white, headless figures were more agreeable company to her than any middle-of-the-night television movie.

Valentine worked industriously for several hours. The worst of the labor on *Legend* was almost finished, Wells Cope had approved all her sketches, and only another half dozen costumes were left to be worked on next week and then translated from gauze into actual cloth. Melanie Adams would have to bring her precious self here in person for the last costume fittings, but that particular problem was one she would leave to Mr. Cope to cope with, Valentine thought sleepily, for she was pleased with her work and ready to stop. Exhausted, she stretched out on the old chaise and lit a Gauloise Bleu, so redolent of Paris, from the package she always kept there. As Valentine lay back and puffed, she felt delightfully relaxed . . . yes, definitely, she must have a studio in their new house, she thought just before she plunged into a deep sleep.

The burning cigarette dropped from her hand and landed on a pile of brittle photographs, which caught fire instantly. The photographs ignited one of the old newspapers, and within seconds the entire studio was ablaze, the gauze on the dressmaker's dummies going up in flares of flame, the paper that filled the room feeding the roaring fire that quickly consumed Valentine's studio. The fire raced through the newly painted offices down the newly painted central staircase and attacked the piles of lumber left everywhere by the carpenters. It was fueled by the cans of paint that were standing about in every corner, some of them carelessly closed by the painters who were to return the next morning. Hungrily the roaring blaze destroyed floors and walls and newly varnished display cases, rushed to attack the paneling in the Edwardian Winter Garden, and leapt through the freshly papered walls of the dressing rooms that stood with their doors propped open for the workmen's convenience.

In just a few fierce, catastrophic minutes, well before the Beverly Hills Fire Department arrived, Scruples was gutted, its interior burned to the ground within its setting of formal gardens that kept the store separate from Rodeo Drive. Valentine was dead, quickly asphyxiated long before she could have known what was happening.

9

Almost a year after the fire, in the spring of 1981, Josh Hillman, for all his lawyerly attention to detail, felt that no matter how carefully he looked for a still-unfinished piece of business, the Scruples file could be closed. Too agitated to sit down, he paced about his own office in the imposing Century City offices of Strassberger, Lipkin and Hillman, unable to feel the usual relief of a man who knows that a difficult job of work is behind him.

Billy had never laid eyes on the site of the Beverly Hills Scruples again, he thought, remembering how she had come to him straight from the airport and given her orders in a state of grief that he would not have believed possible during their years of a close business relationship.

"Bulldoze the outside walls to the ground," she had said, in a parched, ragged, all-but-unrecognizable voice, "bulldoze the gardens, clean it up and sell the land immediately."

He'd nodded assent and made a note, but then she continued to pour out instructions that simply didn't make any sense to him.

"Sell the Chicago store, sell the New York store, the Munich store, the Honolulu store, the Hong Kong store; stop construction on all the other stores that are underway, sell all the parcels of land that I bought for future construction, get rid of them as quickly as possible, Josh."

"Billy, I understand how you feel about the Beverly Hills store," he'd told her gently, "but selling Chicago and New York? That's going too far, Billy, much too far. As your lawyer I have to advise you that it's the worst possible business decision you could make. Both of those stores are doing amazing business and their locations can never again be duplicated. Nobody in his right mind would sell them in today's boom market. I know how deeply upset you feel, but, believe me, this is not the time to make any long-range plans. We'll talk about it in a few weeks if you still—"

"Josh! Shut up! I've made up my mind and I'm not interested in profit or loss."

"Look, you've got to absorb some of the shock. You're not rational now, it's normal to feel this way but if these orders are carried out, you'll ruin the Scruples empire."

"The sooner the better," she'd said in a tone of such arid, corrosive intensity that he'd stared at her incredulously, for no one knew better than he how much the triumphant success of the Scruples boutiques meant to her.

"Billy, forgive me, but I just don't understand," he'd said, utterly at a loss.

"Valentine would be alive today if I hadn't asked her to design the costumes for *Legend*. I'm sure that was what she must have been doing in the store—she was overworked and trying to meet the deadline. It was my fault, Josh, and that's all I'm ever going to say about it to anybody but you. The only reason I'm telling you is so that you'll stop objecting and get to work. *It was my fault.* This is the only thing I can think of to do—I know it won't bring her back, but . . . somehow . . . . it's right."

"Billy—" he'd stopped, arrested in mid-protestation by her ghastly voice.

"Josh, I expect you to work with the Ikehorn estate lawyers in New York, I want nothing more to do with it, I leave it in your hands. Pay six months' salary to everyone who had worked in the Beverly

Hills Scruples, two months' to the people from Chicago and New York, and pay every outstanding bill of whatever nature at once, without discussion, Josh, without discussion. Never, under any circumstances do I intend to talk to you about this again. *Scruples must cease to exist.*"

Billy had disappeared from his office even before he'd had a chance to tell her that he would follow her orders. He had accepted her crazed haste, her irrational feelings of guilt, but he had not acted without his customary thoughtful precision. It had been a year before all those orders could be carried out and finalized, down to the last comma on the last sheet of legal paper. Josh Hillman had liquidated the Scruples holdings, wherever they existed, at an efficient but businesslike pace. He knew that the market for choice retail locations had never been higher and was growing by the minute. By the time he'd finished disposing of the stores and the land he was able to take a grim satisfaction in the fact that the destruction of the Scruples empire had realized a substantial net profit, particularly in the case of the Chicago and New York stores, which he was able to sell immediately. The rest of the work was completed now and all that remained, although no one in the world knew it, was the piece of apricot marble with the Scruples name carved on it that had been fixed to the front door of the boutique on Rodeo Drive. It had been routinely delivered to him by the Beverly Hills Fire Department, in his capacity as Billy's legal representative, and he had not been able to part with it.

The nameplate was all that was left to him of Valentine, Valentine whom he had loved from the first instant he laid eyes on her; Valentine for whom he had divorced his wife of many years; Valentine who had intended to marry him, so he believed, until the very day she eloped with Spider Elliott. No one had ever known of their love, not even Joanne, his ex-wife. Josh Hillman had had to accept Valentine's marriage in the same stoic, terrible silence in which he had grieved for her after her death. It was the only thing he could do for the woman who had given him such joy.

Josh Hillman looked east from the windows of his twenty-second-story office. It was a smogless day and he could see as far as the outline of the tall apartment house in which Valentine had lived, first alone, and later, after her marriage with Spider. Where was Spider now, he wondered.

The check for ten million dollars, which represented Spider and Valentine's share of their partnership with Billy, had been delivered to Spider by messenger while he was still in Los Angeles, but no one had seen him since the memorial service for Valentine. Through a yacht broker at Marina del Rey who had called him before he accepted Spider's check, hastily written on a local bank, Josh had learned that Spider had bought an oceangoing vessel, a battered, third-hand, but basically sound old sailing boat with no frills, a boat that could properly be termed anything from a yacht to a hulk. It was some fifty-five feet long, carried a reliable motor besides its sails, and possessed four cabins, enough for a small crew as well as the owner. Within the week Spider had moved a few belongings on board, hired two seasoned crew members, stocked the boat, and simply disappeared in the direction of Hawaii. Twice there had been word that someone had glimpsed him, but he communicated with nobody. He had been spotted at an anchorage off Kauai, and then he had been lost to view for months until he anchored at Raiatea, in the Society Islands of French Polynesia. There, in a region as large as western Europe, Josh supposed that Spider had remained, for lack of other news.

He wished he could do the same, Josiah Isaiah Hillman thought, he wished he could just tell the world to continue on its way to perdition without him and sail away and try to come to some bearable terms with life, but he was forty-seven, the senior partner of a great law firm, a man with three children and duties to the community. The only romance in his orderly, upright, achieving life, a life of responsibility and probity, had been his passion for Valentine, and now that she was gone he would continue on as he had before he met her, knowing that he could count on habit to keep him going.

Thank God, he thought, no one had dreamed of asking him to speak at the memorial service that had been held for Valentine in Billy's gardens. He would not have been able to utter a word without breaking down, any more than Billy or Spider, who had sat withdrawn from each other and everyone else. He had not dared to look at Spider, but he had glanced at Billy and seen that her face was almost entirely hidden by the wide brim of the black hat with which she had sheltered herself from view. Dolly Moon had spoken, telling them of her magical experiences with Valentine with such overflowing love, and the control of the great actress that she was, that her words had been healing. And Jimbo Lombardi, Valentine's great pal from her days as a New York fashion designer, had remembered her with his saving humor, recounting a trove of whimsical memories of the years in which Valentine had been the most vivid member of the coterie that swirled around her former employer, John Prince. Wells Cope had spoken too, in a grave, eloquent appreciation of Valentine's talent, and finally Gigi had uttered a few short phrases in her clear, unfaltering voice, although she trembled visibly, speaking of the first day on which she had met Valentine, and of the other days on which they had been together, only happy days, only days of joy. And then it was over.

Billy had closed the house on Charing Cross Road, leaving Josie Speilberg and Burgo O'Sullivan in charge of supervising its upkeep. A cleaning crew went in once a week, to keep the unused rooms spotless, the gardens continued to be tended, but Billy seemed to have deserted California forever when she had gone away a year ago, taking Gigi with her to spend the rest of the summer with Jessica Thorpe Strauss and her family in East Hampton.

And he, Josh Hillman thought, had to go home now and dress for another dinner party at Susan Arvey's, because, according to her, he was now the most eligible single man in Hollywood. He wished on no other man such a dreary, useless, pathetic fate.

"I can't believe the Labor Day weekend's coming up," Jessica said mildly, her famously sad lavender eyes wide, her famously enchanting mouth drooping in its famously irresistible way. She looked up from her book in the last week of August 1980, through the cloud of baby hair that still retained its Pre-Raphaelite vagueness. She and Billy had been sitting silently, reading on a screened porch. All summer long, from the time Billy and Gigi had arrived after Valentine's funeral until today, two months later, Jessica had avoided any hint of a word that might seem to raise the question of Billy's future activities, but now the end of summer was upon them, and something had to be settled.

Three years older than Billy, Jessica had seen Billy through the most important changes of her adulthood, but never in sixteen years had she known her friend to be closed off from her in this granitelike grief, an inaccessible statue of a woman who had come half alive only when she threw herself into sailing and playing tennis with Jessica's own five kids and Gigi, as if Billy had come to East Hampton instead of going to summer camp, seeking nothing more than the adolescents' youthful spirits and joking company. She had avoided being alone with Jessica as much as possible.

As if I'd ask her questions, Jessica thought, as if I'd try to give her sensible advice, as if I don't know that there are some things that words can't touch and that I can't do anything to help her.

But after Labor Day the Strausses would have to begin to think about packing up and organizing their yearly return to Manhattan, for the junior members of the family would all be returning to their various schools in September and there were clothes to be bought and arrangements by the dozen to be made.

"Labor Day . . . oh, Jessie, no, not the end of the summer . . . I've always hated Labor Day, but this year . . ." Billy said slowly, lowering her book reluctantly. "I can't remember when the approach of any holiday has made me so anxious."

"Hmmm." Jessica made a neutral noise. She wasn't going to interrupt, Jessica thought, not when it seemed as if Billy might finally be ready to have the discussion that was inevitable.

"Jessie," Billy said, sitting up straight and pushing the book aside, "I've been taking advantage of you all summer, don't waste your time saying it isn't true and other nice, well-meaning crap because we both know that all I've been doing here is trying to get myself back together. I'm so sick of kids I could scream, so I guess I'll have to talk to you."

"Hmmm."

Billy smiled faintly. "You can go 'hmmm' all day, I won't mind, so spare yourself, you need to save that energy for shopping for shoes with the twins, they've told me they plan to refuse to wear anything but sneakers all winter—oh, I know all your kids' secrets, Jessie, including that David junior is insanely in love with Gigi, but since they're the same age he might just as well have a crush on Jeanne Moreau in the maturity department, but I swore not to tell you, so promise you'll pretend that you don't know, all right?"

"Hmmmmmmmm."

"However, he's so cute that she does let him make love to her."

"*What!*"

"I knew I could get a rise out of you." Billy actually laughed at the expression on Jessica's face, and Jessica, hearing the laugh, relaxed. If Billy could tease her, things were beginning to get back to normal.

"So what am I going to do with my life? That's the question you're asking yourself, aren't you?"

"It has crossed my mind," Jessica said with mild encouragement.

"Listen to this," Billy said, " 'you just have to *go on* when it is worst and most helpless—there is just one thing to do . . . and that is to go straight on through to the end of the damn thing.' Doesn't that sound like good advice?"

"For what? Navigating the Amazon?"

"It's some advice given to F. Scott Fitzgerald when he was having trouble with *Tender is the Night*. I think it could apply to just about anything except eating a chocolate cake. So I'm going to follow it and just go 'straight on through.' "

"Through what?"

"Through life, you know perfectly well that's what I mean," Billy said with such bravado that she sounded shrill. "I'm going to pretend that I'm an appallingly rich, not half-bad-looking, single and still young woman who can buy literally anything in the world that she wants. I'm going to own houses in the right places, meet the right people, fuck the right men, give the right parties, and be photographed at the right places at the right time of the year." She paused, scrutinized Jessica's unjudgmental expression and continued in a lower voice. "Only a very few people will know that I've utterly failed with my life because I refuse, from now on, to collaborate in my ruin. What people think about you ultimately depends on what you admit, and henceforth I admit nothing unless it looks, smells and sounds like triumph."

"Good grief," Jessie murmured.

"Well, what do you think?" Billy's question was uneasy, defiant and touched with panic.

"Why ask me? Nobody that triumphant would need my opinion."

"I mean it, Jessie, I really do intend to do just what I said, because I've got to have a plan and it's the only one I can seem to imagine that won't hurt anybody but myself. I'm aware that it's not the prescription for getting to heaven—"

"It involves only three of the Seven Deadly Sins, actually," Jessica said thoughtfully. "Lust, greed and pride."

"What are the others?"

"Envy, gluttony, sloth and anger, according to Saint Thomas Aquinas, although I don't know who appointed him . . . . but looked at that way, you're marginally—just barely—on the side of the angels."

"I wouldn't care if I committed six out of the seven. I couldn't possibly do gluttony . . . . I just want to get out of this place I'm stuck at in my head, and the high life is all I can think of. I know I should be devoting myself to the betterment of humanity, but I can't kid myself that I'd last long at that . . . I've given Josh carte blanche to use my money to do it for me, he's so good about knowing how to give money where it's needed."

"What about Gigi?"

"We've talked quite a bit. She doesn't really want to go to college, and I can't blame her, I never went either, and I certainly can't force her. She's impatient to become independent as soon as possible, so she's gotten herself an entry-level job with the fanciest caterer in New York, it's called Voyage to Bountiful, Cora Middleton suggested them. Of course I'd like to keep her on a chain so that she'd never get far from me, but officially what can I do but be in favor of it, given Gigi's abilities?"

"But where will she live?"

"I've rented an apartment for her in the building with the best security I could find. She's going to share it with a girl named Sasha Nevsky. Sasha's a very grown-up, responsible twenty-two, and her mother was friendly with Gigi's mother. I arranged the whole thing over the phone with Mrs. Nevsky . . . she was thrilled because Sasha's been living in a walk-up in a dubious neighborhood. Now the two girls will be almost around the corner from you, so at least I know Gigi can always drop in on you for advice when she needs it, and when she has a vacation she'll come and visit me or I'll come to New York to visit her."

"Coming to visit from where, for heaven's sake? How come your high life doesn't start in Manhattan?" Jessica asked, alarmed for the first time in this conversation.

"I want to live outside of the United States for a while, Jessie," Billy said slowly.

"Oh, Billy, don't go away," Jessica pleaded. "Why do you have to leave New York?"

"Ah, come on, I need a fresh start and New York is too public, I feel I've used it up, everyone knows everything about me . . . you understand, don't you?"

"Unfortunately, yes."

"And I won't be any farther away than I was when I was in California," Billy said in her most persuasive voice, "at least not at first. It's the same three thousand miles either way, Paris or L.A."

"Paris! You're *not* going back to live in Paris! Wilhelmina Hunnenwell Winthrop, I don't believe it!"

"French is the only foreign language I speak, and anyway I have unfinished business there."

"I'll just bet I know what it is."

"Oh, Jessie, you don't know everything, you only know almost everything . . . . oh, so what, maybe you're right, I did leave Paris when I was poor and rejected, with my tail between my legs, and it is tempting to think of a grand return . . . and if you're going to go in for the high life, you look for it where they've known how to do it right for hundreds of years, no?"

"I suppose that was Cora's idea too, no?"

"She's horrified. She wanted me to stay right here, just like you."

"Oh Christ. I'm being abandoned again. As if it weren't tough enough being the discontinued woman."

"Huh?"

"My glove size was the first to go," tiny Jessica said mournfully, "or maybe it was my bra, it was so long ago I hardly remember. Nobody wears a 34A cup anymore, that I guarantee. Then came my panties . . . they stopped making size-four panties and didn't even warn me so I could stock up. Forget shoes, they stopped designing size-five shoes for grownups years ago, and I even have to buy my tennis socks in the children's department. As for clothes, what used to realistically be labeled a size eight is now called a size four or six, you'd never believe my alteration bills. Am I shrinking, I wonder, or is there some growing prejudice against divinely delicate women? Just about the only thing I can still be sure of getting in the right size is prescription reading glasses. You *can* be too rich . . . like you . . . or too thin . . . . like me . . . . but you can never have enough reading glasses. They discontinued my lipstick color and my favorite mascara and—oh, there are the children."

"If a magnificent six-foot-two-inch lad can be termed a child. What's David junior singing?"

"His new ode to Gigi. It's sung to the tune of 'I've Grown Accustomed to Her Face' . . . 'I've grown accustomed to her shoes, her heels, her soles, her mules, hold no mystery for me now, her infinite variety is on the wane, it's time I looked for different cooze again, I've grown accustomed to her shoes.' Sweet, isn't it, even if it doesn't quite scan?" Jessica sang in her high, pure soprano, enjoying her revenge for Billy's joke about Gigi and David.

"Jessica! *Cooze?* How dare he? And where did he hear that word?

Gigi didn't say he was making love to her, but she didn't say he *wasn't*, either," Billy hissed.

"Then I guess we'll never know, will we?"

"Mothers of sons are insufferably smug!"

"I have daughters to worry about, too."

"Don't waste time worrying," Billy said, suddenly serious. "It doesn't help. The things you pick to worry about don't happen, and then you find out that you wish they had, because they wouldn't have been that bad after all compared to what did happen."

Sasha Nevsky sat on the floor, surrounded by half-packed suitcases, and gave herself up to a gloomy fit of disappointment and anticipated disaster. She had many reasons not to want to leave her pleasantly messy room-and-a-half without a view on a rundown street off West End Avenue. She had been coerced into giving up her very own inviolate place, by God, to move across town to a newly furnished, luxurious apartment in the very center of the best part of the East Side that she was going to have to share, *share*, with Gigi Orsini, who was almost four years younger than she, a girl whom she barely remembered as a sort of Munchkin with pounds of awful hair, a girl who looked as if she hadn't reached puberty. Sasha was perfectly aware that her mother had sold her down the river to Billy Ikehorn, and all for the sake of solicitous, round-the-clock doormen, a guarded service entrance and an elevator that was still run by a real live man, not just by pushbuttons. She was going to have to give up her privacy, her priceless, hard-won privacy so necessary for her complicated life, just because her mother wanted her to live in a good neighborhood in a safe building.

But when Sasha's mother, Tatiana Orloff Nevsky, that terrorist gypsy, took to a notion, no member of her family dared to cross her, a fact Sasha accepted bleakly. It had been difficult enough getting permission to move out on her own, and she was still keeping a discreetly low profile, because of the nature of her particular calling. Her mother had opposed her job for a year, before giving in and letting Sasha exercise her talent, but, as she reminded her daughter regularly, her permission had been given on a temporary basis.

How could one tiny, bright-eyed woman manage to be so powerful as to prevent her daughter from using her own abilities for so long?

Sasha wondered. What gave her mother the unquestioned and absolute rule she enjoyed in the wide family circle? If she could ever figure out what invisible but unquestioned moral authority made her mother the unrivaled boss lady of six families, each one of them headed by one of her mother's five younger sisters, all born Orloffs, she'd look for those qualities in herself, develop them, Sasha resolved, and take over the world.

Glumly, sorting out panty hose by color, Sasha reviewed her twenty-two years of life. She was the Nevsky misfit, the all-but-disgrace to the entire close-knit Russian Jewish tribe of the Orloff sisters, the only one among the host of her talented cousins who couldn't sing, couldn't act, couldn't play any musical instrument and, tragedy of tragedies, couldn't dance. She couldn't tap, couldn't attempt ballet, couldn't even manage a simple time step, she had no fucking *rhythm* in a family in which babies were born auditioning for Hal Prince.

Family Thanksgivings had been the worst, Sasha decided. She'd have to sit there, hating her too-tall, too-skinny, untalented self and listen to tales of musicals past and musicals present and future, on Broadway or off, revivals or tours, for old musicals never died. When they stopped swapping musical stories, she'd heard endless accounts of her cousins' lessons and recitals and triumphs in dance and music school, of her aunts' hopes and plans for them, all the while wondering what she would do in life, for academically she had nothing much to boast of either. Her native shrewdness, her quick mind, had never translated into the good marks that might have commanded a little respect.

She knew what the rest of the family thought of her. They pitied her in their boisterous, good-natured way if they ever bothered to think about her at all; she was their family wet sparrow shivering on a branch, a harmless stick of a girl, Tatiana's one failure, overlooked and unconsidered, without any of the necessary juices that went into the rich Orloff-Nevsky stew. She used to look at herself in the mirror and persuade herself that there was nothing really wrong with the way she looked, but as soon as she found herself within the Orloff-Nevsky circle, Sasha became so uncomfortable that she made herself as inconspicuous as possible, withdrawing into whatever corner she could find. Whatever looks she possessed she hid, hunching her shoulders forward and slumping, making herself as plain and small as possible, with the instinct of the outsider for protective coloration. She knew that if any of the family were to notice evidence of the smallest attempt to make herself attractive, it would become the major news of the day, sure to be commented on with a deluge of too much well-meant surprise, too much encouragement, too much advice. Only the constant loving reassurance of her brilliant older brother, Zachary, a many-talented boy five years older than she, had kept up Sasha's self-esteem during those formative years.

Until. Until she'd grown into her splendid set of assets at a much later age than usual. Maybe the Orloff-Nevskys, a naturally lean and fairly flat-chested group, with typical dancers' well-muscled legs and spinal flexibility, didn't think it was an asset to have the prettiest pair of perfectly shaped tits and the most delicately emphatic of rounded asses and the most desirably tiny waist in the world, but another group of people did, and would pay for them, and so she, formerly an ungifted, hopeless, skinny wretch, she, Sasha Nevsky, had turned into the top lingerie model on Seventh Avenue.

The top. A lingerie showroom was as close to a theater as she'd ever get, Sasha realized, but if there had still been a Ziegfeld, she'd have been his lead showgirl because she walked like a divinity. Sasha Nevsky, she mused, thinking of herself in the third person as she often did, walked with a pure inspiration no dance lessons could have taught, she walked with a natural and inimitable mixture of exactly enough sass and exactly enough sexiness and exactly enough dignity to display the expensive panties and bras and slips and nightgowns manufactured by Herman Brothers, in a way that caused them to jump out of the showroom into department stores and specialty shops all over America.

The fact that Herman Brothers had been in business for almost a hundred years and was one of the most solid and respected lingerie firms in the United States, hadn't been enough to convince her mother that working there wasn't a form of white slavery. It had taken a visit to their impressive offices and a long talk with Mr. Jimmy, son of one of the original Herman brothers and now the stout, white-haired, bon-vivant owner of the firm, a man known for his benevolence and kindliness, to persuade Tatiana Nevsky to allow her daughter to take a job that paid her as much as any gypsy earned in a month, and, more important, paid it regularly.

Sasha had been working for Mr. Jimmy for over a year, and the same sense of drama that served her in the Herman Brothers showroom had been translated into her daily life. She straightened up to her full height of five feet nine, threw back her glorious shoulders, learned the minimum she needed to know about hair and makeup to give her native beauty full play, and carefully began to buy the kinds of clothes she had always dreamed about when she read fashion magazines. However, she never allowed the new Sasha to go to family parties, for her mother's worst fears about the immorality of the lingerie world would only have been confirmed by the sight of such a sinister difference in her quiet but safely innocent and unblemished daughter.

But now, just when she'd totally settled into her new job, Sasha thought, where the working hours were not too demanding, the colleagues pleasant and the gossip splendidly instructive, now, when she'd just about acclimated her plants to the gloom of her room and a half, now that she was on the verge of planning to straighten out her closets, now that her cat, Marcel, was finally housebroken, now that her three most favored dates had been allotted their time in her strict schedule, she, Sasha Nevsky, the magnificent one, was to be uprooted and moved to a place so classy that it wasn't even near a subway!

Of course, she could take the bus crosstown and change on Eighth Avenue, she could even take taxis on her salary, but she was saving her money fervently so that one day she could open her own lingerie shop. If there was one thing Sasha Nevsky knew about, she told herself, it was what women wanted to wear under their clothes.

She couldn't dance, but there was a future for her in retailing, she'd bet on it. She'd also bet that Gigi Orsini wore white cotton underpants and didn't even need a bra. Obviously, with Billy Ikehorn as her stepmother, the dumpy nonentity she remembered must have become a spoiled bossy brat. And probably still a virgin.

Gigi explored her new apartment tentatively, opening and closing linen and china and glassware closets filled with unfamiliar wares, including a sterling silver service for twelve and a complete Limoges tea service. Every shelf in the kitchen was crowded with supplies, the fridge was bulging. What had Billy been thinking of? Did she expect her to be giving dinner parties?

Gigi felt like a burglar casing the joint, rather than the legitimate occupant. She'd slept here alone last night, on one of the two new beds in her room, after seeing Billy off to Paris, and no place had ever seemed so frighteningly quiet, although she knew that the building was as well guarded as a harem at the height of the Ottoman Empire. It was the first time in her life she'd been alone at night, all on her own, she realized, wondering uneasily when Sasha Nevsky would arrive.

The last time they'd seen each other must have been something like five years ago, Gigi thought, counting backwards to another life, and if they had talked she didn't remember it, for the almost-four-year age gap that separated them had been all but unbridgeable. However, she remembered Sasha because she'd been so silent, visibly not at home in her skin, gawky and ill at ease, not one of the bubblingly attractive and competitively lively offspring of the Orloff sisters.

At least Sasha had the retiring and backward qualities that were desirable in a roommate, since Billy had decreed with all of her authority that she couldn't be allowed to live on her own in New York without one. Gigi had put on her most disgraceful jeans and T-shirt, her oldest and dirtiest sneakers, so that she wouldn't frighten the timid girl with any of the sensational new clothes that Billy had bought her before she took off for Paris. However, self-respect demanded that she put on a great deal more mascara than usual and add a few touches of new color to her hair, since this was New York and Sasha Nevsky was, if nothing else, a New Yorker.

A roommate should be invisible . . . . a mere presence . . . . a shadow . . . a neutral ghost who left you alone, whom you left alone, someone who respected your privacy, as you would respect hers. In 1980 it seemed bizarrely anachronistic that two girls who had nothing in common should be coerced by others into the enforced intimacy of living together. The only thing that connected them was Gigi's mother, Mimi O'Brian, who had long ago been a friend of Tatiana Nevsky's, and once a year Mrs. Nevsky would phone Gigi in California to find out how she was getting along.

Gigi shook her head in dismay. She was convinced that establishing Sasha Nevsky as her roommate was Billy's way of making sure that she had a chaperone. Although she had understood Gigi's desire to start to earn a living, once she'd found a suitable apartment for her, Billy had attached the Nevsky girl to the deal, a girl who had undoubtedly been instructed to watch over her, just because she was older. Who knows? Sasha might even be reporting to Billy every time she had a date, if anybody ever asked her out. Fortunately there was so much room in the apartment that they would each have a widely separated bedroom and bath. She'd simply have to work out a way to keep Sasha Nevsky at a distance.

Nervously, for she didn't expect Sasha for an hour and she had nothing else to keep her occupied, Gigi did the first thing that came to hand in the unnaturally neat apartment, and mixed up a batch of her own bittersweet Dutch chocolate-chip cookies and put them to bake in the new oven. She was trying to take inventory of the contents of the fridge when the doorbell rang shrilly. She jumped at the sound, and wiping her hands on her apron she went to answer it, a deeply skeptical frown on her face.

"Yes?" she said irritably to the magnificent brunette who stood there, a tall, imposing creature of frightening sophistication, her black hair piled high, wearing a superbly fitted black suit, a suspicious look on her face, a modern-day Gibson Girl of lush Edwardian beauty, tapping her high-heeled shoe impatiently and holding a gigantic white Angora cat in the crook of her arm.

"Does Gigi Orsini live here?"

"Why?" Gigi asked, looking up through the filigree of her bangs.

"Does she or doesn't she?" Sasha asked.

"Who wants to know?"

"Sasha Nevsky." It was true, Gigi realized with a sinking heart, seeing something in the intruder's face that looked familiar. Her impressively tilted nose was pert but haughty, her full upper lip seemed to curl upward in an expression of inborn superiority and her out-of-fashion noble brow was splendidly courageous.

"I'm Gigi," she admitted reluctantly.

"No way," Sasha said flatly.

"I am," Gigi insisted, outraged.

"Prove it. Tell me my mother's maiden name."

"Stalin. And you're just as impossible as she is."

"Maybe we'll get along," Sasha laughed, walking uninvited into the apartment, "if you like cats."

"Nobody mentioned one word about cats," Gigi sputtered. "A cat is no part of this arrangement."

"Like hell it's not. Those two unindicted co-conspirators, my mother and your stepmother, would have agreed on my being your roommate even if I'd brought a small zoo. You're lucky it's just my dear little cat."

"Ha! That thing's as big as a dog, and it's walking around like it owns this place."

"It does, cats own every place they go. And his name is Marcel. Where do you get your hair dyed?"

"I do it myself . . . peroxide on a comb."

"It's sensational. Do you do the collars and cuffs too?"

"Huh?"

"Pubic hair, so guys will think you're a natural tangerine-head."

"No . . . but I will . . . damn! I should have thought of that my-self, it's a dead giveaway."

"So you're not a virgin?"

"Of course not," Gigi said indignantly. "Are you?"

"My dear," said Sasha grandly, "you are trying, rather patheti-cally, to insult the Great Slut of Babylon."

"Wow! The ideal chaperone. Do you do it for a living?"

"Merely an avocation."

"What makes you think you're so great?"

"My reviews . . . all raves." Sasha sat down and gestured at Gigi to sit down too, with the air of a gracious hostess. "If Sasha Nevsky's reviews could be printed, I'd be world-famous. My God! Marcel likes you! He never does that!"

Gigi looked at the long-haired animal that had jumped into her aproned lap. His purring seemed more aggressive than friendly. She hoped she wasn't allergic to cats.

"How many men," Gigi asked curiously, "does it take to be a Great Slut?"

"Three. Always three, never less, never more. You have to know exactly where to draw the line or you're just an ordinary slut."

"Three at once?"

"Really, Gigi! Consecutively, and not on the same night. Each one gets two nights a week and on Sunday I sleep alone."

"That's an active sex life, but what exactly makes you a Great Slut instead of just a bimbo or a tramp?" Gigi asked, fascinated.

"Attitude, the key is all attitude. It's entirely a mental concept. I make all my own rules. I'm capricious, I'm arbitrary, and when I'm feeling unusually kind and at my best, I'm still erratic and wayward."

"Inconstant, fickle, temperamental—maybe verging on . . . cruel?" Gigi suggested.

"You've got it," Sasha said approvingly. "Gigi, *Men Must Suffer*. Those are the three key words. Remember them. Without them you're nothing but another girl, extremely cute, I admit, in fact I'd go so far as to say way beyond cute, into individual, into special, but still just a girl. If you were a Great Slut you couldn't lose. What's that wonderful smell?"

"Oh shit, I forgot!" Gigi jumped up and ran into the kitchen and rescued the cookies just in time. Sasha followed her curiously, and Marcel jumped up on the kitchen table and hovered meaningfully over the cookie pan.

"As soon as they cool a bit, we can eat them," Gigi said.

"I should have known. Marcel was sucking up to you because he could tell you'd been making cookies. I wonder . . . hmmm . . . did you make them from a mix?"

"A mix? Look, Sasha, you may know everything about being a Great Slut, but can't you recognize homemade cookies when you see them? I happen to be a superb cook, and I'm only telling you that because you don't exactly hide your own light under a bushel."

"Really great?"

"One of the best."

"A superb cook who masters the arts of the Great Slut would be the *Ultimate* Slut," Sasha said thoughtfully. "If you can teach me to cook, I'll teach you how to be a Slut . . . there are a million vital details you'd never be able to imagine on your own, but you'll have to get some decent clothes."

"I have decent clothes. I just wore this old stuff so I wouldn't intimidate you."

"Maybe I can't dance, Gigi, but you're talking to a Nevsky here, and the daughter of an Orloff. We don't intimidate."

"I noticed," Gigi said. "Somehow that came across."

"I like you," Sasha said. "And when I like someone, she stays liked. I'll never make you suffer."

"I like you too," Gigi said, throwing her arms around Sasha's waist and giving her a kiss on the shoulder.

"This could be fun," Sasha said.

"It's fun already," Gigi declared. "Do any of your victims have a friend for me? I lost a lot of time before I met you."

Perhaps, she thought, one day in the distant future she'd know Sasha well enough to confide in her about Quentin Browning and the mass of black-and-blue tissue she used to think of as her heart. After he'd decamped, Gigi found that some essential sense of faith in herself had vanished, some conviction about her own worth that she didn't know she'd possessed until she'd lost it. She became convinced that she'd asked for the kick in the teeth she'd received; she'd set herself up for it, given herself to a stranger, without using any of the armor a girl was supposed to protect herself with, without pretense or holding back or coyness or any of the arts of flirtation that were taught in the movies and even at Uni High. She'd literally flung herself at him that first night, she'd latched on to Quentin like a leech, and finally he'd been driven to show her how little she meant to him, how little he respected her. No, she wasn't a virgin, and she intended to learn as much about making men suffer as she could, but she couldn't imagine that she'd ever be able to trust a man again. She could be a Great Slut even without a sex life. It was, as Sasha said, all in the attitude. She'd learned her lesson early, perhaps too early, but it had been necessary for the future. Her motto still held true; she regretted nothing.

During Christmas of 1980, Billy returned to New York to spend the holidays with Gigi. She'd been invited to the Nevskys' for a fairly small family dinner of a mere two dozen people, and there she'd discovered how lucky she'd been in finding the demure, tongue-tied and unthreatening Sasha Nevsky as a roommate for Gigi. The girl could be an arresting beauty, Billy thought, but unfortunately she was unaware of her potential; she presented herself so mousily that you could easily miss her among the colorful cousins. Sasha held herself shyly apart, jumping and mumbling whenever Billy tried to draw her out in conversation, clinging to Gigi as her sponsor even within her own family, all of whom had embraced Gigi as an adopted Orloff-Nevsky. Better, far better a colorless and dependable roommate for Gigi than a hip New Yorker. As far as she was concerned, the later Gigi grew up, the better.

Billy had poked around Gigi's apartment, asking indirect questions to find out just what their boyfriend situation was, but both girls seemed stuck, not at all unhappily, in that age of innocence which lasts from that final visit to the pediatrician to the first visit to the gynecologist to get a supply of the Pill. Since Marcel had given Billy an attack of hives, she couldn't return for more in-depth investigation, but she was satisfied that Gigi was learning a great deal at Voyage to Bountiful, and Sasha's job, which apparently was something to do with bookkeeping in a Seventh Avenue lingerie house, obviously kept her gainfully occupied. And the two girls kept the apartment immaculately; it almost looked as if it had never been slept in.

* * *

Early in 1981, soon after the New Year, Billy returned to Paris, where she occupied a vast four-room suite, as luxuriously spacious as a house, on the second floor of the Ritz, the suite in which the Duke and Duchess of Windsor had lived for long enough to give it their name. Billy sat curled up on one of the rose damask sofas in her favorite of the two sitting rooms, thinking that at last she was ready to start house-hunting. The briskly burning, well-tended fires of the Ritz fireplaces were, for all their warmth, hotel fires; the flowers everywhere had the rich but stiff impersonality of hotel flowers; the atmosphere of the rooms, as cozy and perfumed as the interior of a giant muff, was nevertheless a hotel atmosphere. She had managed to impose some of her personal presence on the rooms: the writing table was covered with her pads and pens and books of phone numbers; her favorite photographs of Gigi and Dolly and Jessica in their heavy silver frames stood on the mantel and on the end tables; books, magazines and newspapers were piled everywhere; the firelight was reflected from a dozen personal surfaces, from her highly buffed fingernails to the deep, almost greenish luster of the long string of black pearls she'd just taken off and was playing with idly—but she wasn't truly at home here. Los Angeles was over, New York was over, Paris must provide her with a new home base.

Fortunately, Cora Middleton was in Paris too. She had arrived only yesterday, on some legal business connected with her husband's estate, and when she'd telephoned, Billy had invited her to tea. Cora had offered to help Billy find a real-estate agent.

"There are so many of them," Cora had said, "that it's all but impossible to tell the good ones from the bad, but luckily I know someone I trust entirely. Her name is Denise Martin, and if you'd like I can manage to put you in touch with her. The best way to work with real-estate people, whether you're buying or selling, is to use only one. If she knows you have three other competitors looking for places for you, she won't break her back for you the way she will when you're exclusive to her. Since you're a serious buyer, one agent will show you absolutely everything on the market, even if she has to split the commission with another agent. As far as she's concerned, fifty per-cent of a sure thing is better than working for a hundred percent of a commission that may not happen."

As always, Cora's advice had been excellent, Billy realized, in the weeks to come, as Denise Martin and she combed the Seventh Arrondissement together. This ancient, noble quarter of the Faubourg

Saint-Germain on the Left Bank was the only part of Paris in which Billy would consider living. Like Madame de Staël, who once said that she would willingly give up her beautiful country house and view of the mountains in Switzerland for "the gutter of the Rue du Bac," Billy felt that the Seventh offered the only chance to be a part of the secret, well-guarded charm of a Paris in which history was still alive. However, the rare private houses that became available there sold through personal relationships, almost never reaching the open market. People whose ancestors had lived in the Faubourg Saint-Germain long before the time of Louis XV had been known to languish for decades waiting for a small apartment in the Seventh.

Nevertheless, in less than two months Denise managed to hear a rumor that concerned an *hôtel particulier* whose owner had just died, a private house on the Rue Vaneau that none of the half dozen heirs could afford to buy from the others and keep up on their own. It was not palatial, a mere twenty rooms, but nevertheless the owners were asking the price of a palace: eight million dollars. Several days after she saw the house on the Rue Vaneau, Billy found herself in a musty office, surrounded by a pair of *notaires,* one acting for her and one for the owner, as well as a pair of real-estate agents who could only try, unsuccessfully, to conceal their eagerness.

The purchase of property was one of the areas in which Billy had, through the years, become a seasoned, tough businesswoman. Although she had never before consummated a deal without having the final legal papers vetted by Josh Hillman, she knew the steps of the process thoroughly and prided herself on always getting her money's worth. As she sat at a large table, with everyone's eyes on her, her pen in her hand, she hesitated.

She was about to sign the check for the *promise de vente,* a check for ten percent of the price of the house, a check for eight hundred thousand dollars, nonrefundable if she didn't go through with the purchase for any reason whatsoever, including her death. Billy was keenly aware that no matter how desirable the house was, no one had ever dreamed that she would pay the asking price, as she was about to bind herself to do. The price, like all property prices, had been set unrealistically high to allow room for bargaining. In addition, it was customary, in fact essential, for a buyer to have an inspection made by a qualified expert to find out if the structure was sound, before signing anything. No Frenchwoman, not the richest and most capricious in the country, would dream of buying, at its inflated asking price, a house she'd seen only days before, no, never, it was unheard of under any circumstances. The *notaires* and real-estate agents would have every reason to consider her the biggest sucker they'd ever come across. She would be letting herself be nailed, pronged, hustled, rustled and whatever was the French equivalent of screwed, blued and tattooed.

"If you don't sign today, someone else will certainly come along, and quickly too, on the Rue Vaneau," Denise said to her in a low voice, as Billy sat without moving. "The heirs' acceptance of the *promise de vente* means that they must, legally, sell to you, no matter what happens. And what if this afternoon someone else sees the house —there are so many rich people buying in Paris now, attempting to establish themselves—and offers them more than their asking price? Without the *promise de vente,* you could lose the house. It happens all the time when people hesitate."

Utter rot, Billy thought. She had never quite trusted Denise's judgment, and now she knew she'd been right. The trust Cora put in her was mistaken, that of a woman who was accustomed to buying small objects, not large properties. No *hôtel particulier,* even in the best of locations, would sell in an afternoon; the house would cost a fortune to maintain, it had been allowed to go to seed by its elderly owner, and there would be many months of hugely expensive renovation before she could start to decorate. She could safely negotiate for weeks.

Ah, but hundreds of years ago that particular house—not a mansion but a manor house—on the Rue Vaneau had been built for her, Billy thought. It had waited more than two centuries to capture her. A chord had been struck in her deepest fantasies from the minute someone had opened the high grilled gates set into walls over which ivy clambered densely and showed its glossy tips on the street side. Billy stepped into a large courtyard irregularly set with cobblestones and looked at a supremely pleasant house that immediately invited her to enter. She walked forward toward the welcoming double doors set above four semicircular steps, barely glancing at the two flanking wings of the house, one of which, guarded by a statue of a prancing horse, was obviously the stable wing. Even in her eagerness she had time to note the distinctive, finely cut gray stones of the unimposing two-story house, the peeling gray-white shutters, the shell-headed carvings over the French windows, the air of rustic calm that had fallen over her as soon as the gate to the street had been closed. In a dream she walked into a circular entrance hall with inlaid, sagging parquet floors and ideally discreet measurements that spoke to the sense of proper human dimensions lodged somewhere in her brain. The noise of Paris disappeared entirely as she wandered through the shabby, interconnecting rooms that all possessed such a happy wastefulness of space, such a multitude of windows and fireplaces, that she knew that once the house had been surrounded by country gardens, once it had been a very fine house—though never a coldly grand house—in which generations had lived and died in grace and dignity.

Billy had stepped into a glorious past, where the patient passage of time was confirmed by every room: cobwebs glinted in the corners like mathematical drawings in spun silver; tall, dim mirrors set into paneling showed her dreamlike reflections splotched with gold; floors creaked with intrigue and intimate recognition of her step; every window seat, spilling stuffing, invited her to kneel and observe the fanciful play of creepers on the windowpanes. If she looked outside she felt she would see brave, arrogant horsemen with feathers in their velvet caps and beautiful women in powdered wigs, whose vast skirts concealed a happy amorality, whose titles illuminated the pages of old books. She didn't care if every pipe in the house had to be replaced, if every piece of slate on the roof let in rain, if there were rats in the wine cellars and mice in the top floor and dry rot in the moldings.

She was in the mood to buy, and buy instantly, buy big and buy recklessly, a mood she'd believed she'd never feel again, with the listless, empty indifference of someone who has outgrown a vice. But now she felt herself being lured into the thrilling undertow of her old passion to own, to possess, to acquire; she was being filled by the old covetousness, the frenzied impatience to make something hers. Caution and common sense were equally absurd, for she was feeling desire again, desire, that life-giving force; desire, that need that can't be called up by any force of will; desire, by whose rules she had lived for so long; desire, the pleasure that had given her up after her divorce.

Billy signed the check slowly, forming each letter of her name with mounting pleasure, utterly indifferent to the exorbitant fees of the *notaires,* the twelve different taxes she deliberately hadn't asked about, the commissions on commissions that would curl Josh's hair when he saw the documents.

Christ, it was bliss to spend too much money again.

* * *

From the street, Billy's high gates presented an impenetrable façade that was as properly gray and austere as the other eighteenth-century houses in the neighborhood. Like the many old palaces in the neighborhood, the manor house on the Rue Vaneau was built *entre cour et jardin,* possessing the traditional *cour d'honneur* in front and a spacious garden at the back. Every one of its rear windows looked out on the parkland of the Hôtel Matignon, the official residence of the Prime Minister of France, which stood, guarded by police, several hundred feet away on the Rue de Varenne, at right angles to Billy's house. The Matignon's splendid park, for it was far too vast to be called a garden, stretched for many acres, and only a wall separated Billy's garden from the great trees and wide lawns of the Prime Minister. In the *Plan Turgot,* drawn in 1738, Billy's house didn't exist, nor did the Rue Vaneau. The entire area had been covered with trees, lawns and flower gardens as far as the eye could see. Now the Matignon's rural possessions had been reduced in size, and a number of the most desirable old houses in Paris lined the Rue Vaneau, an aristocratic street so quiet that the only transportation back and forth was by foot, bicycle or private car.

Once the renovation of the house was under way, but before she decided on a decorator, Billy had gone to Monsieur Moulie, the brilliant landscape designer who also owned Moulie-Savart, the most chic of Parisian flower shops in the Place du Palais Bourbon. She asked the droll, bouncy and agreeably flirtatious young Monsieur Moulie to redesign her conventional and overgrown garden into something rare and fine, knowing that full-grown trees would have to be carried straight through the house with their root balls intact, a project that had to be completed before the decoration was begun. Monsieur Moulie had given her a garden in which the trees and shrubs were chosen because they would stay green through the long, rarely freezing winters, until the vines and flowers he planted so cleverly began to bloom.

Billy continued to live at the Ritz, but she spent a large part of every weekday at the Rue Vaneau, supervising the work of renovation. She had learned that the progress of contractors the world over demands constant watchfulness to keep it on track. In the case of a French contractor, whose crews were allowed by their unions to work no more than thirty-nine hours a week, the work was further complicated by the early-Friday-afternoon disappearance of essential workmen, pleasure-bent, as well as the frequent long holiday weekends on which the entire construction crew expected, like the rest of France, to *faire le pont,* "make a bridge," an arrangement that gave them off the day before the holiday and the day after.

The house on the Rue Vaneau totally consumed her. She had become willingly fixated on every detail of making the old house structurally sound again. With far less personal involvement and emotion than she now expended on one old manor house, she had been able to ride herd on the construction of half a dozen new stores in half a dozen countries.

Every night she returned to the Ritz, peeled off her clothes and plunged into a hot bath in the deep white tub. As she looked tiredly around at the white marble bathroom with its sink and tub faucets in the shape of golden swans, and piles of peach-colored Porthault towels, Billy admitted to herself that if she had done the sensible, normal thing and started to work with a great Parisian decorator, a Henri Samuel or a François Catroux or a Jacques Grange, as soon as she'd bought the house, it would now be as much her decorator's concern as her own. He would have set someone in charge of all this basic construction, he would make weekly inspections, he would report to her only when it was necessary. She could be off skiing or lying on the beach of some private island or looking for a country place in England or buying racehorses or . . . but no, she might as well admit it, there was nothing else that she wanted to do except stay in Paris.

As Billy dressed for dinner she looked at herself in the mirror and laughed at her glowing face. She was as possessive as a doting mother of a new baby. She didn't want any decorator near her house yet, she didn't want to share it with a single soul, she didn't want advice, no matter how good, she didn't want help, no matter how necessary. It was *her* house, by God, and she'd spend her energy gladly to bring it back to life. Hanging about supervising the renovation of a neglected manor on the Left Bank was not why she'd told Jessica she had moved to Paris, not what she'd planned on before finding the house, but now she knew that even if she wanted to release her grip on the project, she wouldn't be able to make herself do so. She was hooked.

10

*Q*uickly a full life in Paris built itself around Billy, taking her out of the seductive cocoon of the Ritz, where every comfort could be attained by touching a button, and sending her off in many directions, accompanied by her driver, Robert, who expertly maneuvered the inconspicuous black Citroën that was appropriate to Paris, as if he had radar.

Invitations had started arriving almost before her suitcases had been unpacked. Her arrival had been unheralded by anything more than her reservation of the Windsor Suite, yet somehow it was mentioned in Maggie Nolan's well-read English-language society newsletter. Her purchase of one of the last of the beautiful houses of the Ancien Régime that had remained in private hands merited a small squib in the *International Herald Tribune*. Billy suspected that Denise Martin and probably someone at the reception desk at the Ritz were a key station on the underground circuit of Parisian gossip.

At first the bulk of her invitations came from the established business and social leaders of international society to whom Ellis had introduced her on former visits, and from the American Ambassador to Paris. Each party she went to brought more hospitable people into her life until the mantel of her fireplace was piled with "stiffies," as Billy had once heard an Englishwoman call engraved invitations. She was frequently engaged for lunch, during which no work took place at the house in any case, for the workmen all consumed a serious picnic, complete with much red wine, at an improvised table in her future kitchen.

The French version of the ladies' lunch serves the purpose of bringing eight or ten close friends together to engage in close inspection of all attractive newcomers. Keeping to her intention to go to all the right parties, Billy accepted invitations right and left, only stopping short at agreeing to spend weekends at various châteaux in the surrounding countryside. After a diet of two or three lunches and some four dinner parties or balls a week, Billy wanted her weekends to herself.

She had made dozens of the right new acquaintances. The descendants of the noblest names in France, although some of them had always remained unbendingly aloof to Cora Middleton de Lioncourt, melted into wholehearted welcome at the arrival of Billy Ikehorn. Her celebrity piqued their interest; well-known foreigners, long before Benjamin Franklin, have always been a hot ticket in Paris; her money fascinated them, for aristocratic Parisians are as materialistic a group as has ever existed. With her beauty and her perfect command of French, Billy instantly became French society's equivalent of the hottest new girl on the block.

One or two of the clever, glossy women she had met might possibly become more than mere acquaintances, Billy judged, although her social life was growing almost too quickly for real friendship to develop. In addition she was too deeply involved in her right and necessary folly of a house to have the time to cultivate intimacy. Now, Billy realized, the only things missing, to make her life the triumph she had prescribed for herself to Jessica, were more time to shop and the right man to fuck. Sex and shopping . . . where had she heard that catchy, promising phrase before? In a song? In a book?

Sex? Perhaps she had been too sanguine? The men she'd met in Paris were a disappointment. They were married and faithful, or married with a mistress, or married and casting about for a casual affair, or unmarried and looking for a fortune, or professional "extra" men. For a woman of thirty-seven the prospects of finding the right man were just as dim as they had been in Los Angeles and New York. Never mind, Billy thought, as she tore herself away, from time to time, from the tunnels of scaffolding and the forest of new pipes on the Rue Vaneau, to hurry to a fitting at Saint Laurent or Givenchy, never mind, there was always shopping floating in the air of Paris, and where there was shopping, sex would somehow follow.

On those weekends she guarded for herself, Billy indulged a new addiction that was linked directly to the future she so clearly saw herself leading in her house. A Saturday or Sunday didn't feel complete without a visit to the huge flea market, the Marché aux Puces at the Porte de Clignancourt, where she discovered the minor, personal, amusing things that no decorator could choose for her.

With experience, Billy learned how to dress to shop effectively in the Marchés Biron, Vernaison or Serpette, the areas of the Puces where such small treasures could be discovered. Over the plaster-spattered jeans she wore at the construction site, she wore a heavy gray sweater she had bought for its evident cheapness, and wrapped a battered beige raincoat over the result. She used no makeup and tied a plain scarf in a nondescript shade of maroon under her chin. She laced up her oldest tennis shoes and carried plastic shopping bags from the Monoprix chain store in which to bring home her booty. She tucked a tube of lip gloss and a wad of cash in a deep inside pocket of her raincoat, but she left her handbag at the Ritz.

She looked truly disgraceful, Billy thought, immoderately pleased with her all-but-unrecognizable reflection as she stalked through the Ritz lobby very early on weekend mornings. The three courtly concierges behind their desk, the gentle, hulking Yugoslavian guard who prevented the merely curious from wandering more than a few feet into the hotel, and the squad of doormen and package carriers who could always get a taxi when there were none to be had, were thoroughly accustomed to such garb when their more experienced clients headed to the Puces.

Such a disguise was necessary in order to bargain with any chance of success. Billy, who had so often surrendered herself to spending with an abandon so total that it felt omnipotent, now found that living in France gave her a new attitude toward a different kind of spending. She was fascinated by the Puces because it provided the opportunity to spend money with miserly caution, with tightfisted reluctance, small sums paid in small bills with a fine and exhilaratingly guilty feeling of parting with *real* money, money she managed to believe, just before the moment she gave it up, that she really couldn't afford—an authentic twinge of sweet sin that she hadn't known since her youth. When she wrote a check on funds she knew to be bottomless, the money simply wasn't real. The only way she could experience her money as actual and palpable was when she had to pay in cash, to peel off each bill and see it counted out after a long transaction that involved the game of bargaining.

She was not fool enough to flatter herself that any Puces dealer would let her get away with a genuine bargain, but at least she looked so far from rich that she could haggle until she had reached somewhere near the lowest price the dealer would happily accept, coming away feeling that both of them were satisfied with the transaction and that the business had been concluded as properly as if she were a Frenchwoman.

One clear, chilly April morning in 1981, Billy stumbled out of the long, shop-lined streets of the Marché Biron, worn down by many hours of all-but-fruitless search. The antiques dealers, heartened by the arrival of the first free-spending tourists of spring, had been unusually stubborn today, and she had reacted with the resistance of the native who feels she's being treated as a sucker in her own country. She had bought only one tiny, mysterious ivory bottle, and as she sat in a crowded sidewalk café drinking coffee and hungrily eating a croissant, she unwrapped the bottle from its layers of protective newspaper and placed it carefully on the table to give herself something, no matter how small, to gloat over. She loosened her raincoat belt and slumped back in the wicker chair, with her tired feet sticking straight out in front of her, and carefully surveyed the two-inch-high bottle. She didn't really crave it, Billy realized suddenly. The ivory was unquestionably old, but she had no idea what it was, nor did she care. But it would be a souvenir of the freedom she felt sitting here so anonymously, the freedom that came from being in a disguise that would attract no one's attention, of being part of a crowd in which no one knew her, of being a stranger in a strange land, yet one in which she felt at home. She hadn't felt so free in years, Billy mused, her eyes glazing over . . . . Feeling free was the same as feeling young.

"That's a damn good shape," said a man's voice from the table behind her.

"Are you talking to me?" Billy asked wearily, over her shoulder.

"Yeah. Would you mind if I took a better look at it?"

"Sure," she said. He was American, certainly a tourist. Billy turned, holding the bottle, and gave it to the tall man who was seated behind her, an empty coffee cup in front of him. He put on a pair of glasses and turned it over in his hands, running his fingers over and over its tapered cylindrical shape slowly and carefully. He twisted its tiny, rounded stopper experimentally, removed it and replaced it.

"It's a beaut. How did you find a Chinese apothecary bottle here? It must have held something fairly lethal, judging by the size of the stopper."

"Do you collect bottles?" Billy asked, thinking that since she'd spent over four hours at the greatest Parisian bazaar of antiques and managed to emerge with an ivory bottle that wasn't even French, she must either know something arcane or be very stupid.

"Collect?" His deep voice was humorous, speculative and leisurely. "Occasionally I accumulate junk, or rather it tends to accumulate around me, but that's not collecting. I'm a sculptor—it was the shape of this bottle that attracted me . . . . it's kind of wonderful."

"Please keep it," Billy heard herself saying.

"What!"

"Really . . . I'd like you to have it. You appreciate it more than I do."

He thrust the bottle back at her, shaking his head. "Hey, thanks, babe, but no thanks, you're a little nuts, did you know that? You look as wiped out as if you've just fought your way through the trenches of no-man's-land to find it, you can't possibly give it away." Now the humor in his voice turned to concern.

"I'm probably hungry," Billy said, suddenly self-conscious. She knew all too well what she must look like.

"I'm getting you a ham sandwich on a baguette. Or cheese. That's all they have here, babe, unless you want pastry."

"No thanks," Billy refused automatically. Pastry!

"Mind if I join you? At least let me buy you another coffee." He stood up, without waiting for her assent, and sat down next to her. She'd eaten that croissant so quickly that she must be ravenous, he thought. She was ridiculously generous too, for she was obviously a tourist, a working girl who'd probably saved for a long time to come to Paris in April, and old ivory like that couldn't have cost less than fifty bucks. Didn't she know she'd be better off spending her money on a decent sweater than buying a useless bottle and offering it to a stranger? The sculptor in him cried out against seeing such authentic beauty muffled by such clothes.

Billy drank the coffee he ordered, glancing at him sideways. She had never talked to a stranger in a café before, or allowed herself to be picked up, not even during the year she'd spent in Paris when she was twenty. She'd been too shy then, and later, when she'd visited Paris, she'd been with Ellis. Yet what were French cafés for?

This sculptor person, who called her "babe" so casually, was noticeably lean and decidedly angular, and probably in his late thirties. He had exceptionally thick red-brown hair, cut very short, so that his handsomely shaped skull was clearly outlined. Under his cheekbones his cheeks went in instead of out, so that there was a patrician gauntness to the shape of his face. His long, battered nose gave him a tough, capable profile. He'd taken off the large horn-rimmed glasses he'd put on to examine the bottle, and she could see now that his thick eyebrows overhung deep-set gray eyes that looked at her as if she were funny. Comic, for Christ's sake. His long mouth was quirky, with a good-natured twist, yet he looked like a man who could take care of himself in a fight. In fact he gave out so much physical strength just sitting there that he'd probably welcome a fight. On the other hand he had something of the unmistakably scholarly mien, the furrowed forehead of a professor crossing the Harvard Yard, she realized, remembering her Boston years, and the arrogant young section men who made a fetish out of sporting jackets in such bad shape they couldn't be given to Goodwill. This man wore his beat-up tweed jacket, work shirt and jeans in a way that told her they were his daily garb, not put on for a visit to the Puces, but he wore them with brio. He was clearly something of a roughneck, and just as clearly Ivy League.

"Sam Jamison," he said, introducing himself, offering his hand.

Billy murmured hello, shook his hand, and said, "Honey Winthrop." She had decided, while taking her inventory of his face, that she couldn't tell this man she was Billy Ikehorn. Any American would almost certainly recognize her name. She wouldn't use the name Billy Orsini either, for she had been famous under that name too recently for comfort. Honey had been her despised nickname as a child, but she couldn't think of anything else and she didn't want him to know anything about her except what he saw. She was deeply curious to find

out what it would be like to talk to a man who knew nothing about the
endless baggage train of wealth that followed behind her, heaped with
a load of invisible but acknowledged treasure, wherever she went in
her nighttime Paris.

"Where did you come from, generous Miss Winthrop?"

"Seattle," Billy said. "What about you?"

"Marin County, outside of San Francisco. How long are you here
for?"

"Oh . . . quite a while . . . it's my sabbatical year . . . I'm a
teacher." Good God, what had made her say that? She knew almost
nothing about anything. Why hadn't she said she was a sales clerk?

"What do you teach?" he asked, his nearsighted eyes intent on
her face.

"French?"

"Is that a question? Because if it is, I feel sorry for your pupils.
Listen, you didn't mind being called 'babe,' did you? When I get to
know you better, I'll call you Honey, but right now . . . it sounds
weird, like an . . . endearment, as if we really know each other."

"No, I mean, that's fine, babe's fine. I definitely teach French.
That's why I took my sabbatical year here, obviously. But let's not
talk about it . . . it's boring to everyone but me . . . studying the life
and times of Voltaire at the Bibliothèque Nationale . . . you don't
want to know. Are you living in Paris or just visiting?"

"I'm not sure, babe. I've always wanted to come here, and this
year I finally did something about it, found a studio to sublet in the
Marais, around the corner from the Place des Vosges, and came on
over. I don't ever want to go back. This place has gotten to me. I wish
I knew more French, though. Living here must be easy for you. I can
get around, but I don't have any ease."

"It's not hard to learn," Billy assured him earnestly. She pulled
her forgotten scarf off her head and was running her fingers artfully
through her flattened curls. Christ, she thought, I'd promise to give
this guy a crash course in French slang if he'd just shut the fuck up,
drag me to his studio by my hair and throw me in his bed.

"You don't look like a teacher," Sam Jamison said, and, to his
horror, found that he was blushing to his forehead, the redhead's curse
that he'd thought he'd outgrown. "That's a dumb thing to say, isn't
it?" he added hastily. "How should a teacher look, anyway? It's typical of the kind of remark men make that women hate." How could
anyone so beautiful waste her life teaching kids a language they'd

probably never use? Look at the way she wanted to give him her precious bottle, look at the hideous way she covered her body—why, she wasn't even comfortable accepting a sandwich from a stranger or talking about her work. She needed to be taught to be self-assured and even selfish, to demand whatever she wanted which would be no less than she deserved. A girl like this must want to be fucked, or there was no justice, no mercy, no use in being in Paris in the spring.

"Not necessarily," Billy murmured.

"What's not necessarily?" What had he said, he wondered. He'd lost track. She'd done something to her hair with her fingers that had taken his mind off his words.

"Women don't necessarily hate being told that they don't look like what they do. In my case, teach." She'd never seen a man blush before. Or if she had, she hadn't noticed. It would be heaven if she could get him to do it again. Absolute heaven. His skin was so creamy and fine-grained for such a tough-looking guy.

"What do women like to be told?" Did she not own a lipstick, or did she go around that way to tempt every man who saw her with the natural pink of her mouth? Could he ask her without blushing again?

"Ah, the old question. Even Freud didn't know . . . especially Freud." Why had she mentioned Freud? It sounded so academic, so musty, nobody even talked about Freud anymore. Jung maybe, but not that old creep Freud, who underestimated the clitoris just because he didn't have one.

"He said he didn't know what women wanted, babe," Sam corrected her.

"A quibble. Wanting, telling, what's the difference?"

"You've got me. Anyway, how about lunch? The restaurants are just opening."

"Well . . . these sneakers . . ."

"We could find a bistro. A very small bistro." Or a small hotel, for the love of God, with a very small room and a very big bed. "Or are you expected somewhere for lunch? Husband? Boyfriend?"

"Neither of the above. I'm happily divorced."

"Me too. Kids?"

"A little stepdaughter, who lives in New York. What about you?"

"Nobody . . . just me and my work and Paris and generous Miss Winthrop. Come on, have lunch with me," he pleaded, putting on his glasses and looking into her eyes with the intense scrutiny he had given the ivory bottle.

"I'm really not hungry right this minute, but I am curious about, well, actually . . . . as a matter of fact . . . . I'm curious . . . . about your work . . . I'd love to see it," Billy said faintly, helplessly, her questing eyes downcast under the power of his gaze.

"Oh. Sure. Absolutely. In fact. That's a great idea. It's in my studio . . . well . . . . obviously that's where it'd be." Shit! He could feel himself blushing again.

"Is it far?"

"No. Actually not . . . we can grab a cab . . ."

They sat silently side by side in the cab, walked silently up the five flights of stairs to Sam's studio, silently entered his large, light studio, silently ignored the large geometric shapes that stood everywhere, and silently walked straight into his small, darker bedroom, where they put their arms around each other and began to kiss, standing up, with a violence and a yearning and a need that surprised neither of them.

They kissed for a long time, trembling violently, still without words, until finally Billy shrugged out of her raincoat and kicked off her sneakers and pulled out of his arms so that he could take off his jacket. Suddenly they had no more time for undressing as they were overcome with the mounting necessity of a desire so vast that it was appalling. They fell to the bed, Billy still wearing her sweater, ripping open her jeans and pulling them off, Sam managing to shuck his jeans and his shoes. He entered her without a word, without hesitation, severely, and she accepted him with a lack of control that met his inevitability, a wildly indecent openness that wanted him to fill her and take her without tenderness. He cared nothing for her satisfaction, she nothing for his, and together they met in a place of pure lust where they took what they needed, giving and taking part of one single act in which they lost themselves completely. When they both came at the same time, it was such a surprise that when it was over they lay laughing helplessly, for that wasn't the way it was supposed to happen, not ever, not without at least a modicum of thoughtfulness, and then they managed to cast off the rest of their clothes and fell asleep in each other's arms, still without a word.

"Darling babe, if you're not hungry now, you're not human."

Billy opened her eyes, blinked in confusion and realized that she was in a warm bed with a wonderful-smelling, naked man she'd met only hours before. That's more like it, she thought lazily, good show, very very good show. Sam was rocking her gently awake, nibbling tenderly at her lips.

"I was hungry before, but I didn't want to wait . . . I couldn't . . . have lasted through lunch . . ." She yawned twice, groaning with the pleasure of it. "How could you keep going on and on about food?"

"I couldn't just say, 'let's fuck,' could I?"

"Why not? I couldn't, but you could."

"Why couldn't you say it?" he asked, finding her breasts under the sheets.

"Old American tradition, man has to ask first. Now it's my turn. Let's fuck."

Billy Ikehorn, widowed, divorced, rich, famous, always observed and judged, couldn't say "let's fuck" to anybody, but Honey Winthrop, schoolteacher on the loose in Paris, could say anything that came into her mind. Her students back in Seattle could hardly object. "Let's fuck," she repeated buoyantly.

"Oh, babe, let me see you first." He pulled back the sheets and blanket, looking in the deepest pleasure at her body, a superb female body that had reached perfection. Billy had always possessed a secret lushness of flesh that was hidden in clothes because of her height. Naked, the rich ripeness and swelling, supple mounds of her soft breasts and the voluptuous span of her white thighs were astonishingly evident. Her nipples were so deep in color that they looked as if she had rubbed them with rouge. She was a cornucopia of intoxicating volumes and curves. For long, reverent minutes Sam ran his fingers over the shapes of Billy's body, reveling in finding the soft places and the firm places, the succulent, throbbing bounty he had not had time to look at earlier.

"Oh, Sam, Sam, couldn't you do that later . . . . or are you measuring me to see if you want to sculpt me?" Billy was proud of her body and she felt no false modesty, but if he kept touching her like this much longer, she risked losing her mind.

"I . . . do . . . nonfigurative . . . stuff," he said, tracing the outline of her bellybutton in total absorption.

"Turn over on your stomach," Billy suggested, dry-mouthed, filled with madcap inspiration.

"Huh? What?"

"Fair's fair. I want to look at you the way you looked at me."

He followed her wish, and intoxicated, in a dream, Billy straddled him at his waist so that she could run both of her hands down through his hair and along his spinal column. She trailed her fingertips over the tenderness of his sides, drifting over the wonderfully smooth skin that ran down from his armpits to his waist, brushing him there with her burning touch until she could hear his breath come more and more roughly. Now she shifted her body, sitting across his lean, muscular thighs. She traced a light line of fire very slowly from his waistline to his coccyx and back. He moaned and shifted on the bed, lifting his ass quickly and spreading his legs slightly apart before he lay back again. Billy slid down so that she was sitting on his calves and looked her fill at the juncture of his legs. His penis was already so hard that it had risen up under his stomach, but the heavy globes of his testicles lay on the mattress between his legs. Lawlessly she bent forward and hovered over them, her mouth dry as she realized how completely he trusted her. Finally, with an open mouth, she began to puff little teasing breaths just above his testicles, warming them and watching the clenching of the muscles of his ass as he cried out in wordless desire.

"Now turn over," she whispered as she released him from the weight of her body. He obeyed, lying utterly exposed, his eyes closed, all of his taut, thin length revealed. Billy intended to touch him slowly and lingeringly on all his most sensitive parts, his furrowed forehead, his temples, under his jaw, inside his elbows, his nipples, all the places that men love to have caressed as much as women do, but when she saw how rampantly distended he was, she instantly abandoned that idea. She had to have his cock in her again, right now, and she moved lithely, flinging one of her legs back over his body and balancing on the bed on her knees while she held his robust penis, swollen savagely now, in both hands so that she could guide him inside her. His eyes were open and he watched her face until the tip of his penis just nuzzled at the lips he'd entered so brutally before, watched as she gradually pushed him into the warm, quivering place between her legs. He didn't stir as Billy gradually eased the pliant column of her body down until he was enfolded deep, deep into her flesh. She lay forward on his chest so that her head was pillowed in his neck. He allowed her to set her own pace, rising and falling above him for a few crucial inches, using his penis as her plaything, her possession. He held himself back brutally and gave himself utterly to her, delighting in the increasing rapidity of her movements, avidly watching the purposeful, building tension of her body as she drove herself closer and closer to the sought-after moment after which there was no turning back. At last she threw back her head in sightless ecstasy, her whole body shuddering uncontrollably, gasping in a fine heedlessness, until she collapsed back onto his chest, pulsating in the still spasmodic aftermath of her orgasm. Only then did he lift her in his powerful arms and turn her over so that she was lying on her back, only then, like a heathen worshiping a deity, did he smoothly reenter the pasture of her body and, with an exquisite concentration and sternly controlled fierceness, slowly allow himself to possess her again.

"Order something you can eat with one hand," Sam told Billy, "because I'm not going to let go of this one."

"Not even if I promise to let you have it back?"

"No. I don't trust you that much. You're a bossy babe."

"Is that why you picked a pizzeria?"

"Maybe. Or maybe because there are four of them on this street. I eat in this one almost every night."

"The French would call it your *cantine*." Billy was divinely disheveled, although she'd tried to do something about her hair with Sam's hairbrush. She had managed to brush her teeth with his toothbrush, and take half a bath in his tiny tub. She wore one of his sweaters, an ancient, yellow, V-necked Shetland that covered one shoulder and fell off the other. It was cinched in at the waist with an old blue tie she'd found in his closet, but nothing had erased the traces of lovemaking that left her cheeks patched with red where his whiskers had rubbed her and her lips swollen and her dark eyes huge and bright and heavy with gratification.

"I knew you'd get around to giving me a French lesson if I waited long enough," he said.

"Don't count on it, I have other things planned for you."

"Could you describe them?"

"Not here, Sam, not in a public place."

"Nobody's listening. Anyway, they're all French."

"Do you want to get hard again?" Billy's voice was soft and certain.

"It's not about want. I *need* to eat two or three pizzas . . . but after dinner, yeah, that's just exactly what I want."

"After dinner, Sam—if you think you can handle it."

"Are you sure this is a sabbatical year, or were you run out of town by the PTA?"

"You'll never know," she laughed. "I have my little secrets."

"Babe, let's go to your place first, wherever it is, and pick up anything you need to spend the night and tomorrow and tomorrow night and—"

"Oh . . . no . . . let's not. That would . . . oh, you know . . . take too long. There's a drugstore open at the corner. All I need is my own toothbrush and a comb. I have simple tastes."

"You look better in my clothes than in yours."

"I don't always dress the way I did today. You can't teach in jeans and sneakers."

"We can go to your hotel tomorrow, then, and get your clothes and stuff."

"Sam, wait a minute! I'm not planning to move in with you."

"Why not?"

"It's . . . well, it's just not a good idea. It's too soon to do anything like that, in the first place, and besides, I have to be independent. That's just the way I am."

"You mean I'm rushing you."

"Sort of. It just isn't—sensible."

"You're not a sensible girl, babe."

"True, I'm not, I never have been. It's one of my major fatal flaws . . . and if I move in, you'll find out all the other ones."

"Okay, I'm willing to find them out one day at a time. But the invitation's open. My house is your house, my clothes are your clothes, my bed is your bed."

"Sam, how could any woman let you get away? How come you got divorced?"

"We married too young, right out of college. I didn't have the brains to know that sculpture doesn't pay unless you happen to hit it just right . . . and by the time I had a dealer and started to sell enough to support us, she'd lost patience. I never blamed her. And you, Honey, darling—no, I simply can't deal with that name—babe, darling, why did you dump your husband?"

"I found out that he was a basic shit. A first-class basic shit, mind you. I guess you can't blame a man for his character—you have to blame yourself for your choice. But to hell with it, if I were still married I wouldn't be here, and that idea—the very possibility of missing this particular day of my life—it's . . . . *unthinkable* . . . entirely out of the question! Oh, Sam, what if I hadn't bought that bottle?'' Billy asked, suddenly appalled at how much had depended on her last-minute purchase.

''Come on, you know I'd have found a way to talk to you, once I saw you sitting there alone. The bottle was the perfect excuse.''

''Is it or isn't it a Chinese apothecary bottle, Sam?''

''Look at it this way, why shouldn't it be? If you really want to know, darling, we should ask an expert. I haven't got a clue.''

Billy returned to the Ritz early Monday morning, leaving Sam, who had been working in his studio since shortly after dawn, as was his habit. She found a large pile of phone messages and invitations waiting for her on the desk in her sitting room. She read through them impatiently, threw them back on the desk and settled down on a couch to think. All these pieces of paper represented an entire life that she could no longer lead and still be with Sam. He thought she was going to spend the day at the Bibliothèque Nationale, but she'd promised to return with a bathrobe and a few clothes at four o'clock when he always quit work.

She picked up the Michelin green guide to Paris that she kept handy for planning the museum excursions for which she still hadn't found time. On one of the first pages she pounced on the map she needed. Billy put a red X in each of three places, the Place des Vosges, the Place Vendôme, where the Ritz was located, and the Rue Vaneau. The X's formed a greatly elongated triangle with the Place des Vosges at its longest point, to the north of the Seine. It was the easternmost square of historic Paris, as far distant from the Ritz, on the Right Bank, as it was from the Rue Vaneau, on the Left. She drew a circle around the Marais, stopping short of the Pont Neuf, that popular stop on the tourist circuit of Paris. Many people she knew would be taking that inevitable stroll across the Pont Neuf as spring advanced, she thought, wishing desperately that nobody had ever decreed that a visit to Paris in the spring was an obligatory part of the good life.

Wouldn't you just know, Billy thought, that a new vogue for living in the dilapidated, formerly royal quarter of the Marais had just come into existence? The glory of the Marais as a residential quarter had reached its height during the seventeenth century, but during the reign of Louis XVI the nobility had started to move westward. After the French Revolution the Marais had been abandoned for almost two hundred years. Wasn't it just her luck that when she'd found a man who loved her for herself, he'd be living smack in the center of the newest chic place in Paris for finding an old apartment and renovating it?

Still, the interest in the Marais was just beginning, it wasn't as if Sam had a studio established opposite Dior, and he'd told her that after his long working days he found more than enough café and bistro life in the Marais to keep him there almost all of the time, particularly since getting from the Marais to anywhere else in Paris was difficult by bus or Métro and damn near impossible by taxi. This morning it had taken her taxi three-quarters of an hour to fight its way up the Rue de Rivoli to the Ritz.

Wilhelmina Hunnenwell Winthrop, *think,* she commanded herself. You lied yourself into this double life and now you've got to stick with it. If only she weren't so rampagingly giddy, so dizzily euphoric, so flushed with the kind of dangerous erotic excitement that brooked no consequences. She had to stop thinking about Sam, stop thinking about the firmness, already so dear, of his lips and the amused, slow sound of his voice and those impossibly fascinating hollows under his cheekbones, she had to stop, stop it this very second, stop and figure out what she was going to do.

The woman Sam had met two days ago was a woman no other man had seen with clear eyes since Ellis Ikehorn had stopped to take another look at her when she was a twenty-year-old secretary. Sam had met a woman who was no more, no less than a plain human being, the essential human being of seventeen years ago whom nobody alive now knew besides Jessica and Dolly . . . . and yes, to be fair, Spider Elliott, who'd never paid the slightest homage to the fact that she was Billy Ikehorn and could buy the Ritz itself if the Sultan of Brunei, the richest man in the world, who had just bought it for himself, wanted to sell.

Billy Ikehorn, the life she led and everything she represented, didn't exist for Sam Jamison. He probably wouldn't have anything to say to such a person and certainly wouldn't dream of getting involved with her.

Involved. That was what they were. Intimately involved. In love? In love with love? In love with that ever-young legend of Paris in April? She couldn't say exactly, she was afraid to be any more impulsive than she'd already been—it had been the most impulsive forty-eight hours of her impulsive life—but nothing in the world could stop her from being with him tonight and tomorrow and the day after, and that was enough for now. She felt total interest in Sam Jamison. It wasn't just sex. Since her divorce she'd had a few cautious flings, but sex hadn't survived her fear of being a mark, of being a target. Sex had never been enough to keep her with a man she suspected was an opportunist. And, Wilhelmina Winthrop, if you don't stop thinking about tonight with Sam, you're never going to get your plans made.

Billy jumped as there was a light tap on her door. Almost immediately, even before she could answer the knock, the door opened and a *gouvernante* entered, carrying a large vase full of the first pale peach tulips from Holland that the Ritz buys by the thousands each week. Each section of the hotel has its own *gouvernante,* a young, good-looking, smartly dressed, highly efficient woman who speaks at least six languages and whose function in life is to see that all the staff are performing their tasks impeccably and that all the clients are well taken care of in every detail.

"Oh, Mrs. Ikehorn, forgive me, I thought this room was empty. The maids said they'd just made it up and they'd noticed that some of your flowers weren't quite fresh."

"I just came in, Mademoiselle Hélène," Billy said. "Thank you. Please put them down on the table."

Mademoiselle Hélène's eyes flicked longingly over the roses on the mantel, and Billy knew that left to her own devices she'd check out the absolute freshness of every last one of the arrangements with which the Windsor suite was automatically filled. But her training was too good for her to be unaware that Billy wanted to be alone, and she left with a quick smile.

As soon as the room was empty, Billy jumped up and started pacing back and forth between the windows that looked out over the Place Vendôme. The Ritz, she thought, the bloody wonderful Ritz! It was like living at home with your parents and two hundred servants, all of whom want nothing more than to please you, a matter that merely requires that they know where you are at all times.

She'd been living here for eight months, since last September, leaving only for Christmas in New York, during which time her suite had, of course, been kept vacant. This morning the maids who made up the rooms must have noticed that her bed hadn't been slept in. They would have assumed she had been away for the weekend. If she spent nights with Sam, the *gouvernante* would probably not be notified that she wasn't sleeping at the Ritz for another week, possibly less. It might be a few days more before Mademoiselle Hélène would become uneasy. It was her profession to worry about the guests. Anything unusual would inevitably come to her notice, particularly since the rate on the four-room Windsor Suite was so high that few people left it unoccupied overnight. Mademoiselle Hélène would be far too tactful to dream of asking Madame Ikehorn why she was spending several thousand dollars a night on a hotel suite she didn't use, but no tact could keep her quick mind from drawing the right conclusion. Billy sighed as she realized that there was no way of preventing the news from spreading through the hotel.

The familiar room-service waiters who brought her breakfast every morning and the second set of waiters who brought her strong tea as she dressed for dinner at night would exchange notes. The men at the reception desk who were in charge of the safe deposit boxes would begin to wonder what had happened to her when she didn't emerge from the elevator almost every night, fully dressed except for her jewels, which she removed as she needed them, signing a receipt each time she opened her safe deposit box and each time she returned her treasures to the vault. Robert, her driver, who was outside the hotel this very minute waiting for her, would expect to drive her to the Rue Vaneau as usual, to wait for her there and drive her back to the Ritz to dress. Later he would be ready to drive her out to dinner and back again to the Ritz. At the concierge's desk, messages would continue to pile up; carbons of these messages, as well as all letters and invitations would be routinely sent upstairs and slid under the door. The three concierges of the day shift and the three of the night shift, all six of whom she saw every day, would soon put their heads together. Within a week everyone from the top management of the Ritz down to the sous-sous-chef in the kitchen, who scrambled her eggs every morning just the way she liked them, would know that she was spending her nights on the tiles.

No one would say a word. No one would even *look* a word. As long as her bills were paid, the Ritz provided her complete freedom to come and go as she pleased, dressed as she pleased. There was nothing in the area of acceptance and physical comfort that money couldn't buy immediately at the Ritz, except for two things, Billy thought. They'd need a few hours' advance notice to manage a typically American Thanksgiving dinner, since turkey, cranberry sauce and sweet potatoes were rarely eaten in France. And at no price in the world could she buy privacy.

What *was* she going to do, she asked herself, inhaling the fresh tulips and discovering that, as usual, they had no scent at all. Of course she could disappear from the world of the Ritz and move to another luxury hotel, without any explanation. However, the concierges of all the top hotels in Paris knew one another by their first names, they all belonged to the same professional organization of the *Clefs d'Or*, and it would only be a short while before the staffs of not one but two great hotels were aware of her doings.

How could she even transport her luggage, her dozens of suitcases, without everyone knowing? What's more, she'd have to notify Gigi, Jessica, Josh Hillman, her contractor and at least a few of her new friends, or, unable to get in touch with her, they'd think that she had disappeared from the face of the world. Eventually Josh would bombard the hotel with inquiries, and if he was not satisfied he'd be on the next plane. Another hotel merely added complications. *Unless.* Unless it was the kind of hotel where no one would pay attention to her, where no one would notice her, where her name on her passport, which was demanded on registration by all French hotels, would be meaningless. Either a very large commercial hotel or a small, unknown hotel on a little street.

Billy considered the possibilities. Sam would have to know where she lived eventually; she couldn't flit away, as she had this morning, to some hotel whose name she had managed to forget to tell him. A teacher on a sabbatical year would be unlikely to live in a large commercial chain hotel, a Hilton or a Sofitel. It would be too expensive, even if she had a tiny room, and most of the large hotels were located in the center of Paris. That added to the chance of meeting someone she knew, someone who might wonder what she was doing out of context. If, God forbid, she ran into Susan Arvey at the Ritz, it would be entirely natural. But if she ran into Susan Arvey coming out of a Sofitel! It would take half an hour of lying to make it seem unimportant.

Why did people want to be rich and famous? It sounded so desirable until you needed to disappear and just love and be loved without your lover knowing who you were in real life.

A small hotel, then. She'd take a room in the kind of small hotel that was too understaffed to care who came or went, the kind of hotel in which Sam would expect her to be living. She'd keep her suite at the Ritz in order to receive messages and to maintain the façade of the life she'd constructed in Paris. Sam could be told that she lived in the small hotel, and the Ritz, where she'd actually sleep for two nights a week, would remain her base.

She truly didn't care that the staff and management of the Ritz would know that she kept the Windsor Suite and rarely slept in it. On those nights she'd maintain her Paris social life, greatly reduced in scope. People would say she was a snob or perhaps merely exclusive. Whatever they said, it didn't matter, for her world was newly made and they had no importance to her. As far as the Ritz personnel were concerned, she was sure that they had all seen far stranger and more suspicious behavior on the part of their clients, and that once the fact that she spent many nights away had been thoroughly discussed, it would be forgotten as just another sexual caprice.

The small hotel would be a kind of dressing room, a way station between identities. She'd keep her teacher clothes and cosmetics there, and if Sam ever wanted to see her place, he could do so without surprise or suspicion. She'd keep books and magazines there, trinkets, underwear and shoes . . . all appropriate, all things she could buy in a few hours.

Blowing out a breath of relief, Billy got undressed so that she could take a long, hot bath. She watched the tub fill, wrapped in a peignoir, too relaxed by her solution of her problem to do anything but watch the water spill out of the golden swans, when suddenly, after two days of utter forgetfulness, she remembered the house on the Rue Vaneau.

Shit, no! She'd missed an appointment with the contractor to see the man who had drawn up a final floor plan for the new kitchen; the expert in charge of restoring the molding throughout the house was expected in an hour; the dreaded inspectors from the city electrical department were coming today to check the new wiring—and that was only the beginning of the things that she had undertaken to supervise.

Billy turned off the taps abruptly and ran to a phone barefoot. She'd been avoiding the intrusion of a decorator, but one name had remained in her head, Jean-François Delacroix, a young man who had started out on his own several years ago after intensive training at the side of Henri Samuel, the dean of Parisian decorators. Several women whose taste she respected had waxed enthusiastic about his original-ity. Within minutes, with the aid of her favorite concierge, she had him on the line.

"Monsieur Delacroix, this is Billy Ikehorn. I'm—oh, good, you know who I am, that simplifies things. Now tell me, are you prepared to take over the remaining renovation and all the interior decoration of a good-sized house on the Rue Vaneau, a house of twenty rooms? Can you start right now? Today?"

"But, Madame . . . Madame Ikehorn, surely it is first essential that we meet, that we go over the house and find out if we have a rapport, if we see things in the same light?"

"Not at all," Billy said brusquely. "I've heard excellent things about you. The question is, can you begin *immediately*? If you're occupied with another project, just tell me."

"Madame, I will make the time, but there are so many questions only the client can answer—the parameters of the budget, the questions of contemporary or period, country or urban, minimalist or classical, elegant or informal, understatement or bold, space for art, the role of fantasy—I could go on for hours—"

"Please, Monsieur, do not. I don't want formal French furniture, gilt, minimalist, or anything aggressively modern. As for the budget, use your own judgment. Spend whatever is necessary. I will have my bankers at the Chase open an account for you. Other than that, Monsieur Delacroix, *surprise me!*"

"But, Madame—"

"Yes?"

"We will—meet—one day?"

"Of course. Soon, unquestionably soon, but . . . I can never say in advance. The essential thing is that you take charge at once, today, just as soon as you can get there. I'll call my contractor and he'll be expecting you. I must warn you, the electrical inspectors are coming this afternoon."

"Such functionaries hold no terror for me, Madame."

"Then you're the man I want. Good-bye, Monsieur."

"*A bientôt, Madame,*" Jean-François Delacroix said hopefully, as Billy hung up.

The man probably thinks I'm eccentric, she said to herself, as she turned on the taps again. Which of her skirts and pants could seem suitable for a teacher? Which of her blouses and sweaters were believable? Was her underwear too elegant, or could she say it had been a going-away gift from the other teachers? Her shoes? Could she have inherited a little money to explain her indispensable cosmetic case? Or should she buy plastic bottles and jars, throw them all in a soft carryall and explain her watch, a few pairs of simple earrings and a pearl necklace by inventing a legacy from Aunt Cornelia? Aunt Cornelia would understand. Have understood . . . . *Robert*!

Billy gasped as she contemplated the weak link in the chain. Robert, her driver, who spent the time when he wasn't at the wheel gossiping with the other drivers and the doormen in front of the Ritz. She had to get around town somehow, from the little hotel she had yet to choose, down to the Marais, back to the Ritz, and eventually to the Rue Vaneau, for she couldn't let Monsieur Delacroix begin to wonder out loud about his lunatic client.

Good God, had any woman ever had to extricate herself from so many complications? How did other people manage secret affairs? It would be so much easier if she could be herself, instead of Honey Winthrop. For a minute Billy let herself try to imagine telling Sam the truth, but the picture she attempted to create in her head wouldn't form, the words wouldn't come.

She'd tell him eventually, she couldn't keep this up forever, but not now, not until they knew each other so well that the truth simply wouldn't matter. Or perhaps this love, if it was love, wasn't destined to last and the question of telling him would become moot. In any case she couldn't do it now, which meant that Robert had to go. If she kept her driver, he would be the only person in the world besides herself who knew what she was doing, where and with whom. He'd be quick to put it all together, and who could believe that he wouldn't tell his fellow drivers?

Poor Robert . . . she'd give him a bonus heavy with guilt when she told him she no longer needed his services. And she'd find a new chauffeur from an agency, with a rented car, who would pick her up at various spots she designated, get his instructions about when to pick her up, and watch her vanish around the corner. If she aroused his curiosity, if he ever attempted to follow her, she'd know at once and change drivers that same day. He would be paid in cash, he'd never know her name. She sighed in relief, her problems solved.

Billy found herself standing in the bathroom looking at the half-filled tub, not at all sure whether she'd taken a bath or not. Either way, it didn't matter. She was dizzy with renewed need, hungry with the heavy sexual buzz of excruciating desire, a quivering, newly engorged appetite that only Sam Jamison could slake, that only his authoritative hand and mouth could begin to satisfy, that only his body within her could quiet.

At the top of the page there is faded, illegible text (offset/show-through from another page).

II

Chopped liver. Dolly Moon stood in front of the closed refrigerator door in her kitchen and thought deeply and emotionally about chopped liver. She would never consider dipping into the large covered bowl of chopped liver that sat on the second shelf of the fridge, since it was intended for tonight, when she and Lester were giving the traditional Yom Kippur dinner that broke the fast of the Jewish Day of Atonement. Lester and his parents were all at their synagogue, praying, listening to the rabbi, and, as they had been since sundown the night before, fasting, so how could she even be thinking about chopped liver, Dolly asked herself. How could anybody be depraved enough to stand here and obsess over the thought of a very small taste of the chopped liver she had made this morning?

Using a recipe from *The Celebrity Kosher Cookbook*, her favorite, she had pan-fried three pounds of livers in chicken fat ever so carefully, so that they didn't get tough, pan-fried nine finely chopped onions in more chicken fat, until they reached a point of brownness that was just this side of being burnt. She had chopped the livers and onions with a dozen hard-boiled eggs and much, much more chicken fat, with a double-bladed chopper in a big wooden bowl, until the well-moistened mixture had reached the precise degree of texture that was neither too finely nor too coarsely chopped.

Little tears came into the corners of Dolly's huge blue eyes and dimmed their natural look of perpetually astonished happiness when she thought how incredibly good she'd been. She hadn't even *tasted* the chopped liver to see if it needed more salt. She'd delegated that task to her cook, because she knew what would happen if she got started on the huge mound. Half of it would disappear in minutes, Dolly thought pathetically. *Minutes*.

She was wearing a peignoir of lavender satin and old lace, her blond hair was up in rollers, and she had no makeup on her sad but still rosy face. Her world-famous too-big mouth turned down at the corners; even her too-big breasts and her too-big bottom, without which she would not be the same Dolly Moon, the world's best-loved comic actress, seemed to express melancholy. Behind her the huge kitchen bustled with staff paying no attention to her silent vigil, for tonight's dinner was a joyous occasion and there were briskets to make and roast chickens to stuff, dozens of side dishes to prepare and elaborate pies and cakes to bake. Dolly and Lester had invited a large group of friends to celebrate the breaking of the fast with them, as well as all of Lester's family.

For ten days, Dolly told herself as she visualized the beautiful bowl of beautiful chopped liver, with chopped parsley sprinkled on top, for ten whole days, ever since the beginning of Rosh Hashanah, the Jewish New Year, her in-laws, who were observant of the religious laws, had been taking stock of the ethical quality of their personal lives, seeking atonement for their sins and forgiving those who had wronged them.

She hoped her mother-in-law hadn't included her in that last category. How could she, when Dolly had produced a set of twins last year, legitimate Weinstocks, both boys, Lester junior and Henry. She knew that at the time of her marriage the elder Weinstocks had accepted her and her newborn Wendy Wilhelmina, Billy's godchild, with some natural reservations. Dolly was not the daughter-in-law of their dreams. She didn't come close. Not the same ballpark. No matter that she had just won an Oscar, they had been far from joyful when they attended their only son's wedding to a bride who was still nursing a baby whose father was a rodeo rider she had never bothered to marry.

Yet now, in September of 1981, three-year-old Wendy was their adored darling, and little Lester and Henry were their princes. And they loved Dolly, she was sure, and they were proud of her. Her last movie, in which she'd starred with Dustin Hoffman, had earned the largest grosses of any comedy of the year, and her in-laws had personally accounted for at least twelve of the tickets sold, for they had seen it six times, going to the movie house in Westwood and standing in line just like civilians, because they wanted to watch it with an audience and hear the laughs with their own ears. No, they really loved her, and anyway, the state of her in-laws' affections was not the reason she was standing here in front of the fridge, fighting her compulsion to open the door and sample, just on the tip of a fork, the tiniest bit of that chopped liver.

There was every chance that the cook hadn't salted it properly. No one would criticize it to her face, but after they came home from temple, joyous, mentally cleansed of their sins, physically ravenous, and swallowed the customary glass of orange or tomato juice to replace their electrolytes, drained by twenty-four hours of fasting, and then attacked the chopped liver, wouldn't they be horribly disappointed if it was undersalted?

"Dolly, you're going to be late." The interrupting, self-assured voice came from a young woman who had just walked boldly into the kitchen.

"Please leave me alone for just a few more minutes," Dolly begged her personal publicist, Janie Davis, a skinny brunette who could devour a double order of barbecued ribs and burn them up in half an hour on the phone. But that wasn't amazing, she thought broodingly, all female PR people were aggressively thin, it must be part of the job description.

"But, Dolly, the kids are waking up. You know the twins have only one good hour a day."

"They have twenty-four good hours," Dolly sniffed.

"You know what I mean," Janie insisted, implacable. "One *good* hour—one!"

Dolly considered the facts. Outside on the lawn was a photographer from *Good Housekeeping,* who, with two assistants, was waiting to take the cover photograph for the March 1982 issue, a picture of Dolly and her three children. He had already taken the shots of Dolly herself that would accompany the cover story on Dolly Moon's life, which so brilliantly combined marriage, career and motherhood. Three publicity people from the Arvey Studio, where Dolly was shooting her new film with Robert de Niro, were standing around talking to the photographers and hoping to be helpful. Upstairs, in her dressing room, a makeup man and a hairdresser were waiting to get their hands on her. Hanging on a special hanger in her closet was the dress Nolan Miller had made for her, a delicious dress that would be perfect for the world's sexiest milkmaid, a dress Nolan had delivered in person just an hour ago, after it had required a last-minute adjustment to let it out at the waist.

"Maybe you should stop eating between meals, Dolly," he'd said to her warningly, and she'd looked way, way up into his handsome, kind face and promised, yes promised, to stop eating. Yes, Nolan, yes, you sweet man who told me I was almost as pretty as Jaclyn Smith, I promised you to stop eating between meals, and if I don't, the next time I go to your place to be fitted, you'll know if I did or didn't.

But Nolan wasn't frightening enough, that was the problem. He'd manage to make her look wonderful even if she did taste a tad of the chopped liver right this minute. And he'd been adorable to her, although there was no disputing that she'd gained a half-inch at her waistline, that little waist that, along with her nose, were the only small things about her. God should have arranged it so that when you gained weight the first place to show it would be the tip of your nose, Dolly thought wistfully. A ballooning nose would provide a real incentive to stick to water-packed tuna and fake cheese made of tofu.

She lacked incentive, Dolly admitted morosely. Lester loved to eat, they'd met over her strudel and courted over Chinese food, and slept together the first time when she'd been at least eight months pregnant, so how could he not like her round?

Just thinking about Lester made her feel better. Not less interested in the chopped liver, but more cheerful. He'd given up his publicity job after their wedding and gone to work briefly for his father. However, he'd soon become fascinated by the financial possibilities of tracking down and buying up as many of the great old black-and-white television series as possible. With the aid of a bank loan he'd gone into business for himself, and as she understood it, his future prospects were excellent.

They had far more money than they needed anyway. Dolly couldn't believe how much her agent had managed to get her—on her firm instructions—when she'd recently signed a three-picture contract with the Arvey Studio. It was ridiculous, all that money being paid to her, money that was, in her own unvoiced opinion, basically based on her giggle, no matter how the critics raved on about her acting, but there it was, and here she was, aching, quivering, intent, with the madness of an addict, on obtaining a quick fix of chopped chicken liver. On a Ritz cracker.

Incentive? If Billy were around she'd call her up and get a quick, good old-fashioned lecture on the exact number of very seriously bad calories in one ounce of chopped liver that would set her straight, but Billy hadn't been back in the United States for a year. She wrote from time to time, and phoned on the odd occasion, but somehow she seemed to have . . . floated away . . . for the last six months or so. There had been a slackening off in their communication, nothing to get alarmed about, since Billy seemed to be so delighted with her Parisian life, in fact she seemed downright overjoyed every time she and Dolly talked. There must be something very wonderful about Paris, Dolly decided, for Billy had sounded quite unlike herself. She had sounded *relaxed*, and if there was one thing she knew about Billy Ikehorn, it was that she didn't relax, not ever. She couldn't, it was genetically impossible. Something to do with Boston, perhaps, or having been fat until she was twenty. Oh, Billy, where are you when I need you?

"Dolly, the twins are being dressed. Dolly, come upstairs and get made up and combed out. The photographer is ready, everything is ready, and from three to four Nanny says we can count on the twins to be angels. *Dolly*," Janie Davis demanded, ready to call for help if necessary, "it's two-fifteen now."

"Hold my hand, Janie," Dolly said, closing her eyes tightly on the door to the fridge, behind which stood the ultimate object of her amorous fantasies. "Hold my hand and lead me out of the kitchen. Pull as hard as you have to. I'll be okay as soon as I get upstairs."

Spider Elliott looked up from the letter he was having so much difficulty writing and ordered another bottle of SeyBrew, the local beer he'd discovered in a comfortable café in Victoria, on the island of Mahe, the crossroads of the Seychelles. The islands were scattered throughout an archipelago in the Indian Ocean some thousand nautical miles off the east coast of Africa, and the day before, Spider and his two-man crew had anchored off Victoria with the intention of spending a few nights ashore while they restocked the ship with the excellent local produce.

Although Victoria was a few degrees south of the equator, it was a good place from which to send mail with a certainty that it would be delivered, for the town was an international tourist destination. Mahe was as far away as you could travel, going around the globe from the United States, before you found yourself started on a return route, a dream of still-unspoiled beauty with famous bird sanctuaries and some of the best snorkeling and scuba diving in the world. English, French and other European languages were being spoken by the many visitors sitting at the tables around him.

When he'd dated his letter October 1981, Spider realized that he'd been gone almost a year and a half. He'd trained himself not to keep track of time, although days, weeks, even months had mercifully started to melt for him a long time ago. He had put so much space behind him that he had finally reached that place at which the past was indeed another country, the future was unimportant, only today existed, and even today merely unfolded, minute by minute.

He had still not communicated with anyone, this was the first letter he had written since he'd sailed from Los Angeles. Last night he'd ventured into the casino at the Beau Vallon Bay Hotel, inspired by a minor curiosity about how it would feel to find himself among a crowd again. He'd bought some rupees, played a little roulette, lost the rupees, and discovered that he felt irritated, jumpy and itchily uncomfortable amid so many people. He'd been about to leave when he'd come across a group of people off the cruise ship that was anchored in the harbor. A woman he vaguely remembered had come up to him, greeted him with amazement, and told him her name. Spider had realized that she was a minor Scruples customer, someone who shopped there for Christmas presents. It was from her that he'd first learned that every one of the Scruples, from Munich to Hong Kong, existed no longer.

Spider hadn't been able to sleep that night as he pondered the meaning of this news. He'd finally decided that he wouldn't try to find out any more about it, just let it be, when an idea came into his mind that wouldn't leave, no matter how hard he tried to persuade himself that it wasn't possible. Eventually he'd promised himself to write to Billy so that he could put the idea out of his mind and go on with his life, almost—but not yet entirely—peacefully drugged into painlessness by the sea, the sky and the sun.

Dear Billy,

I'm sending this letter to Josh Hillman since I have no idea where you are, but know he will have it delivered to you. You won't have any idea where I am, although on a nautical map it's all very precise, but I'm told that it's as close to the classic idea of an island paradise as there is left, and so-called paradises are one thing I've become an expert on in the last year. Believe me, most of them are overrated.

In any case, yesterday I was on shore for the first time in many weeks and I bumped into someone who told me that every last one of the Scruples had been closed, not just those in New York and Chicago. It was the first time since I left that I'd met anyone from Beverly Hills . . . I've successfully stayed away from people. When I left I'd heard nothing about this, and naturally I've assumed that you were still busy opening one foreign store after another.

I spent hours trying to figure out why the hell you would have closed down all *the stores, particularly when they were clearly going to do so well, and only one weird idea finally began to make any kind of sense to me. This is probably way off base, I'm probably imagining the whole thing, but just in case it isn't, I felt I had to write and tell you that if you thought that you were in any way responsible for the fire at Scruples, you* must not *believe that for a minute.*

We didn't discuss how the fire happened, in fact we didn't discuss anything at all, but I could have, and probably should have, told you that I believe now that Valentine must have caused it accidentally.

From the time I first met her in New York she had the habit of occasionally smoking French cigarettes when she had finished some hard work and was feeling a little tired or homesick.

Sometimes, when she had trouble sleeping, she used to go to her design studio and work, even when I was at home. It was a habit she'd picked up and I couldn't get her to quit. She said that it was better than wandering around the apartment trying to get back to sleep. What I

*believe must have happened was that she went to Scruples
to work that night, finished work, lit a cigarette, and fell
asleep with it still burning. There's just no other way to
account for the fire.*

*The fact that she had an extra work load because of the
costumes for* Legend *is not something you should think
about. You ought to know that if there hadn't been that
job to do, she would have found something else, since
there was always plenty of work waiting for her, and she
enjoyed getting into it in the middle of the night when she
wouldn't be disturbed.*

*Billy, I know how much Scruples meant to you, maybe
better than anybody in the world. I hope this letter is crazy
and that the idea I had last night is equally crazy. I hope
you just got tired of running so many stores and went on to
something else . . . but somehow that doesn't sound like
you. Anyway, if I am crazy, just disregard this as the
result of too much sun. If not, for the love of God, you
must realize that nothing you did or didn't do could have
caused that fire.*

*I find it hard to believe that Beverly Hills exists. I've
spent most of my time at sea and I've found out that no
matter how big the ocean, you have to keep alert or it will
get you. My crew and I are really in the survival business,
and it keeps us hopping. Maybe I'll weigh anchor
somewhere or other and open a sort of Club Med for kids
safely under the age of puberty.*

*Wherever this letter finds you, I hope you're well and
happy and thriving. I'm very well and as close to happy as
I expect to get for a while . . . but at least I'm not the
same guy who left L.A., and that's a damn good thing.
Give my love to Gigi and Dolly and my regards to Josh
when you see them. I'll be back someday but I just don't
know when. I'm sending a hug for you, Billy, wherever you
are—it would have been great if it had been you I bumped
into last night.*

Spider

"Could you bring me another drink, please?" Spider asked the
waiter as he put the letter in an envelope with a feeling of release. He

looked at the envelope with disbelief that he'd been able to force himself to write it, to actually put on paper thoughts he had fled from in the course of sailing thousands of miles. "This time make it something stronger than beer."

"If I ever get married," Gigi said solemnly to Sasha, as she entered the apartment carrying an oblong cardboard box tied together with string, "I swear by everything that's holy, I'll elope! Nothing, nothing on earth could induce me to be the bride in a real wedding."

"Now what?" Sasha asked mildly, putting another coat of polish on her toenails. It was their sacred never-on-Monday night, and she and Gigi, as usual, were going to be spending it at home together, peacefully organizing themselves for the arduous, man-filled week that lay ahead while Gigi gave Sasha a cooking lesson. It was an autumn evening in late October of 1981, and as Sasha had strolled homeward from the bus stop there was something in the very air that seemed changed since yesterday. Yesterday had still retained a memory of late Indian summer, today had the tempo and flavor of pre-Thanksgiving.

"Emily Gatherum and I had a first planning session this afternoon for a major wedding. I wish you'd been there. The mother of the bride was the kind of uptight perfectionist who has envisioned every splendid princessy detail of her daughter's wedding from the time the poor kid was two. Add one tycoon father, a notorious control freak who doesn't mind paying top dollar for a formal wedding for three hundred people as long he's sure that every penny of it is visible. Ma and Pa haven't spoken since they got divorced three years ago." Gigi peeled off the severely tailored jacket of one of the suits her boss, Emily Gatherum, had decreed that she always wear to work at Voyage to Bountiful, unzipped the straight skirt, unbuttoned her plain white silk blouse and kicked her plain black patent leather pumps toward the ceiling.

"If that wasn't enough," she continued, "immediately after the divorce, Pa married his young executive assistant. She was the only character in this drama who didn't show up today, for obvious reasons. However, we did have the groom's mother, a deeply suspicious, haughty grande dame from the last family in America in which there's never, ever been a divorce, a woman who sat there with her nostrils quivering in well-bred distaste, letting everybody know she thinks her only son is far too good to marry this poor girl. Naturally the future bride was an emotional wreck. I felt so sorry for her, torn between her horrid parents and trying to placate her future mother-in-law at the same time. Imagine having to deal with all the tensions of those three natural enemies! The last item on the agenda today was the bride's own ideas about what she wanted her wedding to be like, although they should have been the first consideration.''

"You worry too much," Sasha said, unperturbed by Gigi's familiar career anxieties. "When you started at Voyage to Bountiful, the only thing la Emily allowed you to do was answer the phone, extract the basic facts from new clients, and then pass on the call to her or one of her assistants—and I'll never forget how you complained that you weren't learning anything. Then, little by little—like in a week— Miz Gatherum realized what a perfect treasure you were, she taught you how the kitchen was run, you got cozy with all the sous-chefs, she trained you to write menus, you learned the details of contracts and commissions and how there's a built-in profit the client doesn't know about on every last sprig of parsley she buys, every tiny teaspoon she rents. Now you've been in charge of small parties from beginning to end, you're sitting in on those all-important first planning sessions, but here you are, still grousing away. Why can't you take a more positive view? I think that it's just a matter of time before Emily Gatherum lets you run a planning session yourself.''

"God forbid," Gigi said fervently. "It's only the planning sessions that still get me nervous . . . . all that wishful, yearning, unspoken romance people bring to them . . . they have such lovely pictures in their minds and no idea of the logistics. They think that as soon as they've taken a deep breath and decided to hire Voyage to do the party, their troubles are all over because they've put themselves into experienced hands. They think we can take all the pain out of entertaining. And the fact is that they bring on all the complications themselves because they won't—they can't—just leave it to us. It's unbearable, literally *unbearable* to them not to get involved in every last detail short of cooking the food and putting it on the plates.''

Gigi gathered up her clothes and took them into her bedroom. She emerged, brushed her hair vigorously, liberating her swaying cap of marigold hair from the neat bell she sprayed it into every morning. Her light green eyes flashed with light and humor under her long lashes on which even Emily Gatherum had never been able to make her stop using three coats of mascara. It had been more than a year during which Gigi had been rapidly learning the catering business, yet she seemed five years older than the girl who had arrived in New York to take possession of her new apartment and meet her new roommate.

She had made that inevitable leap into full adulthood, crossed that invisible and irreversible line that divides young women from real women. The impish quality that had made her seem almost childish well into her teens had disappeared, replaced by a piquant maturity, a lissome, nimble maturity that was illuminated by zest and a peppery sense that life was still a very good kind of game.

Gigi's face had absorbed the individual details that had made her such a pert and impudent-looking girl. The almost-turned-up nose, the almost-pointed ears, the small mouth with the upper lip that promised merriment, the beautifully shaped eyelids under her pointed eyebrows, now belonged to a woman whom some would call beautiful and others would qualify as intensely pretty, but no one would ever again call elfin. Yet one thing had never changed; the 1920s Jazz Baby quality that Billy had first spotted. Something bred into her slim bones and her beautifully formed skull made Gigi, dedicated working girl though she was, seem like a reincarnation of an idealized flapper, a modern version of all the wild, glowing, flirtatious, restlessly naughty, breathlessly dancing, feverishly laughing, flushed young things who once broke hearts as carelessly as they breathed.

"You know the client of my dreams?" Gigi asked dreamily. "An executive, a busy single man. The first words out of his mouth would be the budget, then he'd provide all the vital details, allow us plenty of time to case his apartment so we'd know how to set up, approve one of the three choices of menu and never change his mind, not ask to see ten napkin colors or the size of the wineglasses or a sample flower arrangement, not become hysterical the day of the party . . ."

"And how many clients like that do you have?" Sasha asked interestedly. "Because if they're hanging around, you could at least introduce me to a few."

"Emily said she had one once. It was right after she started Voyage, but she still remembers him. Then he got married to a gourmet cook who did their parties herself with just someone in the kitchen to clean up."

"Single men go to parties, they don't give them, not catered parties anyway."

"But Zach gives parties and he's single."

"Zach?"

"Your older brother, *that* Zach."

"Gigi, you have to understand, Zach's different," Sasha explained kindly. "He's in the theater, he's a director, and on top of that he's a Nevsky, son of an Orloff. To Zach, life *is* a party. For him, a few friends for drinks translates into vodka, wine and dinner for two dozen people and anyone they might bring with them. And they do the dishes."

"I like . . . his attitude."

"Get in line, little one, get in line," Sasha said lazily, leaning back on a heap of pillows to let her toes dry. She was wearing a pair of heavy white satin man-tailored pajamas with a wide collar and deep cuffs made from softly fluted mousseline. On one pocket were embroidered the initials *A.L.* The pajamas, which had been made in 1925, had been Gigi's birthday present to her ten months ago. Gigi had written a card to accompany the present:

> *Surely you don't think anybody ever slept a wink in these pajamas? I happen to know that the lady—some say her name was Antoinette, yet others insist it was Lola— slipped into them only when slumber was the very last thing on her mind. Antoinette-Lola owned a large ebony chest that contained many great jewels, each one of them an emerald to match her eyes. Her yacht, although it had a crew of twenty, had only one master cabin. When she entered a ballroom, the entire orchestra stood up and played "Sweet and Low Down," a song the Gershwin brothers had written just for her. Antoinette-Lola's husband understood that he must never come home between five and seven, but nevertheless he was the happiest of men. What did Antoinette-Lola know? Nothing Sasha hasn't learned. She would have wanted you to wear these pajamas and have only good times.*
>
>

With all my love,
Gigi

Underneath the note Gigi had drawn a little sketch of Sasha at her most arrogant, wearing the pajamas, brandishing a long cigarette holder, her legs entwined with the leashes of three huge white Angora cats.

It was while she was looking for something special to give Sasha that Gigi had found herself becoming fascinated by old-fashioned lingerie. Now, when she had time, she combed the secondhand clothes markets and certain specialized antiques shops of the city, sometimes coming home with a well-preserved treasure of fine linen trimmed with baby Irish or Madeira lace. One by one she found silk chiffon and crepe chemises, knickers, camisoles, boudoir caps, peignoirs, tea gowns, nightgowns, and even corset covers with ribbon threaded through them. She'd put each item on once to see how it looked and then tuck it away carefully in a special drawer, protected by tissue paper, for her own future delectation.

Once, when she'd arrived home in triumph, bearing one of the first lightweight, two-way, all-in-one stretch corsets, a historic object that dated from 1934, Sasha had protested that she should never have bought such a horrifying garment. Gigi insisted that whoever had owned it must have blessed its inventor, who had liberated women from the boned corsets of an earlier day. Each bit of lingerie that she brought home seemed to her to have a history, each one could tell a wondrous story if she could only be alive to its vibrations, and no matter how much Sasha laughed at her and told her she was turning into a fetishist, she stubbornly added to her collection, finding ever more alluring and delicate examples of forgotten styles.

"Sasha," Gigi asked seriously, "do you think I'm getting cynical?"

"You've grown up awfully fast since you started working, but cynical? No, I don't think so. It seems to me that a cynic would sneer at the possibility of human goodness or sincerity . . . you don't sneer, you just keep hoping to find it . . . if anything, you're the opposite of a cynic, a cockeyed optimist or something like that."

"That's what Zach says."

"Does he?"

"Yes," Gigi said, curling up on the pillows near Sasha. "When I told him that every time I worked on a wedding I thought it was a shame to spend so much money when there was only a fifty-percent chance that the couple would stay married, he said I was just being realistic, and that realistic is good."

"Did he?"

"Uh-huh. And when I told Zach that I thought it was disgusting to give elaborate birthday parties for two- and three-year-olds, just so that the parents could show off how much money they had to each other, he said it was my social conscience speaking, and I should be glad I had one, but I should also realize that any party spread money around to lots of different businesses and working people."

"No kidding."

"Yep. And when Zach and I talked about the theater he said that I should think of parties as theatrical productions, that I should divorce them from their emotional quotient. Zach told me not to agonize the way I used to do about whether the hosts were having fun at their own parties, because they were the producers and it wasn't their business to have fun. Zach said I should only worry about how the guests were enjoying it, because the guests were the audience and the entire party was mounted for them. Zach said when a party's successful, the hosts have plenty of time to be happy when it's over, but that there's no way I can hope to eliminate their nervousness while it's going on. His point of view has been a big help to me. Very steadying. Zach knows so much. No wonder he's such a terrific director."

"You think so, do you?"

"Oh yes, Sasha. Zach's truly wise," Gigi assured his sister. "He said that anytime you become a professional, no matter how glamorous your profession seems to the outside world, you have to turn into a worker bee, like him or me. Zach said that on the one hand you have to personally give up the illusion of your profession—which unfortunately is exactly what drew you to it in the first place—because you learn firsthand about the nuts and bolts and grind and sweat that create it, but on the other hand you've made it happen for a lot of other people, and that's your reward . . . that and the fun of the work itself, the process."

"When did you have this conversation with Zach?"

"Oh, every now and then, different times, it wasn't all in one conversation."

"I see. I see." Sasha meticulously tested her toenails and found them dry. "Gigi, what's in that box? Just looking at it, I know you've been lingerie-shopping."

Gigi untied the string of the cardboard box and pulled out a garment unlike any that Sasha had seen before. "That's not lingerie," Sasha declared.

"Yes it is. It's what they called a breakfast jacket," Gigi answered, caressing the soft deep rose velvet from which the supple, hip-length jacket was made. "Look, it's lined in pleated beige chiffon, and this dark fur that trims the edges is something they used to call 'kolinsky,' according to the woman who sold it to me. Isn't it heavenly? Imagine slipping this on for breakfast when the fire hasn't quite warmed the room. Have another kipper, m'dear.''

"It looks as if it's your size," Sasha said. "Come on, try it on.''

Gigi put on the jacket, which was designed with deep armholes and no buttons so that it fell open in an almost oriental way. She twirled around twice, her eyes closed in pleasure. "I thought I'd give it to Jessica for Christmas . . . it might hang a bit on her, but she can always belt it.''

"Why don't you keep it? It's perfect for you.''

"I'm trying to get all my Christmas shopping done by the end of the month. You know how busy we get around Christmas . . . I'll never have time to get away from the office after November hits and people start to think about holiday parties. Groaning-board time is almost upon us.''

"Come to think of it, aren't you dying for dinner? It's been a long time since lunch, and I was on my feet all afternoon, peddling bras and panties.''

"There's lots of Creole chicken stew left over from yesterday,'' Gigi said. "It'll be even better reheated. It won't take any time in the microwave.''

"What!'' Sasha was immobile with shock. "Did you say *re-heated*? *Warmed up*? Did you say *microwave*?''

"I know, Sasha, I know perfectly well that tonight's the night I always teach you to cook something new, but just once couldn't you please, please eat something you didn't make?''

"Oh, I suppose so,'' Sasha conceded unwillingly. "Although it wasn't in our original deal. You don't see me canceling your lessons without notice.''

"Sasha?'' Gigi cleared her throat. "Sasha, I don't think I'm ever going to make it as a Great Slut. Your lessons are being wasted on me.''

"Aha! So that's why you don't want to give me a cooking lesson!''

"No! That's a coincidence. I've been intending to explain for a long time, but I didn't want to spoil our fun. Sasha, I might as well admit that I'm no good at balancing more than one man at a time—it feels . . . oh, I don't know . . . . icky? . . . . there's got to be a better word, but you know what I mean. It goes against my grain. Look at it this way, at least I found it out so I'll never have to wonder if I'm missing something. And, Sasha, I don't really enjoy making men suffer, even though I know how good and necessary it is for them. I've been taking your lessons under false pretenses because I didn't want to let you down. It sounded like a terrific idea when you first explained to me, but . . . well, whatever I thought way back then, I simply don't have what it takes, I keep backsliding and I know you'd disapprove . . . so I think we should give it up."

"This does not mean you are going back on my cooking lessons." Sasha's tone contained no question. It was as good as a contract.

"No, no, no. I'll give you double lessons, as many as you want, I promise," Gigi wailed and disappeared into the bedroom, still wearing the jacket over her underwear.

Sasha put away the implements in her pedicure kit and lay back on the couch, contemplating a microwaved dinner more calmly. In fact it would be rather nice not to have a cooking lesson, not to have to change into jeans and an apron and follow Gigi's complicated instructions. She probably knew more about cooking than any woman would ever need. But she wasn't going to touch that microwave. That was Gigi's department. And she'd make Gigi set the table too, and clean up afterwards, to punish her for her failure to follow through on her opportunities.

Sasha looked up as Gigi slipped into the living room. She was dressed to go out, in high black boots into which she'd tucked dark green, wide-wale corduroy trousers. She'd belted a black cashmere turtleneck sweater tightly around her waist with a wide belt of woven silver and gold, and she wore the rose velvet breakfast jacket tossed gallantly over her shoulders. She looked like a small Russian officer in the army of the Czar, Sasha thought, uncoiling in surprise.

"Just where is your apron, Miss Orsini? I believe there is a chicken stew waiting to be reheated."

"Oh, Sasha, please, would you mind eating alone tonight?" Gigi asked pleadingly.

"On Monday night, the Monday night we keep for each other? I don't believe you said that!"

"I have . . . a sort of appointment . . . more or less of a . . . date." Gigi was backing slowly into the hallway that led to the front door.

"You have a *date*? With a man? Are you mad? You know you need Monday off!" Sasha followed her and cut off her retreat.

"Not if I don't go out with three different men all week long. Not if I'm taking up monogamy," Gigi said defiantly.

"I was afraid of this." Sasha shook her noble head indignantly, her long black hair tumbling over the shoulders of her white satin pajamas. "All my lessons down the drain, all wasted on you. I never should have let you in on my secrets . . . but I blame myself, you never had the makings of a slut, great or otherwise, you don't have the heart for it. So you have a date, do you? Just who is important enough to cause you to stand me up?"

"I'm just going to grab a bite," Gigi said defensively.

"I didn't ask *what* you were going to do, I asked who with?"

"I need some advice, some professional advice, I'm going out to get it."

"I didn't ask *why* you were going out for dinner, I asked who with?"

"Sort of . . . . Zach."

"There is nobody, *nobody* on this earth, who is 'sort of Zach,' " Sasha spat, her dark eyes narrowing in rage. "And you, Gigi Orsini, know it. Don't you?"

"All right, so I have a date with Zach, so what?"

"What have I done? Oh God, where did I go wrong? How can such a thing be happening to me? Abomination! This is an abomination in the eyes of the Lord!"

"Sasha, calm down and stop yelling! What's wrong with my going out with Zach?"

"I heard the word 'monogamy'—I heard the name Zach—and you dare to ask what's wrong? *You slut!*"

"Just tell me what's wrong. You don't have to be insulting."

"Zach's my brother, *mine*, that's what's wrong! I adore him! *I'm jealous!* That's what's wrong!"

"You'll get over it," Gigi said comfortingly. "It won't take you more than a few days to realize that it's better me than a stranger."

"How do you know?" Sasha asked tragically. "How can you possibly be sure?"

"Human nature, Sasha," Gigi said as she left the room. "Even you have some."

12

*O*h, come on, Cora, where's your sense of adventure?'' Billy pulled Cora de Lioncourt down the crowded side street of the Marché Saint-Honoré, a food market near the Ritz, and into the door of Le Rubis, an old-fashioned café-turned-wine bistro where the list of wines sold by the glass took up five feet of wall space. Billy found a paper-covered table in the packed room, installed herself and Cora, and gestured wildly until she caught the eye of the owner. "Léon," she yelled over the din, "two glasses of Beaujolais Nouveau and two of your *rillettes* sandwiches."

Cora de Lioncourt recoiled. "You can't possibly order Beaujolais Nouveau. It's a cabdriver's wine, Billy, nobody drinks it!"

"You've lived in New York too long," Billy laughed. "Cora, this is the biggest celebration since Bastille Day . . . . the Beaujolais Nouveau has arrived! Wake up! It's November fifteenth, 1981, and all over France people are fighting to get the first glass . . . I brought you here as a special treat. My little Beaujol is the most intelligent wine in the world.''

''The cheapest, I'm sure, but what makes it intelligent?''

''No sooner is it harvested than it is *acheté, bu et pissé*—quick and to the point.''

''Bought, drunk and . . . eliminated. Charming. You might as well drink grape juice, in my opinion.''

''Now, now, Cora, don't underestimate my expertise. There is Beaujol and Beaujol, most of it is of inferior quality or mixed with Algerian wine—but Le Rubis is one of the few places you can drink it with confidence—Léon's been buying directly from the same grower forever, with no middlemen involved. He can serve us any Beaujolais in existence, so if you're going to be snooty about *mon petit* Beaujol, I'll buy you a glass of Moulin-à-Vent or Côte de Brouilly, or Saint-Amour—but I'm sticking with the Nouveau. Let's try some of the *fromage fort*, shall we? It's Léon's special mixture of Roquefort and goat cheese—just the right thing to bring out the flavor of the wine.''

Cora's eyes widened in horror as she looked at Billy drinking the fruity, light, almost unfermented wine that could be swilled with impunity. *Fromage fort! Rillettes* indeed! She wouldn't dream of touching that country pâté made from shreds of fresh-cooked pork mixed with cold pork fat—food beloved of the lower classes, food no one had asked Cora to eat in all the years she'd lived in France.

Cora had already been in Paris for ten days, and Billy had been unexpectedly difficult to pin down to a lunch. Now that they were together, she fully expected to be taken to the Relais Plaza, the most fashionable place for two women to lunch in Paris . . . but no, here they were in this tumbledown hideout, not even a decent bistro, elbowed by a jolly mob of laughing patrons, shopgirls, businessmen, workingmen, and even a few street sweepers, who were all already well into the spirit of the long-awaited festivities, passing each other fresh glasses of the newly arrived wine directly over Cora's head.

''I'll eat your *rillettes* if you don't want it, Cora,'' Billy offered. ''Shall I ask Léon for a menu? He does a good omelet.''

''Please.'' She passed Billy her plate quickly.

''Oh, Cora, I'm sorry. You're really not enjoying this at all, are you? I thought it would be amusing for a change. I know it's a bit of a marketing gimmick, this whole Beaujolais madness, but it's the closest the French get to the Halloween spirit. Come on, we'll go somewhere quieter.''

"It's not that I don't like it—it's just that it's so noisy that it's hard to talk here," Cora said, concealing her ruffled relief.

A few minutes later, after a brisk walk back to the Ritz, the two women were installed at a table in the Espadon, the Ritz restaurant.

"Tell me all about the new house," Cora asked eagerly. "When will you move in? Can I visit this afternoon?"

"Oh . . . let's wait till it's finished," Billy responded lightly. "There isn't a stick of furniture in it yet."

"Even empty, I'm dying to see it," Cora replied. Billy was just being evasive. "This is my first trip to Paris since you bought it," Cora added, a hint of reproach in her voice, "and once I leave, I won't be back for months. I simply must have a preview before I go back to New York, or people will make it into even more of a mystery than they have already."

"You mean people in New York have been . . . . gossiping about my place? Why should they bother?"

"Of course they gossip," Cora said, showing her perfect teeth. "It's only to be expected, given who you are. On a certain level, haven't you noticed that when something very intriguing is going on in Paris or London, it seems to be happening in New York too? People feel a part of it, they take a proprietary interest. And you've managed to make them even more curious by turning into a dropout."

"Cora, I have *not* been a dropout," Billy said sharply. "Just last week I went to the Rothschilds' ball and the Polignacs' dinner."

"Two parties in a week? That's the same as being invisible during November. It's the height of the Paris season, Billy, and you've been asked everywhere. You've made a lot of hostesses unhappy with all your refusals." Cora's tone was teasing, but it was clear that she was serious.

"Surely that's my right?" Billy asked, her voice rising. "I hate going out more than twice a week. Even two evenings means spending an eternity on clothes and hair. I can't begin to imagine how the women who do it every night handle the boredom of it."

She put down her soup spoon with a bang, carried away by her words. "They get up, make phone calls and dress for lunch. After lunch they go shopping and have endless fittings. Then they get their hair done for the evening, go home to dress for dinner, put on more makeup, go out for the evening, and come home to take off their clothes and makeup and go to bed in order to start all over again the next morning. That's their life, Cora, their *whole* life! How can they stand it?''

Billy's face was alight with an emotion that Cora de Lioncourt couldn't decipher. Could she possibly be sincerely indignant at a use of time women in society took for granted? Was she merely impatient with the repetitive quality of any social round, no matter how glamorous, how elevated? Or . . . or, and this was more likely, wasn't Billy hiding a disappointment that all the preparations she had made for social occasions hadn't yet produced any man whose name was attached to hers? After all, from everything Cora had heard, Billy herself had led exactly the life she'd just described for six months after arriving in Paris.

''A woman like you, who's used to running a business, would naturally find such a life limited,'' Cora said carefully. ''But I promise you there are many women who would give all they have to lead that life you find so empty.''

''Would you?''

''Good heavens, no,'' Cora said emphatically. ''A collector always wakes up excited by the thrill of the chase—it's like having a full-time job, except that you spend money instead of making it. I've always thought that the only way to be rich and stay interested in life was either to collect with passion—collect anything, it doesn't matter what—or be very competitive at something you do well—some sport, for example. I'm sure that's the explanation for golf.''

''And bridge.''

''Exactly. Now, when do I see this mystery house? Empty or not, I won't be satisfied until I lay eyes on it.''

''We can go after lunch if you like,'' Billy said, realizing that eventually she'd have to show Cora the house, and the sooner she got it done, the less she'd have to juggle her life while Cora was visiting. And Cora could report to anyone who was making a mystery out of the Rue Vaneau that it was just a big empty house in the process of being redecorated, no more, no less.

Merely meeting Cora for lunch today had meant an extra trip to the Ritz in order to transform herself into the Billy Ikehorn Cora expected to see. Changing her clothes for lunch, she'd found herself so rushed that her heart had pounded with anxiety as she abandoned one set of clothes for another. She'd have to go back to the hotel room she'd taken on the Rue Monsieur le Prince, stuff the Saint Laurent dress and coat she was wearing into the back of the closet, and change into something else before she could go back to Sam. No, damn it! That would mean going home in clothes different from those she'd worn when she left Sam this morning. He'd notice—he noticed everything about her. She'd have to return to the fucking Ritz, change fucking back into the fucking clothes she'd put on this fucking morning and then go home. And all this without using her fucking driver because she never let him pick her up at the Ritz or deposit her either at the Rue Vaneau or Sam's studio. What a fucking drag!

"My driver's sick today," Billy added smoothly. "I hope we can find a taxi."

"Jean-François? I thought you were in Aix, buying antiques?" Billy was disagreeably surprised to see her decorator arriving at the Rue Vaneau. She had just given Cora a whirlwind tour of both floors of the restored manor house, and they were on their way out when Jean-François Delacroix entered. Without being impossibly rude, she had to introduce him to Cora, and it was five o'clock already.

"I came back on the TGV this morning, Madame. There wasn't much to be had, and what there was, I bought yesterday."

"Is this Monsieur Delacroix?" Cora asked.

"Oh, forgive me. May I present Jean-François Delacroix? Jean-François, this is the Comtesse de Lioncourt. We're just leaving."

"Everyone knows of the Comtesse and her exquisite taste," the young decorator said, kissing Cora's hand. "I tremble already."

"Nonsense," said Cora, "nothing's installed yet . . . alas, in such a superb house there's nothing for me to see, either to praise or to criticize. It is all potential, but splendid potential."

"Madame, we needed time to perfect the setting, the frame, so that it will be light, flexible and pure throughout, the spirit of the eighteenth century revisited, as it were, by Madame Ikehorn's sensibility. Meanwhile, I am storing the treasures we find in the old stables."

"I wonder," Cora said, quivering with eagerness, "if I could have a quick peek at them."

"It would be my pleasure, Madame, but they are all carefully covered against the damp."

"Oh no!" Cora almost stamped her foot in frustration. The visit had been pure irritation from beginning to end. Visiting bare rooms, with nothing to look at but architectural details and newly restored floors and walls had been a form of torture that had left her feeling murderous, yet she'd been fairly warned beforehand, so she couldn't show how cheated she felt.

"Couldn't you uncover something, something small?" She might yet salvage something from this afternoon.

"I could try, Madame, that is . . . if Madame Ikehorn . . ."

"Go ahead, Jean-François," Billy said with resignation. Once Cora had heard the word "treasures," Billy had known that there would be no avoiding a visit to the stables. "I'll stay here and find out what that gardener is doing. He should have finished planting bulbs days ago. But don't be long, it's getting late and we have to find a taxi before the worst of the rush hour. You have only ten minutes."

"Tell me where you went in Aix, Monsieur," Cora asked, and she and the young decorator plunged into a discussion of the merits of the antiques dealers of Provence as they crossed the courtyard to the stable block. There he threw open the old doors, turned on the lights and revealed the two dozen old horse stalls, packed full.

Cora walked up and down, realizing quickly that each piece of furniture and each object was far too carefully wrapped for her to see anything in a short time.

"Yes, Madame," the decorator shrugged, seeing her face, "I know, it is disappointing. I would like to have your opinion of many of the things I have bought. But, here, at least, I can show you something that has just arrived and has not yet been protected properly." He pulled a tarpaulin away from what seemed to be a picture leaning up against a wall and revealed an oblong mirror, elaborately surrounded by a carved mirror frame, all of it glimmering and glistening dimly like a dark window into a jeweled past.

"Ah . . . lovely! Very lovely indeed. It isn't French, is it? Late seventeenth century."

"Precisely, Madame. It is German and was presented to the ruling House of Orange to celebrate a victory in battle."

"It's marvelously flamboyant. And in perfect condition, I see."

"I intend it for Madame Ikehorn's bedroom. To view oneself in such a mirror is to see oneself reincarnated in another era, do you not think so, Madame?"

"I agree, Monsieur," Cora said, looking without pleasure at her reflection in the old glass. "Is the house to be surpassingly romantic, then?"

"Who can tell, Madame?"

"Surely you, Monsieur," Cora said in surprise.

"I think I may well be the last man in Paris to know." The young decorator spoke with an edge of bitterness that was at odds with his evident desire to show her something beautiful.

"How is that possible?" she probed, smiling as if she thought he meant to be merely modest.

"I must not complain, Madame, but this is not like any other project in which I have been involved." He covered the mirror and started toward the stable door.

"No, wait, Monsieur Delacroix, you seem discouraged. Perhaps I can help. As you may have guessed, Madame Ikehorn relies heavily on my advice."

"You are the first of her friends to visit the house. That gives me some hope that soon there will be others."

"You *are* discouraged. Is my friend difficult to please? Because if she is, you must know that she has always been that way. It is not a reflection on your talents."

"Difficult? No, I could not say that Madame Ikehorn is . . . difficult."

"Then what problem is there? Surely not that of the expense involved in furnishing the house?"

"Nothing like that, Madame. I have carte blanche. From the very first day I was asked to undertake this project, not a single one of my suggestions has been turned down because of its cost."

"Then you have a decorator's dream job."

"Yes, in principle, one would be forced to say so."

"But?"

"Ah, Madame de Lioncourt, you will think that I am complaining . . ."

"Not at all, Monsieur." Cora gave him her lovely smile. "You are not a man who complains, I can see that."

"It is the waste!" he burst out. "This is a marvelous house, one of the most charming in Paris, this is a house that was created at a time when the nobility could lead lives that were an art form. This is no ordinary house, Madame, it is one that demands a greatness of concept. Once I saw it, I knew that if I could bring it back to life I would achieve a dream. For weeks I could not believe how lucky I was to have this rare privilege dropped in my lap, a house that asks in every stone to be opened up to the world, a house whose very walls inform you that within them you are at the peak of Western civilization. I believed that when it was finished there would be dinners, galas, garden parties, large receptions . . . I confess I even entertained the fantasy that it would be photographed for magazines . . ."

"A house like this will make your career," Cora said reassuringly. "Everyone will be talking about it. I don't think you have to worry about that."

"But no! Madame, that is why I am discouraged."

"I don't understand."

"Nor do I. Madame Ikehorn has told me that she does not intend to receive on a large scale, that she does not want me to design the reception rooms with great galas in mind, that she will never allow the house to be photographed. 'Make my house cozy,' she has told me, *cozy*, as if this were an English cottage! Cozy! That is for the bourgeois. The bedrooms, of course, should be intimate and comfortable, but the reception rooms? Impossible!"

"It seems like a contradiction in terms," Cora murmured.

"Exactly that! Only the English in their country houses can combine grandeur and cozy. With them it is the result of ten generations of collectors, each one adding another layer of objects so that eventually even the largest spaces become a three-dimensional tribute to their ancestors, filled with things good and bad, memories—and dogs, especially dogs, is that not true?"

"Dogs do furnish a room," Cora murmured, her mind intent on his words.

"In Paris it is not possible to achieve this cozy effect in a classical building of such perfection. I believe it would violate the spirit of the house. I have tried to explain it to her . . . but she insists. She says it can be done. At first she asked me to surprise her, but that was the last thing she wanted—I discovered that quickly. So I have tried to give her what she wants." Jean-François sighed as he thought of his strong-minded client. "We have found all our treasures together on the few days a week she can spare me. Madame Ikehorn insists on sharing in all the details of the decoration."

"I'm sure you underestimate yourself," Cora said thoughtfully. "You may achieve a new kind of grand coziness that will be just what people are looking for in these difficult days."

"That is what I have told myself, Madame, that is what I hope it will be like. Even if only a few close friends of Madame Ikehorn see it, still, they will tell others . . ."

"I promise to come back when it is finished, and you can be sure that I will spread the word," Cora said.

"I hope Madame is prepared to be patient . . . ."

"But the house is ready for the installation, why shouldn't it proceed?"

"Madame Ikehorn is in no hurry to move in. She does not want me to complete the house yet, she tells me she is in no rush and that once it is installed she will have the problem of finding staff to maintain it. Now she has only the guardian in the gatehouse. So I wait. Sometimes I ask myself if Madame Ikehorn intends *ever* to finish this house? You understand that this is difficult for me? I do not wish to complain, but I too have my sensitivities. If this house were mine, I could not wait to take possession of it."

"Nor could I. I wonder why she is not eager."

"That is what I ask myself. It hurts me to see the house empty, not just professionally but personally. I tell you this in confidence, of course, since you are Madame's intimate friend. I would not speak of it to others. I hope you do not think I'm complaining. I adore Madame Ikehorn, you understand."

"You have every right to complain," Cora said. "In your place I would go mad. But perhaps we should return now."

"You will keep my confidence, I know."

"You may count on me, Monsieur."

Cora de Lioncourt dressed for dinner in a fever of delighted speculation. As she changed from a black suit to a black dinner dress, she made a mental tally of the extraordinary changes in Billy Ikehorn, changes no mere year in Paris could explain.

In the first place, the woman who had been famous for a decade and a half for her unrelenting chic, the woman who always wore the latest styles before anyone else, had been dressed in a dress-and-coat ensemble from a Saint Laurent collection that had been photographed in a half dozen magazines several couture seasons ago. Even if it was her favorite outfit, it was deeply odd for her to be seen still wearing something so dated. And far worse, far, far worse, the dress had been *tight*. Beyond a shadow of a doubt, the dress had been tight at the waistline and over her hips. Six pounds? Seven? Billy, whose past, well-documented public life proved that she had never deviated from the iron discipline that is second nature to the true woman of fashion, had done the unthinkable and put on weight. It hadn't taken her gusto for the revoltingly fattening *rillettes* to prove it—her zipper told the story.

Cora thought back to the lunch in New York with Spider Elliott. Billy had possessed a perfection of grooming then that was missing today. Another woman might not have noticed it, for Billy was as beautiful as before, perhaps more so, but the high gloss that spoke of hours and hours of attention, the varnished finish that only money could buy, had been absent at lunch. Billy's nails had not been polished, nor had they been buffed to a high shine. Her hair had been permitted to grow out of its short blunt cut. Now it reached below her ears, an attractive look, perhaps, but one without style. Her eye makeup seemed to have been put on in a hurry, and she'd worn no earrings. Details . . . vital details.

The entire episode at the wine bar might have passed as the effect of living in France—a severe case of going native—except that a woman like Billy Ikehorn would normally live in France forever and never once enter a place like that. Her *"petit* Beaujol" indeed! It was positively indecent. Not that a liking for Beaujolais was significant in and of itself, Cora told herself, but her ease in the wine bar, her acceptance of a table covered only by paper mats—that was all part of the delicious puzzle.

Cora had known that there was something not right with Billy even before the lunch today that had taken too long to arrange. Many of her friends in Paris had told her that Billy had snubbed their invitations, making excuses for not attending the evening parties and lunches she had been glad to go to when she first arrived. During those first months in Paris, Billy had invited guests to dine in one or another of the great restaurants, in obedience to reciprocity, that most holy rule of social life. Now, Cora was told, she no longer reciprocated even those invitations she deigned to accept, and a single woman, no matter how rich and well placed, must reciprocate or be forgotten.

What could explain Billy Ikehorn's slide? Why was she dragging her feet so that she didn't have to move into the house for which she'd been in such a ridiculous hurry to plunk down far too much money, a sale whose every detail Cora had known, for Denise Martin had paid her a handsome commission?

"She didn't make the grade," Cora said out loud. She sat down in a deep chair in her hotel room, startled by her sudden revelation. Everything added up when she started to think about it. Cora had made it her business to find out as much as possible about Billy Ikehorn, going back to look at the old newspaper clippings of her first marriage. The New York Public Library was a storehouse of information that no one but she seemed to have the wit to use. There she'd uncovered many a glossed-over fact, guessed at many a secret motivation, detected the murky primary sources of certain fortunes, and factored all of them into her business.

After she'd met Billy, Cora had dug out all the old newspaper accounts of the alliance with Ellis Ikehorn that had made Billy one of the richest women in the world. She knew that although Billy was a Boston Winthrop, she came from a poor and undistinguished subsidiary branch of that huge family. A Winthrop, yes, but in the smallest way. Billy's background looked good on paper, but the clear reality was that she had been a secretary who had married her boss, a man whose own antecedents still remained dubious and unknown. Her early life with him had looked brilliant in photographs, but as a couple the Ikehorns had made no secure place for themselves in society. The Scruples era had kept her picture in the fashion sections, but her West Coast social life was almost nonexistent. Billy's short second marriage, to a first-generation Italian-American movie producer, was hardly the stuff of society pages.

Yes, Cora understood it now. Billy's move to Paris had been that of a woman who wanted to make a new start. She understood for the first time why Billy hadn't been tempted to take on the New York establishment. The Old Guard was almost impossible to penetrate. The new people were a tough bunch, battle-hardened women reluctant to part with their own recently won status, more difficult for a single woman to win over than the French, to whom all rich and generous Americans were equally acceptable and equally indifferent.

So. So that was it. Billy had come here with a lavishly open hand and Billy had bought a house that was much too aristocratic for an American and Billy had indiscriminately accepted all her invitations, good and bad, and somewhere, somehow, Billy had seen that she'd failed to quite measure up to the task she'd set for herself. Perhaps she'd made influential enemies among the ten women who ruled Paris, perhaps she'd slept with exactly the wrong men—somewhere she'd made a huge, irreparable mistake that had taken the wind out of her sails. Of course she was invited to the big catchall balls and parties, but she had never mentioned being invited to those intimate gatherings of close friends, those small celebrations that showed true acceptance, those inner-circle parties to which she had not been invited herself, Cora thought with the deeply satisfied sneer of one outsider recognizing another.

So. Billy must have realized that she wasn't going to triumph in the game she'd set out to play with trumpets blaring and cymbals sounding. Now she was in the process of giving it up with a show of sour grapes. *She had let herself go. She hadn't made the grade!* Billy Ikehorn simply didn't have what it took to achieve the brilliant position she had come to Paris to seek. She was a Cinderella who had gone slinking back to her fireside, finding the glass slipper too tight for comfort.

Of course poor Billy was in no hurry to move into her fine house. She would never feel as at home there, no matter how cozy she mistakenly tried to make it, as she did in the rented rooms of a hotel, available to anyone who could pay their price. It was a great pity, Cora thought, smiling bitterly, her expression needlelike. She, Cora, could dwell in the Rue Vaneau in the way the house deserved, and if she'd had Billy's money to spend during her marriage to Robert de Lioncourt, if she hadn't had to manage so courageously to create an impression of ease, *she* would have made the grade. She was certain of it.

"Never again! I promise you, Sam, darling, never again! I'm so sorry I'm late, you weren't worried, were you?" Billy rushed into the studio well past seven o'clock, out of breath from racing up the stairs. "The traffic was worse today than it's been all year. Christmas shopping's started."

"I never gave it a second thought. I figured you were stuck on top of the Eiffel Tower for the night and that you'd be down by morning." She couldn't ignore the tightness of concern in his voice, even though his words were joking.

"It almost came to that." Billy kissed him hastily and sprawled exhausted in one of the rattan chairs that had come with the studio, giving it an incongruous patio touch. "Why is everyone I ever knew back home convinced that I have nothing better to do than spend their one day in Paris with them?"

"I told you you didn't have to say yes, sweetheart, you could have made some excuse," Sam said evenly.

"I'm sorry for them just passing through, but today was too much."

"Did your Cora appreciate her guided tour? Did she say thanks?"

"Not so you'd notice."

"Come back here, sweetheart. You deserve major appreciation. You have that look on your face again, that I'm-too-busy-to-live look."

"Oh, Sam," Billy wailed, and collapsed gratefully in his lap, her arms wound tightly around his neck, letting herself relax for the first time since she'd finally escaped from Cora and started on the zigzag trip home that had been prolonged by her stop at the Ritz to change clothes.

"New shoes?" he asked.

Billy looked down at the expensive Maud Frizon pumps that she'd forgotten to leave at the Ritz.

"Oh. Yes, aren't they nice? Cora couldn't spend a day in Paris without doing some shopping, so I splurged too. I think it was the only time we sat down all day."

"Not even lunch?"

"Lunch, of course. Believe it or not, Cora took me to lunch at the Ritz. But she's always had a bit of money, so I didn't feel guilty."

Billy had long ago realized that the more truth she used with Sam, the easier it was to lead her double life. She had also invented certain major lies that now were so firmly established that they seemed to have become the truth.

Twice a week, on Tuesdays and Fridays, Sam believed that she left her daily work at the Bibliothèque Nationale and went straight to the home of a wealthy, house-bound Frenchwoman who lived in the heart of the faraway Sixteenth Arrondissement. There Billy gave her pupil English lessons and stayed on for a late dinner to engage her in English conversation. When Sam had asked her why she didn't come back to his studio after the lessons, Billy had stubbornly asserted that she must sleep at least two nights in her own bed in her hotel on the Rue Monsieur le Prince to keep her independence.

Her independence. That wretched, miserable, ragged, worn-out excuse for an excuse that had left her hating the mere idea of independence, Billy thought wearily. Her independence, the only subject about which she and Sam disagreed until, as now, they were sick and tired of it. Independence, of which every busy minute was spent working on the house with Jean-François, or catching up on her mail and messages at the Ritz, running a minimum of necessary errands and getting her hair washed. She couldn't find time to shop, she was lucky if she could manage to schedule a pedicure. She rushed through her days and then hurriedly bathed and dressed to go out at night so that her presence in Paris continued to be established. She couldn't risk having curious acquaintances begin to wonder out loud if she had totally disappeared, and if so, where had she gone?

How could she have been so shortsighted, when she'd first met Sam, as to imagine that leading a double life would be a thrilling game? She'd made such clever plans, filled with self-congratulation as she faced down the staff of the Ritz without a blink on anyone's part; she'd been so snappily efficient when she found a perfectly placed, modest hotel room near the Luxembourg Gardens to serve as her supposed home, one that Sam could visit at will. She'd established her system of getting around Paris anonymously; she'd managed to ride tight herd on Jean-François, constantly working to keep his more grandiose ideas in check. Somehow the details had meshed, no one had spotted her in the wrong place with the wrong person, yet every day her double life was becoming more and more distasteful to her. Billy felt fragmented, pulled to pieces, torn between being the animated, elegant, bejeweled woman who kept up her end of a cosmopolitan dinner table conversation, and the carefree schoolteacher from Seattle with a consuming interest in Voltaire and a passionate love for Sam Jamison.

How she loathed having to lie to him! Only weeks after they first met, Sam had asked her to marry him. After their time in Paris was over, he told her, he would move to Seattle and work there if she couldn't get a teaching job in Marin County. His West Coast dealer had sold two large pieces from his last show; he had hopes of receiving an Arts Council grant, and they wouldn't have to live in a garret, he'd promised her. There was no reason for them to be apart ever again.

If she'd been one person, the schoolteacher, Billy would have accepted him immediately, even if it was too soon, even if she barely knew him. But Wilhelmina Hunnenwell Winthrop Ikehorn Orsini, with all her history, had learned some hard lessons about men who had no money and women who had too much. She didn't dare allow herself the bankrupting simplicity of yielding to impulse once again.

She controlled one of the world's great fortunes. She had once told Vito that she couldn't get rid of it even if she wanted to, which she did not. It was as important to her as it had ever been. Billy understood herself clearly enough to know that the habit of being able to utilize great wealth with the same unthinking assurance with which she used her own two hands, had become woven into the very fiber of her identity. The kind of life she'd been leading with Sam was not a life she could endure for long. It was only bearable because it was a stopgap. In fact, to be resolutely honest, it was a form of slumming.

No, it *was* slumming, plain and simple, Billy thought, holding Sam so tightly that she could feel his heart beating. She had to acknowledge, even as she rumpled the back of his hair with her loving touch, that she hated the five flights of steep stairs; she hated the coarse sheets that were washed weekly by a rough-and-ready local laundry; she hated getting out of a warm bed into a cold room and having to wait for the unreliable heat to warm the studio; she hated eating a cheap meal in a restaurant night after night, for there was only a hot plate in the studio; she hated the tiny tub in which she could only scrub herself section by section; she hated sharing a cramped bathroom and she hated not being able to buy armloads of blossoming plants and fresh flowers. She wanted to throw out every one of the inexpensive things she'd bought with such relish in that first raid she'd made on the Galeries Lafayette, looking for an appropriate costume for her new role as Honey Winthrop.

Jessica would understand, Billy thought as she nipped Sam's mouth with little kisses. Jessica would see immediately that Billy didn't insist on an ostentatious life of gilded luxury, but that, on the other hand, living in an uncomfortable studio shouldn't be the price of love.

Billy yearned with all her heart to live with Sam in the spacious, soothing, deep comfort she and Jean-François had planned for the Rue Vaneau, yearned to turn the stables into a suitable studio for Sam. There they would inhabit that gracious old house humming with the quietude of centuries, and fill it with their love. It wouldn't be the brilliant public life she'd raved on to Jessie about, but a truly private life, warmly tuned to their deepest pleasures. They would see only people they both really liked; they could travel whenever they wanted to, they could buy a house on a Greek island or a farm in Tuscany. Or they could stay at home and dig in the garden—she didn't care, so long as they were together. If it amused Sam, they could even lunch at the Ritz, where she knew the predictably pretentious menu by heart.

She had not been ready to guess what their future held until she had enough confidence in him to believe that he could accept her riches and the immense freedom they allowed her—until she had reason to know that he would continue to love her in spite of them.

During those weeks, last spring and summer while he had pressured her to marry him, Billy had retained just enough judgment to know that sex had left her judgment in ruins. She'd used her claim to a need for independence to put him off, bought priceless time with her lies about who she was, so that they had built a foundation together that went beyond the sexual need that continued to grow stronger the more they knew each other.

They'd lived with each other's moods and each other's silences. She knew that Sam Jamison was a quietly obstinate man who had chosen to follow his talent in spite of the knowledge that making a living by sculpture was achieved by very few. She had found that he was a fair man who listened carefully to her reasons for retaining her independence, even though he continued to believe that she was wrong. She'd discovered that he was a profoundly proud man who hated it every time she insisted on paying her share of their bistro meals or the occasional movie they went to in the Latin Quarter. She had faith in him now, this proud man who was as straight as a die, this proud man who respected her as much as she respected him.

Billy had watched Sam work for hours; she'd known him euphoric when his work went right and blackly depressed when it went wrong. They'd seen each other through food poisoning and head colds and allergy attacks. They'd survived a sweltering summer in Paris without air-conditioning; they'd rented a car and taken a week's trip to the Loire, encountering flat tires, terrible hotels, bad meals, impossibly crowded châteaux, and days of downpour. He knew Honey Winthrop at her worst and Billy Ikehorn at her best, Billy thought with a rueful smile, but he still didn't know the truth.

She planned to tell him very soon. In two weeks Sam was having an exhibition at the Daniel Templon Gallery on the Rue Beaubourg, owned by an avant-garde dealer who showed works by Helmut Newton and other sculptors, like Sam, who made shapes Billy could understand only because they pleased her, because they gave her a visceral, nonjudgmental joy.

If there were wise children in other galaxies, surely their toys would be wrought by Sam Jamison, she thought, looking over his shoulder at the series of large double and triple half-arcs, subtly entwined to make indefinable but unforgettable shapes. Each group of arcs rested in fragile yet perfectly balanced equipoise on a flat wooden base. Although she knew how firmly they were attached, Billy found herself keeping a sharp eye on the arcs, as if they had minds of their own and might decide to abandon their monumental equilibrium and start to roll wildly around the sides of the studio, in some sort of giant game played by unknown rules. At night she sometimes crept out of the bedroom to watch the arcs in the moonlight. Perhaps they waited until it was dark to do their thing, whatever it was. Finally she'd confided this concern to Sam. "That's the way I wanted to make you feel," he'd told her, clearly overjoyed.

Sam's brilliant young dealer, balding, bespectacled and charming, was sending for the contents of the studio next week. Once the opening of the show was over, after Sam had stopped worrying, as he now was doing about the reception of his work, Billy had decided that she would tell him everything.

How? When? In what words? She didn't know. The occasion would present itself as occasions always did once you'd finally made up your mind, once you had at last decided that it was safe to place your trust in another human being.

Sam Jamison leaned against the far edge of the long bar in the refreshment foyer at the Paris Opéra, while Henri tried vainly to order drinks. Henri Legrand, his dealer's eager young assistant and a fervent advocate of his work, had been given two tickets to tonight's gala evening, and he'd invited Sam to come with him to celebrate the final installation of Sam's show. From the vantage point of his height, Sam looked with fascination around the crowded room that contained everything he disliked most in architecture and interiors, yet managed to carry off its ultra-ornate Second Empire style by the power of sheer audacity. Never had there been so many varied marbles, such overblown chandeliers, or such an outlandish flood of gilt used before or since in France. The Opéra, Sam thought, made Versailles look like a chicken farm.

The Opéra was a Paris of which he knew almost nothing. When he had first arrived almost a year ago, before he started to work seriously, Sam had given himself a month to explore the city as thoroughly as possible. From morning to night he'd wandered with the Michelin as his guide. He'd walked the length of every great Right Bank boulevard, seen every foot of the Seine from both banks, crossed every bridge to admire the view up and downriver. He'd sauntered along each small Left Bank street, sat in two dozen parks and explored two dozen churches; he'd claimed a hundred tables at sidewalk cafés on the city's most populous corners and watched people for hours. He'd had a drink at the George Cinq and the Plaza Athenée and the Ritz, he'd looked into the windows of Dior and Nina Ricci and Hermès, he'd taken the Paris by Night tour, and seen the city from the top of the Arc de Triomphe. The greatest part of his time had been spent in museums.

Once Sam had covered the main outposts of the tourist's Paris, he had turned his back on it with little regret. It was time to get down to work. Life in the Marais continued to interest and satisfy him with its charming variety, its small, often humble, streets inhabited by artisans and small businesses, just around the corner from many of the noblest buildings of the seventeenth century. There in the air he could feel the ghosts of Madame de Sévigné, Richelieu, Victor Hugo, the ghosts of all the kings and courtesans and seigneurs and great ladies to whom the Marais had once been home. To truly know a city as vast and various as Paris was impossible, Sam had discovered in his month of exploration, but to experience Paris by living intimately the life of one of its neighborhoods was to possess Paris forever.

He was glad that Henri had persuaded him to come to the Opéra gala tonight, the first day of December. It was certainly the only occasion he'd have for wearing the old dinner jacket he'd packed with the rest of his wardrobe, on the theory that if you own one you might as well have it with you. Sam felt invisible, dressed like every other man in the room, and invisible was exactly right for his mood. It made a needed change from the feeling of exposure to the public eye that had rocked him when he'd seen his work installed in the unfamiliar light of Templon's gallery. Not one piece of these bones of his bone had seemed entirely at ease there, disturbed from the spatial relationships with each other that they'd gradually assumed in his studio, but Daniel had been vastly pleased by the look of the show. Sam hugged his long arms to his sides, making room for the crowd, as he visualized the night of the opening, the traditional *vernissage*, with its small drinks and large crowds of invited guests, jostling each other so closely that even if they wanted to see his arcs, they wouldn't be able to do more than glimpse them or be goosed by them. But some of those people were critics and some would return to look at the work seriously and write about it. And collectors, one or two, or perhaps none, would buy. It was impossible to say what the future would hold for this particular show, but Sam was satisfied—almost satisfied—with his new work, and that was the only essential for him.

Henri triumphantly handed him a drink and Sam toasted the gallery assistant, who spoke English well and was eager to improve his slang.

"Thank you, old buddy, for distracting me tonight. If I weren't here I'd be home hitting the bottle in an empty studio. Honey's giving an English lesson tonight, and you've probably saved me from a nervous breakdown."

"You've never been to the Paris Opéra before?"

"Never. And I'm enjoying the intermission better than the first act—more noise and prettier women."

"You realize, Sam, that this monument to bad taste was built to show off the Frenchwoman—the opera is only an excuse—the staircase of honor is the best parade ground for a grand *toilette* in all of Europe, but now, alas, unless it's a gala like tonight, people come here in jeans and sweaters—but not those who sit in the best seats. Not yet, at least. Look at those people coming in right now. Admit it, old buddy, they decorate the room far better than it deserves."

Sam glanced across to a group of people who were being ushered to a reserved table in the center of the room, on which bottles of champagne stood waiting in their ice buckets. The men were in white tie, the women in lavish ball gowns, and everything about the way they moved toward their central position spoke of entitlement. They were so casually certain of special service in a roomful of people who were all trying to attract the overworked waiters, that they hadn't hurried to secure a place, as the others had, but drifted in when they chose, with the languor and grace of peacocks on a lawn. They didn't even glance around to see who else was there because they formed their own tight, superior cosmos in which exceptional territorial rights were taken for granted.

People like that must know, Sam thought, that half of this huge room is staring at them, yet they received such attention by ignoring it, and ignoring it convincingly. You'd think they were having a picnic on a lonely beach from the way they concentrated on each other's witticisms.

"The Beautiful People," Sam remarked to Henri. "They give new meaning to the expression 'the world is your oyster,' whatever that means. Maybe you have to love oysters to get it."

"Just so. Sometimes I wonder what it must be like to be them."

"We'll never know, pal," Sam answered incuriously, looking away.

"What a beauty!" Henri pulled on Sam's arm. "Look! That blonde in the red gown, that's the one for me. What do you think of my taste in broads?"

Sam focused on a luscious blonde who was deep in conversation with the man next to her.

"Not bad, Henri, not to be sneezed at, you wouldn't want to kick her out of bed, but probably not a broad."

"And the redhead in green velvet? Not to be coughed at either, eh, Sam?"

"*Sneezed* at, pal, not *coughed* at, don't try to improve on our slang," Sam grinned.

"I can see one woman at that table who is not a beauty, the older one in black, in profile, and even she is a *jolie laide*. Shall I go and try to pick her up? Perhaps with her I'll be lucky."

"I'll hold your coat, Henri. Only the brave deserve the fair."

A brunette, her back to Sam, who wore her hair pulled up high on her head and caught into a knot of white roses, clinked glasses with the man flanking her. She had on a strapless gown of white satin, the boned bodice clasping her tightly at her waist. As she moved to touch her glass with the man seated on her right, blue-white flecks of light scattered from the huge diamond drops that hung from her ears and glinted from the great clasp of her heavy diamond necklace.

The nape of her neck. The shape of her shoulders. The lift of her arms. *Impossible*.

"Sam!" Henri cried in dismay as his American friend pushed his way through the mob, straight toward the center table. "Sam! Stop! I was just kidding!"

Sam plowed toward the table, unaware of the loud complaints of the people whose glasses he tipped, whose burning cigarettes he knocked aside. He halted abruptly behind the brunette, mute, suddenly unable to move. The girl in red looked up at him curiously.

"Billy," she said in French, "either the monsieur behind you wishes to say good evening or he plans to eat the roses from your hair."

Billy half turned, smiling in amusement, looked up, and froze so completely that only the fragments of light broadcast by her diamonds continued to move.

"Oh no! *No!* Sam, I was going to tell you," she gasped.

"*Who are you? Who the hell are you?*"

"*Sam* . . . . I was going to tell you as soon as the show . . ."

"What the hell are you doing here with these people? What the fuck is going on?"

"Sam, *please*." Billy stood up hastily. "They're listening to every word," she said with difficulty, speaking under the hubbub. "Go away, I beg you, go away, right now! I'll meet you at home in half an hour. For Christ's sake, *go!*"

Sam turned on his heel and fled the room, ran down the vast, endless staircase, and made his way out of the Opéra. He sat in a cab hearing nothing, seeing nothing but Billy's face, her diamonds, her bare shoulders. Nine months, he thought, over and over, counting them on his fingers, nine months, from April till now, nine whole months. At each second he felt his utter bewilderment changing into a pure rage. Whatever the explanation, he'd been played for a fool. A total, utter, complete fool.

Five minutes after Sam had entered his studio, Billy walked through the open door, wrapped in dark sable, her white satin skirts billowing wide over her silver slippers, every diamond still defiantly in place.

"What's your story?" he asked roughly, standing in the middle of the empty studio.

"Sam, you have to listen to me—"

"Let's get this straight right now. I don't have to do anything."

"I know how angry you must be," Billy said, as calmly as she could, "but, Sam, I swear to you that I've been planning for weeks to tell you right after the show, when you wouldn't be dreading the opening—"

"Thanks for your concern. I really appreciate that one hell of a lot. It's always great to be made into a stupid fucking fool on somebody's timetable."

"Does the name Billy Ikehorn mean anything to you?"

"Yeah. Even in Marin County the hicks have heard of Billy Ikehorn."

"I'm Billy Ikehorn. I'm also Honey Winthrop—I was Honey Winthrop for twenty years."

"Okay. Big fucking deal. So I know one true thing about you. That's nothing at all when everything else is a bunch of filthy, stinking lies."

"Sam, you've got it all wrong, the reason—"

"Bullshit! Why didn't you tell me who you were after the first weekend we spent together? Because you never trusted me enough, not for one minute, that's the reason, there's no other possible reason. *Nine months!* How long does it take you to trust somebody? The truth is that it wasn't safe for me to know about Billy Ikehorn and all her damn money. What the fuck did you think I'd do with it if I'd known? Steal it? Spend it? Extort it? Blackmail you?''

"You don't understand how it happened, you're not giving me a fair chance to explain—''

"You don't have to explain the only essential thing. You've never considered me an equal—I'm your fling with bohemia, your secret amusement, your roll in the gutter. The people you were with tonight —that's your crowd. Just look at you, look in the mirror and you'll know who you are! If this whole thing weren't so Stella Dallas, I could laugh. I didn't know women like you had pet sculptors—but live and learn. Just get the fuck out of here and don't come back.''

"Sam, I want to marry you. I love you.''

"What utter crap! How can you stand there and say a thing like that? Even if you meant it, and I'll never believe anything you say again, do you think I'd ever *consider* marrying a woman who didn't trust me enough to tell me who she really was for nine whole months? A woman who played all sorts of sickening games with me, games I can't begin to add up, a woman who didn't dare let me know that she had money and lied over and over about where she was at night? I don't know *one* true thing about you, the person you really are, if there is such a person. Do you think it matters if you call yourself Honey Winthrop or Billy Ikehorn when you never trusted me? How many other times have you done this in your life? How many other men have there been all along? You and your sacred independence—I fell for that line. Have you any idea how *insulted* I feel? How deeply, permanently insulted? I didn't know anyone could make me feel this way. I told you to leave. I'm telling you again. You disgust me. Get out.''

"I won't go! Not until you hear me out—''

Billy stood in the empty studio and listened to the sound of Sam's footsteps clattering down the stairs.

13

She wouldn't dream of spying on her best friend, Sasha told herself as she waited in a nondescript Second Avenue restaurant for Zach to join her for lunch, she was *protecting* her. Last Monday, when Gigi had left for her date with Zach, she had had such a pathetic, vulnerable, trusting look on her dear, innocent little face that, after intense soul-searching and deep thought, Sasha had come to the conclusion that close women friends owed each other a higher, finer loyalty than they owed to mere male members of their families.

If women had developed this kind of admirable solidarity in the past, they wouldn't be stuck with the cads who made up the vast majority of today's male population. Yes, even her darling Zach was a cad, a better kind of cad than most, but, to face facts, deeply spoiled, bad to the core, Sasha thought sadly. It wasn't his fault that he'd been idolized by womankind since the first time his diaper had needed changing. It wasn't his fault that women had been offering themselves to him freely for as long as she could remember. It was worse now than it had been during the years when high school and drama students had taken up yards of space loitering about under his feet for a mere look from him. As a director in the hothouse atmosphere of Off Broadway, he naturally inspired the most potent possible sexual fantasies. What actress didn't want to drag her director into bed? Nor was it Zach's fault that he had so often let himself be entrapped in a series of highly visible love affairs—what red-blooded director could help being aroused by his actresses? Off Broadway was poorly paid but, in compensation, it reeked of sex.

Now that Gigi had realized she didn't have the qualities it took to become a Great Slut, she must not be allowed to become contaminated by Zach. Gigi was too tender, her heart too open to illusions of love. She, Sasha, must take action in her capacity as the older and wiser roommate. As Gigi's duenna, her chaperone, her guardian, her designated barrier against involvement with the wrong kind of man, she had a clear-cut duty to warn off her brother, who, without realizing what he was doing, would take advantage of a sweet, good woman who hadn't been able to effectively put away her old-fashioned romantic ideals. A woman like Gigi.

Zach kissed Sasha lingeringly on the back of her neck and slid into the seat opposite her. "If you weren't my kid sister, I'd say you were a fine-looking figure of a woman."

"But I am, Zach," Sasha said as severely as she could, considering that she worshiped him.

"Then I have to say that you're outtasight gorgeous. Lip-smackin', finger-lickin' good. If Ma could see you now, she'd be a candidate for immediate cardiac care. When are you going to stop showing up for family parties done up like a postulant about to take her final vows?"

"Not till my wedding day, if I ever have one, given that I've never met a man worthy of me. The guys I know are just a bunch of housebroken puppies. I can't imagine marrying any of those brats."

Zach grinned and ignored Sasha's familiar complaint about the immaturity of the male sex. "Kid, Ma knows what you do for a living. Do you think she imagines you wear a body stocking under the undies?"

"She doesn't want to know any more than she has to. Trust me on that. Anyway, Zach, I didn't make this date to discuss my childish boyfriends or my voluntary nonentity status in the Orloff-Nevsky circle.''

"So why are we here? Aside from our normal incestuous urge to be together?" He smiled at her, a man in a billion. He had something rough and ready, something both demanding and kind, something clever and humorous in his dark eyes, that told every woman who looked into them that he was good for a laugh, a fuck, a stage direction, or a shoulder to cry on, or all four, if need be, although not necessarily simultaneously. Zach Nevsky was built like a longshoreman, wide and tall, with a muscular neck that carried his arrogantly set head in a way that made him dominate every group he was in. His nose was big and crooked and would have been the most noticeable feature in his reckless, high-cheekboned face if it hadn't been perfectly counterbalanced by his mouth, which was sardonic, generous and determined. At twenty-eight, Zach Nevsky was a stud with brains.

"Oh, Zach," Sasha sighed, looking at him wistfully, "don't rub it in.''

"Sasha, that little incestuous tickle is the only way for siblings to really appreciate each other as friends, given that they're natural enemies.''

"You and your theories," Sasha said gloomily.

"You sound like a girl with a problem. Tell Daddy.''

"I'm worried about Gigi."

"What about her?" He sounded alarmed, Sasha thought. A guilty conscience, no doubt. She was just in time.

"Zach, you know that Gigi isn't just another girl, don't you?"

"I've never met another Graziella Giovanna Orsini," he said stiffly.

"She told you her names!"

"I asked. Why, are they some kind of secret?"

"It took me months to pry them out of her. She thinks they're too formal.''

"I think they suit her," Zach said with an uneasy defensiveness in his voice. "So what's her problem?"

"She's a very sensitive person, Zach." As if he didn't know, Sasha thought. Men were such shits.

"Sensitive is good. Would you want her to be insensitive? To put on and take off sensitivity like a sweater?"

"Her feelings could easily be hurt."

"That's something you could say about almost every member of the human race. We could all easily be hurt, even you, even me. I'm highly sensitive too. Even Ma's feelings could be hurt. We've just never dared to find out."

"Zach, you're being deliberately dumb. You're trying to stop me from saying what I came here to say because you don't want to listen to it. Now pay attention! Gigi has a lousy father and a mother who went and died on her at a difficult time in her adolescence. Her step-mother seems to have disappeared into the depths or heights of Paris, we're not quite sure which. All Gigi gets from her is an occasional, wildly happy phone call. It sounds as if she'll never be back. So, except for me, she's more or less alone in the world and she's not all that happy with her job—so you and I have an obligation to treat Gigi very, very *carefully*. We have to be *gentle* with her. Am I getting through to you, Zach?"

"A lousy father, huh?"

"The real article. She hasn't heard a word from him in more than a year. Not even a postcard. She's just a babe in the woods. And I think she's developing a little crush on you, a kind of transference."

"No way," Zach said forcefully. "You're imagining things."

"You only say that because you've become hardened to women's finer emotions, Zach. You've had so many easy victories over the female population that you don't even notice it when a demure little person like Gigi starts taking every word from your mouth as if it were coming from an oracle. You have no idea how many times she quotes you to me as the ultimate authority."

"Yeah, sure," Zach said disbelievingly. "Authority on what exactly? Her job problems?"

"Basically, yes, but that's just a smokescreen for her craving to say your name. When you begin to have an irresistible urge to say another person's name, when you drag it into every conversation even when it's not about that person—well, even you have to know what that means. It's a dead giveaway, the absolute sign of a developing crush."

"What is this 'crush' business?" Zach said, deeply irritated. "A schoolgirl inclination? A mild preference? A little bit of pastel non-sense? It's not a word that I ever expected to hear from you, kid. A crush is essentially harmless and juvenile, like something out of *Little Women*."

"I was employing a shorthand way of saying that I think that these conversations you've been having with Gigi about her job are leading her to take you more seriously than you intend."

"Sasha, spit it out! Stop beating around the bush, don't give me long sentences that don't mean anything," Zach exploded.

"If you don't stop listening to her and giving her advice, she'll fall in love with you," Sasha said portentously.

"That's a laugh!"

"I know Gigi and I tell you it's happening. It may even be too late."

"Very funny," Zach said furiously. "This is all part of it, isn't it? This lunch is all part of the plot you two have hatched against me, isn't it?"

"What are you talking about?"

"Sure, Sasha, go ahead and play the innocent friend! She sent you here to say all this, didn't she? Or was it your idea? Which one of you figured out this fiendish twist? Which one of you decided that I wasn't suffering enough? Oh, I know how you two think, I know all about how men must suffer, but I never realized that it applied to your own brother! Don't you have a speck of family loyalty?"

"You . . . you're suffering? Did you say you were suffering?"

"Right, rub salt in my wounds. Stretch me on the rack and listen to my bones crack one by one, bury me in the sand and let the fire ants start in on my eyeballs, enjoy yourself! What did I ever do to you to merit such treatment, that's what I'd like to know!"

"Zach, shut up. I have to think," Sasha said frantically.

"There's nothing to think about. You and your little pal have won. Enjoy your victory, wallow in it, what the hell do I care? 'Men have died from time to time, and worms have eaten them, but not for love.' Well, I have news for Shakespeare, he didn't know for sure, did he? He didn't take a poll, he sure as hell never asked me."

"You're dying for love?" Sasha gasped.

"Not yet, not just yet, but it could go that way if I don't get hold of myself. Not that she hasn't told you all about it! I suppose the two of you sit around and laugh at me, two witches and their victim. Oh, she started out according to the book, all those timid questions, with a sort of quaver in her voice, making me feel so big and protective and important. And that look of hers, as if I knew the secret of the universe, did you train her to zap me with that look? And then asking to come to my place last Saturday night when she was troubled—troubled, honest to God, that was the word she used—and somehow or other, half an hour later I found myself tasting the best food I'd ever had in my life while she sat as far away from me as possible and looked so fucking beautiful in that fucking stage-prop apron that I couldn't even eat—and the whole time she's telling me about what happened with her and that Englishman back in California, the guy who broke her heart when she was a virgin, the lousy bastard who was going to sneak out on her without saying good-bye—she probably invented that whole story just to make me even more jealous than I am already. And then all those nights she told me she couldn't go out with me because she had other dates, but she won't tell me one single word about them, not a breath, not a hint—that's another thing you taught her, didn't you? All I can say is I'll get you for this, Sasha. One day I'll get you!"

"Tell me I'm not hearing what I'm hearing," Sasha implored the heavens.

"That's right, *gloat*! And not letting me lay a hand on her—that's your doing too. I recognize your touch, you ought to be put away. First get the sucker into a condition where he can't see straight, then deny him anything but a kiss on the tip of your wonderful pointed little nose or the top of your silky little tangerine head, and if he's very good, let him kiss your soft little cheek, but that's it! Not another inch! And tell him it's because you're afraid that you might get too fond of him—fond!—if he kissed your lips . . . *lips,* she actually stopped at the lips! Yeah, that was the killer, all right. And what the fuck is so terrible about fond? That blew me out of the water. I've never heard that in my whole life—where do you come up with these tricks? Do you find it in Jane Austen? Henry James? The *Kama Sutra*?"

"Jesus!"

"He never said anything about fond. Sasha, I know your principles, and idiot that I am, I never questioned them, but I don't think that an innocent girl, who must have been a fairly decent human being before she met you, should have been allowed to be contaminated by your sick, manipulative, man-hating ideas. And get that stricken look off your face. You brought this on me all by yourself, so spare me the fake consternation."

"Oh, Zach! Will you ever forgive me?"

"Sure, in a hundred thousand light-years or when I get my hands on Gigi and do all the things I'm dying to do to her, whichever comes sooner. Now eat your lunch, choke on it. I'm going back to the theater.''

Sasha looked blankly at her plate, a tear in each eye. Poor Zach, poor darling, sweet, beloved Zach. Slowly, very slowly, a reluctant smile of triumph spread over her face. Everything Gigi had accomplished she owed to her. Gigi hadn't gone about it the way she would have herself, but nevertheless . . . a win was a win. Poor Zach. Men *must* suffer. It was so good for them.

"You know, I think the first Mormons were on to a good thing," Gigi said to Sasha as she surveyed an assortment of the best of her lingerie trove. She had arranged them carefully, piece by piece, on tissue paper that she'd used to cover their couch.

"You do?" This was not the sort of comment Sasha would normally dignify with her whole attention, but she had a new respect for Gigi. Her friend was playing a deep game with Zach, and although Sasha had resolved not to ask her a single direct question, anything Gigi said might be taken as a clue to her masterful and still mysterious plan of attack.

"You know how their wives always look so beatific and blissed-out in photographs—didn't you see that picture in the papers this morning of that old Mormon who got caught with a dozen wives, even though they're not supposed to do that anymore?"

"What about it?"

"It struck me that they looked more peaceful than any group of women I've seen in years. Then it hit me—Kappa Kappa Mormon! Twelve women and one guy, that's about the right proportion for happiness."

"Gigi, you know how Sasha Nevsky feels—three guys and one girl is the right proportion."

"But has it made you all that happy? You keep complaining that they're all so inexperienced, so un-grown-up, immature, even the best of them. Have you thought about taking your talents to a retirement community? Try to unthink, Sasha, and then *rethink*. Bring the cells of your great brain to bear on this setup. Eleven other women you really like, eleven women you have fun with, eleven women you can talk to the way you can *never* talk to a man—and then you'd have your kids running around freely with a huge bunch of half brothers and sisters, so they'd be taken care of better than any woman could do by herself, and there'd be almost no housework because you've got twelve pairs of hands to do it. On the downside, you'd probably only get laid a few times a month, but so what? Sex is overrated, admit it, and you'd have no reason to be jealous, because the other wives wouldn't get more than you.''

''Hmmm. I don't know. I reserve my judgment on sex, but I bet there'd have to be at least one wife everyone hates,'' Sasha said thoughtfully.

''And the one that everybody else wants to be like—the homecoming queen combined with Miss Congeniality—but she'd be so nice you couldn't envy her.'' Gigi sat cross-legged on the floor, clasping a wide-sleeved bed jacket made of lavender georgette crepe trimmed with cream-colored Margot lace encrusted with French rosebuds that she had destined for Dolly's Christmas present.

''But what about your individuality? You'd lose it, wouldn't you, in the mob?''

''Why? Is having exclusive rights on some man what makes you an individual? You'd be exactly, precisely the same person you are, except that you'd know what the future holds, you'd have no anxiety about men and their wicked wicked ways, no free-floating depression, no possible fear of loneliness, no getting older except with a whole gang who are getting older at the same rate—Sasha, it's ideal! You could stop living a life based on your relationship with men and just live!'' Gigi spoke with such ringing, passionate conviction that Sasha looked at her in alarm.

''You make a convincing case. Do I have some time to think about it before I join?''

''Take as much as you want,'' Gigi said generously. ''It's illegal anyway, but I love the idea.''

Yes, Sasha thought, she could see why being a Mormon wife would appeal to Gigi. Any girl who was pursuing Zach with Gigi's breathtaking success and brilliant dissimulations must have heard about all the broken hearts he'd caused, all the dramas of jealousy. Right now Gigi had the upper hand, even if she didn't know it, but with Zach's history she must be seriously worried about keeping him once she'd got him. Kappa Kappa Mormon, with Zach as the head of the family, might seem like the solution. Maybe it *was* the solution?

''If I don't get my Christmas presents all settled today, I'm not giving any," Gigi said. "I think this is just perfect for Billy." She put down the bed jacket and held up a short, all-but-transparent wisp of delicate black lace hanging from tiny black satin straps, and danced it in front of Sasha's eyes.

"It was made in the early 1920s—they called this 'camiknickers.' See, it's a chemise and wide-leg panties all in one. You'd wear a black garter belt and black silk stockings with it. Hasn't it got that French feeling? I've written the card. Want to hear it?"

"Sure," Sasha said enviously. She and Billy were about the same size, and those camiknickers would be perfect for her.

" 'Where Was She Going?'—that's the title," Gigi started, and began to read:

Her name was Nora. Yes, Nora, such a simple, good name. Complicated, suspicious men—who should have known better, but men are such fools, aren't they?—trusted her because of it. They put their faith in her winsome, shy smile and her huge, guileless eyes and her hesitant blushes, and laid their hearts in her hands. But how could they guess that Nora wore black lace camiknickers under her prim, high-necked blouses and her proper pleated skirts? Nora should have been locked up in a tower and the key thrown away. Why? Because after one of her lovers fell into that deep sleep of total satisfaction that only a night with Nora could give, she slipped out of bed and went dancing in nothing but her camiknickers and a pair of tiny golden shoes, dancing in places the men who loved her didn't dream existed, dancing with men she'd never see again, men who would ship out in the morning still thinking of her, men who could never, ever forget her, dancing until the moon had long set and the sun was about to rise. (Of course, Nora wore a fur cape over the camiknickers so she wouldn't shock the taxi drivers.) Nora was always back in bed before her lover woke up— and she had to be awakened with a kiss. With so many kisses. Oh yes, Nora was too much for any one man, Nora of the dancing feet and the light, faithless, beautiful great heart.

"Gigi!" Sasha burst into tears. "Gigi, you *can't* give that to Billy. You know you meant it for me! Say you did, say you just wanted to see if I liked it!"

"Oh, Sasha, I didn't mean to make you cry! Of course it's for you! It's pure you, not Billy at all. But it isn't even wrapped and I haven't done the drawing."

"You can do all that later," Sasha sniffed, "just let me try it on."

She came back in two minutes, a Nora even Gigi hadn't imagined, swept Gigi into her arms and twirled the two of them around the living room in waltz time.

"It's divine on you," Gigi sighed in satisfaction, when Sasha finally let her go. She'd searched high and low for something that Sasha, who wore lingerie all day long, would respond to. "Now all you need is the fur cape, and you're set for a long night."

"What would my never-jealous Mormon sisters-in-law think about this? Trouble in Mormon paradise, Gigi, that's what it would be. Unless you could find one for everybody."

"It's one of a kind, all my things are."

"What are you actually giving Billy?"

"This." Gigi unfolded a heap of heavy old-gold satin and flung it over her sweater and jeans. It was much too long for her, even without the short train that puddled at her feet. From her shoulders to well below her waist, the satin was covered with a floaty layer of creamy lace that also formed the wide, scalloped sleeves. The lace was attached to the satin here and there by knots of Nattier-blue velvet bows.

"What on earth is that?"

"It's the finest, rarest thing I have. A tea gown actually—in the early 1900s, women wore things like this when they had their intimate friends over for tea. You don't think it's a bit much, do you?"

"It's perfect for Billy. Have you written the card?"

"Not yet. I have to think of just the right kind of thing—it's what I imagine Billy wearing in her new place in Paris, on a winter afternoon like today, pouring tea for direct descendants of the characters who inspired the characters in Proust—or on a houseboat in Kashmir—or maybe in Scotland, one afternoon when it's too rainy to go out grouse shooting . . ."

"Billy doesn't shoot grouse."

"Really, Sasha, the only trouble with you is you're too literal-minded. It's for any place and any time when you want to be particularly glamorous and swoopy. And these pajamas are for Jessica. They're too small for me, so they should be just right for her," Gigi added, shaking out two pieces of palest pink muslin, trimmed at the neck and sleeves and at the bottom of the mid-calf pantlegs in deep tiers of Pierrot-like ruffles. "It's French, from the 1920s . . . . doesn't it look like her?"

"Is it sexy enough?" Sasha sounded dubious as she preened in her black lace.

"Lingerie doesn't always have to be sexy. This is adorable, and that's what Jessica is. And this is for Emily Gatherum,'' Gigi said, showing Sasha an almost conical black bra with holes that allowed the nipples to protrude.

"You wouldn't!"

"No, actually it's for me. Courtesy of Frederick's of Hollywood, 1960. Emily wouldn't understand it."

"What are you going to do with it?"

"Wouldn't you like to know, Miss Nevsky? It was known as 'the courtesan's battle dress'—and don't even bother to try to get it away from me, either. Get that covetous look out of your eye. I need it more than you do. Now go change and give me back your Christmas present so I can finish the card and wrap it. I have these other cards to do for Dolly and Billy and Jessica and Mazie, and there's that wonderful, chocolate-colored, silk-and-chiffon 1930s slip for Josie Speilberg, the only woman I know who still wears a full slip, and all these other linen and lace petticoats and chemises for Emily and my friends at Voyage to Bountiful—oh, how can I finish writing the cards this afternoon? I shouldn't have let you distract me. Look how late it is."

"Gigi, I'll do all the gift wrapping for you—you know I do great wrapping—if you let me take everything—cards and all—to the office to show the other models. Please? They'd only be out of the house for a day, and Christmas isn't for weeks. I'd guard them carefully."

"Do you really think they'd be interested?" Gigi asked, tempted.

"No question. Good lingerie models need more flesh than other models—we have to be plush and luxuriant and ripe, or things would just hang on us—and sometimes, especially around Christmas, we all get depressed, thinking we're not lean and sinewy or sylphlike enough. Yes, even Sasha Nevsky has had her doubts. It would help so much if they knew what women used to wear before panty hose came along."

"All right . . . but just for one day. And you can't take my bra. I may be needing it."

"They've all seen bras like that, Gigi. It's still being made . . . exactly the same style, and half the women in Des Moines have one at home," Sasha said gently. "It's called the 'Saturday Night Special.' "

"It's a well-known phenomenon, the Christmas Blues, I read all about it in Dear Abby, there's nothing wrong with us for feeling this way, there would almost be something wrong if we didn't," Dawn Levine said in an unconvincing voice, tying the belt of the cotton robe she wore in the models' dressing room at Herman Brothers. "But Dear Abby didn't say anything about why I've gained two whole revolting pounds around my waist, with Christmas still weeks away. Maybe Ann Landers will write something about psychological Christmas weight gain . . . couldn't it be like a false pregnancy?" Dawn spoke without conviction, her blond hair falling to her shoulders in bright sheaves, her straight bangs almost in her doleful Irish blue eyes.

"Bah, humbug, and don't try to cop a plea, baby," Sally Smart replied. "If you've gained two pounds, and I can see from here that you have, it's because you ate eight thousand calories of ugly fat that you didn't metabolize—that's the way my mother explains it to me. She says it's her maternal duty to tell me the things other people will be too kind to say." Sally pushed the strands of her brown pageboy behind her ears and wrinkled her freckled nose at Dawn. "Tell that to Dear Abby," Sally advised glumly, "and let her weasel out of it. Let her try to make you believe you're just retaining water, but don't ask me to go along with your pathetic self-delusion."

"Gee, thanks, Sally, you've made me feel a hell of a lot better," Dawn said resentfully. "You deserve your mother, is all I can say. And she deserves an evil daughter like you. Has she told you that the tiny pimple on your chin is getting bigger by the minute and will probably be fully ripe for Christmas Eve, but it doesn't matter since you don't have a date that night anyway? Or for New Year's Eve, for that matter?"

" 'At Christmas play and make good cheer, for Christmas comes but once a year,' didn't either of you two meanies ever learn that jingle in school?" inquired Rosa Modena, the third of the four lingerie models, as she inspected her legs with a harried, horrified look. "I'm getting varicose veins," she told them with breathless conviction. "Oh, Good Lord in Heaven, there goes my career! Quick, one of you, promise me that twenty-two is too young for varicose veins!"

"Not necessarily," Sally assured her. "They could happen anytime. And shut up about good cheer, unless you're willing to shop for the presents I have to find for my sisters' kids, all nine of them, the little fuckers."

"I thought you were crazy about them," Dawn protested.

"Not at Christmas I'm not. The kids get the good presents, they get the excitement of waiting for the big day, they love to sing those stupid carols, and all of us grownups have to go along because we don't have the guts not to. And if you think the pimple on my chin is getting bigger, you should see the one on my ass.''

"If Sasha doesn't get back with our sandwiches pretty soon, I'm going to cry,'' Rosa announced loudly. "I hate Christmas, I hate my legs, I hate myself, I hate my boyfriend, and I particularly hate the two of you!''

"I see I'm just in time,'' Sasha said, rushing into the models' dressing room with the cardboard box of sandwiches that it had been her turn to pick up for their lunch today. "Another minute, and three perfectly decent girls who normally act like ladies would be tearing each other's hair out. Here, eat, for God's sake, and hush that nasty Christmas talk, pretend it's the Fourth of July. Your magnificent Sasha Nevsky, thoughtful as ever, has brought something to cheer you up and get you through the day.''

Sasha had an expectant light in her eyes, the angle of her Gibson Girl nose was more witty than usual, her smile was full of anticipation, and the modified pompadour in which she had arranged her dark hair rose with authority.

While Sally, Rosa and Dawn were eating hungrily, she took from their hiding place in the closet the two small suitcases in which she'd brought Gigi's things that morning. As soon as they'd finished their hasty lunch, she opened the suitcases and removed, one by one, the Christmas presents Gigi had found for her friends. She held up each piece of old lingerie, told them what it was, and then passed it around for them to examine. They handled the old garments reverently, exclaiming over the feel of the fabrics, for everything they wore or modeled was made from cotton or nylon, and none of them had ever owned hand-made lingerie, nor were they familiar with the old styles.

As Sasha read the words of each of Gigi's cards out loud, she saw the expressions of discontent and petulance and worry dissolve from the faces of her co-workers, to be replaced by the starry-eyed, all-but-trancelike enchantment of children listening to a magical story for the first time.

"Could . . . I just . . . ?'' Sharp-tongued Sally touched the satin of the tea gown destined for Billy with the tips of her fingers, and pleaded with her eyes for a chance to put it on.

"Be especially careful,'' Sasha warned her, unable to resist Sally's look, particularly since she knew how gently each of the girls had been trained to handle the original samples they wore in the showroom. Tall Sally took off her robe and slowly arranged the tea gown around her shoulders, slipping her arms into the lace sleeves and taking a few steps so that the train could fan out behind her.

"My God," she breathed, "I feel . . . oh, I can't even say how I feel . . . certainly not like mean, horrid old me. Oh, Sasha, do I ever have to take it off?"

"Eventually, I'm afraid."

"I'm going to read the card again, myself," Sally said, striking a regal pose. "Listen, all of you.

She came from an ancient British family and she was christened Mary-Jane Georgina Charlotte Alberta but she insisted on being called Georgie. Her parents brought her up strictly, because she was so frighteningly beautiful . . . but her riding teacher and her piano professor fought a duel over her before she was fifteen. The Aga Khan gave her winning tips on long shots for the Thousand Guineas at Newmarket, the heir to a dukedom offered her his heart, his hand and his coronet, a great banker gave her a rope of pink pearls that had taken ten years to collect. But Georgie cared nothing for money or jewels or rich and titled men—she wanted true love and she found it at seventeen with the most charming man in London . . . a violinist at the Café de Paris. Her poor parents never recovered! She lost true love at eighteen and found it again at nineteen. In fact, Georgie found true love more than thirty times in her life, and each time was more blissfully unexpected than the last. In Venice she found it with a gondolier, in Argentina with a professional tango dancer, in Grenada with a gypsy, in New York with a welterweight and in Hollywood with a screenwriter. (Even Georgie's greatest admirers had trouble understanding that!) Fortunately, Georgie could afford any amount of true love for she had invented and patented mascara when she was eighteen and a half, during a few idle weeks between the jockey and the police inspector. Every afternoon, cozily wrapped in her favorite tea gown, Georgie spent a long hour over tea and tiny sandwiches. The tea tray was brought to her bedroom by the butler. Did anyone ever notice how often Georgie changed her butlers? Or how young and handsome they all were? When a woman performs a public service like inventing mascara, she is entitled to satisfy all *her fancies. That's what Georgie thought, and that's what Georgie did. And did and did. And the butlers did it too. Lucky Georgie!*

"I'm going to cultivate Georgie's attitude toward life," Sally said, her voice fairly singing as she came to the end of the card. "She knew what was really important. Her butlers couldn't complain either."

"She could never have achieved all that with a name like Mary-Jane," Dawn said thoughtfully, as she eyed the pink Pierrot-ruffled pajamas with longing. While Sally had been reading, Rosa had been lovingly clutching a hemstitched white crepe de chine petticoat and matching camisole, both decorated with bows of white satin ribbon, destined for Emily Gatherum.

"Oh, go on all of you and try everything on," Sasha cried, exasperated at herself for having imagined that she could just show and tell while her friends were visibly aching to put on the lingerie. "Try everything on. *Carefully.* Just give me back the ruffled PJs—they're too small for any of us."

Sasha slipped into her own black lace camiknickers as the others were dressing, all of them deliberately holding back the quick movements of their experienced hands so that they could put on the unfamiliar lingerie with caution. They walked about, getting the feel of the garments, and soon they pranced, paraded and capered, admiring themselves and each other with delighted, flushed faces.

In front of the full-length mirrors, four women with glorious bodies; each felt that she had slipped through a little hole in the fabric of time and seen herself as she might have been in another, far more romantic and provocative life, each of them transformed by the aura of belonging within the circle of an endlessly repeatable moment. Gigi's cards had given them the clues they needed to feel that each garment wasn't merely an example of antique lingerie but a tangible connection to a piquant, attainable dream, sealed with a promise of timelessness, a dream in which they could so easily imagine themselves starring. They felt sensuously alert to another world, in a graceful and right relationship to an erotic sensitivity they hadn't known before.

There was a knock on the door. "You ladies decent?" Mr. Jimmy called.

Rosa, Dawn and Sally froze and looked at Sasha in consternation, as if they'd been caught playing dress-up in the attic.

"Stop it, all of you," Sasha scolded. "It's still our lunch hour, and anyway, he's such a darling, let's give him a treat. Come on in, Mr. Jimmy," she called. "We're no less decent than we usually are."

"In a half hour there'll be some buyers from Higbee's and . . . ."

what's going on here?" Mr. Jimmy asked, looking around in amazement. He had never seen his girls with such dreamy, unbusinesslike, happy faces.

"I'm Nora," Sasha said, stepping forward and kissing him on his forehead, "and tonight you and I have a late date—we're going to dance and dance till dawn."

"I'm Georgie," Sally said, "and I have the feeling that you just may get the job as my new butler."

"I'm Lola-Antoinette," Rosa said, wearing Sasha's white satin pajamas. "And I want to thank you for the emeralds . . . you really shouldn't have . . . but since you did . . . ." She too kissed him on his forehead.

"Hey, come on," Mr. Jimmy grinned, "are you girls trying to put me out of business? Say, where'd you find these things anyway? I can almost remember . . . . well, never mind what I can almost remember, I couldn't be that old."

"My roommate, Gigi, collects antique lingerie," Sasha explained. "She's giving these as Christmas presents. I brought them in to show everybody . . . . oh, and the cards, you've got to read the cards and look at the sketches to understand the concept." She handed him Nora's card and he sat down and read it through.

"We may be dancing tonight, Nora, but I'm not shipping out tomorrow," Mr. Jimmy said, laughing. "Let's see your card, Sally." He read it quickly and gave her the smile that had sold five million girdles. "The new butler, huh? Well, thanks for the thought, Georgie. I'll have to take it up with my accountant."

"Don't worry, Mr. Jimmy," Sally cooed. "Georgie's butlers didn't stay long . . . as I see it, her only problem was she wore out her help."

"Read mine," Rosa and Dawn both clamored together, waving their cards.

"I wish I could, but I came in to tell you that we've got half a dozen buyers coming in who didn't order enough for Christmas even though I warned them, so battle stations, girls, get ready to show the holiday line again. Hey, Sasha, do you think you could get me together with your friend? I'd like to know a little more about this—and you come too, of course."

"I'll work it out," Sasha said, hearing a tone of interest in Mr. Jimmy's benevolent voice that made the hair stand up on the back of her neck.

"Let's do it as soon as we can. I gather that Nora and Georgie went in for immediate gratification, and so do I."

"Aye, aye, Captain."

"Have you done a lot of writing, Gigi?" Mr. Jimmy asked after he had finished ordering for the three of them in the northern Italian restaurant that he had suggested for dinner.

"No, nothing, not unless you count those cards. Sasha probably told you that I'm in the catering business . . . . I'm a food person, basically. I started to get interested in antique lingerie a few years ago, but until Sasha's last birthday I'd never given anyone a piece of my collection—I thought that the white satin pajamas looked like something only Sasha deserved to have. She inspired my first card and my first little drawing."

"That would be Lola-Antoinette, the lady to whom I generously gave the emeralds—the outfit Rosa was wearing?"

"And it looked just right on her, although we're completely different types," Sasha said.

"About how long does it take you to write a card like that?" Mr. Jimmy inquired curiously.

"It depends," Gigi said. "Sometimes I get the idea right away and sometimes I have to think for a while, but once I get going, about half an hour, if it's a long one."

"You did at least six or seven in one afternoon just the other day," Sasha reminded her. "Maybe more."

"Christmas pressure," Gigi said, shrugging modestly. She liked Mr. Jimmy just as much as Sasha had assured her she would. He had the most honest red face she'd ever seen, and an adorable fringe of white hair. He was about her height except that he probably weighed at least a hundred and fifty pounds more than she did. If he had on a red velvet suit he could go to work as the fattest, most cherubic Santa in the bell-ringing business in a second, Gigi thought, watching him drink his second martini. Even his nose had the right red lines in it.

"Gigi . . ." Mr. Jimmy turned to her abruptly. "This is a business dinner and polite people aren't supposed to get to the business part until they've finished their main course, but to hell with that—I have a proposition to make to you."

"About my antique lingerie?"

"Yes, but much more than that. If I'd seen your old things just sitting on a shelf somewhere, I wouldn't have had this idea, but the way Sasha and the girls reacted to them and the cards you wrote came together in my head the other afternoon. I've been looking around for a way to increase our share of the lingerie market. Competition's getting rougher all the time, everybody's ads are getting better and better, but Herman Brothers, big as we are, hasn't been particularly innovative lately. I've been giving it a lot of thought, and you got me thinking along new lines. What if I found a whole bunch of antique lingerie items that could be expertly reproduced to look like the real thing, sized them all the way up the range from four to fourteen, and created an entirely new collection, using advertising that would employ your cards as copy and your drawings as the illustrations? How does that strike you?"

"But . . . but . . . I don't know anything about advertising," Gigi gulped.

"I do, believe me, it's not a sacred mystery. All you'd have to do is write the cards and do the drawings and—"

"Mr. Jimmy, hold on here. Gigi looks through hundreds of garments in dozens of little stores before she finds one that she buys," Sasha interrupted. "She's emotionally involved in them, they speak to her. She couldn't write about lingerie she didn't have a personal feeling for."

"She wouldn't have to. I'd send Gigi out in style with a couple of people to help her and she could find the lingerie herself, or I could send scouts out all over the country to buy exceptional pieces and Gigi could decide which ones she responded to. The collection would always be Gigi's choice . . . she's got the touch. I'd be the one to decide if her choices were too impractical to be reproduced at a price, but basically we'd get together on it and have a meeting of minds, and you, Sasha, could referee the whole process."

"Wait a minute, Mr. Jimmy," Gigi protested, "you keep talking about 'reproducing' them. The whole point to my lingerie is that everything's unique, one of a kind, the real thing."

"Well, they couldn't be that, Gigi," he said resolutely. "Not in a huge business like Herman Brothers. There's no getting around the fact that they'd be reproductions, but look at it this way—they'd be the best reproductions you could ever hope to find, using only natural fibers, real silks, real laces and so on. If they didn't look and feel like the real thing, they wouldn't sell. I'm thinking about a very high-end and exclusive line of garments, for carefully selected stores. The reproductions wouldn't have anything cheap about them, including their price, but we'd be spreading the romance of wearing a piece of almost-antique lingerie to thousands of women who couldn't have it otherwise, because they don't know where to find these items. In fact, they don't even know they want them yet. But they will, they will!"

"Hmmm." Gigi felt torn between his enthusiasm and her reluctance to broadcast something that had been her private, intimate pleasure, something she shared only with a few close friends in mind. " 'Almost-antique'—did you just invent that?"

"I must have," he said proudly. "Not bad, is it?"

"But, excuse me, Mr. Jimmy, is it honest to call something brand-new an almost-antique?"

"Gigi, I think you're being a little overscrupulous here," Sasha broke in. "Nothing is legally antique until it's over a hundred years old. Your lingerie is mostly about sixty years old, maximum eighty. You don't call it 'secondhand underwear,' do you? But that's what it is." Couldn't Gigi hear opportunity when it came knocking at the door? she thought, her mouth watering at the thought of a new line.

"Girls, girls, let's not split hairs, we're getting away from my idea," Mr. Jimmy said expansively. "I couldn't do it without Gigi's choice of lingerie, without her words and drawings. I was thinking of starting small, a collection containing about thirty items. And if the buyers don't go for it, which, frankly, would surprise me, there's no risk, because I'll be putting up all the money to get this thing off the ground."

"Speaking of which . . ." Sasha said meaningfully, dipping her tongue in her sherry like a bear after honey.

"Speaking of which, ladies, Gigi will get a piece of the profit on every piece we sell, but not until I know if this is going to be a success or not."

"I was thinking of another system," Sasha said smoothly, "an advance against royalties, like they have in the book business. Since Gigi'd be picking the lingerie, writing the copy and doing the drawings, she'd be acting in the capacity of editor, author and illustrator. She should get a certain amount when she agrees to put in the time to do this for you, she should get another amount when she's completed all the work so that you're ready to start manufacturing. That way, if you don't make a profit, God forbid, she'd still be paid back fairly for all her hard work. Otherwise she's done it all for nothing. After all, Mr. Jimmy, thirty cards! And drawings! Thirty new women to invent!"

"Interesting approach," Mr. Jimmy grumbled. "But would it make me a gentleman book publisher instead of a garmento?"

Listening intently, Gigi realized that, scruples about authenticity aside, she was excited by Mr. Jimmy's idea. It was pure fun for her to search for lingerie and create cards, but she'd never realized there was a way to make money from it. She cleared her throat.

"My literary agent, Miss Nevsky, has found a solution that I find workable," Gigi announced, sounding exactly like Emily Gatherum at her most authoritative. "Of course, she'll have to negotiate the terms of the advance against royalties with you, Mr. Jimmy, while I'm not present, for which she'll receive the customary agent's fee. The creative person shouldn't have anything to do with the business side. It's bruising to the psyche. Just thinking about it makes me queasy."

"Gigi's the sensitive, fragile one of the two of us, Mr. Jimmy," Sasha said. "I'm the ruthless agent. *Nothing* makes me feel queasy. So shall we discuss the advance tomorrow, in your office? I see our food coming, and I never like to eat lobster Fra Diavolo and talk money at the same time."

14

$\mathcal{M}$ adame Ikehorn?'' Mademoiselle Hélène, the *gouvernante* of the second floor at the Ritz, tapped lightly at Billy's bedroom door for the fourth time that morning. Yesterday the chambermaids had reported that there were Do Not Disturb signs on all of the doors to Billy's suite and they had been unable to make up the room. This in itself was not remarkable—privacy might be highly desirable for such a length of time—but on the other hand such lengthy repose was invariably accompanied by several calls to room service. However, Mademoiselle Hélène had checked with room service and they had filled no orders from the suite since teatime the day before yesterday. The concierge, when she questioned him, answered that Madame Ikehorn had returned from the opera before midnight on Thursday and had not left the hotel since. That meant, Mademoiselle Hélène calculated, that her most curiously erratic guest had remained in her room now for two nights and one full day, as well as this entire morning, without ordering anything to eat, or being seen by any of the staff.

Madame Ikehorn had been at the Ritz for so long, and they were all so accustomed to the irregular hours at which she came and went, that until now her reclusion had been taken to be just another of her varied caprices. Today, however, measures must be taken.

The young woman in her smart black suit tapped once more and then inserted the passkey in the lock. The door was chained shut on the inside.

"Madame Ikehorn," she called through the small opening, "are you all right? Can you hear me? It's Mademoiselle Hélène."

"Go away and leave me alone." Billy's voice came from the bed. The room was totally dark, the shutters closed and the curtains pulled, although it was almost noon in Paris.

"Madame, are you ill? I'll have a doctor come immediately."

"I'm fine. Just leave me alone."

"But, Madame, you have had nothing to eat for almost two days."

"I'm not hungry."

"But, Madame—"

"Stop bothering me! What do I have to do to get some peace and quiet around here?"

The *gouvernante* closed the door softly. At least Madame Ikehorn was alive. She hadn't slipped in the tub and drowned; she hadn't fallen on a wet tile floor, hit her head and bled to death; she wasn't lying unconscious in her bed. For the moment Mademoiselle Hélène's mind was eased, but she was determined to keep a close watch on the situation as she gave her orders to the floor staff. They were to watch the suite and let her know immediately when anyone came out or entered. No one should be allowed to go hungry long at the Ritz in Paris, and even worse, be subjected to sleeping on the same sheets for two nights in a row.

Lying in a tight ball under the frail armor of bedclothes that was her only protection from reality, Billy tried to go back to sleep without success. When she'd returned from Sam's studio she'd taken a massive combination of tranquilizers and sleeping pills to take the edge off her utter anguish. She'd ranted and raved out loud at the walls, still trying to explain to Sam—it was all so monstrously unfair, so bitterly unjust!—and at the same time she'd felt as incredulously abandoned as if Sam had suddenly died in her arms. She'd ached for a single word of understanding as she feverishly paced back and forth through the rooms of her suite, as if one or another room would make any difference to her dry-eyed, impotent despair, offer any comfort, any sign that there was still hope. Finally the pills had started to take effect and she'd rolled into bed for an endless night of hideous, half-awake, fragmented sleep during which she'd kept seeing the look on his face as Sam told her that she disgusted him.

Now, Billy realized, as sleep resisted her completely, she'd worked herself into a state of horrifying clearheadedness. Her mind felt like a bare plain, scoured by wind and rain and a blazing sun, a plain on which no grass could possibly be expected to grow. She seemed to live both on and somehow *in* that plain, where only one thing was absolute: in the matter of men and money she was damned.

Her grief was not a storm of blind emotion. She would have welcomed hours of tears if they had helped to give her some relief, but tears wouldn't come. Something held her mind clamped hard to the facts that had brought her to this place in her life. Obsessively, without forgetting a detail, Billy had been reliving her nine months with Sam and her year with Vito, trying to turn over and examine every detail of her relationships with them. When she separated their very different personalities and considered only the facts, the fatal truth was plain. She was a rich woman, and no man could manage to love a rich woman.

She had stopped being human to Sam the moment he learned she was rich. He had blocked her out, the woman he knew, at that second, or he couldn't have been so uncharacteristically angry, so unkind, so unwilling to even listen. He could never have said that she disgusted him—Sam, whom she had known in such direct passion and the sweet intimacy of love—if she hadn't become *another*, transformed instantly because of wealth. He had refused to acknowledge her, stamped on all the honest emotion she had for him, because he felt insulted, suspected, not trusted. His pride hadn't survived that blow, and his pride was more important than his love.

Vito had resented her money from the beginning. He'd never stopped believing that it gave her an upper hand, a power he wouldn't be able to fight. All her actions had been judged against that power. And he too had turned against her. Had he ever seen her as a plain, unadorned female who loved him? The aura of riches, from which she'd tried to protect Sam, had been inescapable.

Vito had accused her of being an imperious queen bee. Sam had accused her of not considering him an equal. Would they have believed these things of her if it weren't for the money?

Even if she knew the answer, even if she knew exactly what a Billy Ikehorn was like without money, she could never *be* that person to anyone but Jessica and Gigi and Dolly. Only another woman could think of her as a human being like herself. They shared being a woman with her, they knew that no amount of money could change that essentially vulnerable condition. A woman with money has as great a need for love as any other woman. Why couldn't a man see that?

Billy burrowed into her wrinkled heap of pillows and faced the fact that there was no satisfactory solution for a woman with her kind of problem—the kind of problem a hundred women out of a hundred probably believed that they'd like to have, the kind of problem for which many women would trade their own lives without a second thought. She had so much. What right *did* she have to want more? She should give the whole bloody, impossible search up once and for all, she should train herself not to hope for love. She should expect nothing more from any man than she would from a trip to a foreign country: novelty, new food, new scenery, new customs, the sound of a new language. Then when she'd had enough, she would be able to return home untroubled at heart, as she had intended to from the start. That way she couldn't be hurt. Lowered expectations—wasn't that what they called it? Or just reality?

A sound of stealthy voices came from behind her bedroom door. It must be Mademoiselle Hélène, Billy thought, trying to get into her room. She'd put nothing past the woman, including taking the door off its hinges, to make sure her charges were all right. God damn it to hell! Was nothing sacred in the Ritz?

She jumped out of bed and staggered angrily to the door in the darkness, listening to hear what they were up to outside.

"I bet it's a hangover." Billy recognized the voice of one of the chambermaids.

"Or else she's on a binge. There's enough in the minibar to keep you drunk for days," the second chambermaid calculated.

Billy hastily retreated to her bed and looked at the large clock on the wall. It said either noon or midnight. The room was too dark to give her a clue. She went swiftly to a window and tugged impatiently on the heaviest of the three layers of curtains that covered every Ritz window, a vast expanse of green brocade thickly lined and interlined, made more weighty by its four rows of braid in four contrasting shades of green and its trim of fat puffs of green and rose ball-fringe. The curtains parted enough for her to reach the elaborate, rose-colored silk undercurtains. She opened them and peered through the last layer of gauze curtains, outside of which were tightly closed, white-painted metal shutters that rose and fell at the touch of a button on the wall by the window. She pressed the button and immediately streaks of daylight entered the room. Noon. Thank God, Billy thought as she went to the phone to order a large breakfast. She called housekeeping to make up her room, unbolted her doors, and disappeared into the bathroom for a long shower. She washed and dried her hair, brushing it carelessly back from her face, and quickly, automatically put on her makeup, forcing herself through these motions out of an instinct of self-preservation.

When she emerged, still in her pink toweling robe, Billy found the curtains of every window in her suite pulled back, her bed made, vases of fresh white roses standing on every table and bureau, and her covered tray waiting with a copy of the *International Herald Tribune*. Startled, Billy discovered that it was Saturday. No wonder she felt so dizzy and so hungry. She must have taken more pills than she'd meant to—but what suspicious minds those chambermaids had! Too many years at their trade, no doubt, had made them expect the worst. She ate everything on her tray and called down for more croissants and coffee. While she was waiting she looked at the sunlight falling on the floor, that rare, fragile, precious light that sometimes comes to Paris in the winter, reminding Parisians that their city is on the same latitude as Helsinki. Billy's mind floated away from herself and her pain, and with a start she remembered that the opening of Sam's show had taken place the night before. In an instant she found herself on the phone with a concierge.

"Monsieur Georges, could you do me a favor, please? I'd like you to call the Templon Gallery on the Rue Beaubourg and ask if any of the pieces of sculpture from yesterday's opening were sold. Please don't say who you are."

She hung up to await his return call. Surely, after Adam and Eve, God had invented the Ritz concierge.

The phone buzzed within minutes. "Oh no! Five pieces! Yes, yes, Monsieur Georges, it is good news! Thank you."

Billy's head whirled in surprise and dizzying joy. Five pieces the first night! Who had ever heard of a success like that for an American who had never shown in Paris before? Sam must be triumphant beyond triumphant. He must feel . . . . he must . . . . no, *she*, she must seize this opportunity, she must write to him immediately, before his flush of victory could fade—she must make him understand all the things that he hadn't let her explain to him in the shock of discovery. Surely he would be receptive now—more than receptive—he must be dancing on the ceiling, his fears forgotten, his artistic insecurities thrown off—his mind must be open and ready to let her in!

He had already forgiven her! Billy was suddenly convinced of it. And he didn't know how to find her, he hadn't the least idea where to look for her! If she didn't write to him he'd never know. He could be tearing his hair out trying to imagine where she was, desperate to see her, remorseful, hating the words he'd said . . . oh yes! Busy finding pen and paper, she could see him so clearly, see the look on his face as he realized that she'd disappeared, that he'd lost her. Quickly, she must write quickly, for she couldn't approach him again until he'd read her letter.

The idea took complete possession of her and carried her along as she scribbled page after page, vividly describing what it was like to meet every man with the fact of her wealth invisibly pinned on her dress like a price tag. She hadn't been insulting him, she wrote, Sam had to see that, she had merely been waiting for the right time to tell him the truth. She had been tempted to be honest with him so many times, but at first she'd been too happy just being Honey, reveling in being loved for herself. Yes, that delight had been too important to her. She'd been weak with herself—she admitted that freely, but *never* had she suspected him of any of the loathsome things of which he'd accused her. There had been such delicious novelty at first in putting on a mask, an innocent charm that did no one any harm. Then, by the end of the summer, he'd become so deeply involved with the show, growing more and more concerned about it. How could she have disturbed him then, during those four difficult months of mounting nervousness before the show had opened? Oh, surely he must know that she'd believed totally in his success! *But he had to prove it to himself* —so she'd made herself wait until after the exhibition. She saw now that she'd been totally wrong, horribly misguided, but it had been a miscalculation created by the depth of her love. Couldn't he make allowances for her stupidity, based on her past experiences with other men, and couldn't he forgive her for it? Stupidity was her only crime.

How could he not believe her, Billy asked herself as she sealed the letter, shaking with the speed and conviction with which she'd written. How could Sam fail to understand the reality of what had happened once he'd read her explanations? Wasn't truth unanswerable?

Billy called downstairs to have a messenger sent to hand-deliver the letter by taxi to the gallery, where it would be sure to reach him. The minute it was gone and the activity of the past hour abruptly stopped, she was besieged by the doubts she hadn't let herself think about while she was writing. She bent her head, closed her eyes and rested her forehead on her hands, picturing Sam opening the envelope and reading the pages. Had she left anything out, anything that would be conclusive, anything that should have been added to her plea? She couldn't leave this room until he'd had a chance to call, until he'd had a chance to read and reread the letter, and think about it. *And call.* Such a letter could not be left in limbo—no one could be that cruel. There would be an answer soon.

In frantic agitation she looked at the clock again. Saturday, not quite two-thirty. She had no way of knowing where Sam was. He could be out for a hasty lunch with Daniel or Henri, or he could be deep in discussion with gallery-goers. Saturday was the prime day for art collectors to make their rounds, and except for the lunch hour, when most galleries closed, Sam would be expected to remain rooted to the exhibition space, ready to answer any questions that people might ask. The gallery might stay open late tonight, taking advantage of the troops of art lovers who crowded the busy neighborhood of the Beaubourg Museum. The invitations for the opening yesterday had been from seven till ten—Daniel could easily decide to stay open equally late again tonight if the drop-in traffic warranted it.

When would Sam be able to slip away and read her letter? Surely there would be time for that, surely he would find a free minute and take the letter into Daniel's office—by four—or five. Oh, surely by five o'clock! But what if he put the letter away into a pocket and resolved not to read it until he got home? Was it even possible that he would tear it up unread? No, no, that couldn't be. That was a crazy thought. People only did that in movies. Yet if Sam didn't read the letter until the gallery closed . . .

She had to get out of here, Billy realized. She was filled with too much savage uncertainty to stay in any one place. The familiar visual continuity of her suite was nightmarish, reminding her of the past nine months of happiness. Every tall white rose, every pompous cluster of ball-fringe, every settled sign of luxury and placidly well arranged surface irritated her heart as if they were iron filings, scraped into her agony. She was filled with too much wild conjecture, too many unanswered questions, to remain in these quiet, undisturbed rooms. She lived in a world of dread. She had endowed that letter with such importance that she'd drive herself mad, she'd explode with her longing for Sam to understand and forgive her, she'd tear herself up with her irrational hope that happiness was just a phone call away. She couldn't last another fifteen minutes, waiting here like this. When he called, of course he'd leave a message with the concierge and then she could go to him.

In seconds Billy changed into a dark green velvet jumpsuit and pulled on high, black suede, low-heeled boots. She thrust her arms into a double-breasted, dark mink coachman's coat that buttoned with antique gold coins. It fit tightly to the waist and then whirled wide to mid-calf. She grabbed a bag and a watch and automatically put on the pair of huge cabochon emerald earrings she always wore with Sam because the irregular, unfaceted stones didn't reflect light and could easily be taken for fakes.

Where? Where? In less than a minute Billy had reached the first-floor lobby, flown across it, and crossed the Rue de la Paix. There, on the other side of the Place Vendôme, lay Van Cleef and Arpels. She pushed into the store quickly. It was empty for the moment and a salesman immediately stepped forward.

"Good afternoon, Madame. Is there something I can do for you?"

"Yes, yes, I'd like to see . . . ." Billy halted. She had no idea what she wanted, only that she wanted, needed, had to have something, anything, but immediately, right away for God's sake, couldn't he understand that? She looked at the salesman in angry confusion. Idiot, she thought, he's a complete idiot.

"Is it for a gift, Madame?"

"No, no—for me—something unusual, different, exceptional. . . ."

"Something in diamonds, Madame? No? Sapphires, emeralds, rubies—"

"Yes," she almost stuttered as he was about to run on and on, "yes, rubies, Burmese rubies."

"The most difficult stones to find," the salesman said, glancing appreciatively at her earrings. "As it happens, we have several superb examples that have just arrived for Christmas. Madame has come at an excellent time for—"

"Go and get them," Billy said, cutting him short. The fierce look in her eyes informed him of five of the most welcome words in the jewelry business. Rich. American. Woman. Impulse. Shopper.

As he hurried away to search out the few fine pieces set with rare Burmese rubies, he left Billy alone in the small, private, gray velvet and gilt room to which he had led her, as quiet as if it had been soundproofed, a room that had been designed for serious buyers, a room that shut out the bustle of the city. As she waited, tapping one boot in fretful eagerness, Billy met her own eyes in the round mirror that stood on the table next to the black velvet pad on which the jewelry was to be displayed. Stunned, she peered closer. Jesus Christ Almighty, was that the way she looked? She held her breath in shock at the mad avidity marked so clearly on her features. A furrow she didn't know existed had appeared between her eyebrows and her lips were tightened in an impatient grimace, as if she were holding herself back from springing at a piece of raw meat. She was ugly with covetousness and greed. Inside she felt choked by the diffuse cloud of turbulent anticipation that threatened to strangle her with its deadly combination of fear and unreasoning hope, a cloud that she could try to disperse with the soothing ritual of handling, trying on and eventually buying jewels, as in the Middle Ages men opened their veins in an attempt to relieve their fevers.

No! She jumped up and was out of the shop in an instant, taking a deep breath as she hit the frosty air. She was insane, she told herself as she almost ran along the sidewalk in the direction of the Seine. Insane to buy jewelry she didn't want to hold herself together, insane to use this old method of plastering a temporary lid on her need to hear from Sam.

Did she believe that buying hundreds of thousands of dollars' worth of stones could put her back in control of her life? Was this what it took to give her strength? If so, she *was* the sum of what she bought. And, damn it, she had to be better than that! She couldn't be only what she wore, she couldn't be only the glittering things she could pile on herself in the finest shops in the world. She wasn't just that expensive package wrapped in white satin and hung with diamonds that Sam had seen at the Opéra, she wasn't merely that woman all-but-panting for a quick fix that the unfortunate, now-disappointed salesman had encountered in Van Cleef.

As she passed Cartier and Bulgari, Billy imagined all the stock of the jewelry stores within a two-minute walk of the Ritz, imagined tray after tray of blazing wares dumped in a heap at the foot of the Vendôme column, forged from the bronze of twelve hundred cannons captured at the Battle of Austerlitz. How high would the heap become before it equaled her net worth? Eventually, there would be enough of those colored bits of rare mineral, to which men had decided to assign intrinsic value, to equal the Ikehorn holdings. And then what? What words could the stones speak, what actions could they take, what emotions could they feel? All those rich chips of fire wouldn't be worth a damn on a cold night when only a fire of wood or another human being could keep her warm.

Billy came to the vast Place de la Concorde, its eternal nobility of proportion dwarfing the worst traffic jam in Paris, and skirted the Grecian façades of the Jeu de Paume and the Orangerie, crossing to the Left Bank at the Pont de la Concorde, loping along as swiftly as she could among the loitering crowds enjoying the unexpected brightness of the day. She had no destination, no agenda, nothing to do with herself except keep moving until she could make that phone call to the Ritz that would give her a message from Sam. On the peaceful Left Bank she walked a little more slowly, along the bulk of the Palais Bourbon, until she found herself in the small square directly behind the Palais where her florist was located.

Outside Moulie-Savart, covering the street and overflowing into the square itself, was the brilliant, multicolored, pre-Christmas surprise of a garden of flowering plants backed by a tall assortment of green potted plants. Billy stopped dead, her eyes focused on the startlingly gay vision of temptation that had sprung up against the gray stones. Then, unwaveringly, she followed along the perimeter of the square on its opposite side. She didn't intend to be tempted to buy so much as a single amaryllis in a pot.

There was nothing morally wrong with buying things, she told herself as she walked, shopping was rooted in the human psyche, people waited eagerly at every oasis for the sight of camel trains bearing goods, itinerant peddlers had been sure of a welcome wherever they went, cavemen must have held cave swap meets. When in human history had shopping not been a normal human occupation? But not for her, not today. She had to endure the wait until she heard from Sam without recourse to her old ways of keeping from feeling emotion. She didn't know why, only that it was necessary. Not for anyone else, but for her. Perhaps it was superstition? A form of test? If she didn't buy anything, was it a charm to make Sam call the Ritz in the next fifteen minutes?

No, magical thinking of that childish sort didn't work. Did she honestly believe that if she thought about nothing but Sam reading her letter and rushing to a telephone, she'd send a strong enough psychic message to make it happen?

Billy passed a café and hesitated. How did she know that there was nothing to be said for transmission of thoughts? How many times had she phoned someone and been told that they were just about to phone her? She rushed into the café and bought a pay-phone token at the counter. For minutes she waited behind a skinny teenaged boy who was relating to his girlfriend the plot of the movie he'd seen last night, acting out the role of Gérard Depardieu. There should be a law, Billy thought blackly, a law that a woman waiting for a phone automatically gets priority over any male. How could they call this a civilized country? She jostled the vile little creep with the point of her elbow and begged his pardon loudly, several times, until she finally forced him to end his conversation. At the Ritz there were no messages for her, one of the three concierges reported. But it was not even four, that promising afternoon hour between lunch and tea when, all over Paris, gallery-goers would be sauntering into the new shows. It was far too early to expect anything, Billy told herself, and began to walk more quickly, as if speed could allow her to outdistance her inner turmoil, defang the dread that pierced her stomach, allow a ray of light to penetrate the dark hollows of her thoughts.

Soon she found herself in front of the Rodin Museum. Here was a place she dared enter. The government of France or the city of Paris or whoever owned the Hôtel Biron did not put price tags on the bronzes within.

She paid the entrance fee and then found herself unexpectedly unwilling to go into the museum. She couldn't confine herself between any four walls, no matter what masterpieces they contained. She took her unrestful spirit into the oasis of the park that lay behind the museum and wandered among the groups of families who had come to let their children run about under the geometric ranks of trees. She tried to distract the unruly leaping of her mind by concentrating on watching French children at play. Each one of them possessed positive differences from the others, each one was a small and definite person, with an agenda of his own, rather than just another one of a bunch of kids. They formed a group of tiny individuals who had consented to join together for a while, not a pack. Many of them played happily by themselves, absorbed in some private project. And yet, thought Billy, she had read that the worst punishment that could be inflicted on a French child who was disruptive in school was to be verbally ostracized by his classmates, to have his words ignored, allowed to participate in school but not addressed or listened to.

As she sat on a bench she noticed that each time a child was frustrated or angry in play with the others, the child, instead of creating a fuss, made an immediate beeline for its parents, who were watching closely from a nearby bench. There the child poured out its grievances, was listened to closely and calmly, reassured and sent back to the group, happy again.

She had been one and a half when her mother died, Billy mused. Her father, that overworked doctor whose free time he dedicated entirely to research, had never had more than a few minutes to spend with her, and even then his mind was visibly far away. Hannah, the housekeeper, had been her only adult connection to the world. Only after she entered first grade had she become aware that she didn't have a life like other children, just a bunch of snooty cousins who didn't accept her, and a few bossy aunts. Without having performed any bad action, she had been put in the position of an ostracized child. As she watched a tearful, rosy little girl being dusted off, cuddled, kissed, praised and given words of motherly advice before being sent off to the sandbox again, Billy felt a sharp pain pierce her heart and startling tears come to her eyes.

She *had* been a neglected child, Billy realized. She had never thought of herself in that light before, but the sight of the little girl informed her clearly and absolutely that at an age she couldn't remember, she had not been properly valued. She had not been loved in the only way that would have given her the inner sense of selfhood she was still struggling to find.

If you didn't grow up with that sense of selfhood, how could you ever get it? Not from all the Burmese rubies in the world. Not from being given your weight in diamonds on your birthday. She pondered the question fruitlessly until it sent her rushing out of the park. Happy children were not what she needed to see on this endless Saturday afternoon.

At the exit to the museum, Billy found herself on the Rue de Varenne. It wasn't a coincidence, she realized, that if she turned right and followed the one-way street for another ten minutes past the Rue Barbet de Jouy, she'd be standing on the corner of the Rue Vaneau, only steps from her house. The key to the gate was safely in her handbag. Again no coincidence. She had been headed here since she left the Ritz, Billy realized.

Before she turned to the permissible refuge of her house, Billy sought another café. There the pay phone was guarded by a "Madame Pipi," one of the legion of dour Frenchwomen who expect to be tipped by anyone using the rest rooms or the phone. This Madame Pipi was a direct descendant of the women who sat knitting and counting heads at the foot of the guillotine, Billy decided, as the woman bestirred herself grudgingly to condescend to connect her to the Ritz. There were three messages that she asked to have read to her. None of them was from Sam. He must be incredibly distracted, she told herself, quickly tamping down on her alarm, or else he hadn't received the letter. She asked to speak to Monsieur Georges, who assured her that the letter had been delivered as promised and that he was in possession of a receipt from Monsieur Jamison.

Billy fled along the narrow sidewalk, chilled as the afternoon light failed quickly, blocked out by gray stone townhouses. In mad haste she unlocked the gates to her house and closed them behind her, waved a greeting at the surprised *guardien*, crossed the cobbled courtyard and opened the front door by pressing the buttons of the new burglar alarm that responded only to a code.

Finally safe, she pressed her back to the front door and let herself sag forward, bent almost in half, hugging herself for comfort, sobbing bitterly. He could *not* have read the letter yet, that was the only possible explanation. And she couldn't call the gallery, she couldn't go to the gallery, she could do nothing but wait. Billy wept harshly, knowing that there was nobody to hear her, keening in an agony of disappointment that nevertheless still contained every last stubborn bit of hope that had sustained her all day long.

What if Sam had called and not left a message? Billy was electrified as she asked herself the sudden question. Why would he ask to be put through to the concierge when her phone didn't answer? Why would he think of leaving a message? Why had she made that assumption? When the phone rang in her empty room, he would have simply hung up in frustration! That must be it! Even now he might be on his way to the Ritz—or waiting for her in the lobby. But no, of course he couldn't leave the gallery. It was vitally important for him to be there until it closed, and only Daniel could decide that.

Billy dried her eyes as hope returned, and wandered distractedly to the back of the house, where a new winter garden had been built. A long window seat stretched along the three sides of the double-glazed windows, looking out on the evergreen garden behind the house. The new central heating was turned as low as possible, but the room conserved the warmth of today's sun and she was able to take off her coat and fold it into a comfortable pillow that she arranged on the window seat. She leaned on the pile of mink and pressed her nose to the window, trying to decide what to do. The trees in the Prime Minister's park still had sunlight flicking in their top branches, but a fat, full, low winter moon hung in the hyacinth sky over the top of the Hôtel Matignon. From the nearby cathedral of Saint Clotilde came the first clear call of the many church bells of the quarter, each tolling five o'clock in its own time, occasionally achieving a ravishing, unplanned harmony.

She could do nothing better, Billy realized finally, than to rest here for a while. Her long walk and her tormented phone calls had left her exhausted. Gradually she let herself be lulled by the comforting bells, the comforting warmth, the comforting realization that drifted into her head that one word to Jean-François would ensure that within a week she could be living here. Here, right here, next Saturday at this time, she and Sam could inhabit this house, Billy thought dreamily . . . . the installation wouldn't take longer than that . . . down to the first cases of wine in the cellar. There was a perfectly symmetrical fir tree in the garden that they would hang with hundreds of tiny white lights for Christmas. Every night they'd ask for fruitwood fires to be lit in each room; they'd burn dozens of candles as soon as darkness fell; every day, while Sam worked, she'd wander around, shifting and rearranging things on the tables and chests and walls until they found their right places, for objects in a house took their own good time to discover their one predestined location. Her lovely low manor house would glow with firelight through the darkness of this entire winter, a reminder of the past come back to life.

Billy slipped back, exhausted, on the mink and let her mind drift deeper into this vision until the moon rose higher and the sound of bells roused her again. She was hungry, no, *starving*. And terribly cold. How much time had passed? Was it possible that she could have dozed without realizing it, thinking she was awake while she phased out for an hour? She couldn't see her watch in the darkness. Billy unfolded her coat, wrapped it around her and buttoned it tightly. Should she call the Ritz again? No, damn it, damn it to hell, that wouldn't do any good, she'd figured that out earlier. She should have forced herself to spend the day waiting in her suite by the phone, no matter what state her nerves had been in. One thing was sure, whether Sam had read her letter yet or not, he couldn't communicate with her while she stood irresolutely in a dark house he didn't know existed.

The only sensible thing she could do now was to get something to eat before she fainted from hunger. She didn't need Burmese rubies, but, by God, she needed food, Billy thought as she locked the gate carefully behind her. Shivering from the damp, deep chill in the air, she ran as quickly as she could down the Rue du Bac to the Boulevard Saint-Germain, where she turned right in the direction of the Brasserie Lipp. She had never been to the world-famous restaurant, but it was close to the house and offered the two things she needed, warmth and food.

Singlemindedly, Billy entered the crowded, informal brasserie near the crossroads of Saint-Germain-des-Prés and strode hastily through a mass of people who milled about right inside the door, holding drinks. Her cheeks were bright pink with the cold, her dark eyes deeply refreshed from the sleep she hadn't realized had overcome her, her hair whipped in every direction by the wind. Her mink collar stood straight up, framing the vivid drama of her beauty, which was heightened by the pounding mixture of hope and panic she had been carrying all day. The skirt of her coat flared out as she hurried in on a breath of winter air like a Russian princess who had crossed the steppes with a pack of wolves behind her. She headed straight toward a middle-aged, stern, unsmiling man with a mustache who was clearly in charge.

"Good evening, Monsieur," she said, smiling into his eyes, which were level with her own, "I hope you have room for just one."

The man with the mustache, Roger Cazes, the most courted and fawned-over restaurant owner in France, looked at this stranger in his usual expressionless way and made up his mind that there must be room, even at the most crowded time of the most crowded day of the year. All the people seated outside at the jammed, covered café in front of the restaurant as well as the folk inside, standing up with drinks, had already asked him humbly for the benediction of a table and been told to expect to wait for as long as an hour, but this woman by herself, this sublime, wide-eyed unknown who had just asked for the impossible, with unquestioning faith that she would receive it, would be seated at once. Filling such an innocent, lunatic request made owning a restaurant a daily adventure for Monsieur Cazes.

Faithful customers had been coming weekly to *chez* Lipp for ten, even twenty years, thinking one day to finally find themselves seated at one of the best tables, until they finally resigned themselves to the good but lesser tables decreed by his iron rule. However, Billy was led immediately around a glass partition to the narrow room on the far left of the front of the brasserie, the holy of holies, a small, mirrored, noisy nook that was always filled with Monsieur Cazes's pets—politicians, writers, and actresses. No reservations were ever taken *chez* Lipp, no one, not the most powerful men in France, was allowed to occupy the same table twice in a row for fear that they might dare to think that they had established a toehold on it; men took their sons there to eat as soon as they were old enough to hold a knife and fork, in a futile attempt to ensure a table in the boy's future.

Billy found herself squeezed in between two big, laughing groups on a long, black leather banquette, barricaded by a tiny table draped in white linen that had materialized in the magical way that can only happen in certain of the most desirable restaurants in the world. She glanced at the short, unchanging menu printed on a small card.

"Smoked salmon, roast lamb, and a carafe of red wine," Billy told the ancient waiter, unconscious of the glances of the other diners. She drank a glass of wine thirstily while she waited for the salmon to arrive. Suddenly, unexpectedly, Billy felt herself relax into the coziness and the roaring vitality of the restaurant, a relaxation she needed desperately. She sat back into the small space that had been miraculously carved out for her, snuggling into the soothing ambiance that is created in a small room in which strangers eat and drink in convivial anonymity. She drank more wine and felt the fearful tension of agitation and apprehension that she had carried all day diminish slightly.

She sipped wine while around her Frenchwomen with short hair were deciding to let their hair grow and tumble over their faces, and French women with long hair were resolving to cut their hair to her careless, unnameable length and brush it with their fingers as she must have done. People measured her with their eyes, and dark green became the fashionable color and velvet became the fashionable fabric of the winter of 1982 as Billy sat with her eyes casually surveying the people visible through the glass partition in front of her.

A woman is at her most distinguished when she dines alone in a chic restaurant, if her attitude shows that she feels perfectly at home and is unconscious of any embarrassment in being by herself. Billy had never been more distinguished than that Saturday night *chez* Lipp, as she concentrated on her almost-white Norwegian salmon and rare lamb, eating with a sharply focused appetite.

There was a woman sitting opposite her who reminded Billy slightly of Jessica Thorpe, and her lips curved in private amusement in a way that made half the men in the room sit up straight in a jolt of curiosity. She tried to remember the ridiculous shopping list of future plans she'd announced to Jessie way back in East Hampton. Hadn't she said, Billy asked herself, with an abrupt sense of wine-inspired comedy, that since she was a woman who could buy anything in the world, she intended to own houses in the right places, meet the right people, give the right parties, be photographed at the right places at the right time of the year, and fuck the right men?

Billy shook her head slightly in rueful disbelief. Jessie would have every right to be disappointed in her. She had managed to meet many of the right people, but she had found most of them boring; although she had been invited to a host of the right parties, she had found many of them tedious. She had at least managed to buy one wonderful house, but, true to form, she had failed to fuck the right men. She had fallen in love—but that hadn't been on the list.

Billy wrenched her mind away from Sam, determined to finish her meal without a leap of anxiety. Yes, Billy thought, concentrating as hard as she could on those right men she had neglected to fuck, yes, in retrospect, now that it was too late, there was one kind of man who was stunningly appropriate for a woman like her, the most logical solution to the problem of being a woman with money. No one had ever accused her of intelligent premeditation, but now she saw that she should have cast her net wide and caught a charming, cultivated, elegant, worldly European, brought up to marry money, a man whose wife's riches would be as gratifying and necessary an ornament to him as his title would be an ornament to her. She didn't even have to find a European, Billy mused, an Englishman would have done perfectly. More than a hundred years of British fiction had been devoted to the well-regarded, highly traditional and totally serious occupation of marrying an heiress; no English duke would consider her fortune anything more than his due, and right now she could be busily decorating the castle for a grand, old-fashioned Christmas if she'd only had some common sense. But might not this imaginary nobleman have proved to be as disappointing as the right people and the right parties? Wouldn't he have turned out to be shallow and unfulfilling, a bright bauble, a possession rather than a man? Billy distracted herself with these questions as she paid her bill.

She decided to return to the Ritz immediately, but first she had to visit the ladies' room. Her waiter informed her that it was to be found by descending a staircase halfway toward the back of the main restaurant. Billy's way was momentarily blocked by a parade of overburdened waiters coming out of the kitchen.

Finally her path cleared and she was able to edge through a narrow corridor of tables ranged opposite the cashier and turn a corner into the main room. She stopped suddenly as a hasty glance snagged on a detail, the fabric of the edge of a sleeve. It was the tweed of Sam's jacket, the jacket he always wore. Billy stood very still, looking at the sleeve. Seconds passed in ungraspable slowness while she waited to hear him speak her name. She must be mistaken, it couldn't be Sam, she thought, and found the courage to look up. Sam and Henri were seated side by side, facing into the room. Daniel sat opposite them, with his back to her. Sam was leaning forward, frozen in the middle of a word. Billy took an eager step forward, her eyes locked into Sam's gaze, her whole soul gathered into a mute question. He drew back and shook his head with absolute rejection, looking her full in the face without a flicker of expression. Billy knew at once that their connection had been broken forever. He looked at her as if she were a waxwork, not a living woman. Henri gaped. Unconsciously, Billy took one more step toward their table, but Sam warded her off with the steady, blank refusal of his eyes. Then he turned away deliberately and said something to Henri.

Billy turned and walked out of the restaurant with an imperative remainder of dignity that kept her from falling. On the street there was an empty taxi rank where two people waited in line. Her mind utterly emptied by the damage she had just sustained, she joined them automatically. Seconds later, Henri, who had run after her, tugged at her sleeve. Blankly, still clutching her severe composure, she turned to him.

"Honey, he believes it was only your friends who bought his work. Seven were sold by the time we closed . . . incredible! He thinks that you . . . paid for it, arranged it, *faked it,* he is convinced that he had no true success."

"I didn't do that."

"Of course not, we know it, we tried to tell him, but he refused to believe us. Honey, I'm sorry. He's a fool."

"He read my letter?"

"Yes, as soon as he got it. And then the clients started to come . . ." Henri spread his hands apart in explanation.

"Go back, you're shivering. Thank you for telling me, Henri."

She must have known most of the day, Billy thought, from the time she found out that he had received the letter, for if she hadn't known all day, if she hadn't been preparing herself for this final failure, why was she feeling nothing now? Why was she sitting on the bed, still wearing her coat, numb within and without? She had no idea what to do next, no memory of how she had come from Lipp to her suite, she could imagine no future, remember no past, the present didn't exist.

She heard a slight noise under her door and watched a letter emerge on the carpet. She looked at the letter for a half hour before she managed to make herself pick it up. She turned it over and over, a manila envelope from Josh Hillman. Finally, because she had nothing else in the world to do with herself except open this letter, she did so, finding that it contained a second letter, its envelope almost covered with foreign stamps, another communication from Spider Elliott. Automatically she opened it and automatically she read it through.

> *Dear Billy,*
>   *I still don't know where you are or if you got the last letter I sent you, but I woke up this morning in the mood to write to someone, and it's the first time I've felt this way since I left L.A. If I write any of my six sisters, the others will all get jealous, so since you're the only other woman in my life, you get this by default. (And don't nag, I've sent my mother postcards from every port so she wouldn't worry about me.)*
>   *I've made my way to the Aegean Sea and the Greek Islands, in island terms the equivalent of Broadway and*

42nd St.—there are 2,000 of them. Someone from the Greek tourist board has spread the word that the islands have a total of 30,000 beaches. I wonder if they sent out some poor schmuck to count them? Sounds like a marketing gimmick to me . . . that would make 15 beaches to each island! But I'm willing to believe it—I think I've sailed past about 29,000 stretches of golden sand. How come it was such a big deal that Onassis had one private island out of 2,000? If he'd had his own baseball team I'd be impressed, but an island? Give me a break!

I'm anchored off Skala, the port of an island called Astipalaia in the Dodecanese chain of islands. Sound familiar? No, you don't have to feel stupid, Billy, it's practically unknown. However, it has all the advantages, a hill town with a windmill, a fishing village on a lagoon and a Venetian citadel. Did I mention the nudist beach? Seriously, there is one. With 2,000 islands to choose from, I figured that the one with a nudist beach had to have some free-spirited nightlife too, so that's why I'm anchored here.

Amazingly enough, I have the awful suspicion that I'm all sailed out. One more flying fish, one more sunset, one more quaint harbor town, one more gorgeous day on the Aegean, or any other body of water—and I may throw up. Seriously. I didn't know you could get too much sea and too many islands, but believe me, the mania has its limits.

I grew a long, scruffy sort of greenish beard out of sheer boredom and shaved it off for the same reason. I've read so much that I think I need glasses, but since I can still see the type if I hold the book at arm's length, I'm not seriously worried. I've looked at so many stars that I'm ready for a job in a planetarium, but not willing. I can steer a boat in my sleep and I actually do it all the time without getting into trouble, because the ocean is really very big. That's about the most profound truth I've discovered—the ocean is fucking big! I always heard it was in geography class, now I know it is. Major insight. I hope to hell you're impressed, because it took me a lot of time to get this piece of information.

My crew and I are still getting along. I hired a couple of

*confirmed hermits and this is the best gig they've ever had,
no people and damn little talking. At least they can cook. I
realized too late that what I should have done was hire a
couple of communicative Italians. By now I'd be fluent,
the guy with the best tan on the Via Veneto.*

*I think it's about time for me to get out of here and go
home. I don't have any particular plans, but I know that
I've had it with this ship. Maybe I'll go back to
photography. Or maybe I'll open an art gallery and
encourage young painters, or maybe I'll start a new
business. Who knows? It's a funny thing about being rich
. . . it seemed like a huge amount of money when I turned
it over to Josh so he could invest it for me, but now I've
gotten accustomed to the idea of money quietly piling up,
money that means I'll never have to work again . . . and
the idea of no work turns out to be the most horrible
thought I've had in a long time! The question of what to do
with myself and my future is beginning to loom large. I
guess you're one of the few people who can really
appreciate what I mean . . . after all, you weren't in it for
the loot when you started Scruples, were you? In spite of
all the fun—and trauma—the three of us had making
Scruples work, I don't see myself with a future in any
other store . . . I'll never find another partner like you—
there couldn't be anyone else as much fun to fight with—
so what would be the point? Christ, what a frosty bitch you
were when Valentine and I first got out to L.A.,
remember? But I saw that basic creampuff in you and it
didn't take me long to whip you into shape. I think I did a
damn good job on you, if I say so myself.*

*Billy, old friend, I'm sending this off tomorrow with the
wish that it'll get to you in time to convey a big hug for a
merry Christmas. I fully intend to have one, and I hope
you're planning a great holiday too. When I get back to
L.A., I'll be in touch with you as soon as Josh tells me
where the hell you are. I'm thinking of flying back from
Athens. Sailing back would take another year—no way!
Joyeux Noël, my good woman.*

Love and kisses—
Spider

Tears were running fast and hot over Billy's face as she came to the end of the letter. Why on earth was she crying now, she wondered, why was she feeling something at last? Her tears were for Spider, she understood finally, tears of happiness for him. He sounded as if he had healed, as if he had returned to someone very much like his old self.

She felt herself breaking out of the cave of ice in which she had been wandering, lost and uncaring. *If Spider could survive, so could she, by Christ!* The world wasn't lost because one chickenhearted man didn't have enough confidence in himself to see who she really was, money and all. Fuck Sam's artistic angst! Fuck Vito and Sam, those oh-so-vulnerable cowards who had the nerve to pride themselves on the accident of being born male, although they were crippled by their essential lack of belief in themselves and their quivering timidity about their real worth. Fuck ever again pretending to be what she couldn't help being, fuck all men, contemptibly hiding behind the tissue paper– thin veneer of their overrated male hormones, who still didn't have the balls to stand up to her! These men, who thought of women as the weaker sex, were terrified whenever a woman showed strength. What gutless wonders they were at heart!

Billy was galvanized into an emotion that felt like nothing else but a vast and abiding rage, an emotion strong enough to make her phone downstairs and make flight reservations to New York for the next day. She had all night to pack, she realized, as she rang for the maids and dried her tears, more than enough time, for she would not try to sleep again until she was on the plane, leaving Paris and everyone in it behind.

15

This whole mad weekend trip was typical of Zach Nevsky, Nick De Salvo thought in admiration. Just yesterday, on Friday morning, Zach's entire company of actors had been stuck up to their eyeballs in a thick miasma of dullness, a vast, glue-like bog that was rising fast over their heads. Every last one of the performers, even he, the star, was numb with a supreme lack of interest in the playwright's vision. That word, *vision,* made him queasy behind his eyes. Vision, ech!

Was vision-sickness some sort of violently contagious virus that only attacked actors who had been struggling in a rehearsal hall for weeks on end? Maybe it was unshakable, unacknowledged insecurity that made them all secretly wonder why the hell they were involved in this silly business of worrying about the vision of some writer, instead of working at a normal job as their parents had suggested, demanded, implored that they do for as long as they all could remember?

He'd been sitting there, word-perfect as always, but mentally flat on his ass with his sudden lack of curiosity about the subtext of the play. Did he give a flying fuck if Hamlet and his mom had a yen to dance the dirty turkey? Did he care if his uncle had done the nasty on his daddy? Did he give a shit if he'd hurt the feelings of that weird nymph, Ophelia, or if she'd always been around the bend? Talk about a whiner! And what sensible guy could worry that if he died, he might —perchance, as the fellow said, perchance, no less—dream? Weren't bad dreams just about the least of Hamlet's worries, perchance?

Why had he, Nick De Salvo, a dues-paying, seriously major, hot young star, an outstanding member of Young Hollywood, turned down a giant-budget buddy flick at Universal to come back to New York and play Hamlet Off Broadway? So what if all the greatest actors in history had felt they had to have a whack at the greatest play in history? Why hadn't he left it alone, he didn't need to prove to himself that he was as good as Olivier, he knew he wasn't, not yet. Give him time. The guys at Universal weren't exactly hustling him to play Shakespeare, and his agent had all but popped a hernia at the news.

Yeah, yesterday there wasn't an actor in the room who hadn't reminded him of a gloomy, resentful schoolkid kept in unfairly during recess. And then Zach had walked in and strolled around the table without a word, looking at their glum faces in paternal amusement, given each of them a jelly doughnut out of a paper bag, unleashed that big, unguarded laugh of his and told them all to take seventy-two. Not five, not ten, not even the afternoon off, but just to get the hell out of the rehearsal hall and not dare to come back until Tuesday, when they would have had a three-day weekend to recover from too much great language.

"You're all too good to be bad," he'd told them, "you've all got what it takes or I wouldn't let you in the door, but you're forcing it. You can fake an orgasm—yeah, even you guys—but you can't force Shakespeare, so out! Have some laughs before I lay eyes on you again, or I won't let you come play tragedy with me!"

The room had cleared in ten seconds and he had decided to go skiing with Zach. Nothing New York had to offer could be more fun, Nick reflected as he drove along a highway that had been recently cleared of snow after an early, pre-Christmas blizzard. Zach and he had been best friends since grammar school, even though he sometimes got fed up with the guy when he was nudging, kvetching, manipulating, shaking, moving and harping on that vision thing. "I'm not a sieve, Nick," Zach would say, "I'm there to serve the playwright and I can't do it unless I connect to the vision personally. Directing is about allowing creative people to discover the stuff they've got through me."

Well, Zach was right, as usual. The only time he had been spectacularly wrong was back in seventh grade when he'd tried to be an actor himself. Probably because Zach was the tallest guy in the class, he'd been given a part in the spring play. A real lox, act he could not, no way, but he'd memorized everyone's lines by the first rehearsal and started prompting them when they forgot, and then making suggestions and finally shaping the play to his thirteen-year-old vision, leaving poor Miss Levy, their homeroom teacher and official director of the play, wondering what had hit her.

Being in that play with Zach was the reason he was a successful actor now, Nick realized. Even way back then, Zach had encouraged him, even deep into the first year of puberty the guy had time to have vision and to articulate it. What the fuck, admit it, he'd missed hearing people carry on about the vision thing out on the Coast. Like all the rest of Young Hollywood he'd wake up every morning and wonder if his success was due to dumb luck and timing plus the face he couldn't be proud of because he'd been given it, not worked for it, or whether he could maybe, possibly, really act. Actors lived with fear. The whole town ran on fear. Somehow Zach took the fear away and replaced it with courage. A stint with Zach forced him to dig down the way the camera never did, made him touch the core of the talent he had, allowed him to use it to its fullest. His *commodity*. The ability to act was his commodity, the only one he had to offer besides his face, and every once in a while he needed to work with a director who deeply valued that commodity, who recognized it and didn't inhibit his individual creative impulses. Yeah, he had to admit it, he had the vision thing too. Once you'd been exposed to Zach, you couldn't ignore it. He hadn't been back East for a year—he was overdue for a dose of Zach. Invigoration, thy name is Nevsky. When had the guy learned to ski?

What about the girls? How had Pandora Harper, who was playing Ophelia, and who was hopelessly and, as far as he could see, unsuccessfully, drooling for Zach, managed to horn in on this ski trip? He didn't remember inviting her, but she seemed to be with him, sort of. She wasn't his type, he didn't lust to melt her glacial, well-bred blond beauty, although Pandora, to be fair, could act up a storm or Zach wouldn't have cast her. She'd come from an impeccable background, been Deb of the Year or something equally improbable, yet she had a frightening ambition to succeed as an actress and a lot of the equipment. But, good actress or not, he sure as hell wasn't interested in a girl who was manifestly salivating over Zach in a subtle way only another man could see.

What he didn't get was Gigi Orsini. Was she Zach's date or wasn't she? It hadn't been made plain. Zach's sister's roommate? What kind of relationship was that? It didn't explain how come she made the fourth member of their little winter sports group, especially since she'd never been skiing before. He had to get to the bottom of this because if Gigi was not Zach's date, he personally would be deeply interested in teaching her how to, most efficiently and quickly, take off her ski boots, her ski pants, and her ski underwear, all of which she'd told him she'd borrowed for the weekend. She had zing, tang, zest, zip, all that scrumptious springtime stuff. Nothing dumbly traditional there. Gigi'd be all pinky-pointy and spirited, not well-bred and boring. Yes, indeed. Yum!

What she'd like to know, Pandora Harper thought, was how this Gigi somebody, who couldn't even ski, had attached herself to Nick De Salvo, just about the most happening young leading man in Hollywood. Had Zach, in his divinely dictatorial way, simply dragged her along as a blind date for Nick? Improbable as it sounded, in this day and age, people still got fixed up, as they quaintly put it, and there was every chance that his sister had nagged him to do something about her roommate. Tacky.

Gigi-whoever was a perky little thing, you had to admit, if you liked perky, and she very much did not. You couldn't trust the perky ones, they were sneaky and fast, disappearing behind almost any closed door or into any dark closet to rip off a quickie and no one the wiser. They had a kind of animal cunning, or, as Hamlet said, "methinks it is like a weasel."

Darling, gorgeous Zach, hard as it was to credit, was old-fashioned enough to care deeply for his sister. He was sentimental in a world in which men hadn't been sentimental for a hundred years. And an idealist in a world that glorified everything but ideals. If he weren't the most unassailably sexy man she'd ever laid eyes on, she'd steer very clear of him. Useless idealism and outdated sentimentality weren't her thing, any more than perky. Nobody got famous on them. Or rich, for that matter.

Not that money mattered to her, she had more money than anyone would ever need in a dozen lifetimes, thanks to Great-Grammy's trust, and a good thing too, when you considered that another actress would have to be willing to go hungry working Off Broadway. No, money didn't matter. Fame, oh yes, fame, nothing less—that was what she was after, and that was what she intended to have. On her way to fame, how divine to find Zach Nevsky, bull-necked, rugged, boiling with energy, and by reputation possessed of the most reliable hard-on in the entire theatrical world of Greater Manhattan. Every fine young actress must screw her quota of directors, and a few extra if possible. Tradition demanded it, and she'd been brought up to obey tradition, particularly when it agreed with her inclinations.

She'd called Zach as soon as she'd heard that he'd lured Nick De Salvo to town. The Prince of Young Hollywood daring to tackle the Bard was bound to draw a flock of reviewers from every element of the media. They would come to bury Nick—a violently handsome boy, but not her type—and end up raving about her Ophelia. Zach had been directing new work by young playwrights for almost a year. It was a clever shift of pace for him to put Nick into the ultimate classic, and to cast against physical type, a Danish prince played by a smoldering Latin who looked as if he belonged to a biker gang. Maybe it would work, but it didn't matter to her how long the play ran; opening night was the only night that mattered. She'd been letting Zach direct her as he saw Ophelia—that unutterably *dreary* vision thing of his—but on opening night she'd play her as she should be played—Ophelia was clearly a raving nymphomaniac, not just borderline, but seriously bat-shit. She'd get her hands on Nick's cock and caress it in all sorts of deliciously wicked ways during the "get thee to a nunnery" number. There wouldn't be anything anybody could do to stop her; Nick was professional enough to carry on, and she'd make the sensation and get the attention she was expecting. What could Zach do about it at that point, after the critics saw her doing everything but giving Hamlet head while he nattered away at her? Words, words, words indeed! She'd show them. A doublet and hose were perfect for easy access.

Just thinking about it made her ready for Zach. There had been some nonsense mentioned about her sharing a room with Gigi—she'd manage to get around that barrier somehow or her Great-Grammy would be ashamed of her. Harpers didn't let other people make their arrangements for them. Not even directors.

What could Emily Gatherum do when she'd asked for a three-day weekend off but give it to her, Gigi thought righteously. She'd already promised Emily that she'd work Christmas Eve, New Year's Eve and Christmas Day, filling in for two different chefs who had to be at home or risk divorce, so Emily owed her that much. Catering was a business that supposedly never stopped for three hundred sixty-five days a year, but with family men you had to provide some degree of flexibility. When Zach had called this morning and announced that this was finally her chance to learn how to ski, she'd dashed over to Jessica's and borrowed clothes from those of the kids who were more or less her size. She could rent the skis and boots tomorrow when they got on the slopes.

The only thing she didn't understand was, where was the gang? Zach had said something about going with a gang—did he mean just the ice princess, Grace Kelly look-alike Miz Pandora and her precious box, plus much-too-beautiful Nick De Salvo, who was trying to impress her for some reason? In her terms, as she remembered it from Uni, a gang meant a whole bunch of people, not just four. And another thing, how come Pandora had plunked herself down in the backseat next to Zach, where they seemed to be having a high old time, leaving Nick to drive and be Hollywood-charming to her, as if she hadn't been inoculated against that from birth?

She wished Sasha were with them. Sharing a room with Pandora wasn't going to be a thrill, but Zach had said she wasn't a bad kid when you got used to her, not the cold, snobbish minx she seemed to be. It would take more than a weekend to make her go for his theory, Gigi told herself rebelliously. It was so typically Zach to think that and act on it, like his theory about *Hamlet*. He was certain that there was a way of balancing things in Shakespeare so that he could make *Hamlet* available to all kinds of people who didn't honestly expect to enjoy it, who went to the theater because they thought they had to once a year in the name of culture. Zach was like a child building a sand castle and making all the other kids help him, telling them exactly where to empty their pails of sand and urging them to hurry and bring more. Was he a gigantically talented theatrical brat, another flashy wonder boy who'd break your heart eventually and wouldn't even notice, or was he the real thing, a creative artist who also happened to be a good, loving, wonderful man she could dare to fall in love with?

She couldn't judge yet, Gigi decided, but maybe a weekend in the snow would give her an idea. It was hard to really get to know Zach on his native turf because he was always in charge, always surrounded, the chief, the boss, the leader, always worked up in search of his vision—that vision thing of his that she understood so perfectly —but on skis he'd be different. Life-sized. Or almost. He didn't know how to ski either, so they'd start even.

He'd missed a beat somewhere, Zach thought, trying not to listen to Pandora chat away, and that was something that should never happen to him. He'd intended to spend this trip sitting in the backseat with Gigi, watching the moon rise on the snow, while Nick and Pandora were growing increasingly absorbed in each other up front—at the very least, Gigi would let him hold her hand—but Pandora had somehow gotten his perfectly clear signals crossed and slid into the place he'd destined for Gigi. She was a grabby piece of work, that girl, and should go far. She basically belonged in Alfred Hitchcock's Hollywood, but she was too bloody pretentious about the theater to admit it. Still, a highly useful actress who took direction perfectly.

Even with this glitch, his master plan was well under way, his plot to lure Gigi away from New York with him, away from his sister's alarming influence, away to a place where the two of them would find themselves together and alone in the middle of nature. He had faith in nature, maybe because he was strictly a city boy, but he suspected that nature might make Gigi more generous to him than any amount of stagecraft. Of course, blizzard or not, Gigi wouldn't have gone off for a weekend with him by himself, so he'd had to co-opt the others. As for the rest of the company of actors, he would have had to give them three days off, skiing or no, when they hit that wall that they'd been due to hit anyway. It never failed, even with fluff or farce, there was always one stagnant period when the most dedicated actors started going stale, and any smart director had to give them a time-out. But with the devastating richness of Shakespeare, the literally overwhelming language beating on and on in their heads night and day, there usually came more than one time when the circuits broke down and all they wanted to do was go home and watch daytime soaps and eat pizza and take naps.

It was easier for him, he was just a shoemaker cobbling a pair of shoes from scratch, dealing with so many elements besides the words, running a complicated human community, putting on a play, for Christ's sake. *A play*. Directing was the only work in the world that was pure play, and he was the luckiest man in the world to be the playmaster, to have Shakespeare's language in front of him, those most beautiful words in the public domain—although there were those who'd say the Bible—sitting there on the page waiting for him to turn them once again into a piece of reality, a celebration of life, a celebration of man, not an intelligence test or an entrance exam.

There were some directors who made themselves miserable from time to time, thinking that orchestra conductors had better jobs than they did, because the conductor was up on stage, a performer himself as well as the shaper of the composer's vision. He'd had his own moments of frustration, sure, it had sometimes occurred to him that if he was in the business of interpreting the playwright's vision using the creativity of the actors, then who exactly was he, Zach Nevsky? But then he'd realize that he'd a million times rather work with language than sounds, then he'd remember that he was tone deaf, then he'd ask himself if the only job he'd be ready to trade for was God's. When that happened—and the answer to the question was yes, God, or, better still, Actor/Director—he knew he was the one who needed a pizza and a nap as a consolation for his lack of acting talent.

Okay, so you couldn't have absolutely everything. He'd settle for exactly what he had, plus Gigi. If he weren't so sure that Nick would never make a move on his girl, he'd be a little jealous of the way they were talking Hollywood trash together, ever so comfy. He tended to forget that Gigi had a movie-producer father because that incomprehensible bastard had no place in her life. Maybe Vito Orsini seemed to have dropped off the face of the earth, but guys like that never disappeared, they were harder to get rid of than Jimmy Hoffa. One thing he didn't have to worry about was asking Vito for Gigi's hand in marriage, that shit had forfeited all his rights to his daughter. He'd probably have to ask Sasha, if he had to ask anybody. Or maybe Gigi's stepmother, Billy Ikehorn herself, far away in Paris. But first he had to get Gigi out alone in the sparkling snow, all by themselves in the pristine wilderness, with real blue sky and real pine trees and the kind of real air that never made it to Central Park, just the two of them. He'd always wanted to go skiing. It looked like a snap.

They arrived at Killington very late on Friday night and went to bed immediately, Gigi and Pandora sharing a room without discussion because they were so anxious to get to sleep, Zach and Nick in another, one door down the same corridor.

Early the next morning they all ate huge breakfasts of pancakes, bacon and porridge to give them strength, on the advice of Pandora, who had been put on skis before she was three, and Nick, who often skied in Vail and Sun Valley. Gigi and Zach went off together to rent skis and boots and join one of the classes at the ski school. Killington taught beginners on short, three-foot skis, without using poles, an amazingly rapid form of instruction that enabled the skier to experience the feeling of swooshing downhill almost immediately, since they didn't have to cope with the awkwardness of long boards and flailing poles.

The beginners' class was designed to be as easy as possible. The students took the low nursery gradient one swoop at a time, turning up into the hill to stop. There were fifteen of them, and eventually, urged on by their ski instructor, they made several turns in each swoop, checking their speed when they turned. Each move down the crowded hill, on which many other classes were busy, couldn't take place until they each had had an individual turn and regrouped. Before lunchtime the beginners had all had the terrifying joy of standing at the top of a hill, looking way down to the bottom, knowing that they had done it once and could do it again.

Gigi and Zach stood at the bottom of the nursery slope, thrilled with themselves, and looked up to see Nick, a black bullet, and Pandora, a sleek silver arrow, coming straight at them from a great distance up the mountain, gathering speed as they skied dead straight down the hill, stopping just at their feet with a sharp turn uphill accompanied by a snappy flourish.

"Go ahead, show off," Zach said. "We'll learn to do that too."

"It takes time, Zach, skiing the fall line . . . . and dumb guts," Nick answered, releasing his skis.

"What's the fall line, Nick?"

"The straightest way down the hill, without checking your speed. Until you ski the fall line you can't get the full feel of it. You haven't conquered the mountain and you haven't conquered your basic, normal fear of falling. Nobody wants to risk a fall."

"Come on, Nick, look at all those little kids coming straight down just like you and Pandora—half of them are two or three years old," Zach protested.

"Sure, and they've been on skis since they could stand up. It's not as easy as it looks."

"Elitist pig," Zach laughed. "Are you hungry or are you hungry?"

"I'm hungry," said Gigi, as she watched Pandora hoist her long skis effortlessly to her shoulder, take both her poles in one hand, and stride off with a confident wiggle of her tightly encased silver ass. Zach looked after her with an appreciative gleam in his eye. Gigi was wearing baggy navy ski pants and a dark green jacket that looked dull with navy, borrowed from two different Strausses. She felt a sudden pang as she became conscious of how amateurish and clumsy she felt in comparison.

Their hearty lunch was served cafeteria-style, for the afternoon session of ski school started promptly at two. Nick and Pandora took the lift back up to the top of the mountain, waving good-bye to Zach and Gigi with what seemed to both of them to be looks of barely concealed pity.

"Gigi, do you really want to spend the whole afternoon doing the same thing we were doing this morning?" Zach asked her immediately.

"That's the way the school's set up," Gigi answered firmly.

"Gigi, ski school's a business, just like anything else. They hold you back so you'll keep paying them, even when you could perfectly well do it by yourself. We spent most of our time waiting for the rest of the class—didn't it make you feel frustrated?"

"Sure, but how else can I learn?"

"Listen, Gigi, we both know how to ski under control now, right? We've learned how to stop and how to turn, right? Why don't we skip school, go up the mountain, and take the easiest beginner's trail down slowly, doing *exactly* what we learned this morning? That way we'll get ten times more skiing than if we stay in class."

"That might make sense, Zach Nevsky, except I have the nasty suspicion that you lust in your heart to ski the fall line."

"Gigi, I promise, I swear on every precious marigold hair of your precious little head, I will not try to ski the fall line this afternoon. I'm not a moron. I'll do that mother before the weekend's over—but today I just want to cram in as much practice as I can. It's sunny, it's cloudless, how can we waste it?''

She looked appraisingly at Zach. It seemed heartless to fetter such a natural athlete. He'd been far and away the best in the class, imitating the instructor much more exactly and effortlessly than any of the others, catching on naturally to the rhythm of the turns, leaning forward, bending his knees and swinging his arms from side to side with grace. An Orloff-Nevsky, after all, could always pick up a dance step faster than the rest of the chorus line, and Zach was no exception. And he looked so touchingly eager, his straight black hair, too straight and abundant to ever keep a part, falling over his forehead, his eyes squinched up in the yearning for adventure.

"Ah, Gigi, you must be itching to get away from these nursery slopes . . . . even the name's demeaning, and they're as crowded as the subway. In class we're only getting to actually ski a few minutes at a time.'' Zach spoke with all the intrepid persuasiveness that had led so many actors into taking chances with their talent, making leaps into new areas they hadn't believed they were capable of conquering.

"I just don't know.'' Gigi hesitated, enormously tempted against her better judgment, but still unsure.

"The only way to feel truly *here* is to go up the mountain. You know I won't let you get into any trouble . . . come on, Gigi, let's go for it!''

"Oh, Zach . . .'' Gigi looked down at her little red skis and her impressively high-tech plastic boots and something in his tone made her yearn to take a risk.

"I promise I'll take care of you, please, Gigi! I won't go if you don't. It wouldn't be fun by myself.''

"Oh . . . . all right,'' she agreed, as people eventually did when Zach Nevsky challenged them.

Zach had been right, Gigi decided. The beginners' trail was hundreds of yards wide at the top of the mountain, a field of crisp, virgin powder snow. The mountain peak seemed a million miles removed from the trampled, crisscrossed, wet snow of the ski-school slopes, which now lay thousands of feet below, beyond their view. They were on top of the world, a hummingly quiet, strangely thrilling place from which they could see violet-white mountain peaks above them in every direction. Gigi felt as if the air she was breathing contained a rare essence distilled from sunlight and purity. Merely standing there gave her a completely new experience of peace and self that she could never have imagined if she had refused to follow Zach to the top of the mountain.

Gigi skied in Zach's tracks, not at all anxious to make her own path. While dozens of other skiers sped past them he carefully went first, about twenty-five feet at a time, keeping half-horizontal to the pitch of the mountain, checking his speed several times before he stopped and waited for her to catch up with him. Gigi wobbled a bit, trying to coordinate the swing of her arms and knees. Soon, as they crisscrossed the mountain slowly, on the treeless snow field, she gained confidence and ability as she managed to arrest her downhill motion where Zach was waiting for her. He hadn't told her, down at the bottom of the mountain, that he planned to reward her for each successful effort by kissing the top of her head, but there was no way she could evade him on skis, and the top of her head was not a recognized erogenous zone. At least it hadn't been when he'd started, but now it was getting sensitized, or else she had sneaky, highly erotic nerve endings in her scalp she'd never known about.

"Listen, Zach, cut that out!"

"It's like giving a dog a pat when he does a new trick. That's all." He grinned at her in admiration.

"Dogs don't ski . . . and you're patronizing me," Gigi said, shaking her head at him in warning.

"So what parts of you can I kiss? I don't want you to feel your courage and style are going unnoticed or unappreciated."

"None of them, Zach. You know my rules," she said severely.

"All right, Gigi," he replied meekly, and set off down the mountain. Now that they had passed below the wide snow field at the peak, a chilly little wind sprang up. Slowly they continued their laboriously measured progress downhill. As soon as they reached the treeline, the freedom of the snow field disappeared. Fir trees, their branches heavy with snow, grew several dozen feet apart on either side of what had now become a recognizable trail, making it necessary for Zach to angle a bit more sharply downward in his horizontal descent and make more frequent turns.

"Hey, let's rest for a bit, Zach, I'm out of breath," Gigi said as she stopped next to him, laughing shakily with a mixture of pride and excitement. She could ski!

"Just lean uphill against me, I'll hold you. Oh, Gigi, isn't this everything I thought it would be? Aren't you glad you came?" She smiled up at him in agreement, covered with snow from her harmless falls, her cheeks burning, her eyes greener than he'd ever seen them, and he couldn't resist putting both his arms tightly around her and kissing her full on her lips.

"Zach . . . stop," Gigi gasped.

"Just one more kiss," he murmured, "don't want you to get frostbite," and kissed her again, a long, dangerously pleasurable kiss, his lips so warm on her cold mouth that Gigi could feel herself weakening toward him.

"Zach! Stop that and keep going," Gigi insisted, determined that he wasn't going to be allowed to break her rules just because they were on a mountain.

He looked at her with eyes filled with helpless longing, but set off again. As they descended slowly, reaching the middle of the mountain, along the relatively straight trail, the afternoon sun fell still lower in the sky and the snow began to develop an icy crust. The ruts made by earlier skiers were deeper and deeper as the trail grew narrower and there was less room to maneuver. Zach now skied only some fifteen feet before he stopped to wait for Gigi, a painfully plodding process. Ahead of them were more trees, endless trees growing fairly close together, and they had no idea where the trail would open out into another field of snow. No other skiers had passed them for at least a half hour; the waiting silence was almost ominous, as if they were now alone on the mountain.

"I think we should try to go a little faster," Zach said.

"Right," Gigi agreed grimly.

Zach descended thirty feet, making small, short, checking turns to keep from picking up speed, and stopped to wait for Gigi. She didn't possess the natural coordination to waggle the way he did, but she released the tree she'd been holding, bent her knees, spread her arms and followed him determinedly. She teetered dangerously and just managed to regain her balance several times before she stopped by skiing directly into Zach, who was resting by leaning uphill against a tree. He grabbed her and steadied her.

"Great! You're doing great!" he said.

"This has definitely stopped being fun." Gigi felt her legs shaking. She'd give anything to be in a kitchen again, with a dozen hot stoves to slave over, in secure professionalism.

"I know, Gigi, I never thought the beginner's trail would get this narrow. I'm sorry, sweetheart, it was a dumb idea but we're still doing fine. Look, I can feel you getting nervous, uptight. Unclench your muscles or you'll hurt yourself." He took off his mitts and put them under his arm, took her head and clasped it on both sides with his big warm hands. For minutes he just warmed her cheeks and ears and she snuggled into the comforting bulk of his body, feeling safe and relaxed. Zach put his woolen ski cap on her head, for she had forgotten to wear one. "But you're still so cold, darling, so cold," he said, worried, and bent his body as if he could encompass her in his shelter, holding her tightly and kissing her nose and her eyes and finally her lips because he knew they were cold too. "Gigi, sweetheart, my little darling, I love you so terribly much . . . you're my girl, please say you're my girl, Gigi, you know how I love you, there's no one else for me in the world, tell me you're going to be my girl."

Zach continued to cover her face with kisses as he spoke. He, who knew all the great poetry of love, was too moved to find anything more eloquent to say to Gigi. He'd believed that he was self-sufficient, until Gigi. He needed her so much it frightened him, and he fought that fright. Although his words were pleading, he kept his tone demanding, confident, as if all of his power were still intact. Gigi trembled in his massive embrace, trying to release her head from the vise of his hands, feeling herself on the verge of giving in to his insistence, of surrendering finally to his urgency, of agreeing to be his girl. She saw the unmistakable spark of total intention in his eyes and, tensing again, she thought suddenly that it wasn't fair, it just was not fair of him to be attacking her emotions now when she was stuck up here alone with him in this strange, frightening, remote place. *Not fair!*

"No!" Gigi cried, using all her strength to twist her head away. Unexpectedly she broke out of his grasp and immediately started to slide downhill backwards, her skis moving so swiftly that there was no possibility of trying to control them. Stunned into immobility for a second, Zach started after her, but her momentum had carried her too far for him to catch up. Gigi, arms flailing helplessly, shouted in fear.

"Fall down!" Zach yelled. "Fall down!" All of Gigi's lessons left her mind and automatically she screamed and fought to stay upright as she went faster and faster downhill until she crashed at full speed into a tree on the opposite side of the trail. She crumpled in a heap into the high-piled snow on the side of the trail. In seconds, Zach was lying on the snow next to her.

"Gigi!" he implored. "Gigi, are you all right?"

She was sobbing in pain, and unable to speak with the shock.

"Gigi, does anything hurt?" he entreated. "Gigi, talk to me!"

"It's my leg . . . I think it's broken . . . no, don't touch it! Don't try to move me! For Christ's sake, what are we going to do? Oh, I *hurt*!"

"It's all my fault! Oh, Gigi, it's all my fault!"

Gigi's sobbing doubled as the acute pain in her left leg grew worse. His face agonized with remorse and guilt, Zach looked back, as far up the mountain as he could, but all the way up the trail above them there was nobody to be seen or heard. He checked his watch and realized with horror that it was later than he thought, almost four o'clock.

"I'm going to get help. Do you understand, Gigi?"

"Don't leave me here alone!" she sobbed.

"I have to, Gigi," he insisted, "it's too dangerous to wait." Still weeping, she set her teeth resolutely and nodded. Zach stripped off his parka and heavy sweater and managed to bundle Gigi's torso and neck with them without disturbing her legs. He brushed the snow off her cap and pulled its wool down over as much of her face as he could, so that it didn't come into direct contact with the snow. "If you hear anybody coming, scream for help as loud as you can, understand?" Gigi nodded again, tears rolling down her cheeks. Zach struggled upright, wearing only a thin wool shirt tucked into his ski pants, bareheaded and barehanded, for his mitts had been lost up the mountain as he dashed after Gigi. He took a deep breath, looked back at her wordlessly, beseechingly, and set off, skiing under tight control, for he'd be no use to Gigi if he hurt himself. He made no stops as he made his cautious way down the trail through the trees, but as soon as he had reached the open slopes beyond the narrow trail, he leaned forward from his ankles, his knees deeply bent, as he had seen Nick do earlier and skied the steep fall line like a demon, his mind empty of everything but the need to reach help for Gigi. In minutes Zach had reached the bottom of the mountain, shouting as he came to a stop. Within seconds two ski patrolmen were on the lift with a sled to bring Gigi down.

"Jesus, Zach, what's wrong?" Nick yelled, skiing over quickly through the crowd. Zach was standing alone, looking upward desperately, his fists clenched.

"Gigi's leg . . . I think it's broken."

"Shit! The poor kid! But it happens every day on the baby slopes, they're the most dangerous place to be. Too crowded."

"We went up the mountain."

"Zach, you *asshole*! How could you take her up there? You wanted to ski the fall line, that's fucking *criminal*!"

"It wasn't that."

"You just skied the fall line, you shit! I watched you come down, man, totally dumb reckless, but I thought you'd gone up alone."

"To hell with the fall line, Nick, I didn't notice. Do you see the sled yet?"

"They just left, it takes time to get to the top . . . . Christ, how *could* you let her go up with you?"

"I don't know . . . I thought . . . a beginner's trail . . . *stupid, so fucking stupid*! I'll never forgive myself, Nick . . . . I didn't dream it would get so narrow."

"That's why they call it a trail. Come on in the ski hut, you'll freeze out here."

"I'll come in when she's down."

"Christ!" Disgustedly, Nick gave Zach his ski cap, found a blanket to throw over his shoulders, and stood waiting with him until the ski patrol came smoothly down the mountain with Gigi covered with blankets, strapped flat to a wide sled.

"We're taking her to the hospital," one of the ski patrolmen said, tossing Zach his parka and sweater. "Just the leg, she'll be okay."

"We'll follow you," Nick said, seeing that Zach was speechless with relief. The two men followed the ambulance into town to the hospital, where dozens of victims of ski accidents had already been treated that day. They sat in the waiting room, silent and tense. After three-quarters of an hour, a busy nurse came up to them, speaking hurriedly.

"It's a nice, clean fracture of the fibula. Boot-top, mid-shaft. She should heal without problems," the nurse announced. "We've doped her up and she'll be out of pain for hours, the fracture's been set, Doctor put her in a walking cast, these are her crutches. She's badly bruised, but that's normal. Here are more pain pills, one every four hours, enough to last three days. She can navigate, I showed her how to handle the crutches, but she needs rest more than anything now. Here are her X rays. You pay at the desk going out." She rushed off before they had a chance to ask any questions. Zach strode rapidly toward the desk.

An orderly, pushing Gigi in a wheelchair, appeared at the swinging door, skillfully dodging two more skiers who were being carried in by the ski patrol. She had a cast on her left leg from her ankle to below her knee, her ski pant flapping where it had been slit up the front. With her white, exhausted face she looked like a rag doll who'd been forgotten by a careless child.

"How do you feel, you poor kid?" Nick asked as he took the bar of the wheelchair.

"Not too bad. The doctor thought it was one of the cleanest fractures he'd seen all week," Gigi said faintly. "Very complimentary, as if I'd done it nicely on purpose."

"Does it still hurt?"

"No, but I feel goofy . . . must be the drugs. They have an assembly line going in there . . . amazing, orthopedist's heaven . . . but not recommended."

"Did he happen to tell you what the fibula was?"

"Nope, just said I'd been lucky, considering. No big deal."

"Gigi . . . ." Zach, back from the desk, stood holding the X rays, looking down at her abjectly, his hands at his sides. Gigi took absolutely no notice of him. "Gigi?" he asked again, in deepest distress.

She looked straight ahead, right through him. "Nick, can you take me back to the lodge, please?"

The two men exchanged glances and helped Gigi transfer from the wheelchair to the car in silence. At the lodge they steadied her as she insisted on using her crutches, inching along as she practiced walking, putting her weight on her broken leg as briefly as possible.

"Oh, really, what an absolute bloody *bore,*" Pandora groaned as they entered the small bedroom. "I wondered where you'd all got to, so I hitched a ride back. I should have guessed . . . beginner's luck."

"Thanks."

"You'll be fine. Happens all the time," Pandora said briskly.

"Thanks."

"I'll help you off with your clothes," Pandora offered in an exasperated tone.

"Thanks."

"Guys, out. I can manage, I've done it before."

Soon Gigi was settled in bed in her red flannel pajamas. Pandora had cut the left leg short so that there was room for the cast. The room, as are the rooms of most ski lodges, was overheated, and Gigi had declined a sweater. Pandora put on her after-ski velvet trousers, silk

blouse and soft furry boots, took her bag, and went down to the bar of
the lodge, looking for action.

"Where's Zach?" she asked Nick, who was perched on a bar-
stool. She sat down beside him.

"Up in our room."

"How come?"

"He's not in the mood to join this merry throng."

"For pity's sake, why not?"

"He feels responsible because he took Gigi up the mountain."

"Good Lord . . ." Pandora laughed incredulously. "She didn't
tell me that, in fact she didn't say anything much. How absurd of her.
Talk about your know-nothing amateurs! It's just as much her fault as
his. You'll never catch me doing something as clearly stupid as that."

"Have you considered joining the Red Cross?" he asked coldly,
as she ordered herself a drink.

Nick and Pandora sat drinking at the bar in glum silence. It was
typical of Pandora, Nick mused, to regard a broken leg as if it were a
social gaffe she was too well-bred to make. He wished he had never
told her that Zach had taken Gigi up the mountain, although she'd be
bound to learn it sooner or later. The questions he'd asked himself
about Zach's feelings toward Gigi had been resolved by the guy's
absolute anguish over Gigi's accident. The lunk was in love for the
first time in his life. And who could blame him?

A number of the women in the bar were glancing in Nick's direction, recognizing him. Ignoring Pandora, he fell into conversation with
a pretty redhead who was sitting on his right. Irritated, Pandora finished her drink and ordered another. This was going to be a wonderful
evening, Nick flirting with every girl in the lodge, relishing his role of
just-treat-me-like-a-regular-guy, playing it modest and charming to all
the dreary little star-fuckers while Zach lurked about gloomily in his
room.

Zach . . . . all alone, no doubt blaming himself unnecessarily for
Gigi's silly tumble, needing comfort, feeling blue and lonely. Zach,
still being idealistic and old-fashioned and sentimental. Zach at his
most vulnerable. Zach alone and going to waste.

"I'll just go and check on them," Pandora said to Nick. "Have
you got the key to your room?" He handed it to her and she slipped
out of the bar and nipped up the stairs, congratulating herself on recognizing an opportunity when it fell in her lap. That was how Harpers
organized their lives while other people daydreamed profitlessly.

Quietly Pandora stood outside the half-open door to Zach and Nick's room. Why hadn't Nick told her it wasn't locked? The room was so small that she could see almost all of it. Zach lay sprawled on his back on the far bed, lit only by the light on the night table that stood between the twin beds. She could see at once that he had fallen asleep on the edge of the bed in the heat of the room. His ski boots were kicked to one side of the wall, his ski pants were hanging from the bedpost, but he still wore his Jockey shorts. A bathrobe lay on the bed by his hand, as if he anticipated having to fling it on. Pandora stepped through the doorway and closed the door firmly but quietly behind her, tiptoeing noiselessly, in her supple, felt-soled boots, to Zach's bed.

Gigi settled back in bed, feeling oddly comfortable, all things considered. The powerful injections that the doctor had given her before he tried to set her leg had worked immediately, and the pain pills that followed had an effect that showed no sign of beginning to wear off. She was floating pleasantly, and the knowledge that she had an ordinary broken leg seemed more reassuring than otherwise. It could have been so much worse.

Gigi closed her eyes for a while, hoping to sleep, until she became aware that she was trying to push away the uneasy consciousness that she had been deliberately unkind to Zach at the hospital. Could she still maintain that he'd been unfair to her up on the mountain? He'd just told her that he loved her, told her straight out, for the first time, that she was the only girl in the world for him, and kissing—considerable kissing—under those circumstances was understandable, wasn't it? Even Sasha's code would have to allow that at such a time a man didn't deserve to suffer. So what if she'd seen a look of victory in his eyes? Didn't that fairly reflect those long moments in which she'd finally let herself kiss him back as she had yearned to for so long? Did she have to react as violently as an insulted maiden in a Victorian novel?

As Gigi replayed exactly what had happened, as she figured out why she'd gone flying downhill like Harold Lloyd, she knew that she couldn't blame her broken leg only on Zach. Lying there in the snow, waiting in awful pain and loneliness for help to come, she'd been so frightened that she'd turned her fear and pain into rage, building up a case against Zach to take her mind off her terror, but in fact until she had wrenched herself out of his secure grasp, she'd been safe enough up on the mountain. He'd skied carefully and considerately all the way, although he should never, ever have lured her into taking the risk. But recklessness *was* Zach, for him it wasn't even recklessness but a conviction that almost anything could be done if you had the courage to take a chance. She'd known it and she'd had a choice.

Thinking it over in her languid haze, Gigi clearly understood that she was angry at herself, not at Zach. But she'd taken her anger out on him at the hospital. When he'd told her, while he and Nick were helping her upstairs, that he was going to stay in his room next door in case she needed something, she hadn't responded by so much as a nod. Or a blink. Not so much as a disdainful sniff. As if even rejection was too good for him.

He'd been so abjectly miserable. Hadn't she almost . . . . enjoyed? . . . well, yes, *enjoyed* seeing mighty, dominating, all-wise Zach Nevsky reduced almost to tears by her accident?

How had it all started? She'd first met Zach at one of the Nevsky family celebrations, and even though he was Sasha's much-discussed brother, it had seemed excessively flattering to her the way every female, every aunt, niece and cousin in the room had clustered around him, vying for his attention. He'd been involved with an actress then, according to Sasha who monitored his affairs, and then with another actress. No woman could resist Zach, Sasha declared proudly, and no woman could keep his interest for long. Wasn't it then, long ago, that she had set her will against Zach, the red-hot center of his feverish theatrical world, the darling of the drama critics, the unquestioned King of Off Broadway? Wasn't it then that she had determined that if ever, by any chance, they had anything to do with each other, she'd keep him at arm's length? Oh, yes, Gigi told herself, she'd played a stern, hard game with him, as sweetly prudish, as daintily prickly, as demurely standoffish, as any clever virgin fishing for a husband with a substantial income in a Trollope novel. It was a wonder she hadn't insisted that he call her Miss Orsini. She'd played a good game—but played it too long, and she had a broken fibula to prove it. Gigi sighed euphorically. Oh, she wanted Zach, wonderful Zach, she wanted to tell him everything she'd been thinking, she wanted him to know she loved him, and he was just next door. The problem was the room didn't have a phone and Pandora had thoughtlessly closed the door of their bedroom as she left for the bar, too quickly for Gigi to shout after her.

She'd managed fairly well on her crutches before, Gigi thought, consideringly. But then both Nick and Zach had been hovering over her so she'd known she couldn't fall. The doctor had assured her that it was safe to stand on her walking cast, even to go up and down stairs, and Zach was so near. Still, why take a childish chance? What if she slipped in trying to get to the door, and broke her other leg? Hadn't she faced enough danger for one day? She shuddered as she remembered the mountain and closed her eyes, unable to make up her mind. She didn't *feel* sensible, that was the problem.

Pandora stood over Zach and surveyed the situation. He was plunged into the deep sleep of total exhaustion, as wiped out as if he'd taken knockout drops. It was the first time she had seen him without his characteristic expression of energetic command. Her breath caught in her throat as she looked at his splendid body, all but naked, powerful but utterly abandoned to unconsciousness. Oh, she loved having him like this, helpless and defenseless. She loved the big, rounded, passive lump of his limp genitals. She'd never had a man utterly in her power, never before experienced the immediate rush of heat that invaded her at the sight of a man she had wanted, but hadn't yet conquered, delivered so entirely into her rule. An insistent, welcome pulse started to beat heavily between her legs as speedily, and in absolute silence, Pandora stripped off all her clothes and let them slide to the floor, never taking her gaze away from Zach's unprotected nakedness, measuring it with expert, covetous eyes. Softly she removed the bathrobe from the mattress and lightly lowered her slender body into its place, lying sideways, next to Zach but not touching him, supporting herself on one elbow, her chin on her hand, so that she could watch his face.

Zach never moved as she lay down; his deep, regular breathing didn't change. Pandora reached down and inserted her hand stealthily into the fly of his shorts and stretched her right hand out flat over his penis, exerting no pressure at all. It felt downy, wrinkled, and soft-skinned, and as her palm recognized its length she felt herself grow almost unbearably wet. She scrutinized his face as she made her tentative contact with his flesh, and saw no change in his unconsciousness. Curbing herself strictly, she waited until, under the delicate warmth of her motionless hand, Zach's organ began to grow fatter, less limp, unmistakably awakening as he slept. Still he lay quietly, undisturbed, and soon she judged that it was safe to curve her fingers around him and begin to increase the pressure on his penis in the most adroit fashion, faintly, slightly, so that gradually, very gradually, while he slumbered on, his penis rose and nudged her fingers so that she had to spread them to accommodate him. Better and better, Pandora thought, intoxicated but still disciplined, her fingers maintaining their cuddling, feathering motions, better and better than she would ever have imagined. Soon she managed to gently widen the opening of his fly, and his penis, freed from the restriction of the fabric, but still guided by her touch, rose straight into the air. She kept her whole hand lightly circled around it, as it jerked and jumped in irregular beats, continuing to fill and stiffen until it lay on his stomach, pointing upward toward his waist. Zach sighed deeply in his sleep, moved his head, but showed no signs of waking. Pandora waited as long as she could to fully savor the sight of his magnificent arousal. He would never belong so utterly to anyone else, she thought triumphantly. Not like this. Finally, unable to hold herself back any longer, she opened her fingers, softly released his shaft, and shifted her position with the utmost care, so that she held herself spread above Zach's body, straddling him with both her knees, balanced easily on one arm and the flat of her hand, suspended, hovering over him like a slim golden and white predator.

Still he slept, although he mumbled something in his sleep and moved his head from side to side. She looked down to make sure that the entrance to her thighs was poised a little farther down his body than the swollen tip of his organ. Her free hand slowly and expertly lifted the heavy rod and fed it slowly, easily, inch by rigid inch, into her hungry, waiting body. One of Zach's eyelids opened a slit as he almost woke, and then fell shut again. Pandora tightened her inner muscles, relaxed them and tightened them again, just enough to provide a distinct pulsation. Zach started to move within her as both his eyelids opened.

"What?" he gasped, utterly confused and disoriented. Pandora was silent, tense and spellbound with her galloping need as, for the first time, she dared to move her hips and bottom backward and forward in an irresistibly insistent rhythm. Zach, still not entirely awake, rolled over, automatically holding her in his arms, instinctively keeping himself rooted inside her. He pinioned her to the mattress and blinked blankly down at her face. "What the hell . . . ?" he whispered thickly, wonderingly. Still she said nothing, but finally allowed herself to abandon the agonizingly slow, acutely voluptuous curb she had so guilefully imposed on herself. She thrust her pelvis upward in a lawless frenzy so that he would penetrate her as profoundly as possible. Zach, excruciatingly inflamed, rammed into her body in an animalistic reflex. Their bodies were locked together, Pandora's naked legs were wrapped around his back, and Zach was rutting deeply inside her, both of them grunting with unchained hunger, when Gigi pushed open the door. She staggered back against the wall, unable to move or to turn her eyes away. The two on the bed were unaware of everything as they moved quickly toward their rapid, uncomplicated, barbarous climax and fell apart heavily, groaning in relief, eyes closed.

Released from her trance, in a frantic desire to escape, Gigi maneuvered too quickly on her crutches and banged her cast loudly against the door. Zach raised his head, looked up and caught a glimpse of her face just as she managed to turn her back. He gaped at her, stunned into immobility, as she started clumsily to negotiate the corridor, leaving the door swinging open. In unutterable shock he saw himself as Gigi must have seen him. He pulled himself out of Pandora in a huge lurch, struggled to a standing position and futilely attempted to put on his ski pants.

"And just where do you think you're going?" Pandora demanded in silky displeasure, her eyelids still closed. No man had ever left her body with such an ungentlemanly lack of ceremony.

"You crazy bitch! I could kill you for this!"

Her eyes flew open in disbelief. "*What!* What's wrong with you?"

"Gigi saw us."

"So what if she did?"

"Get the hell out of here!" Zach shouted, and slumped into a chair, finally realizing that he couldn't follow his insane determination to run after Gigi. What could he say that she would believe? That anyone would ever believe?

"Zach! Is that any way to treat a lady?" Pandora asked, trying to turn it into a joke. In her confident, reliable and often-reinforced opinion, she'd been unforgettable. But not crazy-bitch-unforgettable. Really, Zach was simply unhinged tonight. To say nothing of ungrateful. "Get out," he repeated, in a tone of such menace that she wiped herself off hastily on the top sheet and dressed as if the floor were on fire. She slammed the door and stood irresolutely in the hallway. She couldn't go back to the room, God knows.

Pandora shrugged her shoulders petulantly, checked her clothes to make sure they were on straight, rearranged her hair in a series of practiced pats and started downstairs in the direction of the bar, her patrician beauty only heightened by the brilliant color in her cheeks and the hungry, unsatisfied appetite in her eyes. Certainly not Nick, she decided, he didn't deserve to get lucky tonight, but the bar was full of great-looking guys. She was just getting started, she thought, with an interior smile. A quickie was never enough, not even what must have been the slowest quickie in history. When Zach started to remember how good she was, he'd be sorry indeed that he'd sent her away. By tomorrow he'd be hanging around like a hungry puppy, begging to be fed again. No chance of that. Harpers are never to be dismissed.

16

I don't understand why she's still so upset,'' Billy said worriedly
as she and Sasha sat in the kitchen of the apartment Sasha shared
with Gigi. It was a Saturday and Sasha wasn't working, so they
had taken advantage of the opportunity to meet in the kitchen for their
first private talk. "She should have started to bounce back by now,
bruises and all, don't you think?"

Gigi had arrived back in New York with her broken leg a few
hours after Billy had arrived from Paris and moved back into her
apartment at the Carlyle. That had been four days ago, days in which
Billy had spent much of her time keeping Gigi company and making
sure that she was fed. In the evenings she'd divided her time between
Gigi and Sasha's place and Jessica's apartment, finding that mere constant, casual communion with three women, who knew nothing of what
had happened with Sam, was like a poultice on her raw pain and anger.

"If it were just her leg, I'd agree with you, but now I know for sure it's got to be something that happened with Zach," Sasha replied. "He hasn't phoned since she got back, that's not like him at all, and she hasn't mentioned his name, which used to be slipped into every sentence she spoke. I suspect a good old-fashioned broken heart and I'd like to break his goddamned head for him, but I'm afraid to ask her straight out—there's something so closed in and hurt and pinched about her face—she's never been like this before—it keeps me from being my usual inquisitive self. And then . . . since it concerns Zach I feel I should stay out of it."

"But, Sasha, you must know exactly what was going on between them. He's your brother, she's your roommate, you two are the same generation, how *can* you not know?"

"Billy, if I had a clue I promise I'd tell you every detail, but I never understood it. Whatever was going on was out of a time warp—"

"Not a love affair?"

"Not what anybody normal would call a love affair. No touching—"

"*No touching?* Come on!"

"They must both be mentally sick. How any woman, given a chance, could not touch Zach . . ."

"Or any man not touch Gigi . . . ."

Billy and Sasha looked at each other in complete understanding, not of Zach and Gigi, but of each other. Over the last few days they had discovered that they were deeply compatible in the mysterious way in which women of different ages, backgrounds and life experience can sometimes find themselves comfortable, even intuitive, with each other, in spite of their not knowing each other well.

"We'd better unpack this lunch hamper from La Grenouille," Billy said, "while it's still hot. I ordered this morning and had my driver pick it up—I thought we could all use a hot lunch, instead of more sandwiches."

"An army travels on its stomach, and three women can make an army . . . even with one walking wounded, one about to be unemployed and one . . . . whatever you are," Sasha said delicately. Billy wasn't her imperious, astonishing self almost as much as Gigi wasn't herself. Or more.

"Maybe someday I'll tell you, if I ever figure it out myself." She couldn't bullshit clear-eyed Sasha, Billy thought, even if she wanted to.

"At least it doesn't involve Zach."

"The Orloffs and the Nevskys are in the clear on this one," Billy said, producing a smile.

"That's lucky. I feel guilty enough as it is. Come on in the living room, Billy. We can have a picnic while I show you a picture of the condo I may decide not to buy in Hawaii. Or then again, I may. I need a bigger audience for my catalog collection."

"Catalog? Do you mean *Previews*? I keep a stack of them at the hotel, to remind me that I can always buy a plantation or a ranch or an island in Maine, or all three, for that matter, as well as a castle in Spain. My escape routes."

"But you don't—you really *could*, after all, and you don't—why not?"

"I guess I'm just not a country girl. I wouldn't know what to do with myself," Billy said thoughtfully. "Most women who have a number of houses use them to lead the kind of heavy-duty social round that doesn't attract me. I like to keep busy, seriously busy. I'd have to learn the cattle business or take up shooting wild ducks or lobster fishing—not my bag. Gigi, are you ready for some of this pâté?"

"No thanks."

"But you should try to eat something, baby. You've been losing weight in front of my eyes and you didn't have any to lose," Billy said, looking at Gigi with worry.

"I promise to have some of the chicken when you both get around to it," she temporized.

"Okay, but I'll hold you to it. Now I have a confession to make. I've been dying to open your Christmas present since I got back, and last night, when I went back to my place for dinner, I gave in to the temptation. Darling, it's so incredibly beautiful, I've never had anything like it! The minute I put it on I felt like another woman, I *became* Georgie—who had a hell of a lot more fun than Billy—and I just couldn't take it off. If I say so myself, I looked divine in it, so romantic, so alluring . . . . even without a butler in sight, alas. I read the card to Jessica over the phone and she insisted that I read it again to David when he came back from the office. They couldn't get over it—the violinist at the Café de Paris . . . the rope of pink pearls . . . Georgie inventing mascara—they never knew you had an imagination like that. I'm taking it over tonight so they can see the robe and the wonderful sketch of me with the three battling butlers. Poor Jessie's dying to open her present, but the Strausses always celebrate an all-out Hanukkah, and after that they do a big Christmas, so she doesn't dare. Thank you, Gigi, truly it's the most enchanting and original present I've ever had.''

"I knew you'd like it when I found it,'' Gigi said, mustering a trace of animation.

"What are you giving Jessie? I promise I won't even hint to her.''

"Ruffled pink pajamas, they're French, circa 1920s, and I'm pretty sure they're just her size.''

"What does the card say?''

"It's in the package now, but Sasha made Xerox copies of all of the cards when we thought we were going to start a lingerie line with Mr. Jimmy.''

"Poor Mr. Jimmy,'' Billy said. "Even though I never knew him, I know I would have doted on him. Imagine, dropping dead of a heart attack in the middle of a poker game, with a winning hand—''

"Here today, gone tomorrow,'' Gigi interrupted. "Maybe it was all for the best. He'd had a good life and he didn't suffer for a second. And since he was a bachelor . . .''

"Really, Gigi, you're absolutely heartless!'' Sasha protested. "What about me? I worked for him for years, I loved the man, I'm the one who misses him desperately. And what about the fact that his only heir, his nephew the shrink, has closed the deal to sell the company to Warner's? Ha! Would that all shrinks moved so fast. And Warner's has all the models they need—what is Sasha Nevsky going to do for a living after the papers are signed? Here today, gone tomorrow—is that all you can say about poor Mr. Jimmy? Really, Gigi, you should be ashamed of yourself!''

"And it was a damn good idea too, copying antique lingerie, nobody's doing it,'' Billy added. "I'm so sorry about your hopes being dashed like that, both of you.''

"If you like the idea, why don't you go into business with us?'' Sasha suggested. "You could start a new company and do just what he was planning to do.''

"What! No. Oh, Sasha, no, I don't think so. I can't possibly imagine myself competing on Seventh Avenue after owning Scruples . . . it feels totally wrong, it *is* totally wrong, and that's an end to it.'' Billy shook her head vigorously. Did Sasha have the slightest idea of what the tight elite of the innerwear industry would think of her as a new entry with Gigi's whimsical idea? She'd be a laughingstock, going from Scruples into such a small, if charming, undertaking. "Why don't you take your idea to another company? I could easily make introductions for you and Gigi.''

''No thanks, Billy,'' Gigi said hastily, before Sasha could answer. ''It was one thing with Mr. Jimmy . . . I felt safe with him, even though it took me a while to agree to it, but it was his idea, not mine. *He* came after *me*. I wouldn't want to propose something so special to a bunch of strangers.''

''I would,'' Sasha said vigorously, preventing her cat from getting into the pâté.

''That's because you're an Orloff,'' Gigi said listlessly.

''If you weren't such a sad case I'd take that as an insult,'' Sasha replied. ''I'll assume you mean that I have more resistance to bad luck than you do, more fortitude, more optimism.''

''Whatever you say.''

''A broken leg won't last forever, and the Gatherum was surprisingly decent about it, even if she did scream at you on the phone for half an hour. After all, she's holding your job for you.''

''That's because she can't find anybody better to work in her vile and odious business,'' Gigi said with abrupt vehemence. ''Arguing with the clients who want the top of the line and don't want to pay for it; steering unsuspecting clients to the most expensive rental places and florists because that way we pick up more money on our percentages of what they charge; the perfectionist hostesses with the holes in their hearts who will never, ever be satisfied; the unending details and paperwork and the phone attached to your ear; the amount of vicious gossip about other caterers from the waiters who work for all of them —so you know that they've got to be gossiping everywhere about you too; the attitude that no matter how tired a kitchen worker is, he or she gets no rest. Did you know that if they so much as lean against something during a lull, somebody will spot them and say, 'If you can lean, you can clean'? That happened to me when I started, and I've never forgotten it. I hate the whole stinking-to-the-core catering business, I don't know why I ever thought I wanted to be in it, and I'll be damned if I'll go back to it! I'd rather get a job as a chef in a private family.''

Billy looked at her defiant face and held her peace. This could only be a momentary rejection of a field in which Gigi had already made brilliant progress, not something to take seriously. It was her broken heart speaking, not her ambition.

''Gloom and doom, doom and gloom,'' Sasha muttered, eating the pâté with an excellent appetite. "What a lousy holiday season. If it weren't for Marcel here, I'd catch your mood, but Marcel is one happy cat. I hoped I'd get some consolation from my catalogs, but even the new Neiman-Marcus Christmas Book has let me down . . . . again. What on earth made them think I'd want an electronic bicycle that's hooked up to a giant TV with two hours of programmed scenery, so you don't get bored while you bike—for twenty thousand dollars in real American money? This has to be a new low. Billy, did you ever see the 'ComRo 1' they offered last year? No? Imagine a big, ugly robot that opens doors, takes out trash, sweeps, waters the plants, and walks the dog, at only fifteen thousand bucks! At those prices I can open my own doors, thank you very much! And look at this! Fourteen thousand dollars for a tunic and pants from Galanos! . . . I'd sooner learn to sew!" Sasha kicked with exasperation at the pile of Christmas catalogs that she'd been collecting for years. "At least the year before last, Neiman's had a cute ostrich that was only fifteen hundred, relatively speaking a bargain . . . if you happen to live on a ranch."

"Why do you hang on to those things, if they make you so mad?" Billy asked, amused and curious. She'd never seen anyone with a catalog collection before.

"Because they're there, I guess. It's some sort of sick addiction. It's not as if I ordered much from them, just an item or two for my aunts to keep me on their lists. They all show the same obvious, predictable Christmas merchandise, whether it's B. Altman or Bonwit's or Sakowitz or Marshall Field or Jordan Marsh or Saks or Bloomie's—excruciatingly dull suits and dresses, overly fluffy blouses, overly fancy sweaters, overly expensive furs—wait a minute, here's a wild Russian Barguzin sable cape for a hundred thousand, no less, which I'd happily take, to warm my wild Russian heart, but only if Mr. Marcus gave it to me for love—excruciatingly dull dresses and suits, just what you would expect every man with a fear of shopping would order for his wife or daughter or sister, but nothing a woman would ever buy for herself, nothing exciting, just reworking of last year's stuff that I know by heart, and boring, boring, boring. Not necessary. *Not young!"*

"You're just not a catalog customer," Billy decided. "You have too much style of your own."

"I could be," Sasha said thoughtfully. "I could be. Anybody could be. Oh well, at least Neiman's is better than the other department stores—they try to be different . . . I kind of craved that ostrich.

The other catalogs, the ones that don't come from the big department stores, concentrate on safe jewelry that wouldn't thrill any woman, or watches—there are a zillion watch catalogs—or gifts from places like Tiffany and Gump's. Maybe I should go realistic and send for Sears, Roebuck. Or I could move to the woods and get L.L. Bean. My problem is I want catalogs to be about *fashion*. To think I'm still silly enough to wait all year long for them to come, as if I somehow believe that this year, finally, I'm going to be surprised. It's pitiful, purely pitiful.''

"Maybe it's like giving yourself a lot of Christmas presents you don't have to pay for or return," Gigi suggested, trying to be responsive to complaints she'd heard many times before, since Sasha ruffled disapprovingly through her catalogs at many odd hours, even in her bath, treating them as if they were a form of literature. Gigi felt she owed it to Sasha to try to show some interest after her awful remarks about Mr. Jimmy. How could she possibly tell Sasha the real reason she'd been so pessimistic, the real reason why she didn't believe in anything anymore? Sasha loved Zach, and she couldn't put her in the position of having to choose between them.

"No," Sasha answered Gigi, between bites of chicken and endive, as Billy listened with interest. "I don't think it's exactly that. Reading catalogs, disappointing as they always are, is more like going shopping when I don't have the time to waste in a crowded store, or the money for impulse buying. It's basically a fantasy trip, I guess. A cheap thrill. See, all this stuff in the catalogs *is* actually available—it's not like a fashion magazine, where they show clothes that aren't in the stores yet. With a catalog, all I have to do is call a toll-free number and it's mine—so even if I don't want it and can't afford it I'm having the fun of being impossibly choosy without a salesgirl glowering at me. I can turn down a diamond necklace and one of those china Boehm birds for almost five hundred dollars, and a Vuitton bag and thirty different velour bathrobes that all look alike—and I can feel that I'm above temptation. It's probably the nun-like, non-consumer side of my personality trying to grow. Next year I'm going to throw them all out unopened because they'll just be more of the same.''

"I bet you don't," Gigi said morosely.

"You're right . . . as I said, I'm an optimist. And would I want to be the last person on my block not to know about the new 1983 Neiman-Marcus His-Her gift? And how come it isn't Her-His?''

"Is a lot of your fascination just curiosity?" Billy asked.

"In the beginning, Billy, when they first arrive, yes, but look how tattered some of these are . . . you'd think they were children's books . . . I swear I know them by heart. It's got to be some sort of character flaw, but at least I share it with a lot of other people. Billy, here's that condo I mentioned I was considering buying." Sasha handed Billy the Neiman's 1982 Christmas Book, and Gigi looked at a photograph of Hanalei Plantation in Kauai, a vast acreage of land set on a blue and emerald bay that had been used as a location for the movie of *South Pacific*.

"What condo?" Billy wondered. "This is a view from the air, it covers dozens of miles."

"Read it! Right down at the bottom of the page it says that they're building furnished condos with what they call 'Bali High' sunset views —isn't it gorgeous?" Sasha sounded deeply possessive.

"*Starting* at one million two hundred thousand? Isn't that . . . ?"

"Expensive? So? It can't ruin Sasha Nevsky to dream. Mark Twain said no girl was ever ruined by a book. Since I'm not going to buy the knee socks with jingle bells or the whipsnake—whipsnake?— sounds kinky—handbag, I can also not buy the condo. It's more fun to *not* buy the condo. It makes me feel richer."

"I think I'm starting to understand, or maybe I'm getting more confused," Billy laughed. Sasha was so spirited that she didn't understand how Gigi couldn't look just a little more cheerful.

"Look at this, Billy," Sasha said, flourishing the B. Altman catalog. "Here's a hostess gown for over four hundred dollars—just two pieces of pure silk, two sleeves, a little smocking and embroidery at the neck, and since it says 'made in India,' you know the labor wasn't expensive. They're getting away with murder."

"Over four hundred? Let me see that," Gigi asked. "Oh, how awful . . . . maybe it's the photo." She examined the picture closely, her pale face alert for the first time since she'd come home with her leg in a cast.

"Maybe it's the style," Sasha answered acidly.

"Maybe . . . ." Gigi said and stopped. "Forget it."

"Maybe what?" Billy insisted. "Come on, Gigi, maybe what?"

"Well . . . . what if . . . just what if . . . . I did get a whole collection together, the way I was going to for Mr. Jimmy, and have it copied and sell it . . . by catalog? No, that's a terrible idea. Me? A catalog? I don't know the first thing about catalogs."

"Of course you do," Sasha objected. "I own every decent catalog published in the last five years, and you've been through every page of every last one of them with me, Gigi Orsini, and a lot of them twice.''

"True, but they're all so big and fancy and only for Christmas. My lingerie is different from what people are used to, and all I have to sell is the lingerie, not all that other stuff—hams and jams and dog's sunglasses—lingerie's not enough to fill a catalog. They put tons of stuff on every page.''

"I think Gigi's right about that, Sasha,'' Billy said. "You need a lot of merchandise and you need a name. Every one of these catalogs you have here is from a famous store; people order from them largely because the gift box has instant name recognition and it comes from a place they consider to have status, like Neiman's or Tiffany. Nobody's ever heard of Gigi Orsini . . . not yet.''

"Wait a minute, Billy, what you just said about recognition, did you hear yourself?'' Gigi asked, suddenly excited. "You're absolutely right, it takes recognition, that's the key—Billy, *what about Scruples*?''

"Scruples?'' Billy said blankly. "What are you talking about?''

"Scruples—*a catalog like Scruples*!''

"Oh please, Gigi!'' Billy said, instantly offended. "Scruples was the most exclusive specialty store in the world. Scruples would never, *never* have had a catalog! I would not have allowed it, not in a million years. And anyway, there are no Scruples anymore. No, absolutely not!''

"But listen, Billy, that's the thing, there are no more stores, but the Scruples name and reputation and mystique and status have never lost their power. It's only been . . . what? . . . not even two years . . . you could bring it back, but in a different form . . . the first really great catalog for fashion!''

"Oh, Gigi, do you have any idea of how expensive we were?'' Billy snapped, deeply irritated. "There were enough women in Beverly Hills and New York and Chicago to support three boutiques, not big department stores, but large boutiques located in the centers of wealthy areas. The other Scruples were all in other countries. Most people never had the kind of money you needed to shop at Scruples, and the ones who did *certainly* don't shop by mail order! Mail order! Even if I liked the idea . . . and I have to say I most definitely don't . . . you could never sell clothes as expensive as Scruples' clothes

without fitting rooms and perfect alterations and personal attention—
no, it couldn't work, it simply can *not* be done.''

"But what if the clothes weren't so expensive?'' Gigi insisted.
"What if they were affordable?''

"Then they wouldn't reflect Scruples. It's out of the question.''
Billy spoke angrily. Gigi simply had no idea why the idea of Scruples
as a catalog assaulted and damaged her memories of her perfect store,
her exquisite, exclusive boutique, the dream she had created to satisfy
no one but herself, the dream that was over forever.

"Billy,'' Gigi said intently, "Scruples was a concept before it
worked—remember how you told me that you started with one concept—to bring the elegance of Dior to Beverly Hills—and then Spider
changed it into a fun Disneyland for grownups? Why couldn't you
change it again? Make it a moderate-priced concept, but with just as
much taste? Call the catalog Scruples Two, so people wouldn't think
it was the same thing . . . . it would be about taste and quality and the
youth and style that Sasha keeps wanting—''

"And it wouldn't have to arrive only at Christmas, like the others,'' Sasha interrupted, galvanized. "It wouldn't have to contain this
gifty-gifty stuff—it could come twice—or maybe even four times—a
year, the way the stores change their merchandise by the season. Oh,
Billy, it could be done! I'm your customer, Gigi's your customer, even
you might find out that you'd be your own customer!''

"Scruples Two,'' Gigi said. "Just the name alone makes it different—the 'Two' part shows that it's not trying to be like the store, it's
its own self.'' She grabbed her crutches and got up to get the photo-
copies of her cards. "Look, Billy, it could have a section for my
antique lingerie, with these cards as copy—come on, read them, Billy.
Hell, I could write the whole catalog if I had to, couldn't I, Sasha?
How hard could it be? I couldn't get the merchandise designed or
made, but you could, Billy, and Sasha could help, and . . . oh, Billy!
You've got to say yes!''

"No.''

"No?'' Gigi asked reflexively. She knew that when Billy said no,
she meant it.

"No, and I'd really rather change the subject.'' Billy got up from
the floor, where she'd been sitting eating lunch from the coffee table.
She was all but trembling with a violent rage she didn't want the girls
to see, a rage she couldn't explain to herself. "I'm supposed to be

getting my hair cut this afternoon and I'm late already. Gigi, you still haven't had anything to eat. I'll call later.'' She wrapped herself hastily in her coachman's mink coat and in seconds the front door had closed behind her.

"Was it something I said?" Sasha asked.

"Something we both said, I guess," Gigi answered. "The last time I saw her that mad, she divorced my father."

"Mrs. Ikehorn, is there something wrong?" Louis, Billy's alarmed hairdresser, finally forced himself to ask. She'd been sitting rigidly in his chair for ten minutes after he'd finished cutting and blowing her wet hair dry, staring straight into the mirror without any expression or a single word.

Billy started. "Oh. No, Louis, as a matter of fact it's the best haircut I've had in years. I was just thinking about something . . . Christmas shopping . . . .''

"Oh, don't say those words, Mrs. Ikehorn, just don't say those awful words," he pleaded. "I haven't started yet. You look smashing. Fabulous. I'd say ten years younger, maybe twelve. You must never let your hair get too long again. Those Paris hairdressers—when did they get off the boat? You made it back here just in time, another sixteenth of an inch and you'd have lost your special look. Two weeks, Mrs. Ikehorn, only two weeks between cuts, promise me?"

"I promise, Louis. Thank you. See you in two weeks."

Billy's limousine was waiting for her in front of the salon, and she rode back to her hotel in a brooding silence, her anger faintly mollified by the job Louis had done on her neglected head. There was probably no fury a really good haircut couldn't diminish, she thought, but what right did those two young twits have to imagine Scruples in the form of a catalog? Who read catalogs anyway? If they came to the house you threw them out . . . junk mail, that's all they were. A soon-to-be unemployed panty model and a reluctant caterer—how could they possibly have the incredible nerve to suggest using the name of Scruples to glorify a catalog of moderately priced clothes? It was sickening, like dancing on a grave, *indecent*!

Deep in thought, Billy stalked forbiddingly into the hotel and asked for her keys at the desk.

"Mrs. Ikehorn," the room clerk said, "a gentleman has been waiting for you for the last three hours."

"I don't have any appointments, not that I remember."

"He's over there, Mrs. Ikehorn." Billy turned as the room clerk pointed toward a man sitting in a chair in the lobby. He immediately got up and approached her.

"Mrs. Ikehorn?"

"Yes?"

"I'm Zach Nevsky."

"What do you expect me to do, congratulate you?"

"Please, Mrs. Ikehorn, you're the only person I can talk to."

"Why should anybody in her right mind want to talk to you?" Billy asked.

"Because I can't expect anybody else to listen to me, and I have to talk to someone."

"Why should I give a damn about your problems?"

"Because you're Gigi's stepmother and guardian," Zach insisted doggedly.

"I don't know what that has to do with it. She hasn't had a legal guardian for years. However, come on up, I'll listen to you because I'm curious and that's the only reason. Sheer curiosity as to what makes vile guys like you tick. I'm collecting lice this year."

In the living room of Billy's suite, Zach, without the aid of so much as a glass of water, told Billy the entire story of his day on the mountain with Gigi.

"After we got back to the lodge, I stayed in my room. I'd told her I'd be there if she needed anything and I left my door open so I could hear her. I must have been beat, absolutely beat, because I fell asleep in the room, it was hot and I couldn't get the window open, and the next thing I knew I woke up and, ah, I was in this sexual mode with Pandora."

"Sexual mode?" Billy asked severely. "Just what is that supposed to mean?"

Zach looked down at his shoes. "I was lying on my back and, well . . . genital arousal had taken place in my sleep and Pandora was . . . she was . . . or rather I was in a posture with her in which . . . intromission had already occurred." He clenched his fists, his voice as matter-of-fact as he could make it. Nick could do this better. Anybody could.

" 'Intromission'? Could you describe that?" Billy asked sternly.

"My . . . male organ was . . . penetrating her body. She was above me. I don't know how she got there and until I woke up I wasn't aware of what had taken place, but motion was taking place between her genitals and mine.''

''Motion?''

''A back-and-forth, up-and-down motion that had started in my sleep. I continued to participate in the motion because I found myself in a highly excited state of . . . . extreme tumescence . . . and I was . . . . that's not important, that's not an excuse, but the thing is I continued the motion without withdrawing until the moment of ejaculation. It was afterwards that I realized that Gigi was watching.''

''Let me get this absolutely straight,'' Billy said. ''In plain Anglo-Saxon, Gigi came into the room and caught you while you were *innocently* fucking Pandora?''

Zach looked up, deeply flushed. ''In plain Anglo-Saxon, that's exactly what happened. But Pandora began it while I was asleep.''

''But you finished it while you were awake? You knew perfectly well who Pandora was, you weren't dreaming?''

''I knew and I was awake. I didn't stop because I couldn't. I know that's not an excuse. But I didn't want to fuck her—I mean I wanted to continue at that particular time, but I would never have sought an opportunity to do so. *She fucked me first.* Jesus, I sound like a little kid. 'He hit me first, Ma, he started it,' but it's the truth.''

''Hmm.'' Billy got up and walked to the window and looked out on Fifth Avenue far below. She didn't want him to see her trying not to laugh. She tried hard to repress the giggles that bubbled up in her, biting her lips and trying to multiply nine by seven, which usually worked.

''But can you believe me?'' Zach asked, unable to endure her silence.

''Oddly enough, I can.''

''You can!'' Zach stood up, knocking over the chair. ''Thank God! I was afraid I'd never find anyone who could understand.''

''Pandora reminds me of someone I knew once, long ago,'' Billy said, remembering the pool house where she'd spent so many afternoons with a succession of men during the last years of Ellis Ikehorn's long fight against death. The rapacious Pandora was chaste compared to the way she'd behaved back then.

''Is that the only reason you believe me?'' Zach demanded.

''No, Zach, it isn't. Perhaps I'm clairvoyant and I can read your thoughts, or perhaps it's because you look and sound like a man who truly loves Gigi—I think people should be given the benefit of the doubt when they've hurt the person they love without meaning to, without intending to, without understanding exactly what they were doing. Your story isn't as strange as . . . some I've heard recently.''

"Will you talk to Gigi for me?" he asked eagerly.

"I don't think that would help, at least not right now. Gigi hasn't the life experience I've had, she's much too upset to listen to anything as improbable as your story, she could never believe it. What's more, just the idea that we've discussed her together, behind her back, might be counterproductive. Give it a little time. At least you know I believe you, and I'll tell Gigi I do when the right moment comes. Give her a little breathing space. It's such a mixed-up mess right now, I don't want to get into the middle of it.''

"You're sure?"

"I'm positive."

Zach turned away, downcast. What good did it do for her to believe him and not tell Gigi? "Look, Mrs. Ikehorn," he said, turning back to Billy, "I know Gigi so well, I refuse to believe that she wouldn't at least attempt to be fair to me. Sure, I understand that you don't want to get into it, at least right now, but you'd be doing such a great thing, such a good deed! She loves me, I know she does, and God knows I love her. Couldn't you just take the risk? You can't possibly know it'd be counterproductive if you don't at least try, and what have you got to lose?''

"Zach, now I understand perfectly how you got Gigi to go up the mountain," Billy said, shaking her head firmly. "But I'm a tougher nut to crack. If you're so sure, then go talk to her yourself. She can't get away from you with a cast on her leg.''

"I deserve that.''

"That's why I said it. Good-bye, Zach. Till we meet again.''

Billy closed the door to the suite behind him. No touching, Sasha had said. No touching? *That man?* Should she have Gigi examined by a board of three shrinks before having her committed to an asylum, or should she just consider it a weird new fad, like swallowing goldfish? No, it couldn't be a fad, swallowing goldfish was something she could almost imagine herself doing, on a dare, if she was totally drunk and carried away by peer pressure in a gang of happy goldfish swallowers . . . but not even *touching*?

On impulse, Billy went to the phone and dialed Josh Hillman's number. It was time to let him know she was back in the United States. After a full day's diet of Gigi and Sasha and Zach, she felt the need to talk to someone settled and wise and safely on the other side of the confusions and misplaced enthusiasms and misunderstandings of the absurdly young. Maybe people like herself, grownups, should never try to make sense of children under thirty. Maybe there was something to the rhetoric of the sixties, after all. "Never trust anybody under thirty," wasn't that how it had gone?

The next afternoon, still surprised by her quick decision, Billy found herself getting off the first plane to leave New York in the morning and arrive in Los Angeles. She hadn't told Josh she was coming, she hadn't even called Josie to tell her to send a car and driver. After she and Josh had finished chatting last night, she'd been overcome by a feeling that she wanted to pop out to L.A. and just take a quick look around, just to get a feel of the place again. Unless you were actually in California you tended to forget it existed, especially when you were plunged into the morass of New York or trying to cope with Paris.

As the taxi drove out of the airport on its way to the Bel Air Hotel and she saw the first cornball, awkward palm trees standing by the side of the highway in the sunlight, Billy began to feel something in her heart open in pleasure. She really hated palm trees. It was so nice to see those goony-looking things, so nice to come to a place where there were so many trees that were green all year long that you could afford to disapprove entirely of some of them. She hadn't seen anything green in winter, except the view from her garden on the Rue Vaneau, and the trees planted there so carefully didn't have the same quality of genuine greenness as California trees. They were too dark, she thought, consideringly, far too dark, gloomy actually, and three-quarters of the time you were watching rain dripping off their grim branches. Why did no one ever admit that it almost always rained in Paris except for July and August when you died of the heat?

At the hotel, Billy changed into a winter-white wool suit, grabbed a scarlet cashmere muffler—the whole hotel was decorated for Christmas and she might as well get into the spirit—and arranged with the front desk for a car and driver.

"Where to, ma'am?" the driver asked as they drove along Stone Canyon Road.

"Drive around a bit, take a right here and just keep on going on up the hill, wherever it looks prettiest," Billy said, knowing that you could stay lost in Bel Air for hours, even if you'd lived there for years.

"You new to the town, ma'am?"

"Yes, I'm sightseeing. But don't explain anything to me, I want to see it as if I didn't know anything."

"Fresh eyes."

"Exactly."

After fifteen minutes of aimlessly looking out of the window and breathing the warm, perfumed midwinter air, Billy came to a decision. She took a slip of paper out of her wallet on which she'd jotted down some information Josh had given her. She consulted it, and gave it to him. "Driver, would you please take me to this number in Mandeville Canyon?"

"Certainly, ma'am." The driver turned the car and headed down-hill toward Sunset, where he left the confines of Bel Air and started out in the direction of the ocean.

The limo pulled up in front of a modern house set so high on the canyon rim that it had an unobstructed view of the Pacific Ocean in the distance. Billy walked up to the front door unhesitatingly and rang the bell. She heard a voice yell, "Coming," and in a few seconds the door was pulled open.

"Hello, Spider," she said.

17

*P*eppone's was the kind of authentically old-fashioned Italian restaurant that might be expected to exist almost anywhere except California, all well-worn leather and candlelight and dark wood, without a ray of sunlight piercing its intimate dimness, an oasis tucked into the corner of an old shopping street on Barrington Place, between Spider's newly rented house and Bel Air. As Billy sipped her drink she remembered how Spider had opened his door, a few hours ago, and lifted her off the ground with a great shout of welcome and such a bone-crushing hug that she still seemed to feel it. He'd whirled her around and around and kissed both her cheeks before he'd finally put her down. In fact, she still felt dizzy.

"I feel deeply weird," Billy observed as she watched the busy waiters discussing the specials of the day with the many customers. "It's the oddest thing, Spider, I'm not quite here, but I'm not quite anywhere else . . . I'm all topsy-turvy."

"By New York time," Spider calculated, "it's ten o'clock at night and in Paris it's six hours later, which would make it four in the morning. You've only been back in the States for five days, so you've still got jet lag from Paris, aggravated by the trip here. You're about to have dinner long before you used to wake up."

"Spider, you do make sense. I never thought of jet lag . . . . that's what comes of staying put for too long. This must be the way they feel in space. I think I've been spaced out since I arrived in L.A.—is spaced out the same as spacey?"

"I think you need that drink, Billy. Maybe it'll ground you and alert your body to the idea that it's almost dinnertime, and then we'll think about looking at the menu, but not yet. I'm still trying to get over opening the door on you—I was expecting the dry cleaner and there you were, Billy, looking like the Spirit of Christmas Future. I called Josh the day I got back last week to find out where you were. Then when I called the Ritz they weren't sure where you'd gone off to, so I figured you were away for Christmas. Somehow I pictured you lying under swaying palm trees in Marrakesh, with three Frenchmen at your feet."

"Not even close."

Billy looked at Spider briefly. Ever since they'd met again, she'd been snatching quick glances at his face, trying to decide why he seemed to have changed so much. Even in the dusk of Peppone's, Spider looked like the Viking mariner of old. His hair, bleached by the sun, was blonder than ever, but there were many visible strands of silver in it now, particularly at his temples, and new lines on his deeply tanned face. He was leaner than she remembered his ever having been, not gaunt, but sinewy, as if he didn't possess a pound to spare, yet he radiated health. He looked as if he would smell of the sea, of tar and rope and fog and a clean wind.

It wasn't these visible and predictable changes that continued to occupy Billy's attention, but something deeper, the disappearance of a quality Billy had always factored into her approach to Spider. Since she'd first known him, he had looked so much the part of the quintessential California Golden Boy that she'd never been able to take him entirely seriously. The combination of his hair and his blue eyes had always vaguely irritated her. It worked so dazzlingly well, in spite of being so obvious, that it deserved to be entirely discounted by any intelligent woman. Behind any thought she had of Spider lingered a subliminal vision of him dropping whatever he was doing and heading for the beach with a surfboard, absorbed in nothing more important than catching the perfect wave. This vivid mental picture had colored her entire perception of him, in spite of the fact that she'd never known Spider to go surfing.

The mind-set in which she'd imprisoned him for years had been suddenly erased and replaced by a strength and a seriousness in his character that was impossible to overlook. He'd always been tough, uncompromising and honest, but now those qualities, which she had taken for granted, had solidified into an emotional density that seemed new to her. He'd kept his irrepressibly pagan quality—Spider was still a free spirit who would never belong to the world of nine-to-five, never settle into a routine or any system of thinking but one of his own choice. He was a man who had, almost from childhood, escaped the bonds of the everyday, the mundane, a man who had always forged his own path without worrying about what people thought. He'd admitted happily to a misspent youth, and Billy had believed that he'd never truly left it.

Now Billy was aware, with her whole consciousness, that Spider was no longer the sensuous, almost happy-go-lucky, lazily good-natured seducer and charmer who had ruled over the hothouse world of Scruples—a dictatorial, loving Pygmalion to hundreds of women. For years Spider had taken all the good things of life as they came to him with a sort of innate innocence and intense pleasure. He had seemed to expect nothing but joy from the world, but now his smile was wise and tempered by experience. Not sad, Billy thought, not bitter, simply no longer *expectant*. Billy felt a prickle of tears at this realization, although the fact that Spider Elliott had finally become a full adult was surely no cause for sorrow.

"How were things at the house?" Spider asked. "Has it been kept up to your standards, or was there a weed in the cabbage patch?"

"My *house*? Do you believe it—it didn't even occur to me to go there. Now I don't have the time. I think I'll go back to New York tomorrow."

"Oh no, you won't! I haven't laid eyes on you in almost two years and you're not going anywhere till I have a chance to find out what's been happening to you. Corresponding with you is like putting letters in bottles, throwing them in the ocean and watching them float off into the horizon."

"Two whole letters? Is that your idea of a correspondence?"

"For me it was. Heavy-duty correspondence—and they were long letters, too. Where have you been besides Paris?"

"Nowhere. I stayed there the whole time, except for Christmas of the first year, when I flew to New York to see Gigi."

"So what kind of guy is the lucky son of a bitch?"

Billy blinked, turned slightly to pick up a bread stick, and took a bite to gain time. Shit! She'd been too busy puzzling out the changes in Spider to remind herself how dangerously sensitive he was to a woman's whole being, how finely tuned he was to anyone female, that bloody mind reader. Too perceptive by half, certainly too much so for her comfort in this reunion.

"I don't know what you're talking about," Billy said calmly.

"The guy you're involved with in Paris. Unhappily, I guess, or you wouldn't have left him alone so soon before Christmas, unless he's married of course, and having a family Noël."

"Spider, you always jumped to conclusions," Billy answered him smoothly, with a reproving nod of her head. "That's one of your problems. Why does there have to be a guy? Isn't Paris, the city, enough to keep a person fascinated for years? I've explained how involved I've been with renovating my house."

"Sure, Billy, but there isn't a house that could glue you in place that long, not even in *La Ville Lumière*. I know my Mrs. Ikehorn, remember? I find it outside of the realm of possibility—or any law of nature—to believe that you could stay unattached in Paris for two years, much less come home looking—hell, you were always one hell of a flagrantly beautiful broad and now you look more . . . alive? . . . more awakened? . . . whatever, there's something so different about you, something less regal, less . . . formidable, more womanly, vulnerable, softer, even . . . yes, you can shoot me for it, but something *sweeter*, you're less of a boss, more of a dame . . . a terrific dame. Oh, there's *gotta be a guy*, I can see it in your eyes, but don't tell me about it, tell Dolly or Jessie or Josie or Gigi or Sasha what's-her-name —tell a woman, why confide in a man, even if he's one of your best friends, he's never going to understand, right?"

"Have it your own way." Billy shrugged, still holding on to her calm and refusing to be drawn. "And why do you persist in calling me a 'broad' and a 'dame,' Spider? In your last letter you even called me a 'frosty bitch'—is that the way you think of me?"

"It's a habit, with you, and not necessarily a bad one, to help keep things in focus. When Valentine and I came out here to work for you, she was scared silly of you just because you were so rich. She was afraid of the power you had to take away that big chance you had given us. I remember one night, before we'd managed to make you see reason, I had to explain to her in graphic detail that no matter how many hundreds of millions of dollars you had, the only thing that mattered about you was that you were basically another female person, not all that different from every other woman in the world. You were demanding, sure, tough, sure, impossible, absolutely, but still ruled by the same needs and worries and anxieties and emotions as all other female persons. I finally managed to get Valentine to realize that simply having money hadn't turned you into Marie Antoinette—of whom, as I recall, you were giving a damn good imitation—and she was never afraid of you again. That's why you two got to be friends, real friends.''

"We were, weren't we?" Billy was silent for a minute and so was Spider. Finally she spoke. "I still can't understand why you think that being rich hasn't made me . . . different. Don't you respect power, Spider? I'm not talking about any personal power or abilities I may have, but at least the power of the money itself? The power of everything I can do with it?''

"Of course I respect power, who on this planet doesn't? But when I think about you, it's because of what you, Billy Ikehorn, *are*, not what you choose to do with something that you happened to inherit. Remember, you weren't born rich, you didn't grow up rich, it didn't form your character from the very start—if it had, that'd be a different story. But if you gave all your dough away, you'd still be you, as far as I can see. So I keep the two things clearly and distinctly separate. You are Billy. Mrs. Ikehorn can do x or y because she can afford it, but that's not what Billy's *about*. Get it? It's kinda like Dick and Jane, real simple. And it's also healthier that way, believe me.''

"I do," Billy said after a thoughtful pause. Dick and Jane? Why were other men unable to think of it so clearly and cleanly? Spider was anything but simple-minded. Perhaps he understood women because he'd grown up with so many sisters?

"Hungry enough to order yet?"

"Not until I have another drink.''

"Fine, if you promise not to leave tomorrow. You'll just add on another three hours of jet lag in the other direction and really get screwed up.''

"You've talked me into it," Billy laughed. "My ability to say no has been severely tried in the last few days. I haven't got the strength to argue with one more person. I wish you could have heard Gigi and Sasha—you've got to meet the belle Sasha, Spider, to believe her—trying to persuade me to go into the catalog business with them. Those two wouldn't take no for an answer.''

"Why the catalog business?"

"Oh, it's too complicated to talk about. And then there was Zach Nevsky . . . now there's a discussion I definitely can't go into . . .'' Billy started to laugh again at the memory.

"All right, keep your secrets. I'll find out everything sooner or later anyway. But why catalogs? Gigi is about as far as you can get from stupid, maybe she's on to something.''

"A catalog called Scruples Two? I do *not* think so, thank you very much,'' Billy said disdainfully, shaking her head in vigorous repudiation.

"Say again?''

"Her idea was to start a new, reasonably priced clothing catalog, and call it Scruples Two since that would give it an immediate name to attract people. And Sasha wanted to come out with it each season, not just at Christmas the way they do now. Of course I told them it was out of the question.''

"Of course. Just like of course Scruples, the original boutique, was all done up to the teeth in deadly Parisian gray silk and gilt and haughty salesladies so that it intimidated shoppers right out of the door.''

"Spider! You *can't* possibly think it's a good idea!''

"Why not, Billy?''

"But . . . listen, Spider, we were about the very best, we were the most exclusive . . . Valentine's custom designs . . . . the elegance . . . Spider, a catalog is so . . . *available*! Anybody, just absolutely anybody could order from it,'' Billy sputtered, outraged at his lack of agreement.

"But Scruples doesn't exist anymore, Billy, Scruples is over. Very much over,'' Spider said patiently, with a touch of grimness. "You put Scruples out of business all by yourself. Now that was a perfect example of the power of money. You used that power and I, for one, was sorry, but it was clearly your prerogative to plow a thriving business underground, even if we ended up with a net profit. On the other hand, you wouldn't be diluting Scruples' name, because the name is only a memory."

"But, Spider—"

"Hell, Billy, even if all the Scruples were still there, you could put out a catalog without going into competition with yourself. You'd be showing a less expensive version of the Scruples *attitude* toward clothes. Our customers never wore only our stuff, Billy, they wore all sorts of things at just about every price range. You were one of the few people who could afford to dress from head to toe at Scruples, and when you wanted anything in denim or jeans, even you had to go elsewhere. We showed the ultimate designers because we were carving out a position for the Scruples name, making it the top store for special occasions. But that was in real life, with money-making boutiques in the most affluent areas in the country. A catalog would have to be much less expensive and very different in its orientation . . . but since I live in the present tense, I see no reason not to think about it."

"I still think it's indecent!"

"No way. It's a good idea, there's nothing wrong with it."

"But, Spider!—"

"Billy, I don't remember how many times I've heard you say, 'but Spider,' whenever I wanted to change your arrangements. Don't 'but Spider' me—as I think my mother used to say, it makes no nevermind."

"Well, I never won an argument with you in my life," Billy said, taking a deep breath and trying to cool down. She was too jet-lagged to stay angry. "So let's talk about something else."

"Let's talk about the catalog."

"I'm not going to do one," she said flatly.

"I accept that. You don't and you won't. Why should you do anything you don't choose to do? But I might be interested. I'd certainly like to know more about it. I wrote you that I was looking for something to get into—maybe this could be it, who knows? I have a pisspot of money to invest, a background in retailing, and, in case you don't remember, before we met I made a living with one hell of a good eye for graphics. The thing is, if it came to anything, we'd have to have your permission to use the name of the store. Without the Scruples association it would be an uphill battle."

"Great! Just great. You and Gigi and Sasha and Scruples. *My Scruples!* Why should I stand still for that?"

"Hey, don't have a shit-fit right here at the table. And don't be a dog in the manger, Billy. If you don't want to do it, butt out, but at least give it a chance. Don't kill this idea because you don't like it. Unlike Scruples, *it doesn't belong to you.* Maybe it can't be done, maybe it won't work under any circumstances, but sitting there on the sacred name of Scruples like a great, big, beautiful, broody bird, guarding it like the crown jewels of England or some enormous egg you're hatching, you're gonna look pretty damn silly."

"That's a mixed metaphor, or a mixed simile, or a mixed analogy," Billy said grumpily, after a long, sulky, thoughtful pause.

"I knew you'd listen to reason! You haven't changed all that much, after all, Billy," Spider said joyously. "It still takes me to explain it to you better. Waiter, bring this female another drink."

"Josie? Yes, Josie, it's me, I'm back. What? I know, I can hear you, come on, stop crying, there's nothing to cry about. Josie, not only can I hear you, but I'm sure everyone in your neighborhood can hear you. That's better . . . . no, I'm not in New York, I'm at the Bel Air. Look, I'll explain why tomorrow, I'll be home in the morning. Do you have a pencil? Oh my God, Josie, I just realized it's almost midnight! I'm sorry, did I wake you up? Good, I'm relieved. It's just that when I make up my mind I get kind of carried away . . . You've noticed? I guess you have. Anyway, please send Burgo over to get me around ten, maybe nine, never mind, I'll call when I'm ready. First thing in the morning, when you wake up, call Gigi at her place and tell her to quit her terrible job and get on out here on the double with Sasha. Oh, and the catalog collection, be sure to say they should bring it with them. Send the plane for them. What do you mean, we sold it? I told you to? Damn! Well, make whatever flight arrangements are necessary, Gigi's leg is broken—no, she's fine, don't worry—but be sure to send limos and look into buying another jet, we'll need it. Maybe two. Get some prices for me. Got that? Okay. Tomorrow, start calling agencies and interviewing a staff. Yep, like before, same number of people, unless you think we need more. I'll leave it up to you. How are the gardens? Wonderful. Now, Josie, I need to set up an office, in an office building, Century City, as close to Josh Hillman as possible.

Room enough for, oh, say ten people to start with. A good-sized office for me, and you'll be there, next to me, and another good-sized office for Spider. Well, of course, Spider Elliott, how many Spiders are there? I wouldn't be doing it without him, would I? Doing what? I'll tell you that tomorrow, too. Paris? I'm definitely not going back to Paris, Josie, you can count on that. No, I don't know what I'll do with the house, but it can't pick itself up and run away, can it? Fax the Ritz to pack all my clothes, everything I left there, and send it all on here, air freight, and tell them they've finally got the Windsor Suite back and send my love and thanks to them all. Tell them they were wonderful. What else? That's about all I can think of now. I'm so jet-lagged it's pathetic, my mind doesn't seem to be working right. Good night, Josie. Oh, I'm sorry you're too excited to get a wink of sleep tonight, it's all my fault . . . but you don't think I'll be able to sleep either, do you? We can sleep next week or something. Next month. Next year. 'Night, Josie.''

"Breaking even" were two of the most miserable words in the language, Vito Orsini thought as he prowled around his bungalow at the Beverly Hills Hotel, but he would gladly have settled for them to describe his last picture. When a picture broke even, no one made a profit, but at least they didn't end up with a loss. His last picture had died at the box office after two weeks, and the loss would be in the millions. Thank God it hadn't been his own money . . . that was a major consolation. He'd been paid two hundred thousand as his producer's fee for a year and a half's intensive work, lasting from preproduction through postproduction. He'd lived high on his per diems, the daily allowance everyone received during the actual production, but what little remained of his two hundred thousand wouldn't pay for this exorbitantly expensive obligatory bungalow at this moth-eaten yet still obligatory hotel where he had to stay in order to keep up the obligatory tap dance of the unemployed, just-on-the-verge-of-the-obligatory-big-deal, about-to-ride-high-again, Oscar-winning producer, back in town to peddle another obligatorily desirable book to Curt Arvey.

"My money's tied up in Switzerland." That had a nice ring to it, if you weren't worrying about the interest you were building up on every credit card you had. It would sound even better if some hard-nosed fucker—God knows who—in the business affairs department at

Arvey's studio hadn't forced him to cross-collateralize *Mirrors* and *The WASP* so that if *Mirrors* continued to make money for his lifetime and beyond, he'd never see a penny's profit from it.

But what the hell, Dominick's and the hotel would still carry him for a long time. The two hundred thousand grand had almost entirely gone, vanished, disappeared, not to Zurich but for good, to pay his necessarily high-living entertainment and travel expenses—he had to keep up a successful front or retire from show business entirely—and to option a new property, a British best-seller. He'd only just managed to get the book by trading on his Oscar until he was ready to strangle the author's agent, a canny Brit who'd held out for fifty thousand dollars up front. If the author hadn't been in love with *Mirrors* and subtle enough to see the inspiration in *The WASP*, it would never have happened, but *Fair Play* was his, a brilliant comedy of contemporary English society that had been a huge literary success and had sold well commercially.

Curt Arvey was his first best bet for backing, Vito thought, no matter how many of the other studios in town could be interested. Always go back first to the guy who lost money on you most recently, he's your best customer because he has the biggest interest in getting that money back. Every independent producer knew this truth that might seem odd in the real world where you'd look to find backing from a fresh sucker, not someone you still owed. Arvey would be the most anxious man in town to have Vito in his power again. More pictures had been financed out of revenge than out of love, and Arvey, *WASP* or no *WASP*, wouldn't be immune to the opportunity for revenge combined with the profit motive.

Vito gave himself a close but unself-conscious inspection in the mirror. A piece of talent, an actor or a director, could afford to dress any way he chose, but the money man, the producer, the "suit," had to look immaculately and expensively well tailored and impeccably groomed. He'd do, he decided, and left his room for the Polo Lounge, where Fifi Hill had invited him for lunch. Fifi had never forgotten that he owed his Best Director Oscar to Vito, and gratitude in Hollywood, with lunch thrown in, was as rare as a whore who gave green stamps.

"Good Lord, Vito's back," Susan Arvey said to Lynn Stockman, an occasional lunchtime companion. The two women were sitting indoors in the Polo Lounge's main room, for only tourists were eating outside in the sunshine of a December day, underneath the flower-filled baskets that hung from every branch of an ancient tree. It was so unseasonably warm that they both wore the jackets of their suits over their shoulders. Susan, in a starkly elegant dark green suit and a simple, pale green silk blouse, looked as compellingly pretty as ever, with her hair, caught up in its smooth chignon, making all the teased and fluffed hairdos of other women look overdone. She possessed a finished, polished perfection that Lynn Stockman, for all her good looks, could only marvel at.

"Where?" Lynn asked.

"Just over there," she said, nodding to her right at a table fifteen feet away. "Don't catch his eye, whatever you do."

"Susan, in this town you can't not say hello to people because of two flops," Lynn said, surprised. "Eli and I spend at least three nights a week eating dinner with people we'd slam the door on in any sane, civilized city, but you never know when you'll need them again. Anyway I've always had a soft spot for Vito."

Susan raised her eyebrows indifferently. Lynn was married to the head of another studio and was one of the few women in Hollywood who dared to consider herself Susan's equal and get away with it. The lively young widow of a multimillionaire East Coast industrialist, Lynn had grown up in a world of steady, serious money that didn't acknowledge the existence of such a local social phenomenon as Hollywood Royalty. When she'd married Eli Stockman she'd blown into Beverly Hills on a wave of natural self-confidence, assuming that she was just as good as anyone she could possibly meet, and probably better. Film society, the world's most notoriously easy nut to crack, provided that you have the right husband, had instantly accepted her at the value she'd placed on herself.

"A soft spot for Vito?" Susan asked. "Why on earth?"

"On the whole I admire his work—forgetting the last two—Vito's not afraid to do something different, even if it doesn't work. He takes chances. How many people can you say that about here?"

"Why don't you write about it for *Interview*?"

"Don't be stuffy, sweetie. *The WASP* didn't send you over the hill to the poorhouse. What's more, he's terribly attractive. I always knew why Billy Ikehorn married him—pure lust. She's back too, did you know?"

"Of course. Lying very low, however. When I called, she said she wasn't accepting invitations for a while—too many Paris parties.

Billy just wants to vegetate for a while and get over jet lag. Jet lag! She's been back at least a week."

"Two weeks and counting, Susan. Do you think that she and Vito might get back together?"

"Oh, please. How long do you think pure lust lasts, Lynn?"

"With Vito I'd give it three, maybe four years, and that's against a score of six months for the average gent. There's something so dark and alluring about him, something . . . hmmm . . . . something . . ."

"Flashy?" Susan Arvey snapped.

"Possibly that *is* the explanation. It's so simple that it just never occurred to me," Lynn said mischievously. "If I weren't a happily married woman . . ."

"Good God, Lynn, why don't you just go on over to Vito's table and send Fifi Hill over to me? Don't let me stand in your way."

"I might at that, but unfortunately I have a hair appointment with Mario after lunch. I'll bet you that Vito could . . . last . . . . longer than any shampoo and set."

"And you might lose your bet. You're just assuming, I trust."

"But of course, sweetie, that goes without saying. Caesar's wife had nothing on me. Interesting, isn't it, that you never heard of Vito being linked to anyone except Maggie MacGregor and that was out in the open, nothing they were trying to keep secret. He's entirely discreet about whatever he does or doesn't do, but then men who have the greatest successes with women don't talk about them, as a rule, do they? Just look at Warren . . . and wouldn't we all like to! Billy wouldn't have married Vito if he hadn't been incredible in bed. He has such an intensely physical quality . . . but of course, a young Vittorio de Sica!"

"Lynn, honestly!"

"Oh, Susan, where's your imagination?" Lynn teased. "Lighten up, sweetie. Just because Curt has been having dental surgery for the last three months and demanding your sympathy and constant attention, doesn't mean you have to come all over scandalized at a spot of harmless speculation." She laughed at Susan's exasperated expression. "Waiter, we're ready to order, please."

As the two women were finishing their lunch, Fifi and Vito walked by their table and stopped to say hello.

"Sit down, both of you," Lynn suggested. "Join us for coffee?"

"I can't, Lynn," Fifi said, "I'm due in a meeting in Burbank. But I wish I could."

"I'd like that," Vito said. The Polo Lounge was still full of people, and an invitation to join the wives of the heads of two studios was not to be declined. He sat down next to Susan, although Lynn was the one who had invited him. Susan moved away slightly, as he had expected. What an utter bitch she was. A condescending bitch who had snubbed him time and time again, a woman who hadn't thought he'd been good enough for Billy, a woman who had actually enjoyed the flop of *The WASP*, although she thought he didn't realize it, a woman who was going to get hers one day, whether she knew it or not.

"What's new in your life, Vito?" Lynn asked curiously.

"I've bought a terrific book called *Fair Play*."

"Aha! I loved it. Eli's English people sent it over in galleys. It isn't out here yet."

"If I'd waited till it was, forget it."

"You really think there's a film in it?"

"I know there is."

"I hope you're right, Vito. *Fair Play* is terribly good. Very stylish, very droll." And, she thought, if satire is what closes on Saturday night, British comedies of manners are what close two days earlier. Unless he could get Streisand and Clint Eastwood, unlikely casting, even for Vito.

"If only the wives ran this town," Vito said, "we could do the deal right here."

"But they don't, more's the pity. Damn, I have to run. Mario's always on time, and I don't dare to keep him waiting. Lunch next week, Susan? I'll call." She scribbled her name on the check and was off with a flashing smile of humor and a touch of malice. It would do Susan Arvey good to have to make polite conversation with Vito Orsini.

"Well, Vito, you're looking well," Susan said. "How was Europe?"

"I hear you shifting into your hostess voice, Susan. You don't have to bother. The interesting thing is that I've known you for ten years or more and I've never talked to you and detected the slightest sign of genuineness. Do you dislike me in particular, or is it nonspecific?" Vito's voice was amused, impregnated with his unclassifiable charm. Susan's lips parted slightly in shock.

"You always stand on ceremony with me, Susan. Even when I won three Oscars for Curt's studio, you didn't let up. I have a theory that when a woman behaves like that with a man who obviously admires her, it's to let him know that there's nothing doing. The thing I don't understand is why you warn me off over and over. I've never made a pass at you."

"Vito, I don't know what gives you the idea that I treat you any differently from most people, and I've got to go too," she said firmly.

"Just a minute, Susan. I'm aware that you have the power structure of Hollywood in the forefront of your mind at all times, but don't you ever give yourself any freedom? Do you know how half-alive you looked all through lunch? I saw a luscious woman going to waste, leading a life that doesn't use up half of her wild energy. I wonder how you discipline yourself to stay so collected? Is it the tennis that does it for you, Susan? Or the art collection? Or the parties? You realize, of course, that you've always been one of the most desirable women around, not the youngest, not the most beautiful—after all, this is Hollywood—but one of the most desirable. There's sexuality written all over you."

"Shut up, Vito. That's enough," she said, but she didn't get up, hypnotized into inaction by his audacity.

"You've always been afraid of me, Susan, that's why you've made yourself believe that you don't like me. You don't have to worry, other people can't see you the way I do, and I keep my perceptions to myself. I like secrets, Susan, and so do you. I like to make my own rules, and so do you. I like to follow my own instincts, Susan, that's why I'm not in the mainstream and never will be. I know that somewhere, somehow, you follow your instincts too. You're the personification of a lady, correct, cool, just the right degree of cordiality for everyone you meet, and not a drop more. But nothing will make me believe I've ever seen the real Susan Arvey."

"That's all very interesting, Vito, but I have a fitting."

"Your fitting can wait," Vito said calmly. There were few women in the world who could resist a discussion of their qualities, Vito knew, and Susan Arvey, who took such extraordinary care of herself, least of all.

"You couldn't look as thoroughly young as you do if it weren't for some other reason than sheer vanity," he continued, thoughtful and measured, certain of his insight. "You couldn't have that wonderful skin, that quite perfect face, you couldn't have the body of an exquisite girl. On the one hand there's Susan Arvey, the conventional wife who's never dropped a stitch, and on the other hand there's Susan Arvey, the exceptional woman who must have her secrets because she's too intelligent and too strong to be merely what she seems. While Fifi and I were having lunch, I kept imagining you the way you were meant to be, as if there were a film running in my mind . . . ." Vito paused for a second, and when she continued to listen to him, although she looked straight ahead, he knew that he'd succeeded in arousing her. There was only one totally satisfactory way to get his revenge. Curt would never know about it, of that he was sure.

"I kept imagining you someplace else, Susan, not here, where everybody knows you, but someplace where you could be yourself, let yourself go with all the volcanic vitality I know you have. For some reason I imagined a little bar in the Valley, a sort of roadhouse, the kind of place nobody we know ever goes. I saw you walking in, looking just the way you do now, unapproachable, collected, and yet incredibly exciting. I saw all the men in the bar becoming instantly aware of you, unable to hide their interest, all of them with only one idea on their minds, giving it to you, Susan, any way you wanted . . . . I wonder . . . *have you ever had it any way you wanted?* Have you ever been able to ask for it straight out? Have you, Susan? I could see you picking and choosing, taking the one who pleased you the most into a back room . . . taking him and allowing him to give you pleasure, and then, if that wasn't enough, taking another. I saw you free, Susan, able to act like a man . . . . it's strange, you're so marvelously feminine and yet I feel a masculine drive in you, a masculine need . . . it's a fascinating contradiction." Vito took her hand and pulled it under the tablecloth and placed it on his crotch. He'd been getting steadily harder from the minute he'd told her how desirable she was, and her face had remained composed. She'd listened to him for too long to turn back now. "Pleasure, Susan . . . do you know how long I've ached to give you pleasure?"

Oh, the bastard, Susan Arvey thought as she bit her lips, the bastard, it had been too many months since she'd been to New York. She needed it, needed it as she had never needed it before, and he smelled it on her, the bastard.

Vito released her hand slightly, and when she didn't put it back on the table immediately, he put his hand back over hers, pressing it firmly down, watching her teeth catch her lower lip. "I'm in the third bungalow to the right along the pathway. I'll leave now. I'll wait for you. If you don't come, I'll understand and I'll never mention it again.

If you do come, no one will ever know. The choice is yours. I want you. I've always wanted you. The real you, the secret you. Come to me, Susan.''

As she walked along the path, there was only one thought in Susan Arvey's mind; whatever happened, he'd have to beg before the afternoon was over. Oh yes, she must reduce him to begging. In Cannes, after Vito had first met Billy, Susan had been stuck at the hotel night after night, listening to Curt sleeping, tormenting herself with pictures of what those two must be doing to each other. He'd be made to pay for those nights of fevered frustration.

As Vito waited, as resolute as a matador waiting for the bull to enter the ring, he resolved that he'd make her want him so badly that she'd have to ask for it, no matter how much she tried not to. Nothing less would satisfy him.

He opened the door to her knock. They didn't smile at each other, but once they were alone inside the living room of the bungalow, where the curtains had been drawn so that a dim golden glow was the only light, the entire history of their long, arm's-length acquaintance was tacitly put aside as entirely irrelevant. Vito locked the door behind her as Susan unpinned her chignon and let her long blond hair fall around her shoulders. He took her in his arms and kissed her perfect mouth without a word or a sound, although she could feel the quickening rhythm of his heart. Strange, she thought, as he continued to kiss her, strange how long it had been since she had kissed a man besides her husband. She didn't allow kissing in New York. She'd forgotten how different one man's mouth was from another. Vito's strongly formed lips were so hard that they could easily be cruel, but his tongue was unexpectedly gentle, tentative as it merely touched the inner rims of her lips, moving slowly without the attempt at invasion that she anticipated.

For minutes he was content to stand there kissing her, supporting her firmly in his muscular arms, concentrating on feeling the suspicious set of her mouth gradually relax under the clever operation of his tongue. Only when he could feel her own tongue moving slightly forward to meet his, did he initiate any contact, probing her half-parted mouth with a deliberate delicacy, little by little establishing an intimacy of touch and taste that she had never expected.

Each kiss sensitized her to the next, each kiss was followed by a studious exploration of her face with his lips, first her earlobes, from which he removed her earrings one by one before he took each dainty lobe and sucked it as if it were a nipple, learning it with his lips, his tongue and his grazing, careful teeth. When he finally returned to her mouth he found it more eager than before but he took no advantage of her quickening, kissing her piercingly, but not for long enough, before he removed his lips and wandered to her eyelids, taking his time as he covered her lids and her brows and her lashes with the very lightest possible brushes of his languorous tongue. This time, when his tongue entered her mouth she held it there, matching him thrust for thrust, until finally, with triumph, Vito felt her tongue impatiently move forward into his mouth, while her arms reached up so that she could run her fingers upward on his neck. He pulled away, bent his head, evading her fingers, and kissed her throat, from the pulse at its base, all the way up to her jawline, tracing the slender column over and over from right to left with a quick, nibbling, maddeningly light use of his lips.

At last he picked Susan up easily, and sat down in a deep couch, holding her on his lap. She closed her eyes and leaned back against him passively, refusing to allow herself to utter any demands since he must be the one to beg, although she was having difficulty keeping herself still as she felt the heavy length of his penis against her thigh. Still kissing her neck, Vito began to unbutton her blouse, from neck to waist, slowly freeing her breasts, those succulent breasts on which he had watched the large nipples harden and pucker while they were still sitting at the lunch table. He made no attempt to free her arms from the silk, preferring to keep the whiteness of her body framed by the pale green fabric. He shifted beneath her so that he held her lying across his thighs, her legs supported by the couch, enabling him to devote his entire attention to her firm, blossoming, swelling flesh. Not her nipples, he thought, not her nipples until she starts to rub her legs together, and he took first one and then the other heavy breast in both his hands, and softly clasped and unclasped them until Susan was focused entirely on the discriminating attention of his warm fingers, which flattered her more than she had ever been flattered in her lifetime. She arched her ribcage, not realizing that she was beginning to move her hips.

When he felt her tensing on his thighs, Vito allowed his fingers to move from her breasts to his mouth. She heard him licking the tips of each of his fingers before he began to caress her nipples with such a discreet touch that their wetness made it almost unendurable. She wanted his mouth on them desperately, yet still he used his wet finger-tips, all five of them gathered together to surround each nipple with a circle of painful sweetness until the tips were pointed, fully erect and dark pink with blood. Gauging the instant exactly, Vito finally bent his head and took one nipple into his hot mouth, listening with delight to the sigh that escaped her as he sucked, increasing the pull of his mouth and the strength of his plundering tongue. She pushed her breasts together with her hands, as if she wanted him to take both nipples into his mouth together, but her breasts were far too big for that, and he devoted his attention to each in turn, always leaving one before it had been stimulated to its peak, so that she was never satisfied but kept hanging on the brink of the full-blown sensation of being suckled that he knew she wanted. This wasn't about what she wanted, he thought as he felt her breasts swell and grow fuller under his educated torment, and this wasn't about what he wanted, because he'd wanted to take her on the floor from the first kiss, take her quick and dirty and leave her there without finishing her off.

Vito got off the couch and arranged a cushion under Susan's head. He fell to his knees on the carpet, still fully clothed, and removed her skirt and her underwear, so that she lay fully exposed to his gaze, her only clothing the blouse that still clung to her arms. Her eyes were half open so that she could see the look on his face when he saw her body, the body she knew was so ripe, so strong and so ready to be looted. He looked her over steadily, with an expressionless scrutiny, as he took off his tie, his jacket and his shirt. Susan held her breath as he began to unfasten his belt, and watched with bewilderment as he changed his mind and refastened it.

Vito, still kneeling, inclined his head between her legs and soon she felt the brush of his lips on her pubic hair, just a whisper of a touch as the skin of his subtle lips barely made contact with the soft, fine hairs of the blond triangle. At first he only used his lips and his nose to browse questingly in that hair, nuzzling her and inhaling her fragrance. She felt herself becoming engorged with desire, she knew that her lower lips were becoming more visible as they grew pinker and more prominent, but she held herself rigid, waiting for his tongue. Her eyes closed when she finally felt the point of his tongue barely touching her outer lips, running delicately along their rim, leaving a wet trail in their wake. Over and over his tongue retraced its path, ignoring her inner lips that were pouting in expectation like the petals of a flower. Susan wouldn't allow herself to move her legs, although she felt like screaming when the tip of his tongue descended cautiously into the channel that lay between her inner and outer lips, parting them with the utmost care, its heat traveling moistly between them as he lapped his fill, carefully avoiding making any contact with her clitoris. That small, deep pink, blunt arrow of her living flesh grew larger and harder. Surely, surely he must take it in his mouth, she thought as she waited fruitlessly for that essential prize, reduced to one excruciating need.

Disbelievingly, just as she was about to put her hands on his head and push her clitoris up into his mouth, she felt Vito take her in his arms and turn her over so that she lay facedown on the couch. He began to explore each inch of her backbone, as now, newly disciplined, she proudly refused to move or speak, schooling herself to lie still even when his lips dawdled cannily as they descended toward the fine globes of her bottom. He took them in his hands and pressed them from the outside of her hips toward the downy line that separated them. She didn't allow herself to rub against the fabric of the couch as she heard Vito's breathing grow harsher, but she waited, waited sternly, knowing full well how beautiful she must look, how lush and full. Even when she felt his fingers parting the globes so that he could insert his tongue between them, she didn't move, even when his tongue probed ever more deeply, she didn't raise herself to allow him more access than was possible in her prone position. She kept herself resolutely unclenched, knowing that the lubrication between her legs was moistening the couch. Even when he withdrew his tongue and she felt his middle finger reach between her legs, pressing toward her tumid, aching lips, she lay still. Her head was turned away from him, so that he couldn't see her mouth on which agonized desire was so clearly written, so that he couldn't see the determination in her eyes, so that he couldn't see the victorious expression she knew she wore when she felt him at last put one arm under her belly and raise her high off the couch so that he was able to push his head between her legs. She was burningly distended, there was nothing she could do to deny that, she was as open as she'd ever been, but she let Vito finally suck her clitoris deeply into his mouth, bathing it with his tongue, without a sound of satisfaction or moan of desire. She neither resisted nor responded until, insane with her taste and her smell he turned her over on her back, ripping off his trousers and shorts in frantic haste. He rose and flung himself on the couch, so that he was bestride her on his knees, his straining penis clasped in one hand, the other holding her thighs apart roughly. Their eyes met and held.

"Ask for it," Vito said.

"Never."

"Ask for it."

She used all the muscles of her strong legs to push them together, so forcefully that he was unable to keep them apart with only one hand.

"You ask," Susan whispered, putting her own fingers over her tautly swollen clitoris and rubbing with a flickering expertise, seeming to be absorbed in the pleasure she was giving herself, watching him grow more avid as her rhythm quickened. Helplessly Vito saw her approaching an orgasm without him.

"Stop that!"

"Ask me nicely," she panted without stopping.

"You win, you bitch!" he gasped. She took away her hand, opened her legs and tilted upward so that he could enter her immediately, both of them so consumed with each other and so inflamed by their long duel that they gripped each other and used each other more violently, more brutally, than they had ever used another person. They came together ferociously, in racking spasms that happened too soon, but lasted and lasted until they were weak and totally drained.

They lay together for many slow minutes, without speaking, half-asleep.

"Game, set and match, Susan Arvey," Vito murmured at last.

"Well played, Vito."

"Can I see you tomorrow?"

"No, I'm busy all day. But come for dinner, I'm having a party."

He looked at her pink face, at the tumbled strands of hair, wet at the roots, at all the delectable disarray of a satisfied woman, and he covered the sticky hair of her mound with the palm of his hand and pressed down on it possessively.

"I'll come for dinner, but you won't be this Susan, I'll see another person."

"You'll have your memories," she said tauntingly.

"That won't do. You know that. You know this is only the beginning."

Mutely she nodded her assent, her eyes brilliant with anticipation.

"That roadhouse in the Valley, it really exists. I'm going to take you there next. And we're going to sit at a table in the corner of a crowded bar and I'm going to make you come just using my fingers, no matter who's watching, you know that, don't you?"

Susan nodded again. She knew two tricks for every one of his. He had no idea of how she was going to enslave him.

As he watched Susan dress, Vito wondered if it was going to be more or less of a challenge to make Curt Arvey put up eleven million dollars to finance his next film. He'd never done business before with a man whose wife had already begun to obsess him. She was a thrillingly bad girl, a thoroughly naughty girl, and her long carnal punishment was going to be the most exciting experience of their lives. He knew already that there was nothing he and Susan wouldn't do to each other before they had finished.

Susan pinned up her chignon, thinking of how she was going to instruct Curt to deal with Vito, for he had asked her advice about the appointment he had with Vito tomorrow. Curt must not say yes under any circumstances, no matter how taken he was with Vito's potentially interesting and just as potentially impossible project. Nor must he give him a quick and merciful no. *Maybe*. It must be *maybe* for a long, long time. Only a tantalizing, elusive but very real and possible *maybe* would keep Vito exactly where she wanted him until she decided to end it—one way or another. She'd won today, but their tournament was only beginning, and one element must be missing in the wonderfully challenging months to come. There would be no fair play.

*S*pider, was this really necessary?'' Billy asked rebelliously as she marched into his office, carrying a large shopping bag from Saks. "I feel like a fool playing parlor games."

"Humor me, Billy, sit down, put the bag down, and we'll wait for the others."

"Don't tell me I'm the first?"

"Actually, you're a few minutes early."

"Probably because I'm the only one who didn't cheat," Billy said suspiciously, as she settled herself on one of the two large semicircular sofas that faced each other at one end of the office high in the same Century City office tower that housed the law firm of Strassberger, Lipkin and Hillman.

"I heard that," Sasha said, rushing into the large room in a flurry. "I didn't cheat, Spider said five minutes and I took five minutes exactly." She carefully deposited her bulging shopping bag next to Billy's. "I've been terrified that this thing would burst wide open all the way here."

"You should use two bags, one inside the other, like I did," Billy said. "Two identical shopping bags have roughly the tensile strength of a piece of luggage."

"Really?" Sasha asked, impressed.

"I have no scientific proof, but it works."

"Oh, don't tell me you're all here already," Gigi wailed plaintively, as she came into the office, swinging a shopping bag from her arm. "I had to stop to get gas." She was enveloped in an almost floor-length garment and she moved rather stiffly, although the cast on her leg had been removed two weeks ago. She sat down next to Sasha, put her bag on the rug, and waited expectantly.

"All present and accounted for," Spider announced as he closed the door to his office and sat down opposite the three women. "Now, isn't this nice? Which of you gentlewomen wants coffee?"

"This is not 'nice,' " Billy muttered, "it's like some kind of sick New Age consciousness-raising coven or an AA meeting. Why don't you get up and say, 'My name is Spider and I'm addicted to cross-dressing'?"

"Coffee, Billy?" Spider asked. "Maybe a Danish?"

"No thanks, I've finished breakfast," she snapped.

"Gigi, Sasha?"

Both of them declined, too eager to see the contents of the others' shopping bags to be interested in anything that would require waiting.

"Who wants to go first?" Spider asked. None of them answered. "Sasha, how about you?"

"Why me?"

"Well . . . let's see . . . in the first place, because I said so. In the second place, because you're the one who collects catalogs. If it weren't for you, none of us would be here. In the third place, you have the fattest shopping bag, and it's splitting down the side as I speak."

"All right," Sasha agreed, "but you all have to realize that I still haven't bought any clothes for California, so I had to pick from a completely urban closet."

"Look, gentlewomen all, this is not a competition. I simply suggested—" Spider said.

"Suggested?" Billy said, with a cranky toss of her dark curls. "You insisted."

"Correct. I *insisted* that you each spend exactly five minutes in your closets, imagining that a fire was approaching rapidly, and you had to choose whatever absolutely indispensable items of clothing you could pack into one paper shopping bag. The Five-Minute Fire Drill Wardrobe. It doesn't matter where you live, Sasha, or for what climate you dress, or for what kind of life, the only thing that matters is what *kinds* of things you picked. As I said yesterday, you will not be judged on the contents of your bag.''

He'd never expected Billy to be so resistant to his idea, Spider thought, but then he'd never seen the size of Billy's closet. Or was it that she didn't like doing exactly what he'd asked Gigi and Sasha to do? Was she so used to being the boss of any enterprise that she felt uncomfortable as a team player? This February morning was their first official day in the planning phase of Scruples Two, and maybe she was just nervous, afraid of failure, although failure in the shopping-bag experiment wasn't possible. Perhaps he should have suggested having this meeting in her office, but since his contained the comfortable circle of couches, and since he and Billy were equal financial partners in this venture, he hadn't thought it mattered.

Sasha was gingerly extracting from her bag a black vinyl trench coat lined in bright red. She sighed in relief. ''Here's what was making it so bulky. I packed the smallest things first, so I'd know how much space I had left for the big things. The coat goes over everything, rain or shine, day or night, I've had it three years.'' She laid it on the rug in front of her feet. Next she pulled out a black cardigan sweater in a medium-weight wool. ''This goes over everything too, you can use it as a jacket or by itself, over pants or a skirt. You can dress it up or down. If you unbutton the three top buttons, belt it and wear lots of necklaces, you can go anywhere at night in it, or you can wear it backwards and it makes a tunic top.''

''How long have you had it?'' Spider asked, as she placed it next to the trench coat.

''More or less forever. Maybe five years, maybe six, it's seen better days, but in a fire I'd take it because I don't know where I could get another.''

''What else is in there?'' Gigi asked.

''My favorite black pants,'' Sasha said, hauling each item out one by one as she spoke, ''my favorite gray pants, my one and only ancient glen plaid blazer that never goes out of style, the only pair of black high-heeled pumps I've ever been comfortable in, my two favorite plain white silk shirts, because with the pants, the cardigan, the coat, and shirts I could go around the world, if I had to, and my lucky dress." She held up a limply dangling rag of red jersey. "This can't guarantee a peak experience, but it tends to operate in my favor."

"How old *is* that thing?" Billy wondered, as impressed by Sasha's presentation as she was by the way the girl looked. She was wearing beautifully cut navy trousers and a true red turtleneck sweater that brought out the jet of her hair and eyes. She'd matched her lipstick perfectly to the sweater. Did they come more passionately alluring than Sasha Nevsky? Billy wondered. If so, she didn't want to know about it.

"Four years old, but that doesn't matter. Only the neckline matters to me in a dressy dress, and the fit."

"Sasha, did you just go into your closet and haul these things out in five minutes, or did you think about it beforehand?" Spider inquired.

"Are you kidding? I made a list first. It took about twenty minutes, maybe more. I always make lists, doesn't everybody?" Sasha asked. "And," she added, "when I moved here last month I gave away everything I didn't really wear a lot anymore, so there's almost nothing left in my closet, anyway. It took me the whole five minutes to fold these things neatly and cram them into the bag. You never said we shouldn't think about it, Spider. Actually, if I only had five minutes to think *and* pack, I'd take my jewelry, my cash, my credit cards, my driver's license, my bankbook and my cat."

"Bravo, you get the Forbes Four Hundred humanitarian award," Billy murmured. She knew she'd been right about Sasha. She had a rock-solid sensible brain under all those lashings of hair, that theatrically femme-fatale witchery and her deliberate use of exaggeration.

"Great, Sasha, leave it all right there, please," Spider directed. "Now Gigi."

She got up and turned around slowly. "I'm wearing all the bulky stuff," she announced. "You didn't say anything about getting dressed, Spider, so I used four minutes to put on my best underwear, a plum-colored pullover in a color I know I'll never find again because there must have been a mistake in the dye vat, my turquoise turtleneck cashmere sweater that I got on Orchard Street for almost nothing, my finally broken-in white jeans, my antique silver-and-turquoise Mexican belt that cost a fortune, my favorite silver earrings, my best cowboy boots, a great pink blazer I got on sale, and this eggplant-colored cape that looks as if I stole it from Beau Brummell. It's from a secondhand store in Hackensack.''

"Is that fair?'' Billy demanded heatedly. "Gigi didn't pack. No wonder she can hardly walk, she's wearing sixteen layers of clothes.''

"Everything's fair if I didn't say not to,'' Spider decreed. "What's in your shopping bag, Gigi?''

"Since I only had a minute left, I grabbed a pair of decent brown velvet pants for places you can't wear jeans, about a dozen different scarves, all different sizes, because they give me a dozen different looks, my best belts, the art deco costume jewelry I've been collecting, and the black velvet vest Billy gave me years ago because it's still my favorite thing of all. Oh, and here's a dear little bunch of artificial violets I couldn't bear to leave behind.''

"No shirts?'' Spider asked.

"I figured I could always buy a shirt or T-shirts—this fire isn't going to destroy the stores too, is it?''

"No.''

"Actually . . . it took me . . . . well, about twelve minutes to pack my bag because I couldn't decide which were my very favorite belts and scarves and I got hung up trying them on . . . I should have just taken them all,'' Gigi confessed sheepishly. "I guess I flunk. I spent sixteen minutes all together. I could have spent two hours in there.''

"How long did it take to put in the pants and the vest?'' Spider asked.

"Less than a minute.''

"Okay, I'm writing that all down.'' He grinned at the culprit. "You can take off your cape now.'' She looked so adorably guilty in her bulky clothes, covered by an eighteenth-century cape that could have been rented from a costume supply house, that he had a fugitive desire to give her a kiss of reassurance. He hadn't realized that they were all going to take him so seriously or to try to figure out ways to get around his fire-drill suggestion. Were women more literal-minded than men? Or just *these* women?

"Well,'' Billy sniffed indignantly, "I see I'm the only one who stuck to the rules. I had Josie with a stopwatch inside my closet and I didn't think about it first and make a list, or wear what I should have packed.''

She thought of herself racing around her thirty-foot-square dressing room, practically caroming off its lavender silk walls, barefoot on the ivory carpet, banging herself black and blue on the Lucite accessory island in her haste to find the few indispensable clothes among the hundreds and hundreds of garments, so many of them never worn, that hung on the long racks. Of course, she told herself wrathfully, if the girls hadn't taken an apartment together in West Hollywood, claiming that they were too accustomed to their independence to move into her house, she could have supervised the way in which they did their shopping bags, to make sure they didn't cheat, as they both most certainly had.

"Good for you, Billy. I knew you'd play fair. Now let's see what you brought," Spider said, as coaxingly as a first-grade teacher to a timid child on show-and-tell day, for he'd finally realized that her irascibility came from shyness rather than from anger. He'd always known Billy was shy, ever since he'd had to do all the inviting for the first Scruples party, but she managed to hide it, even from him. It was one of her most endearing qualities, although she'd never believe him if he told her, which he wouldn't, on reflection.

She was just barely thirty-nine, he knew, since he was eleven months younger, which made them officially the same age each year for the month between his birthday in October and hers in November, and she was probably finding it embarrassing to be placed in the same position as these younger women. Billy was used to traveling with piles of expensive luggage, she probably hadn't packed for herself since she married Ellis Ikehorn, and she would have trouble limiting herself to a shopping bag's worth of clothes.

"I decided to take everything from one designer so it'd be coordinated," Billy said, poking in her bag. "Saint Laurent, he's the most practical. Here's a pants suit, black, a cashmere sweater set, black, a chiffon blouse, black, a white silk shirt, a red suede boxy jacket that goes over everything like a short coat, and a matching skirt, plus a long plaid trench coat made of waterproof silk lined in quilted red satin. I don't know how old they are exactly, but they all work together."

"That's almost the same as what I have, except it's the real thing and not the knock-off," Sasha said in surprise.

"And no one would know the difference," Billy added, "unless they looked at the labels, because I picked the simplest and most classic things I have, and so did you. We could go around the world together, as a twin act, the red-and-black team."

"Doesn't anyone want to see what I brought?" Spider asked.

"You? This catalog is only for women," Billy said, surprised.

"It seemed only fair," Spider responded, getting a shopping bag from behind his desk and putting it on the floor. "Okay, here's my double-breasted blazer, a dress shirt, and my gray flannel trousers, that's as dressed up as I ever get, and I hate to go shopping so I brought them; here's my Burberry trench coat, a cable-stitched navy sweater my mother gave me five years ago, that I live in, a couple of favorite V-necked cashmere pullovers, three work shirts and a pair of jeans. And my reading glasses. Didn't anybody else bring reading glasses?"

"I've got them in my handbag," Billy said as the two girls looked at each other in amazement. Reading glasses?

"Right, handbags give you gentlewomen the advantage."

"If you stop calling us gentlewomen, we'll each pay you a quarter," Billy said, laughing for the first time that morning.

"What can I call you collectively that no one will jump on me for?"

"Women," Billy said.

"Ladies," Sasha offered.

"Guys," Gigi said. "Call us, 'you guys,' it's the only safe way to go."

"Okay, guys, what does this mess on the rug tell us?"

Gigi, who by this time had added her cape, blazer, belt and turtle-neck sweater to the pile of clothes, spoke up.

"It tells me that you're all a bunch of unsentimental, practical-minded, color-blind copycats who wouldn't know what to do with an accessory if it wrapped itself around your neck, like poor Isadora Duncan's scarf."

"So noted." Spider grinned at her indulgently. Gigi had tucked the thin, plum-colored, long-sleeved pullover, which fit her slender frame closely, into her jeans, and pinned the bunch of violets at her throat. Her intricate silver earrings dangled to her shoulders, and her orange hair stood away from her face as indignantly as if she were a badly surprised cat. Half of her looked ready to play the harp on the concert stage, he thought, the other half to ride the range.

"Well," Sasha said, "aside from the fact that Billy and I think alike, only she does it on her feet five times quicker than I do, I'm the only one who brought a dress. After a fire destroyed your apartment, you'd be eating out a lot—didn't anybody realize that but me?"

"I've got the skirt to my red suit, and two shirts, the black chiffon and the white silk—that makes the equivalent of two dresses for me," Billy observed.

"And I've got my blazer," Spider said, "and a dress shirt. No tie, but I could always buy one if I had to. I could join you guys in the restaurant without causing you shame."

"And so could I," Gigi said, "if I put on my velvet pants. The cowboy boots go *anywhere*."

"By a dress," Sasha insisted, "I mean a sexy dress. Your blouses aren't specifically sexy, Billy, and neither is Gigi's sweater."

"Sasha's right," Spider said. "And Sasha's wrong. Sexy isn't what's low-cut or fits like your second skin, sexy is your attitude when you wear it."

"Oh, Spider, don't start trying to sell us our own old clothes," Billy said, remembering how he used to tutor women in what to wear and how to wear it.

"Just making an observation for the record, Billy. Anybody else got anything else to say?"

"Yes," Billy said. "With the exception of Sasha's dress, every single thing we each packed is a separate. Pants, jackets, sweaters, blouses. Only one skirt, mine. Only Sasha and Gigi thought about their feet. We could all wear Spider's wardrobe, if his things were cut for women. What we have here, with the exception of Gigi's accessories, and Sasha's dress, is a theme. Am I following your thought process, Spider?"

"Uh-huh."

"I don't get it," Gigi said. "Are you talking unisex?"

"I think I get it, but I don't think I like it. I think you're talking boring and safe, Billy," Sasha said plaintively. "I hate gifty clothes, but I hate dull clothes just as much."

"No," Billy said, getting up and prowling around the circle of couches, picking her words thoughtfully and slowly, "what I'm talking about is concentrating on a collection of the *best possible separate pieces* that we'll totally *rethink* to give them a unique twist . . . let's think of them as *new classics* that can be combined in dozens of different ways to make capsule wardrobes for most ordinary, real-life situations. You don't want to even try to sell special-occasion dresses by catalog . . . women like to shop for them. Or fitted, tailored suits either. Of course, we'll hire our own designers—but yes, totally *versatile separates* that can be dressed up or down."

"I couldn't have put it better myself," Spider said.

"Thank you, Mr. Elliott. In France they call people who say things like that 'inspectors of finished work.' "

"Classics?" Gigi asked, her face falling in disappointment. "I never wear classics."

"But you do, Gigi," Sasha said, "only you wear them in weird colors and weird combinations and they're always too big or too small or eleventh-hand, but you've got a jacket, pants, and sweaters, just like everybody else."

"Oh. So I do." Gigi looked crestfallen. Classics! "What about accessories?" she demanded.

"That's where I think you let the catalog customers do their own thing," Spider said.

"Oh no, that's where I think you should give them an idea of what to do," Gigi replied, incensed. "Take Sasha's black cardigan—I could make it look fifteen or twenty-five different ways with the right accessories. If we sold the ultimate, perfect, best black cardigan in the world and didn't have a double spread of pictures of different ways in which you could wear it, we wouldn't be giving our customers the service they deserve!"

"And when we get someone to design our ultimate cardigan, the Scruples Two cardigan," Billy said, "we should offer it in a range of colors. Not everybody wants to wear black, lots of women can't. We need at least six basic colors . . . gray, navy, camel—"

"Deep, deep purple, heartbroken lavender, sort of an autumnal mossy-misty green, a blissful blue, between delphinium and the sky at twilight, a kind of ultimate pink, not shocking pink, not baby pink or raspberry, but definitely an important pink, a smoky beige that isn't too yellow or too brown . . ." Gigi stopped, waiting for more inspiration.

"Guys! Hold it for a second," Spider said. "Before we get bogged down in details, are we agreed on the main thrust of Scruples Two: classic, versatile, newly imagined separates? Real clothes for real women? It has *never* been done before in the long history of catalogs."

"One minute! What about my antique lingerie?" Gigi protested.

"And I promised Jessica to do a section for the discontinued woman, all those things she can't find anymore," Billy said.

"I told three of my aunts that I guaranteed them a section where they could find wonderful things for themselves. They're all still beautiful and they love clothes and are willing to pay good money for them, but they weigh over two hundred pounds," Sasha informed them. "Each."

"All those things will be included," Spider said. "Isn't that right, Billy? But the meat and potatoes of Scruples Two, the part where we make most of our money, is, as I see it, the separates you need year in and year out."

"Will it be published four times a year?" Sasha asked, not willing to give up her hobby horse.

"I hadn't started to think about frequency," Spider admitted.

"I think it's essential or it isn't fashion," Sasha insisted.

"Sasha's right," Billy said. "We've got to be thinking in terms of the next selling season long, long before we send the first one out."

"For those technical details we need a catalog person," Spider said firmly. "We have to hire the best person in the catalog world, somebody who's lived a catalog life. None of us knows what kind of pricing we're talking about, what kind of mailing lists, what inventory problems we might have. Guys, we don't know fuck-all about catalogs, we just know that Scruples Two is going to be a howling success."

"We can hire ten people who know that stuff, Spider," Billy assured him, "but we can't hire somebody who invented the Five-Minute Fire Drill Wardrobe. You *were* getting us to lead you to the theme that way, weren't you?"

"Sort of."

"I love that 'ah, shucks, it weren't nothin', ma'am,' look you get, Spider," Gigi said.

"Just a hunch, Gigi," Spider said modestly.

Spider's desk phone buzzed. Startled out of his concentration on the catalog, he picked it up with annoyance. "Who? Oh, okay, sure, send him in.

"It's Josh Hillman," he said, turning to Billy. "He's got those papers we're supposed to sign today; they have to be witnessed."

"Why would one of the top lawyers in L.A. leave his office to bring them here himself?" Billy asked.

"It's got to be pure curiosity. He's dying to know exactly what we're up to."

"Oh, I haven't seen Josh in years!" Gigi cried. "Is he still the most eligible man in Beverly Hills?"

"So I understand," Billy answered, shrugging, as Sasha quickly slipped out of the room by another door that led to a ladies' room.

Gigi rushed to give Josh a big hug and kiss, realizing as she saw him that she'd never really looked at him as a man before. She must have been too much of a kid, or too hung up on her imaginary visions of the young Marlon Brando, to realize that a man in his forties wasn't too old to fall into the handsome category. His eyes were many shades grayer than the sprinkling of gray in his short hair; he was as lithe as ever, even taller than Spider, and his high cheekbones, quizzical glance, clever mouth and sardonic smile all combined to make him a man of clear distinction.

"Garage sale?" Josh asked Billy, holding Gigi by the waist and looking at the mountain of clothes.

"It's a kind of contest," she said protectively. She still hadn't told Josh exactly what business she was going into with Spider, but had just asked him to draw up the partnership papers.

"Josh, you're the first to see the seed of Scruples Two," Spider announced.

"I thought it was going to be another store, there's an awful lot of money being spent on designer clothes these days."

"Not a store, and not a lot of money," Spider said like a proud father, not noticing that Billy was trying to signal him with her eyes to keep quiet about their plans. "We're going to create the first great fashion catalog based on the essential clothes no woman can live without. The twenty percent of the stuff she buys that she wears ninety percent of the time."

"Where'd you get that statistic?" Josh asked, raising his eyebrows dubiously.

"*Pravda*. But ask any woman, Josh, and she'll confirm it. And we're going to publicize it in a way no one has ever dreamed of publicizing a catalog before. Billy's going to be on every national television show that has a female audience, from 'Good Morning America' and 'Today' to Phil to Oprah, and on all the major local shows, the way writers tour for new books, showing people how our pieces work together—"

"I am going to do *what!*" Billy almost shouted, astonished. What the hell made him think she'd go on television?

"Of course—with three models to show the clothes while you explain the theme—with the fire drill this morning, I forgot to mention it. The idea came to me last night after we looked over your new jet. The travel wouldn't be tough, and shows will be fighting over a chance to get you. Of course we've got to give a huge press party, the way we did for Scruples, long before the first catalog is mailed, maybe one here, one in New York and one in Chicago—maybe Dallas?—I'll work that out with our PR people—"

"What PR people?" Billy gasped.

"The ones we're going to hire, of course," Spider said briskly, getting up and striding around the room in excitement. "Another thing, we should send out specially designed Scruples Two clothes hangers with every piece of merchandise that needs one, nothing more annoying than not enough hangers, isn't that right, Josh? And I've just realized that Gigi should do a lot of TV too with her accessory ideas, television producers are always looking for show-and-tell stuff."

"Spider!" Gigi squeaked, but he paid no attention to her, carried away by his ideas. "We're going to advertise in selected markets in national magazines—no catalog has ever advertised—and Scruples Two is free, so we'll get a terrific response."

"How about skywriters, Spider?" Billy asked, "and the Goodyear blimp saying, 'Welcome home, January'?"

"On target, Billy, on target," he said, looking as if he were about to burst into a chorus of "Seventy-six Trombones." "Maybe a little too cute, but I like your thinking. I always liked your thinking." He stopped to blow her a kiss, before he continued. "We'll send a special Scruples Two tape measure and a life-size wall chart to every new customer so we can establish their exact size, and then we'll have fewer returns—of course we'll take returns without question—"

"Nobody, nobody does that!" Billy said, outraged.

"That's why we have to. The only way to capture a mail-order customer with a new kind of catalog she's never seen before is to give her the chance to return what she doesn't like without any valid reason. If she doesn't have that option, she'll look but not order. Billy, I know it might cost us a lot at first, but we'll build our customers' trust, we'll learn what merchandise works and what doesn't, and we'll more than make it back in the long run. Right, Billy, do we agree?"

"We agree," she smiled, finally won over by his enthusiasm. Why shouldn't they use the Goodyear blimp? Before the football games? No, that would probably be too expensive, but the blimp didn't only work on Super Bowl Sunday. And why not TV commercials? Lester Weinstock had bartered his old television shows for tons of commercial time, and she could buy it from him at a substantial discount. Absolutely TV!

"And," Spider went on, "at least in the first issue, we ought to run a major contest, maybe customers could send us pictures of how they combine our separates and the winner gets to come out here in Billy's jet and go on a shopping spree with all you guys on Rodeo Drive and also gets one of everything in the catalog—we ought to have more than one winner, what about a baker's dozen?—and Sasha could—''

"Sasha could what?" Sasha asked as she came back into the room wearing her lucky red dress and high-heeled black pumps into which she'd just changed. A total silence fell as she moved toward them with the walk of dignified yet delicately wanton energy that had sold enough panties and bras to reach to the moon, a creature of sheen and luster, dark fire and dark, dark red rubies, her limp jersey dress transformed into the most perfectly cut garment in the world, its long sleeves only adding to the shock of the deeply cut neckline from which her breasts rose halfway in their white splendor.

Wrong, Spider thought, how wrong can a man be? On Sasha, sexy isn't attitude, sexy is what is low-cut and fits like a second skin. *And* attitude. Women could always surprise him.

She's up to something, Gigi thought in diverted apprehension . . . that Orloff-Nevsky magic they should all be arrested and put away for, she's turned it up as far as I've ever seen it.

"Sasha, this is Josh Hillman," Billy said, the only one of them with enough presence of mind to remember that they hadn't met. "Josh, this is Sasha Nevsky, Gigi's roommate and our co-conspirator in this project."

"How do you do?" Sasha and Josh each said at the same time as they shook hands. They paused and then said again in chorus, "Fine, thank you."

"Have we run out of small talk so quickly?" Sasha asked, looking up into Josh's face with a breathtakingly intimate smile Gigi had never seen before.

"Uh . . . no . . . uh . . . I hope not . . . not so soon," Josh stammered.

He looked as if he'd been hit over the head by a two-by-four, Billy noted with a touch of enchanted mischief. Her conservative lawyer could use a good shaking up, in her opinion, as could every other man, except Spider, who was like quicksilver.

"You're Gigi's roommate?" Josh asked Sasha, as if there were no one else in the room.

"We shared an apartment in New York for over two years. I'm

so very, very much older than Gigi that I was acting as her chaperone.''

"How much older?" he asked, as if it were a matter of life or death.

"It feels like a decade," Sasha sighed, swaying slightly closer to him. "Several decades, as a matter of fact."

Why doesn't she swoon? Gigi asked herself gleefully. Why doesn't she just swoon dead away into his arms, when she tells lies like that?

"Where do you live?" Josh asked urgently.

"Gigi and I share a place in West Hollywood . . ." Sasha replied, her voice a private, unexpected note, like a cello string gently touched for the first time.

"Josh," Gigi said, feeling mercy for him, "why don't you come by for a drink tonight? Everybody's seen our apartment but you, and we're feeling house-proud at the moment."

"That's a great idea, Gigi," Spider said crisply. This courtship ritual was wasting his time. "Maybe we'd better look at those papers now, Josh?"

"Papers?"

"The papers you brought to be signed?"

"Oh, those papers . . . . I have them right here. Ah . . . look, Spider, there's no rush, I'll just leave them with you and Billy. Gigi and . . . Sasha . . . I'll come by for that drink tonight, if I may," he said, and fled the room.

"He doesn't know our address," Gigi said.

"I think he'll manage to find it out," Billy laughed. "Back to work, ladies? Oh, and gentlemen . . . come on, back to work, you guys."

"Will you stop fiddling with the ice bucket and get out!" Sasha ordered Gigi impatiently.

"He's not even due for fifteen minutes," Gigi pointed out.

"What if he's early? I don't want that ghastly pink car of yours anywhere in the neighborhood!"

"I'm going, I'm going, but first you have to explain why you're not wearing your lucky dress. If ever there was a time—"

"I don't need it anymore."

Gigi eyed Sasha wearing a high-necked black dress that was the most conservative and expensive item in her wardrobe, an utterly simple, clinging column of silk crepe.

"That dress makes you look . . . ."

"How?"

"Like a . . . oh, my God! Like a *nice girl*! Sasha, I accept that you're the Great Slut of all time, but don't do this, you can't be so cruel," Gigi implored. "I know men must suffer, but why victimize that sweet, kind, good man—he's never in his life done anything half bad enough for you to make him think you're a nice girl!"

"Never mind," Sasha said loftily.

"And putting your hair up on top of your head in that prim way, you look *ancient*," Gigi said wrathfully, giving a severe poke to the fire she'd lit in their fireplace.

"How ancient?"

"Almost . . . thirty-five."

A gratified smile briefly illuminated Sasha's ardent face.

"Good. Now *out*, Isadora, before I strangle you with your least favorite scarf."

"Okay, okay, but first tell me . . . or I won't leave," Gigi said, backing away, "tell me, was it the words 'top lawyer' or the word 'eligible' that made you change into your lucky dress?"

"I honestly don't remember. I think it was instinct, a reflex action, something about that name, Josh Hillman—it *resonated*. Oh, will you just please leave?"

"Sasha, you're not, no, you can't be . . . *nervous* . . . ?" Gigi came close and peered at her friend.

"Sasha Nevsky doesn't even know how nervous feels," Sasha said threateningly, "but you will if you're still here in the next five seconds."

"We're out of wood," Josh said as he and Sasha sat in front of the low-burning fire. "How can that be? There was plenty when I arrived."

"What time is it?"

"It's . . . almost ten. What happened to the time?"

"Did we spend it on the Hillmans?"

"And the Orloffs and the Nevskys?"

"I can't sort it out," Sasha answered dreamily. "The Hillmans sound exactly like a bunch of Nevskys who don't happen to dance. It's all a blur."

"But we missed dinner," Josh said in concern. "I made an eight-thirty reservation at Le Chardonnay."

"For three?"

"For two. I was planning to separate you from Gigi one way or another. We've got to eat. I'll call Robert and tell him we're on our way."

"Would you think I was crazy if I said I was in the mood for deli?"

Josh looked at this peerless woman in astonishment. He'd been craving a corned beef on rye for the last few minutes. He'd never before talked so much and so personally, never found such a sympathetic, understanding audience, and only Jewish soul food would hit the spot in his state of exaltation.

"I'm taking you to Art's in the Valley, it's the best deli in L.A.," he promised her. "Say good-bye to Marcel."

No one at Art's was surprised to see the elegantly dressed couple enter. From spiffed-up teenagers after their proms to babies six weeks old; from groups of hale and well-nourished senior citizens to film-star refugees from celebrity restaurants—all forms of humanity eventually beat a path to Art's. There, Art himself presided over his famous establishment decorated in a calming combination of beiges, walls hung with enormous photographs of each of its sandwiches, roomy booths spaced so that diners could eat in a privacy and relative quiet unknown in the other delicatessens of Hollywood.

Sasha and Josh were given a semicircular booth in a corner and presented with open menus that offered, besides eighteen appetizers, forty-four sandwiches and eight soups, six different kinds of hamburgers, thirty-eight varieties of hot or cold plates, thirteen salads, eighteen side orders, eight kinds of potatoes and eighteen desserts.

"Oh." Sasha looked bewildered. "Gee whiz."

"Shall I order for you?"

"Please. I wouldn't know where to start."

"How hungry are you?"

"I'm not sure, but logically I must be perishing. I've barely eaten a thing since breakfast . . . the plans for the catalog were too exciting."

Josh scanned the menu. "Do you like smoked fish?" he asked Sasha, and when she nodded assent, he looked up at the waitress. "First bring us some appetizers; sturgeon, lox, whitefish and, let's see, oh, the herring in sour cream . . . hmmm . . . . and then a corned beef sandwich for me and a—Sasha, is corned beef okay for you? Right, make that two corned beefs, and maybe a brisket dip on a French roll with gravy, and one of your combo sandwiches—the Art's Special, the triple-decker with rare roast beef, pastrami and Swiss. That should do to start. And potato pancakes with sour cream and plenty of applesauce. Maybe you'd better bring us a few extra plates so we can share. To drink? Club soda, Sasha? White wine? Beer? Champagne? It's something called Rocar, must be Californian? Fine, a bottle of Rocar, please, and some plain water."

As they waited for their appetizers, Josh and Sasha sipped their champagne thoughtfully, hunger a convenient explanation for the sudden silence that had fallen between them. Sasha was cursing herself for suggesting deli; even a hungry woman should remember that the harshest overhead light in the world is to be found in delicatessens. But he was so wonderful that she'd forgotten everything except the way his eyes slanted upward. To kiss him right there, on the outer corner of each eye, right on the laugh lines that appeared each time he smiled . . . oh, nothing like this had ever happened to her, and fluorescent lights or no, nothing like this would ever happen again. Her career was over, she thought in amazement, years of dedicated application to masculine torment brought to a dead stop by one grownup man for whom she felt ready, if need be, to stop a bullet.

Sasha brought an inner spotlight with her, Josh thought, trying not to stare. No matter how beautiful she'd been by firelight, she was more entrancing when he could see her clearly. When he'd been lucky enough to catch a glimpse of her this morning, taken off-guard and looking wild and wicked, he hadn't dreamed that she was perfection itself. No wonder Billy had confided Gigi to her—she had such modesty, such dignity, and a beautifully serene reserve, a deeply mysterious quality that only a rare woman still preserved in this blaring day and age. He felt that he had already glimpsed her personal signature of flowering grace combined with a crisp, adult clarity, an intense, soothingly silent, precise listening quality. But, my God, that upper lip, that lush upper lip, that pouting, curling upper lip . . . a man could stand only so much . . . .

"Here you go," the waitress said, putting down four generous plates of smoked fish, accompanied by a heap of sliced rye bread, a plate of sliced tomatoes, onions and lemons, and an oval dish of pickles.

"You start," Josh said, giving Sasha a serving fork. She transferred a slice of smoked sturgeon to an empty plate, added a piece of the smoked salmon, a bit of whitefish and a piece of lemon. She nibbled on a crust of rye bread while he served himself. Sasha took a morsel of whitefish, chewed with determination, and washed it down with champagne. Josh speared a bit of smoked salmon and managed to swallow it by sheer willpower.

"It's odd, when you get too hungry . . . sometimes you can't eat right away," she murmured.

"I know . . . I think I may have over-ordered."

"It just looks like so much . . . . food."

"They're famous for their large portions . . ."

"It's not that the whitefish isn't delicious . . ."

"Try some salmon," Josh suggested.

"Oh, I couldn't—I'm saving myself for the sandwich."

"Herring?"

"No, thank you," she said piteously.

"Have you ever been married?" His voice was calm.

"No, thank you."

"I asked if you've ever been married."

"Oh. No."

"Why not?"

"I've never met the right man. Only boys, immature boys. At least that was the way they seemed to me."

"How could that be?"

"I haven't any idea," Sasha said in a bewildered voice, "I suppose they were all just too young for me. But you've been married. Why did you get divorced?"

"I wasn't in love with my wife."

"Was that enough reason?"

"I . . . fell in love with somebody else."

"Who was she?" Sasha asked, feeling a sharply pointed shaft of pure jealousy slam into her stomach.

"Valentine, before she married Spider," Josh said.

"I'm sorry," Sasha said softly.

"It's all right now. I've never told anyone but you." His voice was blankly amazed as he heard his admission.

"Is there something wrong with the fish, Mr. Hillman?" the waitress asked in a worried tone.

"No, we're just not as hungry as we thought."

"What should I do about the sandwiches?"

"Oh, go ahead and bring them. Maybe they'll inspire us."

The waitress cleared the table and returned to the kitchen, stopping to have a word with Art as she went. She returned laden with a large tray from which she deposited the four plates of sandwiches and the platter of potato pancakes. Each sandwich was a tower of thinly sliced meat, at least five inches high, mounded on specially baked rye bread, garnished with more pickles and onion slices.

"Good Lord," Sasha said, appalled, "I've never seen anything like this in New York."

"I split them in half and eat them like open-faced sandwiches, otherwise you can't get them into your mouth. Here, I'll fix yours for you."

"I . . . could I just start with the applesauce?"

"Without the pancakes?"

She nodded, rapt in contemplation of his hands as they moved amid the plates, lifted the saucer of applesauce and placed it in front of her. She took a spoon and dipped it in. Babies eat applesauce, she told herself, little tiny babies with their undeveloped digestive tracts can do away with a ton of the stuff. Why couldn't she?

"Sasha, eat your applesauce," Josh commanded, and she put the spoon in her mouth. It went down fairly easily, and with diligence and champagne, she made herself swallow four small spoonfuls.

"There's a picture at the bottom of the plate," Josh said coaxingly, watching her eat.

"You must have children."

"Three. They're good kids."

Sasha was skewered anew by a flight of visceral arrows of jealousy. A man with children had to maintain a relationship with their mother. She wished she hadn't asked, she thought, putting her spoon down with a definite gesture of rejection. She looked at his cornedbeef sandwich and at the sight of it her heart lifted. It hadn't been touched. Not so much as one bite.

"Josh, eat something."

"I'm not hungry . . . . unless . . . you're really not going to finish that applesauce . . ."

"It's all yours."

He took a few spoonfuls and put down his spoon. Skillfully avoiding the sandwiches, he took both of her hands in his.

"I can't eat. It's hopeless. I'm in love with you."

"Me too," Sasha said faintly.

"You can't eat or you're in love with me?"

"Both," she whispered.

"Will you marry me?"

"Of course."

"Look at me," he demanded, but she couldn't make herself meet his eyes.

"We've got to get out of here," Josh said, grabbing the passing waitress. "I can't wait for the check." He put five twenty-dollar bills down on the table. "I think that should be enough. Thank you for your service."

"But your doggy bags!"

"Never mind." He extracted Sasha gently from the booth and they walked, hand in hand, to the door.

"They didn't eat, they didn't even want doggy bags," the waitress reported to Art.

"What'd I tell you, Irma? I spotted it right away. Love. It's the only thing that doesn't go with deli. But they'll be back. Sooner or later they're going to get hungry again."

"Stop it," Gigi muttered, "go away. I was in the middle of a wonderful dream."

"Your alarm is about to go off anyway—I waited five whole minutes to wake you."

"Sasha, you're impossible," Gigi said, opening her eyes. "First you throw me out of my own house and now you invade my bedroom at the crack of dawn to gloat over a new conquest—" She closed her eyes again.

"We're going to get married."

"Sure you are . . ."

"You heard me. Josh and I are going—"

"You can't marry a man you met yesterday," Gigi said, sleepily dismissing Sasha's newest form of torture.

"Where is that written?"

Gigi opened her eyes wide, sat up and peered speechlessly at Sasha. She was still wearing the black dress, but her hair was down around her shoulders and her makeup had all but disappeared, replaced by a look of such pure and utter happiness that it brought tears to Gigi's eyes.

"Sasha!" She threw her arms around her and kissed her cheeks. "My God! It's wonderful—wonderful beyond words—when?"

"Well, not right away. It takes time to organize a big wedding."

"But . . . but . . ." Gigi stopped, too confused to know what to ask next.

"Someday you'll meet a man too, Gigi, someone you can't stand to see suffer," Sasha said compassionately.

"Thank you, Sasha, I appreciate knowing that. Thanks for sharing. It gives me hope. This big wedding, does Josh want that?"

"He wants whatever I want," Sasha said in blissful, justified confidence.

"And you'll wear a long white dress?"

"With a long train and a long veil, and I know what you're leading up to, Gigi. There's a reason why the six Orloff sisters never disagree. They don't *dare*. You see, there's something called the Dreaded Orloff Curse, and if anyone ever puts the Orloff Curse on you, it's good-bye, Charlie."

"Isn't it more like 'good-bye, Great Slut'?"

"Gigi! I'm warning you—"

"You don't scare me. My two Orsini grandmothers, Giovanna and Graziella, were both from Florence. This descendant of two very dominating old ladies, from a place where a lot of very bad things happened hundreds of years ago—ever heard of Savonarola?—can take on the six Orloff sisters anytime—so I'll just forget the past. It's a blank, for Josh's sake—I've known him a bit longer than you have. Oh, Sasha, I'm so glad! You deserve him! Congratulations!"

"You don't congratulate the bride, you congratulate the groom," Sasha said, falling back on the bed in a heap of joy. "You tell the bride that you know she'll be very happy."

"I know you'll be very happy, Sasha darling. Does *he* know how old you are?"

"We never actually got around to that. I don't know how old he is, either. What does it matter?"

"Maybe after the wedding?" Gigi suggested.

"Good thinking. There's hope for you yet."

19

ow, darling," Billy said with distilled sweetness to John Prince, the richest of the top American fashion designers, "don't explode until I've had a chance to explain it to you, we've known each other too well and too long for that."

"I don't do cheap clothes, Billy. I never have and I never will. I'm stunned, actually stunned, that you would come to me, of all people, with this proposition. A catalog! Good grief!" Prince was genuinely offended. All the lines of his square, agreeably reassuring face were set in a disapproving frown, and even his carefully cultivated, English-country-squire manner had been dropped and replaced by his native Midwestern bluntness.

"Moderately priced, Prince, darling, never 'cheap.' "

"I don't care what adjectives you use," Prince said, as he and Billy sat together in his New York office, on a bitterly cold day in early

February. "You can call them whatever keeps you from blushing, but you're talking about a skirt that would sell for fifty dollars."

"Why not?"

"Just look at yourself in a mirror, for pity's sake. That suit of mine cost two thousand two hundred dollars, look at the fabric, look at the workmanship, look at—"

"The markup," Billy insisted in winsomely smiling disagreement. "Prince, I used to run a store, so I know what this suit really cost. Let's see, if I remember correctly, and I do, your cost to produce it, including fabric, trim, labor and a percentage of what you pay to keep your business running, like rent, couldn't have been more than four hundred fifty-five bucks. You sold it to Bergdorf's for a thousand dollars, since that average markup is a little more than double your cost. Now, Bergdorf's markup is also a little more than double, making their price tag two thousand two, plus, I might add, more for alterations. So here I stand, dressed in less than five hundred dollars' worth of real value, having paid four times that at retail. I can afford it, but damn few people can. You probably didn't sell more than a dozen of these suits in the whole country, if you sold that many."

"Billy, what kind of point are you trying to make?" Prince asked heatedly. He dreaded the fortunately rare customers who knew the pricing structure of the garment business, something with which they had no business being acquainted, a secret that stripped away the glamour of beautiful clothes. How could you enjoy wearing an expensive suit if you knew what it was really worth, and why was Billy Ikehorn tormenting him? Why didn't she go and inform the jewelers from whom she bought her diamonds that their markup was four hundred percent and leave him alone?

"I'm simply pointing out," Billy said, resuming an air of appealing innocence, "that if you sold twenty of these suits, you made a profit of roughly ten thousand dollars. If you were designing moderate-priced clothes, you'd be taking orders in the hundreds or thousands of each item, making less per unit, but more, very much more, in the long run."

"Do you think I don't know that, Billy?" Prince responded in disdain. "The idea doesn't tempt me for a second. My name stands for the very top of the market in ready-to-wear. I've made all the money anyone could need . . . . 'thousands' of anything is not what the John Prince label is about. People would be horrified if I started to design moderate-priced clothes. I'd lose my ladies, my lovely ladies."

Billy repressed a sigh of exasperation. Prince's cherished ladies, who vied for him as an indispensable extra man at every one of their parties, were nothing more than a small handful of women in Manhattan who depended on Prince as if he were a magic amulet against the powers of social oblivion. They, and their counterparts in perhaps fifteen other American cities, armed in their always becoming, always suitable, always stylish and self-evidently expensive Princes, could move confidently among their friends and enemies, secure in the knowledge that whatever else might be said about them, no one could accuse them of lack of taste or the inability to spend money freely.

Getting Prince to design for Scruples Two was worth any amount of persuasion, Billy thought, her resolve hardening. He had a particular talent she needed, even if he had never valued it, and, equally important, he had become, over the last twenty years, thoroughly famous throughout the entire country thanks to licensing his name. If Prince were instantly recognizable only to the three or four hundred thousand women who read *Vogue, Fashion and Interiors* and *Harper's Bazaar,* it would mean little to the future customers of Scruples Two, but the words "By John Prince" could be found on top lines of bedsheets and bath towels, belts, shoes, costume jewelry, sunglasses, watches and handbags. His two perfumes were both wildly successful. His name had been so widely advertised, for so long, that he had become an institution, as well known in the United States as Dior or Saint Laurent in France. Getting John Prince to design the capsule collections for Scruples Two would be an instantaneous imprimatur of fashion authority to millions of women.

Billy knew perfectly well that in reality Prince created his expensive ready-to-wear, as well as his licensees' designs, with the indispensable assistance of an entire troupe of unknown assistants, of whom Valentine had been the favorite for three years.

Billy and Prince were sitting, each with a cup of coffee, on the oversized tufted Chesterfield that was one of the Anglophile glories of Prince's office. From Prince himself to the last rare, leather-bound volume on his polished mahogany bookshelves, nothing in the magnificent room betrayed that they were not in some privileged private house in the heart of the designer's London fantasy land, a Henry Jamesian world he had created around him from the first days of his success. If she looked out his windows, Billy thought fleetingly, instead of crowded Seventh Avenue, she'd expect to see Hyde Park on a perfect June day a century ago, with perfectly turned-out riders on perfect thoroughbreds proceeding down the wide bridle path of the Row, some at a stately walk, some at a gallop, all pursuing a favorite pastime of a world in which splendid leisure was the norm.

She turned to look speculatively at Prince as he sat as interestingly clad as the Duke of Windsor had ever been. "Nobody puts his own clothes together better than you do, Prince," Billy observed truthfully. "It's such a miracle of systematic disagreement, each item so clearly independent and yet so right with the others, that I can only wonder how you manage to make the choices every morning. How *do* you decide to put together your own checks and plaids and polka dots and herringbones and flannels? They're a symphony of the most sublime discords. Do you keep a chart on the wall of your closet?"

"I just throw everything together and it comes out like this," Prince answered, "it's a little knack. And you can't butter me up, Billy, because everything I'm wearing was custom-tailored for me, to my choice of fabrics, and it all cost the earth."

"I'm not buttering you up, darling. Sometimes I do, but not about business." Billy moved closer to him on the couch. "Now take this red paisley tie," she said as she admiringly flicked a finger at it, "just look at what it does for that brown and blue striped shirt you're wearing. And the shirt is oddly perfect with your checked jacket, and the jacket's the most exceptional partner to your taupe twill trousers. I saw your toggle-fastened pea coat when I came in—the ideal thing to wear over all this. That's no mere 'little knack,' sweetheart, it's a major talent for separates. You choose to use your knack in the way you dress yourself, but not your rich lady customers. That knack, Prince, is *exactly* the reason I want you to design my capsule collections."

"Billy, will you never learn to take no for an answer?" Prince asked, his good nature restored. He and Billy went back a long way, after all, and during the time that Scruples had been in business, it had been one of his most profitable accounts.

"Never!" Her answer was launched with such profound conviction, such a martial spirit, that it took possession of the air and made him regard her with new interest. He remembered when she'd started Scruples—he hadn't believed an amateur could make a success out of a boutique, but the fact that she'd proved him utterly wrong didn't make her catalog notion any more appealing.

"Prince, listen to me," Billy commanded, getting up and perching on the edge of his desk, her slim, claret-red suit, with its matching crushed-velvet collar and cuffs, as perfect as only three fittings could make it. She wore a small, romantic hat of dark sable, almost the color of her eyes, tilted so far forward that it grazed her eyebrows, allowing her curls to spring freely away from her ears. She looked at the designer with a concentration he had never seen on her face before. "I don't think you see the point of the capsule collections. We're going to start with four of them, small but edited so well that there isn't a single wasted or unnecessary idea. They're directed toward young women who have, in *Vogue*'s immortal words, 'more taste than money.' One will take a woman through a week at her job, one will take her traveling, one will give her everything she needs for weekends —great-looking sportswear—and the fourth will be for after-hours— dates, restaurants, business dinners, all that. Everything in each individual collection has to work with just about anything in the other three collections. In other words, your easy office blazer is designed to be worn over your weekend pants and your restaurant shirt— clever, dressed-down designs that give a woman a hundred choices— letting her dress the way you dress, Prince."

"Billy, stop selling me."

"I'm just thinking out loud. You will admit that the women who don't have the money to buy your ready-to-wear would love to be able to buy Scruples Two Prince exclusives?"

"The whole point, pet, is that they can't. If they can't afford Prince, well . . ." He threw up his hands. "I wish they could, but some things will always be out of reach except for the happy few."

"You know, when I was buying tons of clothes, during my first marriage, I didn't buy yours. I always admired them, but I thought I'd wait until I was over thirty to wear them. Has it occurred to you that women in their twenties, no matter how much money they have, aren't your customers?"

"Until they grow up," Prince observed from a lofty height, "they're not ready for me. And I don't lose anything, because how many young women can afford my clothes anyway?"

"There are lots of smashing rich young women who won't even consider your things, Prince, because you've been designing for the same group of women ever since you started. They're getting older and older, always photographed in Prince—your look is inextricably associated with them, the wealthy matron's badge of office: the Prince ballgown, the important jewelry, the blond bouffant hairdo and the ten-thousand-dollar facelift. Where are your new customers going to come from? All those bright young designers, not just the Calvin Kleins and the Ralph Laurens, but others we haven't heard from yet, will capture women who would otherwise graduate toward you, sweetie. On the other hand, if you designed for Scruples Two, you'd have to give yourself a good shaking-up and dusting-off, you'd have to challenge yourself to do something you've never yet proved you can do—versatile clothes at a humane price. Everyone would be talking about your new look, your new attitude. Why repeat yourself when you can *renew* yourself, Prince, you can *feed your legend* in a way nothing else ever will."

"You're shining me on."

"I didn't know you knew that expression, darling. Of course I am. There are other major designers who'd jump at this—they know it won't affect their regular customers, they know that one thing has nothing to do with the other, but none of them has your particular talent. They make *outfits*."

"So do I."

"But you don't *wear* outfits," Billy said on a true, fresh note. "You wear separates, by choice. I've never once seen you in two pieces that matched unless it's black tie, and even then you always add something different—a tweed waistcoat, plaid inside the cuffs and under the collar of your dinner jacket, a cotton batik cummerbund."

"I'll give you that," he said, pleased in spite of himself. "I like to enjoy myself when I get dressed."

"Oh, Prince! That's it! That's exactly it! Clothes that work like dogs but continue to give you a divine little *high* each time you put them on. Just tell me this, even if you won't do it, is there anything you don't like about my idea except the price?"

"I'm afraid you're trying to reinvent the wheel, pet. Separates have always been with us. A woman can go to any department store and buy them, she doesn't need me."

"But it's just not that easy! What if her job doesn't leave her time to shop? What if she doesn't have the ability to pull things together? What if she doesn't live near a big store with a good selection of clothes? What if she doesn't like the newest styles? What if she's a busy young mother juggling baby, husband and career? Shopping's a *nightmare* for most women!"

"Very depressing indeed, dear."

Billy laughed out loud. "You're such a good-hearted guy, Prince, but I'd never know it to listen to you now."

"Oh, just don't play the 'Where is your sense of social responsibility?' card. I do my bit. Why do *you* want to be in trade, pet? I've never understood it. Why, you could be a duchess, even an *English* duchess," he said reverently, unable to imagine a station in life that he would rather occupy or for which he was better suited.

"I'm basically a working girl, Prince, just like you're a working man. And right now I'm anxious to get a jump-start that will put my new project on the map quickly. You—or another top designer—are the key to a necessary edge. It's not that I doubt the success of Scruples Two, I know I'm on the verge of something huge, but as usual, I'm impatient. If you're going to offer the ultimate pleated skirt in the world, for example—at a price—you have to give it a special twist, a certain something that makes it stand out from every other skirt. If I knew what I wanted, believe me, I'd design it myself, but I haven't a clue. Oh well, I should have known that you couldn't be motivated. And it's a shame, really. I've always felt I owed you something for taking Valentine away. She'd have worked for you forever if I hadn't lured her out to Scruples."

"Just how would letting you con me," he chuckled, "repay me for taking Valentine away?"

"The money, darling. The loot," Billy said as she got up to go. "But, as you said, you feel you have as much as you need. I guess you're immune from the horrid little secret of the very, very rich. Well, good-bye, Prince, darling, I have to make another pitch at lunch."

Prince got up to accompany her to the door. "What horrid little secret?" he asked lightly.

"Oh, you know—it's a bit shame-making really, but most people never feel they have *enough* money, do they? . . . . And yet we all have so much more than we can ever spend. It must be something in human nature, this unending drive for *more*. I've been on that list of the ten richest women in America since Ellis died, yet now I'm determined to make Scruples Two a Fortune 500 Company. You own this big dress business, but you're not on the list of the Forbes 400—you can't build a private fortune in the hundreds of millions making expensive clothes, even with your licenses—I guess it's a game, really, always wanting *more* when one has so much . . . ."

"Your guess is as good as mine . . ." He shrugged in irritation.

"Just look at me with a lovely house in Paris that I don't even use but I love too much to sell. It's too absurd, darling, when I could have a magnificent yacht and estates here and there, and spend my time having glorious fun, transporting my friends from one perfect vacation to another.'' Billy paused and seemed to be considering her prospects with the attention of a woman in a brimming rose garden, pruning shears in hand, trying to choose the one perfect bud among a superfluity of marvelous blooms.

"But no," she said finally, "here I am, darling, on good old Seventh Avenue, beavering away at this catalog because I'm so certain that the time is right for it and I'm going to prove it, Prince, come what may. Perhaps I'm a workaholic . . . but it's so exciting that it can't be bad for me. And the royalties on Scruples Two will be immense . . . I just felt I'd rather you had them than somebody else."

"Royalties?"

"Well, obviously whoever designs the capsule collections will get a royalty on every single piece sold. You understood that, of course . . . I did remember to say that, didn't I? I suppose I could save the money and hire a crack design team, but I'd rather pay the royalties and have a giant name attached to the collections. There'll be more in the end for everybody, including little me."

"Billy?"

"Yes?"

"You are a totally evil little girl, you know that, don't you?"

"Sweetheart, the *worst*!"

"Sit down. Let's talk."

"Oh, Prince!" Billy rushed into his arms. She hadn't been sure she'd have to pay royalties, she'd hoped to get away with a huge design fee, but when it came down to the wire, if that was what it took, it was worth it. Some people really were only interested in money, and Prince, thank God, had always been one of them.

Her return, or rather her retreat, to her native land seemed to suit Billy Ikehorn, Cora de Lioncourt decided, as she and Billy had tea together at Billy's apartment. The semi-rural ease, the downright unapologetic sloppiness—or was it slovenliness?—that she understood was a permissible way of life in California, obviously agreed with Billy in a way that the electric elegance of Paris had not. Of course, making the grade in Los Angeles would take no effort for her at all. It must be such a relief for her to give up on New York and Paris and slink back home. It was the only explanation she could think of that would account for Billy's air of excited happiness on a dreary day in a dreary month on which the only appointment she had mentioned having was one with John Prince to look at his new spring collection.

Cora observed Billy closely, noticing that not only had she lost the weight she'd gained in Paris, and had her hair cut short again, but that her personal style, her carelessly brilliant chic mixed with sensuality, was once more intact. Today, in addition, Billy seemed to be suppressing some secret triumph, Cora realized with irritation, as she nibbled at a tea sandwich. Other people's secrets were *impermissible*.

"You're looking extraordinarily well, Billy," she said, her enticing voice honeyed and faintly reproachful, as if looking too well were something that had to be explained.

"Thank you, Cora. It's your city that does it. I love a good stiff jolt of New York every now and then. It's a tonic to my system."

"But you still don't plan to buy a place here?"

"Why bother? An apartment hotel's so convenient."

"Will you be moving into your house in Paris in the spring?"

"I haven't decided yet," Billy said with an impenetrable smile.

"But what do you *do* with yourself in Los Angeles? You made such a speech at the Ritz about women who don't do anything but shop and go to parties, and now you're living in a place where there's far less going on than there is here or in Paris."

"Oh, I keep busy with this and that, Cora, it's amazing how the days fly by," Billy said evasively. She had no intention of telling Cora about Scruples Two. Winning Prince over had been a necessary struggle, but there was no reason to expose her fledgling project to a woman of such overly refined standards that she would dump cold water on the mere idea of a fashion catalog.

More secrets, Cora thought. Billy Ikehorn and her secrets truly infuriated her. Billy had an unsubdued independence that made Cora want to see her shatter into pieces, like a shop window hit by a well-thrown rock. Billy had refused to be guided by any one of Cora's recommendations except in the matter of her Parisian real-estate agent. Her own percentage of that deal had been a meager, unacceptable return for her trouble. She had groomed Billy Ikehorn to be the catch of her lifetime of manipulation. By all rights Billy should have become a cash cow, yet she continued to elude Cora, as un-bovine as an eel in mud. Her buoyant high spirits were no more than deliberate provocation.

Oh, Billy knew exactly how enviable she was, Cora thought, consumed by bitterness, as she watched her sitting there in that brilliantly chosen sable hat, her large sable muff held in her lap, as carelessly luxurious as a latter-day Anna Karenina before she came to grief. This woman to whom riches came without effort, this woman who had been born to beauty, this woman who could, by lifting a finger, instantly acquire better objects than those Cora had worked a lifetime for, drove her mad with envy. Just by existing, Billy made her feel shabby, as if the careful, clever cultivation and accumulation of her own life were a small and unremarkable achievement.

She gave up on Billy Ikehorn, there was no reason to dance around her any longer, no reason to continue to protect their relationship in hope of future gain.

"I had the oddest experience in Paris, after I saw you last at the Opéra," Cora remarked.

"Did you?"

"Remember that man who came over to our table and made that awful scene, that tall, angry, redheaded man who asked you who the hell you were?"

"That? Of course, how could I forget? An old beau with a grievance, nothing more."

"But you see, that's exactly what's so odd. A few days later, I saw him again. I was doing the new exhibitions, and there he was, in the Templon gallery with some very interesting work, if you happen to like modern sculpture." She observed Billy with the watchful quietude of a panther.

"He would be there," Billy said calmly. "That's where he showed his work."

"Of course I didn't try to talk to him, but after he left the gallery with the dealer, I fell into conversation with an assistant, Henri somebody, a great admirer of your sculptor . . . Sam Jamison? . . . . yes, that was his name, wasn't it?"

"Yes."

"And Henri, rather a charming fellow who grabs any chance to speak English, told me that he'd been with your old beau, as you call him, at the Opéra that night. He even remembered seeing me at your table. He said that the sculptor . . . . Sam . . . . had disappeared after he saw you . . . missed the second act entirely."

"We all saw him rush away." Billy shrugged, sweating under her blouse.

"And we all saw you rush after him," Cora said, her most brilliant smile flickering on her lips, baring her perfect teeth.

Billy confronted Cora directly, impatiently letting her muff drop to the floor, folding her arms, her smoky eyes defiant. "Cora, what are you driving at? What business is it of yours? Am I not permitted a private life?"

"Now, Billy, of course you are. Don't be silly. It's merely that Henri what's-his-name thought you were somebody else entirely, somebody named Honey Winthrop. I didn't know you still used your maiden name."

Billy continued to fix Cora with a dangerous gaze. "I think that there are things friends shouldn't ask each other about, don't you?"

"You're right, of course," Cora agreed, lightly. "Yes, another sandwich, please, they're so good I can't resist. Tell me, did you order a lot from Prince?"

"Much too much," Billy said. "The new collection was particularly good."

As Cora bit into her tiny watercress sandwich, she thought of the deeply interesting lunch to which she had invited charming young Henri Legrand. He had been just as curious about Billy as she was about Sam Jamison, and between the two of them they had pieced together the whole incredibly juicy story. Billy had her secrets, true, but not as many as she believed, and the most intriguing of them now belonged to Cora de Lioncourt.

"Gigi, look at this photo," Spider asked, as he walked into her office with the sleeves of his blue denim work shirt rolled up, "and tell me what you think about it." He passed her an enlargement of a color photograph of a group of women, all but one of whom seemed to be in their late twenties or early thirties. They were standing in a garden in a laughing group around an older woman, seated on a garden seat, whom they were toasting with flutes of champagne.

"Who are they?" Gigi asked curiously, sitting behind her desk.

"I'll tell you, but that's not important, just give me your off-the-cuff reaction."

Gigi studied the photo closely before she answered. "They're happy," she said, "genuinely happy, that's the first thing I notice, and they're really glad to be together. They're relaxed, carefree—oh!— they have a strong family resemblance, they've all got to be related one way or another. Come on, Spider, who are they?" Gigi looked up at him through her bangs in her most singularly coaxing way, both frank and slightly comical, as unable to keep a restless, native flirtatiousness out of her eyes as she was to change the way her ears were so delicately pointed.

"Keep talking," he said. "So far I haven't heard anything profound from the person who's announced that she thinks she can write all the copy for Scruples Two."

Gigi bent her bright, silky head attentively over the photograph. "They're not New Yorkers, but they're not country girls either, they're too sophisticated for that. I don't know how I know, but I'm sure of it, San Francisco, Chicago, Dallas, L.A.? They're sophisticated in a casual sort of way, as if they don't have to work at it . . . it comes naturally to them. They all know how to dress but they're not copycats. Two of them—these two in jeans," she said, pointing, "are definitely underdressed compared to the others, but they look just fine anyway. They're all nice-looking women, a couple of them are very nice looking, but not one is what I'd call a real beauty. If I had to guess —do I have to guess, Spider?—okay, okay, I'd say that they're probably married and have kids . . . but," Gigi paused and pondered before she continued, "most likely they aren't full-time housewives. Maybe one or two are, but I think most of them work, or teach, or do heavy-duty volunteer work . . . what I mean is that they look as if they're busy with a lot of interesting things and they're having such a good time! I wish I knew them. Actually the best looking of them is the older woman—why are they all toasting her?"

"It was her birthday lunch," Spider said proudly. "That's my mom."

"Oh . . . Spider," Gigi sighed, and unexpected tears flooded her eyes. "You're so *lucky*."

Appalled, Spider leaned down and put a comforting arm around her shoulders. "Damn it, Gigi, I forgot about your mother. Hell, I shouldn't have sprung it on you like that. I just forgot entirely. *I'm so sorry*. Here's a Kleenex," he said contritely.

"It's okay, Spider, honestly." Gigi blew her nose and blotted her eyes, recovering herself. "I never do that—I don't know what came over me. Your mother's stunning, and of course those are your famous sisters—I was so busy getting a general impression of the picture that I completely missed the fact that I was looking at three sets of twins . . . their features were the last thing I was thinking about, and anyway they try to look individual."

"Actually, that's why I didn't tell you who they were. If you'd known, you'd have been too busy trying to figure out which twin belonged with which, to have concentrated on the general look of them all together."

"Did I get them right, as far as what I said?"

"On the nose. Of course, they're not all that carefree, who is? But they're a happy bunch of sweeties and busy full-time with many things besides their husbands and kids. I took that picture three years ago. I remembered it last night and dug it out to show everybody. You're the first to see it—I thought that the look, not my sisters specifically, but the look they have, was right for Scruples Two."

"You mean kind of easygoing sophisticated?"

"That absolutely, and more. I've been up to my elbows in every catalog ever published. There isn't one of them that isn't a disaster, an art director's or fashion editor's nightmare, graphically fifteen years behind the times. I've been analyzing every magazine on the newsstands, looking at the models, the locations and the layouts, and the one thing that I've decided is that we have to establish a single type of woman who embodies the Scruples Two look. Then we'll choose our models from those who have our look naturally, loud and clear. Instead of hiring top models and dressing them in our clothes, we've got to find models who look the way our customers would and *can* look if they try. Not just in their wildest dreams, but in reality. We shouldn't show them something they *can* afford to buy, being worn by someone they automatically dismiss as being too beautiful to relate to. You said you wished you knew my sisters . . . . I want our customers to wish they knew our models."

"They're awfully . . . ."

"Awfully what?"

"Well . . ." Gigi hesitated. She agreed with Spider in principle, but his sisters were so WASPy it hurt Italian-Irish teeth she hadn't known she possessed.

"Very naturally . . . ah . . . blond and blue-eyed?" she ventured.

"Shit, yes. They're ultra-WASPs, come by it naturally, my mother's family was from Sweden and my father's from England, that's not what I mean." Spider laughed at Gigi's delicacy. His sisters would have been chosen as pin-up girls in the Third Reich, God forbid. "I'm just using them as an example of real women, not beauties. Well-educated but not society. Middle class but not noticeably lower or upper. Urbane but not necessarily urban. Outdoorsy when necessary, but never horsy. Clean-cut but not chiseled. Grown up. Relaxed but animated, with some character in their faces. *Intelligence* in their eyes —that's essential. They could be black, white, Oriental or Hispanic, so long as they have the right look.''

"Where are we going to find these models?'' Gigi sounded skeptical as she observed the visionary light fill Spider's eyes.

"We'll use unknowns, probably the gals who can't make the grade at the model agencies because they're not knockouts or because they're not early-flowering, ten-foot-tall teenagers. Or maybe women who've never planned to model.''

"Spider, aren't you looking for the deliberately *average*?'' Gigi worried. "That doesn't sound like a hell of a lot of fun . . . . looking at clothes on real, average women.''

"I'm looking for gals who are way above average, but *not* so you'd notice it before you notice the clothes. A fine distinction Gigi, but one that I have down cold. Once, way back in history, models used to be my avocation, my hobby, my reason for getting up in the morning and definitely for going to bed at night. Trust me on picking models, Gigi.''

"You're the expert,'' Gigi conceded. "I'm more into excess, as in 'Why can't we use the most beautiful girls in the world to make our clothes look good?' ''

"Because it's a big turnoff. I don't know if women even realize it, but after they've seen too many beautiful girls in magazines they get to feeling a nasty little low-level depression, a fretfulness, a dissatis-faction, that they don't understand is *directly* connected to the models. They keep right on reading magazines, sure, because they're curious about fashion and beauty, but a steady diet of top models makes any woman feel subliminally unattractive in comparison. Women who feel unattractive aren't going to be in the mood to call up and order clothes over the phone at midnight. I want our customers feeling *euphoric*!''

"Midnight?''

"Well, sure. We have to have round-the-clock phone ordering . . . get them when they're in the mood. What if a woman wakes up at three A.M. with an anxiety attack? Could there be a better way to cure it than to catalog shop? She doesn't even have to get out of bed, only reach for her phone and her catalog. She can chat with her Scruples Two phone pal, order a little something, and go back to sleep feeling a whole lot better.'' Spider inspected Gigi's desk, piled high with discarded sheets of typing paper. "Working on something?''

"Just fiddling,'' Gigi said. "Trying to set the tone, work out a sort of introduction to the catalog in general terms, so people will know what we're about.''

"Read it to me?''

"It's still awfully rough, but . . . oh, all right,'' Gigi said, squirming with the fearful, hesitant timidity of authorship. She had to get some feedback or burst, and Spider was the only person left in the office.

I know some secrets you hide in your closet that you won't tell your best friend about . . . well, maybe you would, if she'd sympathize, instead of giving you that wise-ass, smarter-than-thou look, but how can you count on it? As for telling your sister, you know better! For example there's that beautiful, ruffled, real lace blouse you bought because you were feeling so romantic that you couldn't resist it, and when you got it home and tried it with all your skirts, it made you look weirdly like your mother. But it's too good to give away and too small to give her. And then there's that good wool suit, too expensive even when you bought it on sale, but it was exactly what your boss would approve of and you knew you could wear it forever. Except that you found out that it's too hot and too uncomfortable to wear all day long in the office and too conservative to wear at night, and the jacket just looks wrong with a pair of pants and a T-shirt.

I understand about that low-cut sweater you bought because you thought it would look marvelous with simple pants for one of those invitations to a don't-bother-to-get-dressed-up party. (Don't you hate it when the hostess says that? Why give a party unless people can dress?) Of course it makes you look as if you had a severely split personality. I have three of them and I haven't got it right yet.

I know about those elephant-retreating-into-the-jungle pants that you bought without checking in a three-way mirror and I know about that practical, sensible coat you wore for two years, hating every minute of it, because you're practical and sensible only to a point— and it went too far!

But enough of these tales of closet woe. Why torture yourself about that bright red, sparkly cocktail dress you bought for Christmas parties and regretted even before you had it shortened—and that was three years ago!

My point is that we all make mistakes. Everyone. *People who boast that they never make the same mistake twice make new ones all the time. The best-dressed man I know once told me that two out of three things he bought were mistakes and he only wore the one that wasn't. I don't know anyone who can* afford *to make mistakes like that. But you can afford to take all the things in your closet that make you feel a nasty little "yucch" in your heart, and give them away to the Salvation Army, because, face it, you're* never *going to wear them again anyway.*

And then, as a reward for cleaning house, you can take a look at the clothes in this catalog and think about owning some of them. Just call us and we'll get them in the mail to you right away and we pay the shipping. They're not too expensive, they're beautifully made, they work, *together and separately, and best of all, if you don't absolutely love them when you try them on, just send them right back to us without excuses and we guarantee your money back. No strings. I want you to enjoy opening your closet door. Clothes should make you feel happy, never,* ever *guilty.*

"Don't stop reading," Spider said.

"That's it . . . I was just looking for places to cut."

"Cut one word, change one single word, and you'll have to answer to me," Spider said threateningly.

"You . . . like it?"

"Gigi, it's fucking perfect! Damn! I wish Billy were here to read it. She's gonna be so thrilled. Let's call her in New York and you read it to her over the phone . . . no, it's after seven here, after ten in New York, she won't be in. Oh, baby, you are one talented copywriter! We *have* to celebrate. I know, I'm taking you right out to a wonderful dinner. You deserve the best, in fact even I deserve a treat for finally figuring out the model problem."

Gigi lay back in her desk chair, her arms and legs flopping loosely, looking up at him wide-eyed with a flood of relief. She'd been so worried about the tone of the introduction to the catalog that she'd made six false starts in the last few days, and what she'd just read Spider had been written in desperation in the last two hours.

"Oh, I don't want to go to a restaurant," she said. "Not now. I'm too wound up to sit still . . . let me cook, I haven't had anyone to cook for since Sasha deserted me for Josh, and my idea of a celebration is eating my own food, but not eating it alone."

"It's too much work for you," he protested halfheartedly.

"I have to calm down from my literary crisis, and cooking's the best way."

"Okay, but you've got to let me help."

"Done, you can open the wine."

"That was the best pasta primavera, the best veal with wild mushrooms, the best spinach salad, the best . . . what was the dessert?"

"We haven't reached it yet," Gigi said. "We've had seconds on everything, finished a bottle of wine—"

"Whatever dessert is, it's gonna go to waste, I want to eat more but I can't. Did you and Sasha eat like this all the time?"

"Even better," Gigi said, "when we didn't have dates. That wasn't often, or we'd have been twice our size."

"And she left you for a man? No gratitude, that girl, none."

"But an excellent, indisputable sense of timing."

"She's got that," Spider said, stretching luxuriously and sipping from the glass of brandy Gigi had poured for him. "I'll grant her that. Talk about striking while the iron is hot."

"She said it was *beshert*, that's Yiddish for fated, destined, written in the stars."

"I'm inclined to agree with her. Josh is another person, transformed, transfixed, transfigured, transported, all the "trans" words. I never knew a man could be so happy, and even his kids approve of her. Are they going to get married here or back East?"

"They're not sure yet. The great white wedding of the year will require transportation of one family or another from one coast to another, and there seem to be more Hillmans than Orloff-Nevskys, which I wouldn't have believed possible. Sasha's clan are professional nomads, they can be packed and ready to jump on a plane in five minutes. The Hillmans are stick-in-the-muds . . . so probably here."

"And of course you're going to be the maid of honor?"

"You bet your ass. Maid of honor and private-eye catering consultant so they get the best of everything and don't get persuaded to have anything they don't want."

"Don't you ever relax?" Spider asked curiously, as he observed Gigi. He felt languid, lazy and utterly pleased with life, after making himself comfortable on the inviting, slightly rump-sprung, faded flowered couch that had come with the furnished apartment, but Gigi was still clearing the table, a job she had insisted on doing herself. She moved economically, with the same effortless, quick precision with which she'd prepared their meal. At least Gigi had been persuaded to let him tend the fire as well as open the wine, jobs she'd conceded were men's work.

How long ago had she been Billy's newly hatched chick, he wondered dreamily. Five years, six years, more? And now Gigi was more adult, in some ways, than Billy herself, just as capable of the bravura gesture as Billy, if you took into account the differences in their ages and means, just as hardworking when possessed by an idea or a goal, yet somehow Billy had an impulsive quality that Gigi didn't seem to possess. Billy rushed into things recklessly and sometimes unwisely. Gigi, he'd bet, would proceed with all due dispatch and a lot fewer emotional bruises.

"The last time I relaxed I broke my leg," Gigi said ruefully, as she came and sat down next to him.

"I'll take you skiing some day," Spider offered. "You can't let one bad experience cheat you out of the greatest sport in the world."

"I don't think so," Gigi said seriously. "That's one invitation I can be counted on to refuse."

"Did it hurt that much?"

"It still hurts," she murmured, so softly that he barely caught the words.

"I'm sorry, Gigi, I'd never let you get hurt."

"Oh, you'd say that, of course, but you can't guarantee it, can you?" Gigi shook her head in wise negation.

"I guess not," he admitted. "Mountains . . . they're perilous by nature. You can break a leg standing on the lift line if some dumb snow bunny skis into you."

"You've just convinced me never to go skiing again . . . not that I needed another lesson." There was something in Gigi's voice that made Spider look at her closely. More had been broken than her leg, he realized, more than he'd ever been allowed to know. Gigi, for all her droll, spicy, heartbreaker's charm, for all the almost arrogant impudence of her merrily shaped mouth, was a private person, a deeply private person he didn't really understand at all. And he didn't like that, not one bit, he couldn't accept it, it went against all of his nature to allow a girl he'd known for years to have a mysterious life he knew nothing about. Suddenly he found that he wanted her desperately.

"Gigi," Spider said, and held her by her shoulders, "darling

Gigi . . . if you don't want me to kiss you, I don't know how I'll stand it.''

Gigi stared at him. He wasn't pulling her forward, just touching her lightly with his big, firm hands, leaving the decision up to her. As if she could resist one kiss, just one kiss, from a man who'd been her hero from the day she'd met him, as if she weren't yearning for the comfort of his arms after all her profoundly wounded disillusionment, after feeling totally bereft and loveless for months. Gigi swayed forward, only two inches, but he needed no other signal to pull her tightly against him and seek her lips.

At the first touch of his mouth, Gigi was stunned by the depth of her need. Spider kissed her over and over, tentatively at first, and then, as she responded, more and more passionately, until she felt herself reeling with delight. She lay in his arms as he bent over her, his mouth the center of her world, his searching, seeking, impetuous mouth, his sighs of pleasure, his eagerness, his arms trembling as he clasped them so tightly around her that she felt he would never let her go. To kiss, to kiss like this forever, he tasted so good, he smelled so good, she wanted nothing more from life, Gigi told herself with half of her mind, as she was tossed in a sea of soul-restoring kisses, her arms wrapped as tightly around Spider's neck as if he were rescuing her from a shipwreck. I'm being swept away, she assured herself, swept away . . . and she attempted to abandon herself to him, in spite of a dim swarm of disturbing thoughts that refused to be chased out of her mind.

Suddenly, Gigi felt the touch of Spider's hand at her breast. She held her breath, shocked out of her trance. She moved for the first time since he'd begun to kiss her, trying to sit up.

"No, no, baby, don't be frightened," Spider said softly, "don't be frightened. I said I'd never hurt you."

"Spider—*let me go!*"

"But . . . but . . . . Gigi, darling, *why?*"

"It's wrong . . ."

Gigi's inflection was so urgent that he moved reluctantly away from her, until they were both sitting almost upright side by side on the couch, his arms keeping her turned toward him.

"Gigi, how could it be wrong? Don't you want me?"

"Of course I do . . . who wouldn't?" she asked simply. "But it *is* wrong, don't ask me how I know, don't ask me to make sense, don't ask me for a single good reason, just believe me."

"Wow," Spider said shakily, "you want a lot."

"I know."

"I don't have a choice, do I?" His voice was rueful.

"Thank you, Spider."

"Oh boy . . . . 'thank you, Spider' . . . you'd better promise me that we'll always stay very good friends, darling, after I let you get away so easily." He couldn't help but smile at her anxious, imploring, half-guilty, but totally defiant expression.

"It wasn't all that easy for me."

"Now it's my turn to say 'I know.' I guess that's some satisfaction. Better than nothing, right? Good night, my baby. Don't forget to punch the time clock when you get to the office in the morning. And thank you for dinner. An exceptional dinner. Dinner with Gigi—as lovely—and as perilous—as any damn Alp I've ever skied in my life."

20

*H*e has a twinkle in his eye," Sasha remarked quietly to Billy, as Joe Jones, the newly hired marketing chief of Scruples Two, walked into Billy's office, in which everyone working on the catalog was gathered, including Sasha's four new assistants, sitting expectantly in a cluster of well-turned-out, ambitious young femininity.

You would too, Billy thought, if you had the deal Joe has. In order to lure one of the top marketing wizards of L.L. Bean to work for her, she'd had to quadruple his salary, to match each of the four seasons. For a man who worked as hard as he did, Joe Jones was deeply attached to leisure-time activities. She'd listened as patiently as she could as he described the joys of watching the leaves change in autumn, the pleasures of walking in fresh snow in winter, the fascination of the slow awakening of the woods in the spring, and the delights of summer sailing from Camden Harbor, all of which he'd have to abandon to come to California. When she'd agreed to his salary she'd also had to agree to move him and his wife to Los Angeles, pay the rent on a house for them for a year and sign an ironclad five-year employment contract that would continue to be paid no matter what happened to the business. John Prince had been a pushover compared to the gnomelike gent from Down East, but the harder Joe had made it for her, the more Billy had respected him, for he was leaving arguably the best job at the best-run company in the catalog business, and she admired him for driving the toughest deal possible. He was the kind of man she needed.

With Joe she'd managed to hire his almost equally expensive brother, Hank, one of several men who ran something called "operations" for the giant Spiegel people. Just thinking about operations made Billy squirm. She didn't want to know about them; they were the vital plumbing of the catalog business, where words like "returns" were tossed about with a freedom that would make any sensitive person shudder. Just let Scruples Two get off the ground, she prayed, and she'd make herself find out exactly what operations involved . . . but not till then. That's what Hank got paid for.

"You've all met Joe before," Billy said when everyone had settled down. "I'm going to let him speak for himself."

"Thanks, Billy," he said, his pink cheeks, round face, spectacles and white hair making him look as innocently reassuring as if he ran an old-fashioned general store. "Folks, you all probably know that about ninety-nine percent of new catalog businesses go under in eight months," Joe began. "That's the bad news. The good news is that if you're a success, you can expect to break even in two, three years, maybe a little less. So we're talking about a capital-intensive business, and I'm satisfied that there's enough capital here to keep going till the break-even point. My job is basically to get you the customers to reach that point and push beyond it. Far beyond it." He twinkled steadily as he looked around the crowded room.

"Circulation," Joe announced. "That's the name of the game. Unless your catalog reaches the right people, it doesn't matter how good your merchandise is. I know what kind of people you've got to reach, I know where the lists of those people are. I know how to buy those lists, I know how to use those lists and what to look for in them, and I know how often you need to hit people with new catalogs so that you finally connect with them and stay connected. Repetition, repetition, repetition! We hit them with five or six mailings for the fall-

winter catalog, and the same for spring-summer. Plus the Christmas book, of course. Every catalog has a different cover, every one contains a percentage of new merchandise, we constantly drop what doesn't work, but primarily we repeat the big sellers in different combinations photographed differently. *Repetition*, folks, you can't live without it."

Sasha nodded in agreement. Joe Jones was on her wavelength.

"Now your cost of doing business is in two places. First, inventory. That's what mail order is all about. You can't send out a catalog without physically owning the inventory and having it in the warehouse. Inventory's all *guesswork*. You can be wrong in two ways," he said benevolently, looking at their worried faces. "You guess wrong and you're stuck with overstock. Overstock is what ruins most everybody. You guess wrong the other way, you understock and you can't fill your orders. If you do that twice, you've lost a customer," he said with the cheer of a magician who pulls out a string of rabbits from a toadstool. "Either way, you can't expect to guess right most of the time without a couple of years of experience under your belt, and even then it's *still* a crapshoot."

Should I thank him for not telling me this sooner? Billy asked herself, not daring to look at anyone's face.

"Excuse me, Joe," Gigi said, "but why do you look so happy?"

"I love a crap game, kid, poker too. What's the fun otherwise?"

"Poker Saturday night, my house?" Gigi offered.

"You're on, kid. I'll only warn you once—my wife's considered a pretty good player. It's those long Down East winters brings out hidden talent. Now the other cost of doing business is in putting out the catalog. Paper costs, mailing costs, printing costs, photography costs—they can all kill you. Spider here is going to worry with me about that. Right, Spider?"

"Right, Joe," Spider said. Billy decided to peek at him and see how he was surviving Joe Jones with gloves off. She looked at Spider sitting next to Gigi and saw them exchanging a complicated, amused, somehow intimate glance. Maybe they both liked crap games, she thought, because they seemed to be enjoying themselves far more than she was. Come to think of it, in the weeks since she'd been back from her trip to New York, Maine, and then back to New York again to keep an eye on Prince and make sure he was producing sketches and finding fabrics as quickly as possible, she'd noticed that a new friendliness had sprung up between Spider and Gigi.

Working together in the same office, it was only natural, Billy speculated, particularly since, in the absence of actual finished samples, Spider and Tommy Tether, the superb young art director he'd hired away from Ralph Lauren, were experimenting with different ways of laying out Scruples Two, working from the best ads and editorial pages in actual fashion magazines, since Spider had decreed that the catalog was to give all the visual pleasure of a magazine, and depart completely from current catalog design. Gigi was working with them, trying to fit her kind of personal, chatty copy into the space they made available. Proximity always made for palship, Billy thought sagely as she listened to Joe talk about something called "sell ratio" that he'd already explained to her a number of times without totally getting through.

Proximity. No, it was impossible, absolutely impossible, Billy told herself. Spider was a hundred years too old for Gigi. Gigi was just a child . . . well, almost a child . . . . no older than . . . she had been herself when . . . she'd met Ellis Ikehorn. Who had been sixty. Spider was only thirty-eight. And she, Billy Ikehorn, must be insane.

"You'll know in two months after your first mailing," Joe Jones was telling them as he finished speaking. "Average industry response is two percent. If you don't do that, forget it. If you do better, the sky's the limit. When my brother Hank gets back from Virginia, he'll brief you all on the new warehouse, the phone operations, and the packing and shipping setup. And returns. He can do that better than I can. Anybody got any questions?"

"I don't get Virginia," Sasha complained. "I can't understand why we're going to create the catalog here, design the capsule collections in New York, manufacture the stuff in factories all over the place, and then keep it all in Virginia."

"When you're building a half-million-square-foot warehouse you don't want to buy land in California, Sasha. When you're counting on your phone operators to be patient, helpful and thoroughly informed, in other words, act as the best salespeople possible, you want to hire nice folks with kind voices, and so you look for a place in the South, where there's a solid, more or less unbreakable tradition of patience and good manners. And lower salaries. Now you wouldn't want to do that in New York City, would you?"

"Not really," Sasha said, laughing. She'd been working as Billy's assistant, staying blessedly put in L.A. while Billy whisked around in her jet, lighting fires under Prince and luring key men away from other

companies, a Lorelei with an open checkbook. Sasha's job was working on the antique lingerie collection with Gigi and Gigi's old friend
Mazie Goldsmith, as well as on the Discontinued Woman petite collection and on the designs for dumpling-shaped women for which no one
yet had found exactly the right name. Her four busy assistants were
all experienced, sharp young women, and a good thing too that they
worked as hard as they did, since her wedding plans were taking several hours a day of her time, and she couldn't attend to them at night
because at night there was Josh. And she'd better start paying attention, because after all, it if weren't for her, this whole thing would
never have happened. Or had it started with Gigi? No matter . . . her
mind always meandered and gallivanted into the future when she
thought about Josh, and he'd had to get Strassberger and Lipkin to
handle a lot of his own work for the same reason.

"I guess that's it," Billy said as Joe stopped speaking. "Thank
you, Joe, it's been an education."

"The thing to remember, folks, is that it's not nearly as complicated as I've made it sound," Joe said, eyes positively dancing with
anticipation. "It's one hell of a lot worse."

"Billy, you've been out of town so much that I feel as if you never
really came back from Paris," Dolly Moon complained, as the two of
them sat out by her swimming pool in the late-April sun, near a bed of
blooming tulips.

"Oh, Dolly, I know. W.W.'s growing so fast—poor thing, I'm a
lousy godmother. She's almost five and I haven't done anything about
her religious education yet. Isn't that the main thing a godmother's
supposed to be responsible for?"

"She'll manage, she's got a God-fearing grandmother, it's me
who's stuck without you," Dolly fretted. "Just look at me, for God's
sake! I'm the one who should be God-fearing—maybe then I'd be able
to diet. Give me some of that good, old-time religion! Fire, Billy,
hellfire and brimstone, please, Billy, I'm counting on you," Dolly
implored pitiably. "I've got to lose twenty-five pounds in the next six
weeks. We start shooting in June. Dustin and I are doing the sequel to
the movie we made together, and as of right now I think I outweigh
him two to one. He won't be able to reach my lips when he kisses me,
and if I sat on his lap, he'd be squashed flat. I love him, but why does
he have to be so puny?"

"Dolly, you know I can't help you anymore," Billy said sternly. "You've got to go to some sort of group, Weight Watchers or Overeaters Anonymous or something like that. I've told you a thousand times that you need to have other dieters to call and talk to when you get those urges. It's no good calling me, I'm compulsive about staying thin, so it's easy for me."

"But you've got to have some little . . . tips? Tricks? Or don't you even want to eat anymore?"

"Sure, I want to. I'm human. Take chocolate. You know I adore it."

"Yeah, but you don't touch it. You wouldn't eat a bite of the chocolate cake at lunch."

"Well . . ." Billy said hesitantly.

"Well?"

"Actually, chocolate's easy. Fortunately, chocolate looks like turds . . . real turds. It's the same color, after all. So whenever I see chocolate, I tell myself that it's turd sculpture. A wedge of turds, a circle of turds, a square of turds, a sauce of melted turds—"

"I get it! I love it! I'll never eat another ounce of chocolate anything—but, Billy, what about white food? Mashed potatoes, vanilla ice cream, white bread with butter on it—?"

"*Butter* on it? I simply don't believe you said that! Dolly, forget turds, you're in deep shit. A group's the only answer. Twenty-five pounds in six weeks? That's almost a pound a day." Billy shook her head in dismay. "You'd better go to a good nutritionist immediately and find out what's the fastest safe way. And stop eating off your children's plates. You know that's where half the trouble is. Tell yourself that every time you do it, you're depriving them, taking the food out of their little mouths."

"But I know it isn't true, the cook always makes too much. And they never even finish, they have picky appetites," Dolly said miserably.

"Oh, Dolly, it's not as if you didn't look absolutely wonderful," Billy said truthfully. "The real trouble is that being plump is so becoming to you, and you have so little vanity that you're not motivated to keep your weight down between pictures."

"I know," Dolly wailed. "I turn down a hundred scripts for every one I accept. But I want time to be with the kids and Lester."

"What's the point of being one of the biggest stars in the world if you have to miss out on them? If you weren't a working actress you could forget about the whole thing. Sasha Nevsky—you met her, remember?—has three aunts who are twice as overweight as you, and they've been that way almost all their lives, happy, healthy and well-loved. We're designing a whole bunch of really wonderful clothes for them in Scruples Two, the 'Dumpling Collection' we call it, until we find the right name."

"What do they look like? The clothes, not the aunts," Dolly asked morosely.

"They're based on elastic waistbands. Unlike you, most plump women don't have waists, so they end up buying things that just start at the top and keep getting wider and wider. With the elastic waistbands we can build fairly wide shoulders into the clothes, and an illusion of a waistline, and work with an interesting drape."

"Call them 'Dolly Moons,' " Dolly sighed. "They sound like a good idea."

"But why on earth would you want clothes designed specifically for plump women to have your name on them?" Billy asked incredulously.

"So I could stay out of them! Billy, that's it! I don't want to have to wear your Dolly Moons, I want to wear divine Nolan Millers. That's my motivation! Oh, Billy, I knew you'd help me. You've got to call them 'Dolly Moons' or it won't work for me. Oh, Billy, thank you! You've saved my life!"

"Your reason, maybe, but hardly your life," Billy said, laughing at her friend. "If you really mean it, it's a sensational boost for us. But better ask Lester first, see if it's all right with him. And talk to your agent and your lawyer, they may not like the idea, and I don't want to take advantage of you."

"Billy, hon, no one, and I mean no one, takes advantage of me," Dolly said in a tone of voice that made Billy sit up in astonishment. "You don't think I let my agent make my business decisions for me, do you?"

"I guess I did," Billy said slowly, suddenly aware that her old friend's native shrewdness was almost always camouflaged by the shock of the sheer extravagance of her Renoir-esque presence. Even she had allowed herself to drift into making the mistake of underestimating Dolly.

"Once I got my career on track, I promised myself that no man was ever going to tell me how to run my life again, not even Lester," Dolly said, her astonished blue eyes wider than ever in their seriousness. "A woman in this business has to think for herself or else she'll become the captive of a business manager, an agent, the hidden agenda of the agency he works for—those guys could teach the CIA and the Mafia a lesson or two—and at least three different lawyers plus her husband, if she has one. A bunch of guys who think they have the answers. Ha! As they say in Brooklyn, *fuhgedaboudit*! I trust my own decision-making powers, Billy, the way you do. It was the Oscar that allowed me to take this position, and after I'd seized it, I never let it go. I owe a lot to Vito, when you stop to think about it."

"I never have. But you're right, until you were cast in that part in *Mirrors*, nobody appreciated you properly, they couldn't see the actress beneath the tits and ass."

"Don't say those words! I'd forgotten about them for a minute. All right, all right, tomorrow I'll put myself into the hands of a nutritionist. A female nutritionist. Okay? You satisfied now?"

"Do it today," Billy said grimly. "Butter!"

"Today. I promise. Oof! I feel thinner already. Now tell me about Gigi. I haven't seen her in ages. How's she doing?"

"Brilliantly. She's writing the most original catalog copy you've ever read, and she and Mazie are hunting down antique lingerie all over L.A. and San Francisco. Then she does her own illustrations for those pages. They're enchanting, funny . . . well, you saw the one she sent you for Christmas, so you know. If I didn't bump into her at the office now and then, I'd hardly ever see her myself."

"Don't you miss her?"

"Of course I do, but what can I do about it? She's too grown-up to live with me. I suppose it would be like . . . living at home with your mother."

"That's ridiculous! If I were her age I'd jump at the chance."

"It's easy for you to say, because we're friends, peers. But Gigi and I are . . . sort of related, well, not really related, not really mother and daughter at all, but . . . something," Billy said, struggling, as she had for a long time, to figure out what she and Gigi were to each other now that she wasn't her legal guardian, now that Gigi wasn't an unadopted, teenaged almost-daughter she'd taken under her wing. She'd referred to her as her stepdaughter, but that had never really been true.

"Well, I hope she's making good use of her privacy," Dolly said, wiggling her eyebrows like Harpo Marx.

"That's the thing, her privacy means I don't have a clue. I had this crazy idea . . ."

"Hmm?"

"No, it's something that couldn't be. Put it out of your mind, as they say in Boston."

"Billy," Dolly said warningly, "you shouldn't have brought it up if you weren't going to tell. You know I won't let you get away with doing that to me."

"Oh, it's too stupid. But there's this kind of . . . thing . . . between her and Spider."

" 'Thing'? What kind of thing?"

"An *attitude,* nothing more. At least nothing I know about. It's as if they . . . shared . . . something nobody knows about. I must be certifiable, unbalanced, ready to be removed by little men in white to even dignify it by bringing it up. What's more, it's none of my fucking business."

"You take the high road, I'll take the low road," Dolly said, almost bouncing as she leaned forward in eager interest. "Gigi and Spider? Well, it wouldn't be impossible, would it? He's a man, she's a woman, that gives them something to work on right there."

"Dolly, you're disgusting."

"I'm realistic, and realistic is often disgusting. He's free, she's free, she's his type, he's every woman's type—"

"What do you mean, 'she's his type'?"

Dolly looked at Billy as if she were simple-minded.

"Red hair, green eyes, small bones, slightly pixified, full of adorable impertinence—like Valentine."

"But Gigi *dyes* her hair!" Billy cried in outrage.

"Right, like I'm not a natural blonde, so how can I be thought of as one of the all-time ultimate blondes from here to Tibet?"

" 'Like Valentine,' " Billy said slowly. "It never occurred to me. Valentine was unique—so French . . ."

"Half-Irish, like Gigi, if you're going to count country of origin. Gigi's mother was Irish and so was Valentine's father. Irish genes are potent stuff."

"Dolly? Do you really see a resemblance?"

"Enough of one for his subconscious to latch onto it," Dolly replied.

"That bloody, *bloody* subconscious stuff again, I've never been any good at it,'' Billy said ferociously. "It's done nothing but get me into trouble all my life. Nobody really knows what goes on in there, how it works, it could be just a lot of imagination! The whole thing should be abolished!''

"Even you, Billy hon, can't do anything about it.''

"Well, as I said, it's none of my business.''

"Of course not,'' Dolly agreed. "Just because Gigi's something sort of like, but not exactly like, your own kid, and Spider, well, he's your business partner, for one thing, and he's the best male friend you've ever had, and you've been working closely together for longer than I've known either of you—''

"Dolly, you've made your point. Get off it!''

"Okay.'' She'd get off it, Dolly thought, but she hadn't made her point. She hadn't come close. Billy was even worse than she'd realized at the subconscious stuff.

Was her father listening to her at all, Gigi wondered, or was he just responding to her words automatically, according to his notion of how a man should behave with a daughter? Vito's responses, all through dinner, had been intelligent and comprehending as she told him details of her own work and described the rapid progress that was being made on the catalog, but there hadn't been one instant in which she'd been able to see an unmistakable flicker of real concentration or interest behind his eyes. He was listening, she decided, but with half a brain, certainly not well enough to conceal from her that he was deeply worried. And with him, what else was there to worry about but the film business?

The two of them had met for one other dinner like this in the last few months, now that they were both back in California, and Vito had not been entirely there for that one either. He talked a good game, Gigi thought, as she considered him closely over her coffee cup, and he looked a good game, he'd retained his physical authority, with that flashing commander-in-chief aura she remembered so well from every rare childhood encounter. Right now, if he had happened to be talking business, no one would be able to discern that he was uneasy and preoccupied, Gigi decided, but as she rattled on, keeping him up to date on Sasha's wedding plans, his attention wandered and he let his guard down far enough for her to see that all was far from well with him.

She felt curiously protective of her father, Gigi realized, watching his preoccupation. He didn't deserve it, that was for damn sure, and there was no reason for her to have much feeling for a man who had taken almost no interest in her life, but nevertheless *protective* was the only word she could find to describe her emotions. She wished she could do something to help him with whatever was bothering him, but when she questioned him, he assured her that getting *Fair Play* into a studio schedule was no more than the usual hassle it always had been on every film he'd ever produced.

As she observed Vito so essentially detached and remote, in spite of his approximation of a paternal figure, Gigi was seized by an irresistible impulse to talk about Zach Nevsky to the one person she was sure wouldn't take an interest in him. Sasha and she avoided the subject by tacit agreement, and Billy knew nothing about him. But talking to Vito right now would be like talking to an echo chamber.

"In New York I met some theater people," she said, as a pause developed in the wedding conversation.

"Anybody I know?"

"Nick De Salvo?"

"He's not a theater person, he's a movie actor. From what I've seen of him on film, that guy's going all the way," Vito said.

"Nick happened to be in New York because he was playing Hamlet Off Broadway for Sasha's brother, Zach Nevsky." As she said Zach's name, Gigi felt a trembling awareness of stepping into a forbidden zone, a perilous place where she could only come to grief, yet there was a terrible sweetness of surrender in just uttering his name that she couldn't deny herself in spite of what Zach had done to her.

"I read the reviews. Amazing coverage for a practically nonprofit venture like Off Broadway. I guess having Nick De Salvo in it accounted for its being such a giant success," Vito responded judiciously. "How did you get mixed up with those wide-eyed idealists? Through Sasha?"

"Exactly. Do you really think that they're just naïve idealists? Isn't there a future for a director like Zach? Every review gave him the credit, they all called him extraordinary, they all mentioned his vision and daring." Gigi tried to speak dispassionately, despite the thumping of her heart. "The consensus was that Zach's far and away the most exciting and innovative of the young new theater directors— at least that's what they said—I'm no judge."

"Look, Gigi, this Zach Nevsky can be all of those things and more, but what good will it do him? Off Broadway? Come on, use your head. It's hopeless financially, and getting more hopeless every year. Unless he's making movies, he's never going to find a big enough audience to make an impact."

"But couldn't Zach be another Joseph Papp? I know that's what Sasha is hoping for, that one day Zach Nevsky will mean as much to theater as Papp does."

"There's only room for one Papp," Vito pronounced. "How well did you get to know De Salvo?"

"Not well, but he was awfully sweet. I met him that weekend I broke my leg. He's Zach's oldest friend."

"If he's a friend, he should tell Zach Nevsky to leave Off Broadway and come on out here and learn the difference between a grip and a gaffer," Vito said indifferently, not hearing Gigi's sudden, oddly irrelevant little sigh.

He'd been kept dangling by Arvey since before Christmas, Vito thought as he talked to Gigi, and now it was April, four months later. They were no closer to an agreement than they'd been at any time, and yet their negotiations had not yet broken down. If another studio in town had been interested, he'd have taken the project away from Arvey immediately, but everyone had passed on *Fair Play*.

Vito had met with the heads of all the studios and each one of them had assured him that they personally had taken the time to read the coverage of *Fair Play* that had come in from their readers. The notion that they might have actually read the original material themselves was something so out of the question that it never entered their minds or Vito's expectations. Their readers' opinions were based on a three- or four-sentence "log line" summary of the plot, several pages of detailed analysis of the story, a character breakdown, and a final recommendation.

The recommendations had all been variations on the same theme: the book was a gem, a rare treat, a joy to read, its best-seller status was entirely understandable. But as a film? *Commercially?* No. It had too many negatives. It was not recommended. There was nothing in it, absolutely nothing, that would appeal to the young audience that kept them in business. As far as the adult audience was concerned, from whom unexpected support could come when a movie was made that appealed to them, no again. A qualified but definite no. Too risky. Far from a sure thing. The two main characters were just a shade too British, too completely embedded in the British class structure, not people who belonged in a contemporary Noel Coward romp on one hand, nor as powerfully wrong for each other as those in *Sunday, Bloody Sunday,* on the other. No, regretfully, no.

Only Curt Arvey hadn't turned him down. Only Curt Arvey could see the potential in the project, but he wanted Vito to make the film at the unrealizably low price of seven million dollars. "You brought in *Mirrors* at two million two, Vito, seven million is more than three times that," Arvey said stubbornly, not willing to give in an inch on the fact that every single cost of making a film had gone up enormously in the last four years. He discounted entirely the indisputable record that Vito had worked a one-time-only miracle in obtaining the cut-rate services of a great scriptwriter, a superb director and a legendary cameraman for *Mirrors* by collecting on long-due favors and giving away chunks of his share of the profits. Most important of all, Vito had not used a single star in his Oscar-winning picture. To make *Fair Play* work, two stars were vital. There was no reasonable or even rational chance that Vito could pull it off with unknown actors; eleven million dollars was the minimum the picture had to cost. With no room for error. And at that it would still be a low-budget picture for 1982.

He had not used his last card, Vito thought, he had not asked Susan to help him. They were locked in the grip of a passion so complicated, so grave, so far beyond anything that either of them had expected in the beginning, that it transcended Vito's grasp. Susan and he were equally matched; every time they met she fought him to a draw and left him more in her thrall than ever. Yet she never refused any of his demands, never said *enough*. They wanted each other endlessly. The more they had each other, the more they craved. But their connection had turned into something that was no longer only sexual. It now involved Vito in his deepest sense of himself, in his very identity. He was sure of only one thing; if he asked Susan for help, whether she gave it to him or not, their merciless, miraculous, absolutely necessary adventure would end and he would forever think of himself as a defeated man. His back was to the wall, he was living on credit and a loan from Fifi Hill.

"Gigi," he said, taking a difficult breath, "there's something you could do for me . . . you asked me about *Fair Play* earlier. I haven't wanted to tell you what the problem is, but in fact Curt Arvey is being completely unreasonable about the budget. We're only four million dollars apart, but it might as well be forty. Susan Arvey owns stock in Arvey's studio. That means that she's more than just his wife, she has real power. As it happens, Billy is probably the only woman in this town who has influence with Susan. I know how close you and Billy are. If . . . if Billy could put in a good word with Susan, if she could say how much she thinks of the project, it might move things along.''

"I could certainly try,'' Gigi said slowly. "The worst that could happen is that she'd say no.''

"I know I have no right to ask you . . .''

"Don't say that,'' Gigi protested. "It's not a big deal. I'm glad you asked. I know Billy's read the book and I know she loved it. I'm having lunch with her on Sunday, the day after tomorrow, and I'll speak to her then. I just don't know . . . well, I have no idea if . . . I mean, what Billy would be willing to do for you.''

"Thank you, Gigi,'' Vito said, smiling. "I appreciate it.''

It's not a question of what she's willing to do for me, he thought, it's what she's willing to do for you.

"Do you remember the first time we ate here, four years ago?'' Billy asked Gigi as they sat at the table on the terrace. "I'll never forget how amazed you were that people lived like this.''

"I managed to get used to it,'' Gigi said reflectively, vividly remembering her first impressions of that day, yet unable to fit herself into an ever dimmer, almost unrecognizable mental picture she had of the girl to whom it had all happened. "Still, every time I'm back, I'm stunned all over again. The gardens . . . they're so wonderful with all the roses starting to bloom.''

"I know—it's frustrating just seeing them in the morning as I go to the office. I've started to get up an hour earlier so I have time to wander around and notice what's happening—by the time I get home it's too dark. I'm missing this whole springtime, but it's my own fault, I listened to Spider Elliott. I should know by now that he can talk me into anything.''

"Billy? You're not sorry about doing the catalog? You're not having second thoughts, are you?'' Gigi asked. "We're far past the point of no return now.''

"No, not second thoughts. I just didn't realize how all-consuming it would be, how exciting, how . . . almost frightening. A store, even a number of stores, was bite-sized, essentially known territory, something I was sure I could handle, but this is different.'' Billy shook her head ruefully. She looked too thin, Gigi thought, tense, even nervous, although Billy had made an effort to look relaxed, wearing white linen trousers and an oversized white turtleneck from which her dark, casually curly head rose on her long neck in the offhandedly queenly manner she always presented to the world.

"The catalog means going public such a different way than a store," Billy continued. "It reflects its creators, puts their taste on the line. Last night I woke up at three. I'd had a nightmare that the whole thing flopped and I was a laughingstock. *Laughingstock.* I've been haunted all my life by that possibility. Naturally I couldn't get back to sleep, so I read till morning."

"I wake up in a cold sweat," Gigi said, "wondering if anybody is going to buy antique lingerie from my copy and sketches—how do I even know if sketches will work when the rest of the catalog is photos?"

"Do you stay up all night the way I do?"

"I tell myself that if it doesn't work, I can always go back to cooking," Gigi admitted. "I try to remember very complicated French recipes, and by the time I get to the fifth or sixth ingredient, I'm dead to the world."

"I wonder if Spider suffers from middle-of-the-night catalog anxiety attacks?" Billy asked.

"I don't know, he's never mentioned it."

"Then I guess that means he doesn't. That's typical. 'Who, me, worry?' " Billy said astringently.

"Maybe he's just as worked up as we are, but won't admit it. After all, I'm not the final authority on Spider."

"As a matter of fact, Gigi, I rather think you are," Billy said, her tone evenly pitched on the clear borderline between a joke and an unimportant speculation.

"What makes you say that?" Gigi asked, struck by Billy's strange words. She suddenly shifted in her chair so that she faced Billy directly, her hair swinging away from her face with the abruptness of her motion, her pointed, startled eyebrows lifted so far that they were hidden in her bangs. Every feature in the perfect oval of her face, from her straight little nose to her full upper lip, seemed to echo the question in her green eyes.

"Oh, Gigi . . ." Billy shrugged her shoulders indifferently, carefully moving the saltcellar and pepper mill around on the yellow linen tablecloth, as if overcome with a search for perfect symmetry.

" 'Oh, Gigi,' *what*?" Gigi queried sharply, pursuing the remark.

"Billy, what on earth makes you think I'm the final authority on Spider?"

"Well, you work so closely with him, copy and layout are totally tied together," Billy said, backpedaling quickly. "If he were having doubts, he'd tell you about them."

"Why me? You and he are the investors in Scruples Two, I'm just a hired hand, except for my royalties on the antique lingerie. I have nothing to lose and everything to gain. But you two have worked together for years, you'd certainly be the one he'd talk to."

Billy hesitated, so slightly that it was barely visible. "Well, I see what you mean . . . but," she insisted, "that's not necessarily the case."

"I don't understand," Gigi said bluntly, struck by Billy's persistence.

"It's not important."

"It is to me," Gigi insisted.

"Gigi . . . really, I'm sorry I said anything."

"Well, you did. And I can't let it lie there," Gigi said defiantly.

"It's nothing . . ." Billy said airily, speaking with a dismissive, smiling voice, but unable to further evade the subject that had haunted her for weeks, the subject she hadn't been able to keep from mentioning. "Really nothing . . . I've simply noticed that you and Spider have a kind of . . . friendliness or understanding or relationship or whatever —that isn't exactly . . . invisible. There's some kind of intimacy, a bond between you and Spider . . . . something . . . new . . . and, well, who knows? . . . it could be something, oh, you know . . . something meaningful." Billy stopped abruptly, aware that the forced lightness had been flattened out of her voice. She flashed a quick, unconvincing smile at the pepper mill, unable to look at Gigi's face.

Gigi moved awkwardly in her chair and took an abrupt bite of a cookie. An uncomfortable silence grew between them, and yet neither of them moved to break it.

"I didn't realize that it showed," Gigi said finally. "There is something new, yes, but unless you call simple friendship meaningful, it's not meaningful."

"I do call simple friendship meaningful. There's too little of it in the world not to be. But between a man and a woman—oh, forget a man and a woman, Gigi, between you and Spider, I don't think for a second that friendship could possibly be 'simple.' "

"Why not?" Gigi asked mildly, springing up from her chair and walking toward the stone balustrade that separated the terrace from a bed of yellow roses. She gazed out at the far acres of trees, without seeming to see them, waiting for Billy's answer. When it didn't come, she walked back to the table as if she were returning from a far greater distance than a few feet. Hot red spots had ignited on each of her cheeks. Billy's eyes were looking at her in an inexorable question that refused to accept her forced, uncharacteristic blandness.

"We had dinner one night, when you were in New York, right after I'd finished the introduction copy," Gigi said rapidly, as she stood in front of Billy, trying to sound matter-of-fact. "Dinner to celebrate. Afterwards, we were talking and . . . then, Spider kissed me . . . for a few minutes, and then we stopped. That's all that happened, a few kisses, but it dissolved some barrier between us—probably that of a giant generation gap—and we decided that we were going to be real friends from now on. Whatever you've noticed, simple friendship is what it boils down to."

"Do you and Spider still have dinner together?" Billy asked, her face rigidly nonjudgmental. She was horrified as she heard how prying her words sounded, but Gigi answered easily.

"Sure, from time to time, when we work particularly late, usually with Tommy, but sometimes alone. He hasn't tried to kiss me again and he never will."

"How can you possibly sound so sure? *Never* is a big word. Never is a long time."

"Because I told him it was completely wrong!"

"Well," Billy said briskly, getting up from the table. "That's that, then. Shall we take a stroll around the orchid house? My Jill St. Johns are just starting to bloom."

"Billy, come back here and talk to me," Gigi pleaded. "I want you to know why it was wrong."

"It's none of my business, Gigi, you don't have to explain anything to me," Billy said stiffly, with the nearest approach to coldness that Gigi had ever heard in her voice, but she turned toward Gigi and sank back into her chair. Gigi too sat down and took Billy's hand, holding it tightly.

"Oh, Billy, I need someone to talk to so badly. I haven't got a soul in the world anymore I can discuss things with but you, and I miss it! When I first came here, a little bedraggled mess, and you took me in and changed my life, there was nothing I couldn't say to you, nothing I couldn't bring to your doorstep, but after the fire at Scruples,

when you went off to Europe—since then we just haven't been together, just the two of us, in one place long enough to have any time
alone. This is the first time in I don't know how long—'' Gigi bent her
head to hide her emotion, the tears that were visibly rising in her eyes,
and Billy found herself smoothing the bright strands of hair and making
little comforting noises, as if Gigi were sixteen again, and wrapped in
towels.

"You can talk to me about anything, darling, you know that,"
Billy murmured. "I thought that Sasha had taken my place . . . it's
only normal, you're the same generation."

"No one could ever, *ever* take your place, Billy, don't you understand that? And I couldn't possibly tell Sasha about Spider. She'd
think it was funny or she wouldn't really hear me, she's living in
another dimension, Josh is the only thing that matters to her now."

"I'm listening. You matter to me."

"When Spider kissed me, after the first shock, because I didn't
know he was going to do it, he really took me by surprise, there was a
moment when it seemed okay and then . . . Billy, the only way I can
think of to describe it is that the room we were in was *full of people*.
We weren't alone. Spider wasn't really all there, it wasn't *me* he really
wanted, I realized that almost immediately. I can't guess what he was
thinking, but I knew it was just a combination of circumstances that
caused him to kiss me—a good dinner, wine, a fire, all the stuff that
leads up to a kiss, but he hadn't planned it. For example, if you'd been
in L.A. instead of in New York, it would never have happened, it
would have been the three of us having dinner . . . in fact, the first
thing he thought of after I read him the copy was to call you so you
could hear it, but it was too late in New York. I'm trying to say that
there's nothing *inevitable* between us, there never has been, and for
me, kissing should be inevitable, not just because you're at a certain
place at a certain time and it seems like an amusing or interesting
option."

"How did you ever get so serious?" Billy said in wonder. "In this
day and age, Gigi, a little kissing isn't supposed to be something as
momentous as 'inevitable,' for heaven's sake."

"A little kissing with Spider . . . it isn't just like a little kissing,"
Gigi muttered, "it's like a lot of kissing."

"I'll bet it is," Billy said dryly. "But you talked about a room full
of people. I don't understand that at all, unless you mean Valentine."

"No . . . no," Gigi said, considering deeply. "I didn't think he could possibly get me mixed up with Valentine. I was so lonely that night, I was feeling so bummed out, I just needed some human contact, I guess. But in that roomful of people, Valentine wasn't there at all. I think Spider's mourned her, and he'll always adore her memory, but he's in another part of his life now. I guess what I meant was that . . . . the other people were mostly all the dozens of girls, the models he'd just been telling me about, the gorgeous girls he used to have flings with, before Valentine, and then, mainly . . . the most important thing for me was someone else . . . someone I met in New York. It didn't work out, to put it mildly, but I can't get over it. I know I have to, I tell myself it's just a question of time, but while Spider was kissing me I couldn't stop thinking of . . . this other person. That's why I knew it was wrong."

"Zach Nevsky," Billy said with gentle authority.

Gigi gaped and turned red. "Sasha told you! Well, she doesn't know fuck-all about it! Nobody does!"

"Sasha only told me that she was mystified by your relationship with Zach. Remember, Gigi, when we were looking at her catalogs before Christmas? That's the only time she mentioned him, because she thought it was very strange that he hadn't called all week to find out about your leg."

"Then where'd you get that crazy idea?" Gigi demanded violently.

"Zach told me."

"*What!*" Gigi was stricken with utter confusion. "Why are you smiling like that!" she cried accusingly at Billy. "There's nothing to smile about. Zach talked to you? I don't believe this! But whatever he told you, it's a lie!"

"Oh, Gigi, you and Zach are so pathetically screwed up. I'm sorry, I shouldn't be laughing," Billy gasped, biting her lips.

"Billy, if you don't stop turning this into a joke, I'll . . . I'll . . ."

"Now just shut up and listen to me. Zach came to see me a few days after the ski accident. He decided I was the closest thing you had to a mother, and he wanted to clear things up—"

"Oh, sure, make excuses," Gigi shouted. "How dare that vile, promiscuous, sickeningly hypocritical sex fiend, that tin-pot dictator who doesn't give a shit about anything but himself, have the *nerve* to try to lie to you!"

"Because he loves you. *He loves you.* Gigi! Don't go off like a rocket again, Zach does love you, I'm convinced of it, and I know exactly what happened when you found him with that blonde. Will you shut up and listen to the whole story and just not interrupt until I've finished?"

"A pack of lies! Zach can talk anybody into anything, but I can't believe you didn't see through him!" Gigi was sputtering in her fury.

"Are you going to listen, or aren't you?" There was something in the combination of Billy's inescapably dancing eyes and obdurate, uncompromising attitude that made Gigi finally subside into grudging, unwilling silence.

"Okay," she said unbendingly, and listen she did, as Billy told her everything that had been said from the moment Zach had introduced himself to her in the hotel lobby.

"Gigi, don't you see that it wasn't Zach's fault?" Billy pleaded as she finished the story.

"I don't *know* that it happened exactly like that . . . but, yes, I suppose it's not impossible . . . I guess," Gigi responded, as if she were talking to herself, thinking intently. "The one thing I'm sure of is that Pandora is quite capable of anything. That girl . . . I hate the idea, but I suppose that if he woke up . . . with her like that . . . he probably couldn't have stopped. And up on the mountain—Zach did say he loved me and I believed him . . ." Gigi spoke reluctantly, but her face was opening like a flower in the sun after a shower of rain. "Why didn't he tell me himself?"

"Would you have listened to him then?"

"I wouldn't have let him in the door."

"There hasn't been a single opportunity to tell you sooner, or I'd have grabbed it," Billy said. "It isn't the kind of 'oh, by the way' sort of thing you drop into a conversation, and anyway I thought you'd forgotten him, consoled yourself with Spider."

"I've never stopped brooding about Zach, *that poor dumb idiot.*" Gigi stopped for a fit of the giggles. " 'Intromission'? He actually said he was in a 'posture in which intromission had already occurred'? Do you suppose he made up that word?"

"I checked the dictionary," Billy said, "it's in there all right, it means penetration."

"I'd never have believed he knew such a . . . . dainty way to describe it." Gigi doubled over in an unstoppable outburst of mirth.

"Anyway," she said when she'd recovered, mopping at her face with her napkin, "Spider's too old for me, for heaven's sake, he's as old as . . ." she stopped in confusion.

"As I am," Billy calmly completed the phrase.

"I don't mean you're old, you know that, but you're almost exactly the same age as Spider, you're the same age my mother was, even if you look twenty-seven, a too-thin, nervous twenty-seven, and Spider could have been my father, give or take a few months, if he'd started early . . . it's not the same as Sasha and Josh at all. Josh could be her father theoretically, but she couldn't possibly be his daughter, if you see what I mean."

"You make your point perfectly."

"Oh!" Gigi said. "Fathers. I almost forgot. I had dinner with mine the other night, and he asked me to ask you to put in a good word with Susan Arvey about *Fair Play*. He wanted you to tell her it was a movie that should be made, use your influence with her."

"I simply do not believe the sheer callousness of that man," Billy said flatly.

"I thought it was odd, his asking you for a favor, you'd be the last person—but apparently the Arveys really have him over a barrel. He's never admitted that anything was going badly before, he even told me that they were only four million dollars apart on the deal, but it might as well be forty. That's the first time he's ever mentioned money to me, he likes to act as if it's raining down from heaven. I've never seen him so deeply worried. I told him I'd pass on the request, but I couldn't say that I thought you'd do it. Under the circumstances."

"I'll think about it," Billy said briefly. "Now what are you going to do about Zach? Will you write or phone?"

"Oh no," Gigi protested, shocked. "Not out of the blue. He's coming out for the wedding next month. When I see him, I'll know. What if he's found somebody else?"

"Want to bet on it?" Billy offered. "I'll give you interesting odds, if he's found somebody else, you get a million. Cool cash. If he hasn't, you owe me one dollar. You'll never get a better bet than that."

"It would be a nice consolation prize . . . but I only bet on cards, dice and horses. Men are too tricky." Gigi looked at her watch. "My God, Billy, this has been the longest lunch in history. I promised Sasha she could bring her cat to spend a few days at my place. He's developed a nervous condition, he's losing his hair from severe jealousy of

Josh—she wants me to see if I can live with Marcel. I don't think it's going to work, but I've got to get home because she'll be coming by with him any minute. You don't happen to want a cat, do you?''

"If I did, it wouldn't be Marcel. Give me a kiss, you darling,'' Billy said tenderly. "We must never, ever lose each other again, Gigi, not for a minute.''

After Gigi left, Billy went restlessly up to her room. It was rather late in the afternoon, but there was a sky punctuated by small, puffy pink clouds that reflected the setting sun. She couldn't possibly stay indoors with so much on her mind, she realized, and she quickly made her way back outside, heading for her walled garden.

She strolled around it, searching for a dead leaf to pick off a geranium, or a drooping rose that needed to be pruned, finding nothing in all the swaying sheaves of bloom that needed any attention. "Too many gardeners,'' she murmured to herself, taking a single fully open white rose and studying it absently as she thought over her complicated conversation with Gigi. The usual clarification of her thoughts that she hoped would come to her in the secret garden didn't take place. She couldn't see far enough in front of her, Billy decided, to know which way she was headed, but there was one definite thing she could do, only one, and she decided to get it over with immediately. With a look of resolution she made her way back to the house, a huntress pursuing her prey through the forest, repeating to herself that there was no time like the present, never any time quite like it. On the terrace she picked up a phone.

"Mr. Orsini, please,'' she said to the operator at the Beverly Hills Hotel.

"Hello, Vito, it's Billy,'' she said rapidly. "Fine, thank you. Look, Gigi asked me to call Susan Arvey. I'm sorry, but I'd rather not. I can't stand that woman, never could. There's something about her that gives me the creeps. I don't trust her. I know . . . . I know I used to see a lot of her, that doesn't mean I liked her, and frankly I don't think she ever liked me. She just liked knowing me, being my hostess, I can tell the difference. What's the situation on the film? Come on, Vito, don't waffle, just give me the bottom line, the whole story, as nasty as it comes. Never mind why I want to know, if you don't want to talk about it I'll hang up now. Right. Right . . . I see. How much is the grand total? Eleven? Is that final, or is that a budget you can live with? Uh-huh. Uh-huh. A definite twelve? You're sure it won't be thirteen? All right, I'll finance the picture . . . yes, of course I mean the whole thing, you don't think I want to be in business with Curt Arvey, do you? I'll call Josh tomorrow and you can go see him in the afternoon, get a deal memo, so you can go ahead with preproduction. He'll work out all the gruesome details, my profit percentage and all that, just don't put my name on it. Oh, Vito, for Christ's sake, don't thank me, I'm not doing this for you. Of course I liked the book, that doesn't have anything to do with it either. Why? Because I've always dreamed of being in show business, isn't that enough for you? What? You 'insist' on knowing? I don't fucking believe you! All right, I'm grateful to you. You don't merit my gratitude, but that doesn't mean I don't feel it. You have the great, good, totally undeserved luck to have Gigi for a daughter. No, I'm not doing it because she asked me, don't you think I saw through that ploy? I know you, Vito, remember? I know exactly how your mind works. It's because Gigi *is,* because I've had her in my life, because I'll always have her, because I love her . . . and if you hadn't been her father, she wouldn't be here. Just accept it. No, you don't owe me anything . . . you still don't get it, do you, Vito? *I owe you.* Oh, Vito, just one thing, there's a terrific New York theater director named Zach Nevsky—oh, you know about him already? I want him to direct the picture. Get him out here as soon as possible. Tomorrow if you can. Yes, Vito, that's all the interference I'm planning on. But it's a condition. A definite condition. I don't care if he's never used a camera before—get a smart cinematographer— you'll be planning the shots yourself anyway. No, Vito, he's not 'uncredentialed'—*he knows me.* Fine, I'm glad we can agree. Good-bye, Vito, just don't call to let me know how things are going.''

21

A fashion show?" Billy asked coldly, repeating Spider's words. She hadn't seen him since her lunch with Gigi until this minute, when he burst into her office filled with his new idea. "I've never even considered that."

"I hadn't either, it came to me in the middle of the night," Spider explained. "I'd been dreaming about the catalog, and when I woke up the whole thing was as clear as if it had already happened: we'd show only Prince's clothes for the four capsule collections, each collection shown complete in itself, and then all the separate pieces reassembled and put back together in the endless different ways you've been working on, to demonstrate how versatile they are. We'd need at least eighteen runway models working at top speed, maybe more, considering Gigi's accessory ideas."

"It's not impossible, every last one of the samples is finally here, but who would we be putting on the show for?"

"That's the point," Spider said, his enthusiasm flaring sharply. He'd slouched on the corner of Billy's desk, lanky and graceful, but now he leaned forward eagerly. "The cream of the fashion press, the top editors of the big papers' style sections, the wire service ladies, the fashion editors of every magazine women read, and TV of course, the fashion editors of the national daytime morning shows, the afternoon talk shows, and the people who book segments on the big local morning shows in the top markets—there are literally hundreds of people important enough to invite."

"Invite?" Billy said, sounding almost quenched by the magnitude of his plans. "Invite where?"

"I thought we'd have a junket, a whole weekend, so we can fly them all here to Beverly Hills, plan some special events, and then show the Scruples Two Prince collections on Saturday night at a gala party, maybe on a studio soundstage—we'd get professional party planners to work that part out—but do you like the idea?"

"Give me a split second to think about it," Billy said, leaning her elbows on her desk and supporting her head on her fingertips. It was well past seven o'clock on the Monday evening following her lunch with Gigi, and she'd been working without a break all day, munching a sandwich as she supervised the unpacking of the precious, finished "counter samples" that had arrived by courier after one of Prince's chief assistants had spent months making sure that each sample was reproduced exactly to Prince's specifications and to the quality of his original sample.

"Isn't it too soon, Spider?" Billy asked, raising her head wearily. "We still have to manufacture our stock, produce the catalog, and get it in the mail—that's months away. Why would we want the publicity now?"

"Buzz, Billy, *buzz*. We gotta arouse curiosity, get the customers' juices flowing. Movie studios always start to show trailers of their big Christmas films in the middle of the summer to begin to build buzz. Scruples Two is so absolutely different from anything else in the catalog world that we need major PR far in advance of mailing. Hey, are you listening to me?"

"I was thinking of the Scruples ball . . . the first Saturday of November in 1976, remember? And now we're talking about another party almost seven years later . . . such a different kind of party . . . it was sheer magic back then . . . the media was there too, but the guests were mostly stars, celebrities, society, the most beautiful women in their biggest ball gowns, the full moon, the dancing that never stopped . . . they called it the Last Great Party, but of course it wasn't . . .''

"Billy, that's over," Spider said, almost harshly. "Stop hankering for something that can't be reproduced. Get with it, kid. Scruples Two is appealing to a different kind of customer, and so we're gonna give a different kind of party."

"I thought you were asking my opinion," Billy retorted caustically, rudely jolted out of her brief bout of nostalgia. "But I see you've made up your mind—asking me was just pro forma, wasn't it, Spider? How far have your plans progressed? Have you already made a list of guests, hired a party planner, picked a date? No, wait! Let me guess, your first move was to hire the models, all eighteen of them. That would be true to form."

"I just got the idea last night," he said, astonished at the sudden venom of her tone. "You're the first person I've mentioned it to—why do you have a bug up your ass?"

"Lovely! You express yourself with such elegance, Spider, such a rare and choice vocabulary—"

"Billy, cool it, sweetheart," he said teasingly. "You're not exactly one to talk . . . . there are career marines who've never used some of the words you throw around—did I say 'used'? They may never even have *heard* of them."

"Maybe not, Spider, maybe not, but then they don't go around making moves on girls young enough to be their daughters either, do they?"

"Just what are you talking about?" Spider asked, straightening up abruptly.

"I think you know," Billy said in a searing voice. "You're awfully young to be a dirty old man, aren't you? Getting in practice early, is that it? Or do you just have an uncontrollable itch to screw every single female in the world who happens to be momentarily available, emotionally vulnerable, lonely and helpless? How many hundreds of women had you nailed, Spider, before you decided to add Gigi to your long and squalid list?"

"Jesus! So that's what this is all about. Come on, Billy, that was one isolated incident, months ago, and it never went further than a couple of kisses. And why the hell do I have to explain my private life to you?"

"It's not your life," Billy shouted. "I don't give a flying fuck about your life, it's *her* life, you confused her, you got her all upset, she's been going through all sorts of traumas because you couldn't keep your filthy paws to yourself!"

"You've gone batshit! Gigi and I are buddies. If she felt that way about me, I'd damn well know it. She's too honest to hide anything, she'd have let me know."

"Oh, of course you'd know, even if she didn't say a word, everybody's heard about you and your famous intuition, your legendary ability to understand women. What a sick joke! You can't even tell if a woman is thinking about you when you kiss her, or about somebody else. Why do you think Gigi stopped you from taking advantage of her, from fucking her, to be precise? And you would have, Spider, don't even try to deny it—she's in love with somebody, you asshole, and you don't have the sensitivity of an orangutan or you'd have known it."

"Billy . . . look . . . I'm trying hard to understand this . . . you're protecting your whelp, I see that, but this is ridiculous . . . . for the love of heaven, would you stop making me out to be worse than I am?"

"Are you trying to tell me that you weren't going to fuck Gigi that night if she'd let you? With your reputation as an indiscriminate stud? You, Spider, the cheap male version of the good time that was had by all? Don't make me puke. Of course that's the way it would have ended!"

"You weren't there," Spider said, finally aroused to fury. "You weren't standing around watching. You don't know what I was thinking or what I would never have done. You're sitting in judgment, in retrospect, on something that never even took place! But you've appointed yourself accuser, prosecutor, judge and jury, all in one—"

"Are you trying to deny it?" Billy's rage, feeding on itself, opened up a vast gulf of unnavigable space between them.

"I do deny it!"

"Go ahead. Play the innocent. You're nothing but a cock without a conscience. *I know what you wanted to do.*"

"I don't give a tiny fart for what you think you know. You're dead wrong. I'm outta here."

* * *

Just to say that she was certifiable, Spider thought, as he padded ceaselessly around his big, sparsely furnished house in the darkness, was not enough. He'd dealt with a number of crazy women in his life, most of them only temporarily nuts, although Melanie Adams, one true loony, had slipped past him, to his everlasting regret, but Billy was beyond anything he'd ever experienced. She'd come at him out of nowhere, guns blazing, every word as wounding as she could make it, damn near accusing him of being a child molester and absolutely refusing to listen to him, after years and years of knowing what kind of person he was. Didn't she have any reservoir of decent feelings toward him, after all they'd been through together?

The awfulness had hit him so quickly, he realized, that he was having a delayed reaction to it, like walking away from a serious car accident that should have killed him but hadn't broken a single bone. He felt clammily cold and shaken and sick to his stomach. He'd never dreamed that Billy had the power to hurt him so much. He'd never seen her in such an unholy fury—and for what? For what, for Christ's sake? For the straying emotion of a moment, a moment that had been over months ago, a mutual drawing together—at least he'd thought it was mutual—and a quick drawing away, the kind of thing that could happen to just about any two people on any given night, something that had left him and Gigi with a warm, appreciative feeling for each other, and a lovely but essentially unimportant memory. Or at least that's what he'd thought.

Whatever he'd thought, it obviously wasn't reliable anymore. Californians were used to anticipating an earthquake, he'd lived with that easily overlooked but omnipresent expectation in the back of his mind all his life, but Billy made him feel as if the foundations of his life had tumbled in on him in a few seconds, burying him alive. He'd actually thought she was joking at first, until she'd accused him of being a dirty old man. Jesus! Just remembering it was nauseating him.

The thing of it was, it just didn't add up, didn't make any sense. He knew, Spider told himself, he absolutely knew for dead certain that Gigi couldn't have reported any traumas, serious or otherwise, to Billy. Even if Gigi had told her about that night at her apartment in every detail, nothing had happened to her that should make Billy freak out completely. As far as he knew, there hadn't been any unfinished business to linger on in Gigi's mind, and if she was in love with some unknown guy, whoever he was, well, then, didn't that *prove* that there couldn't have been any damage done?

Okay, okay, he shouldn't have kissed her at all, he'd give Billy that much. He was sorry he'd done it. Sorry wasn't the right word, but it would have to do. If he was going to go all the way back and pick the whole thing apart, it had been a very bad idea to start something with Gigi just because she looked so cute and interesting that night . . . because, oh fuck, because he'd been in the mood, and for no other good reason. He'd known Gigi since she was a kid—she was still a darling kid in some ways—and he should never have kissed a kid he'd known for years. For any reason. Or maybe he should have, if he'd been in love with her, but first, to be fair, he'd have had to tell her and find out how she felt about it—but he wasn't in love with Gigi, never had been, never would be.

If that made him an utter and complete and irredeemable shit, so be it. There wasn't anything he could think of to do or say that would change things with Billy. She had been so totally accusatory that it was hopeless. She didn't just despise him, she must genuinely *hate* him. As that thought established itself in his mind, Spider discovered that it was possible to feel ten times worse than he had been feeling until now.

Would he have made love to Gigi if she hadn't stopped him? Well, wouldn't he?

"You miserable bastard," Spider groaned out loud. Who was he kidding?

Billy hadn't even been able to consider dinner, she couldn't find a single place in the whole house where she could sit down for thirty seconds, she knew that even her hidden garden would hold no comfort for her tonight. Finally she'd come upstairs and huddled up on the window seat of the bay window of her dressing room, wrapped in the old afghan she'd had for more than twenty years. Her refuge of last resort, Billy thought. Did every woman have one private place to which she went when she faced the worst moments of her life, or were most women condemned to lock themselves in a bathroom with teenagers trying to get in? And why was she asking herself things she already knew? She was so deeply ashamed, so horrified at herself, that thinking about other people helped to take her mind off herself and her awfulness, that's why.

Even when she'd been most bitter, most angry about Vito, she'd never allowed herself to carry on like that, in that indescribably odious, ghastly . . . she'd never even felt like it, come to think about it. She'd never wanted to utterly destroy Vito with words, she'd never wanted to cover him with slime, she'd tried her best to rise above their problems, not throw herself into the gutter and roll around in it like a demented . . . thing. A vile thing she didn't recognize, with vile words, words she didn't know she was going to say, spewing out of her mouth at Spider, who stood there looking so stunned, trying to treat it as if it were one of their typically good-natured, fake-aggressive, mock-hostile encounters, until he'd realized . . . . and even then he hadn't gotten really angry until she'd goaded and goaded him until he had to protect himself.

Who did she think she was, the morals squad? The thought police? The Boston Watch and Ward Society? Gigi was more than mature enough to make her own decisions, she had been independent far beyond her age when she'd arrived in California long ago, and at this point in her life she'd been living on her own for years, in the biggest of big bad cities, with nothing more than a temporarily unconsummated romance with Zach Nevsky to make her miserable. Concern for Gigi was no excuse for becoming, without warning, a damned effective death ray of a woman.

A frosty bitch. That's what Spider's first impression of her had been. Mild, favorable, *generous,* compared to the reality.

Oh God, she must be still angry at Spider, Billy thought. She didn't have a single good reason, but she felt, deep in her gut, that she wouldn't be satisfied until she could hurt him and hurt him, until she'd reduced him to tears. Yes, to tears. Nothing less. He was so fucking invulnerable, so sure of himself, so at ease with life, so comfortable with people, so unshy, so . . . . everything she wasn't. How could she be this kind of person, this loathsome dog in the manger, envying him his personality and lashing out at him so unforgivably because he was just being himself?

Couldn't it be stress, she asked herself, deep in misery. Couldn't stress, which was blamed for everything that went wrong from death to pimples, be the real reason she'd been so hideous to Spider? The stress of producing this wretched, *bloody* catalog? Yes, it was all the fault of the catalog, Billy told herself, as she had a piercing memory of the moment when she'd been swept up in Spider's arms and greeted as joyously as if she were the one and only person in the world he'd really wanted to see. There had been no catalog then, no horde of employees, no business partnership . . . just a simple, happy relation-ship that she'd ruined for all time. *Never.* They could never go back after the words she'd said.

Billy pulled the old afghan up over her curls so that she was enfolded by it from head to toe, and gave herself up completely to a storm of hot, brokenhearted tears.

There should be an escalator, or even a fireman's ladder, between the two floors occupied by Scruples Two, Josie Speilberg told herself as she stood waiting impatiently for the arrival of one of the four elevators that serviced the Century City office tower in which the company was located. How did they expect her to run this whole enterprise when she had to waste a good twenty-five minutes a day traveling from floor to floor?

The years during which she'd worked at Mrs. Ikehorn's house were like a long, lazy luxury cruise on board an ocean liner compared to the white-water rapids, the electric, nonstop hurly-burly of the cat-alog. She'd always thought she wanted a more active job, she'd always felt that her talents were greater than she needed to run any house, no matter how big, but now, as office manager of Scruples Two, she was stretched in a dozen different directions. Of course the status and salary that went with it had changed her life, but still, had nobody any consideration for her? As if she hadn't enough to do, acting as the essential liaison between merchandise and catalog production, she also had to keep track of marketing and operations and the rapid progress of the vast Virginia operation.

Everybody was a boss of something, all the departments had their own heads, but in effect, Josie estimated, she was the boss of the bosses, keeping them informed of what was going on from minute to minute. They'd all formed the habit of calling her on the office inter-com to see where they could reach this one or that one—no question about it, she was paying the price of being the most efficient and organized person in the whole operation.

She was the only essential person at Scruples Two, Josie Speil-berg decided as she stepped into the empty elevator, smiling prudently and contentedly to herself. Ultimately essential, and to think that she'd once believed no one was indispensable. Particularly now, with the fashion show weekend almost upon them and everybody plain silly with nerves. Who but she had hired the travel agents to arrange all the incredibly complicated plans that guaranteed that three hundred members of the national and local media would all arrive here tomorrow, early on Friday afternoon, and be transported back to their home bases by Monday evening? Who had located all the hotel rooms and arranged for all the limos and buses? Who had worked with the party planners and the PR people to coordinate every detail of the festivities, since Mrs. Ikehorn was too busy to give it a minute and Spider was out of the office on location photo shoots almost all the time? Who delivered the messages from one of them to the other? She would really like to know how they thought they could have communicated if she weren't around. By satellite?

Surely her title should be changed. Office managers worried about stationery and telephones and payrolls and replacing carpets—she had two assistants to handle that. Vice-president in charge of—what? *Sanity*. Yes, it might be a new position in any company, but there must be a few other unsung women all over the world who deserved to wear that title, besides herself. She'd make corporate history, Josie resolved.

She'd speak to Mrs. Ikehorn about it as soon as the weekend was over. Now would not be a good time, in fact now would be a singularly stupid time, with Mrs. Ikehorn uncharacteristically down in the dumps, yet gritting her teeth and visibly gearing herself up to acting as hostess for the entire three days. Hating the limelight as she did, as fundamentally shy and antisocial as she was—did Mrs. Ikehorn think that she'd kept that particular little secret hidden from her? She had nevertheless recognized and bowed to the fact that it was her physical presence, her newsworthiness, that had made the across-the-board acceptance of her invitations so prompt. Her reclusiveness after the death of Ellis Ikehorn had only whetted the appetite of the press for new material about her. No one knew yet that Scruples Two was a catalog, not a new boutique. The secret had been amazingly well kept, there had been no leaks in the press.

Josie Speilberg, Vice-President in Charge of Sanity. Yes, it had a nice ring to it. And there would undoubtedly be members of the press who would want to interview her one day, not the same way they were clamoring for time with Mrs. Ikehorn, of course . . . . but nevertheless.

* * *

Nothing she had told Sasha about the sheer hell of weddings had penetrated, Gigi reflected. Not one word. There must be some sort of basic human instinct, as impervious to the thinking process as reproduction, that caused otherwise perfectly sensible people to feel that they wouldn't be satisfactorily or even legally married unless they did it in the most public way possible.

The wedding itself was still six weeks away, but Sasha and her mother, the wee and terrorizing Tatiana Nevsky, had been on the phone with each other for hours every day. Apparently, chieftainess Tatiana was as pleased with this marriage as she would have been if Sasha had married Prince Andrew—never a real possibility, even with Charles taken—and Sasha was basking in the unusual glow of her mother's approval. Josh, of course, like all grooms, was just along for the ride. Nobody cared that all he wanted was to get it over with.

The combination of the fashion show weekend and the looming wedding was enough to make anybody but a veteran of the catering wars lose her head, Gigi told herself with a measure of pride. There was nothing that wasn't under control. Each model would go down the runway properly accessorized. They'd rehearsed and rehearsed; each pair of girls shared one professional dresser and each had an individual rack of accessories, all clearly marked, as well as a list of the dozen outfits each of them would wear. The assembly of all the different combinations simply wouldn't have been possible if Prince hadn't hand-tailored a flock of additional samples, but he had come through handsomely. In fact he was so tickled with himself over his enlightened, young, image-busting designs for Scruples Two that he was arriving tonight, Thursday, so that he could work the fashion press all weekend, in addition to narrating the actual show himself. It would all go smoothly, in spite of Billy's apprehension, which must be the reason for the dismal depression she couldn't seem to get over, Gigi assured herself in a flurry of worry, or her name wasn't Graziella Giovanna Orsini. Oy!

It was the fucking maid-of-honor dress that had been the final straw. Leave it to Tatiana Nevsky to dictate, from three thousand miles away, the dresses that she and the bridesmaids, who included Josh's daughter, were going to wear! Talk about interference! This surpassed, in sheer undue influence, anything any bride's grande-dame mother had pulled at Voyage to Bountiful, Gigi thought wrathfully, as she drove her shocking pink Volvo to Josh's condo in a new high-rise on Wilshire Boulevard, to which the dress had been air-expressed.

Gigi had never seen a maid-of-honor dress she didn't loathe. There was some sort of collusion in the fashion industry which dictated that all female members of a wedding, except the bride, must become martyrs. Something constipated the designers of these garments so that they were never what any woman would willingly choose to wear, particularly anyone with a sense of her own style. They were as predictably stiff and ceremonious as costumes from a grammar school historical pageant, without the excuse of tradition. Perhaps the designers, like the schoolteachers, knew that they could get away with it, since they counted on the indulgence of the audience. Personally, she'd rather come as Pocahontas.

Gigi left her car with the parking attendant and took the elevator up to Josh's luxurious apartment, where Sasha opened the door for her so quickly that she must have been listening for the sound of the elevator door to open.

Grumpily, Gigi gave Sasha a kiss. "Where's the masterpiece that we couldn't have found right here? Does your mother think there are no decent stores in Beverly Hills?" she inquired.

"You've always had a sour attitude about my darling little mother," Sasha said, far more merrily than the situation warranted.

"And you didn't? Spare me. You disguised yourself every time you were destined to fall under her eye. She's going to get the shock of her life when she gets out here and discovers you in full flower, unless you're planning to wear your usual 'Look, Ma, I'm invisible and flat-chested' drag on your wedding day."

"You worry too much," Sasha said airily, with a lack of any sympathy, as if Gigi had no right to worry even a little, even with all the things going on that depended on her, from the fashion show to the wedding. Sasha had absolutely insisted that Gigi come to try on her dress today, of all days, the day before the press was descending, pointing out, incontestably, that the dress would need alterations because Gigi was so short, and, what's more, she knew that Gigi was so organized that she'd have nothing left to do at this late date and would need to be distracted.

"Let's see it," Gigi said with resignation, as she spotted the large carton sitting on a table in Josh's large, modern living room. Sasha opened the box and took out a dress that had been packed in dozens of sheets of tissue paper.

"At least it's lavender," Gigi said, circling it warily.

"My mother said that the color would set off your hair. Oh, for

Pete's sake, go into the bedroom and put the thing on, don't just sniff at it suspiciously like Marcel does at Josh. Will you hurry? I can't stand this suspense!''

"He still shedding?'' Gigi asked over her shoulder, as she took the dress away from Sasha and moved reluctantly toward the bedroom.

"No, he's resigned himself, except for the odd nasty glare. His visit to you cured him. The poor thing came back home pathetically happy, you didn't give him enough attention. Will you go? I tell you I'm shaking!''

"Sorry about that,'' Gigi laughed, and disappeared. In the bedroom she stripped down to her panty hose, took off her boots, and exchanged them for the pair of silver slippers she'd brought so that they could measure the hem. She stepped carefully into the cloudlike mass of lavender chiffon, not sure where some unseen zipper might be lurking. It went on lightly, in spite of its many layers of skirt, and zipped up surprisingly easily. Gigi turned to look at herself in the full-length mirror inside the closet.

Well. Maybe Tatiana Nevsky wasn't as bad as Sasha had led her to believe. Maybe the woman was even a genius, Gigi thought excitedly, as she wrapped the wide velvet sash, in a deep shade of Parma violet, around her waist and expertly tied it in a large bow. The dress fit perfectly. It was a good six inches off the ground, the off-the-shoulder neckline hit her at exactly the right place, as low as humanly possible but snugly enough not to slip. The simple bodice was as slender as the skirt was full, the softly pleated sleeves were perfect, widening from the neckline to the wrist, so that they'd fall back in a graceful line when she held her bouquet at waist level. And, wonder of wonders, miracle of miracles, that was all there was to it, no trim, no sequins, no paillettes, nothing but a bell-shaped flutter of dozens of yards of chiffon that anyone could see immediately belonged on a ballet stage. A dress without time or place or season, with no excuse for existing but beauty. Gigi whirled around and around, her freshly streaked hair flying upward in a silken web, and watched the skirt rise and fall, forgetting Sasha, who seemed to be outside waiting for the verdict in tactful silence. She looked . . . . she looked . . . . like a Balanchine-inspired butterfly? . . . a flower with wings? . . . an ideal version of herself?

"Oh, Sasha, I take back all the awful things I've ever said about your mother,'' she cried as she rushed back into the living room.

"I'll tell Ma," Zach said, standing in the center of the room, squarely facing her.

Gigi stopped dead, teetered on her high heels, and barely regained her balance, too shocked to move or speak. She turned so frighteningly pale that Zach took two hasty paces forward and grasped her by her arms so that she wouldn't fall. "I told Sasha to warn you, but she thought—"

"You're early," Gigi heard herself say with lunatic logic. "The wedding . . . it's weeks away . . ."

"That's not why I'm here," he said, putting one of his fingers under her chin and gently turning her face up toward him.

"Zach . . . oh, Zach . . ." she whispered, opening her arms wide and stretching them up to him, utterly bewildered but suddenly entirely certain that whatever was happening was right. Gigi was overwhelmed by a thunderous wave of welcome. This was far more than right, it was inevitable. Necessary, as nothing else had ever been.

"Do you have any idea how much I love you?" Zach asked her anxiously, not daring to kiss her until he'd heard her answer.

"So I've heard," Gigi managed to reply. "So I've been informed . . . reliably informed."

He kissed her then, holding her delicate body close to his splendid bulk, kissed her until the lavender dress wilted and their entire beings were abandoned to each other, hearts and souls overcome, astonished by perfect wonder, yet somehow deeply unsurprised.

"You've never told me you love me," Zach demanded at last, leaving her lips for an instant.

"I don't think you ever asked," Gigi answered. "Not exactly like that, not in so many words."

"Do you love me?" he asked, his voice more humble than she'd ever heard it. Gigi hesitated for a moment, savoring what she knew was doomed to be only momentary uncertainty in Zach Nevsky.

"Yes," she said finally, wholeheartedly giving up reluctance.

"That's good enough for now." He looked down at her and laughed his unguarded, triumphant laugh. " 'Yes' . . . that's all I wanted to hear."

The front door opened in the hall and was closed with a loud slam as Marcel strolled pompously into the room, his tail in the air.

"That's Sasha, trying to be discreet," Zach said. "I made her go out to do some grocery shopping. She wanted to wait in the kitchen, but I wouldn't allow it."

"Is everything all right in there?" Sasha called, still not coming into the living room.

"Go away and shop some more," Zach answered.

"I will not," she said indignantly, as she entered the room. "You've had plenty of time. I just sat in the lobby, I never go grocery shopping, Zach, for your information. Gigi, are you okay?"

"I think so," Gigi said shakily, peeping out from the massive barrier of Zach's arms.

"Oh, my God, Gigi! You've wrinkled the dress! I knew I should never have left you two alone!"

Although John Prince had not accepted Billy's invitation to spend the fashion show weekend as her houseguest, preferring the convenience of a hotel switchboard, she had sent her plane to bring him to Los Angeles, and her car and driver to transport him to the hotel, wait while he checked in, and bring him back to her house for a private dinner. They'd both be so busy over the weekend that Billy thought they might never see each other except in a crowd, and she wanted to discuss the introduction she was going to make before he began to narrate the show.

She waited for Prince in front of the fireplace in one of the twin living rooms. Although it was May, the nights were still cool enough to make a fire inviting. Billy heard Prince's familiar rumble as he entered the house, and she walked quickly forward to greet him with the biggest smile she could muster and kisses on both cheeks. Just the sight of Prince in his tweedy glory made her feel a little less woebegone. He scrutinized her face as she led him toward the couch in front of the fireplace, and seemed reassured by what he saw.

"Well, ducky, I'm glad you're ignoring this," Prince said, tossing a copy of *Fashion and Interiors* on the coffee table. Billy looked at him in surprise. "Ducky" was ominous, that was his term of greatest affection, ten times more meaningful than "pet." She eyed the glossy magazine with concern. Somehow they must have gotten wind of Scruples Two and broken the surprise in "P.D.Q.," their notorious front-of-the-book column. "P.D.Q.," anonymously written, and lavishly illustrated with deliberately embarrassing photographs, could be counted on to be an unapologetic fount of the latest and most malicious gossip of the worlds of society and fashion. It was as juicy and flavorsome as a perfectly ripe melon, and since its inception it had established itself as far and away the liveliest, nastiest and most titillating section of the influential magazine. "P.D.Q." was the first thing every subscriber turned to when the magazine was delivered.

"My copy hasn't arrived yet," Billy said. "What am I ignoring?"

"I brought this from New York. It came late yesterday. Ducky, there's an unfortunate 'P.D.Q.' story. I was hoping you'd seen it and managed to ignore it," Prince said.

"Damn! After we'd managed to stay top-secret for months! I should have known. It couldn't be worse timing, they've scooped everybody," Billy wailed.

"No. It's not about Scruples Two," Prince said somberly.

Alarmed, Billy picked up the glossy magazine and scanned the cover. "P.D.Q.'s Special: Billy Ikehorn's Romantic Caper."

"What the devil . . . ?"

"He's the right one to ask."

With suddenly trembling fingers Billy turned to the "P.D.Q." pages and scanned the story while Prince poured himself a drink and stood with his back to her, studying the fire.

> *You've all heard the one about the pathetic Poor Little Rich Girl who didn't know whether she was loved for her money or herself? "P.D.Q." has discovered that Beverly Hills's own Billy Ikehorn has been trying desperately to find out while leading a double life in Paris.*
>
> *Pay attention, MI-5! Would you believe that our fabulously well dressed Billy managed to pass herself off for almost a year as a simple schoolteacher from Seattle? (A French teacher, of course. What else?) Yes, one of the world's richest women actually convinced the handsome San Francisco sculptor, Sam Jamison, that she was a poor but honest working girl during their long idyll in his Marais studio. Sorry, Sam, but did you ever get a wrong number!*
>
> *Checking with the Paris Ritz, "P.D.Q." learned that Billy officially occupied their Windsor Suite all of last year, but Henri Legrand, of the Galerie Templon, where the sculptor's work made a sensation last fall, told "P.D.Q." that he knew our Billy only as one "Honey Winthrop," Jamison's very much live-in inamorata of many months' duration.*
>
> *Would this make it the first time that a blue-blooded Bos-*

ton Winthrop (our Billy was born Wilhelmina Hunnenwell Winthrop, lest we forget) used the venerable family name to cover up a secret love affair?

Isn't it passing curious that only by pretending to be someone she is not, can Billy seem to find a man? Everyone remembers her short-lived second marriage to film producer, Vito (The WASP) Orsini, quickly interrupted by his big-time affair with Maggie MacGregor. Maggie dumped Vito when it was clear that The WASP was going to be the disaster of the decade, quickly replacing him with Fred Greenspan, her married boss, who soon decided that show-biz news queen MacGregor's show was worthy of an additional half hour of the network's time. Maggie, as everyone knows, got to the top professionally by knowing how to use the right men at the right time. Shouldn't Billy beg smart Maggie for tips on picking men who can do a girl good? Since Billy lost Vito, there has been no one in her life except duped Sam Jamison. It would seem to "P.D.Q." that no amount of money (worse, not even the lack of it!), can buy ỏur Billy lasting love.

How did it end? Many eyewitnesses saw our intrepid heroine make the mistake of being caught with all her diamonds on one gala night at the Opera. (Well, not all of them, of course, but enough to blow that schoolteacher story.) Sam Jamison recognized his Cinderella-in-reverse and made a very public scene, followed the next day by his giving Billy the "cut direct" chez Lipp, where she had tracked him down.

Our Billy decamped in a hurry, fleeing Paris for forgiving Beverly Hills, her old stomping ground, where she remains in mysterious, but understandable (n'est-ce pas?), seclusion. Tennis pro, anyone? "P.D.Q." 's advice for our unlucky-in-love, Poor Little Rich Girl: Next time, "Honey," try to get a man with his own money. To Tell the Truth, will the real Wilhelmina Hunnenwell Winthrop Ikehorn Orsini please stand up? Or isn't there one?

"Well, ducky, at least the photographs are good, particularly the one of you in that bikini," Prince said, turning when he heard Billy throw the magazine down. "And they spelled your name right," he added as he measured the raw bleakness of her face. "Billy, I know it's bad, but it's not life-threatening."

"No."

"What did you ever do to Harriet Toppingham to arouse such vileness? This is lower than they ever get."

"I met her once . . . only once . . . at a party," Billy answered with difficulty, through stiff lips. "Cora de Lioncourt did this, she's the only one who could have put the pieces together."

"Then what did you do to *her*?"

"Nothing . . . nothing I know of," Billy said in a voice as white and rigid as her face.

"Ducky, I know it's a bromide, but when something like this happens, you just have to face it down, get right out there and pretend it never happened. It's not as if you've done anything to be ashamed of."

"You don't understand."

"I won't kid you, Billy, of course people will enjoy this, they'll dine out on it for a week or two, but they'll forget it by the time the next issue comes around."

"No, they won't. People never forget stories as good as this. Never, not as long as I live."

"Well . . . maybe," he admitted, knowing she was right. "But realistically, there's nothing you can do about it."

"No one," Billy said slowly, "literally no one I've ever met or will ever meet won't have heard about this and remember it when they see me . . . I'll always know what they're thinking. I'm a *laughingstock,* someone to be *pitied.*"

"Oh, ducky, please try not to take it so hard. So they laugh, so what? They can't take away all the things they envy about you. Just look in the mirror, just look around you. Billy, you have a triumphant life."

He couldn't understand, Billy realized numbly, he couldn't possibly understand that throughout every day of every week of the formative years of her life she had suffered from being a laughingstock. No matter how high and mighty she seemed today, her deepest perceptions of herself had been formed by the neglect of her parents, by the endlessly cruel mockery of her schoolmates, by the pity of her aunts and the contemptuous rejection of her cousins. She tried to tell herself that it was a familiar story for a lot of people—maybe everyone's self-esteem had been damaged in their youth—but this story in "P.D.Q."

was the pure, distilled, poisonous essence of the nightmares that woke her up in the middle of the night, worried about the reception of Scruples Two. Each sickeningly pointed word was burned into her mind. It was too accurate to deny. She felt as if she'd tumbled backwards for decades, she felt the way that fat freak, Honey Winthrop, had felt year after year after year.

"Prince, I can't . . . I'm simply not capable of facing the media this weekend. Spider can introduce you. I'm staying right here. I won't leave my house, I don't care what anyone says . . . I just can't do it."

"Billy, that's the wrong way to handle this," Prince said sternly.

"There's nothing else I can do. Prince, I'm sorry, but I have to be by myself." Her austere conviction was unanswerable.

"Ducky!" Prince began to follow Billy upstairs, stopped, shrugged helplessly, and decided to leave. Even a room-service dinner alone at the hotel would be more cheerful than having to look at Billy's tormented face any longer. He hated to admit that the whole thing sounded intriguingly spicy, although he certainly wished it had happened to somebody else. The hotel bar would be full of people he knew, every one of them dying to dish about Billy, incognito, fucking her brains out in Paris. Of course he wouldn't linger too long talking in the bar. After all, he was genuinely fond of Billy.

22

*D*o you know where I can find Billy?'' Josh Hillman asked Spider very late on Thursday afternoon.

"Haven't seen her," Spider answered, quickly closing the copy of *Fashion and Interiors* in which he'd just finished reading the "P.D.Q." article. "Why?"

"There's something I want to give her, a good-luck souvenir, for tomorrow." Josh placed the marble nameplate from Scruples that had been saved from the fire on Spider's desk.

"Christ!" Spider recoiled. "You think she wants to see *that*? Jesus, Josh, where'd you get it?"

"The fire department gave it to me after Billy left. I've been hanging on to it for years, didn't know what to do with it. But now, well, I was cleaning out my desk and I came across it and I thought maybe Billy should have it."

"I can't think of anything she'd rather *not* have. It'd just remind her of the fire."

"I don't agree at all, Spider. It will remind her of the success of Scruples. I know she's worried about Scruples Two—I've noticed her looking very down lately. You've seen a million photos of people who lose their entire homes in fires going back to poke in the ashes. They're trying to find something, absolutely anything, to keep as a remembrance of what they used to have. It always seems to comfort them, they'll carry away the damnedest things, it gives them the courage to go on. It's strange, but it happens all the time, I truly know it helps."

"Yeah." Spider looked at Josh in a rush of pity. The lawyer had no reason to suspect that his love for Valentine had not been a secret to Spider. While he'd been sailing from island to island, letting the sea and the sky and the wind slowly deal with his grief, Josh had been forced to stick to business as usual, unable to admit to anyone that he too had lost Valentine.

"Why don't you give it to Billy yourself, Josh?"

"I have to meet Sasha in ten minutes, and I'm late already."

"Okay, Josh, leave it with me and I'll manage to get it to Billy somehow. One thing I'm sure of, she's not in the office. Josie told me that a minute ago, and Josie would know."

As Josh left, Spider realized why he had instinctively hid the "P.D.Q." article, although Josh would unquestionably know all about it long before the day was over. He couldn't endure watching anyone, anyone at all, read it, even someone as totally devoted to Billy as Josh Hillman. He touched the apricot marble with one tentative finger, and traced the beautifully swirling letters of the word *Scruples* that had been chiseled into the stone. Was it possible that this reminder of a past triumph would give Billy something to hang on to through the shipwreck of that unspeakably sickening article? The vomit that Harriet Toppingham had published? Unquestionably the nameplate had somehow helped Josh, that much was sure, or he would never have kept it all this time. Thank God the guy no longer needed it.

"Let me speak to Burgo O'Sullivan," Spider said to the gateman who had refused him admittance to the Ikehorn house.

"Yes sir." He handed Spider the phone.

"Burgo, it's Spider Elliott. Yeah, I know she's closed the house to visitors, the gateman told me. But, Burgo, you know as well as I do it's not a good idea to be alone when you need a friend to talk to. I've tried to find Gigi—I called her apartment but no one answered. Look, Burgo, there really isn't anyone else but me right now, is there? Someone has got to be better than no one. Sure. Will you tell him that? Thanks, Burgo.''

Spider handed the receiver to the gateman, who listened and promptly opened the electric gates for him. Spider pulled up in front of the house, where Burgo was waiting to greet him.

''Where is she?'' Spider asked as he got out of his car, the piece of marble under his arm.

''After Mr. Prince left, she went upstairs for about an hour. Her maid said she was locked in her dressing room. Then she came down in her old cape and went out to walk around,'' Burgo replied with a deeply worried look. ''She hasn't come in since. My hunch is that she's in her private garden. I'll show you where it is. If she's not there, your guess is as good as mine. All the garden lights are on, you can look around as much as you like. I'll let the guards know you're here so they won't bother you.''

Silently, without any small talk, Burgo led the way along the most direct path that cut through an olive grove and eventually came to a stop before the barrier of sentinel cypresses that concealed the stone walls of the garden. It was a chilly, windy night, the trees bending and rustling under the force of a dry Santa Ana wind that drove a full moon across the starry sky. Burgo parted the branches of two old cypress trees and revealed the door to the hidden garden. He gestured briefly and walked away before Spider could knock.

Faced with the uncompromisingly blank, well-made wooden door, Spider hesitated. He could leave Billy alone, in the privacy she had asked for and expected to be accorded her. He could stand here quietly, then wander around the grounds for a decent interval, and drive away, telling Burgo that he hadn't been able to find her. He knew he must be absolutely the last person Billy would want to see, tonight or any other night; she hadn't spoken a single word to him since their fight, she had even contrived never to be in the same room with him. In the course of the last month they had not laid eyes on each other once. But if there was any comfort on earth he could bring to Billy, if this fragment of marble had one-hundredth of the power Josh said it had, he had to give it to her. He knocked.

''What is it, Burgo?'' Billy's voice called.

''It's me, Spider.''

A minute passed. Then another. "It's not locked," she said finally, in an absolutely neutral tone.

Spider pushed open the door and stood still, suddenly robbed of the power to move, bewildered by the magical whiteness of the enclosed garden, lit so softly that no source of light was visible. The passage through the somber screen of cypress into this square of concentrated enchantment made him feel as if he had stumbled into the heart of an awe-inspiring mystery. A living carpet of small white flowers eddied around his feet like surf foam, white tulips grew thickly around his knees, taller lilies tickled the backs of his hands, white roses climbed above his head and thrust their blooms so high that night was all but banished. The mingled sweetness of the climbing jasmine and roses startled him with its power; the moon's reflection, a shivering shimmer, was the only adornment of the small center pool set so tightly into banks of fairy primroses that it seemed to have been dropped from the sky. He looked around for Billy, but he couldn't find her.

"You've never been here," she commented without any inflection, from her concealed seat across the garden under the arbor laden with twisted ropes of white wisteria.

At the sound of her voice, Spider located her barely visible form. "I never knew it existed," he said, not daring to move.

"Since you're here, come in."

"Thank you." He followed the curve of the path and stopped three feet away from the arbor seat, awkwardly putting the marble nameplate down behind him. Now that he was closer he could see that Billy was sitting far back, closely wrapped in some sort of dark, ample covering. Her head was shadowed by a hood, and he could barely make out the slight gleam of her dark eyes. He couldn't give her the nameplate now, Spider thought, not here. He had expected to find Billy indoors, expected to repeat Josh's words, deliver Josh's gift and retreat, but in this sweet, blowing company of blazing, fragile whiteness, his solid hunk of marble seemed out of place.

Billy herself, in the shadows she had chosen, was suddenly inscrutable. He felt a great confusion fall over him. What did he truly know of the woman who sat here so quietly, whose retreat he had dared to invade? What could she have been thinking as she looked out at her garden, as if from a box at the theater, on a performance of private splendor? Suddenly he remembered Billy as she had sat with him at lunch one day in New York, in Le Train Bleu. She had worn high-spirited red, he thought, seeing her vividly, and she had been in total command of her electrifying self, her eyes carrying an empire within them, her strong throat a stalk more beautiful than anything in this garden. That day he had taken fresh measure of the depth of the intensely feminine tenderness that lived in her side by side with an autocratic impulsiveness. He understood her better now, after their intense partnership on Scruples Two, yet as well as he comprehended women, she still managed to elude him. More than in any woman he'd ever met, something about Billy remained fundamentally unknowable on the most basic level. He appreciated the depth of her shyness, yet she could be dauntless and daring far beyond other women. She'd managed to screw up her life, yet she'd maintained a powerful authority as she did so. She was sweet—oh, so sweet—but somehow unaware of the power of her own sweetness. He had come only to bring her comfort. He needed, more than anything, to heal her hurt somehow, to take away her pain, but he didn't know how to begin, because of all the trouble between them.

"I came—" He faltered, and sought a new phrase.

"No, don't," Billy said, holding up a hand in prohibition. "I . . . I have to apologize to you. The things I said, they were totally unforgivable, I can't explain them . . . I don't expect you to forgive me, but—"

"No!" Spider was appalled at her words. "No! Don't apologize! I was out of line, a hundred percent wrong, and you were right. But tell me you don't think of me as a louse. I can't endure your thinking I'm contemptible. Even if you do, *say you don't*! Christ, Billy, I've missed you so! You'll never have any idea how much I've missed you. We can never fight like that again, no matter what happens, it hurts too much. Jesus, I've cried myself to sleep, that's how bad it's been." He stopped suddenly, amazed that he'd told her so much. He'd sworn to himself that no one would ever know how childish he'd been.

"But," Billy said in a tiny voice, "but . . ."

"What does that mean?" Spider asked, confused.

"I . . . missed you too," she answered, in an even smaller voice.

"You mean you don't hate me?"

"Unfortunately . . . not. That would make it easy." She shrank back farther into the protection of the folds of her old, sable-lined cape.

"I don't get it—can't we be friends again the way we used to be?" he asked, refusing to accept a note of unqualified farewell in her voice that terrified him. He moved toward her, bent down and took her cold hands in his, and tried to warm them.

"Friends? Oh no, Spider, not friends . . . not the way we used to be . . . I'm going away . . . back to Paris . . . . or maybe somewhere else . . . I'm not sure yet."

"Billy, for God's sake, you can't leave! I won't let you! It's that lying garbage in the magazine, isn't it?" he asked, trying to peer down at her face, almost hidden by the hood of the cape. Unable to see her and afraid to ask permission, he sat down gingerly on the edge of the narrow garden seat.

"No, not that," Billy said. "It wasn't a lie, you know. It happened, not exactly the way they said, but close enough. That's why I didn't tell you about Sam when you asked. I wasn't proud of it, although, on balance, I believe I made an honest mistake. At first, after I read what they wrote, I was so assaulted by the tone of it—the *sneer*—that I felt like a poor, shriveled thing, someone without an identity except the one they pinned on me. And then, as I read it over and over, unable to leave it alone, it became thinner and thinner until the words became unreal. That thing wasn't about me at all. I discovered that I don't *perceive myself* as a pathetic person. Not anymore. Somewhere, somehow, I seem to have picked up some unmistakable self-esteem—high time, too, as my Aunt Cornelia would say, but never too late. I did have a bad time as a girl . . . growing up . . . but since then I've had a real life with real love and real friends and real achievements. Real ups, real downs, like everyone else. *There is a real me*—even if I don't suit everyone's taste. Don't worry, Spider, I'll survive that miserable magazine, I would never run away and give them the satisfaction of thinking they'd driven me out of town—"

"Then why are you even talking of leaving?" Spider interrupted fiercely. "How can you? It's simply not possible, I won't let you go."

"It's . . . it's . . . because we can't be friends again."

"Why not?" Spider demanded in anguish.

Billy was silent, struggling to gather together all her powers, willing herself to speak, to be honest at last, to say the inadmissible words, get them out and over with and put them behind her for once and for all, to give herself a chance to get on with her life. She couldn't live like this, tasting her lonely love on her tongue, drawing it in on her breath, breathing it out in each sigh.

"Because . . . because you can't keep a friend if you're . . . jealous of him."

"Jealous?" Spider asked blankly.

"Oh, my God, Spider, do I really have to spell it out for you? What do you think made me say those cruel things? Didn't you even guess? I was jealous . . . yes, of Gigi . . . yes, of all the other . . . . women in your life. Of all the women . . . . you've . . . . loved."

Billy abruptly pulled her hands away from his and pushed her hood farther forward so that he couldn't see her face at all, burrowing into her cape for protection.

" 'Jealous,' " Spider repeated slowly, in wonderment and the confused but unmistakable dawning of an impatient, rising hope that he knew far, far less about Billy than he had dreamed, unbelievably less, beautifully less. "Jealous. You wouldn't be jealous if—"

"Don't! Don't say it! Have some decency, don't rub it in. It's bad enough as it is! I have to get over it and *I intend to*," Billy said with pitiless determination.

"Oh no, you won't!" he cried, taking her in his arms and pulling back her hood so that he could see her desolate, pain-filled eyes and her trembling, determined, ardent mouth. He cradled her astonished face in his big hands, keeping himself from kissing her with a heroic effort. First he had to explain things so that she would understand. "If you make a move," Spider told her solemnly, no hesitancy in his voice, "if you take one step, I'll follow you, wherever you go, I'll camp out on your doorstep, if you want privacy you can have it, but I'll always be there for you, waiting patiently. You must never go away from me again, you can't leave me, we've been apart for too long, we've wasted too much time. Now listen to me carefully, Billy, this is the important part. About a year and a half ago you rang my doorbell, and the second I opened my door and saw it was you, I fell in love. But the insane, awful thing is that I didn't understand it until just now. Billy, I've been hopelessly in love with you right from that moment, but it never occurred to me that you could love me—you'd never seemed . . . well, to care about me that much, we'd never had a flicker of an underground romance, so I didn't *allow* myself to know it, I never let myself even imagine . . . never started to even wonder . . . . *oh, but you do love me,* I know it—I can't be that wrong now, can I?" he implored. "Not when I love you so much. Oh, say you're not going anywhere without me, Billy, please say you'll never desert me, say you couldn't be that unkind." Spider pleaded with her with all his heart, as a man might beg for his life, still not entirely sure he was right, for Billy's few, almost enigmatic words had taken him utterly by

surprise. "Say you'll never be jealous again because there'll never be a reason, say you know I'll be true to you forever, because I will be—for God's sake, Billy, *say something!*"

"I don't know where to start," she whispered, her face awakening to the birth of a transforming happiness. "Ask me more questions."

"Oh!" He kissed her over and over in a fury of relief and sudden certitude and discovery. "I'll ask you more questions, don't you worry about that, we can go back and start this right, back to basics, like in the olden days, I'll ask you out on a date and I'll come by and pick you up and take you out for dinner and—and then I'll bring you home and ask if I can see you again sometime, maybe next Saturday night, or even better, tomorrow, and then I'll ask if I can kiss you good night, like this and like this and like—"

"Do we have to start so far back?" Billy managed to whisper between his needful, poignant kisses, kisses that had obsessed her for so long that she could scarcely comprehend their warmth, their breathtaking reality, their indisputable substance, scarcely believe that this was not just another daydream. "I'm much too . . . sophisticated . . . . to start dating again."

"Anywhere you want . . . oh, darling, I'm so much in love with you I don't know what to do. Can't we get married? Come on, Billy," Spider urged her, his voice becoming almost unrecognizable with impatience. "I can't stand waiting around for all that in-between stuff when I'm absolutely sure what's going to happen in the end—there's no other possible way for us to exist except married to each other. Darling, what can I say to make you understand?"

"There's always been this one particular thing about you, Spider," Billy said, laughing in profligate bliss as she looked up into his eyes. She caressed his lips possessively, borne strongly aloft on a surge of happiness so pure that it was crystalline, so powerful that it felt like riding the swell of a mighty ocean, so indivisible that she trusted it fearlessly. "You have the most amazing ability to talk me into anything, anything at all. Are you going to miss it when you discover that everything you want, I want too? Because if you prefer, I can always put up a fight, but wouldn't it be simpler if I said yes, in advance, to everything?"

"Sure," said Spider, transcendently joyous but not blinded, "yeah, right, Billy, yes in advance to everything. Oh, my darling, that'll be the day."

Epilogue

One Year Later

*T*here are many cunning ways in which to wake up a sleeping man without his ever knowing that he's been deliberately aroused, Billy told herself, as she lay wide awake next to Spider in her big bed. You can move as vigorously as possible from side to side, until the mattress begins to feel like a rough sea; you can twitch the sheets and blankets up so far that they cover his mouth and nose and he has to wake up to get some air; you can tickle him sneakily in any number of tender places, until he's irritated enough to open his eyes; you can even choose one hair on his head and pull it out so that his efforts to remain unconscious are doomed. Or you can shout "Boo!" into his ear and immediately lie back, feigning drowsy innocence, as he bolts upright in surprise.

But was it fair to wake someone who was sleeping as profoundly as he was? Spider was probably enjoying REM sleep, the deepest *stage, in which dreams come, that restorative phase of sleep, deprived of which for days at a time, people soon become disoriented and unhappy and start having delusions. But hadn't he had more than enough sleep for anybody's needs, Billy asked herself fretfully, while she'd been up all night, trotting to her flower-filled bathroom every hour, walking miles around the enormous bedroom to stop her legs from cramping, getting carefully back into bed and composing herself once again for the rest that hadn't come? Wide awake, she stared upward in the predawn dimness as she tried to decide whether Spider would be angry if she neglected to wake him up and share the saga of her disturbed night with him?*

Yet there was an advantage to her being conscious while he slept. Even if she couldn't look into the limitless blue of his eyes, even if she wasn't listening to his voice or watching his pagan smile, in sleep he belonged entirely to her, and she could bask in uninterrupted contemplation of the heaven of sharing a bed with him. She could dote on him, that's what she could do, dote as much as she liked, dote in an unashamed, unobserved orgy of being helplessly in love, a condition she'd learned was not for public display.

As hard as she tried, she hadn't mastered the art of entirely avoiding doting at the office. She'd noticed those amused little nudges people gave each other when Spider was running a meeting, and she'd become so mesmerized by him that she lost track of the subject under discussion and couldn't produce a sensible opinion when it was asked of her. Heather, the most intellectual of Spider's six sisters, had told her that the two of them were a model of uxoriousness. When she'd looked it up in the dictionary, pleased at the implied praise but not wanting to admit that she didn't know what it meant, she'd found an illustrative quotation affixed to the word describing a woman who had "melted into absolute uxorial imbecility." And another of a man who, according to Tennyson, was "a prince whose manhood was all gone, and molten down in mere uxoriousness." Well! If that old prude Tennyson were around, she'd set him straight pretty damn quick on the manhood question, and as for Heather, she couldn't have possibly meant it that way, she must have been trying to show off her vocabulary, missing by a mile.

Marrying a man with six sisters was a continuing revelation, Billy mused. Ellis had had no family, and Vito, if he had one back East in Riverdale, had never bothered to introduce her to them. But Spider's parents lived nearby in Pasadena, four of his sisters were scattered around in Los Angeles, and the two others weren't farther than an hour's plane or car ride from their childhood home. Their reunions were frequent—how had she managed not to hear more about the Elliott family before she married Spider, Billy wondered—demonstrative, wildly good-natured, uninhibitedly verbal, and revolving around Spider in a way that stopped just short of going slightly overboard. The only son, the only brother . . . it was natural that they all adored him. They actually flirted with him, if she was any judge, and who better? Thank goodness she couldn't be jealous of her husband's very own sisters, or was there another horrid, little-known word, like uxorious, that she didn't know about, Billy asked herself suspiciously—a word that might explain why, as much as she was charmed by the warm, happy feeling of becoming an instant member of a huge, loving family, a feeling she'd never known before and had always missed until her marriage, she was never too unhappy to see them all go home and leave her and Spider alone together?

It wasn't as if her sisters-in-law didn't treat her lovingly, Billy thought, smiling at the thought of them. They each had children of their own, more than a dozen all together, but they hovered with anticipation and veneration over her belly as if, in six more weeks, she could be counted on to produce another Shakespeare and another Mozart, instead of merely twin boys who would be merely the only other male Elliotts in existence except for Spider and his father. Her mother-in-law had vainly produced three sets of female twins, trying to give birth to another Spider, but she had accomplished the trick first crack out of the barrel, so to speak, as easily as taking a stroll in the woods, a roll off a log, a shot in the dark—something about fecundity seemed to lead directly to clichés, heartburn, sciatica and insomnia.

Spider moved slightly and she turned toward him hopefully, but he was as fast asleep as ever, his face hidden by one arm. Billy raised herself on her elbows, leaned closer to him and inhaled the smell of his hair. It was better than buttered popcorn, and ten times as tempting. Bravely she resisted the urge to ruffle it, and lay back on her pillows, meditating on motherhood.

Dolly had assured her that twins were no trouble at all, not really much more of a problem to raise than a single baby, but then, on the subject of her boys, Dolly lied like a bandit with the excuse that sticking to her diet took all the strength of mind she possessed. She was using hypnosis, acupuncture, crystals and channeling to bolster her resolve, as well as the thought of having to wear the Dolly Moons that sold in such huge numbers. Could it be Dolly's own lack of willpower that caused her twins to be such free spirits, to put it kindly, Billy wondered. What would she do if her own babies turned out to be as stubborn as Dolly's, Billy asked herself, as she patiently endured them duking it out in her womb. Didn't they realize that there was room in there for both of them? Why did they have to try to trade places all night long? Or were they merely dancing a companionable tango? Perhaps she shouldn't be so anxious for them to be born, perhaps she should be making the most of the last weeks of relative peace she'd have for a long while, but she felt as if she'd been put breathtakingly on hold with this enormous, mysterious, life-changing event looming in the near future.

The only things she'd been able to concentrate on lately had been the designs for the new Scruples Two maternity collection and the line of baby clothes, none of which would exist as finished samples until July.

How could they have imagined a catalog without those essential categories? Even without looking at statistics: she was pregnant; Sasha, with her customary efficiency, was two weeks more pregnant than she; two of Spider's sisters, Petunia and January, were pregnant yet again; to say nothing of Dolly, who had just had to cancel a film in which she brought a lovelorn Arnold Schwarzenegger to his knees, because she too was going to have another baby in seven months. Four pregnant women besides herself in her immediate circle was enough to indicate a trend—or was it an epidemic?—and Scruples Two was nothing if not on top of trends, Billy thought with satisfaction. With hundreds of employees, most of them married women, they'd built model day care facilities in Virginia and Los Angeles so that their carefully trained staff could opt for motherhood, keep their jobs and work out flexible schedules . . . nothing less made any sense.

The entire catalog industry had been revolutionized by the stunning success of Scruples Two and its unprecedented swiftness of growth, right from the first mailing. They'd hit the market at exactly the right time with the right idea; millions of women with no time to go shopping needed well-priced, well-made, cleverly versatile clothes. The graphics Spider had worked out were so different from other catalogs that they'd grabbed an immediate audience, while Gigi's copy had all but created a cult. Oh, they'd had their problems; one essential Prince scarf, intended to be worn with four different outfits, had been *delivered in so jarring a combination of blues that not even Prince himself would have dared to wear them together; sixteen of their most carefully trained, friendly and helpful phone operators had quit in a single week to marry men they'd met via long distance when they'd called up to order antique lingerie as gifts; a wrong guess had left them short thirty-five thousand dark green velvet trousers; the single most popular Dolly Moon caused super-sensitive women to itch and had been returned by the tens of thousands—the list was longer, but through the quarterly sale catalogs they got rid of their mistakes and returns, and still made a healthy profit, with a customer base that was growing as quickly as their expertise and sense of the market.*

Joe Jones and his brother had both bought houses before their first year in California was over, and were busy putting in pools, buying boats and looking for weekend getaways in the nearby mountains of Idyllwild, as tangible a sign of total confidence as she could hope for. Josie Speilberg had resisted an alluring kidnap attempt from L.L. Bean when she'd received her VP in Charge of Sanity title; Prince was in a state of permanent slow burn because he hadn't thought of doing moderate-priced clothes himself, instead of being bound to them by contract for five more years—in short, business as usual, Billy thought, stuffing another pillow in the aching small of her back. Business as usual, that is, except for Cora de Lioncourt. Strange, how violently upset Maggie MacGregor had been at the swipe at her professionalism in that "P.D.Q." article, revengeful enough to make it her business to find out who actually was responsible for the column. When she discovered through her network of informers that Cora had provided the information, although she hadn't written the offending words, Maggie had exposed Cora's secret traffic in kickbacks in a television half-hour devoted to the phenomena that was just beginning to be known as Nouvelle Society. "The Ten Percent Empress of Social Climbers" she'd called the show, and it had ended Cora's usefulness to anybody with a crash. Well, you couldn't blame Maggie for being angry at being accused of sleeping her way to the top when her success had been based on hard work and talent, but that didn't mean she liked Maggie any more than she ever had. Actually, come to think of it, if it hadn't been for that horrid article, if it hadn't been for Spider coming to find her that night to comfort her, it would have taken them longer to find out that they loved each other . . . . although nothing could have kept them apart . . . . sooner or later love, like a cough, makes itself known, Billy thought, happily philosophic, in spite of a discomfort that no well-placed pillow could cure.

She would give just about anything to be able to lie flat on her stomach, Billy thought with longing. Facedown, cheek pressed to the bottom sheet, blankets pulled up over the back of her neck, utterly relaxed, drifting off to sleep . . . she could remember it dimly, no, she could imagine it; memory was too fleeting to capture that delicious state, but imagination was powerful enough to work.

Imagination . . . . Zach Nevsky's imagination had persuaded Vito to transpose an English comedy of manners to a San Francisco setting, thereby solving all the tricky nuances of the British class structure that had threatened to make Fair Play *inaccessible to the mass audience. Nick De Salvo, playing the tough young owner of a restaurant on Fisherman's Wharf, had starred with Meryl Streep, cast as a discreet, very-much-married society woman from Nob Hill, the two of them generating enough forbidden heat to make* The French Lieutenant's Woman *seem downright unisex. Even the teenagers were going to see it, the make-out movie of the year. Vito had his first giant success in a long time.*

The critics had singled Zach out for particular praise, forgetting the producer's role, as usual, but the industry knew that even if Zachary Nevsky was on top of the most-wanted list of new directors in town, Vito Orsini was back in business in a big way. Curt Arvey was reported to be furious that he'd missed the chance to finance Fair Play, *and was openly blaming Susan's advice for his loss. Obviously she was busy trying to reel Vito back into the studio, even being spotted lunching here and there with him, although, Billy thought with a mental grimace, no amount of imagination could conjure up a situation in which Susan's uptight, frigid, judgmental manner could influence Vito one way or another. Beginner's luck, Billy told herself, she'd had beginner's luck in her one fling in show business and she didn't plan to risk it again. Impulsiveness had to stop somewhere.*

Spider sighed and turned over so that his back was toward her. Billy, alert, stared at the outline of his body wistfully and edged herself closer, so that her abdomen came into warm contact with his backbone. Now, just when a major bout of kick-boxing would be welcome, the twins had perversely chosen to make peace. There was a rosy glow outside the drawn curtains that told her the sun was rising. What would happen if she opened them and let in a flood of light? Would even that wake her husband? Was ever a man so gifted at unconsciousness as Spider? So gifted at loving, so gifted at living, so gifted at being gifted? Was ever a woman as unselfish as she, Billy wondered, to allow such a gifted man to waste his time sleeping?

She sighed deeply and plaintively a half-dozen times without result, gave up sighing—it took too much energy—and turned her busy mind to Gigi and Zach. He had been in San Francisco on location for months, and now he was directing a big film in Texas, but when he was in Los Angeles the two of them lived together in her apartment, Zach quickly turning her place into a West Coast version of the ongoing, crowded party of devoted friends he'd created in New York.

Billy approved of Gigi's decision—unshared by Zach—not to rush into marriage. Gigi felt that since she was barely twenty-two, there was plenty of time to think about settling down to serious domesticity after they had actually lived together for a lengthy period of time. But, oh, Gigi was marvelously happy! She was able to handle her job at Scruples Two so routinely that she was considering a tempting offer to work as a copywriter at a rapidly growing advertising agency. She could manage to do both jobs, since the copy for Scruples Two didn't have to be rewritten for each repeat catalog mailing, and her ambition had grown with the wildly enthusiastic acceptance of her antique lingerie, even though men bought it for women in far greater quantities than women bought it for themselves.

Sasha was planning to combine motherhood with a part-time career after a maternity leave of at least four months—she'd already hired a nanny who would help her out from the day she brought the baby home from the hospital. Yes, Sasha had all her bases covered, Billy thought, but she herself couldn't seem to manage to make any firm plans at all besides finding a warmhearted and experienced nurse to help with the twins. How could she possibly know in advance what balance of motherhood and work would be right for her? She still felt very much a working woman by deep temperament and Scruples Two was in its early days, yet surely she'd want some solid time out to plunge into all the experiences of maternity? On the other hand, wasn't it possible that too heavy a dose of the nursery might drive her up the wall? Nothing in her life had prepared her for a sensible compromise about the wonders and problems of motherhood. They were as unpredictable right now as the rest of her surprising tumble through life . . . . she knew only how lucky she was to be able to afford the inestimable luxury of choice.

The future was far too exciting, complicated and full of magic to contemplate for long, Billy concluded, closing her eyes at last, since even the back of Spider's neck was so fascinating to look at that she was bedeviled by the desire to nuzzle it and there was no possibility of maneuvering herself that close to him. It had been so different only a year ago, she remembered dreamily . . . . the weekend of the fashion show, when she and Spider had barely managed to pry themselves apart long enough to shake hands with everybody from the press, much less make sense when they were interviewed. He'd been at her side during every jubilant day, his arm tightly around her waist or thrown around her shoulders, proudly and possessively, the two of them so intensely aware of each other that everything else had been an illusion, a fiction mounted for shadows. Their rapture had been contagious, too strong not to be visible, and soon Gigi suspected and Sasha, of course, took one look and knew right away, and then Prince caught on and rushed to inform all of his closest contacts in the media, which quickly meant that half a hundred relative strangers felt the right to ask them the most amazingly personal questions . . . . professionally intuitive questions . . . . somehow impossible to effectively . . . . deny . . . . even if . . . . she'd wanted to . . . .

"Wake up, my darling," Spider urged her four hours later, so persistently that Billy finally blinked in protest and opened her eyes.

"I didn't want to wake you earlier," he said, leaning over and kissing her, "but I've been wandering in and out of the bedroom like a lost soul, watching you sleep so sweetly—for more than four whole hours—and I just couldn't stand it any longer. I felt too lonely for you. Anyway, it's lunchtime and I'm positive it's not good for the boys when you miss a meal, they need their nourishment, and if you sleep so late during the day, how will you get back to sleep at night?"

"Good question," she murmured, yawning, stretching and feeling wonderfully refreshed.

"Aren't you glad I woke you up?" he asked anxiously, gently pushing her blunt curls away from her forehead so that he could look at her more closely.

"Oh, I am," Billy answered truthfully, on a wave of flawless, untroubled peace. "I'm so glad, sweetheart . . . sleeping is highly overrated, a complete waste of time, when we could be doing something else, like kissing or touching or talking or maybe . . . . even . . . ." she added hopefully, "trying to hug . . . ?"

"You don't look seriously undernourished to me after all, my *beautiful girl, now that your eyes are open,"* Spider said as he started to unbutton his shirt. *"If sleeping is overrated, so is lunch. How about a little kissing and hugging while my arms are still long enough to get around you?"*

"You have an admirable sense of priorities," Billy sighed happily, as she made room for him in bed.

To be continued...